THREE CLASSIC
AFRICAN-AMERICAN
NOVELS

THREE CLASSIC AFRICAN-AMERICAN NOVELS

**Clotel; or,
The President's Daughter**
by William Wells Brown

Iola Leroy, or Shadows Uplifted
by Frances E. W. Harper

The Marrow of Tradition
by Charles W. Chesnutt

*Edited and with an Introduction
by Henry Louis Gates, Jr.*

VINTAGE CLASSICS
VINTAGE BOOKS
A DIVISION OF RANDOM HOUSE, INC.
NEW YORK

A Vintage Classics Original, August 1990
FIRST EDITION

Library of Congress Cataloging-in-Publication Data
Three classic African-American novels / edited and with an
introduction by Henry Louis Gates, Jr.
p. cm.—(Vintage classics)
Contents: Clotel, or, The president's daughter / by
William Wells Brown—Iola Leroy, or, Shadows uplifted / by Frances E. W.
Harper—The Marrow of Tradition /
by Charles W. Chesnutt.
ISBN 0-679-72742-6
1. American fiction—Afro-American authors.
2. Afro-Americans—
Fiction. I. Brown, William Wells, 1818–1884. Clotel, or, The
president's daughter. II. Harper, Frances Ellen Watkins,
1825–1911. Iola Leroy, or, Shadows uplifted. III. Chesnutt,
Charles Weddell, 1858–1932. The Marrow of tradition.
IV. Series.
PS647.A35T47   1990
813.008′0896073—dc20   89-40704
CIP

Book design by Claudia Carlson

Manufactured in the United States of America

20 19 18 17 16 15 14 13

Contents

Introduction

> Fiction is of great value to any people as a preserver of manners and customs—religious, political and social. It is a record of growth and development from generation to generation. No one will do this for us; we must ourselves develop the men and women who will faithfully portray the inmost thoughts and feelings of the Negro with all the fire and romance which lie dormant in our history, and, as yet, unrecognized by writers of the Anglo-Saxon race.
>
> —PAULINE HOPKINS, 1900

By the turn of the century the tradition of African-American fiction was almost four decades old, commencing, as we believe it did, in 1853 with the publication by William Wells Brown of *Clotel; or, The President's Daughter. A Narrative of Slave Life in the United States.* Before 1865 novels by Frank Webb, Martin R. Delany, and Harriet E. Wilson had sought to record in fiction both the political and moral justifications for the freeing of the slaves, and by the time Hopkins called for a new generation of writers who would chart for a new century of readers "the inmost thoughts and feelings of the Negro," African-American novels had begun to appear in quantity, with no fewer than fourteen appearing between 1890 and 1900. Hopkins's was an appeal for the consolidation of a literary movement that had established fictional narrative as the dominant genre in African-American literature.

The stories that blacks would fabricate, Hopkins argued, would be the stories "twice-told" but not yet written, canonical tales of the largely unrecorded Negro cultural milieu "which lie[s] dormant in our history." The narration of these stories was the cultural and political imperative for a people still fighting tenaciously for their most basic rights. *L'Art pour l'art* was not a luxury they could afford, and these fictions would, necessarily, be engagements with history, acts of imaginative literature fueled with "fire and romance," yet functioning as allegories of the American Negro's historical experiences.

The three texts collected here are historical novels that bind themselves to a depiction of the three crucial epochs in African-American history before 1900: slavery (*Clotel*), Reconstruction (*Iola Leroy*), and the Jim Crow era of the 1890s (*The Marrow of Tradition*). Rather than submit their testimony to the still skeptical, and quite hostile, historical profession, these authors turned to fiction to make what each hoped would become crucial interventions in the war against American racism. Through the mediating agency of allegory, they seem to have felt, both white and black Americans could recognize the nature of their historical confrontation over economics and ethnicity, and, sufficiently educated, would construct a new society out of the horrors of the past.

We are only beginning to understand the sheer depth and extent of a form of oppression based upon one's ethnicity, an ethnicity not thought to have been constructed, but which was believed to be both biologically determined and determining, along the lines of "racial character" or "personality," as if social condition had been endowed and preordained by nature. What havoc this biological determinism wreaked on the African-American sensibility is only now being reconstructed by literary historians as we unearth and reprint the hundreds of books that black women and men managed, against enormous odds, to publish, in a collective effort to testify in the face of the terror of a most efficient system of racial oppression. What is astonishing to me, rereading these three texts almost one hundred and fifty years after the first one was published, is how demanding it must have been for these writers to engage in the attempt to speak indirectly to their immediate and pressing social problems through the guise and voice of allegorical historical fictions. What is equally as astonishing is how compelling these novels remain today, both as fictional tales and as social documents.

I have chosen to present *Clotel, Iola Leroy,* and *The Marrow of Tradition* in an attempt to suggest something of the range of black fiction published between the middle of the nineteenth century and the early twentieth century. While other novels could have been chosen, these three, it seems to me, best represent both the variety of sensibilities and of experimentation with fictional form at work within the literary tradition as it unfolded. Tracing three aspects of the effort of Negro intellectuals to define a measure of freedom for themselves, they move from slavery, to freedom, to the organized agitation against legal segregation at the century's end.

CLOTEL

William Wells Brown was born a slave in approximately 1814 near Lexington, Kentucky, and died in 1884 in Chelsea, Massachusetts. Following his escape from slavery on New Year's Day of 1834, in the course of which he named himself "William Wells Brown" (reclaiming the name that his mother had given him at birth, and adopting the surname of a Quaker who befriended him during his escape), Brown enjoyed a remarkable career. A highly respected and extraordinarily popular lecturer in both the antislavery and temperance campaigns, Brown published no less than sixteen books, including the first black novel (*Clotel*), the first published play (*The Escape; or, A Leap for Freedom,* 1858), and one of the first travel memoirs published by a black person (*Three Years in Europe,* 1852). Brown was a remarkably popular author: the first four editions of his slave narrative of 1847 sold ten thousand copies in two years, and five British editions appeared in the next four.* He was also a major figure in international reform circles: he was elected as a delegate to the World Peace Congress held at Paris in 1849, and he lectured widely in England and France, where he met such well-known figures as Victor Hugo, Alexis de Tocqueville, Charles Dickens, Thomas Babington Macaulay, and Alfred, Lord Tennyson.

Brown enjoys the distinction of being the first American of African descent who earned a living as a writer; his books of the 1840s outsold those of such illustrious compatriots as Hawthorne and Melville. Overshadowed by the awesome presence of Frederick Douglass, however, Brown's career and significance to the tradition have not fully or adequately been assessed.

Brown wrote four distinct versions of *Clotel*, the first of which, curiously enough, was not published in America until 1969, perhaps because of its claim that Thomas Jefferson had kept a mistress who was a slave, Sally Hemmings, that she had borne his children, and that Jefferson had sold them. References to Jefferson's paternity disappear completely in the other American editions of *Clotel*.

Brown fully acknowledged that his decision to write *Clotel* was inspired by the enthusiastic reception and powerful influence of Harriet Beecher Stowe's *Uncle Tom's Cabin* (1851–2), which in turn had been inspired in part by Brown's slave narrative of 1847. Like Stowe's book, *Clotel* is a melodramatic novel, constructed around an intricate plot full of dramatic twists and turns that are meant to unmask the horrors of slavery in particular and extensive detail. The novel is replete with portentous moral and political arguments against slavery, reflecting the author's concern that fiction be utilized as an important weapon in the abolitionist movement's arsenal against "the peculiar institution." The novel is episodic in structure and, as several critics have noted, consists

---

* *Narrative of William W. Brown, A Fugitive Slave, Written by Himself.* Boston: Anti-Slavery Office, 1847; enlarged, 1848; London: Charles Gilpin, 1849.

of enough subplots to serve several books, for *Clotel* is as much a narrative of melodramatic events as it is an abolitionist polemic. Here, plot and preachments are everything; characters stand as types.

The novel's plot turns upon the interrelations of six principal characters: Currer, a female mulatto slave, once Thomas Jefferson's housekeeper and mistress; their two quadroon daughters, Clotel, sixteen, and Althesa, fourteen; Horatio Green, a wealthy and prominent citizen of Richmond, Virginia; Mary, Clotel's daughter by Green; and Dick Walker, an evil slave trader. The novel is concerned with dramatizing slavery's perversion of the family unit, the hypocrisy of those who own other human beings, and the vulnerability of black women who are held as slaves.

Clotel is important to the history of the African-American novel not merely because it was the first of its genre; it is important as well because of its representation of the vernacular English that black people speak in its pages, its emphasis on the disruptions of family bonds that slavery depended upon, and its historical scope in tracing the lives and fates of three generations of African-American women. The novel thus demonstrates the direct connections between the construction of individual histories and the larger rhetorical structures of antislavery discourse. *Clotel* was not a novel meant to be read to escape reality; rather, it was intended to present a large chunk of the reality confronting the slave and ex-slave, rendered as dramatically as possible for those white American citizens whose votes and voices alone could prove human slavery incompatible with American ideals of democracy. Brown's novel was an abolitionist's sermon, full of woe and warnings to those who felt themselves somehow removed from the "crisis" of American slavery and color prejudice. Written just eight years before the Civil War, *Clotel* is a remarkable beginning for African-American fiction and remains a fascinating intellectual document of its age.

IOLA LEROY

Frances Ellen Watkins Harper (1824–1911), who enjoyed the honor of being the first African-American professional woman of letters, knew slavery as a text, through the oral and written testimonies of former slaves and the published polemics of the abolitionists. Born of free parents in Baltimore, Harper began her career as a distinguished lecturer against slavery and for temperance. She was educated at her uncle's school for free blacks, and at a bookstore in Baltimore, where she obviously read broadly and deeply. In 1850, at the age of twenty-six, she became the first woman to teach at the Union Seminary, a school founded for free blacks in 1847 near Columbus, Ohio, by the African Methodist Episcopal Church, and shortly thereafter accepted a second teaching position in Little York, Pennsylvania. In 1854 she joined the Underground Railroad Station in Philadelphia, under the direction of William Grant Still, who had been influential in her decision to become a reformer. She delivered her first antislavery lecture, "Education and the Colored Race," in New Bedford, Massachusetts, in 1854 and became a lecturer for the Maine Antislavery Society. Harper was widely praised as an orator, and lectured and read her poems in Maine, Massachusetts, Pennsylvania, New York, Ohio, New Jersey, Vermont, Delaware, Michigan, and Canada until her marriage to Fenton Harper in 1860. Her career was then at a high point: in 1859 she had published "The Two Offers," the first short story by a black woman; her second volume of poems, *Poems on Miscellaneous Subjects*, had sold twelve thousand copies; and her poems, letters, and speeches were appearing regularly in the abolitionist press.

Between 1860 and 1864 Harper "retired" to a farm in Ohio, where she gave birth to a daughter, Mary. Her husband's death in 1864 led her back to the lecture circuit, and she traveled widely throughout the South in the early years of Reconstruction, advocating Negro suffrage and women's rights and publishing prolifically. She settled in Philadelphia and in 1872 created a YMCA Sabbath School of which she was an assistant superintendent. Soon she proved an active agent of the growing women's movement, becoming identified with the Women's Christian Temperance Union, the National Council of Women, the American Woman's Suffrage Association, the American Equal Rights Association, the International Council of Women, and the National Association of Colored Women. Indeed, Harper was probably the most visible black female public figure in the second half of the nineteenth century.

Known as "the Brown Muse," Harper was both a productive and popular author: her *Poems* (1854) was enlarged and reprinted several times, including an 1871 edition listed as its twentieth. By 1878, according to William Grant Still, who wrote the introduction to *Iola Leroy*, her two books of poems had sold some fifty thousand copies. *Iola Leroy* was reprinted three times during Harper's lifetime. Written for "Negro Sunday School Youth," *Iola Leroy, or Shadows Uplifted* is, as Sterling A. Brown has noted, a direct revision of Brown's *Clotel*. It was long thought to be the first novel published by a black woman, and is, in any case, the first black novel to treat the historical period of Reconstruction (1867–1876).

In *Iola Leroy*, Harper emphasizes the capacity of the freed black slaves for social and intellectual "elevation" or "uplift," two key terms in African-American discourse in the latter half of the nineteenth century. For Harper, ethnic identity is a *choice* rather than an immutable fact of nature; Iola and Frank Lattimer decide to "become" black Americans rather than to "pass" for white. *Iola Leroy* is thus a call to arms to the still small but emerging black middle class to avoid the temptation of believing that they could "escape" the social condition of "blackness" in American society and, instead, to dedicate their lives to the betterment of the entire ethnic group.

The novel is also noteworthy for its use of black vernacular speech and for its skill at narrating action and commenting, often with great sensitivity and a delicate sense of irony, upon the significance of their lives. Indeed, *Iola Leroy* contains the richest and fullest representation of black dialect to be found in the nineteenth-century novel. At the same time, its characterization of the mulatto protagonist as an independent, self-conscious agent is a bold critique of the standard conventions of representing mulattoes in the American novel as ambivalent, tortured, or unreliable. The female protagonist of *Iola Leroy* is the most noble and compelling black woman character in black fiction before the turn of the century. As an account of black life during Reconstruction, as an indictment of racial discrimination in the North and the South, and in its technical experimentation with both dialogue and black vernacular speech as a counterpoint to standard English, *Iola Leroy* has a major place in the history of African-American fiction.

THE MARROW OF TRADITION

Charles Chesnutt (1858–1932) was born in Cleveland, Ohio, of free black parents who had, of their own choice, emigrated from North Carolina in 1856. Chesnutt was educated in public elementary schools in Cleveland, then at the normal school for Negroes founded by the Freedman's Bureau in Fayetteville, North Carolina, when his family returned to the South in 1866. By the age of fifteen, Chesnutt's formal schooling had ended and he had become a schoolteacher, working in South Carolina, then returning to North Carolina to teach, first in Charlotte and then in Fayetteville. By 1880, at the age of twenty-two, he was the principal of the black normal school there, a teacher of reading and writing, and had been keeping a literary journal for six years.

After three years, Chesnutt resigned his position as principal and moved to New York City where he served as a reporter for the *New York Mail and Express* and as a stenographer, a trade he had learned in Fayetteville. Less than a year later, he moved to Cleveland and worked as a bookkeeper and then as a stenographer. In 1887 he passed the bar examination in Ohio.

The law, for Chesnutt, was a means of supporting his family; his desire, as he confided to his journal, was to be a writer. And a writer he became. Although he would not prove able to support himself as a writer exclusively for more than a three-year span (1899 to 1902), Charles Chesnutt was, the scholar William L. Andrews argues, the first African-American writer "to enlist the white-controlled publishing industry in the service of his social message, touching a significant portion of the white reading audience with his indictment of American racism." Publishing his essays and short stories in such prominent American journals as the *Independent* and, especially, the *Atlantic Monthly*, Chesnutt, after 1887, was the dominant African-American fiction writer until the Harlem Renaissance. In a sense, he desegregated mainstream American literary magazines and publishing companies, enabling the emergence of other authors such as the poet Paul Laurence Dunbar, who emerged at the end of the century as a second strong voice in black creative letters.

We can scarcely imagine, today, the importance of the publication in August 1887 of "The Goophered Grapevine," Chesnutt's first short story to appear in the *Atlantic Monthly*. Scarcely twenty-two years after the end of the Civil War, and eleven years after the demise of Reconstruction, Chesnutt's and Dunbar's literary productions stood as outstanding examples of the potential of "the race" for "improvement," or "elevation." The literary arts, for these authors, were an implicit political and intellectual statement on behalf of their entire ethnic group.

Between 1899, when he published *The Conjure Woman*, a collection of short stories, and 1905 Chesnutt published six books, including five works of fiction and a short biography of Frederick Douglass. Of these, the work that for many scholars stands as his greatest achievement is his novel *The Marrow of Tradition*. Based upon the 1898 race riot at Wilmington, North Carolina, which Chesnutt researched for two years, *The Marrow of Tradition* is one of the earliest explorations of literary naturalism in the black tradition. Here, character and fate are determined by heredity and custom. Post-Reconstruction southern social conventions, customs, and mores, Chesnutt shows us, were not as they had been represented in the neoplantation fictions so popular in the last two decades of the nineteenth century, which sought to rewrite the history of slavery with nostalgia and romanticism, through a hazy filter of "moonbeams and magnolia blossoms." No, the South that emerged after Reconstruction was just as corrupt, dishonest, and racist as southern society had been before the war. While the forms of a supposedly "new" South might differ in outward appearance from the old, in substance the two were fundamentally the same.

Indeed, the book is profoundly pessimistic, as contemporary novelist John Wideman has remarked, "since the individual Negro, no matter how resolutely he proves his equality, is crushed just as utterly as his most ignorant, underprivileged brother once the Manichean fury of race war begins. History as a lie and a cage is vividly symbolized in the novel by the self-delusions which underlie the lives of Wellington's citizens." And yet Chesnutt's narrative skill enables him to limn this world with nuance and intelligence. As Wideman further notes, Chesnutt's "comprehension of national and international politics, stylistic details such as the sustained imagery of disguise and masquerade, the variety of narrative modes ranging from intrusive essay-commentary to naturalistic dialogue, the use of dialect, folk maxims, parodies of newspaper propaganda create a context for examining the question of Negro-ness that is subtle, complex, and suggestive."

Disappointed with the book's sales and its critical reception (William Dean Howells, who had championed his earlier work, found *The Marrow* to be "bitter, bitter"), Chesnutt in 1902 abandoned his dream of supporting his family on his writings alone and returned to the legal profession, still writing, albeit in his spare time. And while he enjoyed a prosperous existence, became a prominent citizen of Cleveland, and was widely recognized as a founding figure in African-American literature, Chesnutt never enjoyed the popular success of his writings for which he had longed. Never again would his fiction achieve the level of authority and force that it realized in *The Marrow of Tradition*, certainly the most sophisticated rendering of life in the historical period of the post-Reconstruction South that we have. And yet there is a certain force in William Andrew's judgment that "it was he who taught white America for the first time to respect a black fiction writer as a critical realist, even if this meant it could not embrace him as a literary native son."

These three novels, finally, trace the history of the African-American community from slavery to freedom to the disillusionment of a racist order that failed to die. Together they attest to the strong historical impulse of black literature in the nineteenth century, its commitment to social critique, its advocacy of social change, its compulsion to testify to the life of the Negro mind beyond the veils of racial and sexual injustice. Allegories of the historical experiences of Afro-Americans before the twentieth century, these novels confirm the richness and variety of black literary tradition, reveal the formal interconnections of the texts that comprise that tradition, and affirm the culture's collective belief that the will to social change was the will to create literature.

HENRY LOUIS GATES, JR.
April 1990

THREE CLASSIC
AFRICAN-AMERICAN
NOVELS

CLOTEL;

OR,

THE PRESIDENT'S DAUGHTER:

𝔄 𝔑𝔞𝔯𝔯𝔞𝔱𝔦𝔳𝔢 𝔬𝔣 𝔖𝔩𝔞𝔳𝔢 𝔏𝔦𝔣𝔢

IN

THE UNITED STATES

BY

WILLIAM WELLS BROWN

A FUGITIVE SLAVE, AUTHOR OF "THREE YEARS IN EUROPE."

𝔚𝔦𝔱𝔥 𝔞 𝔖𝔨𝔢𝔱𝔠𝔥 𝔬𝔣 𝔱𝔥𝔢 𝔄𝔲𝔱𝔥𝔬𝔯'𝔰 𝔏𝔦𝔣𝔢.

———

"WE hold these truths to be self-evident: that all men are created equal; that they are endowed by their Creator with certain inalienable rights, and that among these are LIFE, LIBERTY, and the PURSUIT OF HAPPINESS."—*Declaration of American Independence.*

———

Preface

More than two hundred years have elapsed since the first cargo of slaves was landed on the banks of the James River, in the colony of Virginia, from the West coast of Africa. From the introduction of slaves in 1620, down to the period of the separation of the Colonies from the British Crown, the number had increased to five hundred thousand; now there are nearly four million. In fifteen of the thirty-one States, Slavery is made lawful by the Constitution, which binds the several States into one confederacy.

On every foot of soil, over which *Stars and Stripes* wave, the Negro is considered common property, on which any white man may lay his hand with perfect impunity. The entire white population of the United States, North and South, are bound by their oath to the constitution, and their adhesion to the Fugitive Slave Law, to hunt down the runaway slave and return him to his claimant, and to suppress any effort that may be made by the slaves to gain their freedom by physical force. Twenty-five millions of whites have banded themselves in solemn conclave to keep four millions of blacks in their chains. In all grades of society are to be found men who either hold, buy, or sell slaves, from the statesmen and doctors of divinity, who can own their hundreds, down to the person who can purchase but one.

Were it not for persons in high places owning slaves, and thereby giving the system a reputation, and especially professed Christians, Slavery would long since have been abolished. The influence of the great "honours the corruption, and chastisement doth therefore hide his head." The great aim of the true friends of the slave should be to lay bare the institution, so that the gaze of the world may be upon it, and cause the wise, the prudent, and the pious to withdraw their support from it, and leave it to its own fate. It does the cause of emancipation but little good to cry out in tones of execration against the traders, the kidnappers, the hireling overseers, and brutal drivers, so long as nothing is said to fasten the guilt on those who move in a higher circle.

The fact that slavery was introduced into the American colonies, while they were under the control of the British Crown, is a sufficient reason why Englishmen should feel a lively interest in its abolition; and now that the genius of mechanical invention has brought the two countries so near together, and both having one language and one literature, the influence of British public opinion is very great on the people of the New World.

If the incidents set forth in the following pages should add anything new to the information already given to the Public through similar publications, and should thereby aid in bringing British influence to bear upon American slavery, the main object for which this work was written will have been accomplished.

22, Cecil Street, Strand, London.   W. Wells Brown

Narrative
of the Life and Escape
of William Wells Brown

"Shall tongues be mute when deeds are wrought
Which well might shame extremest Hell?
Shall freemen lack th' indignant thought?
Shall Mercy's bosom cease to swell?
Shall Honour bleed?—shall Truth succumb?
Shall pen, and press, and *soul* be dumb?"

WHITTIER

William Wells Brown, the subject of this narrative, was born a slave in Lexington, Kentucky, not far from the residence of the late Hon. Henry Clay. His mother was the slave of Doctor John Young. His father was a slaveholder, and, besides being a near relation of his master, was connected with the Wicklief family, one of the oldest, wealthiest, and most aristocratic of the Kentucky planters. Dr. Young was the owner of forty or fifty slaves, whose chief employment was in cultivating tobacco, hemp, corn, and flax. The Doctor removed from Lexington, when William was five or six years old, to the state of Missouri, and commenced farming in a beautiful and fertile valley, within a mile of the Missouri river.

Here the slaves were put to work under a harsh and cruel overseer named Cook. A finer situation for a farm could not have been selected in the state. With climate favourable to agriculture, and soil rich, the products came in abundance.

At an early age William was separated from his mother, she being worked in the field, and he as a servant in his master's medical department. When about ten years of age, the young slave's feelings were much hurt at hearing the cries of his mother, while being flogged by the Negro driver for being a few minutes behind the other hands in reaching the field. He heard her cry, "Oh, pray! oh, pray! oh, pray!" These are the words which slaves generally utter when imploring mercy at the hands of their oppressors. The son heard it, though he was some way off. He heard the crack of the whip and the groans of his poor mother. The cold chill ran over him, and he wept aloud; but he was a slave like his mother, and could render her no assistance. He was taught by the most bitter experience, that nothing could be more heart-rending than to see a dear and beloved mother or sister tortured by unfeeling men, and to hear her cries, and not be able to render the least aid. When William was twelve years of age, his master left his farm and took up his residence near St. Louis. The Doctor having more hands than he wanted for his own use, William was let out to a Mr. Freeland, an inn-keeper. Here the young slave found himself in the hands of a most cruel and heartless master. Freeland was one of the real chivalry of the South; besides being himself a slave-holder, he was a horse-racer, cock-fighter, gambler, and, to crown the whole, an inveterate drunkard. What else but bad treatment could be expected from such a character? After enduring the tyrannical and inhuman usage of this man for five or six months, William resolved to stand it no longer, and therefore ran away, like other slaves who leave their masters, owing to severe treatment; and not knowing where to flee, the young fugitive went into the forest, a few miles from St. Louis. He had been in the woods but a short time, when he heard the barking and howling of dogs, and was soon satisfied that he was pursued by the Negro dogs; and, aware of their ferocious nature, the fugitive climbed a tree, to save himself from being torn to pieces. The hounds were soon at the trunk of the tree, and remained there, howling and barking, until those in whose charge they were came up. The slave was ordered down, tied, and taken home. Immediately on his arrival there, he was, as he expected, tied up in the smoke-house, and whipped till Freeland was satisfied, and then smoked with tobacco stems. This the slaveholder called *"Virginia play."* After being well whipped and smoked, he was again set to work. William remained with this monster a few months longer, and was then let out to Elijah P. Lovejoy, who years after became the editor of an abolition newspaper, and was murdered at Alton, Illinois, by a mob of slaveholders from the adjoining state of Missouri. The system of letting out slaves is one among the worst of the evils of slavery. The man who hires a slave, looks upon him in the same light as does the man who hires a horse for a limited period; he feels no interest in him, only to get the worth of his money. Not so with the man who owns the slave; he regards him as so much property, of which care should be taken. After being let out to a steamer as an under-steward, William was hired by James Walker, a slave-trader. Here the subject of our memoir was made superintendent of the gangs of slaves that were taken to the New Orleans market. In this capacity, William had opportunities, far greater than most slaves, of acquiring knowledge of the different phases of the *"peculiar institution."* Walker was a Negro speculator, who was amassing a fortune by trading in the bones, blood, and nerves, of God's children. The thoughts of such a traffic causes us to exclaim with the poet,

> "—Is there not some chosen curse,
>   Some hidden thunder in the stores of heaven,
>   Red with uncommon wrath, to blast the man
>   Who gains his fortune from the blood of souls?"

Between fifty and sixty slaves were chained together, put on board a steam-boat bound for New Orleans, and started on the voyage. New and strange scenes began to inspire the young slave with the hope of escaping to a land of freedom.

There was in the boat a large room on the lower deck in which the slaves were kept, men and women promiscuously, all chained two and two together, not even leaving the poor slaves the privilege of choosing their partners. A strict watch was kept over them, so that they had no chance of escape. Cases had occurred in which slaves had got off their chains and made their escape at the landing-places, while the boat stopped to take in wood. But with all their care they lost one woman who had been taken from her husband and children, and having no desire to live without them, in the agony of her soul jumped overboard and drowned herself. Her sorrows were greater than she could bear; slavery and its cruel inflictions had broken her heart. She, like William, sighed for freedom, but not the freedom which even British soil confers and inspires, but freedom from torturing pangs, and overwhelming grief.

At the end of the week they arrived at New Orleans, the place of their destination. Here the slaves were placed in a Negro pen, where those who wished to purchase could call and examine them. The Negro pen is a small yard surrounded by buildings, from fifteen to twenty feet wide, with the exception of a large gate with iron bars. The slaves are kept in the buildings during the night, and turned into the pen during the day. After the best of the gang were sold off, the balance was taken to the Exchange coffee-house auction-rooms, and sold at public auction. After the sale of the last slave, William and Mr. Walker left New Orleans for St. Louis.

After they had been at St. Louis a few weeks another cargo of human flesh was made up. There were amongst the lot several old men and women, some of whom had grey locks. On their way down to New Orleans William had to prepare the old slaves for market. He was ordered to shave off the old men's whiskers, and to pluck out the grey hairs where they were not too numerous; where they were, he coloured them with a preparation of blacking with a blacking brush. After having gone through the blacking process, they looked ten or fifteen years younger. William, though not well skilled in the use of scissors and razor, performed the office of the barber tolerably. After the sale of this gang of Negroes they returned to St. Louis, and a second cargo was made up. In this lot was a woman who had a child at the breast, yet was compelled to travel through the interior of the country on foot with the other slaves. In a published memoir of his life, William says, "The child cried during the most of the day, which displeased Mr. Walker, and he told the mother that if her child did not stop crying, he would stop its mouth. After a long and weary journey under a burning sun, we put up for the night at a country inn. The following morning, just as they were about to start, the child again commenced crying. Walker stepped up to her and told her to give the child to him. The mother tremblingly obeyed. He took the child by one arm, as any one would a cat by the leg, and walked into the house where they had been staying, and said to the lady, 'Madam, I will make you a present of this little nigger; it keeps making such a noise that I can't bear it.' 'Thank you, sir,' said the lady. The mother, as soon as she saw that her child was to be left, ran up to Mr. Walker, and falling on her knees, begged of him in an agony of despair, to let her have her child. She clung round his legs so closely, that for some time he could not kick her off; and she cried, 'O my child, my child. Master, do let me have my dear, dear child Oh! do, do. I will stop its crying, and love you for ever if you will only let me have my child again.' But her prayers were not heeded, they passed on, and the mother was separated from her child for ever.

"After the woman's child had been given away, Mr. Walker rudely commanded her to retire into the ranks with the other slaves. Women who had children were not chained, but those who had none were. As soon as her child was taken she was chained to the gang."

Some time after this, Walker bought a woman who had a blind child; it being considered worthless, it was given to the trader by the former owner of the woman on the score of

humanity, he saying that he wished to keep mother and child
together. At first Walker declined taking the child, saying
that it would be too much trouble, but the mother wishing
to have her boy with her, begged him to take it, promising
to carry it the whole distance in her arms. Consequently he
took the child, and the gang started on their route to the
nearest steamboat landing, which was above one hundred
miles. As might have been expected, the woman was unable
to carry the boy and keep up with the rest of the gang. They
put up at night at a small town, and the next morning, when
about to start, Walker took the little boy from its mother
and sold it to the innkeeper for the small sum of *one dollar*.
The poor woman was so frantic at the idea of being separated
from her only child, that it seemed impossible to get her to
leave it. Not until the chains were put upon her limbs, and
she fastened to the other slaves, could they get her to leave
the spot. By main force this slave mother was compelled to
go on and leave her child behind. Some days after, a lady
from one of the free states was travelling the same road and
put up at the same inn: she saw the child the morning after
her arrival, and heard its history from one of the slaves, which
was confirmed by the innkeeper's wife. A few days after, the
following poem appeared in one of the newspapers, from the
pen of the lady who had seen the blind child:—

"Come back to me, mother! why linger away
From thy poor little blind boy, the long weary day!
I mark every footstep, I list to each tone,
And wonder my mother should leave me alone!
There are voices of sorrow and voices of glee,
But there's no one to joy or to sorrow with me;
For each hath of pleasure and trouble his share,
And none for the poor little blind boy will care.

"My mother, come back to me! close to thy breast
Once more let thy poor little blind one be pressed;
Once more let me feel thy warm breath on my cheek,

And hear thee in accents of tenderness speak!
O mother! I've no one to love me—no heart
Can bear like thy own in my sorrows a part;
No hand is so gentle, no voice is so kind!
Oh! none like a mother can cherish the blind!

"Poor blind one! no mother thy wailing can hear,
No mother can hasten to banish thy fear;
For the slave-owner drives her, o'er mountain and wild,
And for one paltry dollar hath sold thee, poor child!
Ah! who can in language of mortals reveal
The anguish that none but a mother can feel,
When man in his vile lust of mammon hath trod
On her child, who is stricken and smitten of God?

"Blind, helpless, forsaken, with strangers alone,
She hears in her anguish his piteous moan,
As he eagerly listens—but listens in vain,
To catch the loved tones of his mother again!
The curse of the broken in spirit shall fall
On the wretch who hath mingled this wormwood and gall
And his gain like a mildew shall blight and destroy,
Who hath torn from his mother the little blind boy."

The thought that man can so debase himself as to treat a
fellow-creature as here represented, is enough to cause one
to blush at the idea that such men are members of a civilised
and Christian nation.

Nothing was more grievous to the sensitive feelings of
William, than seeing the separation of families by the slave-
trader: husbands taken from their wives, and mothers from
their children, without the least appearance of feeling on the
part of those who separated them. While at New Orleans,
on one occasion, William saw a slave murdered. The circumstances were as follows:—In the evening, between seven and
eight o'clock, a slave came running down the levee, followed
by several men and boys. The whites were crying out, "Stop
that nigger! stop that nigger!" while the poor panting slave,

in almost breathless accents, was repeating, "I did not steal the meat—I did not steal the meat." The poor man at last took refuge in the river. The whites who were in pursuit of him, ran on board of one of the boats to see if they could discover him. They finally espied him under the bow of the steamboat "Trenton." They got a pike-pole, and tried to drive him from his hiding-place. When they struck at him he would dive under the water. The water was so cold, that it soon became evident that he must come out or be drowned.

While they were trying to drive him from under the boat or drown him, he in broken and imploring accents said, "I did not steal the meat; I did not steal the meat. My master lives up the river. I want to see my master. I did not steal the meat. Do let me go home to master." After punching and striking him over the head for some time, he at last sunk in the water, to rise no more alive.

On the end of the pike-pole with which they had been striking him was a hook, which caught in his clothing, and they hauled him up on the bow of the boat. Some said he was dead; others said he was "playing 'possum;" while others kicked him to make him get up; but it was of no use—he was dead.

As soon as they became satisfied of this they commenced leaving one after another. One of the hands on the boat informed the captain that they had killed the man, and that the dead body was lying on the deck. The captain, whose name was Hart, came on deck, and said to those who were remaining, "You have killed this nigger; now take him off my boat." The dead body was dragged on shore and left there. William went on board of the boat where the gang of slaves were, and during the whole night his mind was occupied with what he had seen. Early in the morning he went on shore to see if the dead body remained there. He found it in the same position that it was left the night before. He watched to see what they would do with it. It was left there until between eight and nine o'clock, when a cart, which took up the trash from the streets, came along, and the body was thrown in, and in a few minutes more was covered over with dirt, which they were removing from the streets.

At the expiration of the period of his hiring with Walker, William returned to his master, rejoiced to have escaped an employment as much against his own feelings as it was repugnant to human nature. But this joy was of short duration. The Doctor wanted money, and resolved to sell William's sister and two brothers. The mother had been previously sold to a gentleman residing in the city of St. Louis. William's master now informed him that he intended to sell him, and, as he was his own nephew, he gave him the privilege of finding some one to purchase him, who would treat him better than if he was sold on the auction block. William tried to make some arrangement by which he could purchase his own freedom, but the old Doctor would hear nothing of the kind. If there is one thing more revolting in the trade of human flesh than another, it is the selling of one's own blood relations.

He accordingly set out for the city in search of a new master. When he arrived there, he proceeded to the gaol with the hope of seeing his sister, but was again disappointed. On the following morning he made another attempt, and was allowed to see her once, for the last time. When he entered the room where she was seated in one corner, alone and disconsolate, there were four other women in the room, belonging to the same man, who were bought, the gaoler said, for the master's own use.

William's sister was seated with her face towards the door when he entered, but her gaze was transfixed on nothingness, and she did not look up when he walked up to her; but as soon as she observed him she sprang up, threw her arms around his neck, leaned her head upon his breast, and without uttering a word, in silent, indescribable sorrow, burst into tears. She remained so for some minutes, but when she recovered herself sufficiently to speak, she urged him to take his mother immediately, and try to get to the land of freedom. She said there was no hope for herself, she must live and die a slave. After giving her some advice, and taking a ring from his finger, he bade her farewell for ever. Reader, did ever a fair sister of thine go down to the grave prematurely, if so, perchance, thou hast drank deeply from the cup of sorrow? But how infinitely better is it for a sister to "go into the silent land" with her honour untarnished, but with bright hopes, than for her to be sold to sensual slaveholders.

William had been in the city now two days, and as he was to be absent for only a week, it was well that he should make the best use of his time if he intended to escape. In conversing with his mother, he found her unwilling to make the attempt to reach the land of liberty, but she advised him by all means to get there himself if he possibly could. She said, as all her children were in slavery, she did not wish to leave them; but he loved his mother so intensely, that he could not think of leaving without her. He consequently used all his simple eloquence to induce her to fly with him, and at last he prevailed. They consequently fixed upon the next night as the time for their departure. The time at length arrived, and they left the city just as the clock struck nine. Having found a boat, they crossed the river in it. Whose boat it was he did not know; neither did he care: when it had served his purpose, he turned it adrift, and when he saw it last, it was going at a good speed down the river. After walking in the main road as fast as they could all night, when the morning came they made for the woods, and remained there during the day, but when night came again, they proceeded on their journey with nothing but the North Star to guide them. They continued to travel by night, and to bury themselves in the silent solitudes of the forest by day. Hunger and fatigue could not stop them, for the prospect of freedom at the end of the journey nerved them up. The very thought of leaving slavery, with its democratic whips, republican chains, and bloodhounds, caused the hearts of the weary fugitives to leap with joy. After traveling ten nights and hiding in the woods during the day for fear of being arrested and taken back, they thought they might with safety go the rest of their way by daylight. In nearly all the free states there are men who make a business of catching runaway slaves and returning them to their owners for the reward that may be offered; some of these were on the alert for William and his mother, for they had already seen the runaways advertised in the St. Louis newspapers.

All at once they heard the click of a horse's hoof, and looking back saw three men on horseback galloping towards them. They soon came up, and demanded them to stop. The three men dismounted, arrested them on a warrant, and showed them a handbill, offering two hundred dollars for their apprehension and delivery to Dr. Young and Isaac Mansfield in St. Louis.

While they were reading the handbill, William's mother looked him in the face, and burst into tears. "A cold chill ran over me," says he, "and such a sensation I never experienced before, and I trust I never shall again." They took out a rope and tied him, and they were taken back to the house of the individual who appeared to be the leader. They then had something given them to eat, and were separated. Each of them was watched over by two men during the night. The religious characteristic of the American slaveholder soon manifested itself, as before the family retired to rest they were all called together to attend prayers; and the very man who, but a few hours before, had arrested poor panting, fugitive slaves, now read a chapter from the Bible and offered a prayer to God; as if that benignant and omnipotent One consecrated the infernal act he had just committed.

The next morning they were chained and handcuffed, and started back to St. Louis. A journey of three days brought the fugitives again to the place they had left twelve days previously with the hope that they would never return. They were put in prison to await the orders of their owners. When a slave attempts to escape and fails, he feels sure of either being severely punished, or sold to the Negro traders and taken to the far south, there to be worked up on a cotton, sugar, or rice plantation. This William and his mother dreaded. While they were in suspense as to what would be their fate, news came to them that the mother had been sold to a slave speculator. William was soon sold to a merchant residing in the city, and removed to his new owner's dwelling. In a few days the gang of slaves, of which William's mother was one, were taken on board a steamer to be carried to the New Orleans market. The young slave obtained permission from his new owner to go and take a last farewell of his mother. He went to the boat, and found her there, chained to another woman, and the whole number of slaves, amounting to some fifty or sixty, chained in the same manner. As the son approached his mother she moved not, neither did she weep; her emotions were too deep for tears. William approached her, threw his arms around her neck, kissed her, fell upon his knees begging her forgiveness, for he thought he was to blame for her sad condition, and if he had not persuaded her to accompany him she might not have been in chains then.

She remained for some time apparently unimpressionable, tearless, sighless, but in the innermost depths of her heart moved mighty passions. William says, "She finally raised her head, looked me in the face, and such a look none but an angel can give, and said, 'My dear son, you are not to blame for my being here. You have done nothing more nor less than your duty. Do not, I pray you, weep for me; I cannot last long upon a cotton plantation. I feel that my heavenly Master will soon call me home, and then I shall be out of the hands of the slaveholders.' I could hear no more—my heart struggled to free itself from the human form. In a moment she saw Mr. Mansfield, her master, coming toward that part of the boat, and she whispered in my ear, 'My child, we must soon part to meet no more on this side of the grave. You have ever said that you would not die a slave; that you would be a freeman. Now try to get your liberty! You will soon have no one to look after but yourself!' and just as she whispered the last sentence into my ear, Mansfield came up to me, and with an oath said, 'Leave here this instant; you have been the means of my losing one hundred dollars to get this wench back'—at the same time kicking me with a heavy pair of boots. As I left her she gave one shriek, saying, 'God be with you!' It was the last time that I saw her, and the last word I heard her utter.

"I walked on shore. The bell was tolling. The boat was about to start. I stood with a heavy heart, waiting to see her leave the wharf. As I thought of my mother, I could but feel that I had lost

> 'The glory of my life,
> My blessing and my pride!
> I half forgot the name of slave,
> When she was by my side.'

"The love of liberty that had been burning in my bosom had well-nigh gone out. I felt as though I was ready to die. The boat moved gently from the wharf, and while she glided down the river, I realised that my mother was indeed

> 'Gone—gone—sold and gone,
> To the rice swamp, dark and lone!'

"After the boat was out of sight I returned home; but my thoughts were so absorbed in what I had witnessed, that I knew not what I was about. Night came, but it brought no sleep to my eyes." When once the love of freedom is born in the slave's mind, it always increases and brightens, and William having heard so much about Canada, where a number of his acquaintances had found a refuge and a home, he heartily desired to join them. Building castles in the air in the daytime; incessantly thinking of freedom, he would dream of the land of liberty, but on waking in the morning would weep to find it but a dream.

> "He would dream of Victoria's domain,
> And in a moment he seemed to be there;

But the fear of being taken again,
Soon hurried him back to despair."

Having been for some time employed as a servant in an hotel, and being of a very active turn, William's new owner resolved to let him out on board a steamboat. Consequently the young slave was hired out to the steamer St. Louis, and soon after sold to Captain Enoch Price, the owner of that boat. Here he was destined to remain but a short period, as Mrs. Price wanted a carriage-driver, and had set her heart upon William for that purpose.

Scarcely three months had elapsed from the time that William became the property of Captain Price, ere that gentleman's family took a pleasure trip to New Orleans, and William accompanied them. From New Orleans the family proceeded to Louisville. The hope of escape again dawned upon the slave's mind, and the trials of the past were lost in hopes for the future. The love of liberty, which had been burning in his bosom for years, and which at times had been well nigh extinguished, was now resuscitated. Hopes nurtured in childhood, and strengthened as manhood dawned, now spread their sails to the gales of his imagination. At night, when all around was peaceful, and in the mystic presence of the everlasting starlight, he would walk the steamer's decks, meditating on his happy prospects, and summoning up gloomy reminiscences of the dear hearts he was leaving behind him. When not thinking of the future his mind would dwell on the past. The love of a dear mother, a dear and affectionate sister, and three brothers yet living, caused him to shed many tears. If he could only be assured of their being dead, he would have been comparatively happy; but he saw in imagination his mother in the cotton-field, followed by a monster task-master, and no one to speak a consoling word to her. He beheld his sister in the hands of the slave-driver, compelled to submit to his cruelty, or, what was unutterably worse, his lust; but still he was far away from them, and could not do anything for them if he remained in slavery; consequently he resolved, and consecrated the resolve with a prayer, that he would start on the first opportunity.

That opportunity soon presented itself. When the boat got to the wharf where it had to stay for some time, at the first convenient moment Brown made towards the woods, where he remained until night-time. He dared not walk during the day, even in the state of Ohio; he had seen so much of the perfidy of white men, and resolved, if possible, not to get into their hands. After darkness covered the world, he emerged from his hiding-place; but he did not know east from west, or north from south; clouds hid the North Star from his view. In this desolate condition he remained for some hours, when the clouds rolled away, and his friend, with its shining face—the North Star—welcomed his sight. True as the needle to the pole he obeyed its attractive beauty, and walked on till daylight dawned.

It was winter-time; the day on which he started was the 1st of January, and, as it might be expected, it was intensely cold; he had no overcoat, no food, no friend, save the North Star, and the God which made it. How ardently must the love of freedom burn in the poor slave's bosom, when he will pass through so many difficulties, and even look death in the face, in winning his birth-right, freedom. But what crushed the poor slave's heart in his flight most was, not the want of food or clothing, but the thought that every white man was his deadly enemy. Even in the free states the prejudice against colour is so strong, that there appears to exist a deadly antagonism between the white and coloured races.

William in his flight carried a tinder-box with him, and when he got very cold he would gather together dry leaves and stubble and make a fire, or certainly he would have perished. He was determined to enter into no house, fearing that he might meet a betrayer.

It must have been a picture which would have inspired an artist, to see the fugitive roasting the ears of corn that he found or took from barns during the night, at solitary fires in the deep solitudes of woods.

The suffering of the fugitive was greatly increased by the cold, from the fact of his having just come from the warm climate of New Orleans. Slaves seldom have more than one name, and William was not an exception to this, and the fugitive began to think of an additional name. A heavy rain of three days, in which it froze as fast as it fell, and by which the poor fugitive was completely drenched, and still more chilled, added to the depression of his spirits already created by his weary journey. Nothing but the fire of hope burning within his breast could have sustained him under such overwhelming trials,

> "Behind he left the whip and chains,
> Before him were sweet Freedom's plains."

Through cold and hunger, William was now ill, and he could go no further. The poor fugitive resolved to seek protection, and accordingly hid himself in the woods near the road, until some one should pass. Soon a traveller came along, but the slave dared not speak. A few moments more and a second passed, the fugitive attempted to speak, but fear deprived him of voice. A third made his appearance. He wore a broad-brimmed hat and a long coat, and was evidently walking only for exercise. William scanned him well, and though not much skilled in physiognomy, he concluded he was the man. William approached him, and asked him if he knew any one who would help him, as he was sick. The gentleman asked whether he was not a slave. The poor slave hesitated; but, on being told that he had nothing to fear, he answered, "Yes." The gentleman told him he was in a pro-slaving neighbourhood, but, if he would wait a little, he would go and get a covered waggon, and convey him to his house. After he had gone, the fugitive meditated whether he should stay or not, being apprehensive that the broad-brimmed gentleman had gone for some one to assist him: he however concluded to remain.

After waiting about an hour—an hour big with fate to him—he saw the covered waggon making its appearance, and no one on it but the person he before accosted. Trembling with hope and fear, he entered the waggon, and was carried to the person's house. When he got there, he still halted between two opinions, whether he should enter or take to his heels; but he soon decided after seeing the glowing face of the wife. He saw something in her that bid him welcome, something that told him he would not be betrayed.

He soon found that he was under the shed of a Quaker, and a Quaker of the George Fox stamp. He had heard of Quakers and their kindness; but was not prepared to meet with such hospitality as now greeted him. He saw nothing but kind looks, and heard nothing but tender words. He began to feel the pulsations of a new existence. White men always scorned him, but now a white benevolent woman felt glad to wait on him; it was a revolution in his experience. The table was loaded with good things, but he could not eat. If he were allowed the privilege of sitting in the kitchen, he thought he could do justice to the viands. The surprise being over his appetite soon returned.

"I have frequently been asked," says William, "how I felt upon finding myself regarded as a man by a white family; especially having just run away from one. I cannot say that I have ever answered the question yet. The fact that I was, in all probability, a freeman, sounded in my ears like a charm. I am satisfied that none but a slave could place such an appreciation upon liberty as I did at that time. I wanted to see my mother and sister, that I might tell them that "I was free!" I wanted to see my fellow-slaves in St. Louis, and let them know that the chains were no longer upon my limbs. I wanted to see Captain Price, and let him learn from my own lips that I was no more a chattel, but a MAN. I was anxious, too, thus to inform Mrs. Price that she must get another coachman, and I wanted to see Eliza more than I did Mr. Price or Mrs. Price. The fact that I was a freeman—

could walk, talk, eat, and sleep as a man, and no one to stand over me with the blood-clotted cow-hide—all this made me feel that I was not myself."

The kind Quaker, who so hospitably entertained William, was called Wells Brown. He remained with him about a fortnight, during which time he was well fed and clothed. Before leaving, the Quaker asked him what was his name besides William. The fugitive told him he had no other. "Well," said he, "thee must have another name. Since thee has got out of slavery, thee has become a man, and men always have two names."

William told him that as he was the first man to extend the hand of friendship to him, he would give him the privilege of naming him.

"If I name thee," said he, "I shall call thee Wells Brown, like myself."

"But," said he, "I am not willing to lose my name of William. It was taken from me once against my will, and I am not willing to part with it on any terms."

"Then," said the benevolent man, "I will call thee William Wells Brown."

"So be it," said William Wells Brown, and he has been known by this name ever since.

After giving the newly-christened freeman "a name," the Quaker gave him something to aid him to get "a local habitation." So, after giving him some money, Brown again started for Canada. In four days he reached a public-house, and went in to warm himself. He soon found that he was not out of the reach of his enemies. While warming himself, he heard some men in an adjoining bar-room talking about some runaway slaves. He thought it was time to be off, and, suiting the action to the thought, he was soon in the woods out of sight. When night came, he returned to the road and walked on; and so, for two days and two nights, till he was faint and ready to perish of hunger.

In this condition he arrived in the town of Cleveland, Ohio, on the banks of Lake Erie, where he determined to remain until the spring of the year, and then to try and reach Canada. Here he was compelled to work merely for his food. "Having lived in that way," said he in a speech at a public meeting in Exeter Hall, "for some weeks, I obtained a job, for which I received a shilling. This was not only the only shilling I had, but it was the first I had received after obtaining my freedom, and that shilling made me feel, indeed, as if I had a considerable stock in hand. What to do with my shilling I did not know. I would not put it into the bankers' hands, because, if they would have received it, I would not trust them. I would not lend it out, because I was afraid I should not get it back again. I carried the shilling in my pocket for some time, and finally resolved to lay it out; and after considerable thinking upon the subject, I laid out 6d. for a spelling-book, and the other 6d. for sugar candy or barley sugar. Well, now, you will all say that the one 6d. for the spelling-book was well laid out; and I am of opinion that the other was well laid out too; for the family in which I worked for my bread had two little boys, who attended the school every day, and I wanted to convert them into teachers; so I thought that nothing would act like a charm so much as a little barley sugar. The first day I got my book and stock in trade, I put the book into my bosom, and went to saw wood in the wood-house on a very cold day. One of the boys, a little after four o'clock, passed through the wood-house with a bag of books. I called to him, and I said to him, 'Johnny, do you see this?' taking a stick of barley sugar from my pocket and showing it to him. Says he, 'Yes; give me a taste of it.' Said I, 'I have got a spelling-book too,' and I showed that to him. 'Now,' said I, 'if you come to me in my room, and teach me my A, B, C, I will give you a whole stick' 'Very well,' said he, 'I will; but let me taste it.' 'No; I can't.' 'Let me have it now.' Well, I thought I had better give him a little taste, until the right time came; and I marked the barley sugar about a quarter of an inch down, and told him to bite that far and no farther. He made a grab, and bit half the stick, and ran off laughing. I put the other piece in my pocket, and after a little while the other boy, little David, came through the wood-house with his books. I said nothing about the barley sugar, or my wish to get education. I knew the other lad would communicate the news to him. In a little while he returned, and said, 'Bill, John says you have got some barley sugar.' 'Well,' I said, 'what of that?' 'He said you gave him some; give me a little taste.' 'Well, if you come to-night and help me to learn my letters, I will give you a whole stick.' 'Yes; but let me taste it.' 'Ah! but you want to bite it.' 'No, I don't, but just let me taste it.' Well, I thought I had better show it to him. 'Now,' said he, 'let me touch my tongue against it.' I thought then that I had better give him a taste, but I would not trust him so far as I trusted John; so I called him to me, and got his head under my arm, and took him by the chin, and told him to hold out his tongue; and as he did so, I drew the barley sugar over very lightly. He said, 'That's very nice; just draw it over again.' 'I could stand here and let you draw it across my tongue all day.' The night came on; the two boys came out of their room up into the attic where I was lodging, and there they commenced teaching me the letters of the alphabet. We all laid down upon the floor, covered with the same blanket; and first one would teach me a letter, and then the other, and I would pass the barley sugar from one side to the other. I kept those two boys on my sixpenny worth of barley sugar for about three weeks. Of course I did not let them know how much I had. I first dealt it out to them a quarter of a stick at a time. I worked along in that way, and before I left that place where I was working for my bread, I got so that I could spell. I had a book that had the word *baker* in it, and the boys used to think that when they got so far as that, they were getting on pretty well. I had often passed by the school-house, and stood and listened at the window to hear them spell, and I knew that when they could spell *baker* they thought something of themselves; and I was glad when I got that far. Before I left that place I could read. Finally, from that I went on until I could write. How do you suppose I first commenced writing? for you will understand that up to the present time I never spent a day in school in my life, for I had no money to pay for schooling, so that I had to get my learning first from one and then from another. I carried a piece of chalk in my pocket, and whenever I met a boy I would stop him and take out my chalk and get at a board fence and then commence. First I made some flourishes with no meaning, and called a boy up, and said, 'Do you see that? Can you beat that writing?' Said he, 'That's not writing.' Well, I wanted to get so as to write my own name. I had got out of slavery with only one name. While escaping, I received the hospitality of a very good man, who had spared part of his name to me, and finally my name got pretty long, and I wanted to be able to write it. 'Now, what do you call that?' said the boy, looking at my flourishes. I said, 'Is not that *William Wells Brown?*' 'Give me the chalk,' says he, and he wrote out in large letters '*William Wells Brown,*' and I marked up the fence for nearly a quarter of a mile, trying to copy, till I got so that I could write my name. Then I went on with my chalking, and, in fact, all board fences within half a mile of where I lived were marked over with some kind of figures I had made, in trying to learn how to write. I next obtained an arithmetic, and then a grammar, and I stand here tonight, without having had a day's schooling in my life." Such were some of the efforts made by a fugitive slave to obtain for himself an education. Soon after his escape, Brown was married to a free coloured woman, by whom he has had three daughters, one of whom died in infancy. Having tasted the sweets of freedom himself, his great desire was to extend its blessing to his race, and in the language of the poet he would ask himself,

> "Is true freedom but to break
> Fetters for our own dear sake
> And with leathern hearts forget
> That we owe mankind a debt?

"No! true freedom is to share
All the chains our brothers wear,
And with heart and hand to be
Earnest to make others free."

While acting as a servant to one of the steamers on Lake Erie, Brown often took fugitives from Cleveland and other ports to Buffalo, or Detroit, from either of which places they could cross to Canada in an hour. During the season of 1842, this fugitive slave conveyed no less than *sixty-nine* runaway slaves across Lake Erie, and placed them safe on the soil of Canada. The following interesting account of Brown's first going into business for himself, which we transcribe from his "Three Years in Europe," will show the energy of the man. He says, "In the autumn of 1835, having been cheated out of the previous summer's earnings by the captain of the steamer in which I had been employed running away with the money, I was, like the rest of the men, left without any means of support during the winter, and therefore had to seek employment in the neighbouring towns. I went to the town of Monroe in the state of Michigan, and while going through the principal streets looking for work, I passed the door of the only barber in the town, whose shop appeared to be filled with persons waiting to be shaved. As there was but one man at work, and as I had, while employed in the steamer, occasionally shaved a gentleman who could not perform that office himself, it occurred to me that I might get employment here as a journeyman barber. I therefore made immediate application for work, but the barber told me he did not need a hand. But I was not to be put off so easily, and after making several offers to work cheap, I frankly told him, that if he would not employ me, I would get a room near him, and set up an opposition establishment. This threat, however, made no impression on the barber; and as I was leaving, one of the men, who were waiting to be shaved, said, 'If you want a room in which to commence business, I have one on the opposite side of the street.' This man followed me out; we

went over, and I looked at the room. He strongly urged me
to set up, at the same time promising to give me his influence. I took the room, purchased an old table, two chairs,
got a pole with a red stripe painted around it, and the next
day opened, with a sign over the door, 'Fashionable Hair-
dresser from New York, Emperor of the West.' I need not
add that my enterprise was very annoying to the 'shop over
the way,' especially my sign, which happened to be the most
extensive part of the concern. Of course I had to tell all who
came in, that my neighbour on the opposite side did not
keep clean towels, that his razors were dull, and, above all,
he never had been to New York to see the fashions. Neither
had I. In a few weeks I had the entire business of the town,
to the great discomfiture of the other barber. At this time,
money matters in the Western States were in a sad condition. Any person who could raise a small amount of money
was permitted to establish a bank, and allowed to issue notes
for four times the sum raised. This being the case, many
persons borrowed money merely long enough to exhibit to
the bank inspectors, and the borrowed money was returned,
and the bank left without a dollar in its vaults, if indeed, it
had a vault about its premises. The result was, that banks
were started all over the Western States, and the country
flooded with worthless paper. These were known as the 'Wild
Cat Banks.' Silver coin being very scarce, and the banks not
being allowed to issue notes for a smaller amount than one
dollar, several persons put out notes of from 6 to 75 cents in
value; these were called 'Shinplasters.' The Shinplaster was
in the shape of a promissory note, made payable on demand.
I have often seen persons with large rolls of these bills, the
whole not amounting to more than five dollars. Some weeks
after I had commenced business on my "own hook,' I was
one evening very much crowded with customers; and while
they were talking over the events of the day, one of them
said to me, 'Emperor, you seem to be doing a thriving business. You should do as other business men, issue your Shinplasters.' This of course, as it was intended, created a laugh;

but with me it was no laughing matter, for from that moment I began to think seriously of becoming a banker. I accordingly went a few days after to a printer, and he, wishing to get the job of printing, urged me to put out my notes, and showed me some specimens of engravings that he had just received from Detroit. My head being already filled with the idea of the bank, I needed but little persuasion to set the thing finally afloat. Before I left the printer the notes were partly in type, and I studying how I should keep the public from counterfeiting them. The next day, my Shinplasters were handed to me, the whole amount being twenty dollars; and, after being duly signed, were ready for circulation. The first night I had my money, my head was so turned and dizzy, that I could not sleep. In fact, I slept but little for weeks after the issuing of my bills. This fact satisfied me, that people of wealth pass many sleepless hours. At first my notes did not take well; they were too new, and viewed with a suspicious eye. But through the assistance of my customers, and a good deal of exertion on my part, my bills were soon in circulation; and nearly all the money received in return for my notes was spent in fitting up and decorating my shop. Few bankers get through this world without their difficulties, and I was not to be an exception. A short time after my money had been out, a party of young men, either wishing to pull down my vanity, or to try the soundness of my bank, determined to give it 'a run.' After collecting together a number of my bills, they came one at a time to demand other money for them; and I, not being aware of what was going on, was taken by surprise. One day as I was sitting at my table, stropping some new razors I had just purchased with the avails of my Shinplasters, one of the men entered and said, 'Emperor, you will oblige me if you will give me some other money for these notes of yours.' I immediately cashed the notes with the most worthless of the Wild Cat money that I had on hand, but which was a lawful tender. The young man had scarcely left, when a second appeared with a similar amount, and demanded payment. These were cashed, and soon a third came with his roll of notes. I paid these with an air of triumph, although I had but half a dollar left. I began now to think seriously what I should do, or how to act, provided another demand should be made. While I was thus engaged in thought, I saw the fourth man crossing the street, with a handful of notes, evidently my Shinplasters. I instantaneously shut the door, and looking out of the window said, 'I have closed business for to-day: come to-morrow and I will see you.' In looking across the street, I saw my rival standing at his shopdoor, grinning and clapping his hands at my apparent downfall. I was completely 'done *Brown*' for the day. However, I was not to be 'used up' in this way; so I escaped by the back door, and went in search of my friend, who had first suggested to me the idea of issuing my notes. I found him, told him of the difficulty I was in, and wished him to point out a way by which I might extricate myself. He laughed heartily at my sad position, and then said, 'You must act as all bankers do in this part of the country.' I inquired how they did; and he said, 'when your notes are brought to you, you must redeem them, and then send them out and get other money for them; and, with the latter, you can keep cashing your own Shinplasters.' This was, indeed, a new idea for me. I immediately commenced putting in circulation the notes which I had just redeemed, and my efforts were crowned with such success, that, together with the aid of my friend, who, like a philanthropist and Western Christian as he was, before I slept that night, my Shinplasters were again in circulation, and my bank once more on a sound basis."

In proportion as his mind expanded under the more favourable circumstances in which Brown was placed, he became anxious, not merely for the redemption of his race from personal slavery, but for the moral and religious elevation of those who were free. Finding that habits of intoxication were too prevalent among his coloured brethren, he, in conjunction with others, commenced a temperance reformation in their body. Such was the success of their efforts that, in three

31

years, in the city of Buffalo alone, a society of upwards of 500 members was raised out of a coloured population of less than 700. Of that society Mr. Brown was thrice elected president. The intellectual powers of our author, coupled with his intimate acquaintance with the workings of the slave system, early recommended him to the Abolitionists, as a man eminently qualified to arouse the attention of the people of the Northern States to the great national sin of America. In 1843, he was engaged by the Western New York Anti-Slavery Society as a lecturing agent. From 1844 to 1847, he laboured in the Anti-Slavery cause in connection with the American Anti-Slavery Society; and from that period up to the time of his departure for Europe, in 1849, he was an agent of the Massachusetts Anti-Slavery Society. The records of these societies furnish abundant evidence of the success of his labours. From the Massachusetts Anti-Slavery Society he early received the following testimonial. "Since Mr. Brown became an agent of this society, he has lectured in very many of the towns of this commonwealth, and gained for himself, the respect and esteem of all whom he met. Himself a fugitive slave, he can experimentally describe the situation of those in bonds as bound with them; and he powerfully illustrates the diabolism of that system which keeps in chains and darkness a host of minds, which, if free and enlightened, would shine among men like stars in the firmament." Another member of that society speaks thus of him:—"I need not attempt any description of the ability and efficiency which characterised the speeches of William Wells Brown throughout the meeting. To you who know him so well, it is enough to say that his lectures were worthy of himself. He has left an impression on the minds of the people, that few could have done. Cold indeed must be the hearts that could resist the appeals of so noble a specimen of humanity, in behalf of a crushed and despised race."

In 1847, Mr. Brown wrote a narrative of his life and escape from slavery, which rapidly ran through several editions. A copy of this he forwarded to his old master, from whom he had escaped, and soon after a friend of Mr. Brown's received the following letter:

"*St. Louis, Jan. 10th, 1848*

"Sir,—I received a pamphlet, or a narrative, so called on the title-page, of the Life of William W. Brown, a fugitive slave, purporting to have been written by himself; and in his book I see a letter from you to the said William W. Brown. This said Brown is named William; he is a slave belonging to me, and ran away from me the first day of January, 1834.

"I purchased him of Mr. S. Willi, the last of September, 1833. I paid six hundred and fifty dollars for him. If I had wanted to speculate on him, I could have sold him for three times as much as I paid for him. I was offered two thousand dollars for him in New Orleans at one time, and fifteen hundred dollars for him at another time, in Louisville, Kentucky. But I would not sell him. I was told that he was going to run away, but I did not believe the man, for I had so much confidence in William. I want you to see him, and see if what I say is not the truth. I do not want him as a slave, but I think that his friends, who sustain him and give him the right hand of fellowship, or he himself, could afford to pay my agent in Boston three hundred and twenty five dollars, and I will give him free papers, so that he may go wherever he wishes to. Then he can visit St. Louis, or any other place he may wish.

"This amount is just half what I paid for him. Now, if this offer suits Mr. Brown, and the Anti-Slavery Society of Boston, or Massachusetts, let me know, and I will give you the name of my agent in Boston, and forward the papers, to be given to William W. Brown as soon as the money is paid.

"Yours respectfully,
"To Edmund Quincy, Esq."   "ENOCH PRICE."

While Mr. Brown would most gladly have accepted manumission papers, relieving him from all future claim of the slaveholder, and thereby making his freedom more secure, he yet felt that he could not conscientiously purchase his liberty, because, by so doing, he would be putting money into the pockets of the manstealer which did not justly belong to him. He therefore refused the offer of Mr. Price. Notwithstanding the celebrity he had acquired in the North, as a man of genius and talent, and the general respect ·his high character had gained him, the slave spirit of America denied him the rights of a citizen. By the constitution of the United States he was every moment liable to be arrested, and returned to the slavery from which he had fled. His only protection from such a fate was the anomaly of the ascendancy of the public opinion over the law of the country.

It has been for years thought desirable and advantageous to the cause of Negro emancipation in America, to have some talented man of colour always in Great Britain, who should be a living refutation of the doctrine of the inferiority of the African race; and it was moreover felt that none could so powerfully advocate the cause of "those in bonds" as one who had actually been "bound with them." Mr. Brown having received repeated invitations from distinguished English Abolitionists to visit Great Britain, and being chosen a delegate to the Paris Peace Congress of 1849 by the American Peace Society, and also by a convention of the coloured people of Boston, he resolved to acquiesce in the wishes of his numerous friends, and accordingly sailed from the United States on the 18th of July, 1849.

On leaving America he bore with him the following testimony from the Board of Managers of the Massachusetts Anti-Slavery Society:—

"In consequence of the departure for England of their esteemed friend and faithful co-labourer in the cause of the American slave, William W. Brown, the Board of Management of the Massachusetts Anti-Slavery would commend him to the confidence, respect, esteem, and hospitality of the friends of emancipation wherever he may travel:—

"1. Because he is a fugitive slave from the American house of bondage, and on the soil which gave him birth can find no spot on which he can stand in safety from his pursuers, protected by law.

"2. Because he is a man, and not a chattel; and while as the latter, he may at any time be sold at public vendue under the American star-spangled banner, we rejoice to know that he will be recognised and protected as the former under the flag of England.

"3. Because, for several years past, he has nobly consecrated his time and talents, at great personal hazard, and under the most adverse circumstances, to the uncompromising advocacy of the cause of his enslaved countrymen.

"4. Because he visits England for the purpose of increasing, consolidating, and directing British humanity and piety against that horrible system of slavery in America, by which three millions of human beings, by creation the children of God, are ranked with four-footed beasts, and treated as marketable commodities.

"5. Because he has long been in their employment as a lecturing agent in Massachusetts, and has laboured with great acceptance and success; and from the acquaintance thus formed, they are enabled to certify that he has invariably conducted himself with great circumspection, and won for himself the sympathy, respect, and friendship of a very large circle of acquaintance."

The Coloured convention unanimously passed the following resolution:

"*Resolved*,—That we bid our brother, William Wells Brown, God speed in his mission to Europe, and commend him to the hospitality and encouragement of all true friends of humanity."

In a letter to an American journal, announcing his arrival at Liverpool, he speaks as follows:—

"No person of my complexion can visit this country without being struck with the marked difference between the English and the Americans. The prejudice which I have experienced on all and every occasion in the United States, and to some degree on board the *Canada*, vanished as soon as I set foot on the soil of Britain. In America I had been bought and sold as a slave, in the Southern States. In the so-called Free States I had been treated as one born to occupy an inferior position; in steamers, compelled to take my fare on the deck; in hotels, to take my meals in the kitchen; on coaches, to ride on the outside; in railways, to ride in the 'Negro car;' and in churches, to sit in the 'Negro pew.' But no sooner was I on British soil than I was recognised as a man and an equal. The very dogs in the streets appeared conscious of my manhood. Such is the difference, and such is the change that is brought about by a trip of nine days in an Atlantic steamer. *** For the first time in my life, I can say 'I am truly free.' My old master may make his appearance here, with the constitution of the United States in his pocket, the fugitive slave law in one hand and the chains in the other, and claim me as his property; but all will avail him nothing. I can here stand and look the tyrant in the face, and tell him that I am his equal! England is, indeed, the 'land of the free, and the home of the brave.'"

The reception of Mr. Brown at the Peace Congress in Paris was most flattering. He admirably maintained his reputation as a public speaker. His brief address upon that "war spirit of America which holds in bondage nearly four millions of his brethren," produced a profound sensation. At its conclusion the speaker was warmly greeted by Victor Hugo, the Abbé Duguerry, Emile de Girardin, Richard Cobden, and every man of note in the assembly. At the soirée given by M. de Tocquerelle, the Minister for Foreign Affairs, and the other fêtes given to the members of the Congress, Mr. Brown was received with marked attention.

Having finished his Peace Mission in France, he returned to England, where he was received with a hearty welcome by some of the most influential abolitionists of this country. Most of the fugitive slaves, and in fact nearly all of the coloured men who have visited Great Britain from the United States, have come upon begging missions, either for some society or for themselves. Mr. Brown has been almost the only exception. With that independence of feeling, which those who are acquainted with him know to be one of his chief characteristics, he determined to maintain himself and family by his own exertions—by his literary labours, and the honourable profession of a public lecturer. From nearly all the cities and large provincial towns he received invitations to lecture or address public meetings. The mayors, or other citizens of note, presided over many of these meetings. At Newcastle-upon-Tyne a soirée was given him, and an address presented by the citizens. A large and influential meeting was held at Bolton, Lancashire, which was addressed by Mr. Brown, and at its close the ladies presented to him the following address:—

"An address, presented to Mr. William Wells Brown, the fugitive slave from America, by the ladies of Bolton, March 22nd, 1850:—

"Dear friend and brother,—We cannot permit you to depart from among us without giving expression to the feelings which we entertain towards yourself personally, and to the sympathy which you have awakened in our breasts for the three millions of our sisters and brothers who still suffer and groan in the prison-house of American bondage. You came among us an entire stranger; we received you for the sake of your mission; and having heard the story of your personal wrongs, and gazed with horror on the atrocities of slavery as seen through the medium of your touching descriptions, we are resolved, henceforward, in reliance on divine assistance, to render what aid we can to the cause which you have so eloquently pleaded in our presence.

"We have no words to express our detestation of the crimes which, in the name of liberty, are committed in the country which gave you birth. Language fails to tell our deep abhorrence of the impiety of those who, in the still more sacred name of religion, rob immortal beings not only of an earthly citizenship, but do much to prevent them from obtaining a heavenly one; and, as mothers and daughters, we embrace this opportunity of giving utterance to our utmost indignation at the cruelties perpetrated upon our sex, by a people professedly acknowledging the equality of all mankind. Carry with you, on your return to the land of your nativity, this our solemn protest against the wicked institution which, like a dark and baleful cloud, hangs over it; and ask the unfeeling enslavers, as best you can, to open the prison doors to them that are bound, and let the oppressed go free.

"Allow us to assure you that your brief sojourn in our town has been to ourselves, and to vast multitudes, of a character long to be remembered; and when you are far removed from us, and toiling, as we hope you may be long spared to do, in this righteous enterprise, it may be some solace to your mind to know that our name is cherished with affectionate regard, and that the blessing of the Most High is earnestly supplicated in behalf of yourself, your family, and the cause to which you have consecrated your distinguished talents."

A most respectable and enthusiastic public meeting was held at Sheffield, to welcome Mr. Brown, and the next day he was invited to inspect several of the large establishments there. While going through the manufactory of Messrs. Broadhead and Atkin, silver and electroplaters, &c., in Love-street, and whilst he was being shown through the works, a subscription was hastily set on foot on his behalf, by the workmen and women of the establishment, which was presented to Mr. Brown in the counting-house by a deputation of the subscribers. The spokesman (the designer to Messrs. Broadhead and Atkin) addressing Mr. Brown on behalf of the workpeople, begged his acceptance of the present as a token of esteem, as well as an expression of their sympathy in the cause he advocates, viz, that of the American slave. Mr. Brown briefly thanked the parties for their spontaneous free will offering, accompanied as it was by a generous expression of sympathy for his afflicted brethren and sisters in bondage.

Mr. Brown has been in England nearly four years, and since his arrival he has travelled above twenty thousand miles through Great Britain, addressed one hundred and thirty public meetings, lectured in twenty-three mechanics and literary institutions, and given his services to many of the benevolent and religious societies on the occasion of their anniversary meetings. After a lecture, which he delivered before the Whittington Club, he received from the managers of that institution the following testimonial:

> *"Whittington Club and Metropolitan Athenaeum,*
> *"189, Strand, June 21, 1850*

"My dear sir,

I have much pleasure in conveying to you the best thanks of the Managing Committee of this institution for the excellent lecture you gave here last evening, and also in presenting you in their names with an honorary membership of the club. It is hoped that you will often avail yourself of its privileges by coming amongst us. You will then see, by the cordial welcome of the members, that they protest against the odious distinctions made between man and man, and the abominable traffic of which you have been the victim.

"For my own part, I shall be happy to be serviceable to you in any way, and at all times be glad to place the advantages of the institution at your disposal.

> "I am, my dear sir,
> "Yours truly,
> "WILLIAM STRUDWICKE,

"Mr. W. Wells Brown."   "Secretary."

On the 1st of August, 1851, a meeting of the most novel character was held at the Hall of Commerce, London, the chief actors being American fugitive slaves. That meeting was most ably presided over by Mr. Brown, and the speeches made on the occasion by fugitive slaves were of the most interesting and creditable description. Although a residence in Canada is infinitely preferable to slavery in America, yet the climate of that country is uncongenial to the constitutions of the Negroes, and their lack of education is an almost

insuperable barrier to their social progress. The latter evil
Mr. Brown attempted to remedy by the establishment of
Manual Labour Schools in Canada for fugitive slaves. A public meeting, attended by between 3,000 and 4,000 persons,
was held on the 6th of January 1851, in the City Hall, Glas-
gow, which was presided over by Alexander Hastie, Esq.,
M.P., at which resolutions were unanimously passed, approv-
ing of Mr. Brown's scheme; which scheme, however, never
received that amount of support which would have enabled
him to bring it into practice; and the plan at present only
remains as an evidence of its author's ingenuity and desire
for the elevation of his oppressed and injured race. Mr. Brown
subsequently made, through the columns of the *Times*, a
proposition for the emigration of American fugitive slaves,
under fair and honourable terms, from Canada to the West
Indies, where there is a great lack of that labour which they
are so capable of undertaking. These efforts all show the willingness of this fugitive slave to aid those of his race. Last
year Mr. Brown published his "Three Years in Europe; or,
Places I have seen and People I have met." And his literary
abilities may be partly judged of from the following commen-
dations of that ably written work:—

"The extraordinary excitement produced by 'Uncle Tom's
Cabin' will, we hope, prepare the public of Great Britain
and America for this lively book of travels by a real fugitive
slave. Though he never had a day's schooling in his life, he
has produced a literary work not unworthy of a highly educated gentleman. Our readers will find in these letters much
instruction, not a little entertainment, and the beatings of a
manly heart, on behalf of a down-trodden race, with which
they will not fail to sympathise."—*The Eclectic.*

"When he writes on the wrongs of his race, or the events
of his own career, he is always interesting or amusing."—*The
Athenaem.*

"The appearance of this book is too remarkable a literary
event to pass without a notice. At the moment when atten-

tion in this country is directed to the state of the coloured people in America, the book appears with additional advantage; if nothing else were attained by its publication, it is well to have another proof of the capability of the Negro intellect. Altogether Mr. Brown has written a pleasing and amusing volume. Contrasted with the caricature and bombast of his white countrymen, Mr. Willis's description of 'People he has met,' a comparison suggested by the similarity of the title, it is both in intellect and in style a superior performance, and we are glad to bear this testimony to the literary merit of a work by a Negro author."—*The Literary Gazette.*

"That a man who was a slave for the first twenty years of his life, and who has never had a day's schooling, should produce such a book as this, cannot but astonish those who speak disparagingly of the African race."—*The Weekly News and Chronicle.*

"This remarkable book of a remarkable man cannot fail to add to the practical protests already entered in Britain against the absolute bondage of 3,000,000 of our fellow creatures. The impression of a self-educated son of slavery here set forth, must hasten the period when the senseless and impious denial of common claims to a common humanity, on the score of colour, shall be scouted with scorn in every civilised and Christian country. And when this shall be attained, among the means of destruction of the hideous abomination, his compatriots will remember with respect and gratitude the doings and sayings of William Wells Brown. The volume consists of a sufficient variety of scenes, persons, arguments, inferences, speculations, and opinions, to satisfy and amuse the most *exigeant* of those who read *pour se desennuyer;* while those who look deeper into things, and view with anxious hope the progress of nations and of mankind, will feel that the good cause of humanity and freedom, of Christianity, enlightenment, and brotherhood, cannot fail to be served by such a book as this."—*Morning Advertiser.*

"He writes with ease and ability, and his intelligent observations upon the great question to which he has devoted, and is devoting his life, will be read with interest, and will command influence and respect."—*Daily News*.

Mr. Brown is most assiduous in his studies even at the present time. The following extract from his writings will show how he spends most of his leisure hours:—

"It was eight o'clock before I reached my lodgings. Although fatigued by the day's exertions, I again resumed the reading of Roscoe's 'Leo X.,' and had nearly finished seventy-three pages, when the clock on St. Martin's Church apprised me that it was two. He who escapes from slavery at the age of twenty years without any education, as did the writer of this letter, must read when others are asleep, if he would catch up with the rest of the world. 'To be wise,' says Pope, 'is but to know how little can be known.' The true searcher after truth and knowledge is always like a child; although gaining strength from year to year, he still 'learns to labour and to wait.' The field of labour is ever expanding before him, reminding him that he has yet more to learn; teaching him that he is nothing more than a child in knowledge, and inviting him onward with a thousand varied charms. The son may take possession of the father's goods at his death, but he cannot inherit with the property the father's cultivated mind. He may put on the father's old coat, but that is all; the immortal mind of the first wearer has gone to the tomb. Property may be bequeathed but knowledge cannot. Then let him who would be useful in his generation be up and doing. Like the Chinese student who learned perseverance from the woman whom he saw trying to rub a crowbar into a needle, so should we take the experience of the past to lighten our feet through the paths of the future."

The following testimonial to Mr. Brown's abilities, from an American journal of which Frederick Douglas [*sic*] is editor, shows that his talents are highly appreciated in that country:—

"We have the pleasure to lay before our readers another interesting letter from W. Wells Brown. We rejoice to find our friend still persevering in the pursuit of knowledge, and still more do we rejoice to find such marked evidence of his rapid progress as his several letters afford. But a few years ago he was a despised, degraded, whip-scarred slave, knowing nothing of letters; and now we find him writing accounts of his travels in a distant land, of which a man reared under the most favourable educational advantages might be proud."

We should have said that it was Mr. Brown's intention to have returned to the United States to his family ere this. But the passage of the infamous "Fugitive Slave Law" prevented his returning.

Mr. Brown's wife died in Buffalo N. Y. in Jan. 1851. He has two daughters who are now in this country, being trained for teachers. Of course we need not add that for their education they are entirely dependent on their father's exertions. During last year, the Rev. Edward Hore, of Ramsgate, through a willingness to assist Mr. Brown in returning to the United States, wrote to his former owner, and offered him £50, if he would relinquish all claim to him, and furnish the fugitive with papers of emancipation, but the following note from the slaveowner speaks for itself:—

"*St. Louis, Feb. 16th, 1852*

"Rev. Sir,—I received your note, dated Jan 6th, concerning a runaway slave of mine now known by the name of William Wells Brown. You state that I offered to take three hundred and twenty five dollars for him, and give him free papers, in 1848. I did so then, but since that time the laws of the United States are materially changed. The Fugitive Slave Bill has passed since then. I can now take him anywhere in the United States, and I have everything arranged for his arrest if he lands at any port in the Untied States. But I will give him papers of emancipation, properly authenticated by our statutes, for the sum of five hundred dollars (or £100) that will make him as free as any white person. If this suits your views, you can let me know, and I will have the papers made out and forwarded to Boston, to Joseph Gruley, of the firm of Charles Wilkins and Co., 33, Long Wharf. The money must be paid before the papers are handed over to your agent.

"Respectfully your obedient servant,

"To the Rev. Edward Hore."   "ENOCH PRICE"

CHAPTER I

The Negro Sale

"Why stands she near the auction stand,
That girl so young and fair?
What brings her to this dismal place,
Why stands she weeping there?"

With the growing population of slaves in the Southern States of America, there is a fearful increase of half whites, most of whose fathers are slaveowners, and their mothers slaves. Society does not frown upon the man who sits with his mulatto child upon his knee, whilst its mother stands a slave behind his chair. The late Henry Clay, some years since, predicted that the abolition of Negro slavery would be brought about by the amalgamation of the races. John Randolph, a distinguished slaveholder of Virginia, and a prominent statesman, said in a speech in the legislature of his native state, that "the blood of the first American statesmen coursed through the veins of the slave of the South." In all the cities and towns of the slave states, the real Negro, or clear black, does not amount to more than one in every four of the slave population. This fact is, of itself, the best evidence of the degraded and immoral condition of the relation of master and slave in the United States of America.

In all the slave states, the law says:—"Slaves shall be deemed, sold [held], taken, reputed, and adjudged in law to be chattels personal in the hands of their owners and possessors, and their executors, administrators and assigns, to all intents, constructions, and purposes whatsoever. A slave is one who is in the power of a master to whom he belongs.

The master may sell him, dispose of his person, his industry, and his labour. He can do nothing, possess nothing, nor acquire anything, but what must belong to his master. The slave is entirely subject to the will of his master, who may correct and chastise him, though not with unusual rigour, or so as to maim and mutilate him, or expose him to the danger of loss of life, or to cause his death. The slave, to remain a slave, must be sensible that there is no appeal from his master." Where the slave is placed by law entirely under the control of the man who claims him, body and soul, as property, what else could be expected than the most depraved social condition? The marriage relation, the oldest and most sacred institution given to man by his Creator, is unknown and unrecognised in the slave laws of the United States. Would that we could say, that the moral and religious teaching in the slave states were better than the laws; but, alas! we cannot. A few years since, some slaveholders became a little uneasy in their minds about the rightfulness of permitting slaves to take to themselves husbands and wives, while they still had others living, and applied to their religious teachers for advice; and the following will show how this grave and important subject was treated:—

"Is a servant, whose husband or wife has been sold by his or her master into a distant country, to be permitted to marry again?"

The query was referred to a committee, who made the following report; which, after discussion, was adopted:—

"That, in view of the circumstances in which servants in this country are placed, the committee are unanimous in the opinion, that it is better to permit servants thus circumstanced to take another husband or wife."

Such was the answer from a committee of the "Shiloh Baptist Association;" and instead of receiving light, those who asked the question were plunged into deeper darkness!

A similar question was put to the "Savannah River Association," and the answer, as the following will show, did not materially differ from the one we have already given:—

"Whether, in a case of involuntary separation, of such a character as to preclude all prospect of future intercourse, the parties ought to be allowed to marry again."

Answer—

"That such separation among persons situated as our slaves are, is civilly a separation by death; and they believe that, in the sight of God, it would be so viewed. To forbid second marriages in such cases would be to expose the parties, not only to stronger hardships and strong temptation, but to church-censure for acting in obedience to their masters, who cannot be expected to acquiesce in a regulation at variance with justice to the slaves, and to the spirit of that command which regulates marriage among Christians. The slaves are not free agents; and a dissolution by death is not more entirely without their consent, and beyond their control, than by such separation."

Although marriage, as the above indicates, is a matter which the slaveholders do not think is of any importance, or of any binding force with their slaves; yet it would be doing that degraded class an injustice, not to acknowledge that many of them do regard it as a sacred obligation, and show a willingness to obey the commands of God on this subject. Marriage is, indeed, the first and most important institution of human existence—the foundation of all civilisation and culture—the root of church and state. It is the most intimate covenant of heart formed among mankind; and for many reasons the only relation in which they feel the true sentiments of humanity. It gives scope for every human virtue, since each of these is developed from the love and confidence which here predominate. It unites all which ennobles and beautifies life,—sympathy, kindness of will and deed, gratitude, devotion, and every delicate, intimate feeling. As the only asylum for true education, it is the first and last sanctuary of human culture. As husband and wife, through each other become conscious of complete humanity, and every human feeling, and every human virtue; so children, at their first awakening in the fond covenant of love between parents, both of whom are tenderly concerned for the same object, find an image of complete humanity leagued in free love. The spirit of love which prevails between them acts with creative power upon the young mind, and awakens every germ of goodness within it. This invisible and incalculable influence of parental life acts more upon the child than all the efforts of education, whether by means of instruction, precept, or exhortation. If this be a true picture of the vast influence for good of the institution of marriage, what must be the moral degradation of that people to whom marriage is denied? Not content with depriving them of all the higher and holier enjoyments of this relation, by degrading and darkening their souls, the slaveholder denies to his victim even that slight alleviation of his misery, which would result from the marriage relation being protected by law and public opinion. Such is the influence of slavery in the United States, that the ministers of religion, even in the so-called free states, are the mere echoes, instead of the correctors, of public sentiment.

We have thought it advisable to show that the present system of chattel slavery in America undermines the entire social condition of man, so as to prepare the reader for the following narrative of slave life, in that otherwise happy and prosperous country.

In all the large towns in the Southern States, there is a class of slaves who are permitted to hire their time of their owners, and for which they pay a high price. These are mulatto women, or quadroons, as they are familiarly known, and are distinguished for their fascinating beauty. The handsomest usually pays the highest price for her time. Many of these women are the favourites of persons who furnish them with the means of paying their owners, and not a few are dressed in the most extravagant manner. Reader, when you take into consideration the fact, that amongst the slave population no safeguard is thrown around virtue, and no inducement held out to slave women to be chaste, you will not be surprised when we tell you that immorality and vice pervade the cities of the Southern States in a manner unknown in the cities and towns of the Northern States. Indeed most of the slave women have no higher aspiration than that of becoming the finely-dressed mistress of some white man. And at Negro balls and parties, this class of women usually cut the greatest figure.

At the close of the year——the following advertisement appeared in a newspaper published in Richmond, the capital of the state of Virginia:—"Notice: Thirty-eight Negroes will be offered for sale on Monday, November 10th, at twelve o'clock, being the entire stock of the late John Graves, Esq. The Negroes are in good condition, some of them very prime; among them are several mechanics, able-bodied field hands, ploughboys, and women with children at the breast, and some of them very prolific in their generating qualities, affording a rare opportunity to any one who wishes to raise a strong and healthy lot of servants for their own use. Also several mulatto girls of rare personal qualities: two of them very superior. Any gentleman or lady wishing to purchase, can take any of the above slaves on trial for a week, for which no charge will be made." Amongst the above slaves to be sold were Currer and her two daughters, Clotel and Althesa; the latter were the girls spoken of in the advertisement as "very superior." Currer was a bright mulatto, and of prepossessing appearance, though then nearly forty years of age. She had hired her time for more than twenty years, during which time she had lived in Richmond. In her younger days Currer had been the housekeeper of a young slaveholder; but of later years had been a laundress or washerwoman, and was considered to be a woman of great taste in getting up linen. The gentleman for whom she had kept house was Thomas Jefferson, by whom she had two daughters. Jefferson being called to Washington to fill a government appointment, Currer was left behind, and thus she took herself to the business of washing, by which means she paid her master, Mr. Graves, and supported herself and two children. At the time of the decease of her master, Currer's daughters, Clotel and Althesa, were aged respectively sixteen and fourteen years, and both, like most of their own sex in America, were well grown. Currer early resolved to bring her daughters up as ladies, as she termed it, and therefore imposed little or no work upon them. As her daughters grew older, Currer had to pay a stipulated price for them; yet her notoriety as a laundress of the first class enabled her to put an extra price upon her charges, and thus she and her daughters lived in comparative luxury. To bring up Clotel and Althesa to attract attention, and especially at balls and parties, was the great aim of Currer. Although the term "Negro ball" is applied to most of these gatherings, yet a majority of the attendants are often whites. Nearly all the Negro parties in the cities and towns of the Southern States are made up of quadroon and mulatto girls, and white men. These are democratic gatherings, where gentlemen, shopkeepers, and their clerks, all appear upon terms of perfect equality. And there is a degree of gentility and decorum in these companies that is not surpassed by similar gatherings of white people in the Slave States. It was at one of these parties that Horatio Green, the son of a wealthy gentleman of Richmond, was first introduced to Clotel. The young man had just returned from college, and was in his twenty-second year. Clotel was sixteen, and was admitted by all to be the most beautiful girl, coloured or white, in the city. So attentive was the young man to the quadroon during the evening that it was noticed by all, and became a matter of general conversation; while Currer appeared delighted beyond measure at her daughter's conquest. From that evening, young Green became the favourite visitor at Currer's house. He soon promised to purchase Clotel, as speedily as it could be effected, and make her mistress of her own dwelling; and Currer looked forward with pride to the time when she should see her daughter emancipated and free. It was a beautiful moonlight night in August, when all who reside in tropical climes are eagerly gasping for a breath of fresh air, that Horatio Green was seated in the small garden behind Currer's cottage, with the object of his affections by his side. And it was here that Horatio drew from his pocket the newspaper, wet from the press, and read the advertisement for the sale of the slaves to which we have alluded; Currer and her two daughters being of the number. At the close of the evening's visit, and as the young man was leaving, he said to the girl, "You shall soon be free and your own mistress."

As might have been expected, the day of sale brought an unusual large number together to compete for the property to be sold. Farmers who make a business of raising slaves for the market were there; slave-traders and speculators were also numerously represented; and in the midst of this throng was one who felt a deeper interest in the result of the sale than any other of the bystanders; this was young Green. True to his promise, he was there with a blank bank check in his pocket, awaiting with impatience to enter the list as a bidder for the beautiful slave. The less valuable slaves were first placed upon the auction block, one after another, and sold to the highest bidder. Husbands and wives were separated with a degree of indifference that is unknown in any other relation of life, except that of slavery. Brothers and sisters were torn from each other; and mothers saw their children leave them for the last time on this earth.

It was late in the day, when the greatest number of persons were thought to be present, that Currer and her daughters were brought forward to the place of sale. Currer was first ordered to ascend the auction stand, which she did with a trembling step. The slave mother was sold to a trader. Althesa, the youngest, and who was scarcely less beautiful than her sister, was sold to the same trader for one thousand dollars. Clotel was the last, and, as was expected, commanded a higher price than any that had been offered for sale that day. The appearance of Clotel on the auction block created a deep sensation amongst the crowd. There she stood, with a complexion as white as most of those who were waiting with a wish to become her purchasers; her features as finely defined as any of her sex of pure Anglo-Saxon; her long black wavy hair done up in the neatest manner; her form tall and graceful, and her whole appearance indicating one superior to her position. The auctioneer commenced by saying that "Miss Clotel had been reserved for the last, because she was the most valuable. How much, gentlemen? Real Albino, fit for a fancy girl for any one. She enjoys good health, and has a sweet temper. How much do you say?"

"Five hundred dollars."

"Only five hundred for such a girl as this? Gentlemen, she is worth a deal more than that sum; you certainly don't know the value of the article you are bidding upon. Here, gentlemen, I hold in my hand a paper certifying that she has a good moral character."

"Seven hundred."

"Ah; gentlemen, that is something like. This paper also states that she is very intelligent."

"Eight hundred."

"She is a devoted Christian, and perfectly trustworthy."

"Nine hundred."

"Nine fifty."

"Ten."

"Eleven."

"Twelve hundred." Here the sale came to a dead stand. The auctioneer stopped, looked around, and began in a rough manner to relate some anecdotes relative to the sale of slaves, which, he said, had come under his own observation. At this juncture the scene was indeed strange. Laughing, joking, swearing, smoking, spitting, and talking kept up a continual hum and noise amongst the crowd; while the slave-girl stood with tears in her eyes, at one time looking towards her mother and sister, and at another towards the young man whom she hoped would become her purchaser.

"The chastity of this girl is pure; she has never been from under her mother's care; she is a virtuous creature."

"Thirteen."

"Fourteen."

"Fifteen."

"Fifteen hundred dollars," cried the auctioneer, and the maiden was struck for that sum. This was a Southern auction, at which the bones, muscles, sinews, blood, and nerves of a young lady of sixteen were sold for five hundred dollars; her moral character for two hundred; her improved intellect for one hundred; her Christianity for three hundred; and her chastity and virtue for four hundred dollars more. And this, too, in a city thronged with churches, whose tall spires look like so many signals pointing to heaven, and whose ministers preach that slavery is a God-ordained institution!

What words can tell the inhumanity, the atrocity, and the immorality of that doctrine which, from exalted office, commends such a crime to the favour of enlightened and Christian people? What indignation from all the world is not due to the government and people who put forth all their strength and power to keep in existence such an institution? Nature abhors it; the age repels it; and Christianity needs all her meekness to forgive it.

Clotel was sold for fifteen hundred dollars, but her purchaser was Horatio Green. Thus closed a Negro sale, at which two daughters of Thomas Jefferson, the writer of the Declaration of American Independence, and one of the presidents of the great republic, were disposed of to the highest bidder!

"O God! My every heart-string cries,
    Dost thou these scenes behold
In this our boasted Christian land,
    And must the truth be told?

"Blush, Christian, blush! for e'en the dark,
    Untutored heathen see
Thy inconsistency; and, lo!
    They scorn thy God, and thee!"

CHAPTER II

Going to the South

"My country, shall thy honoured name,
   Be as a bye-word through the world?
Rouse! for, as if to blast thy fame,
   This keen reproach is at thee hurled;
The banner that above the waves,
   Is floating o'er three million slaves."

Dick Walker, the slave speculator, who had purchased Currer and Althesa, put them in prison until his gang was made up, and then, with his forty slaves, started for the New Orleans market. As many of the slaves had been brought up in Richmond, and had relations residing there, the slave-trader determined to leave the city early in the morning, so as not to witness any of those scenes so common where slaves are separated from their relatives and friends, when about departing for the Southern market. This plan was successful; for not even Clotel, who had been every day at the prison to see her mother and sister, knew of their departure. A march of eight days through the interior of the state, and they arrived on the banks of the Ohio river, where they were all put on board a steamer, and then speedily sailed for the place of their destination.

Walker had already advertised in the New Orleans papers, that he would be there at a stated time with "a prime lot of able-bodied slaves ready for field service; together with a few extra ones, between the ages of fifteen and twenty-five." But, like most who make a business of buying and selling slaves for gain, he often bought some who were far advanced in years, and would always try to sell them for five or ten years younger than they actually were. Few persons can arrive at anything like the age of a Negro, by mere observation, unless they are well acquainted with the race. Therefore the slave-trader very frequently carried out this deception with perfect impunity. After the steamer had left the wharf, and was fairly on the bosom of the Father of Waters, Walker called his servant Pompey to him, and instructed him as to "getting the Negroes ready for market." Amongst the forty Negroes were several whose appearance indicated that they had seen some years, and had gone through some services. Their grey hair and whiskers at once pronounced them to be above the ages set down in the trader's advertisement. Pompey had long been with the trader, and knew his business; and if he did not take delight in discharging his duty, he did it with a degree of alacrity, so that he might receive the approbation of his master. "Pomp," as Walker usually called him, was of real Negro blood, and would often say, when alluding to himself, "Dis nigger is no countefit; he is de genewine artekil." Pompey was of low stature, round face, and, like most of his race, had a set of teeth, which for whiteness and beauty could not be surpassed; his eyes large, lips thick, and hair short and woolly. Pompey had been with Walker so long, and had seen so much of the buying and selling of slaves, that he appeared perfectly indifferent to the heartrending scenes which daily occurred in his presence. It was on the second day of the steamer's voyage that Pompey selected five of the old slaves, took them in a room by themselves, and commenced preparing them for the market. "Well," said Pompey, addressing himself to the company, "I is de gent-man dat is to get you ready, so dat you will bring marser a good price in de Orleans market. How old is you?" addressing himself to a man who, from appearance, was not less than forty.

"If I live to see next corn-planting time I will either be forty-five or fifty-five, I don't know which."

"Dat may be," replied Pompey; "But now you is only thirty years old; dat is what marser says you is to be."

"I know I is more den dat," responded the man.

"I knows nothing about dat," said Pompey; "but when you get in de market, an anybody axe you how old you is, an you tell 'em forty-five, marser will tie you up an gib you de whip like smoke. But if you tell 'em dat you is only thirty, den he wont."

"Well, den, I guess I will only be thirty when dey axe me," replied the chattel.

"What your name?" inquired Pompey.

"Geemes," answered the man.

"Oh, Uncle Jim, is it?"

"Yes."

"Den you must have off dem dare whiskers of yours, an when you get to Orleans you must grease dat face an make it look shiney." This was all said by Pompey in a manner which clearly showed that he knew what he was about.

"How old is you?" asked Pompey of a tall, strong-looking man.

"I was twenty-nine last potato-digging time," said the man.

"What's your name?"

"My name is Tobias, but dey call me 'Toby.' "

"Well, Toby, or Mr. Tobias, if dat will suit you better, you is now twenty-three years old, an no more. Dus you hear dat?"

"Yes," responded Toby.

Pompey gave each to understand how old he was to be when asked by persons who wished to purchase, and then reported to his master that the "old boys" were all right. At eight o'clock on the evening of the third day, the lights of another steamer were seen in the distance, and apparently coming up very fast. This was a signal for a general commotion on the Patriot, and everything indicated that a steamboat race was at hand. Nothing can exceed the excitement attendant upon a steamboat on the Mississippi river.

By the time the boats had reached Memphis, they were side by side, and each exerting itself to keep the ascendancy in point of speed. The night was clear, the moon shining brightly, and the boats so near to each other that the passengers were calling out from one boat to the other. On board the Patriot, the firemen were using oil, lard, butter, and even bacon, with the wood, for the purpose of raising the steam to its highest pitch. The blaze, mingled with the black smoke, showed plainly that the other boat was burning more than wood. The two boats soon locked, so that the hands of the boats were passing from vessel to vessel, and the wildest excitement prevailed throughout amongst both passengers and crew. At this moment the engineer of the Patriot was seen to fasten down the safety-valve, so that no steam should escape. This was, indeed, a dangerous resort. A few of the boat hands who saw what had taken place, left that end of the boat for more secure quarters.

The Patriot stopped to take in passengers, and still no steam was permitted to escape. At the starting of the boat cold water was forced into the boilers by the machinery, and, as might have been expected, one of the boilers immediately exploded. One dense fog of steam filled every part of the vessel, while shrieks, groans, and cries were heard on every hand. The saloons and cabins soon had the appearance of a hospital. By this time the boat had landed, and the Columbia, the other boat, had come alongside to render assistance to the disabled steamer. The killed and scalded (nineteen in number) were put on shore, and the Patriot, taken in tow by the Columbia, was soon again on its way.

It was now twelve o'clock at night, and instead of the passengers being asleep the majority were gambling in the saloons. Thousands of dollars change hands during a passage from Louisville or St. Louis to New Orleans on a Mississippi steamer, and many men, and even ladies, are completely ruined. "Go call my boy, steward," said Mr. Smith, as he took his cards one by one from the table. In a few moments a fine looking, bright-eyed mulatto boy, apparently about fifteen years of age, was standing by his master's side at the table. "I will see you, and five hundred dollars better," said Smith, as his servant Jerry approached the table.

"What price do you set on that boy?" asked Johnson, as he took a roll of bills from his pocket.

"He will bring a thousand dollars, any day, in the New Orleans market," replied Smith.

"Then you bet the whole of the boy, do you?"

"Yes."

"I call you, then," said Johnson, at the same time spreading his cards out upon the table.

"You have beat me," said Smith, as soon as he saw the cards. Jerry, who was standing on top of the table, with the bank notes and silver dollars round his feet, was now ordered to descend from the table.

"You will not forget that you belong to me," said Johnson, as the young slave was stepping from the table to a chair.

"No, sir," replied the chattel.

"Now go back to your bed, and be up in time to-morrow morning to brush my clothes and clean my boots, do you hear?"

"Yes, sir," responded Jerry, as he wiped the tears from his eyes.

Smith took from his pocket the bill of sale and handed it to Johnson; at the same time saying, "I claim the right of redeeming that boy, Mr. Johnson. My father gave him to me when I came of age, and I promised not to part with him."

"Most certainly, sir, the boy shall be yours, whenever you hand me over a cool thousand," replied Johnson.

The next morning, as the passengers were assembling in the breakfast saloons and upon the guards of the vessel, and the servants were seen running about waiting upon or looking for their masters, poor Jerry was entering his new master's state-room with his boots.

"Who do you belong to?" said a gentleman to an old black man, who came along leading a fine dog that he had been feeding.

"When I went to sleep last night, I belonged to Governor Lucas; but I understand dat he is bin gambling all night, so I don't know who owns me dis morning." Such is the uncertainty of a slave's position. He goes to bed at night the property of the man with whom he has lived for years, and gets up in the morning the slave of some one whom he has never seen before! To behold five or six tables in a steamboat's cabin, with half-a-dozen men playing at cards, and money, pistols, bowie-knives, &c. all in confusion on the tables, is what may be seen at almost any time on the Mississippi river.

On the fourth day, while at Natchez, taking in freight and passengers, Walker, who had been on shore to see some of his old customers, returned, accompanied by a tall, thin-faced man, dressed in black, with a white neckcloth, which immediately proclaimed him to be a clergyman. "I want a good, trusty woman for house service," said the stranger, as they entered the cabin where Walker's slaves were kept.

"Here she is, and no mistake," replied the trader.

"Stand up, Currer, my gal; here's a gentleman who wishes to see if you will suit him."

Althesa clung to her mother's side, as the latter rose from her seat.

"She is a rare cook, a good washer, and will suit you to a T, I am sure."

"If you buy me, I hope you will buy my daughter too," said the woman, in rather an excited manner.

"I only want one for my own use, and would not need another," said the man in black, as he and the trader left the room. Walker and the parson went into the saloon, talked over the matter, the bill of sale was made out, the money paid over, and the clergyman left, with the understanding that the woman should be delivered to him at his house. It seemed as if poor Althesa would have wept herself to death, for the first two days after her mother had been torn from her side by the hand of the ruthless trafficker in human flesh. On the arrival of the boat at Baton Rouge, an additional number of passengers were taken on board; and, amongst them, several persons who had been attending the races. Gambling and drinking were now the order of the day. Just as the ladies and gentlemen were assembling at the supper-table, the report of a pistol was heard in the direction of the Social Hall, which caused great uneasiness to the ladies, and took the gentlemen to that part of the cabin. However, nothing serious had occurred. A man at one of the tables where they were gambling had been seen attempting to conceal a card in his sleeve, and one of the party seized his pistol and fired; but fortunately the barrel of the pistol was knocked up, just as it was about to be discharged, and the ball passed through the upper deck, instead of the man's head, as intended. Order was soon restored; all went on well the remainder of the night, and the next day, at ten o'clock, the boat arrived at New Orleans, and the passengers went to the hotels and the slaves to the market!

> "Our eyes are yet on Afric's shores,
> Her thousand wrongs we still deplore;
> We see the grim slave trader there;
> We hear his fettered victim's prayer;
> And hasten to the sufferer's aid,
> Forgetful of *our own 'slave trade.'*

> "The Ocean 'Pirate's' fiend-like form
> Shall sink beneath the vengeance-storm;
> His heart of steel shall quake before
> The battle-din and havoc roar:
> *The knave shall die*, the Law hath said,
> While it protects our own *'slave trade.'*

> "What earthly eye presumes to scan
> The wily Proteus-heart of man?—
> What potent hand will e'er unroll
> The mantled treachery of his soul!—
> O where is he who hath surveyed
> The horrors of *our own 'slave trade?'*

"There is an eye that wakes in light,
  There is a hand of peerless might;
  Which, soon or late, shall yet assail
  And rend dissimulation's veil:
  Which *will* unfold the masquerade
  Which justifies *our own 'slave trade.'* "

CHAPTER III

The Negro Chase

We shall now return to Natchez, where we left Currer in the hands of the Methodist parson. For many years, Natchez has enjoyed a notoriety for the inhumanity and barbarity of its inhabitants, and the cruel deeds perpetrated there, which have not been equalled in any other city in the Southern States. The following advertisements, which we take from a newspaper published in the vicinity, will show how they catch their Negroes who believe in the doctrine that "all men are created free."

"NEGRO DOGS.—The undersigned, having bought the entire pack of Negro dogs (of the Hay and Allen stock), *he now proposes to catch runaway Negroes*. His charges will be three dollars a day for hunting, and fifteen dollars for catching a runaway. He resides three and one half miles north of Livingston, near the lower Jones' Bluff Road.

"Nov. 6, 1845." "WILLIAM GAMBREL."

"NOTICE.—The subscriber, living on Carroway Lake, on Hoe's Bayou, in Carroll parish, sixteen miles on the road leading from Bayou Mason to Lake Providence, is ready with a pack of dogs to hunt runaway Negroes at any time. These dogs are well trained, and are known throughout the parish. Letters addressed to me at Providence will secure immediate attention. My terms are five dollars per day for hunting the trails, whether the Negro is caught or not. Where a twelve hours' trail is shown, and the Negro not taken, no charge is made. For taking a Negro, twenty-five dollars, and no charge made for hunting.

"Nov. 26, 1847."   "JAMES W. HALL."

These dogs will attack a Negro at their master's bidding and cling to him as the bull-dog will cling to a beast. Many are the speculations, as to whether the Negro will be secured alive or dead, when these dogs once get on his track. A slave hunt took place near Natchez, a few days after Currer's arrival, which was calculated to give her no favourable opinion of the people. Two slaves had run off owing to severe punishment. The dogs were put upon their trail. The slaves went into the swamps, with the hope that the dogs when put on their scent would be unable to follow them through the water. The dogs soon took to the swamp, which lies between the highlands, which was now covered with water, waist deep: here these faithful animals, *swimming* nearly all the time, followed the zigzag course, the tortuous twistings and windings of these two fugitives, who, it was afterwards discovered, were lost; sometimes scenting the tree wherein they had found a temporary refuge from the mud and water; at other places where the deep mud had pulled off a shoe, and they had not taken time to put it on again. For two hours and a half, for four or five miles, did men and dogs wade through this bushy, dismal swamp, surrounded with grim-visaged alligators, who seemed to look on with jealous eye at this encroachment of their hereditary domain; now losing the trail—then slowly and dubiously taking it off again, until they triumphantly threaded it out, bringing them back to the river, where it was found that the Negroes had crossed their own trail, near the place of starting. In the meantime a heavy shower had taken place, putting out the trail. The Negroes were now at least four miles ahead.

It is well known to hunters that it requires the keenest scent and best blood to overcome such obstacles, and yet these persevering and sagacious animals conquered every difficulty. The slaves now made a straight course for the Baton Rouge and Bayou Sara road, about four miles distant.

Feeling hungry now, after their morning walk, and perhaps thirsty, too, they went about half a mile off the road, and ate a good, hearty, substantial breakfast. Negroes must eat, as well as other people, but the dogs will tell on them. Here, for a moment, the dogs are at fault, but soon unravel the mystery, and bring them back to the road again; and now what before was wonderful, becomes almost a miracle. Here, in this common highway—the thoroughfare for the whole country around—through mud and through mire, meeting waggons and teams, and different solitary wayfarers, and, what above all is most astonishing, actually running through a gang of Negroes, their favourite game, who were working on the road, they pursue the track of the two Negroes; they even ran for eight miles to the very edge of the plain—the slaves near them for the last mile. At first they would fain believe it some hunter chasing deer. Nearer and nearer the whimpering pack presses on; the delusion begins to dispel; all at once the truth flashes upon them like a glare of light; their hair stands on end; 'tis Tabor with his dogs. The scent becomes warmer and warmer. What was an irregular cry, now deepens into one ceaseless roar, as the relentless pack rolls on after its human prey. It puts one in mind of Acteon and his dogs. They grow desperate and leave the road, in the vain hope of shaking them off. Vain hope, indeed! The momentary cessation only adds new zest to the chase. The cry grows louder and louder; the yelp grows short and quick, sure indications that the game is at hand. It is a perfect rush upon the part of the hunters, while the Negroes call upon their weary and jaded limbs to do their best, but they falter and stagger beneath them. The breath of the hounds is almost upon their very heels, and yet they have a vain hope of escaping these sagacious animals. They can run no longer; the dogs are upon them; they hastily attempt to climb a tree, and as the last one is nearly out of reach, the catch-dog seizes him by the leg, and brings him to the ground; he sings out lustily and the dogs are called off. After this man was secured, the one in the tree was ordered to come down; this, however, he refused to do, but a gun being pointed at him, soon caused him to change his mind. On reaching the ground, the fugitive made one more bound, and the chase again commenced. But it was of no use to run and he soon yielded. While being tied, he committed an unpardonable offence: he resisted, and for that he must be made an example on their arrival home. A mob was collected together, and a Lynch court was held, to determine what was best to be done with the Negro who had had the impudence to raise his hand against a white man. The Lynch court decided that the Negro should be burnt at the stake. A Natchez newspaper, the *Free Trader*, giving an account of it says,

"The body was taken and chained to a tree immediately on the banks of the Mississippi, on what is called Union Point. Faggots were then collected and piled around him, to which he appeared quite indifferent. When the work was completed, he was asked what he had to say. He then warned all to take example by him, and asked the prayers of all around; he then called for a drink of water, which was handed to him; he drank it, and said, 'Now set fire—I am ready to go in peace!' The torches were lighted, and placed in the pile, which soon ignited. He watched unmoved the curling flame that grew, until it began to entwine itself around and feed upon his body; then he sent forth cries of agony painful to the ear, begging some one to blow his brains out; at the same time surging with almost superhuman strength, until the staple with which the chain was fastened to the tree (not being well secured) drew out, and he leaped from the burning pile. At that moment the sharp ringing of several rifles was heard: the body of the Negro fell a corpse on the ground. He was picked up by some two or three, and again thrown into the fire, and consumed, not a vestige remaining to show that such a being ever existed."

Nearly 4,000 slaves were collected from the plantations in

the neighbourhood to witness this scene. Numerous speeches were made by the magistrates and ministers of religion to the large concourse of slaves, warning them, and telling them that the same fate awaited them, if they should prove rebellious to their owners. There are hundreds of Negroes who run away and live in the woods. Some take refuge in the swamps, because they are less frequented by human beings. A Natchez newspaper gave the following account of the hiding-place of a slave who had been captured:—

"A runaway's den was discovered on Sunday, near the Washington Spring, in a little patch of woods, where it had been for several months so artfully concealed under ground, that it was detected only by accident, though in sight of two or three houses, and near the road and fields where there has been constant daily passing. The entrance was concealed by a pile of pine straw, representing a hog-bed, which being removed, discovered a trap-door and steps that led to a room about six feet square, comfortably ceiled with plank, containing a small fire-place, the flue of which was ingeniously conducted above ground and concealed by the straw. The inmates took the alarm, and made their escape; but Mr. Adams and his excellent dogs being put upon the trail, soon run down and secured one of them, which proved to be a Negro-fellow who had been out about a year. He stated that the other occupant was a woman, who had been a runaway a still longer time. In the den was found a quantity of meal, bacon, corn, potatoes, &c. and various cooking utensils and wearing apparel."

—*Vicksburgh Sentinel*, Dec. 6th, 1838.

Currer was one of those who witnessed the execution of the slave at the stake, and it gave her no very exalted opinion of the people of the cotton growing district.

CHAPTER IV

The Quadroon's Home

"How sweetly on the hill-side sleeps
The sunlight with its quickening rays!
The verdant trees that crown the steeps,
Grow greener in its quivering blaze."

About three miles from Richmond is a pleasant plain, with here and there a beautiful cottage surrounded by trees so as scarcely to be seen. Among them was one far retired from the public roads, and almost hidden among the trees. It was a perfect model of rural beauty. The piazzas that surrounded it were covered with clematis and passion flower. The pride of China mixed its oriental looking foliage with the majestic magnolia, and the air was redolent with the fragrance of flowers, peeping out of every nook and nodding upon you with a most unexpected welcome. The tasteful hand of art had not learned to imitate the lavish beauty and harmonious disorder of nature, but they lived together in loving amity, and spoke in accordant tones. The gateway rose in a gothic arch, with graceful tracery in iron work, surmounted by a cross, round which fluttered and played the mountain fringe, that lightest and most fragile of vines. This cottage was hired by Horatio Green for Clotel, and the quadroon girl soon found herself in her new home.

The tenderness of Clotel's conscience, together with the care her mother had with her and the high value she placed upon virtue, required an outward marriage; though she well knew that a union with her proscribed race was unrecognised by law, and therefore the ceremony would give her no legal hold on Horatio's constancy. But her high poetic nature regarded reality rather than the semblance of things; and when he playfully asked how she could keep him if he wished to run away, she replied, "If the mutual love we have for each other, and the dictates of your own conscience do not cause you to remain my husband, and your affections fall from me, I would not, if I could, hold you by a single fetter." It was indeed a marriage sanctioned by heaven, although unrecognised on earth. There the young couple lived secluded from the world, and passed their time as happily as circumstances would permit. It was Clotel's wish that Horatio should purchase her mother and sister, but the young man pleaded that he was unable, owing to the fact that he had not come into possession of his share of property, yet he promised that when he did, he would seek them out and purchase them. Their first-born was named Mary, and her complexion was still lighter than her mother. Indeed she was not darker than other white children. As the child grew older, it more and more resembled its mother. The iris of her large dark eye had the melting mezzotinto, which remains the last vestige of African ancestry, and gives that plaintive expression, so often observed, and so appropriate to that docile and injured race. Clotel was still happier after the birth of her dear child; for Horatio, as might have been expected, was often absent day and night with his friends in the city, and the edicts of society had built up a wall of separation between the quadroon and them. Happy as Clotel was in Horatio's love, and surrounded by an outward environment of beauty, so well adapted to her poetic spirit, she felt these incidents with inexpressible pain. For herself she cared but little; for she had found a sheltered home in Horatio's heart, which the world might ridicule, but had no power to profane. But when she looked at her beloved Mary, and reflected upon the avoidable and dangerous position which the tyranny of society had awarded her, her soul was filled with anguish. The rare loveliness of the child increased daily, and was evidently ripening into most marvellous beauty. The father seemed to rejoice in it with unmingled pride; but in the deep tenderness of the mother's eye, there was an indwelling sadness that spoke of anxious thoughts and fearful foreboding. Clotel now urged Horatio to remove to France or England, where both her [sic] and her child would be free, and where colour was not a crime. This request excited but little opposition, and was so attractive to his imagination, that he might have overcome all intervening obstacles, had not "a change come over the spirit of his dreams." He still loved Clotel; but he was now becoming engaged in political and other affairs which kept him oftener and longer from the young mother; and ambition to become a statesman was slowly gaining the ascendancy over him.

Among those on whom Horatio's political success most depended was a very popular and wealthy man, who had an only daughter. His visits to the house were at first purely of a political nature; but the young lady was pleasing, and he fancied he discovered in her a sort of timid preference for himself. This excited his vanity, and awakened thoughts of the great worldly advantages connected with a union. Reminiscences of his first love kept these vague ideas in check for several months; for with it was associated the idea of restraint. Moreover, Gertrude, though inferior in beauty, was yet a pretty contrast to her rival. Her light hair fell in silken ringlets down her shoulders, her blue eyes were gentle though inexpressive, and her healthy cheeks were like opening rosebuds. He had already become accustomed to the dangerous experiment of resisting his own inward convictions; and this new impulse to ambition, combined with the strong temptation of variety in love, met the ardent young man weakened in moral principle, and unfettered by laws of the land. The change wrought upon him was soon noticed by Clotel.

CHAPTER V

The Slave Market

"What! mothers from their children riven!
    What! God's own image bought and sold!
Americans to market driven,
    And barter'd as the brute for gold."

WHITTIER

Not far from Canal-street, in the city of New Orleans, stands a large two story flat building surrounded by a stone wall twelve feet high, the top of which is covered with bits of glass, and so constructed as to prevent even the possibility of any one's passing over it without sustaining great injury. Many of the rooms resemble cells in a prison. In a small room near the "office" are to be seen any number of iron collars, hobbles, handcuffs, thumbscrews, cowhides, whips, chains, gags, and yokes. A back yard inclosed by a high wall looks something like the playground attached to one of our large New England schools, and in which are rows of benches and swings. Attached to the back premises is a good-sized kitchen, where two old Negresses are at work, stewing, boiling, and baking, and occasionally wiping the sweat from their furrowed and swarthy brows.

The slave-trader Walker, on his arrival in New Orleans, took up his quarters at this slave pen with his gang of human cattle; and the morning after, at ten o'clock, they were exhibited for sale. There, first of all, was the beautiful Althesa, whose pale countenance and dejected look told how many sad hours she had passed since parting with her mother at Natchez. There was a poor woman who had been separated from her husband and five children. Another woman, whose looks and manner were expressive of deep anguish, sat by her side. There, too, was "Uncle Geemes," with his whiskers off, his face shaved clean, and the grey hair plucked out, and ready to be sold for ten years younger than he was. Toby was also there, with his face shaved and greased, ready for inspection. The examination commenced, and was carried on in a manner calculated to shock the feelings of any one not devoid of the milk of human kindness. "What are you wiping your eyes for?" inquired a fat, red-faced man, with a white hat set on one side of his head, and a cigar in his mouth, of a woman who sat on one of the stools.

"I s'pose I have been crying."

"Why do you cry?"

"Because I have left my man behind."

"Oh, if I buy you I will furnish you with a better man than you left. I have lots of young bucks on my farm."

"I don't want, and will never have, any other man," replied the woman.

"What's your name?" asked a man in a straw hat of a tall Negro man, who stood with his arms folded across his breast, and leaning against the wall.

"My name is Aaron, sir."

"How old are you?"

"Twenty-five."

"Where were you raised?"

"In old Virginny, sir."

"How many men have owned you?"

"Four."

"Do you enjoy good health?"

"Yes, sir."

"How long did you live with your first owner?"

"Twenty years."

"Did you ever run away?"

"No, sir."

"Did you ever strike your master?"

"No, sir."

"Were you ever whipped much?"

"No, sir, I s'pose I did not deserve it."

"How long did you live with your second master?"

"Ten years, sir."

"Have you a good appetite?"

"Yes, sir."

"Can you eat your allowance?"

"Yes, sir, when I can get it."

"What were you employed at in Virginia?"

"I worked in de terbacar feel."

"In the tobacco field?"

"Yes, sir."

"How old did you say you were?"

"I will be twenty-five if I live to see next sweet potater-digging time."

"I am a cotton planter, and if I buy you, you will have to work in the cotton field. My men pick one hundred and fifty pounds a day, and the women one hundred and forty, and those who fail to pick their task receive five stripes from the cat for each pound that is wanting. Now, do you think you could keep up with the rest of the hands?"

"I don't know, sir, I 'spec I'd have to.'

"How long did you live with your third master?"

"Three years, sir."

"Why, this makes you thirty-three, I thought you told me you was only twenty-five?"

Aaron now looked first at the planter, then at the trader, and seemed perfectly bewildered. He had forgotten the lesson given him by Pompey as to his age, and the planter's circuitous talk (doubtless to find out the slave's real age) had the Negro off his guard.

"I must see your back, so as to know how much you have been whipped, before I think of buying," said the planter.

Pompey, who had been standing by during the examination, thought that his services were now required, and stepping forward with a degree of officiousness, said to Aaron, "Don't you hear de gentman tell you he want to zamon your limbs. Come, unharness yeself, old boy, an don't be standing dar."

Aaron was soon examined and pronounced "sound"; yet the conflicting statement about the age was not satisfactory.

Fortunate for Althesa she was spared the pain of undergoing such an examination. Mr. Crawford, a teller in one of the banks, had just been married, and wanted a maid-servant for his wife; and passing through the market in the early part of the day, was pleased with the young slave's appearance and purchased her, and in his dwelling the quadroon found a much better home than often falls to the lot of a slave sold in the New Orleans market. The heartrending and cruel traffic in slaves which has been so often described, is not confined to any particular class of persons. No one forfeits his or her character or standing in society, by buying or selling slaves; or even raising slaves for the market. The precise number of slaves carried from the slave-raising to the slave-consuming states, we have no means of knowing. But it must be very great, as more than forty thousand were sold and taken out of the state of Virginia in one year. Known to God only is the amount of human agony and suffering which sends its cry from the slave markets and Negro pens, unheard and unheeded by man, up to his ear; mothers weeping for their children, breaking the night-silence with the shrieks of their breaking hearts. From some you will hear the burst of bitter lamentation, while from others the loud hysteric laugh, denoting still deeper agony. Most of them leave the market for cotton or rice plantations.

> "Where the slave-whip ceaseless swings,
> Where the noisome insect stings,
> Where the fever demon strews
> Poison with the falling dews,
> Where the sickly sunbeams glare
> Through the hot and misty air."

CHAPTER VI

The Religious Teacher

"What! preach and enslave men?
Give thanks—and rob thy own afflicted poor?
Talk of thy glorious liberty, and then
Bolt hard the captive's door?"

WHITTIER

The Rev. John Peck was a native of the state of Connecticut, where he was educated for the ministry, in the Methodist persuasion. His father was a strict follower of John Wesley, and spared no pains in his son's education, with the hope that he would one day be as renowned as the great leader of his sect. John had scarcely finished his education at New Haven, when he was invited by an uncle, then on a visit to his father, to spend a few months at Natchez in the state of Mississippi. Young Peck accepted his uncle's invitation, and accompanied him to the South. Few young men, and especially clergymen, going fresh from a college to the South, but are looked upon as geniuses in a small way, and who are not invited to all the parties in the neighbourhood. Mr. Peck was not an exception to this rule. The society into which he was thrown on his arrival at Natchez was too brilliant for him not to be captivated by it; and, as might have been expected, he succeeded in captivating a plantation with seventy slaves, if not the heart of the lady to whom it belonged. Added to this, he became a popular preacher, had a large congregation with a snug salary. Like other planters, Mr. Peck confided the care of his farm to Ned Huckelby, an overseer of high reputation in his way. The Poplar Farm, as it was called, was situated in a beautiful valley nine miles from Natchez, and near the river Mississippi. The once unshorn face of nature had given way, and now the farm blossomed with a splendid harvest, the neat cottage stood in a grove where Lombardy poplars lift their tufted tops almost to prop the skies; the willow, locust, and horse-chestnut spread their branches, and flowers never cease to blossom. This was the parson's country house, where the family spent only two months during the year.

The town residence was a fine villa, seated upon the brow of a hill at the edge of the city. It was in the kitchen of this house that Currer found her new home. Mr. Peck was, every inch of him, a democrat, and early resolved that his "people," as he called his slaves, should be well fed and not overworked, and therefore laid down the law and gospel to the overseer as well as the slaves.

"It is my wish," said he to Mr. Carlton, an old schoolfellow, who was spending a few days with him, "it is my wish that a new system be adopted on the plantations in this estate. I believe that the sons of Ham should have the gospel, and I intend that my Negroes shall. The gospel is calculated to make mankind better, and none should be without it."

"What say you," replied Carlton, "about the right of man to his liberty?"

"Now, Carlton, you have begun again to harp about man's rights; I really wish you could see this matter as I do. I have searched in vain for any authority for man's natural rights; if he had any, they existed before the fall. That is, Adam and Eve may have had some rights which God gave them, and which modern philosophy, in its pretended reverence for the name of God, prefers to call natural rights. I can imagine they had the right to eat of the fruit of the trees of the garden; they were restricted even in this by the prohibition of one. As far as I know without positive assertion, their liberty of action was confined to the garden. These were not 'inalienable rights,' however, for they forfeited both them and life with the first act of disobedience. Had they, after

this, any rights? We cannot imagine them; they were condemned beings; they could have no rights, but by Christ's
gift as king. These are the only rights man can have as an
independent isolated being, if we choose to consider him in
this impossible position, in which so many theorists have
placed him. If he had no rights, he could suffer no wrongs.
Rights and wrongs are therefore necessarily the creatures of
society, such as man would establish himself in his gregarious
state. They are, in this state, both artificial and voluntary.
Though man has no rights, as thus considered, undoubtedly
he has the power, by such arbitrary rules of right and wrong
as his necessity enforces."

"I regret I cannot see eye to eye with you," said Carlton.
"I am a disciple of Rousseau, and have for years made the
rights of man my study; and I must confess to you that I can
see no difference between white men and black men as it
regards liberty."

"Now, my dear Carlton, would you really have the Negroes enjoy the same rights with ourselves?"

"I would, most certainly. Look at our great Declaration of
Independence; look even at the constitution of our own
Connecticut, and see what is said in these about liberty."

"I regard all this talk about rights as mere humbug. The
Bible is older than the Declaration of Independence, and
there I take my stand. The Bible furnishes to us the armour
of proof, weapons of heavenly temper and mould, whereby
we can maintain our ground against all attacks. But this is
true only when we obey its directions, as well as employ its
sanctions. Our rights are there established, but it is always
in connection with our duties. If we neglect the one we
cannot make good the other. Our domestic institutions can
be maintained against the world, if we but allow Christianity
to throw its broad shield over them. But if we so act as to
array the Bible against our social economy, they must fall.
Nothing ever yet stood long against Christianity. Those who
say that religious instruction is inconsistent with our peculiar
civil polity, are the worst enemies of that polity. They would

drive religious men from its defence. Sooner or later, if these views prevail, they will separate the religious portion of our community from the rest, and thus divided we shall become an easy prey. Why, is it not better that Christian men should hold slaves than unbelievers? We know how to value the bread of life, and will not keep it from our slaves."

"Well, every one to his own way of thinking," said Carlton, as he changed his position. "I confess," added he, "that I am no great admirer of either the Bible or slavery. My heart is my guide: my conscience is my Bible. I wish for nothing further to satisfy me of my duty to man. If I act rightly to mankind, I shall fear nothing."

Carlton had drunk too deeply of the bitter waters of infidelity, and had spent too many hours over the writings of Rousseau, Voltaire, and Thomas Paine, to place that appreciation upon the Bible and its teachings that it demands. During this conversation there was another person in the room, seated by the window, who, although at work upon a fine piece of lace, paid every attention to what was said. This was Georgiana, the only daughter of the parson. She had just returned from Connecticut, where she had finished her education. She had had the opportunity of contrasting the spirit of Christianity and liberty in New England with that of slavery in her native state, and had learned to feel deeply for the injured Negro. Georgiana was in her nineteenth year, and had been much benefited by a residence of five years at the North. Her form was tall and graceful; her features regular and well defined; and her complexion was illuminated by the freshness of youth, beauty, and health. The daughter differed from both the father and his visitor upon the subject which they had been discussing, and as soon as an opportunity offered, she gave it as her opinion, that the Bible was both the bulwark of Christianity and of liberty. With a smile she said, "Of course, papa will overlook my differing from him, for although I am a native of the South, I am by education and sympathy a Northerner." Mr. Peck laughed and appeared pleased, rather than otherwise, at the manner in which his daughter had expressed herself.

From this Georgiana took courage and said, "We must try the character of slavery, and our duty in regard to it, as we should try any other question of character and duty. To judge justly of the character of anything, we must know what it does. That which is good does good, and that which is evil does evil. And as to duty, God's designs indicate his claims. That which accomplishes the manifest design of God is right; that which counteracts it, wrong. Whatever, in its proper tendency and general effect, produces, secures, or extends human welfare, is according to the will of God, and is good; and our duty is to favour and promote, according to our power, that which God favours and promotes by the general law of his providence. On the other hand, whatever in its proper tendency and general effect destroys, abridges, or renders insecure, human welfare, is opposed to God's will, and is evil. And as whatever accords with the will of God, in any manifestation of it should be done and persisted in, so whatever opposes that will should not be done, and if done, should be abandoned. Can that then be right, be well doing—can that obey God's behest, which makes a man a slave? which dooms him and all his posterity, in limitless generations, to bondage, to unrequited toil through life? 'Thou shalt love thy neighbour as thyself.' This single passage of Scripture should cause us to have respect to the rights of the slave. True Christian love is of an enlarged, disinterested nature. It loves all who love the Lord Jesus Christ in sincerity, without regard to colour or condition."

"Georgiana, my dear, you are an abolitionist; your talk is fanaticism," said Mr. Peck in rather a sharp tone; but the subdued look of the girl, and the presence of Carlton, caused the father to soften his language. Mr. Peck having lost his wife by consumption, and Georgiana being his only child, he loved her too dearly to say more, even if he felt displeased. A silence followed this exhortation from the young

Christian. But her remarks had done a noble work. The father's heart was touched; and the sceptic, for the first time, was viewing Christianity in its true light.

"I think I must go out to your farm," said Carlton, as if to break the silence.

"I shall be pleased to have you go," returned Mr. Peck. "I am sorry I can't go myself, but Huckelby will show you every attention; and I feel confident that when you return to Connecticut, you will do me the justice to say, that I am one who looks after my people, in a moral, social, and religious point of view."

"Well, what do you say to my spending next Sunday there?"

"Why, I think that a good move; you will then meet with Snyder, our missionary."

"Oh, you have missionaries in these parts, have you?"

"Yes," replied Mr. Peck; "Snyder is from New York, and is our missionary to the poor, and preaches to our 'people' on Sunday; you will no doubt like him; he is a capital fellow."

"Then I shall go," said Carlton, "but only wish I had company." This last remark was intended for Miss Peck, for whom he had the highest admiration.

It was on a warm Sunday morning, in the month of May, that Miles Carlton found himself seated beneath a fine old apple tree, whose thick leaves entirely shaded the ground for some distance round. Under similar trees and near by, were gathered together all the "people" belonging to the plantation. Hontz Snyder was a man of about forty years of age, exceedingly low in stature, but of a large frame. He had been brought up in the Mohawk Valley, in the state of New York, and claimed relationship with the oldest Dutch families in that vicinity. He had once been a sailor, and had all the roughness of character that a sea-faring man might expect to possess; together with the half-Yankee, half-German peculiarities of the people of the Mohawk Valley. It was nearly eleven o'clock when a one-horse waggon drove up in haste, and the low squatty preacher got out and took his place at the foot of one of the trees, where a sort of rough board table was placed, and took his books from his pocket and commenced.

"As it is rather late," said he, "we will leave the singing and praying for the last, and take our text, and commence immediately. I shall base my remarks on the following passage of Scripture, and hope to have that attention which is due to the cause of God:—'All things whatsoever ye would that men should do unto you, do ye even so unto them'; that is, do by all mankind just as you would desire they should do by you, if you were in their place and they in yours.

"Now, to suit this rule to your particular circumstances, suppose you were masters and mistresses, and had servants under you, would you not desire that your servants should do their business faithfully and honestly, as well when your back was turned as while you were looking over them? Would you not expect that they should take notice of what you said to them? that they should behave themselves with respect towards you and yours, and be as careful of everything belonging to you as you would be yourselves? You are servants: do, therefore, as you would wish to be done by, and you will be both good servants to your masters and good servants to God, who requires this of you, and will reward you well for it, if you do it for the sake of conscience, in obedience to his commands.

"You are not to be eye-servants. Now, eye-servants are such as will work hard, and seem mighty diligent, while they think anybody is taking notice of them; but, when their masters' and mistresses' backs are turned they are idle, and neglect their business. I am afraid there are a great many such eye-servants among you, and that you do not consider how great a sin it is to be so, and how severely God will punish you for it. You may easily deceive your owners, and make them have an opinion of you that you do not deserve, and get the praise of men by it; but remember that you cannot deceive Almighty God, who sees your wickedness and deceit, and will punish you accordingly. For the rule is, that you must obey your masters in all things, and do the work they set you about with fear and trembling, in singleness of heart as unto Christ; not with eye-service, as men-pleasers, but as the servants of Christ, doing the will of God from the heart; with good-will doing service as to the Lord, and not as to men.

"*Take care that you do not fret or murmur, grumble or repine at your condition; for this will not only make your life uneasy, but will greatly offend Almighty God.* Consider that it is not yourselves, it is not the people that you belong to, it is not the men who have brought you to it, but *it is the will of God who hath by his providence made you servants, because, no doubt, he knew that condition would be best for you in this world, and help you the better towards heaven, if you would but do your duty in it.* So that any discontent at your not being free, or rich, or great, as you see some others, is quarrelling with your heavenly Master, and finding fault with God himself, who hath made you what you are, and hath promised you as large a share in the kingdom of heaven as the greatest man alive, if you will but behave yourself aright, and do the business he hath set you about in the world honestly and cheerfully. Riches and power have proved the ruin of many an unhappy soul, by drawing away the heart and affections from God, and fixing them on mean and sinful enjoyments; so that, when God, who knows our hearts better than we know them ourselves, sees that they would be hurtful to us, and therefore keeps them from us, it is the greatest mercy and kindness he could show us.

"You may perhaps fancy that, if you had riches and freedom, you could do your duty to God and man with greater pleasure than you can now. But pray consider that, if you can but save your souls through the mercy of God, you will have spent your time to the best of purposes in this world; and he that at last can get to heaven has performed a noble journey, let the road be ever so rugged and difficult. Besides, you really have a great advantage over most white people, who have not only the care of their daily labour upon their hands, but the care of looking forward and providing necessaries for to-morrow and next day, and of clothing and bringing up their children, and of getting food and raiment for as many of you as belong to their families, which often puts them to great difficulties, and distracts their minds so as to break their rest, and take off their thoughts from the affairs of another world. Whereas you are quite eased from all these cares, and have nothing but your daily labour to look after, and, when that is done, take your needful rest. Neither is it necessary for you to think of laying up anything against old age, as white people are obliged to do; for the laws of the country have provided that you shall not be turned off when you are past labour, but shall be maintained, while you live, by those you belong to, whether you are able to work or not.

"There is only one circumstance which may appear grievous, that I shall now take notice of, and that is correction.

"Now, when correction is given you, you either deserve it, or you do not deserve it. But whether you really deserve it or not, it is your duty, and Almighty God requires that you bear it patiently. You may perhaps think that this is hard doctrine; but, if you consider it right, you must needs think otherwise of it. Suppose, then, that you deserve correction, you cannot but say that it is just and right you should meet with it. Suppose you do not, or at least you do not deserve so much, or so severe a correction, for the fault you have committed, you perhaps have escaped a great many more, and are at last paid for all. Or suppose you are quite innocent of what is laid to your charge, and suffer wrongfully in that particular thing, is it not possible you may have done some other bad thing which was never discovered, and that Almighty God who saw you doing it would not let you escape without punishment one time or another? And ought you not, in such a case, to give glory to him, and be thankful that he would rather punish you in this life for your wickedness than destroy your souls for it in the next life? But suppose even this was not the case (a case hardly to be imagined), and that you have by no means, known or unknown, deserved the correction you suffered, there is this great comfort in it, that, if you bear it patiently, and leave your cause in the hands of God, he will reward you for it in heaven, and the punishment you suffer unjustly here shall turn to your exceeding great glory hereafter.

"Lastly, you should serve your masters faithfully, because of their goodness to you. See to what trouble they have been on your account. Your fathers were poor ignorant and barbarous creatures in Africa, and the whites fitted out ships at great trouble and expense and brought you from that benighted land to Christian America, where you can sit under your own vine and fig tree and no one molest or make you afraid. Oh, my dear black brothers and sisters, you are indeed a fortunate and a blessed people. Your masters have many troubles that you know nothing about. If the banks break, your masters are sure to lose something. If the crops turn out poor, they lose by it. If one of you die, your master loses what he paid for you, while you lose nothing. Now let me exhort you once more to be faithful."

Often during the delivery of the sermon did Synder cast an anxious look in the direction where Carlton was seated; no doubt to see if he had found favour with the stranger. Huckelby, the overseer, was also there, seated near Carlton. With all Synder's gesticulations, sonorous voice, and occasionally bringing his fist down upon the table with the force of a sledge hammer, he could not succeed in keeping the Negroes all interested: four or five were fast asleep, leaning against the trees; as many more were nodding, while not a few were stealthily cracking and eating hazelnuts. "Uncle Simon, you may strike up a hymn," said the preacher as he closed his Bible. A moment more, and the whole company (Carlton excepted) had joined in the well known hymn, commencing with

"When I can read my title clear
To mansions in the sky."

After the singing, Sandy closed with prayer, and the following questions and answers read, and the meeting was brought to a close.

"Q. What command has God given to servants concerning obedience to their masters?—A. 'Servants, obey in all things your masters according to the flesh, not with eye-service as men-pleasers, but in singleness of heart, fearing God.'

"Q. What does God mean by masters according to the flesh?—A. 'Masters in this world.'

"Q. What are servants to count their masters worthy of?—A. 'All honour.'

"Q. How are they to do the service of their masters?—A. 'With good will, doing service as unto the Lord, and not unto men.'

"Q. How are they to try to please their masters?—A. 'Please him well in all things, not answering again.'

"Q. Is a servant who is an eye-servant to his earthly master an eye-servant to his heavenly master?—A. 'Yes.'

"Q. Is it right in a servant, when commanded to do any thing, to be sullen and slow, and answer his master again?—A. 'No.'

"Q. If the servant professes to be a Christian, ought he not to be as a Christian servant, an example to all other servants of love and obedience to his master?—A. 'Yes.'

"Q. And, should his master be a Christian also, ought he not on that account specially to love and obey him?—A. 'Yes.'

"Q. But suppose the master is hard to please, and threatens and punishes more than he ought, what is the servant to do?—A. 'Do his best to please him.'

"Q. When the servant suffers wrongfully at the hands of his master, and, to please God, take it patiently, will God reward him for it?—A. 'Yes.'

"Q. Is it right for the servant to run away, or is it right to harbour a runaway?—A. 'No.'

"*Q.* If a servant runs away, what should be done with him?—*A.* 'He should be caught and brought back.'

"*Q.* When he is brought back, what should be done with him?—*A.* 'Whip him well.'

"*Q.* Why may not the whites be slaves as well as the blacks?—*A.* 'Because the Lord intended the Negroes for slaves.'

"*Q.* Are they better calculated for servants than the whites?—*A.* 'Yes, their hands are large, the skin thick and tough, and they can stand the sun better than the whites.'

"*Q.* Why should servants not complain when they are whipped?—*A.* 'Because the Lord has commanded that they should be whipped.'

"*Q.* Where has He commanded it?—*A.* 'He says, He that knoweth his master's will, and doeth it not, shall be beaten with many stripes.'

"*Q.* Then is the master to blame for whipping his servant?—*A.* 'Oh, no! he is only doing his duty as a Christian.' "

Snyder left the ground in company with Carlton and Huckelby, and the three dined together in the overseer's dwelling.

"Well," said Joe, after the three white men were out of hearing, "Marser Snyder bin try hesef to-day."

"Yes," replied Ned; "he want to show de strange gentman how good he can preach."

"Dat's a new sermon he gib us to-day," said Sandy.

"Dees white fokes is de very dibble," said Dick; "and all dey whole study is to try to fool de black people."

"Didn't you like de sermon?"asked Uncle Simon. "No," answered four or five voices.

"He rared and pitched enough," continued Uncle Simon. Now Uncle Simon was himself a preacher, or at least he thought so, and was rather pleased than otherwise, when he heard others spoken of in a disparaging manner. "Uncle Simon can beat dat sermon all to pieces," said Ned, as he was filling his mouth with hazelnuts.

"I got no notion of dees white fokes, no how," returned Aunt Dafney. "Dey all de time tellin' dat de Lord made us for to work for dem, and I don't believe a word of it."

"Marser Peck give dat sermon to Snyder, I know," said Uncle Simon.

"He jest de one for dat," replied Sandy.

"I think de people dat made de Bible was great fools," said Ned.

"Why?" asked Uncle Simon.

" 'Cause dey made such a great big book and put nuttin' in it, but servants obey yer masters."

"Oh," replied Uncle Simon, "thars more in de Bible den dat, only Snyder never reads any other part to us; I use to hear it read in Maryland, and thar was more den what Snyder lets us hear."

In the overseer's house there was another scene going on, and far different from what we have here described.

CHAPTER VII

The Poor Whites, South

"No seeming of logic can ever convince the American people, that thousands of our slave-holding brethren are not excellent, humane, and even Christian men, fearing God, and keeping His commandments."

REV. DR. JOEL PARKER

"You like these parts better than New York," said Carlton to Snyder, as they were sitting down to dinner in the overseer's dwelling.

"I can't say that I do," was the reply; "I came here ten years ago as missionary, and Mr. Peck wanted me to stay, and I have remained. I travel among the poor whites during the week, and preach for the niggers on Sunday."

"Are there many poor whites in this district?"

"Not here, but about thirty miles from here, in the Sand Hill district; they are as ignorant as horses. Why it was no longer than last week I was up there, and really you would not believe it, that people were so poor off. In New England, and, I may say, in all the free states, they have free schools, and everybody gets educated. Not so here. In Connecticut there is only one out of every five hundred above twenty-one years that can neither read nor write. There is not a single newspaper taken in five of the counties in this state. Last week I was at Sand Hill for the first time, and I called at a farmhouse. The man was out. It was a low log-hut, and yet it was the best house in that locality. The woman and nine children were there, and the geese, ducks, chickens, pigs, and children were all running about the floor. The woman seemed scared at me when I entered the house. I inquired if I could get a little dinner, and my horse fed. She said, yes, if I would only be good enough to feed him myself, as her 'gal,' as she called her daughter, would be afraid of the horse. When I returned into the house again from the stable, she kept her eyes upon me all the time. At last she said, 'I s'pose you aint never bin in these parts afore?' 'No,' said I. 'Is you gwine to stay here long?' 'Not very long,' I replied. 'On business, I s'pose.' 'Yes,' said I, 'I am hunting up the lost sheep of the house of Israel.' 'Oh,' exclaimed she, 'hunting for lost sheep is you? Well, you have a hard time to find 'em here. My husband lost an old ram last week, and he aint found him yet, and he's hunted every day.' 'I am not looking for four-legged sheep,' said I, 'I am hunting for sinners.' 'Ah'; she said, 'then you are a preacher.' 'Yes,' said I. 'You are the first of that sort that's bin in these diggins for many a day.' Turning to her eldest daughter, she said in an excited tone, 'Clar out the pigs and ducks, and sweep up the floor; this is a preacher.' And it was some time before any of the children would come near me; one remained under the bed (which, by the by, was in the same room), all the while I was there. 'Well,' continued the woman, 'I was a tellin' my man only yesterday that I would like once more to go to meetin' before I died, and he said as he should like to do the same. But as you have come, it will save us the trouble of going out of the district.' "

"Then you found some of the lost sheep," said Carlton.

"Yes," replied Snyder, "I did not find anything else up there. The state makes no provision for educating the poor: they are unable to do it themselves, and they grow up in a state of ignorance and degradation. The men hunt and the women have to go in the fields and labour."

"What is the cause of it?" inquired Carlton.

"Slavery," answered Snyder, "slavery,—and nothing else. Look at the city of Boston; it pays more taxes for the support of the government than this entire state. The people of Boston do more business than the whole population of Mississippi put together. I was told some very amusing things while at Sand Hill. A farmer there told me a story about an old woman, who was very pious herself. She had a husband and three sons, who were sad characters, and she had often prayed for their conversion but to no effect. At last, one day while working in the cornfield, one of her sons was bitten by a rattlesnake. He had scarce reached home before he felt the poison, and in his agony called loudly on his Maker.

"The pious old woman, when she heard this, forgetful of her son's misery, and everything else but the glorious hope of his repentence, fell on her knees, and prayed as follows,— 'Oh! Lord, I thank thee, that thou hast at last opened Jimmy's eyes to the error of his ways; and I pray that, in thy Divine mercy, thou wilt send a rattlesnake to bite the old man, and another to bite Tom, and another to bite Harry, for I am certain that nothing but a rattlesnake, or something of the kind, will ever turn them from their sinful ways, they are so hard-headed.' When returning home, and before I got out of the Sand Hill district, I saw a funeral, and thought I would fasten my horse to a post and attend. The coffin was carried in a common horse cart, and followed by fifteen or twenty persons very shabbily dressed, and attended by a man whom I took to be the religious man of the place. After the coffin had been placed near the grave, he spoke as follows,—

" 'Friends and neighbours! you have congregated to see this lump of mortality put into a hole in the ground. You all know the deceased—a worthless, drunken, good-for-nothing vagabond. He lived in disgrace and infamy, and died in wretchedness. You all despised him—you all know his brother Joe, who lives on the hill? He's not a bit better though he has scrap'd together a little property by cheating his neighbours. His end will be like that of this loathsome creature, whom you will please put into the hole as soon as possible. I won't ask you to drop a tear, but brother Bohow will please raise a hymn while we fill up the grave.' "

. . .

"I am rather surprised to hear that any portion of the whites in this state are in so low a condition."

"Yet it is true," returned Snyder.

"These are very onpleasant facts to be related to ye, Mr. Carlton," said Huckelby; "but I can bear witness to what Mr. Snyder has tole ye." Huckelby was from Maryland, where many of the poor whites are in as sad a condition as the Sand Hillers of Mississippi. He was a tall man, of iron constitution, and could neither read nor write, but was considered one of the best overseers in the country. When about to break a slave in, to do a heavy task, he would make him work by his side all day; and if the new hand kept up with him, he was set down as an able bodied man. Huckelby had neither moral, religious, or political principles, and often boasted that conscience was a matter that never "cost" him a thought. "Mr. Snyder aint told ye half about the folks in these parts," continued he; "we who comes from more enlightened parts don't know how to put up with 'em down here. I find the people here knows mighty little indeed; in fact, I may say they are univarsaly onedicated. I goes out among none on 'em, 'cause they aint such as I have been used to 'sociate with. When I gits a little richer, so that I can stop work, I tend to go back to Maryland, and spend the rest of my days."

"I wonder the Negroes don't attempt to get their freedom by physical force."

"It aint no use for 'em to try that, for if they do, we puts 'em through by daylight," replied Huckelby.

"There are some desperate fellows among the slaves," said Snyder.

"Indeed," remarked Carlton.

"Oh, yes," replied the preacher. "A case has just taken place near here, where a neighbour of ours, Mr. J. Higgerson, attempted to correct a Negro man in his employ, who resisted, drew a knife, and stabbed him (Mr. H.) in several places. Mr. J. C. Hobbs (a Tennessean) ran to his assistance. Mr. Hobbs stooped to pick up a stick to strike the Negro, and, while in that position, the Negro rushed upon him, and caused his immediate death. The Negro then fled to the woods, but was pursued with dogs, and soon overtaken. He had stopped in a swamp to fight the dogs, when the party who were pursuing him came upon him, and commanded him to give up, which he refused to do. He then made several efforts to stab them. Mr. Roberson, one of the party, gave him several blows on the head with a rifle gun; but this, instead of subduing, only increased his desperate revenge. Mr. R. then discharged his gun at the Negro, and missing him, the ball struck Mr. Boon in the face, and felled him to the ground. The Negro, seeing Mr. Boon prostrated, attempted to rush up and stab him, but was prevented by the timely interference of some one of the party. He was then shot three times with a revolving pistol, and once with a rifle, and after having his throat cut, he still kept the knife firmly grasped in his hand, and tried to cut their legs when they approached to put an end to his life. This chastisement was given because the Negro grumbled, and found fault with his master for flogging his wife."

"Well, this is a bad state of affairs indeed, and especially the condition of the poor whites," said Carlton.

"You see," replied Snyder, "no white man is respectable in these slaves states who works for a living. No community can be prosperous, where honest labour is not honoured. No society can be rightly constituted, where the intellect is not fed. Whatever institution reflects discredit on industry, whatever institution forbids the general culture of the understanding, is palpably hostile to individual rights, and to social well-being. Slavery is the incubus that hangs over the Southern States."

"Yes," interrupted Huckelby; "them's just my sentiments now, and no mistake. I think that, for the honour of our country, this slavery business should stop. I don't own any, no how, and I would not be an overseer if I wern't paid for it."

CHAPTER VIII

The Separation

"In many ways does the full heart reveal
   The presence of the love it would conceal;
   But in far more the estranged heart lets know
   The absence of the love, which yet it fain would
   show."

At length the news of the approaching marriage of Horatio met the ear of Clotel. Her head grew dizzy, and her heart fainted within her; but, with a strong effort at composure, she inquired all the particulars, and her pure mind at once took its resolution. Horatio came that evening, and though she would fain have met him as usual, her heart was too full not to throw a deep sadness over her looks and tones. She had never complained of his decreasing tenderness, or of her own lonely hours; but he felt that the mute appeal of her heart-broken looks was more terrible than words. He kissed the hand she offered, and with a countenance almost as sad as her own, led her to a window in the recess shadowed by a luxuriant passion flower. It was the same seat where they had spent the first evening in this beautiful cottage, consecrated to their first loves. The same calm, clear moonlight looked in through the trellis. The vine then planted had now a luxuriant growth; and many a time had Horatio fondly twined its sacred blossoms with the glossy ringlets of her raven hair. The rush of memory almost overpowered poor Clotel; and Horatio felt too much oppressed and ashamed to break the long deep silence. At length, in words scarcely audible, Clotel said: "Tell me, dear Horatio, are you to be married next week?"

He dropped her hand as if a rifle ball had struck him; and it was not until after long hesitation, that he began to make some reply about the necessity of circumstances. Mildly but earnestly the poor girl begged him to spare apologies. It was enough that he no longer loved her, and that they must bid farewell. Trusting to the yielding tenderness of her character, he ventured, in the most soothing accents, to suggest that as he still loved her better than all the world, she would ever be his real wife, and they might see each other frequently. He was not prepared for the storm of indignant emotion his words excited. True, she was his slave; her bones, and sinews had been purchased by his gold, yet she had the heart of a true woman, and hers was a passion too deep and absorbing to admit of partnership, and her spirit was too pure to form a selfish league with crime.

At length this painful interview came to an end. They stood together by the Gothic gate, where they had so often met and parted in the moonlight. Old remembrances melted their souls.

"Farewell, dearest Horatio," said Clotel. "Give me a parting kiss."

Her voice was choked for utterance, and the tears flowed freely, as she bent her lips toward him. He folded her convulsively in his arms, and imprinted a long impassioned kiss on that mouth, which had never spoken to him but in love and blessing. With efforts like a death-pang she at length raised her head from his heaving bosom, and turning from him with bitter sobs, "It is our last. To meet thus is henceforth crime. God bless you. I would not have you so miserable as I am. Farewell. A last farewell."

"The last?" exclaimed he, with a wild shriek. "Oh God, Clotel, do not say that"; and covering his face with his hands, he wept like a child. Recovering from his emotion, he found himself alone. The moon looked down upon him mild, but very sorrowfully; as the Madonna seems to gaze

upon her worshipping children, bowed down with consciousness of sin. At that moment he would have given worlds to
have disengaged himself from Gertrude, but he had gone so
far, that blame, disgrace, and duels with angry relatives would
now attend any effort to obtain his freedom. Oh, how the
moonlight oppressed him with its friendly sadness! It was like
the plaintive eye of his forsaken one, like the music of sorrow
echoed from an unseen world. Long and earnestly he gazed
at that cottage, where he had so long known earth's purest
foretaste of heavenly bliss. Slowly he walked away; then
turned again to look on that charmed spot, the nestling-place
of his early affections. He caught a glimpse of Clotel, weeping beside a magnolia, which commanded a long view of the
path leading to the public road. He would have sprung toward her but she darted from him, and entered the cottage.
That graceful figure, weeping in the moonlight, haunted him
for years. It stood before his closing eyes, and greeted him
with the morning dawn. Poor Gertrude, had she known all,
what a dreary lot would hers have been; but fortunately she
could not miss the impassioned tenderness she never experienced; and Horatio was the more careful in his kindness,
because he was deficient in love. After Clotel had been separated from her mother and sister, she turned her attention
to the subject of Christianity, and received that consolation
from her Bible that is never denied to the children of God.
Although it was against the laws of Virginia for a slave to
be taught to read, Currer had employed an old free Negro,
who lived near her, to teach her two daughters to read and
write. She felt that the step she had taken in resolving never
to meet Horatio again would no doubt expose her to his
wrath, and probably cause her to be sold, yet her heart was
too guileless for her to commit a crime, and therefore she
had ten times rather have been sold as a slave than do wrong.
Some months after the marriage of Horatio and Gertrude
their barouche rolled along a winding road that skirted the
forest near Clotel's cottage, when the attention of Gertrude
was suddenly attracted by two figures among the trees by the

wayside; and touching Horatio's arm, she exclaimed, "Do look at that beautiful child." He turned and saw Clotel and Mary. His lips quivered, and his face became deadly pale. His young wife looked at him intently, but said nothing. In returning home, he took another road; but his wife seeing this, expressed a wish to go back the way they had come. He objected, and suspicion was awakened in her heart, and she soon after learned that the mother of that lovely child bore the name of Clotel, a name which she had often heard Horatio murmur in uneasy slumbers. From gossiping tongues she soon learned more than she wished to know. She wept, but not as poor Clotel had done; for she never had loved, and been beloved like her, and her nature was more proud: henceforth a change came over her feelings and her manners, and Horatio had no further occasion to assume a tenderness in return for hers. Changed as he was by ambition, he felt the wintry chill of her polite propriety, and sometimes, in agony of heart, compared it with the gushing love of her who was indeed his wife. But these and all his emotions were a sealed book to Clotel, of which she could only guess the contents. With remittances for her and her child's support, there sometimes came earnest pleadings that she would consent to see him again; but these she never answered, though her heart yearned to do so. She pitied his young bride, and would not be tempted to bring sorrow into her household by any fault of hers. Her earnest prayer was, that she might not know of her existence. She had not looked on Horatio since she watched him under the shadow of the magnolia, until his barouche passed her in her rambles some months after. She saw the deadly paleness of his countenance, and had he dared to look back, he would have seen her tottering with faintness. Mary brought water from a rivulet, and sprinkled her face. When she revived, she clasped the beloved child to her heart with a vehemence that made her scream. Soothingly she kissed away her fears, and gazed into her beautiful eyes with a deep, deep sadness of expression, which poor Mary never forgot. Wild were the thoughts that passed round her aching heart, and almost maddened her poor brain; thoughts which had almost driven her to suicide the night of that last farewell. For her child's sake she had conquered the fierce temptation then; and for her sake, she struggled with it now. But the gloomy atmosphere of their once happy home overclouded the morning of Mary's life. Clotel perceived this, and it gave her unutterable pain.

> "Tis ever thus with woman's love,
>   True till life's storms have passed;
> And, like the vine around the tree,
>   It braves them to the last."

CHAPTER IX

The Man of Honour

"My tongue could never learn sweet
    soothing words,
But now thy beauty is propos'd, my fee,
My proud heart sues, and prompts my
    tongue to speak."

SHAKSPEARE

James Crawford, the purchaser of Althesa, was from the green mountains of Vermont, and his feelings were opposed to the holding of slaves. But his young wife persuaded him into the idea that it was no worse to own a slave than to hire one and pay the money to another. Hence it was that he had been induced to purchase Althesa. Henry Morton, a young physician from the same state, and who had just commenced the practice of his profession in New Orleans, was boarding with Crawford when Althesa was brought home. The young physician had been in New Orleans but a few weeks, and had seen very little of slavery. In his own mountain home he had been taught that the slaves of the Southern states were Negroes, if not from the coast of Africa, the descendants of those who had been imported. He was unprepared to behold with composure a beautiful young white girl of fifteen in the degraded position of a chattel slave. The blood chilled in his young heart as he heard Crawford tell how, by bantering with the trader, he had bought her for two hundred dollars less than he first asked. His very looks showed that the slave girl had the deepest sympathy of his heart. Althesa had been brought up by her mother to look after the domestic concerns of her cottage in Virginia, and knew well the duties imposed upon her. Mrs. Crawford was much pleased with her new servant, and often made mention of her in [the] presence of Morton. The young man's sympathy ripened into love, which was reciprocated by the friendless and injured child of sorrow. There was but one course left; that was, to purchase the young girl and make her his wife, which he did six months after her arrival in Crawford's family. The young physician and his wife immediately took lodgings in another part of the city; a private teacher was called in, and the young wife taught some of those accomplishments which are necessary for one's taking a position in society. Dr. Morton soon obtained a large practice in his profession, and with it increased in wealth—but with all his wealth he never would own a slave. Mrs. Morton was now in a position to seek out and redeem her mother, whom she had not heard of since they parted at Natchez. An agent was immediately despatched to hunt out the mother and to see if she could be purchased. The agent had no trouble in finding out Mr. Peck: but all overtures were unavailable; he would not sell Currer. His excuse was, that she was such a good housekeeper that he could not spare her. Poor Althesa felt sad when she found that her mother could not be bought. However, she felt a consciousness of having done her duty in the matter, yet waited with the hope that the day might come when she should have her mother by her side.

CHAPTER X

The Young Christian

"Here we see *God dealing in slaves*; giving them to his
own favourite child [Abraham], a man of superlative
worth, and as a reward for his eminent goodness."
                              REV. THEODORE CLAPP,
                              OF NEW ORLEANS

On Carlton's return the next day from the farm, he was
overwhelmed with questions from Mr. Peck, as to what he
thought of the plantation, the condition of the Negroes,
Huckelby and Snyder; and especially how he liked the sermon of the latter. Mr. Peck was a kind of a patriarch in his
own way. To begin with, he was a man of some talent. He
not only had a good education, but was a man of great eloquence, and had a wonderful command of language. He too
either had, or thought he had, poetical genius; and was often
sending contributions to the *Natchez Free Trader,* and other
periodicals. In the way of raising contributions for foreign
missions, he took the lead of all others in his neighbourhood.
Everything he did, he did for the "glory of God," as he said:
he quoted Scripture for almost everything he did. Being in
good circumstances, he was able to give to almost all benevolent causes to which he took a fancy. He was a most loving
father, and his daughter exercised considerable influence over
him, and owing to her piety and judgment, that influence
had a beneficial effect. Carlton, though a school-fellow of
the parson's, was nevertheless nearly ten years his junior; and
though not an avowed infidel, was, however, a free-thinker,
and one who took no note of to-morrow. And for this reason

Georgiana took peculiar interest in the young man, for Carlton was but little above thirty and unmarried. The young Christian felt that she would not be living up to that faith that she professed and believed in, if she did not exert herself to the utmost to save the thoughtless man from his downward career; and in this she succeeded to her most sanguine expectations. She not only converted him, but in placing the Scriptures before him in their true light, she redeemed those sacred writings from the charge of supporting the system of slavery, which her father had cast upon them in the discussion some days before.

Georgiana's first object, however, was to awaken in Carlton's breast a love for the Lord Jesus Christ. The young man had often sat under the sound of the gospel with perfect indifference. He had heard men talk who had grown grey bending over the Scriptures, and their conversation had passed by him unheeded; but when a young girl, much younger than himself, reasoned with him in that innocent and persuasive manner that woman is wont to use when she has entered with her whole soul upon an object, it was too much for his stout heart, and he yielded. Her next aim was to vindicate the Bible from sustaining the monstrous institution of slavery. She said, "God has created of one blood all the nations of men, to dwell on all the face of the earth. To claim, hold, and treat a human being as property is felony against God and man. The Christian religion is opposed to slaveholding in its spirit and its principles; it classes menstealers among murderers; and it is the duty of all who wish to meet God in peace, to discharge that duty in spreading these principles. Let us not deceive ourselves into the idea that slavery is right, because it is profitable to us. Slaveholding is the highest possible violation of the eighth commandment. To take from a man his earnings, is theft; but to take the earner is a compound, life-long theft; and we who profess to follow in the footsteps of our Redeemer, should do our utmost to extirpate slavery from the land. For my own part, I shall do all I can. When the Redeemer was about to ascend to the bosom of the Father, and resume the glory which he had with him before the world was, he promised his disciples that the power of the Holy Ghost should come upon them, and that they should be witnesses for him to the uttermost parts of the earth. What was the effect upon their minds? 'They all continued with one accord in prayer and supplication with the women.' Stimulated by the confident expectation that Jesus would fulfil his gracious promise, they poured out their hearts in fervent supplications, probably for strength to do the work which he had appointed them unto, for they felt that without him they could do nothing, and they consecrated themselves on the altar of God, to the great and glorious enterprise of preaching the unsearchable riches of Christ to a lost and perishing world. Have we less precious promises in the Scriptures of truth? May we not claim of our God the blessing promised unto those who consider the poor: the Lord will preserve them and keep them alive, and they shall be blessed upon the earth? Does not the language, 'Inasmuch as ye did it unto one of the least of these my brethren, ye did it unto me,' belong to all who are rightly engaged in endeavouring to unloose the bondman's fetters? Shall we not then do as the apostles did? Shall we not, in view of the two millions of heathen in our very midst, in view of the souls that are going down in an almost unbroken phalanx to utter perdition, continue in prayer and supplication, that God will grant us the supplies of his Spirit to prepare us for that work which he has given us to do? Shall not the wail of the mother as she surrenders her only child to the grasp of the ruthless kidnapper, or the trader in human blood, animate our devotions? Shall not the manifold crimes and horrors of slavery excite more ardent outpourings at the throne of grace to grant repentance to our guilty country, and permit us to aid in preparing the way for the glorious second advent of the Messiah, by preaching deliverance to the captives, and the opening of the prison doors to those who are bound?"

Georgiana had succeeded in riveting the attention of Carlton during her conversation, and as she was finishing her last sentence, she observed the silent tear stealing down the cheek of the newly born child of God. At this juncture her father entered, and Carlton left the room.

"Dear papa," said Georgiana, "will you grant me one favour; or, rather, make me a promise?"

"I can't tell, my dear, till I know what it is," replied Mr. Peck. "If it is a reasonable request, I will comply with your wish," continued he.

"I hope, my dear," answered she, "that papa would not think me capable of making an unreasonable request."

"Well, well," returned he; "tell me what it is."

"I hope," said she, "that in your future conversation with Mr. Carlton, on the subject of slavery, you will not speak of the Bible as sustaining it."

"Why, Georgiana, my dear, you are mad, aint you?" exclaimed he, in an excited tone.

The poor girl remained silent; the father saw in a moment that he had spoken too sharply; and taking her hand in his he said, "Now, my child, why do you make that request?"

"Because," returned she, "I think he is on the stool of repentance, if he has not already been received among the elect. He, you know, was bordering upon infidelity, and if the Bible sanctions slavery, then he will naturally enough say that it is not from God; for the argument from internal evidence is not only refuted, but actually turned against the Bible. If the Bible sanctions slavery, then it misrepresents the character of God. Nothing would be more dangerous to the soul of a young convert than to satisfy him that the Scriptures favoured such a system of sin."

"Don't you suppose that I understand the Scriptures better than you? I have been in the world longer."

"Yes," said she, "you have been in the world longer, and amongst slaveholders so long that you do not regard it in the same light that those do who have not become so familiar with its every-day scenes as you. I once heard you say, that you were opposed to the institution, when you first came to the South."

"Yes," answered he, "I did not know so much about it then."

"With great deference to you, papa," replied Georgiana, "I don't think that the Bible sanctions slavery. The Old Testament contains this explicit condemnation of it, 'He that stealeth a man, and selleth him, or if he be found in his hand, he shall surely be put to death'; and 'Woe unto him that buildeth his house by unrighteousness, and his chambers by wrong; that useth his neighbour's service without wages, and giveth him not for his work'; when also the New Testament exhibits such words of rebuke as these, 'Behold the hire of the labourers who have reaped down your fields, which is of you kept back by fraud, crieth; and the cries of them who have reaped are entered into the ears of the Lord of Sabaoth.' 'The law is not made for a righteous man, but for the lawless and disobedient, for the ungodly and for sinners, for unholy and profane, for murderers of fathers and murderers of mothers, for manslayers, for whoremongers, for them that defile themselves with mankind, for *menstealers*, for liars, for perjured persons.' A more scathing denunciation of the sin in question is surely to be found on record in no other book. I am afraid," continued the daughter, "that the acts of the professed friends of Christianity in the South do more to spread infidelity than the writings of all the atheists which have ever been published. The infidel watches the religious world. He surveys the church, and lo! thousands and tens of thousands of her accredited members actually hold slaves. Members 'in good and regular standing,' fellowshipped throughout Christendom except by a few antislavery churches generally despised as ultra and radical, reduce their fellow men to the condition of chattels, and by force keep them in that state of degradation. Bishops, ministers, elders, and deacons are engaged in this awful business, and do not consider their conduct as at all inconsistent with the precepts of either the Old or New Testaments. Moreover, those ministers and churches who do not themselves hold slaves, very generally defend the conduct of those who

CLOTEL; OR, THE PRESIDENT'S DAUGHTER

do, and accord to them a fair Christian character, and in the way of business frequently take mortgages and levy executions on the bodies of their fellow men, and in some cases of their fellow Christians.

'Now is it a wonder that infidels, beholding the practice and listening to the theory of professing Christians, should conclude that the Bible inculcates a morality not inconsistent with chattelising human beings? And must not this conclusion be strengthened, when they hear ministers of talent and learning declare that the Bible does sanction slaveholding, and that it ought not to be made a disciplinable offence in churches? And must not all doubt be dissipated, when one of the most learned professors in our theological seminaries asserts that the Bible 'recognises that the relation may still exist, *salva fide et salva ecclesia*' (without injury to the Christian faith or church) and that only 'the *abuse* of it is the essential and fundamental wrong?' Are not infidels bound to believe that these professors, ministers, and churches understand their own Bible, and that, consequently, notwithstanding solitary passages which appear to condemn slaveholding, the Bible sanctions it? When nothing can be further from the truth. And as for Christ, his whole life was a living testimony against slavery and all that it inculcates. When he designed to do us good, he took upon himself the form of a servant. He took his station at the bottom of society. He voluntarily identified himself with the poor and the despised. The warning voices of Jeremiah and Ezekiel were raised in olden time, against sin. Let us not forget what followed. 'Therefore, thus saith the Lord—ye have not harkened unto me in proclaiming liberty every one to his brother, and every one to his neighbour—behold I proclaim a liberty for you, saith the Lord, to the sword, to the pestilence, and to the famine.' Are we not virtually as a nation adopting the same impious language, and are we not exposed to the same tremendous judgments? Shall we not, in view of those things, use very laudable means to awaken our beloved country from the slumbers of death, and baptize all our efforts with tears and with prayers, that God may bless them? Then, should our labour fail to accomplish the end for which we pray, we shall stand acquitted at the bar of Jehovah, and although we may share in the national calamities which await unrepented sins, yet that blessed approval will be ours—'Well done, good and faithful servants, enter ye into the joy of your Lord.'"

"My dear Georgiana," said Mr. Peck, "I must be permitted to entertain my own views on this subject, and to exercise my own judgment."

"Believe me, dear papa," she replied, 'I would not be understood as wishing to teach you, or to dictate to you in the least; but only grant my request, not to allude to the Bible as sanctioning slavery, when speaking with Mr. Carlton."

"Well," returned he, "I will comply with your wish."

The young Christian had indeed accomplished a noble work; and whether it was admitted by the father, or not, she was his superior and his teacher. Georgiana had viewed the right to enjoy perfect liberty as one of those inherent and inalienable rights which pertain to the whole human race, and of which they can never be divested, except by an act of gross injustice. And no one was more able than herself to impress those views upon the hearts of all with whom she came in contact. Modest and self-possessed, with a voice of great sweetness, and a most winning manner, she could, with the greatest ease to herself, engage their attention.

CHAPTER XI

The Parson Poet

"Unbind, unbind my galling chain,
And set, oh! set me free:
No longer say that I'll disdain
The gift of liberty."

Through the persuasion of Mr. Peck, and fascinated with the charms of Georgiana, Carlton had prolonged his stay two months with his old school-fellow. During the latter part of the time he had been almost as one of the family. If Miss Peck was invited out, Mr. Carlton was, as a matter of course. She seldom rode out, unless with him. If Mr. Peck was absent, he took the head of the table; and, to the delight of the young lady, he had on several occasions taken part in the family worship.

"I am glad," said Mr. Peck, one evening while at the tea table, "I am glad, Mr. Carlton, that my neighbour Jones has invited you to visit him at his farm. He is a good neighbour, but a very ungodly man; I want that you should see his people, and then, when you return to the North, you can tell how much better a Christian's slaves are situated than one who does nothing for the cause of Christ."

"I hope, Mr. Carlton," said Georgiana, "that you will spend the Sabbath with him, and have a religious interview with the Negroes."

"Yes," replied the parson, "that's well thought of, Georgy."

"Well, I think I will go up on Thursday next, and stay till Monday," said Carlton; "and I shall act upon your suggestion, Miss Peck," continued he; "and try to get a religious interview with the blacks. By-the-by," remarked Carlton, "I saw an advertisement in the *Free Trader* to-day that rather puzzled me. Ah, here it is now; and," drawing the paper from his pocket, "I will read it, and then you can tell me what it means:

> 'TO PLANTERS AND OTHERS.—*Wanted fifty Negroes.* Any person having *sick Negroes,* considered *incurable* by their respective physicians, (their owners of course,) and wishing to dispose of them, Dr. Stillman will pay cash for Negroes affected with scrofula or king's evil, confirmed hypochondriacism, apoplexy, or diseases of the brain, kidneys, spleen, stomach and intestines, bladder and its appendages, diarrhoea, dysentery, &c. *The highest cash price will be paid as above.*'

When I read this to-day I thought that the advertiser must be a man of eminent skill as a physician, and that he intended to cure the sick Negroes; but on second thought I find that some of the diseases enumerated are certainly incurable. What can he do with these sick Negroes?"

"You see," replied Mr. Peck, laughing, "that he is a doctor, and has use for them in his lectures. The doctor is connected with a small college. Look at his prospectus, where he invites students to attend, and that will explain the matter to you."

Carlton turned to another column, and read the following:

> "Some advantages of a peculiar character are connected with this institution, which it may be proper to point out. No place in the United States offers as great opportunities for the acquisition of anatomical knowledge. Subjects being obtained from among the coloured population in sufficient numbers *for every purpose,* and proper dissections carried on *without offending any individuals in the community!*"

"These are for dissection, then?" inquired Carlton with a trembling voice.

"Yes," answered the parson.

"Of course they wait till they die before they can use them."

"They keep them on hand, and when they need one they bleed him to death," returned Mr. Peck.

"Yes, but that's murder."

"Oh, the doctors are licensed to commit murder, you know; and what's the difference, whether one dies owing to the loss of blood, or taking too many pills? For my own part, if I had to choose, I would rather submit to the former."

"I have often heard what I considered hard stories in abolition meetings in New York about slavery; but now I shall begin to think that many of them are true."

"The longer you remain here the more you will be convinced of the iniquity of the institution," remarked Georgiana.

"Now, Georgy, my dear, don't give us another abolition lecture, if you please," said Mr. Peck. "Here, Carlton," continued the parson, "I have written a short poem for your sister's album, as you requested me; it is a domestic piece, as you will see."

"She will prize it the more for that," remarked Carlton; and taking the sheet of paper, he laughed as his eyes glanced over it.

"Read it out, Mr. Carlton," said Georgiana, "and let me hear what it is; I know papa gets off some very droll things at times." Carlton complied with the young lady's request, and read aloud the following rare specimen of poetical genius:

"MY LITTLE NIG.

"I have a little nigger, the blackest thing alive,
He'll be just four years old if he lives till forty-five;
His smooth cheek hath a glossy hue, like a new polished boot,
And his hair curls o'er his little head as black as any soot.
His lips bulge from his countenance—his little ivories shine—
His nose is what we call a little pug, but fashioned very fine:

Although not quite a fairy, he is comely to behold,
And I wouldn't sell him, 'pon my word, for a hundred all in
   gold.

"He gets up early in the morn, like all the other nigs,
And runs off to the hog-lot, where he squabbles with the pigs—
And when the sun gets out of bed, and mounts up in the sky,
The warmest corner of the yard is where my nig doth lie.
And there extended lazily, he contemplates and dreams,
(I cannot qualify to this, but plain enough it seems;)
Until 'tis time to take in grub, when you can't find him there,
For, like a politician, he has gone to hunt his share.

"I haven't said a single word concerning my plantation,
Though a prettier, I guess, cannot be found within the nation;
When he gets a little bigger, I'll take and to him show it,
And then I'll say, 'My little nig, now just prepare to go it!'
I'll put a hoe into his hand—he'll soon know what it means,
And every day for dinner, he shall have bacon and greens."

CHAPTER XII

A Night
in the Parson's Kitchen

"And see the servants met,
Their daily labour's o'er;
And with the jest and song they set
The kitchen in a roar."

Mr. Peck kept around him four servants besides Currer, of whom we have made mention: of these, Sam was considered the first. If a dinner-party was in contemplation, or any company to be invited to the parson's, after all the arrangements had been talked over by the minister and his daughter, Sam was sure to be consulted upon the subject by "Miss Georgy," as Miss Peck was called by the servants. If furniture, crockery, or anything else was to be purchased, Sam felt that he had been slighted if his opinion had not been asked. As to the marketing, he did it all. At the servants' table in the kitchen, he sat at the head, and was master of ceremonies. A single look from him was enough to silence any conversation or noise in the kitchen, or any other part of the premises. There is, in the Southern States, a great amount of prejudice against colour amongst the Negroes themselves. The nearer the Negro or mulatto approaches to the white, the more he seems to feel his superiority over those of a darker hue. This is, no doubt, the result of the prejudice that exists on the part of whites towards both mulattoes and blacks. Sam was originally from Kentucky, and through the instrumentality of one of his young masters whom he had to take to school, he had learned to read so as to be well understood; and, owing to that fact, was considered a prodigy among the slaves, not only of his own master's, but those of the town who knew him. Sam had a great wish to follow in the footsteps of his master, and be a poet; and was, therefore, often heard singing doggrels of his own composition. But there was one great drawback to Sam, and that was his colour. He was one of the blackest of his race. This he evidently regarded as a great misfortune. However, he made up for this in his dress. Mr. Peck kept his house servants well dressed; and as for Sam, he was seldom seen except in a ruffled shirt. Indeed, the washerwoman feared him more than all others about the house.

Currer, as we have already stated, was chief of the kitchen department, and had a general supervision of the household affairs. Alfred the coachman, Peter, and Hetty made up the remainder of the house servants. Besides these, Mr. Peck owned eight slaves who were masons. These worked in the city. Being mechanics, they were let out to greater advantage than to keep them on the farm. However, every Sunday night, Peck's servants, including the bricklayers, usually assembled in the kitchen, when the events of the week were freely discussed and commented on. It was on a Sunday evening, in the month of June, that there was a party at Mr. Peck's, and, according to custom in the Southern States, the ladies had their maid-servants with them. Tea had been served in "the house," and the servants, including the strangers, had taken their seats at the tea table in the kitchen. Sam, being a "single gentleman," was usually attentive to the "ladies" on this occasion. He seldom or ever let the day pass without spending at least an hour in combing and brushing up his "hare." Sam had an idea that fresh butter was better for his hair than any other kind of grease; and therefore, on churning days, half a pound of butter had always to be taken out before it was salted. When he wished to appear to great advantage, he would grease his face, to make it "shiny." On the evening of the party therefore, when all the servants were at the table, Sam cut a big figure. There he sat with his wool well combed and buttered, face nicely greased, and his ruffles extending five or six inches from his breast. The parson in his own drawing-room did not make a more imposing appearance than did his servant on this occasion.

"I jist bin had my fortune told last Sunday night," said Sam, as he helped one of the girls to some sweet hash.

"Indeed," cried half-a-dozen voices.

"Yes," continued he; "Aunt Winny told me I is to hab de prettiest yaller gal in town, and dat I is to be free."

All eyes were immediately turned toward Sally Johnson, who was seated near Sam.

"I speck I see somebody blush at dat remark," said Alfred.

"Pass dem pancakes and molasses up dis way, Mr. Alf, and none of your insinawaysion here," rejoined Sam.

"Dat reminds me," said Currer, "dat Dorcas Simpson is gwine to git married."

"Who to, I want to know?" inquired Peter.

"To one of Mr. Darby's field-hands," answered Currer.

"I should tink dat dat gal would not trow herself away in dat manner," said Sally. "She good enough looking to get a house servant, and not to put up wid a fiel' nigger," continued she.

"Yes," said Sam, "dat's a wery insensible remark of yours, Miss Sally. I admire your judgment wery much, I assure you. Dah's plenty of suspectible and well-dressed house servants dat a gal of her looks can get, wid out taken up wid dem common darkies."

"Is de man black or a mulatto?" inquired one of the company.

"He's nearly white," replied Currer.

"Well den, dat's some exchuse for her," remarked Sam; "for I don't like to see dis malgemation of blacks and mulattoes, no how," continued Sam. "If I had my rights I would be a mulatto too, for my mother was almost as light-coloured as Miss Sally," said he.

Although Sam was one of the blackest men living, he

nevertheless contended that his mother was a mulatto, and no one was more prejudiced against the blacks than he. A good deal of work, and the free use of fresh butter, had no doubt done wonders for his "hare" in causing it to grow long, and to this he would always appeal when he wished to convince others that he was part of an Anglo-Saxon.

"I always thought you was not clear black, Mr. Sam," said Agnes.

"You are right dahr, Miss Agnes. My hare tells what company I belong to," answered Sam. Here the whole company joined in the conversation about colour, which lasted for some time, giving unmistakeable evidence that caste is owing to ignorance. The evening's entertainment concluded by Sam's relating a little of his own experience while with his first master in old Kentucky.

Sam's former master was a doctor, and had a large practice among his neighbours, doctoring both masters and slaves. When Sam was about fifteen years of age, his old master set him to grinding up the ointment, then to making pills. As the young student grew older and became more practised in his profession, his services were of more importance to the doctor. The physician having a good business, and a large number of his patients being slaves, the most of whom had to call on the doctor when ill, he put Sam to bleeding, pulling teeth, and administering medicine to the slaves. Sam soon acquired the name amongst the slave of the "Black Doctor." With this appellation he was delighted, and no regular physician could possibly have put on more airs than did the black doctor when his services were required. In bleeding, he must have more bandages, and rub and smack the arm more than the doctor would have thought of. We once saw Sam taking out a tooth for one of his patients, and nothing appeared more amusing. He got the poor fellow down on his back, and he got astraddle of the man's chest, and getting the turnkeys on the wrong tooth, he shut both eyes and pulled for his life. The poor man screamed as loud as he could, but to no purpose. Sam had him fast. After a great effort, out came the sound grinder, and the young doctor saw his mistake; but consoled himself with the idea that as the wrong tooth was out of the way, there was more room to get at the right one. Bleeding and a dose of calomel was always considered indispensable by the "Old Boss"; and, as a matter of course, Sam followed in his footsteps.

On one occasion the old doctor was ill himself, so as to be unable to attend to his patients. A slave, with pass in hand, called to receive medical advice, and the master told Sam to examine him and see what he wanted. This delighted him beyond measure, for although he had been acting his part in the way of giving out medicine as the master ordered it, he had never been called upon by the latter to examine a patient, and this seemed to convince him that, after all, he was no sham doctor. As might have been expected, he cut a rare figure in his first examination, placing himself directly opposite his patient, and folding his arms across his breast, and looking very knowingly, he began, "What's de matter wid you?"

"I is sick."

"Where is you sick?"

"Here," replied the man, putting his hand upon his stomach.

"Put out your tongue," continued the doctor. The man ran out his tongue at full length.

"Let me feel your pulse," at the same time taking his patient's hand in his, placing his fingers on his pulse, he said, "Ah, your case is a bad one; if I don't do something for you, and dat pretty quick, you 'ill be a gone coon, and dat's sartin." At this the man appeared frightened and inquired what was the matter with him: in answer, Sam said, "I done told you dat your case is a bad one, and dat's enough."

On Sam's returning to his master's bedside, the latter said, "Well, Sam, what do you think is the matter with him?"

"His stomach is out of order, sir," he replied.

"What do you think had best be done for him?"

"I think I better bleed him and give him a dose of calomel," returned Sam. So to the latter's gratification the master let him have his own way. We need not further say, that the recital of Sam's experience as a physician gave him a high position amongst the servants that evening, and made him a decided favourite with the ladies, one of whom feigned illness, when the black doctor, to the delight of all, and certainly to himself, gave medical advice. Thus ended the evening amongst the servants in the parson's kitchen.

CHAPTER XIII

A Slave Hunting Parson

" 'Tis too much prov'd—that with devotion's visage,
And pious action, we do sugar o'er the devil himself."
SHAKSPEARE

"You will, no doubt, be well pleased with neighbour Jones," said Mr. Peck, as Carlton stepped into the chaise to pay his promised visit to the "ungodly man."

"Don't forget to have a religious interview with the Negroes," remarked Georgiana, as she gave the last nod to her young convert.

"I will do my best," returned Carlton, as the vehicle left the door.

As might have been expected, Carlton met with a cordial reception at the hands of the proprietor of the Grove Farm. The servants in the "Great House" were well dressed, and appeared as if they did not want for food. Jones knew that Carlton was from the North, and a non-slaveholder, and therefore did everything in his power to make a favourable impression on his mind. "My Negroes are well clothed, well fed, and not over worked," said the slaveholder to his visitor, after the latter had been with him nearly a week.

"As far as I can see your slaves appear to good advantage," replied Carlton. "But," continued he, "if it is a fair question, do you have preaching among your slaves on Sunday, Mr. Jones?"

"No, no," returned he, "I think that's all nonsense; my Negroes do their own preaching."

"So you do permit them to have meetings."

"Yes, when they wish. There's some very intelligent and clever chaps among them."

"As to-morrow is the Sabbath," said Carlton, "if you have no objection, I will attend meeting with them."

"Most certainly you shall, if you will do the preaching," returned the planter.

Here the young man was about to decline, but he remembered the parting words of Georgiana, and he took courage and said, "Oh, I have no objection to give the Negroes a short talk." It was then understood that Carlton was to have a religious interview with the blacks the next day, and the young man waited with a degree of impatience for the time.

In no part of the South are slaves in a more ignorant and degraded state than in the cotton, sugar, and rice districts.

If they are permitted to cease labour on the Sabbath, the time is spent in hunting, fishing, or lying beneath the shade of a tree, resting for the morrow. Religious instruction is unknown in the far South, except among such men as the Rev. C. C. Jones, John Peck, and some others who regard religious instruction, such as they impart to their slaves, as calculated to make them more trustworthy and valuable as property. Jones, aware that his slaves would make rather a bad show of intelligence if questioned by Carlton, resolved to have them ready for him, and therefore gave his driver orders with regard to their preparation. Consequently, after the day's labour was over, Dogget, the driver, assembled the Negroes together and said, "Now, boys and gals, your master is coming down to the quarters to-morrow with his visitor, who is going to give you a preach, and I want you should understand what he says to you. Now many of you who came of Old Virginia and Kentuck, know what preaching is, and others who have been raised in these parts do not. Preaching is to tell you that you are mighty wicked and bad at heart. This, I suppose, you all know. But if the gentleman should ask you who made you, tell him the Lord; if he ask if you wish to go to heaven, tell him yes. Remember that you are all Christians, all love the Lord, all want to go to heaven, all love your masters, and all love me. Now, boys and gals, I want you to show yourselves smart to-morrow: be on your p's and q's, and, Monday morning, I will give you all a glass of whiskey bright and early." Agreeable to arrangement the slaves were assembled together on Sunday morning under the large trees near the great house, and after going through another drilling from the driver, Jones and Carlton made their appearance. "You see," said Jones to the Negroes, as he approached them, "you see here's a gentleman that's come to talk to you about your souls, and I hope you 'ill all pay that attention that you ought." Jones then seated himself in one of the two chairs placed there for him and the stranger.

Carlton had already selected a chapter in the Bible to read to them, which he did, after first prefacing it with some remarks of his own. Not being accustomed to speak in public, he determined, after reading the Bible, to make it more of a conversational meeting than otherwise. He therefore began asking them questions. "Do you feel that you are a Christian?" asked he of a full-blooded Negro that sat near him.

"Yes, sir," was the response.

"You feel, then, that you shall go to heaven."

"Yes, sir."

"Of course you know who made you?"

The man put his hand to his head and began to scratch his wool; and, after a little hesitation, answered, "De overseer told us last night who made us, but indeed I forgot the gentmun's name."

This reply was almost too much for Carlton, and his gravity was not a little moved. However, he bit his tongue, and turned to another man, who appeared, from his looks, to be more intelligent. "Do you serve the Lord?" asked he.

"No, sir, I don't serve anybody but Mr. Jones; I neber belong to anybody else."

To hide his feeling at this juncture, Carlton turned and walked to another part of the grounds, to where the women were seated, and said to a mulatto woman who had rather an anxious countenance, "Did you ever hear of John the Baptist?"

"Oh yes, marser, John de Baptist; I know dat nigger bery well indeed; he libs in old Kentuck, where I come from."

Carlton's gravity here gave way, and he looked at the planter and laughed right out. The old woman knew a slave near her old master's farm in Kentucky, and was ignorant enough to suppose that he was the John the Baptist inquired about. Carlton occupied the remainder of the time in reading Scripture and talking to them.

"My niggers aint shown off very well to-day," said Jones, as he and his visitor left the grounds.

"No," replied Carlton.

"You did not get hold of the bright ones," continued the planter.

"So it seems," remarked Carlton.

The planter evidently felt that his neighbour, Parson Peck, would have a nut to crack over the account that Carlton would give of the ignorance of the slaves, and said and did all in his power to remove the bad impression already made; but to no purpose. The report made by Carlton, on his return, amused the parson very much. It appeared to him the best reason why professed Christians like himself should be slave-holders. Not so with Georgiana. She did not even smile when Carlton was telling his story, but seemed sore at heart that such ignorance should prevail in their midst. The question turned upon the heathen of other lands, and the parson began to expatiate upon his own efforts in foreign missions, when his daughter, with a child-like simplicity, said,

> "Send Bibles to the heathen;
>   On every distant shore,
>   From light that's beaming o'er us,
>   Let streams increasing pour
>   But keep it from the millions
>   Down-trodden at our door.

"Send Bibles to the heathen,
  Their famished spirits feed;
Oh! haste, and join your efforts,
  The priceless gift to speed;
Then flog the trembling Negro
  If he should learn to read."

"I saw a curiosity while at Mr. Jones's that I shall not forget soon," said Carlton.

"What was it?" inquired the parson.

"A kennel of bloodhounds; and such dogs I never saw before. They were of a species between the bloodhound and the foxhound, and were ferocious, gaunt, and savage-looking animals. They were part of a stock imported from Cuba, he informed me. They were kept in an iron cage, and fed on Indian corn bread. This kind of food, he said, made them eager for their business. Sometimes they would give the dogs meat, but it was always after they had been chasing a Negro."

"Were those the dogs you had, papa, to hunt Harry?" asked Georgiana.

"No, my dear," was the short reply: and the parson seemed anxious to change the conversation to something else. When Mr. Peck had left the room, Carlton spoke more freely of what he had seen, and spoke more pointedly against slavery; for he well knew that Miss Peck sympathised with him in all he felt and said.

"You mentioned about your father hunting a slave," said Carlton, in an undertone.

"Yes," replied she; "papa went with some slave-catchers and a parcel of those nasty Negro-dogs, to hunt poor Harry. He belonged to papa and lived on the farm. His wife lives in town, and Harry had been to see her, and did not return quite as early as he should; and Huckelby was flogging him, and he got away and came here. I wanted papa to keep him in town, so that he could see his wife more frequently; but he said they could not spare him from the farm, and flogged him again, and sent him back. The poor fellow knew that the overseer would punish him over again, and instead of going back he went into the woods."

"Did they catch him?" asked Carlton.

"Yes," replied she. "In chasing him through the woods, he attempted to escape by swimming across a river, and the dogs were sent in after him, and soon caught him. But Harry had great courage and fought the dogs with a big club; and papa seeing the Negro would escape from the dogs, shot at him, as he says, only to wound him, that he might be caught; but the poor fellow was killed." Overcome by relating this incident, Georgiana burst into tears.

Although Mr. Peck fed and clothed his house servants well, and treated them with a degree of kindness, he was, nevertheless, a most cruel master. He encouraged his driver to work the field-hands from early dawn till late at night; and the good appearance of the house-servants, and the preaching of Snyder to the field Negroes, was to cause himself to be regarded as a Christian master. Being on a visit one day at the farm, and having with him several persons from the Free States, and wishing to make them believe that his slaves were happy, satisfied, and contented, the parson got out the whiskey and gave each one a dram, who in return had to drink the master's health, or give a toast of some kind. The company were not a little amused at some of the sentiments given, and Peck was delighted at every indication of contentment on the part of the blacks. At last it came to Jack's turn to drink, and the master expected something good from him, because he was considered the cleverest and most witty slave on the farm.

"Now," said the master, as he handed Jack the cup of whiskey; "now, Jack, give us something rich. You know," continued he, "we have raised the finest crop of cotton that's been seen in these parts for many a day. Now give us a toast on cotton; come, Jack, give us something to laugh at." The Negro felt not a little elated at being made the hero of the

occasion, and taking the whiskey in his right hand, put his
left to his head and began to scratch his wool, and said,

> "The big bee flies high,
> The little bee make the honey;
> The black folks makes the cotton,
> And the white folks gets the money."

CHAPTER XIV

A Free Woman
Reduced to Slavery

Althesa found in Henry Morton a kind and affectionate husband; and his efforts to purchase her mother, although unsuccessful, had doubly endeared him to her. Having from the commencement resolved not to hold slaves, or rather not to own any, they were compelled to hire servants for their own use. Five years had passed away, and their happiness was increased by two lovely daughters. Mrs. Morton was seated, one bright afternoon, busily engaged with her needle, and near her sat Salome, a servant that she had just taken into her employ. The woman was perfectly white; so much so, that Mrs. Morton had expressed her apprehensions to her husband, when the woman first came, that she was not born a slave. The mistress watched the servant, as the latter sat sewing upon some coarse work, and saw the large silent tear in her eye. This caused an uneasiness to the mistress, and she said, "Salome, don't you like your situation here?"

"Oh yes, madam," answered the woman in a quick tone, and then tried to force a smile.

"Why is it that you often look sad, and with tears in your eyes?" The mistress saw that she had touched a tender chord, and continued, "I am your friend; tell me your sorrow, and, if I can, I will help you." As the last sentence was escaping the lips of the mistress, the slave woman put her check apron to her face and wept. Mrs. Morton saw plainly that there was cause for this expression of grief, and pressed the woman more closely. "Hear me, then," said the woman calming herself: "I will tell you why I sometimes weep. I was born in Germany, on the banks of the Rhine. Ten years ago my father came to this country, bringing with him my mother and myself. He was poor, and I, wishing to assist all I could, obtained a situation as nurse to a lady in this city. My father got employment as a labourer on the wharf, among the steamboats; but he was soon taken ill with the yellow fever, and died. My mother then got a situation for herself, while I remained with my first employer. When the hot season came on, my master, with his wife, left New Orleans until the hot season was over, and took me with them. They stopped at a town on the banks of the Mississippi river, and said they should remain there some weeks. One day they went out for a ride, and they had not been gone more than half an hour, when two men came into the room and told me that they had bought me, and that I was their slave. I was bound and taken to prison, and that night put on a steamboat and taken up the Yazoo river, and set to work on a farm. I was forced to take up with a Negro, and by him had three children. A year since my master's daughter was married, and I was given to her. She came with her husband to this city, and I have ever since been hired out."

"Unhappy woman," whispered Althesa, "why did you not tell me this before?"

"I was afraid," replied Salome, "for I was once severely flogged for telling a stranger that I was not born a slave."

On Mr. Morton's return home, his wife communicated to him the story which the slave woman had told her an hour before, and begged that something might be done to rescue her from the situation she was then in. In Louisiana as well as many others of the slave states, great obstacles are thrown in the way of persons who have been wrongfully reduced to slavery regaining their freedom. A person claiming to be free must prove his right to his liberty. This, it will be seen, throws the burden of proof upon the slave, who, in all probability, finds it out of his power to procure such evidence. And if any free person shall attempt to aid a freeman in regaining his freedom, he is compelled to enter into security in the sum of one thousand dollars, and if the person claiming to be free shall fail to establish such fact, the thousand dollars are forfeited to the state. This cruel and oppressive law has kept many a freeman from espousing the cause of persons unjustly held as slaves. Mr. Morton inquired and found that the woman's story was true, as regarded the time she had lived with her present owner; but the latter not only denied that she was free, but immediately removed her from Morton's. Three months after Salome had been removed from Morton's and let out to another family, she was one morning cleaning the door steps, when a lady passing by, looked at the slave and thought she recognised some one that she had seen before. The lady stopped and asked the woman if she was a slave.

"I am," said she.

"Were you born a slave?"

"No, I was born in Germany."

"What's the name of the ship in which you came to this country?" inquired the lady.

"I don't know," was the answer.

"Was it the *Amazon?*"

At the sound of this name, the slave woman was silent for a moment, and then the tears began to flow freely down her care-worn cheeks.

"Would you know Mrs. Marshall, who was a passenger in the *Amazon,* if you should see her?" inquired the lady.

At this the woman gazed at the lady with a degree of intensity that can be imagined better than described, and then fell at the lady's feet. The lady was Mrs. Marshall. She had crossed the Atlantic in the same ship with this poor woman. Salome, like many of her countrymen, was a beautiful singer, and had often entertained Mrs. Marshall and the other lady passengers on board the *Amazon.* The poor woman was raised from the ground by Mrs. Marshall, and placed upon the door step that she had a moment before been cleaning. "I will do my utmost to rescue you from this horrid life of a slave," exclaimed the lady, as she took from her pocket her pencil, and wrote down the number of the house, and the street in which the German woman was working as a slave.

After a long and tedious trial of many days, it was decided that Salome Miller was by birth a free woman, and she was set at liberty. The good and generous Althesa had contributed some of the money towards bringing about the trial, and had done much to cheer on Mrs. Marshall in her benevolent object. Salome Miller is free, but where are her three children? They are still slaves, and in all human probability will die as such.

This, reader, is no fiction; if you think so, look over the files of the New Orleans newspapers of the years 1845-6, and you will there see reports of the trial.

CHAPTER XV

To-day A Mistress, To-morrow A Slave

"I promised thee a sister tale
Of man's perfidious cruelty;
Come, then, and hear what cruel wrong
Befel the dark ladie."

COLERIDGE

Let us return for a moment to the home of Clotel. While she was passing lonely and dreary hours with none but her darling child, Horatio Green was trying to find relief in that insidious enemy of man, the intoxicating cup. Defeated in politics, forsaken in love by his wife, he seemed to have lost all principle of honour, and was ready to nerve himself up to any deed, no matter how unprincipled. Clotel's existence was now well known to Horatio's wife, and both her [sic] and her father demanded that the beautiful quadroon and her child should be sold and sent out of the state. To this proposition he at first turned a deaf ear; but when he saw that his wife was about to return to her father's roof, he consented to leave the matter in the hands of his father-in-law. The result was, that Clotel was immediately sold to the slave-trader, Walker, who, a few years previous, had taken her mother and sister to the far South. But, as if to make her husband drink of the cup of humiliation to its very dregs, Mrs. Green resolved to take his child under her own roof for a servant. Mary was, therefore, put to the meanest work that could be found, and although only ten years of age, she was often compelled to perform labour, which, under ordinary

128

circumstances, would have been thought too hard for one much older. One condition of the sale of Clotel to Walker was, that she should be taken out of the state, which was accordingly done. Most quadroon women who are taken to the lower countries to be sold are either purchased by gentlemen for their own use, or sold for waiting-maids; and Clotel, like her sister, was fortunate enough to be bought for the latter purpose. The town of Vicksburgh stands on the left bank of the Mississippi, and is noted for the severity with which slaves are treated. It was here that Clotel was sold to Mr. James French, a merchant.

Mrs. French was severe in the extreme to her servants. Well dressed, but scantily fed, and overworked were all who found a home with her. The quadroon had been in her new home but a short time ere she found that her situation was far different from what it was in Virginia. What social virtues are possible in a society of which injustice is the primary characteristic? in a society which is divided into two classes, masters and slaves? Every married woman in the far South looks upon her husband as unfaithful, and regards every quadroon servant as a rival. Clotel had been with her new mistress but a few days, when she was ordered to cut off her long hair. The Negro, constitutionally, is fond of dress and outward appearance. He that has short, woolly hair, combs it and oils it to death. He that has long hair, would sooner have his teeth drawn than lose it. However painful it was to the quadroon, she was soon seen with her hair cut as short as any of the full-blooded Negroes in the dwelling.

Even with her short hair, Clotel was handsome. Her life had been a secluded one, and though now nearly thirty years of age, she was still beautiful. At her short hair, the other servants laughed, "Miss Clo needn't strut round so big, she got short nappy har well as I," said Nell, with a broad grin that showed her teeth.

"She tinks she white, when she come here wid dat long har of hers," replied Mill.

"Yes," continued Nell; "missus make her take down her wool so she no put it up to-day."

The fairness of Clotel's complexion was regarded with envy as well by the other servants as by the mistress herself. This is one of the hard features of slavery. To-day the woman is mistress of her own cottage; to-morrow she is sold to one who aims to make her life as intolerable as possible. And be it remembered, that the house servant has the best situation which a slave can occupy. Some American writers have tried to make the world believe that the condition of the labouring classes of England is as bad as the slaves of the United States.

The English labourer may be oppressed, he may be cheated, defrauded, swindled, and even starved; but it is not slavery under which he groans. He cannot be sold; in point of law he is equal to the prime minister. "It is easy to captivate the unthinking and the prejudiced, by eloquent declamation about the oppression of English operatives being worse than that of American slaves, and by exaggerating the wrongs on one side and hiding them on the other. But all informed and reflecting minds, knowing that bad as are the social evils of England, those of Slavery are immeasurably worse." But the degradation and harsh treatment that Clotel experienced in her new home was nothing compared with the grief she underwent at being separated from her dear child. Taken from her without scarcely a moment's warning, she knew not what had become of her. The deep and heartfelt grief of Clotel was soon perceived by her owners, and fearing that her refusal to take food would cause her death, they resolved to sell her. Mr. French found no difficulty in getting a purchaser for the quadroon woman, for such are usually the most marketable kind of property. Clotel was sold at private sale to a young man for a housekeeper; but even he had missed his aim.

CHAPTER XVI

Death of the Parson

Carlton was above thirty years of age, standing on the last legs of a young man, and entering on the first of a bachelor. He had never dabbled in matters of love, and looked upon all women alike. Although he respected woman for her virtues, and often spoke of the goodness of heart of the sex, he had never dreamed of marriage. At first he looked upon Miss Peck as a pretty young woman, but after she became his religious teacher, he regarded her in that light, that every one will those whom they know to be their superiors. It was soon seen, however, that the young man not only respected and reverenced Georgiana for the incalculable service she had done him, in awakening him to a sense of duty to his soul, but he had learned to bow to the shrine of Cupid. He found, weeks after he had been in her company, that when he met her at table, or alone in the drawing-room, or on the piazza, he felt a shortness of breath, a palpitating of the heart, a kind of dizziness of the head; but he knew not its cause.

This was love in its first stage. Mr. Peck saw, or thought he saw, what would be the result of Carlton's visit, and held out every inducement in his power to prolong his stay. The hot season was just commencing, and the young Northerner was talking of his return home, when the parson was very suddenly taken ill. The disease was the cholera, and the physicians pronounced the case incurable. In less than five hours John Peck was a corpse. His love for Georgiana, and respect for her father, had induced Carlton to remain by the bedside of the dying man, although against the express order of the physician. This act of kindness caused the young orphan henceforth to regard Carlton as her best friend. He now felt it his duty to remain with the young woman until some of her relations should be summoned from Connecticut. After the funeral, the family physician advised that Miss Peck should go to the farm, and spend the time at the country seat; and also advised Carlton to remain with her, which he did.

At the parson's death his Negroes showed little or no signs of grief. This was noticed by both Carlton and Miss Peck, and caused no little pain to the latter. "They are ungrateful," said Carlton, as he and Georgiana were seated on the piazza.

"What," asked she, "have they to be grateful for?"

"Your father was kind, was he not?"

"Yes, as kind as most men who own slaves; but the kindness meted out to blacks would be unkindness if given to whites. We would think so, should we not?"

"Yes," replied he.

"If we would not consider the best treatment which a slave receives good enough for us, we should not think he ought to be grateful for it. Everybody knows that slavery in its best and mildest form is wrong. Whoever denies this, his lips libel his heart. Try him! Clank the chains in his ears, and tell him they are for him; give him an hour to prepare his wife and children for a life of slavery; bid him make haste, and get ready their necks for the yoke, and their wrists for the coffle chains; then look at his pale lips and trembling knees, and you have nature's testimony against slavery."

"Let's take a walk," said Carlton, as if to turn the conversation. The moon was just appearing through the tops of the trees, and the animals and insects in an adjoining wood kept up a continued din of music. The croaking of bull-frogs, buzzing of insects, cooing of turtle-doves, and the sound from a thousand musical instruments, pitched on as many different keys, made the welkin ring. But even all this noise did not drown the singing of a party of the slaves, who were seated near a spring that was sending up its cooling waters.

"How prettily the Negroes sing," remarked Carlton, as they were wending their way towards the place from whence the sound of the voices came.

"Yes," replied Georgiana; "master Sam is there, I'll warrant you: he's always on hand when there's any singing or dancing. We must not let them see us, or they will stop singing."

"Who makes their songs for them?" inquired the young man.

"Oh, they make them up as they sing them; they are all impromptu songs."

By this time they were near enough to hear distinctly every word; and, true enough, Sam's voice was heard above all others. At the conclusion of each song they all joined in a hearty laugh, with an expression of "Dats de song for me;" "Dems dems."

"Stop," said Carlton, as Georgiana was rising from the log upon which she was seated; "stop and let's hear this one." The piece was sung by Sam, the others joining in the chorus, and was as follows:

Sam.

"Come, all my brethren, let us take a rest,
    While the moon shines so brightly and clear;
Old master is dead, and left us at last,
    And has gone at the Bar to appear.
Old master has died, and lying in his grave,
    And our blood will awhile cease to flow;
He will no more trample on the neck of the slave;
    For he's gone where the slaveholders go.

Chorus.

"Hang up the shovel and the hoe—
    Take down the fiddle and the bow—

Old master has gone to the slaveholder's rest;
He has gone where they all ought to go.

Sam.

"I heard the old doctor say the other night,
    As he passed by the dining-room door—
'Perhaps the old man may live through the night,
    But I think he will die about four.'
Young mistress sent me, at the peril of my life,
    For the parson to come down and pray,
For says she, 'Your old master is now about to die,'
    And says I, 'God speed him on his way.'

"Hang up the shovel, &c.

"At four o'clock at morn the family was called
    Around the old man's dying bed;
And oh! but I laughed to myself when I heard
    That the old man's spirit had fled.
Mr. Carlton cried, and so did I pretend;
    Young mistress very nearly went mad;
And the old parson's groans did the heavens fairly rend;
    But I tell you I felt mighty glad.

"Hang up the shovel, &c.

"We'll no more be roused by the blowing of his horn,
    Our backs no longer he will score;
He no more will feed us on cotton-seeds and corn;
    For his reign of oppression now is o'er.
He no more will hang our children on the tree,
    To be ate by the carrion crow;
He no more will send our wives to Tennessee;
    For he's gone where the slaveholders go.

"Hang up the shovel and the hoe,
Take down the fiddle and the bow,
We'll dance and sing,

And make the forest ring,
With the fiddle and the old banjo."

The song was not half finished before Carlton regretted that he had caused the young lady to remain and hear what to her must be anything but pleasant reflections upon her deceased parent. "I think we will walk," said he, at the same time extending his arm to Georgiana.

"No," said she; "let's hear them out. It is from these unguarded expressions of the feelings of the Negroes, that we should learn a lesson."

At its conclusion they walked towards the house in silence: as they were ascending the steps, the young man said, "They are happy, after all. The Negro, situated as yours are, is not aware that he is deprived of any just rights."

"Yes, yes," answered Georgiana: "you may place the slave where you please; you may dry up to your utmost the fountains of his feelings, the springs of his thought; you may yoke him to your labour, as an ox which liveth only to work, and worketh only to live; you may put him under any process which, without destroying his value as a slave, will debase and crush him as a rational being; you may do this, and *the idea that he was born to be free will survive it all*. It is allied to his hope of immortality; it is the ethereal part of his nature, which oppression cannot reach; it is a torch lit up in his soul by the hand of Deity, and never meant to be extinguished by the hand of man."

On reaching the drawing-room, they found Sam snuffing the candles, and looking as solemn and as dignified as if he had never sung a song or laughed in his life. "Will Miss Georgy have de supper got up now?" asked the Negro.

"Yes," she replied.

"Well," remarked Carlton, "that beats anything I ever met with. Do you think that was Sam we heard singing?"

"I am sure of it," was the answer.

"I could not have believed that that fellow was capable of so much deception," continued he.

"Our system of slavery is one of deception; and Sam, you see, has only been a good scholar. However, he is as honest a fellow as you will find among the slave population here. If we would have them more honest, we should give them their liberty, and then the inducement to be dishonest would be gone. I have resolved that these creatures shall all be free."

"Indeed!" exclaimed Carlton.

"Yes, I shall let them all go free, and set an example to those about me."

"I honour your judgment," said he. "But will the state permit them to remain?"

"If not, they can go where they can live in freedom. I will not be unjust because the state is."

CHAPTER XVII

Retaliation

"I had a dream, a happy dream;
I thought that I was free:
That in my own bright land again
A home there was for me."

With the deepest humiliation Horatio Green saw the daughter of Clotel, his own child, brought into his dwelling as a servant. His wife felt that she had been deceived, and determined to punish her deceiver. At first Mary was put to work in the kitchen, where she met with little or no sympathy from the other slaves, owing to the fairness of her complexion. The child was white, what should be done to make her look like other Negroes, was the question Mrs. Green asked herself. At last she hit upon a plan: there was a garden at the back of the house over which Mrs. Green could look from her parlour window. Here the white slave-girl was put to work, without either bonnet or handkerchief upon her head. A hot sun poured its broiling rays on the naked face and neck of the girl, until she sank down in the corner of the garden, and was actually broiled to sleep. "Dat little nigger ain't working a bit, missus," said Dinah to Mrs. Green, as she entered the kitchen.

"She's lying in the sun, seasoning; she will work better by and by," replied the mistress.

"Dees white niggers always tink dey sef good as white folks," continued the cook.

"Yes, but we will teach them better; won't we, Dinah?"

"Yes, missus, I don't like dees mularter niggers, no how;

dey always want to set dey sef up for something big." The cook was black, and was not without that prejudice which is to be found among the Negroes, as well as among the whites of the Southern States. The sun had the desired effect, for in less than a fortnight Mary's fair complexion had disappeared, and she was but little whiter than any other mulatto children running about the yard. But the close resemblance between the father and child annoyed the mistress more than the mere whiteness of the child's complexion. Horatio made proposition after proposition to have the girl sent away, for every time he beheld her countenance it reminded him of the happy days he had spent with Clotel. But his wife had commenced, and determined to carry out her unfeeling and fiendish designs. This child was not only white, but she was the granddaughter of Thomas Jefferson, the man who, when speaking against slavery in the legislature of Virginia, said,

"The whole commerce between master and slave is a perpetual exercise of the most boisterous passions; *the most unremitting despotism on the one part, and degrading submission on the other.* With what execration should the statesman be loaded who, permitting one half the citizens thus to trample on the rights of the other, transforms those into despots and these into enemies, destroys the morals of the one part, and the *amor patriae* of the other! For if the slave can have a country in this world, it must be any other in preference to that in which he is born to live and labour for another; in which he must lock up the faculties of his nature, contribute as far as depends on his individual endeavours to the evanishment of the human race, or entail his own miserable condition on the endless generations proceeding from him. And can the liberties of a nation be thought secure when we have removed their only firm basis, a conviction in the minds of the people that these liberties are the gift of God? that they are not to be violated but with his wrath? Indeed, I tremble for my country when I reflect that God is just; that his justice cannot sleep for ever; that, considering numbers, nature, and natural means only, a revolution of the wheel of fortune, an exchange of situation, is among possible events; that it may become probable by supernatural interference! The Almighty has no attribute which can take side with us in such a contest.

. . .

"What an incomprehensible machine is man! Who can endure toil, famine, stripes, imprisonment, and death itself, in vindication of his own liberty, and the next moment be deaf to all those motives, whose power supported him through his trial, and inflict on his fellow-men a bondage, *one hour of which is fraught with more misery than ages of that which he rose in rebellion to oppose!* But we must wait with patience the workings of an overruling Providence, and hope that that is preparing the deliverance of these our suffering brethren. When the measure of their tears shall be full—when their tears shall have involved heaven itself in darkness—doubtless a God of justice will awaken to their distress, and by diffusing light and liberality among their oppressors, or at length by his exterminating thunder, manifest his attention to things of this world, and that they are not left to the guidance of blind fatality."

The same man, speaking of the probability that the slaves might some day attempt to gain their liberties by a revolution, said,

"I tremble for my country, when I recollect that God is just, and that His justice cannot sleep for ever. The Almighty has no attribute that can take sides with us in such a struggle."

But, sad to say, Jefferson is not the only American statesman who has spoken high-sounding words in favour of freedom, and then left his own children to die slaves.

CHAPTER XVIII

The Liberator

"We hold these truths to be self-evident, that all men are created free and equal; that they are endowed by their Creator with certain inalienable rights; among these are life, *liberty*, and the pursuit of happiness."

DECLARATION OF AMERICAN INDEPENDENCE

The death of the parson was the commencement of a new era in the history of his slaves. Only a little more than eighteen years of age, Georgiana could not expect to carry out her own wishes in regard to the slaves, although she was sole heir to her father's estate. There were distant relations whose opinions she had at least to respect. And both law and public opinion in the state were against any measure of emancipation that she might think of adopting; unless, perhaps, she might be permitted to send them to Liberia. Her uncle in Connecticut had already been written to, to come down and aid in settling up the estate. He was a Northern man, but she knew him to be a tight-fisted yankee, whose whole counsel would go against liberating the Negroes. Yet there was one way in which the thing could be done. She loved Carlton, and she well knew that he loved her; she read in it his countenance every time they met, yet the young man did not mention his wishes to her. There were many reasons why he should not. In the first place, her father was just deceased, and it seemed only right that he should wait a reasonable time. Again, Carlton was poor, and Georgiana was possessed of a large fortune; and his high spirit would not, for a moment, allow him to place himself in a position to be regarded as a fortune-hunter. The young girl hinted, as best she could, at the probable future; but all to no purpose. He took nothing to himself. True, she had read much of "woman's rights;" and had even attended a meeting, while at the North, which had been called to discuss the wrongs of woman; but she could not nerve herself up to the point of putting the question to Carlton, although she felt sure that she should not be rejected. She waited, but in vain. At last, one evening, she came out of her room rather late, and was walking on the piazza for fresh air. She passed near Carlton's room, and heard the voice of Sam. The Negro had just come in to get the young man's boots, and had stopped, as he usually did, to have some talk. "I wish," said Sam, "dat Marser Carlton an Miss Georgy would get married; den, 'speck, we'd have good times."

"I don't think your mistress would have me," replied the young man.

"What make tink dat, Marser Carlton?"

"Your mistress would marry no one, Sam, unless she loved them."

"Den I wish she would lub you, cause I tink we have good times den. All our folks is de same 'pinion like me," returned the Negro, and then left the room with the boots in his hands.

During the conversation between the Anglo-Saxon and the African, one word had been dropped by the former that haunted the young lady the remainder of the night—"Your mistress would marry no one unless she loved them." That word awoke her in the morning, and caused her to decide upon this important subject. Love and duty triumphed over the woman's timid nature, and that day Georgiana informed Carlton that she was ready to become his wife. The young man, with grateful tears, accepted and kissed the hand that was offered to him. The marriage of Carlton and Miss Peck was hailed with delight by both the servants in the house and the Negroes on the farm. New rules were immediately announced for the working and general treatment of the slaves on the plantation. With this, Huckelby, the overseer, saw his reign coming to an end; and Snyder, the Dutch preacher, felt that his services would soon be dispensed with, for nothing was more repugnant to the feelings of Mrs. Carlton than the sermons preached by Snyder to the slaves. She regarded them as something intended to make them better satisfied with their condition, and more valuable as pieces of property, without preparing them for the world to come. Mrs. Carlton found in her husband a congenial spirit, who entered into all her wishes and plans for bettering the condition of their slaves. Mrs. Carlton's views and sympathies were all in favour of immediate emancipation; but then she saw, or thought she saw, a difficulty in that. If the slaves were liberated, they must be sent out of the state. This, of course, would incur additional expense; and if they left the state, where had they better go?

"Let's send them to Liberia," said Carlton.

"Why should they go to Africa, any more than to the Free States or to Canada?" asked the wife.

"They would be in their native land," he answered.

"Is not this their native land? What right have we, more than the Negro, to the soil here, or to style ourselves native Americans? Indeed it is as much their home as ours, and I have sometimes thought it was more theirs. The Negro has cleared up the lands, built towns, and enriched the soil with his blood and tears; and in return, he is to be sent to a country of which he knows nothing. Who fought more bravely for American independence than the blacks? A Negro, by the name of Attucks, was the first that fell in Boston at the commencement of the revolutionary war; and, throughout the whole of the struggles for liberty in this country, the Negroes have contributed their share. In the last war with Great Britain, the country was mainly indebted to the blacks in New Orleans for the achievement of the victory at that place; and even General Jackson, the commander in chief, called the Negroes together at the close of the war, and addressed them in the following terms:—

"Soldiers!—When on the banks of the Mobile I called you to take up arms, inviting you to partake the perils and glory of your *white fellow citizens, I expected much from you;* for I was not ignorant that you possess qualities most formidable to an invading enemy. I knew with what fortitude you could endure hunger and thirst, and all the fatigues of a campaign. *I knew well how you loved your native country,* and that you, as well as ourselves, had to defend what *man* holds most dear—his parents, wife, children, and property. *You have done more than I expected.* In addition to the previous qualities I before knew you to possess, I found among you a noble enthusiasm, which leads to the performance of great things.

" 'Soldiers! The President of the United States shall hear how praiseworthy was your conduct in the hour of danger, and the representatives of the American people will give you the praise your exploits entitle you to. Your general anticipates them in applauding your noble ardour.'

"And what did these noble men receive in return for their courage, their heroism? Chains and slavery. Their good deeds have been consecrated only in their own memories. Who rallied with more alacrity in response to the summons of danger? If in that hazardous hour, when our homes were menaced with the horrors of war, we did not disdain to call upon the Negro to assist in repelling invasion, why should we, now that the danger is past, deny him a home in his native land?"

"I see," said Carlton, "you are right, but I fear you will have difficulty in persuading others to adopt your views."

"We will set the example," replied she, "and then hope for the best; for I feel that the people of the Southern States will one day see their error. Liberty has always been our watchword, as far as profession is concerned. Nothing has been held so cheap as our common humanity, on a national average. If every man had his aliquot proportion of the injustice done in this land, by law and violence, the present freemen of the northern section would many of them commit suicide in self-defence, and would court the liberties awarded by Ali Pasha of Egypt to his subjects. Long ere this we should have tested, in behalf of our bleeding and crushed American brothers of every hue and complexion, every new constitution, custom, or practice, by which inhumanity was supposed to be upheld, the injustice and cruelty they contained, emblazoned before the great tribunal of mankind for condemnation; and the good and available power they possessed, for the relief, deliverance and elevation of oppressed men, permitted to shine forth from under the cloud, for the refreshment of the human race."

Although Mr. and Mrs. Carlton felt that immediate emancipation was the right of the slave and the duty of the master, they resolved on a system of gradual emancipation, so as to give them time to accomplish their wish, and to prepare the Negro for freedom. Huckelby was one morning told that his services would no longer be required. The Negroes, ninety-eight in number, were called together and told that the whip would no longer be used, and that they would be allowed a certain sum for every bale of cotton produced. Sam, whose long experience in the cotton-field before he had been taken into the house, and whose general intelligence justly gave him the first place amongst the Negroes on the Poplar Farm, was placed at their head. They were also given to understand that the money earned by them would be placed to their credit; and when it amounted to a certain sum, they should all be free.

The joy with which this news was received by the slaves, showed their grateful appreciation of the boon their benefactors were bestowing upon them. The house servants were called and told that wages would be allowed them, and what they earned set to their credit, and they too should be free. The next were the bricklayers. There were eight of these, who had paid their master two dollars per day, and boarded and clothed themselves. An arrangement was entered into with them, by which the money they earned should be placed to their credit; and they too should be free, when a certain amount should be accumulated; and great was the change amongst all these people. The bricklayers had been to work but a short time, before their increased industry was noticed by many. They were no longer apparently the same people. A sedateness, a care, an economy, an industry, took possession of them, to which there seemed to be no bounds but in their physical strength. They were never tired of labouring, and seemed as though they could never effect enough. They became temperate, moral, religious, setting an example of innocent, unoffending lives to the world around them, which was seen and admired by all. Mr. Parker, a man who worked nearly forty slaves at the same business, was attracted by the manner in which these Negroes laboured. He called on Mr. Carlton, some weeks after they had been acting on the new system, and offered 2,000 dollars for the head workman, Jim. The offer was, of course, refused. A few days after the same gentleman called again, and made an offer of double the sum that he had on the former occasion. Mr. Parker, finding that no money would purchase either of the Negroes said, "Now, Mr. Carlton, pray tell me what it is that makes your Negroes work so? What kind of people are they?"

"I suppose," observed Carlton, "that they are like other people, flesh and blood."

"Why, sir," continued Parker, "I have never seen such people; building as they are next door to my residence, I see and have my eye on them from morning till night. You are never there, for I have never met you, or seen you once at the building. Why, sir, I am an early riser, getting up before day; and do you think that I am not awoke every morning in my life by the noise of their trowels at work, and their singing and noise before day; and do you suppose, sir, that they stop or leave off work at sundown? No, sir, but they work as long as they can see to lay a brick, and then carry up brick and mortar for an hour or two afterward, to be ahead of their work the next morning. And again, sir, do you think that they walk at their work? No, sir, they run all day. You see, sir, those immensely long ladders, five stories in height; do you suppose they walk up them? No, sir, they run up and down them like so many monkeys all day long. I never saw such people as these in my life. I don't know what to make of them. Were a white man with them and over them with a whip, then I should see and understand the cause of the running and incessant labour; but I cannot comprehend it; there is something in it, sir. Great man, sir, that Jim; great man; I should like to own him."

Carlton here informed Parker that their liberties depended upon their work; when the latter replied, "If niggers can work so for the promise of freedom, they ought to be made to work without it." This last remark was in the true spirit of the slaveholder, and reminds us of the fact that, some years since, the overseer of General Wade Hampton offered the niggers under him a suit of clothes to the one that picked the most cotton in one day; and after that time that day's work was given as a task to the slaves on that plantation; and, after a while, was adopted by other planters.

The Negroes on the farm, under "Marser Sam," were also working in a manner that attracted the attention of the planters round about. They no longer feared Huckelby's whip, and no longer slept under the preaching of Snyder. On the Sabbath, Mr. and Mrs. Carlton read and explained the Scriptures to them; and the very great attention paid by the slaves showed plainly that they appreciated the gospel when given to them in its purity. The death of Currer, from yellow fever, was a great trial to Mrs. Carlton; for she had not only become much attached to her, but had heard with painful interest the story of her wrongs, and would, in all probability, have restored her to her daughter in New Orleans.

CHAPTER XIX

Escape of Clotel

"The fetters galled my weary soul—
A soul that seemed but thrown away;
I spurned the tyrant's base control,
Resolved at least the man to play."

No country has produced so much heroism in so short a time, connected with escapes from peril and oppression, as has occurred in the United States among fugitive slaves, many of whom show great shrewdness in their endeavours to escape from this land of bondage. A slave was one day seen passing on the high road from a border town in the interior of the state of Virginia to the Ohio river. The man had neither hat upon his head or coat upon his back. He was driving before him a very nice fat pig, and appeared to all who saw him to be a labourer employed on an adjoining farm. "No Negro is permitted to go at large in the Slave States without a written pass from his or her master, except on business in the neighbourhood."

"Where do you live, my boy?" asked a white man of the slave, as he passed a white house with green blinds.

"Jist up de road, sir," was the answer.

"That's a fine pig."

"Yes, sir, marser like dis choat berry much."

And the Negro drove on as if he was in great haste. In this way he and the pig travelled more than fifty miles before they reached the Ohio river. Once at the river they crossed over; the pig was sold; and nine days after the runaway slave passed over the Niagara river, and, for the first time in his life, breathed the air of freedom. A few weeks later, and, on the same road, two slaves were seen passing; one was on horseback, the other was walking before him with his arms tightly bound, and a long rope leading from the man on foot to the one on horseback.

"Oh, ho, that's a runaway rascal, I suppose," said a farmer, who met them on the road.

"Yes, sir, he bin runaway, and I got him fast. Marser will tan his jacket for him nicely when he gets him."

"You are a trustworthy fellow, I imagine," continued the farmer.

"Oh yes, sir; marser puts a heap of confidence in dis nigger."

And the slave travelled on. When the one on foot was fatigued they would change positions, the other being tied and driven on foot. This they called "ride and tie." After a journey of more than two hundred miles they reached the Ohio river, turned the horse loose, told him to go home, and proceeded on their way to Canada. However they were not to have it all their own way. There are men in the Free States, and especially in the states adjacent to the Slave States, who make their living by catching the runaway slave, and returning him for the reward that may be offered. As the two slaves above mentioned were travelling on towards the land of freedom, led by the North Star, they were set upon by four of these slave-catchers, and one of them unfortunately captured. The other escaped. The captured fugitive was put under torture, and compelled to reveal the name of his owner and his place of residence. Filled with delight, the kidnappers started back with their victim. Overjoyed with the prospect of receiving a large reward, they gave themselves up on the third night to pleasure. They put up at an inn. The Negro was chained to the bed-post, in the same room with his captors. At dead of night, when all was still, the slave arose from the floor upon which he had been lying, looked around, and saw that the white men were fast asleep. The brandy punch had done its work. With palpitating heart and trembling limbs he viewed his position. The door was fast, but the warm weather had compelled them to leave the window open. If he could but get his chains off, he might escape through the window to the piazza, and reach the ground by one of the posts that supported the piazza. The sleeper's clothes hung upon chairs by the bedside; the slave thought of the padlock key, examined the pockets and found it. The chains were soon off, and the Negro stealthily making his way to the window: he stopped and said to himself, "These men are villains, they are enemies to all who like me are trying to be free. Then why not I teach them a lesson?" He then undressed himself, took the clothes of one of the men, dressed himself in them, and escaped through the window, and, a moment more, he was on the high road to Canada. Fifteen days later, and the writer of this gave him a passage across Lake Erie, and saw him safe in her Britannic Majesty's dominions.

We have seen Clotel sold to Mr. French in Vicksburgh, her hair cut short, and everything done to make her realise her position as a servant. Then we have seen her re-sold, because her owners feared she would die through grief. As yet her new purchaser treated her with respectful gentleness, and sought to win her favour by flattery and presents, knowing that whatever he gave her he could take back again. But she dreaded every moment lest the scene should change, and trembled at the sound of every footfall. At every interview with her new master Clotel stoutly maintained that she had left a husband in Virginia, and would never think of taking another. The gold watch and chain, and other glittering presents which he purchased for her, were all laid aside by the quadroon, as if they were of no value to her. In the same house with her was another servant, a man, who had from time to time hired himself from his master. William was his name. He could feel for Clotel, for he, like her, had been separated from near and dear relatives, and often tried to console the poor woman. One day the quadroon observed to him that her hair was growing out again.

"Yes," replied William, "you look a good deal like a man with your short hair."

"Oh," rejoined she, "I have often been told that I would make a better looking man than a woman. If I had the money," continued she, "I would bid farewell to this place." In a moment more she feared that she had said too much, and smilingly remarked, "I am always talking nonsense."

William was a tall, full-bodied Negro, whose very countenance beamed with intelligence. Being a mechanic, he had, by his own industry, made more than what he paid his owner; this he laid aside, with the hope that some day he might get enough to purchase his freedom. He had in his chest one hundred and fifty dollars. His was a heart that felt for others, and he had again and again wiped the tears from his eyes as he heard the story of Clotel as related by herself. "If she can get free with a little money, why not give her what I have?" thought he, and then he resolved to do it. An hour after, he came into the quadroon's room, and laid the money in her lap, and said, "There, Miss Clotel, you said if you had the means you would leave this place; there is money enough to take you to England, where you will be free. You are much fairer than many of the white women of the South, and can easily pass for a free white lady."

At first Clotel feared that it was a plan by which the Negro wished to try her fidelity to her owner; but she was soon convinced by his earnest manner, and the deep feeling with which he spoke, that he was honest. "I will take the money only on one condition," said she; "and that is, that I effect your escape as well as my own."

"How can that be done?" he inquired.

"I will assume the disguise of a gentleman and you that of a servant, and we will take passage on a steamboat and go to Cincinnati, and thence to Canada." Here William put in several objections to the plan. He feared detection, and he well knew that, when a slave is once caught when attempting to escape, if returned is sure to be worse treated than before. However, Clotel satisfied him that the plan could be carried out if he would only play his part.

The resolution was taken, the clothes for her disguise procured, and before night everything was in readiness for their departure. That night Mr. Cooper, their master, was to attend a party, and this was their opportunity. William went to the wharf to look out for a boat, and had scarcely reached the landing ere he heard the puffing of a steamer. He returned and reported the fact. Clotel had already packed her trunk, and had only to dress and all was ready. In less than an hour they were on board the boat. Under the assumed name of "Mr. Johnson," Clotel went to the clerk's office and took a private state room for herself, and paid her own and servant's fare. Besides being attired in a neat suit of black, she had a white silk handkerchief tied round her chin, as if she was an invalid. A pair of green glasses covered her eyes; and fearing that she would be talked to too much and thus render her liable to be detected, she assumed to be very ill. On the other hand, William was playing his part well in the servants' hall; he was talking loudly of his master's wealth. Nothing appeared as good on the boat as in his master's fine mansion. "I don't like dees steamboats no how," said William; "I hope when marser goes on a journey agin he will take de carriage and de hosses." Mr. Johnson (for such was the name by which Clotel now went) remained in his room, to avoid, as far as possible, conversation with others. After a passage of seven days they arrived at Louisville, and put up at Gough's Hotel. Here they had to await the departure of another boat for the North. They were now in their most critical position. They were still in a slave state, and John C. Calhoun, a distinguished slave-owner, was a guest at this hotel. They feared, also, that trouble would attend their attempt to leave this place for the North, as all persons taking Negroes with them have to give bail that such Negroes are not runaway slaves. The law upon this point is very stringent: all steamboats and other public conveyances are liable to a fine for every slave that escapes by them, besides paying the full value for the slave. After a delay of four hours, Mr. Johnson and servant took passage on the steamer Rodolph, for Pittsburgh. It is usual, before the departure of the boats, for an officer to examine every part of the vessel to see that no slave secretes himself on board.

"Where are you going?" asked the officer of William, as he was doing his duty on this occasion.

"I am going with marser," was the quick reply.

"Who is your master?"

"Mr. Johnson, sir, a gentleman in the cabin."

"You must take him to the office and satisfy the captain that all is right, or you can't go on this boat."

William informed his master what the officer had said. The boat was on the eve of going, and no time could be lost, yet they knew not what to do. At last they went to the office, and Mr. Johnson, addressing the captain, said, "I am informed that my boy can't go with me unless I give security that he belongs to me."

"Yes," replied the captain, "that is the law."

"A very strange law indeed," rejoined Mr. Johnson, "that one can't take his property with him."

After a conversation of some minutes, and a plea on the part of Johnson that he did not wish to be delayed owing to his illness, they were permitted to take their passage without further trouble, and the boat was soon on its way up the river. The fugitives had now passed the Rubicon, and the next place at which they would land would be in a Free State. Clotel called William to her room, and said to him, "We are now free, you can go on your way to Canada, and I shall go to Virginia in search of my daughter." The announcement that she was going to risk her liberty in a Slave State was unwelcome news to William. With all the eloquence he could command, he tried to persuade Clotel that she could not escape detection, and was only throwing her freedom away. But she had counted the cost, and made up her mind for the worst. In return for the money he had

furnished, she had secured for him his liberty, and their engagement was at an end.

After a quick passage the fugitives arrived at Cincinnati,
and there separated. William proceeded on his way to Canada, and Clotel again resumed her own apparel, and prepared
to start in search of her child. As might have been expected,
the escape of those two valuable slaves created no little sensation in Vicksburgh. Advertisements and messages were sent
in every direction in which the fugitives were thought to
have gone. It was soon, however, known that they had left
the town as master and servant; and many were the com-
munications which appeared in the newspapers, in which the
writers thought, or pretended, that they had seen the slaves
in their disguise. One was to the effect that they had gone
off in a chaise; one as master, and the other as servant. But
the most probable was an account given by a correspondent
of one of the Southern newspapers, who happened to be a
passenger in the same steamer in which the slaves escaped,
and which we here give:—

"One bright starlight night, in the month of December last,
I found myself in the cabin of the steamer Rodolph, then lying
in the port of Vicksburgh, and bound to Louisville. I had gone
early on board, in order to select a good berth, and having
got tired of reading the papers, amused myself with watching
the appearance of the passengers as they dropped in, one after
another, and I being a believer in physiognomy, formed my
own opinion of their characters.

"The second bell rang, and as I yawningly returned my
watch to my pocket, my attention was attracted by the appearance of a young man who entered the cabin supported by
his servant, a strapping Negro.

"The man was bundled up in a capacious overcoat; his face
was bandaged with a white handkerchief, and its expression
entirely hid by a pair of enormous spectacles.

"There was something so mysterious and unusual about the
young man as he sat restless in the corner, that curiosity led
me to observe him more closely.

"He appeared anxious to avoid notice, and before the steamer had fairly left the wharf, requested, in a low, womanly voice, to be shown his berth, as he was an invalid, and must retire early: his name he gave as Mr. Johnson. His servant was called, and he was put quietly to bed. I paced the deck until Tybee light grew dim in the distance, and then went to my berth.

"I awoke in the morning with the sun shining in my face; we were then just passing St. Helena. It was a mild beautiful morning, and most of the passengers were on deck, enjoying the freshness of the air, and stimulating their appetites for breakfast. Mr. Johnson soon made his appearance, arrayed as on the night before, and took his seat quietly upon the guard of the boat.

"From the better opportunity afforded by daylight, I found that he was a slight build, apparently handsome young man, with black hair and eyes, and of a darkness of complexion that betokened Spanish extraction. Any notice from others seemed painful to him; so to satisfy my curiosity, I questioned his servant, who was standing near, and gained the following information.

"His master was an invalid—he had suffered for a long time under a complication of diseases, that had baffled the skill of the best physicians in Mississippi; he was now suffering principally with the 'rheumatism,' and he was scarcely able to walk or help himself in any way. He came from Vicksburgh, and was now on his way to Philadelphia, at which place resided his uncle, a celebrated physician, and through whose means he hoped to be restored to perfect health.

"This information, communicated in a bold, off-hand manner, enlisted my sympathies for the sufferer, although it occurred to me that he walked rather too gingerly for a person afflicted with so many ailments."

After thanking Clotel for the great service she had done him in bringing him out of slavery, William bade her farewell. The prejudice that exists in the Free States against coloured persons, on account of their colour, is attributable solely to the influence of slavery, and is but another form of slavery itself. And even the slave who escapes from the Southern plantations, is surprised when he reaches the North, at the amount and withering influence of this prejudice. William applied at the railway station for a ticket for the train going to Sandusky, and was told that if he went by that train he would have to ride in the luggage-van.

"Why?" asked the astonished Negro.

"We don't send a Jim Crow carriage but once a day, and that went this morning."

The "Jim Crow" carriage is the one in which the blacks have to ride. Slavery is a school in which its victims learn much shrewdness, and William had been an apt scholar. Without asking any more questions, the Negro took his seat in one of the first-class carriages. He was soon seen and ordered out. Afraid to remain in the town longer, he resolved to go by that train; and consequently seated himself on a goods' box in the luggage-van. The train started at its proper time, and all went on well. Just before arriving at the end of the journey, the conductor called on William for his ticket.

"I have none," was the reply.

"Well, then, you can pay your fare to me," said the officer.

"How much is it?" asked the black man.

"Two dollars."

"What do you charge those in the passenger-carriage?"

"Two dollars."

"And do you charge me the same as you do those who ride in the best carriages?" asked the Negro.

"Yes," was the answer.

"I shan't pay it," returned the man.

"You black scamp, do you think you can ride on this road without paying your fare?"

"No, I don't want to ride for nothing; I only want to pay what's right."

"Well, launch out two dollars, and that's right."

"No, I shan't; I will pay what I ought, and won't pay any more."

"Come, come, nigger, your fare and be done with it," said

the conductor, in a manner that is never used except by Americans to blacks.

"I won't pay you two dollars, and that enough," said William.

"Well, as you have come all the way in the luggage-van, pay me a dollar and a half and you may go."

"I shan't do any such thing."

"Don't you mean to pay for riding?"

"Yes, but I won't pay a dollar and a half for riding up here in the freight-van. If you had let me come in the carriage where others ride, I would have paid you two dollars."

"Where were you raised? You seem to think yourself as good as white folks."

"I want nothing more than my rights."

"Well, give me a dollar, and I will let you off."

"No, sir, I shan't do it."

"What do you mean to do then—don't you wish to pay anything?"

"Yes, sir, I want to pay you the full price."

"What do you mean by full price?"

"What do you charge per hundred-weight for goods?" inquired the Negro with a degree of gravity that would have astonished Diogenes himself.

"A quarter of a dollar per hundred," answered the conductor.

"I weigh just one hundred and fifty pounds," returned William, "and will pay you three eighths of a dollar."

"Do you expect that you will pay only thirty-seven cents for your ride?"

"This, sir, is your own price. I came in a luggage-van, and I'll pay for luggage."

After a vain effort to get the Negro to pay more, the conductor took the thirty-seven cents, and noted in his cash-book, "Received for one hundred and fifty pounds of luggage, thirty-seven cents." This, reader, is no fiction; it actually occurred in the railway above described.

Thomas Corwin, a member of the American Congress, is one of the blackest white men in the United States. He was once on his way to Congress, and took passage in one of the Ohio river steamers. As he came just at the dinner hour, he immediately went into the dining saloon, and took his seat at the table. A gentleman with his whole party of five ladies at once left the table. "Where is the captain?" cried the man in angry tone. The captain soon appeared, and it was sometime before he could satisfy the old gent, that Governor Corwin was not a nigger. The newspapers often have notices of mistakes made by innkeepers and others who undertake to accommodate the public, one of which we give below.

On the 6th inst., the Hon. Daniel Webster and family entered Edgartown, on a visit for health and recreation. Arriving at the hotel, without alighting from the coach, the landlord was sent for to see if suitable accommodation could be had. That dignitary appearing, and surveying Mr. Webster, while the hon. senator addressed him, seemed woefully to mistake the dark features of the traveller as he sat back in the corner of the carriage, and to suppose him a *coloured man*, particularly as there were two coloured servants of Mr. W. outside. So he promptly declared that there was no room for him and his family, and he could not be accommodated there—at the same time suggesting that he might perhaps find accommodation at some of the huts "up back," to which he pointed. So deeply did the prejudice of looks possess him, that he appeared not to notice that the stranger introduced himself to him as Daniel Webster, or to be so ignorant as not to have heard of such a personage; and turning away, he expressed to the driver his astonishment that he should bring *black* people there for *him* to take in. It was not till he had been repeatedly assured and made to understand that the said Daniel Webster was a real live senator of the United States, that he perceived his awkward mistake and the distinguished honour which he and his house were so near missing.

In most of the Free States, the coloured people are disfranchised on account of their colour. The following scene, which we take from a newspaper in the state of Ohio, will give some idea of the extent to which this prejudice is carried.

"The whole of Thursday last was occupied by the Court of Common Pleas for this country in trying to find out whether one Thomas West was of the VOTING COLOUR, as some had very *constitutional doubts* as to whether his colour was orthodox, and whether his hair was of the official crisp! Was it not a dignified business? Four profound judges, four acute lawyers, twelve grave jurors, and I don't know how many venerable witnesses, making in all about thirty men, perhaps, all engaged in the profound, laborious, and illustrious business, of finding out whether a man who pays tax, works on the road, and is an industrious farmer, has been born according to the republican, Christian constitution of Ohio—so that he can vote! And they wisely, gravely, and 'JUDGMATICALLY' decided that he should not vote! What wisdom—what research it must have required to evolve this truth! It was left for the Court of Common Pleas for Columbian county, Ohio, in the United States of North America, to find out what Solomon never dreamed of—the courts of all civilised, heathen, or Jewish countries, never contemplated. Lest the wisdom of our courts should be circumvented by some such men as might be named, who are so near being born constitutionally that they might be taken for white by sight, I would suggest that our court be invested with SMELLING powers, and that if a man don't exhale the constitutional smell, he shall not vote! This would be an additional security to our liberties."

William found, after all, that liberty in the so-called Free States was more a name than a reality; that prejudice followed the coloured man into every place that he might enter. The temples erected for the worship of the living God are no exception. The finest Baptist church in the city of Boston has the following paragraph in the deed that conveys its seats to pewholders:

"And it is a further condition of these presents, that if the owner or owners of said pew shall determine hereafter to sell the same, it shall first be offered, in writing, to the standing committee of said society for the time being, at such price as might otherwise be obtained for it; and the said committee shall have the right, for ten days after such offer, to purchase said pew for said society, at that price, first deducting therefrom all taxes and assessments on said pew then remaining unpaid. And if the said committee shall not so complete such purchase within said ten days, then the pew may be sold by the owner or owners thereof (after payment of all such arrears) to any one respectable *white person*, but upon the same conditions as are contained in this instrument; and immediate notice of such sale shall be given in writing, by the vendor, to the treasurer of said society."

Such are the conditions upon which the Rowe Street Baptist Church, Boston, disposes of its seats. The writer of this is able to put that whole congregation, minister and all, to flight, by merely putting his coloured face in that church. We once visited a church in New York that had a place set apart for the sons of Ham. It was a dark, dismal looking place in one corner of the gallery, grated in front like a hen-coop, with a black border around it. It had two doors; over one was B. M.—black men; over the other B. W.—black women.

CHAPTER XX

A True Democrat

"Who can, with patience, for a moment see
The medley mass of pride and misery,
Of whips and charters, manacles and rights,
Of slaving blacks and democratic whites,
And all the piebald policy that reigns
In free confusion o'er Columbia's plains?
To think that man, thou just and gentle God!
Should stand before thee with a tyrant's rod,
O'er creatures like himself, with souls from thee,
Yet dare to boast of perfect liberty!"

THOMAS MOORE

Educated in a free state, and marrying a wife who had been a victim to the institution of slavery, Henry Morton became strongly opposed to the system. His two daughters, at the age of twelve years, were sent to the North to finish their education, and to receive that refinement that young ladies cannot obtain in the Slave States. Although he did not publicly advocate the abolition of slavery, he often made himself obnoxious to private circles, owing to the denunciatory manner in which he condemned the "peculiar institution." Being one evening at a party, and hearing one of the company talking loudly of the glory and freedom of American institutions, he gave it as his opinion that, unless slavery was speedily abolished, it would be the ruin of the Union. "It is not our boast of freedom," said he, "that will cause us to be respected abroad. It is not our loud talk in favour of liberty that will cause us to be regarded as friends of human freedom;

but our acts will be scrutinised by the people of other countries. We say much against European despotism; let us look to ourselves. That government is despotic where the rulers govern subjects by their own mere will—by decrees and laws emanating from their uncontrolled will, in the enactment and execution of which the ruled have no voice, and under which they have no right except at the will of the rulers. Despotism does not depend upon the number of rulers, or the number of the subjects. It may have one ruler or many. Rome was a despotism under Thirty Tyrants; under her Four Hundred Tyrants; under her Three Thousand Tyrants. It has been generally observed that despotism increases in severity with the number of despots; the responsibility is more divided, and the claims more numerous. The triumvirs each demanded his victims. The smaller the number of subjects in proportion to the tyrants, the more cruel the oppression, because the less danger from rebellion. In this government, the free white citizens are the rulers—the sovereigns, as we delight to be called. All others are subjects. There are, perhaps, some sixteen or seventeen millions of sovereigns, and four millions of subjects.

"The rulers and the ruled are of all colours, from the clear white of the Caucasian tribes to the swarthy Ethiopian. The former, by courtesy, are all called white, the latter black. In this government the subject has no rights, social, political, or personal. He has no voice in the laws which govern him. He can hold no property. His very wife and children are not his. His labour is another's. He, and all that appertain to him, are the absolute property of his rulers. He is governed, bought, sold, punished, executed, by laws to which he never gave his assent, and by rulers whom he never chose. He is not a serf merely, with half the rights of men like the subjects of despotic Russia; but a native slave, stripped of every right which God and nature gave him, and which the high spirit of our revolution declared inalienable—which he himself could not surrender, and which man could not take from him. Is he not then the subject of despotic sway?

"The slaves of Athens and Rome were free in comparison. They had some rights—could acquire some property; could choose their own masters, and purchase their own freedom; and, when free, could rise in social and political life. The slaves of America, then, lie under the most absolute and grinding despotism that the world ever saw. But who are the despots? The rulers of the country—the sovereign people! Not merely the slaveholder who cracks the lash. He is but the instrument in the hands of despotism. That despotism is the government of the Slave States, and the United States, consisting of all its rulers—all the free citizens. Do not look upon this as a paradox, because you and I and the sixteen millions of rulers are free. The rulers of every despotism are free. Nicholas of Russia is free. The grand Sultan of Turkey is free. The butcher of Austria is free. Augustus, Anthony, and Lepidus were free, while they drenched Rome in blood. The Thirty Tyrants—the Four Hundred—the Three Thousand, were free while they bound their countrymen in chains. You, and I, and the sixteen millions are free, while we fasten iron chains, and rivet manacles on four millions of our fellow-men—take their wives and children from them—separate them—sell them, and doom them to perpetual, eternal bondage. Are we not then despots—despots such as history will brand and God abhor?

"We, as individuals, are fast losing our reputation for honest dealing. Our nation is losing its character. The loss of a firm national character, or the degradation of a nation's honour, is the inevitable prelude to her destruction. Behold the once proud fabric of a Roman empire—an empire carrying its arts and arms into every part of the Eastern continent; the monarchs of mighty kingdoms dragged at the wheels of her triumphal chariots; her eagle waving over the ruins of desolated countries;—where is her splendour, her wealth, her power, her glory? Extinguished for ever. Her mouldering temples, the mournful vestiges of her former grandeur, afford a shelter to her muttering monks. Where are her statesmen, her sages, her philosophers, her orators, generals? Go to their solitary tombs and inquire. She lost her national character, and her destruction followed. The ramparts of her national pride were broken down, and Vandalism desolated her classic fields. Then let the people of our country take warning ere it is too late. But most of us say to ourselves,

> " 'Who questions the right of mankind to be free?
> Yet, what are the rights of the *Negro* to me?
> I'm well fed and clothed, I have plenty of pelf—
> I'll care for the blacks when I turn black myself.'

"New Orleans is doubtless the most immoral place in the United States. The theatres are open on the Sabbath. Bull-fights, horse-racing, and other cruel amusements are carried on in this city to an extent unknown in any other part of the Union. The most stringent laws have been passed in that city against Negroes, yet a few years since the State Legislature passed a special act to enable a white man to marry a coloured woman, on account of her being possessed of a large fortune. And, very recently, the following paragraph appeared in the city papers:—

" 'There has been quite a stir recently in this city, in consequence of a marriage of a white man, named Buddington, a teller in the Canal Bank, to the Negro daughter of one of the wealthiest merchants. Buddington, before he could be married, was obliged to swear that he had Negro blood in his veins, and to do this he made an incision in his arm, and put some of her blood in the cut. The ceremony was performed by a Catholic clergyman, and the bridegroom has received with his wife a fortune of fifty or sixty thousand dollars.'

"It seems that the fifty or sixty thousand dollars entirely covered the Negro woman's black skin, and the law prohibiting marriage between blacks and whites was laid aside for the occasion."

Althesa felt proud, as well she might, at her husband's taking such high ground in a slaveholding city like New Orleans.

CHAPTER XXI

The Christian's Death

"O weep, ye friends of freedom weep!
Your harps to mournful measures sweep."

On the last day of November, 1620, on the confines of the
Grand Bank of Newfoundland, lo! we behold one little solitary tempest-tost and weather-beaten ship; it is all that can
be seen on the length and breadth of the vast intervening
solitudes, from the melancholy wilds of Labrador and New
England's ironbound shores, to the western coasts of Ireland
and the rock-defended Hebrides, but one lonely ship greets
the eye of angels or of men, on this great throughfare of
nations in our age. Next in moral grandeur, was this ship, to
the great discoverer's: Columbus found a continent; the May-
flower brought the seed-wheat of states and empire. That is
the May-flower, with its servants of the living God, their
wives and little ones, hastening to lay the foundations of
nations in the occidental lands of the setting-sun. Hear the
voice of prayer to God for his protection, and the glorious
music of praise, as it breaks into the wild tempest of the
mighty deep, upon the ear of God. Here in this ship are great
and good men. Justice, mercy, humanity, respect for the
rights of all; each man honoured, as he was useful to himself
and others; labour respected, law-abiding men, constitution-
making and respecting men; men, whom no tyrant could
conquer, or hardship overcome, with the high commission
sealed by a Spirit divine, to establish religious and political
liberty for all. This ship had the embryo elements of all that
is useful, great, and grand in Northern institutions; it was

the great type of goodness and wisdom, illustrated in two and a quarter centuries gone by; it was the good genius of America.

But look far in the South-east, and you behold on the same day, in 1620, a low rakish ship hastening from the tropics, solitary and alone, to the New World. What is she? She is freighted with the elements of unmixed evil. Hark! hear those rattling chains, hear that cry of despair and wail of anguish, as they die away in the unpitying distance. Listen to those shocking oaths, the crack of that flesh-cutting whip. Ah! it is the first cargo of slaves on their way to Jamestown, Virginia. Behold the May-flower anchored at Plymouth Rock, the slave-ship in James River. Each a parent, one of the prosperous, labour-honouring, law-sustaining institutions of the North; the other the mother of slavery, idleness, lynch-law, ignorance, unpaid labour, poverty, and duelling, despotism, the ceaseless swing of the whip, and the peculiar institutions of the South. These ships are the representation of good and evil in the New World, even to our day. When shall one of those parallel lines come to an end?

The origin of American slavery is not lost in the obscurity of by-gone ages. It is a plain historical fact, that it owes its birth to the African slave trade, now pronounced by every civilised community the greatest crime ever perpetrated against humanity. Of all causes intended to benefit mankind, the abolition of chattel slavery must necessarily be placed amongst the first, and the Negro hails with joy every new advocate that appears in his cause. Commiseration for human suffering and human sacrifices awakened the capacious mind, and brought into action the enlarged benevolence, of Georgiana Carlton. With respect to her philosophy—it was of a noble cast. It was, that all men are by nature equal; that they are wisely and justly endowed by the Creator with certain rights, which are irrefragable; and that, however human pride and human avarice may depress and debase, still God is the author of good to man—and of evil, man is the artificer to himself and to his species. Unlike Plato and Socrates, her mind was free from the gloom that surrounded theirs; her philosophy was founded in the school of Christianity; though a devoted member of her father's church, she was not a sectarian.

We learn from Scripture, and it is a little remarkable that it is the only exact definition of religion found in the sacred volume, that "pure religion and undefiled before God, even the Father, is this, to visit the fatherless and widows in their affliction, and to keep oneself unspotted from the world." "Look not every man on his own things, but every man also on the things of others." "Remember them that are in bonds as bound with them." "Whatsoever ye would that others should do to you, do ye even so to them."

This was her view of Christianity, and to this end she laboured with all her energies to convince her slaveholding neighbours that the Negro could not only take care of himself, but that he also appreciated liberty, and was willing to work and redeem himself. Her most sanguine wishes were being realized when she suddenly fell into a decline. Her mother had died of consumption, and her physician pronounced this to be her disease. She was prepared for this sad intelligence, and received it with the utmost composure. Although she had confidence in her husband that he would carry out her wishes in freeing the Negroes after her death, Mrs. Carlton resolved upon their immediate liberation. Consequently the slaves were all summoned before the noble woman, and informed that they were no longer bondsmen. "From this hour," said she, "you are free, and all eyes will be fixed upon you. I dare not predict how far your example may affect the welfare of your brethren yet in bondage. If you are temperate, industrious, peaceable, and pious, you will show to the world that slaves can be emancipated without danger. Remember what a singular relation you sustain to society. The necessities of the case require not only that you should behave as well as the whites, but better than the whites; and for this reason: if you behave no better than they, your example will lose a great portion of its influence.

Make the Lord Jesus Christ your refuge and exemplar. His is the only standard around which you can successfully rally. If ever there was a people who needed the consolations of religion to sustain them in their grievous afflictions, you are that people. You had better trust in the Lord than to put confidence in man. Happy is that people whose God is the Lord. Get as much education as possible for yourselves and your children. An ignorant people can never occupy any other than a degraded station in society; they can never be truly free until they are intelligent. In a few days you will start for the state of Ohio, where land will be purchased for some of you who have families, and where I hope you will all prosper. We have been urged to send you to Liberia, but we think it wrong to send you from your native land. We did not wish to encourage the Colonization Society, for it originated in hatred of the free coloured people. Its pretences are false, its doctrines odious, its means contemptible. Now, whatever may be your situation in life, 'Remember those in bonds as bound with them.' You must get ready as soon as you can for your journey to the North.''

Seldom was there ever witnessed a more touching scene than this. There sat the liberator,—pale, feeble, emaciated, with death stamped upon her countenance, surrounded by the sons and daughters of Africa; some of whom had in former years been separated from all that they had held near and dear, and the most of whose backs had been torn and gashed by the Negro whip. Some were upon their knees at the feet of their benefactress; others were standing round her weeping. Many begged that they might be permitted to remain on the farm and work for wages, for some had wives and some husbands on other plantations in the neighbourhood, and would rather remain with them.

But the laws of the state forbade any emancipated Negroes remaining, under penalty of again being sold into slavery. Hence the necessity of sending them out of the state. Mrs. Carlton was urged by her friends to send the emancipated Negroes to Africa. Extracts from the speeches of Henry Clay, and other distinguished Colonization Society men, were read to her to induce her to adopt this course. Some thought they should be sent away because the blacks are vicious; others because they would be missionaries to their brethren in Africa. "But," said she, "if we send away the Negroes because they are profligate and vicious, what sort of missionaries will they make? Why not send away the vicious among the whites for the same reason, and the same purpose?"

Death is a leveller, and neither age, sex, wealth, nor usefulness can avert when he is permitted to strike. The most beautiful flowers soon fade, and droop, and die; this is also the case with man; his days are uncertain as the passing breeze. This hour he glows in the blush of health and vigour, but the next he may be counted with the number no more known on earth.

Although in a low state of health, Mrs. Carlton had the pleasure of seeing all her slaves, except Sam and three others, start for a land of freedom. The morning they were to go on board the steamer, bound for Louisville, they all assembled on the large grass plot, in front of the drawing-room window, and wept while they bid their mistress farewell. When they were on the boat, about leaving the wharf, they were heard giving the charge to those on shore—"Sam, take care of Misus, take care of Marser, as you love us, and hope to meet us in de Hio (Ohio), and in heben; be sure and take good care of Misus and Marser."

In less than a week after her emancipated people had started for Ohio, Mrs. Carlton was cold in death. Mr. Carlton felt deeply, as all husbands must who love their wives, the loss of her who had been a lamp to his feet, and a light to his path. She had converted him from infidelity to Christianity; from the mere theory of liberty to practical freedom. He had looked upon the Negro as an ill-treated distant link of the human family; he now regarded them as a part of God's children. Oh, what a silence pervaded the house when the Christian had been removed. His indeed was a lonesome position.

" 'Twas midnight, and he sat alone—
The husband of the dead,
That day the dark dust had been thrown
Upon the buried head."

In the midst of the buoyancy of youth, this cherished one had drooped and died. Deep were the sounds of grief and mourning heard in that stately dwelling, when the stricken friends, whose office it had been to nurse and soothe the weary sufferer, beheld her pale and motionless in the sleep of death.

Of what a chill creeps through the breaking heart when we look upon the insensible form, and feel that it no longer contains the spirit we so dearly loved! How difficult to realise that the eye which always glowed with affection and intelligence—that the ear which had so often listened to the sounds of sorrow and gladness—that the voice whose accents had been to us like sweet music, and the heart, the habitation of benevolence and truth, are now powerless and insensate as the bier upon which the form rests. Though faith be strong enough to penetrate the cloud of gloom which hovers near, and to behold the freed spirit safe, *for ever*, safe in its home in heaven, yet the thoughts *will* linger sadly and cheerlessly upon the grave.

Peace to her ashes! she fought the fight, obtained the Christian's victory, and wears the crown. But if it were that departed spirits are permitted to note the occurrences of this world, with what a frown of disapprobation would hers view the effort being made in the United States to retard the work of emancipation for which she laboured and so wished to see brought about.

In what light would she consider that hypocritical priesthood who gave their aid and sanction to the infamous "Fugitive Slave Law." If true greatness consists in doing good to mankind, then was Georgiana Carlton an ornament to human nature. Who can think of the broken hearts made whole, of sad and dejected countenances now beaming with contentment and joy, of the mother offering her free-born babe to heaven, and of the father whose cup of joy seems overflowing in the presence of his family, where none can molest or make him afraid. Oh, that God may give more such persons to take the whip-scarred Negro by the hand, and raise him to a level with our common humanity! May the professed lovers of freedom in the new world see that true liberty is freedom for all! and may every American continually hear it sounding in his ear:—

"Shall every flap of England's flag
　Proclaim that all around are free,
From 'farthest Ind' to each blue crag
　That beetles o'er the Western Sea?
And shall we scoff at Europe's kings,
　When Freedom's fire is dim with us,
And round our country's altar clings
　The damning shade of Slavery's curse?"

CHAPTER XXII

A Ride in a Stage-Coach

We shall now return to Cincinnati, where we left Clotel preparing to go to Richmond in search of her daughter. Tired of the disguise in which she had escaped, she threw it off on her arrival at Cincinnati. But being assured that not a shadow of safety would attend her visit to a city in which she was well known, unless in some disguise, she again resumed men's apparel on leaving Cincinnati. This time she had more the appearance of an Italian or Spanish gentleman. In addition to the fine suit of black cloth, a splendid pair of dark false whiskers covered the sides of her face, while the curling moustache found its place upon the upper lip. From practice she had become accustomed to high-heeled boots, and could walk without creating any suspicion as regarded her sex. It was a cold evening that Clotel arrived at Wheeling, and took a seat in the coach going to Richmond. She was already in the state of Virginia, yet a long distance from the place of her destination.

A ride in a stage-coach, over an American road, is unpleasant under the most favourable circumstances. But now that it was winter, and the roads unusually bad, the journey was still more dreary. However, there were eight passengers in the coach, and I need scarcely say that such a number of genuine Americans could not be together without whiling away the time somewhat pleasantly. Besides Clotel, there was an elderly gentleman with his two daughters—one apparently under twenty years, the other a shade above. The pale, spectacled face of another slim, tall man, with a white neckerchief, pointed him out as a minister. The rough featured, dark countenance of a stout looking man, with a white hat on one side of his head, told that he was from the sunny South. There was nothing remarkable about the other two, who might pass for ordinary American gentlemen. It was on the eve of a presidential election, when every man is thought to be a politician. Clay, Van Buren, and Harrison were the men who expected the indorsement of the Baltimore Convention.

"Who does this town go for?" asked the old gent, with the ladies, as the coach drove up to an inn, where groups of persons were waiting for the latest papers.

"We are divided," cried the rough voice of one of the outsiders.

"Well, who do you think will get the majority here?" continued the old gent.

"Can't tell very well; I go for 'Old Tip,' " was the answer from without. This brought up the subject fairly before the passengers, and when the coach again started a general discussion commenced, in which all took a part except Clotel and the young ladies. Some were for Clay, some for Van Buren, and others for "Old Tip." The coach stopped to take in a real farmer-looking man, who no sooner entered than he was saluted with "Do you go for Clay?"

"No," was the answer.

"Do you go for Van Buren?"

"No."

"Well, then, of course you will go for Harrison."

"No."

"Why, don't you mean to work for any of them at the election?"

"No."

"Well, who will you work for?" asked one of the company.

"I work for Betsy and the children, and I have a hard job

of it at that," replied the farmer, without a smile. This answer, as a matter of course, set the new comer down as one upon whom the rest of the passengers could crack their jokes with the utmost impunity. "Are you an Odd Fellow?" asked one.

"No, sir, I've been married more than a month."

"I mean, do you belong to the order of Odd Fellows?"

"No, no; I belong to the order of married men."

"Are you a mason?"

"No, I am a carpenter by trade."

"Are you a Son of Temperance?"

"Bother you, no; I am a son of Mr. John Gosling."

After a hearty laugh in which all joined, the subject of Temperance became the theme for discussion. In this the spectacled gent. was at home. He soon showed that he was a New Englander, and went the whole length of the "Maine Law." The minister was about having it all his own way, when the Southerner, in the white hat, took the opposite side of the question. "I don't bet a red cent on these teetotlars," said he, and at the same time looking round to see if he had the approbation of the rest of the company. "Why?" asked the minister. "Because they are a set who are afraid to spend a cent. They are a bad lot, the whole on 'em. It was evident that the white hat gent. was an uneducated man. The minister commenced in full earnest, and gave an interesting account of the progress of temperance in Connecticut, the state from which he came, proving, that a great portion of the prosperity of the state was attributable to the disuse of intoxicating drinks. Every one thought the white hat had got the worst of the argument, and that he was settled for the remainder of the night. But not he; he took fresh courage and began again. "Now," said he, "I have just been on a visit to my uncle's in Vermont, and I guess I knows a little about these here teetotlars. You see, I went up there to make a little stay of a fortnight. I got there at night, and they seemed glad to see me, but they didn't give me a bit of anything to drink. Well, thinks I to myself, the jig's up: I sha'n't get any more liquor till I get out of the state." We all sat up till twelve o'clock that night, and I heard nothing but talk about the 'Juvinal Temperence Army,' the 'Band of Hope,' the 'Rising Generation,' the 'Female Dorcas Temperance Society,' 'The None Such,' and I don't know how many other names they didn't have. As I had taken several pretty large 'Cock Tails' before I entered the state, I thought upon the whole that I would not spile for the want of liquor. The next morning, I commenced writing back to my friends, and telling them what's what. Aunt Polly said, 'Well, Johnny, I s'pose you are given 'em a pretty account of us all here.' 'Yes,' said I; 'I am tellin' 'em if they want anything to drink when they come up here, they had better bring it with 'em.' 'Oh,' said aunty, 'they would search their boxes; can't bring any spirits in the state.' Well, as I was saying, jist as I got my letters finished, and was going to the post office (for uncle's house was two miles from the town), aunty says, 'Johnny, I s'pose you'll try to get a little somethin' to drink in town won't you?' Says I, 'I s'pose it's no use.' 'No,' said she, 'you can't; it ain't to be had no how, for love nor money.' So jist as I was puttin' on my hat, 'Johnny,' cries out aunty. 'What,' says I. 'Now I'll tell you, I don't want you to say nothin' about it, but I keeps a little rum to rub my head with, for I am troubled with the headache; now I don't want you to mention it for the world, but I'll give you a little taste, the old man is such a teetotaller, that I should never hear the last of it, and I would not like for the boys to know it, they are members of the "Cold Water Army." '

"Aunty now brought out a black bottle and gave me a cup, and told me to help myself, which I assure you I did. I now felt ready to face the cold. As I was passing the barn I heard uncle thrashing oats, so I went to the door and spoke to him. 'Come in, John,' says he. 'No,' said I; 'I am goin' to post some letters,' for I was afraid that he would smell my breath if I went too near to him. 'Yes, yes, come in.' So I went in, and says he, 'It's now eleven o'clock; that's about the time you take your grog, I s'pose, when you are at home.'

'Yes,' said I. 'I am sorry for you, my lad; you can't get anything up here; you can't even get it at the chemist's, except as medicine, and then you must let them mix it and you take it in their presence.' 'This is indeed hard,' replied I; 'Well, it can't be helped,' continued he: 'and it ought not to be if it could. It's best for society; people's better off without drink. I recollect when your father and I, thirty years ago, used to go out on a spree and spend more than half a dollar in a night. Then here's the rising generation; there's nothing like settin' a good example. Look how healthy your cousins are—there's Benjamin, he never tasted spirits in his life. Oh, John, I would you were a teetotaller.' 'I suppose,' said I, 'I'll have to be one till I leave the state.' 'Now,' said he, 'John, I don't want you to mention it, for your aunt would go into hysterics if she thought there was a drop of intoxicating liquor about the place, and I would not have the boys to know it for anything, but I keep a little brandy to rub my joints for the rheumatics, and being it's you, I'll give you a little dust.' So the old man went to one corner of the barn, took out a brown jug and handed it to me, and I must say it was a little the best cogniac that I had tasted for many a day. Says I, 'Uncle, you are a good judge of brandy.' 'Yes,' said he, 'I learned when I was young.' So off I started for the post office. In returnin' I thought I'd jist go through the woods where the boys were chopping wood, and wait and go to the house with them when they went to dinner. I found them hard at work, but as merry as crickets. 'Well, cousin John, are you done writing?' 'Yes,' answered I. 'Have you posted them?' 'Yes.' 'Hope you didn't go to any place inquiring for grog.' 'No, I knowed it was no good to do that.' 'I suppose a cock-tail would taste good now.' 'Well, I guess it would,' says I. The three boys then joined in a hearty laugh. 'I suppose you have told 'em that we are a dry set up here?' 'Well, I aint told 'em anything else.' 'Now, cousin John,' said Edward, 'if you wont say anything, we will give you a small taste. For mercy's sake don't let father or mother know it; they are such rabid teetotallers, that they would not sleep a wink to-night if they thought there was any spirits about the place.' 'I am mum,' says I. And the boys took a jug out of a hollow stump, and gave me some first-rate peach brandy. And during the fortnight that I was in Vermont, with my teetotal relations, I was kept about as well corned as if I had been among my hot water friends in Tennessee."

This narrative, given by the white hat man, was received with unbounded applause by all except the pale gent. in spectacles, who showed, by the way in which he was running his fingers between his cravat and throat, that he did not intend to "give it up so." The white hat gent. was now the lion of the company.

"Oh, you did not get hold of the right kind of teetotallers," said the minister. "I can give you a tale worth a dozen of yours," continued he. "Look at society in the states where temperance views prevail, and you will there see real happiness. The people are taxed less, the poor houses are shut up for want of occupants, and extreme destitution is unknown. Every one who drinks at all is liable to become an habitual drunkard. Yes, I say boldly, that no man living who uses intoxicating drinks, is free from the danger of at least occasional, and if of occasional, ultimately of habitual excess. There seems to be no character, position, or circumstances that free men from the danger. *I have known* many young men of the finest promise, led by the drinking habit into vice, ruin, and early death. *I have known* many tradesmen whom it has made bankrupt. *I have known* Sunday scholars whom it has led to prison—teachers, and even superintendents, whom it has dragged down to profligacy. *I have known* ministers of high academic honours, of splendid eloquence, nay, of vast usefulness, whom it has fascinated, and hurried over the precipice of public infamy with their eyes open, and gazing with horror on their fate. *I have known* men of the strongest and clearest intellect and of vigorous resolution, whom it has made weaker than children and fools—gentlemen of refinement and taste whom it has debased into brutes—poets of high genius whom it has bound in a bondage worse than the galleys, and ultimately cut short their days. *I have known* statesmen, lawyers, and judges whom it has killed—kind husbands and fathers whom it has turned into monsters. *I have known* honest men whom it has made villains—elegant and Christian *ladies* whom it has *converted into bloated sots.*"

"But you talk too fast," replied the white hat man. "You don't give a feller a chance to say nothin'."

"I heard you," continued the minister, "and now you hear me out. It is indeed wonderful how people become lovers of strong drink. Some years since, before I became a teetotaller I kept spirits about the house, and I had a servant who was much addicted to strong drink. He used to say that he could not make my boots shine, without mixing the blacking with whiskey. So to satisfy myself that the whiskey was put in the blacking, one morning I made him bring the dish in which he kept the blacking, and poured in the whiskey myself. And now, sir, what do you think?"

"Why, I s'pose your boots shined better than before," replied the white hat.

"No," continued the minister. "He took the blacking out, and I watched him, and he drank down the whiskey, blacking, and all."

This turned the joke upon the advocate of strong drink, and he began to put his wits to work for arguments. "You are from Connecticut, are you?" asked the Southerner.

"Yes, and we are an orderly, pious, peaceable people. Our holy religion is respected, and we do more for the cause of Christ than the whole Southern States put together."

"I don't doubt it," said the white hat gent. "You sell wooden nutmegs and other spurious articles enough to do some good. You talk of your 'holy religion'; but your robes' righteousness are woven at Lowell and Manchester; your paradise is high per centum on factory stocks; your palms of victory and crowns of rejoicing are triumphs over a rival party in politics, on the questions of banks and tariffs. If you could, you would turn heaven into Birmingham, make every angel a weaver, and with the eternal din of looms and spindles drown all the anthems of the morning stars. Ah! I know you Connecticut people like a book. No, no, all [old] hoss; you can't come in on me." This last speech of the rough featured man again put him in the ascendant, and the spectacled gent. once more ran his fingers between his cravat and throat.

"You live in Tennessee, I think," said the minister.

"Yes," replied the Southerner, "I used to live in Orleans, but now I claim to be a Tennessean."

"Your people of New Orleans are the most ungodly set in the United States," said the minister. Taking a New Orleans newspaper from his pocket he continued, "Just look here, there are not less than three advertisements of bull fights to take place on the Sabbath. You people of the Slave States have no regard for the Sabbath, religion, morality or anything else intended to make mankind better."

Here Clotel could have borne ample testimony, had she dared to have taken sides with the Connecticut man. Her residence in Vicksburgh had given her an opportunity of knowing something of the character of the inhabitants of the far South.

"Here is an account of a grand bull fight that took place in New Orleans a week ago last Sunday. I will read it to you." And the minister read aloud the following:

"Yesterday, pursuant to public notice, came off at Gretna, opposite the Fourth District, the long heralded fight between the famous grizzly bear, General Jackson (victor in fifty battles), and the Attakapas bull, Santa Anna.

"The fame of the coming conflict had gone forth to the four winds, and women and children, old men and boys, from all parts of the city, and from the breezy banks of Lake Pontchartrain and Borgne, brushed up their Sunday suit, and prepared to see the fun. Long before the published hour, the quiet streets of the rural Gretna were filled with crowds of anxious denizens, flocking to the arena, and before the fight commenced, such a crowd had collected as Gretna had not seen, nor will be likely to see again.

"The arena for the sports was a cage, twenty feet square, built upon the ground, and constructed of heavy timbers and iron bars. Around it were seats, circularly placed, and intended to accommodate many thousands. About four or five thousand persons assembled, covering the seats as with a cloud, and crowding down around the cage, were within each of the bars.

"The bull selected to sustain the honour and verify the pluck of Attakapas on this trying occasion was a black animal from the Opelousas, little and sinewy as a four year old courser, and with eyes like burning coals. His horns bore the appearance of having been filed at the tips, and wanted that keen and slashing appearance so common with others of his kith and kin; otherwise it would have been 'all day' with bruin at the first pass, and no mistake.

"The bear was an animal of note, and called General Jackson, from the fact of his licking up everything that came in his way, and taking 'the responsibility' on all occasions. He was a wicked looking beast, very lean and unamiable in aspect, with hair all standing the wrong way. He had fought some fifty bulls (so they said), always coming out victorious, but that neither one of the fifty had been an Attakapas bull, the bills of the performances did not say. Had he tackled Attakapas first it is likely his fifty battles would have remained unfought.

"About half past four o'clock the performances commenced.

"The bull was first seen, standing in the cage alone, with head erect, and looking a very monarch in his capacity. At an appointed signal, a cage containing the bear was placed alongside the arena, and an opening being made, bruin stalked into the battle ground—not, however, without sundry stirrings up with a ten foot pole, he being experienced in such matters, and backwards in raising a row.

"Once on the battle-field, both animals stood, like wary champions, eyeing each other, the bear cowering low, with head upturned and fangs exposed, while Attakapas stood wondering, with his eye dilated, lashing his sides with his long and bushy tail, and pawing up the earth in very wrath.

"The bear seemed little inclined to begin the attack, and the bull, standing a moment, made steps first backward and then forward, as if measuring his antagonist, and meditating where to plant a blow. Bruin wouldn't come to the scratch no way, till one of the keepers, with an iron rod, tickled his ribs and made him move. Seeing this, Attakapas took it as a hostile demonstration, and, gathering his strength, dashed savagely at the enemy, catching him on the points of his horns, and doubling him up like a sack of bran against the bars. Bruin 'sung out' at this, 'and made a dash for his opponent's nose.'

"Missing this, the bull turned to the 'about face,' and the bear caught him by the ham, inflicting a ghastly wound. But Attakapas with a kick shook him off, and renewing the attack, went at him again, head on and with a rush. This time he was not so fortunate, for the bear caught him above the eye, burying his fangs in the tough hide, and holding him as in a vice. It was now the bull's turn to 'sing out,' and he did it, bellowing forth with a voice more hideous than that of all the bulls of Bashan. Some minutes stood matters thus, and the cries of the bull, mingled with the hoarse growls of the bear, made hideous music, fit only for a dance of devils. Then came a pause (the bear having relinquished his hold), and for a few minutes it was doubtful whether the fun was not up. But the magic wand of the keeper (the ten foot pole) again stirred up bruin, and at it they went, and with a rush.

"Bruin now tried to fasten on the bull's back, and drove his tusks in him in several places, making the red blood flow like wine from the vats of Luna. But Attakapas was pluck to the back bone, and, catching bruin on the tips of his horns, shuffled him up right merrily, making the fur fly like feathers in a gale of wind. Bruin cried 'Nuff' (in bear language), but the bull followed up his advantage, and, making one furious plunge full at the figure head of the enemy, struck a horn into his eye, burying it there, and dashing the tender organ into darkness and atoms. Blood followed the blow, and poor bruin, blinded, bleeding, and in mortal agony, turned with a howl to leave, but Attakapas caught him in the retreat, and rolled him over like a ball. Over and over again this rolling over was enacted, and finally, after more than an hour, bruin curled himself up on his back, bruised, bloody, and dead beat. The thing was up with California, and Attakapas was declared the victor amidst the applause of the multitude that made the heavens ring."

"There," said he, "can you find anything against Connecticut equal to that?" The Southerner had to admit that he was beat by the Yankee. During all this time, it must not be supposed that the old gent. with the two daughters, and even the young ladies themselves, had been silent. Clotel and they had not only given their opinions as regarded the merits of the discussion, but that sly glance of the eye, which is ever given where the young of both sexes meet, had been freely at work. The American ladies are rather partial to foreigners, and Clotel had the appearance of a fine Italian. The old gentleman was now near his home, and a whisper from the eldest daughter, who was unmarried but marriageable, induced him to extend to "Mr. Johnson" an invitation to stop and spend a week with the young ladies at their family residence. Clotel excused herself upon various grounds, and at last, to cut short the matter, promised that she would pay them a visit on her return. The arrival of the coach at Lynchburgh separated the young ladies from the Italian gent., and the coach again resumed its journey.

CHAPTER XXIII

Truth Stranger
Than Fiction

"Is the poor privilege to turn the key
Upon the captive, freedom? He's as far
From the enjoyment of the earth and air
Who watches o'er the chains, as they who wear."
                                        BYRON

During certain seasons of the year, all tropical climates are
subject to epidemics of a most destructive nature. The inhabitants of New Orleans look with as much certainty for
the appearance of the yellow-fever, small-pox, or cholera, in
the hot-season, as the Londoner does for fog in the month
of November. In the summer of 1831, the people of New
Orleans were visited with one of these epidemics. It appeared
in a form unusually repulsive and deadly. It seized persons
who were in health, without any premonition. Sometimes
death was the immediate consequence. The disorder began
in the brain, by an oppressive pain accompanied or followed
by fever. The patient was devoured with burning thirst. The
stomach, distracted by pains, in vain sought relief in efforts
to disburden itself. Fiery veins streaked the eye; the face was
inflamed, and dyed of a dark dull red colour; the ears from
time to time rang painfully. Now mucous secretions sur-
charged the tongue, and took away the power of speech; now
the sick one spoke, but in speaking had a foresight of death.
When the violence of the disease approached the heart, the
gums were blackened. The sleep, broken, troubled by con-
vulsions, or by frightful visions, was worse than the waking

hours; and when the reason sank under a delirium which had its seat in the brain, repose utterly forsook the patient's couch. The progress of the heat within was marked by yellowish spots, which spread over the surface of the body. If, then, a happy crisis came not, all hope was gone. Soon the breath infected the air with a fetid odour, the lips were glazed, despair painted itself in the eyes, and sobs, with long intervals of silence, formed the only language. From each side of the mouth spread foam, tinged with black and burnt blood. Blue streaks mingled with the yellow all over the frame. All remedies were useless. This was the Yellow Fever. The disorder spread alarm and confusion throughout the city. On an average, more than 400 died daily. In the midst of disorder and confusion, death heaped victims on victims. Friend followed friend in quick succession. The sick were avoided from the fear of contagion, and for the same reason the dead were left unburied. Nearly 2000 dead bodies lay uncovered in the burial-ground, with only here and there a little lime thrown over them, to prevent the air becoming infected.

The Negro, whose home is in a hot climate, was not proof against the disease. Many plantations had to suspend their work for want of slaves to take the places of those carried off by the fever. Henry Morton and wife were among the thirteen thousand swept away by the raging disorder that year. Like too many, Morton had been dealing extensively in lands and stocks; and though apparently in good circumstances was, in reality, deeply involved in debt. Althesa, although as white as most white women in a southern clime, was, as we already know, born a slave. By the laws of all the Southern States the children follow the condition of the mother. If the mother is free the children are free; if a slave, they are slaves. Morton was unacquainted with the laws of the land; and although he had married Althesa, it was a marriage which the law did not recognise; and therefore she whom he thought to be his wife was, in fact, nothing more than his slave. What would have been his feelings had he known this, and also known that his two daughters, Ellen and Jane, were his slaves? Yet such was the fact. After the disappearance of the disease with which Henry Morton had so suddenly been removed, his brother went to New Orleans to give what aid he could in settling up the affairs. James Morton, on his arrival in New Orleans, felt proud of his nieces, and promised them a home with his own family in Vermont; little dreaming that his brother had married a slave woman, and that his nieces were slaves. The girls themselves had never heard that their mother had been a slave, and therefore knew nothing of the danger hanging over their heads. An inventory of the property was made out by James Morton, and placed in the hands of the creditors; and the young ladies, with their uncle, were about leaving the city to reside for a few days on the banks of Lake Pontchartrain, where they could enjoy a fresh air that the city could not afford. But just as they were about taking the train, an officer arrested the whole party; the young ladies as slaves, and the uncle upon the charge of attempting to conceal the property of his deceased brother. Morton was overwhelmed with horror at the idea of his nieces being claimed as slaves, and asked for time, that he might save them from such a fate. He even offered to mortgage his little farm in Vermont for the amount which young slave women of their ages would fetch. But the creditors pleaded that they were "an extra article," and would sell for more than common slaves; and must, therefore, be sold at auction. They were given up, but neither ate nor slept, nor separated from each other, till they were taken into the New Orleans slave market, where they were offered to the highest bidder. There they stood, trembling, blushing, and weeping; compelled to listen to the grossest language, and shrinking from the rude hands that examined the graceful proportions of their beautiful frames.

After a fierce contest between the bidders, the young ladies were sold, one for 2,300 dollars, and the other for 3,000 dollars. We need not add that had those young girls been sold for mere house servants or field hands, they would not have brought one half the sums they did. The fact that they were the grand-daughters of Thomas Jefferson, no doubt, increased their value in the market. Here were two of the softer sex, accustomed to the fondest indulgence, surrounded by all the refinements of life, and with all the timidity that such a life could produce, bartered away like cattle in Smithfield market. Ellen, the eldest, was sold to an old gentleman, who purchased her, as he said, for a housekeeper. The girl was taken to his residence, nine miles from the city. She soon, however, knew for what purpose she had been bought; and an educated and cultivated mind and taste, which made her see and understand how great was her degradation, now armed her hand with the ready means of death. The morning after her arrival, she was found in her chamber, a corpse. She had taken poison. Jane was purchased by a dashing young man, who had just come into the possession of a large fortune. The very appearance of the young Southerner pointed him out as an unprincipled profligate; and the young girl needed no one to tell her of her impending doom. The young maid of fifteen was immediately removed to his country seat, near the junction of the Mississippi river with the sea. This was a most singular spot, remote, in a dense forest spreading over the summit of a cliff that rose abruptly to a great height above the sea; but so grand in its situation, in the desolate sublimity which reigned around, in the reverential murmur of the waves that washed its base, that, though picturesque, it was a forest prison. Here the young lady saw no one, except an old Negress who acted as her servant. The smiles with which the young man met her were indignantly spurned. But she was the property of another, and could hope for justice and mercy only through him.

Jane, though only in her fifteenth year, had become strongly attached to Volney Lapuc, a young Frenchman, a student in her father's office. The poverty of the young man, and the youthful age of the girl, had caused their feelings to be kept from the young lady's parents. At the death of his master, Volney had returned to his widowed mother at Mobile, and knew nothing of the misfortune that had befallen his mistress, until he received a letter from her. But how could he ever obtain a sight of her, even if he wished, locked up as she was in her master's mansion? After several days of what her master termed "obstinacy" on her part, the young girl was placed in an upper chamber, and told that that would be her home, until she should yield to her master's wishes. There she remained more than a fortnight, and with the exception of a daily visit from her master, she saw no one but the old Negress who waited upon her. One bright moonlight evening as she was seated at the window, she perceived the figure of a man beneath her window. At first, she thought it was her master; but the tall figure of the stranger soon convinced her that it was another. Yes, it was Volney! He had no sooner received her letter, than he set out for New Orleans; and finding on his arrival there, that his mistress had been taken away, resolved to follow her. There he was; but how could she communicate with him? She dared not trust the old Negress with her secret, for fear that it might reach her master. Jane wrote a hasty note and threw it out of the window, which was eagerly picked up by the young man, and he soon disappeared in the woods. Night passed away in dreariness to her, and the next morning she viewed the spot beneath her window with the hope of seeing the footsteps of him who had stood there the previous night. Evening returned, and with it the hope of again seeing the man she loved. In this she was not disappointed; for daylight had scarcely disappeared, and the moon once more rising through the tops of the tall trees, when the young man was seen in the same place as on the previous night. He had in his hand a rope ladder. As soon as Jane saw this, she took the sheets from her bed, tore them into strings, tied them together, and let one end down the side of the house. A moment more, and one end of the rope ladder was in her hand, and she fastened it inside the room. Soon the young maiden was seen descending, and the enthusiastic lover, with his arms extended, waiting to receive his mistress. The planter had been out on an hunting excursion, and returning home, saw his victim as her lover was receiving her in his arms. At this moment the sharp sound of a rifle was heard, and the young man fell weltering in his blood, at the feet of his mistress. Jane fell senseless by his side. For many days she had a confused consciousness of some great agony, but knew not where she was, or by whom surrounded. The slow recovery of her reason settled into the most intense melancholy, which gained at length the compassion even of her cruel master. The beautiful bright eyes, always pleading in expression, were now so heart-piercing in their sadness, that he could not endure their gaze. In a few days the poor girl died of a broken heart, and was buried at night at the back of the garden by the Negroes; and no one wept at the grave of her who had been so carefully cherished, and so tenderly beloved.

This, reader, is an unvarnished narrative of one doomed by the laws of the Southern States to be a slave. It tells not only its own story of grief, but speaks of a thousand wrongs and woes beside, which never see the light; all the more bitter and dreadful, because no help can relieve, no sympathy can mitigate, and no hope can cheer.

CHAPTER XXIV

The Arrest

"The fearful storm—it threatens lowering,
   Which God in mercy long delays;
Slaves yet may see their masters cowering,
   While whole plantations smoke and blaze!"
CARTER

It was late in the evening when the coach arrived at Richmond, and Clotel once more alighted in her native city. She had intended to seek lodgings somewhere in the outskirts of the town, but the lateness of the hour compelled her to stop at one of the principal hotels for the night. She had scarcely entered the inn, when she recognised among the numerous black servants one to whom she was well known; and her only hope was, that her disguise would keep her from being discovered. The imperturbable calm and entire forgetfulness of self which induced Clotel to visit a place from which she could scarcely hope to escape, to attempt the rescue of a beloved child, demonstrate that overwillingness of woman to carry out promptings of the finer feelings of her heart. True to woman's nature, she had risked her own liberty for another.

She remained in the hotel during the night, and the next morning, under the plea of illness, she took her breakfast alone. That day the fugitive slave paid a visit to the suburbs of the town, and once more beheld the cottage in which she had spent so many happy hours. It was winter, and the clematis and passion flower were not there; but there were the same walks she had so often pressed with her feet, and the same trees which had so often shaded her as she passed through the garden at the back of the house. Old remembrances rushed upon her memory, and caused her to shed tears freely. Clotel was now in her native town, and near her daughter; but how could she communicate with her? How could she see her? To have made herself known, would have been a suicidal act; betrayal would have followed, and she arrested. Three days had passed away, and Clotel still remained in the hotel at which she had first put up; and yet she had got no tidings of her child. Unfortunately for Clotel, a disturbance had just broken out amongst the slave population in the state of Virginia, and all strangers were eyed with suspicion.

The evils consequent on slavery are not lessened by the incoming of one or two rays of light. If the slave only becomes aware of his condition, and conscious of the injustice under which he suffers, if he obtains but a faint idea of these things, he will seize the first opportunity to possess himself of what he conceives to belong to him. The infusion of Anglo-Saxon with African blood has created an insurrectionary feeling among the slaves of America hitherto unknown. Aware of their blood connection with their owners, these mulattoes labour under the sense of their personal and social injuries; and tolerate, if they do not encourage in themselves, low and vindictive passions. On the other hand, the slave owners are aware of their critical position, and are ever watchful, always fearing an outbreak among the slaves.

True, the Free States are equally bound with the Slave States to suppress any insurrectionary movement that may take place among the slaves. The Northern freemen are bound by their constitutional obligations to aid the slaveholder in keeping his slaves in their chains. Yet there are, at the time we write, four millions of bond slaves in the United States. The insurrection to which we now refer was headed by a full-blooded Negro, who had been born and brought up a slave. He had heard the twang of the driver's whip, and saw the warm blood streaming from the Negro's body; he had witnessed the separation of parents and children, and was made aware, by too many proofs, that the slave could expect no justice at the hand of the slave owner. He went by the name of "Nat Turner." He was a preacher amongst the Negroes, and distinguished for his eloquence, respected by the whites, and loved and venerated by the Negroes. On the discovery of the plan for the outbreak, Turner fled to the swamps, followed by those who had joined in the insurrection. Here the revolted Negroes numbered some hundreds, and for a time bade defiance to their oppressors. The Dismal Swamps cover many thousands of acres of wild land, and a dense forest, with wild animals and insects, such as are unknown in any other part of Virginia. Here runaway Negroes usually seek a hiding-place, and some have been known to reside here for years. The revolters were joined by one of these. He was a large, tall, full-blooded Negro, with a stern and savage countenance; the marks on his face showed that he was from one of the barbarous tribes in Africa, and claimed that country as his native land; his only covering was a girdle around his loins, made of skins of wild beasts which he had killed; his only token of authority among those that he led, was a pair of epaulettes made from the tail of a fox, and tied to his shoulder by a cord. Brought from the coast of Africa when only fifteen years of age to the island of Cuba, he was smuggled from thence into Virginia. He had been two years in the swamps, and considered it his future home. He had met a Negro woman who was also a runaway; and, after the fashion of his native land, had gone through the process of oiling her as the marriage ceremony. They had built a cave on a rising mound in the swamp; this was their home. His name was Picquilo. His only weapon was a sword, made from the blade of a scythe, which he had stolen from a neighbouring plantation. His dress, his character, his manners, his mode of fighting, were all in keeping with the early training he had received in the land of his birth. He moved about with the activity of a cat, and neither the thickness of the trees, nor the depth of the water could stop him. He was a bold, turbulent spirit; and from revenge imbrued his hands in the blood of all the whites he could meet. Hunger, thirst, fatigue, and loss of sleep he seemed made to endure as if by peculiarity of constitution. His air was fierce, his step oblique, his look sanguinary. Such was the character of one of the leaders in the Southampton insurrection. All Negroes were arrested who were found beyond their master's threshold, and all strange whites watched with a great degree of alacrity.

Such was the position in which Clotel found affairs when she returned to Virginia in search of her Mary. Had not the slave-owners been watchful of strangers, owing to the out-break, the fugitive could not have escaped the vigilance of the police; for advertisements, announcing her escape and offering a large reward for her arrest, had been received in the city previous to her arrival, and the officers were there-fore on the look-out for the runaway slave. It was on the third day, as the quadroon was seated in her room at the inn, still in the disguise of a gentleman, that two of the city of-ficers entered the room, and informed her that they were authorised to examine all strangers, to assure the authorities that they were not in league with the revolted Negroes. With trembling heart the fugitive handed the key of her trunk to the officers. To their surprise, they found nothing but wom-an's apparel in the box, which raised their curiosity, and caused a further investigation that resulted in the arrest of Clotel as a fugitive slave. She was immediately conveyed to prison, there to await the orders of her master. For many days, uncheered by the voice of kindness, alone, hopeless, desolate, she waited for the time to arrive when the chains were to be placed on her limbs, and she returned to her inhuman and unfeeling owner.

The arrest of the fugitive was announced in all the news-papers, but created little or no sensation. The inhabitants were too much engaged in putting down the revolt among the slaves; and although all the odds were against the insur-gents, the whites found it no easy matter, with all their caution. Every day brought news of fresh outbreaks. Without scruple and without pity, the whites massacred all blacks found beyond their owners' plantations: the Negroes, in return, set fire to houses, and put those to death who attempted to escape from the flames. Thus carnage was added to carnage, and the blood of the whites flowed to avenge the blood of the blacks. These were the ravages of slavery. No graves were dug for the Negroes; their dead bodies became food for dogs and vultures, and their bones, partly calcined by the sun, remained scattered about, as if to mark the mournful fury of servitude and lust of power. When the slaves were subdued, except a few in the swamps, bloodhounds were put in this dismal place to hunt out the remaining revolters. Among the captured Negroes was one of whom we shall hereafter make mention.

CHAPTER XXV

Death Is Freedom

"I asked but freedom, and ye gave
Chains, and the freedom of the grave."
SNELLING

There are, in the district of Columbia, several slave prisons, or "Negro pens," as they are termed. These prisons are mostly occupied by persons to keep their slaves in, when collecting their gangs together for the New Orleans market. Some of them belong to the government, and one, in partic- ular, is noted for having been the place where a number of free coloured persons have been incarcerated from time to time. In this district is situated the capital of the United States. Any free coloured persons visiting Washington, if not provided with papers asserting and proving their right to be free, may be arrested and placed in one of these dens. If they succeed in showing that they are free, they are set at liberty, provided they are able to pay the expenses of their arrest and imprisonment; if they cannot pay these expenses, they are sold out. Through this unjust and oppressive law, many per- sons born in the Free States have been consigned to a life of slavery on the cotton, sugar, or rice plantations of the Southern States. By order of her master, Clotel was removed from Richmond and placed in one of these prisons, to await the sailing of a vessel for New Orleans. The prison in which she was put stands midway between the capitol at Washing- ton and the President's house. Here the fugitive saw nothing but slaves brought in and taken out, to be placed in ships and sent away to the same part of the country to which she herself would soon be compelled to go. She had seen or heard nothing of her daughter while in Richmond, and all hope of seeing her now had fled. If she was carried back to New Orleans, she could expect no mercy from her master.

At the dusk of the evening previous to the day when she was to be sent off, as the old prison was being closed for the night, she suddenly darted past her keeper, and ran for her life. It was not a great distance from the prison to the Long Bridge, which passes from the lower part of the city across the Potomac, to the extensive forests and woodlands of the celebrated Arlington Place, occupied by that distinguished relative and descendant of the immortal Washington, Mr. George W. Custis. Thither the poor fugitive directed her flight. So unexpected was her escape, that she had quite a number of rods the start before the keeper had secured the other prisoners, and rallied his assistants in pursuit. It was at an hour when, and in a part of the city where, horses could not be readily obtained for the chase; no bloodhounds were at hand to run down the flying woman; and for once it seemed as though there was to be a fair trial of speed and endurance between the slave and the slave-catchers. The keeper and his forces raised the hue and cry on her pathway close behind; but so rapid was the flight along the wide avenue, that the astonished citizens, as they poured forth from their dwellings to learn the cause of alarm, were only able to comprehend the nature of the case in time to fall in with the motley mass in pursuit, (as many a one did that night,) to raise an anxious prayer to heaven, as they refused to join in the pursuit, that the panting fugitive might escape, and the merciless soul dealer for once be disappointed of his prey. And now with the speed of an arrow—having passed the avenue—with the distance between her and her pursuers constantly increasing, this poor hunted female gained the *"Long Bridge,"* as it is called, where interruption seemed improbable, and already did her heart begin to beat high with the hope of success. She had only to pass three-fourths of a mile across the bridge, and she could bury herself in a vast forest, just at the time when the curtain of night would close around her, and protect her from the pursuit of her enemies.

But God by his Providence had otherwise determined. He had determined that an appalling tragedy should be enacted that night, within plain sight of the President's house and the capitol of the Union, which should be an evidence wherever it should be known, of the unconquerable love of liberty the heart may inherit; as well as a fresh admonition to the slave dealer, of the cruelty and enormity of his crimes. Just as the pursuers crossed the high draw for the passage of sloops, soon after entering upon the bridge, they beheld three men slowly approaching from the Virginia side. They immediately called to them to arrest the fugitive, whom they proclaimed a runaway slave. True to their Virginian instincts as she came near, they formed in line across the narrow bridge, and prepared to seize her. Seeing escape impossible in that quarter, she stopped suddenly, and turned upon her pursuers. On came the profane and ribald crew, faster then ever, already exulting in her capture, and threatening punishment for her flight. For a moment she looked wildly and anxiously around to see if there was no hope of escape. On either hand, far down below, rolled the deep foamy waters of the Potomac, and before and behind the rapidly approaching step and noisy voices of pursuers, showing how vain would be any further effort for freedom. Her resolution was taken. She clasped her *hands* convulsively, and raised *them*, as she at the same time raised her *eyes* towards heaven, and begged for that mercy and compassion *there*, which had been denied her on earth; and then, with a single bound, she vaulted over the railings of the bridge, and sunk for ever beneath the waves of the river!

Thus died Clotel, the daughter of Thomas Jefferson, a president of the United States; a man distinguished as the author of the Declaration of American Independence, and one of the first statesmen of that country.

Had Clotel escaped from oppression in any other land, in

the disguise in which she fled from the Mississippi to Richmond, and reached the United States, no honour within the gift of the American people would have been too good to have been heaped upon the heroic woman. But she was a slave, and therefore out of the pale of their sympathy. They have tears to shed over Greece and Poland; they have an abundance of sympathy for "poor Ireland"; they can furnish a ship of war to convey the Hungarian refugees from a Turkish prison to the "land of the free and home of the brave." They boast that America is the "cradle of liberty"; if it is, I fear they have rocked the child to death. The body of Clotel was picked up from the bank of the river, where it had been washed by the strong current, a hole dug in the sand, and there deposited, without either inquest being held over it, or religious service being performed. Such was the life and such the death of a woman whose virtues and goodness of heart would have done honour to one in a higher station of life, and who, if she had been born in any other land but that of slavery, would have been honoured and loved. A few days after the death of Clotel, the following poem appeared in one of the newspapers:

"Now, rest for the wretched! the long day is past,
And night on yon prison descendeth at last.
Now lock up and bolt! Ha, jailor, look there!
Who flies like a wild bird escaped from the snare?
    A woman, a slave—up, out in pursuit,
        While linger some gleams of day!
    Let thy call ring out!—now a rabble rout
        Is at thy heels—speed away!

"A bold race for freedom!—On, fugitive, on!
Heaven help but the right, and thy freedom is won.
How eager she drinks the free air of the plains;
Every limb, every nerve, every fibre she strains;
    From Columbia's glorious capitol,
        Columbia's daughter flees

To the sanctuary God has given—
  The sheltering forest trees.

"Now she treads the Long Bridge—joy lighteth her eye—
Beyond her the dense wood and darkening sky—
Wild hopes thrill her heart as she neareth the shore:
O, despair! there are *men* fast advancing before!
  Shame, shame on their manhood! they hear, they heed
    The cry, her flight to stay,
  And like demon forms with their outstretched arms,
    They wait to seize their prey!

"She pauses, she turns! Ah, will she flee back?
Like wolves, her pursuers howl loud on their track;
She lifteth to Heaven one look of despair—
Her anguish breaks forth in one hurried prayer—
  Hark! her jailor's yell! like a bloodhound's bay
    On the low night wind it sweeps!
  Now, death or the chain! to the stream she turns,
    And she leaps! O God, she leaps!

"The dark and the cold, yet merciful wave,
Receives to its bosom the form of the slave:
She rises—earth's scenes on her dim vision gleam,
Yet she struggleth not with the strong rushing stream:
  And low are the death-cries her woman's heart gives,
    As she floats adown the river,
  Faint and more faint grows the drowning voice,
    And her cries have ceased for ever!

"Now back, jailor, back to thy dungeons, again,
To swing the red lash and rivet the chain!
The form thou would'st fetter—returned to its God;
  The universe holdeth no realm of night
    More drear than her slavery—
  More merciless fiends than here stayed her flight—
    Joy! the hunted slave is free!

"That bond-woman's corse—let Potomac's proud wave
Go bear it along *by our Washington's grave*,

CLOTEL; OR, THE PRESIDENT'S DAUGHTER

And heave it high up on that hallowed strand,
To tell of the freedom he won for our land.
  A weak woman's corse, by freemen chased down;
    Hurrah for our country! hurrah!
  To freedom she leaped, through drowning and death—
    Hurrah for our country! hurrah!"

CHAPTER XXVI

The Escape

"No refuge is found on our unhallowed ground,
    For the wretched in Slavery's manacles bound;
    While our star-spangled banner in vain boasts to wave
    O'er the land of the free and the home of the brave!

We left Mary, the daughter of Clotel, in the capacity of a servant in her own father's house, where she had been taken by her mistress for the ostensible purpose of plunging her husband into the depths of humiliation. At first the young girl was treated with great severity; but after finding that Horatio Green had lost all feeling for his child, Mrs. Green's own heart became touched for the offspring of her husband, and she became its friend. Mary had grown still more beautiful, and, like most of her sex in that country, was fast coming to maturity.

The arrest of Clotel, while trying to rescue her daughter, did not reach the ears of the latter till her mother had been removed from Richmond to Washington. The mother had passed from time to eternity before the daughter knew that she had been in the neighbourhood. Horatio Green was not in Richmond at the time of Clotel's arrest; had he been there, it is not probable but he would have made an effort to save her. She was not his slave, and therefore was beyond his power, even had he been there and inclined to aid her. The revolt amongst the slaves had been brought to an end, and most of the insurgents either put to death or sent out of the state. One, however, remained in prison. He was the slave of Horatio Green, and had been a servant in his master's dwelling. He, too, could boast that his father was an American statesman. His name was George. His mother had been employed as a servant in one of the principal hotels in Washington, where members of Congress usually put up. After George's birth his mother was sold to a slave trader, and he to an agent of Mr. Green, the father of Horatio. George was as white as most white persons. No one would suppose that any African blood coursed through his veins. His hair was straight, soft, fine, and light; his eyes blue, nose prominent, lips thin, his head well formed, forehead high and prominent; and he was often taken for a free white person by those who did know him. This made his condition still more intolerable; for one so white seldom ever receives fair treatment at the hands of his fellow slaves; and the whites usually regard such slaves as persons who, if not often flogged, and otherwise ill treated, to remind them of their condition, would soon "forget" that they were slaves, and "think themselves as good as white folks." George's opportunities were far greater than most slaves. Being in his master's house, and waiting on educated white people, he had become very familiar with the English language. He had heard his master and visitors speak of the down-trodden and oppressed Poles; he heard them talk of going to Greece to fight for Grecian liberty, and against the oppressors of that ill-fated people. George, fired with the love of freedom, and zeal for the cause of his enslaved countrymen, joined the insurgents, and with them had been defeated and captured. He was the only one remaining of these unfortunate people, and he would have been put to death with them but for a circumstance that occurred some weeks before the outbreak. The court house had, by accident, taken fire, and was fast consuming. The engines could not be made to work, and all hope of saving the building seemed at an end. In one of the upper chambers there was a small box containing some valuable deeds belonging to the city; a ladder was placed against the house, leading from the street to the window of the room in which the box stood. The wind blew strong, and swept the flames in that direction. Broad sheets of fire were blown again and again over that part of the building, and then the wind would lift the pall of smoke, which showed that the work of destruction was not yet accomplished. While the doomed building was thus exposed, and before the destroying element had made its final visit, as it did soon after, George was standing by, and hearing that much depended on the contents of the box, and seeing no one disposed to venture through the fiery element to save the treasure, mounted the ladder and made his way to the window, entered the room, and was soon seen descending with the much valued box. Three cheers rent the air as the young slave fell from the ladder when near the ground; the white men took him up in their arms, to see if he had sustained any injury. His hair was burnt, eyebrows closely singed, and his clothes smelt strongly of smoke; but the heroic young slave was unhurt. The city authorities, at their next meeting, passed a vote of thanks to George's master for the lasting benefit that the slave had rendered the public, and commended the poor boy to the special favour of his owner. When George was on trial for participating in the revolt, this "meritorious act," as they were pleased to term it, was brought up in his favour. His trial was put off from session to session, till he had been in prison more than a year. At last, however, he was convicted of high treason, and sentenced to be hanged within ten days of that time. The judge asked the slave if he had anything to say why sentence of death should not be passed on him. George stood for a moment in silence, and then said, "As I cannot speak as I should wish, I will say nothing."

"You may say what you please," said the judge. "You had a good master," continued he, "and still you were dissatisfied; you left your master and joined the Negroes who were burning our houses and killing our wives."

"As you have given me permission to speak," remarked George, "I will tell you why I joined the revolted Negroes. I have heard my master read in the Declaration of Independence 'that all men are created free and equal,' and this caused me to inquire of myself why I was a slave. I also heard him talking with some of his visitors about the war with England, and he said, all wars and fightings for freedom were just and right. If so, in what am I wrong? The grievances of which your fathers complained, and which caused the Revolutionary War, were trifling in comparison with the wrongs and sufferings of those who were engaged in the late revolt. Your fathers were never slaves, ours are; your fathers were never bought and sold like cattle, never shut out from the light of knowledge and religion, never subjected to the lash of brutal task-masters. For the crime of having a dark skin, my people suffer the pangs of hunger, the infliction of stripes, and the ignominy of brutal servitude. We are kept in heathenish darkness by laws expressly enacted to make our instruction a criminal offence. What right has one man to the bones, sinews, blood, and nerves of another? Did not one God make us all? You say your fathers fought for freedom— so did we. You tell me that I am to be put to death for violating the laws of the land. Did not the American revolutionists violate the laws when they struck for liberty? They were revolters, but their success made them patriots—we were revolters, and our failure makes us rebels. Had we succeeded, we would have been patriots too. Success makes all the difference. You make merry on the 4th of July; the thunder of cannon and ringing of bells announce it as the birthday of American independence. Yet while these cannons are roaring and bells ringing, one-sixth of the people of this land are in chains and slavery. You boast that this is the 'Land of the Free'; but a traditionary freedom will not save you. It will not do to praise your fathers and build their sepulchres. Worse for you that you have such an inheritance, if you spend it foolishly and are unable to appreciate its worth. Sad if the genius of a true humanity, beholding you with tearful eyes from the mount of vision, shall fold his wings in sorrowing pity, and repeat the strain, 'O land of Washington, how often would I have gathered thy children together, as a hen doth gather her brood under her wings, and ye would not;

behold your house is left unto you desolate.' This is all I have to say; I have done."

Nearly every one present was melted to tears; even the judge seemed taken by surprise at the intelligence of the young slave. But George was a slave, and an example must be made of him, and therefore he was sentenced. Being employed in the same house with Mary, the daughter of Clotel, George had become attached to her, and the young lovers fondly looked forward to the time when they should be husband and wife.

After George had been sentenced to death, Mary was still more attentive to him, and begged and obtained leave of her mistress to visit him in his cell. The poor girl paid a daily visit to him to whom she had pledged her heart and hand. At one of these meetings, and only four days from the time fixed for the execution, while Mary was seated in George's cell, it occurred to her that she might yet save him from a felon's doom. She revealed to him the secret that was then occupying her thoughts, viz. that George should exchange clothes with her, and thus attempt his escape in disguise. But he would not for a single moment listen to the proposition. Not that he feared detection; but he would not consent to place an innocent and affectionate girl in a position where she might have to suffer for him. Mary pleaded, but in vain—George was inflexible. The poor girl left her lover with a heavy heart, regretting that her scheme had proved unsuccessful.

Towards the close of the next day, Mary again appeared at the prison door for admission, and was soon by the side of him whom she so ardently loved. While there the clouds which had overhung the city for some hours broke, and the rain fell in torrents amid the most terrific thunder and lightning. In the most persuasive manner possible, Mary again importuned George to avail himself of her assistance to escape from an ignominious death. After assuring him that she, not being the person condemned, would not receive any injury, he at last consented, and they began to exchange apparel. As George was of small stature, and both were white, there was no difficulty in his passing out without detection; and as she usually left the cell weeping, with handkerchief in hand, and sometimes at her face, he had only to adopt this mode and his escape was safe. They had kissed each other, and Mary had told George where he would find a small parcel of provisions which she had placed in a secluded spot, when the prison-keeper opened the door and said, "Come, girl, it is time for you to go." George again embraced Mary, and passed out of the jail. It was already dark, and the street lamps were lighted, so that our hero in his new dress had no dread of detection. The provisions were sought out and found, and poor George was soon on the road towards Canada. But neither of them had once thought of a change of dress for George when he should have escaped, and he had walked but a short distance before he felt that a change of his apparel would facilitate his progress. But he dared not go amongst even his coloured associates for fear of being betrayed. However, he made the best of his way on towards Canada, hiding in the woods during the day, and travelling by the guidance of the North Star at night.

With the poet he could truly say,

"Star of the North! while blazing day
Pours round me its full tide of light,
And hides thy pale but faithful ray,
I, too, lie hid, and long for night."

One morning, George arrived on the banks of the Ohio river, and found his journey had terminated, unless he could get some one to take him across the river in a secret manner, for he would not be permitted to cross in any of the ferry boats, it being a penalty for crossing a slave, besides the value of the slave. He concealed himself in the tall grass and weeds near the river, to see if he could embrace an opportunity to cross. He had been in his hiding place but a short time, when he observed a man in a small boat, floating near the shore, evidently fishing. His first impulse was to call out to the man and ask him to take him over to the Ohio side, but the fear that the man was a slaveholder, or one who might possibly arrest him, deterred him from it. The man after rowing and floating about for some time fastened the boat to the root of a tree, and started to a neighbouring farmhouse.

This was George's moment, and he seized it. Running down the bank, he unfastened the boat, jumped in, and with all the expertness of one accustomed to a boat, rowed across the river and landed on the Ohio side.

Being now in a Free State, he thought he might with perfect safety travel on towards Canada. He had, however, gone but a very few miles when he discovered two men on horseback coming behind him. He felt sure that they could not be in pursuit of him, yet he did not wish to be seen by them, so he turned into another road leading to a house near by. The men followed, and were but a short distance from George, when he ran up to a farmhouse, before which was standing a farmer-looking man, in a broad-brimmed hat and straight-collared coat, whom he implored to save him from the "slave-catchers." The farmer told him to go into the barn near by; he entered by the front door, the farmer following, and closing the door behind George, but remaining outside, and gave directions to his hired man as to what should be done with George. The slaveholders by this time had dismounted, and were in front of the barn demanding admittance, and charging the farmer with secreting their slave woman, for George was still in the dress of a woman. The Friend, for the farmer proved to be a member of the Society of Friends, told the slave-owners that if they wished to search his barn, they must first get an officer and a search warrant. While the parties were disputing, the farmer began nailing up the front door, and the hired man served the back door in the same way. The slaveholders, finding that they could not prevail on the Friend to allow them to get the slave, determined to go in search of an officer. One was left to see that the slave did not escape from the barn, while the other went off at full speed to Mount Pleasant, the nearest town. George was not the slave of either of these men, nor were they in pursuit of him, but they had lost a woman who had been seen in that vicinity, and when they saw poor George in the disguise of a female, and attempting to elude pursuit, they felt sure they were close upon their victim. However, if they had caught him, although he was not their slave, they would have taken him back and placed him in jail, and there he would have remained until his owner arrived.

After an absence of nearly two hours, the slave-owner returned with an officer and found the Friend still driving large nails into the door. In a triumphant tone and with a corresponding gesture, he handed the search-warrant to the Friend, and said, "There, sir, now I will see if I can't get my nigger."

"Well," said the Friend, "thou hast gone to work according to law, and thou canst now go into my barn."

"Lend me your hammer that I may get the door open," said the slaveholder.

"Let me see the warrant again." And after reading it over once more, he said, "I see nothing in this paper which says I must supply thee with tools to open my door; if thou wishest to go in, thou must get a hammer elsewhere."

The sheriff said, "I will go to a neighbouring farm and borrow something which will introduce us to Miss Dinah;" and he immediately went in search of tools. In a short time the officer returned, and they commenced an assault and battery upon the barn door, which soon yielded; and in went the slaveholder and officer, and began turning up the hay and using all other means to find the lost property; but, to their astonishment, the slave was not there. After all hope of getting Dinah was gone, the slave-owner in a rage said to the Friend, "My nigger is not here."

"I did not tell thee there was any one here."

"Yes, but I saw her go in, and you shut the door behind her, and if she was not in the barn, what did you nail the door for?"

"Can't I do what I please with my own barn door? Now I will tell thee; thou need trouble thyself no more, for the person thou art after entered the front door and went out at the back door, and is a long way from here by this time. Thou and thy friend must be somewhat fatigued by this time; wont thou go in and take a little dinner with me?"

We need not say that this cool invitation of the good Quaker was not accepted by the slaveholders. George in the meantime had been taken to a Friend's dwelling some miles away, where, after laying aside his female attire, and being snugly dressed up in a straight-collared coat, and pantaloons to match, was again put on the right road towards Canada.

The fugitive now travelled by day, and laid by during night. After a fatiguing and dreary journey of two weeks, the fugitive arrived in Canada, and took up his abode in the little town of St. Catherine's, and obtained work on the farm of Colonel Street. Here he attended a night-school, and laboured for his employer during the day. The climate was cold, and wages small, yet he was in a land where he was free, and this the young slave prized more than all the gold that could be given to him. Besides doing his best to obtain education for himself, he imparted what he could to those of his fellow-fugitives about him, of whom there were many.

CHAPTER XXVII

The Mystery

George, however, did not forget his promise to use all the means in his power to get Mary out of slavery. He, therefore, laboured with all his might to obtain money with which to employ some one to go back to Virginia for Mary. After nearly six months' labour at St. Catherine's, he employed an English missionary to go and see if the girl could be purchased, and at what price. The missionary went accordingly, but returned with the sad intelligence that, on account of Mary's aiding George to escape, the court had compelled Mr. Green to sell her out of the state, and she had been sold to a Negro trader, and taken to the New Orleans market. As all hope of getting the girl was now gone, George resolved to quit the American continent for ever. He immediately took passage in a vessel laden with timber, bound for Liverpool, and in five weeks from that time he was standing on the quay of the great English seaport. With little or no education, he found many difficulties in the way of getting a respectable living. However he obtained a situation as porter in a large house in Manchester, where he worked during the day, and took private lessons at night. In this way he laboured for three years, and was then raised to the situation of clerk. George was so white as easily to pass for a white man, and being somewhat ashamed of his African descent, he never once mentioned the fact of his having been a slave. He soon became a partner in the firm that employed him, and was now on the road to wealth.

In the year 1842, just ten years after George Green (for he adopted his master's name) arrived in England, he visited France, and spent some days at Dunkirk. It was towards sunset, on a warm day in the month of October, that Mr. Green, after strolling some distance from the Hotel de Leon, entered a burial ground, and wandered long alone among the silent dead, gazing upon the many green graves and marble tombstones of those who once moved on the theatre of busy life, and whose sounds of gaiety once fell upon the ear of man. All nature around was hushed in silence, and seemed to partake of the general melancholy which hung over the quiet resting-place of departed mortals. After tracing the varied inscriptions which told the characters or conditions of the departed, and viewing the mounds beneath which the dust of mortality slumbered, he had now reached a secluded spot, near to where an aged weeping willow bowed its thick foliage to the ground, as though anxious to hide from the scrutinising gaze of curiosity the grave beneath it. Mr. Green seated himself upon a marble tomb, and began to read Roscoe's *Leo X.,* a copy of which he had under his arm. It was then about twilight, and he had scarcely gone through half a page, when he observed a lady in black, leading a boy, some five years old, up one of the paths; and as the lady's black veil was over her face, he felt somewhat at liberty to eye her more closely. While looking at her, the lady gave a scream, and appeared to be in a fainting position, when Mr. Green sprang from his seat in time to save her from falling to the ground. At this moment, an elderly gentleman was seen approaching with a rapid step, who, from his appearance, was evidently the lady's father, or one intimately connected with her. He came up, and, in a confused manner, asked what was the matter. Mr. Green explained as well as he could. After taking up the smelling bottle which had fallen from her hand, and holding it a short time to her face, she soon began to revive. During all this time the lady's veil had so covered her face, that Mr. Green had not seen it. When she had so far recovered as to be able to raise her head, she again screamed, and fell back into the arms of the old man. It now appeared quite certain, that either the countenance of George Green, or some other object, was the cause of these fits of fainting; and the old gentleman, thinking it was the former, in rather a petulant tone said, "I will thank you, sir, if you will leave us alone." The child whom the lady was leading, had now set up a squall; and amid the death-like appearance of the lady, the harsh look of the old man, and the cries of the boy, Mr. Green left the grounds, and returned to his hotel.

Whilst seated by the window, and looking out upon the crowded street, with every now and then the strange scene in the grave-yard vividly before him, Mr. Green thought of the book he had been reading, and, remembering that he had left it on the tomb, where he had suddenly dropped it when called to the assistance of the lady, he immediately determined to return in search of it. After a walk of some twenty minutes, he was again over the spot where he had been an hour before, and from which he had been so unceremoniously expelled by the old man. He looked in vain for the book; it was nowhere to be found: nothing save the bouquet which the lady had dropped, and which lay half-buried in the grass from having been trodden upon, indicated that any one had been there that evening. Mr. Green took up the bunch of flowers, and again returned to the hotel.

After passing a sleepless night, and hearing the clock strike six, he dropped into a sweet sleep, from which he did not awaken until roused by the rap of a servant, who, entering his room, handed him a note which ran as follows:— "Sir,—I owe you an apology for the inconvenience to which you were subjected last evening, and if you will honour us with your presence to dinner to-day at four o'clock, I shall be most happy to give you due satisfaction. My servant will be in waiting for you at half-past three. I am, sir, your obedient servant, J. Devenant. October 23. To George Green, Esq."

The servant who handed this note to Mr. Green, informed him that the bearer was waiting for a reply. He immediately resolved to accept the invitation, and replied accordingly. Who this person was, and how his name and the hotel where he was stopping had been found out, was indeed a mystery. However, he waited impatiently for the hour when he was to see this new acquaintance, and get the mysterious meeting in the grave-yard solved.

CHAPTER XXVIII

The Happy Meeting

Man's love is of man's life, a thing apart;
'Tis woman's whole existence."

BYRON

The clock on a neighbouring church had scarcely ceased striking three, when the servant announced that a carriage had called for Mr. Green. In less than half an hour he was seated in a most sumptuous barouche, drawn by two beautiful iron greys, and rolling along over a splendid gravel road completely shaded by large trees, which appeared to have been the accumulating growth of many centuries. The carriage soon stopped in front of a low villa, and this too was embedded in magnificent trees covered with moss. Mr. Green alighted and was shown into a superb drawing room, the walls of which were hung with fine specimens from the hands of the great Italian painters, and one by a German artist representing a beautiful monkish legend connected with "The Holy Catherine," an illustrious lady of Alexandria. The furniture had an antique and dignified appearance. High backed chairs stood around the room; a venerable mirror stood on the mantel shelf; rich curtains of crimson damask hung in folds at either side of the large windows; and a rich Turkey carpet covered the floor. In the centre stood a table covered with books, in the midst of which was an old-fashioned vase filled with fresh flowers, whose fragrance was exceedingly pleasant. A faint light, together with the quietness of the hour, gave beauty beyond description to the whole scene.

Mr. Green had scarcely seated himself upon the sofa, when the elderly gentleman whom he had met the previous evening made his appearance, followed by the little boy, and introduced himself as Mr. Devenant. A moment more, and a lady—a beautiful brunette—dressed in black, with long curls of a chestnut colour hanging down her cheeks, entered the room. Her eyes were of a dark hazel, and her whole appearance indicated that she was a native of a southern clime. The door at which she entered was opposite to where the two gentlemen were seated. They immediately rose; and Mr. Devenant was in the act of introducing her to Mr. Green, when he observed that the latter had sunk back upon the sofa, and the last word that he remembered to have heard was, "It is her." After this, all was dark and dreamy: how long he remained in this condition it was for another to tell. When he awoke, he found himself stretched upon the sofa, with his boots off, his neckerchief removed, shirt collar unbuttoned, and his head resting upon a pillow. By his side sat the old man, with the smelling bottle in the one hand, and a glass of water in the other, and the little boy standing at the foot of the sofa. As soon as Mr. Green had so far recovered as to be able to speak, he said, "Where am I, and what does this mean?"

"Wait a while," replied the old man, "and I will tell you all."

After a lapse of some ten minutes he rose from the sofa, adjusted his apparel, and said, "I am now ready to hear anything you have to say."

"You were born in America?" said the old man.

"Yes," he replied.

"And you were acquainted with a girl named Mary?" continued the old man.

"Yes, and I loved her as I can love none other."

"The lady whom you met so mysteriously last evening is Mary," replied Mr. Devenant.

George Green was silent, but the fountains of mingled

grief and joy stole out from beneath his eyelashes, and glistened like pearls upon his pale and marble-like cheeks. At this juncture the lady again entered the room. Mr. Green sprang from the sofa, and they fell into each other's arms, to the surprise of the old man and little George, and to the amusement of the servants who had crept up one by one, and were hid behind the doors, or loitering in the hall. When they had given vent to their feelings, they resumed their seats, and each in turn related the adventures through which they had passed.

"How did you find out my name and address?" asked Mr. Green.

"After you had left us in the grave-yard, our little George said, 'O, mamma, if there aint a book!' and picked it up and brought it to us. Papa opened it, and said, 'The gentleman's name is written in it, and here is a card of the Hotel de Leon, where I suppose he is stopping.' Papa wished to leave the book, and said it was all a fancy of mine that I had ever seen you before, but I was perfectly convinced that you were my own George Green. Are you married?"

"No, I am not."

"Then, thank God!" exclaimed Mrs. Devenant.

"And are you single now?" inquired Mr. Green.

"Yes," she replied.

"This is indeed the Lord's doings," said Mr. Green, at the same time bursting into a flood of tears. Mr. Devenant was past the age when men should think upon matrimonial subjects, yet the scene brought vividly before his eyes the days when he was a young man, and had a wife living. After a short interview, the old man called their attention to the dinner, which was then waiting. We need scarcely add, that Mr. Green and Mrs. Devenant did very little towards diminishing the dinner that day.

After dinner the lovers (for such we have to call them) gave their experience from the time that George left the jail dressed in Mary's clothes. Up to that time Mr. Green's was substantially as we have related it. Mrs. Devenant's was as follows:—"The night after you left the prison," said she, "I did not shut my eyes in sleep. The next morning, about eight o'clock, Peter the gardener came to the jail to see if I had been there the night before, and was informed that I had, and that I had left a little after dark. About an hour after, Mr. Green came himself, and I need not say that he was much surprised on finding me there, dressed in your clothes. This was the first tidings they had of your escape."

"What did Mr. Green say when he found that I had fled?"

"Oh!" continued Mrs. Devenant, "he said to me when no one was near, I hope George will get off, but I fear you will have to suffer in his stead. I told him that if it must be so I was willing to die if you could live." At this moment George Green burst into tears, and threw his arms around her neck, and exclaimed, "I am glad I have waited so long, with the hope of meeting you again."

Mrs. Devenant again resumed her story:—"I was kept in jail three days, during which time I was visited by the magistrates, and two of the judges. On the third day I was taken out, and master told me that I was liberated, upon condition that I should be immediately sent out of the state. There happened to be just at the time in the neighbourhood a Negro-trader, and he purchased me, and I was taken to New Orleans. On the steamboat we were kept in a close room, where slaves are usually confined, so that I saw nothing of the passengers on board, or the towns we passed. We arrived at New Orleans, and were all put into the slave-market for sale. I was examined by many persons, but none seemed willing to purchase me, as all thought me too white, and said I would run away and pass as a free white woman. On the second day, while in the slave-market, and while planters and others were examining slaves and making their purchases, I observed a tall young man, with long black hair, eyeing me very closely, and then talking to the trader. I felt sure that my time had now come, but the day closed without my being sold. I did not regret this, for I had heard that foreigners made the worst of masters, and I felt confident that the man who eyed me so closely was not an American.

"The next day was the Sabbath. The bells called the people to the different places of worship. Methodists sang, and Baptists immersed, and Presbyterians sprinkled, and Episcopalians read their prayers, while the ministers of the various sects preached that Christ died for all; yet there were some twenty-five or thirty of us poor creatures confined in the 'Negro Pen,' awaiting the close of the holy Sabbath, and the dawn of another day, to be again taken into the market, there to be examined like so many beasts of burden. I need not tell you with what anxiety we waited for the advent of another day. On Monday we were again brought out and placed in rows to be inspected; and, fortunately for me, I was sold before we had been on the stand an hour. I was purchased by a gentleman residing in the city, for a waiting-maid for his wife, who was just on the eve of starting for Mobile, to pay a visit to a near relation. I was then dressed to suit the situation of a maid-servant; and upon the whole, I thought that, in my new dress, I looked as much the lady as my mistress.

"On the passage to Mobile, who should I see among the passengers but the tall, long-haired man that had eyed me so closely in the slave-market a few days before. His eyes were again on me, and he appeared anxious to speak to me, and I as reluctant to be spoken to. The first evening after leaving New Orleans, soon after twilight had let her curtain down, and pinned it with a star, and while I was seated on the deck of the boat near the ladies' cabin, looking upon the rippled waves, and the reflection of the moon upon the sea, all at once I saw the tall young man standing by my side. I immediately rose from my seat, and was in the act of returning to the cabin, when he in a broken accent said, 'Stop a moment; I wish to have a word with you. I am your friend.'

I stopped and looked him full in the face, and he said, 'I saw you some days since in the slave-market, and I intended to have purchased you to save you from the condition of a slave. I called on Monday, but you had been sold and had left the market. I inquired and learned who the purchaser was, and that you had to go to Mobile, so I resolved to follow you. If you are willing I will try and buy you from your present owner, and you shall be free.' Although this was said in an honest and off-hand manner, I could not believe the man to be sincere in what he said. 'Why should you wish to set *me* free?' I asked. 'I had an only sister,' he replied, 'who died three years ago in France, and you are so much like her that had I not known of her death, I would most certainly have taken you for her.' 'However much I may resemble your sister, you are aware that I am not her, and why take so much interest in one whom you never saw before?' 'The love,' said he, 'which I had for my sister is transferred to you.' I had all along suspected that the man was a knave, and this profession of love confirmed me in my former belief, and I turned away and left him.

"The next day, while standing in the cabin and looking through the window, the French gentleman (for such he was) came to the window while walking on the guards, and again commenced as on the previous evening. He took from his pocket a bit of paper and put it into my hand, at the same time saying, 'Take this, it may some day be of service to you; remember it is from a friend,' and left me instantly. I unfolded the paper, and found it to be a 100 dollars bank note, on the United States Branch Bank, at Philadelphia. My first impulse was to give it to my mistress, but, upon a second thought, I resolved to seek an opportunity, and to return the hundred dollars to the stranger.

"Therefore I looked for him, but in vain; and had almost given up the idea of seeing him again, when he passed me on the guards of the boat and walked towards the stem of the vessel. It being now dark, I approached him and offered the money to him. He declined, saying at the same time, 'I gave it to you—keep it.' 'I do not want it,' I said. 'Now,' said he, 'you had better give your consent for me to purchase you, and you shall go with me to France.' 'But you cannot buy me now,' I replied, 'for my master is in New Orleans, and he purchased me not to sell, but to retain in his own family.' 'Would you rather remain with your present mistress than be free?' 'No,' said I. 'Then fly with me tonight; we shall be in Mobile in two hours from this, and when the passengers are going on shore, you can take my arm, and you can escape unobserved. The trader who brought you to New Orleans exhibited to me a certificate of your good character, and one from the minister of the church to which you were attached in Virginia; and upon the faith of these assurances, and the love I bear you, I promise before high heaven that I will marry you as soon as it can be done.' This solemn promise, coupled with what had already transpired, gave me confidence in the man; and rash as the act may seem, I determined in an instant to go with him. My mistress had been put under the charge of the captain; and as it would be past ten o'clock when the steamer would land, she accepted an invitation of the captain to remain on board with several other ladies till morning. I dressed myself in my best clothes, and put a veil over my face, and was ready on the landing of the boat. Surrounded by a number of passengers, we descended the stage leading to the wharf, and were soon lost in the crowd that thronged the quay. As we went on shore we encountered several persons announcing the names of hotels, the starting of boats for the interior, and vessels bound for Europe. Among these was the ship Utica, Captain Pell, bound for Havre. 'Now,' said Mr. Devenant, 'this is our chance.' The ship was to sail at twelve o'clock that night, at high tide; and following the men who were seeking passengers, we went immediately on board. Devenant told the captain of the ship that I was his sister, and for such we passed during the voyage. At the hour of twelve the Utica set sail, and we were soon out at sea.

"The morning after we left Mobile, Devenant met me as I came from my state-room, and embraced me for the first time. I loved him, but it was only that affection which we have for one who has done us a lasting favour: it was the love of gratitude rather than that of the heart. We were five weeks on the sea, and yet the passage did not seem long, for Devenant was so kind. On our arrival at Havre we were married and came to Dunkirk, and I have resided here ever since."

At the close of this narrative, the clock struck ten, when the old man, who was accustomed to retire at an early hour, rose to take leave, saying at the same time, "I hope you will remain with us to-night." Mr. Green would fain have excused himself, on the ground that they would expect him and wait at the hotel, but a look from the lady told him to accept the invitation. The old man was the father of Mrs. Devenant's deceased husband, as you will no doubt long since have supposed. A fortnight from the day on which they met in the grave-yard, Mr. Green and Mrs. Devenant were joined in holy wedlock; so that George and Mary, who had loved each other so ardently in their younger days, were now husband and wife.

A celebrated writer has justly said of woman, "A woman's whole life is a history of the affections. The heart is her world; it is there her ambition strives for empire; it is there her avarice seeks for hidden treasures. She sends forth her sympathies on adventure; she embarks her whole soul in the traffic of affection; and, if shipwrecked, her case is hopeless, for it is a bankruptcy of the heart."

Mary had every reason to believe that she would never see George again; and although she confesses that the love she bore him was never transferred to her first husband, we can scarcely find fault with her for marrying Mr. Devenant. But the adherence of George Green to the resolution never to marry, unless to his Mary, is, indeed, a rare instance of the fidelity of man in the matter of love. We can but blush for our country's shame when we recall to mind the fact, that while George and Mary Green, and numbers of other fugitives from American slavery, can receive protection from any of the governments of Europe, they cannot return to their native land without becoming slaves.

CHAPTER XXIX

Conclusion

My narrative has now come to a close. I may be asked, and no doubt shall, Are the various incidents and scenes related founded in truth? I answer, Yes. I have personally participated in many of those scenes. Some of the narratives I have derived from other sources; many from the lips of those who, like myself, have run away from the land of bondage. Having been for nearly nine years employed on Lake Erie, I had many opportunities for helping the escape of fugitives, who, in return for the assistance they received, made me the depositary of their sufferings and wrongs. Of their relations I have made free use. To Mrs. Child, of New York, I am indebted for part of a short story. American Abolitionist journals are another source from whence some of the characters appearing in my narrative are taken. All these combined have made up my story. Having thus acknowledged my resources, I invite the attention of my readers to the following statement, from which I leave them to draw their own conclusions:—"It is estimated that in the United States, members of the Methodist church own 219,363 slaves; members of the Baptist church own 226,000 slaves; members of the Episcopalian church own 88,000 slaves; members of the Presbyterian church own 77,000 slaves; members of all other churches own 50,000 slaves; in all, 660,563 slaves owned by members of the Christian church in this pious democratic republic!"

May these facts be pondered over by British Christians,

and at the next anniversaries of the various religious denominations in London may their influence be seen and felt! The religious bodies of American Christians will send their delegates to these meetings. Let British feeling be publicly manifested. Let British sympathy express itself in tender sorrow for the condition of my unhappy race. Let it be understood, unequivocally understood, that no fellowship can be held with slaveholders professing the same common Christianity as yourselves. And until this stain from America's otherwise fair escutcheon be wiped away, let no Christian association be maintained with those who traffic in the blood and bones of those whom God has made of one flesh as yourselves. Finally, let the voice of the whole British nation be heard across the Atlantic, and throughout the length and breadth of the land of the Pilgrim Fathers, beseeching their descendants, as they value *the* common salvation, which knows no distinction between the bond and the free, to proclaim the Year of Jubilee. Then shall the "earth indeed yield her increase, and God, even our own God, shall bless us; and all the ends of the earth shall fear Him."

Iola Leroy,

or

Shadows Uplifted

BY

FRANCES E. W. HARPER

see 1x intro

TO MY DAUGHTER

MARY E. HARPER,

THIS BOOK IS LOVINGLY DEDICATED

Bob (Robert) Johnson

Thomas Anderson (marster Anderson's Tom)

Introduction

I confess when I first learned that Mrs. Harper was about to write "a story" on some features of the Anglo-African race, growing out of what was once popularly known as the "peculiar institution," I had my doubts about the matter. Indeed it was far from being easy for me to think that she was as fortunate as she might have been in selecting a subject which would afford her the best opportunity for bringing out a work of merit and lasting worth to the race—such a work as some of her personal friends have long desired to see from her graphic pen. However, after hearing a good portion of the manuscript read, and a general statement with regard to the object in view, I admit frankly that my partial indifference was soon swept away; at least I was willing to wait for further developments.

Being very desirous that one of the race, so long distinguished in the cause of freedom for her intellectual worth as Mrs. Harper has had the honor of being, should not at this late date in life make a blunder which might detract from her own good name, I naturally proposed to await developments before deciding too quickly in favor of giving encouragement to her contemplated effort.

However, I was perfectly aware of the fact that she had much material in her possession for a most interesting book on the subject of the condition of the colored people in the South. I know of no other woman, white or colored, anywhere, who has come so intimately in contact with the colored people in the South as Mrs. Harper. Since emancipation she has labored in every Southern State in the Union, save two, Arkansas and Texas; in the colleges, schools, churches, and the cabins not excepted, she has found a vast field and open doors to teach and speak on the themes of education, temperance, and good home building, industry, morality, and the like, and never lacked for evidences of hearty appreciation and gratitude.

Everywhere help was needed, and her heart being deeply absorbed in the cause she willingly allowed her sympathies to impel her to perform most heroic services.

With her it was no uncommon occurrence, in visiting cities or towns, to speak at two, three, and four meetings a day; sometimes to promiscuous audiences composed of everybody who would care to come.

But the kind of meetings she took greatest interest in were meetings called exclusively for women. In this attitude she could pour out her sympathies to them as she could not do before a mixed audience; and indeed she felt their needs were far more pressing than any other class.

And now I am prepared to most fully indorse her story. I doubt whether she could, if she had tried ever so much, have hit upon a subject so well adapted to reach a large number of her friends and the public with both entertaining and instructive matter as successfully as she has done in this volume.

The grand and ennobling sentiments which have characterized all her utterances in laboring for the elevation of the oppressed will not be found missing in this book.

The previous books from her pen, which have been so very widely circulated and admired, North and South—"Forest Leaves," "Miscellaneous Poems," "Moses, a Story of the Nile," "Poems," and "Sketches of Southern Life" (five in number)—these, I predict, will be by far eclipsed by this last effort, which will, in all probability, be the crowning effort of her long and valuable services in the cause of humanity.

While, as indicated, Mrs. Harper has done a large amount

of work in the South, she has at the same time done much active service in the temperance cause in the North, as thousands of this class can testify.

Before the war she was engaged as a speaker by anti-slavery associations; since then, by appointment of the Women's Christian Temperance Union, she has held the office of "Superintendent of Colored Work" for years. She has also held the office of one of the Directors of the Women's Congress of the United States.

Under the auspices of these influential, earnest, and intelligent associations, she has been seen often on their platforms with the leading lady orators of the nation.

Hence, being widely known not only amongst her own race but likewise by the reformers, laboring for the salvation of the intemperate and others equally unfortunate, there is little room to doubt that the book will be in great demand and will meet with warm congratulations from a goodly number outside of the author's social connections.

Doubtless the thousands of colored Sunday-schools in the South, in casting about for an interesting, moral story-book, full of practical lessons, will not be content to be without "IOLA LEROY, OR SHADOWS UPLIFTED."

WILLIAM STILL.

CHAPTER I

Mystery of Market Speech and Prayer-Meeting

"Good mornin', Bob; how's butter dis mornin'?"

"Fresh; just as fresh, as fresh can be."

"Oh, glory!" said the questioner, whom we shall call Thomas Anderson, although he was known among his acquaintances as Marster Anderson's Tom.

His informant regarding the condition of the market was Robert Johnson, who had been separated from his mother in his childhood and reared by his mistress as a favorite slave. She had fondled him as a pet animal, and even taught him to read. Notwithstanding their relation as mistress and slave, they had strong personal likings for each other.

Tom Anderson was the servant of a wealthy planter, who lived in the city of C——, North Carolina. This planter was quite advanced in life, but in his earlier days he had spent much of his time in talking politics in his State and National capitals in winter, and in visiting pleasure resorts and watering places in summer. His plantations were left to the care of overseers who, in their turn, employed negro drivers to aid them in the work of cultivation and discipline. But as the infirmities of age were pressing upon him he had withdrawn from active life, and given the management of his affairs into the hands of his sons. As Robert Johnson and Thomas Anderson passed homeward from the market, having bought provisions for their respective homes, they seemed to be very light-hearted and careless, chatting and joking with each other; but every now and then, after looking furtively around, one would drop into the ears of the other some news of the battle then raging between the North and South which, like two great millstones, were grinding slavery to powder. As they passed along, they were met by another servant, who said in hurried tones, but with a glad accent in his voice:—

"Did you see de fish in de market dis mornin'? Oh, but dey war splendid, jis' as fresh, as fresh kin be."

"That's the ticket," said Robert, as a broad smile overspread his face. "I'll see you later."

"Good mornin', boys," said another servant on his way to market. "How's eggs dis mornin'?"

"Fust rate, fust rate," said Tom Anderson. "Bob's got it down fine."

"I thought so; mighty long faces at de pos'-office dis mornin'; but I'd better move 'long," and with a bright smile lighting up his face he passed on with a quickened tread.

There seemed to be an unusual interest manifested by these men in the state of the produce market, and a unanimous report of its good condition. Surely there was nothing in the primeness of the butter or the freshness of the eggs to change careless looking faces into such expressions of gratification, or to light dull eyes with such gladness. What did it mean?

During the dark days of the Rebellion, when the bondman was turning his eyes to the American flag, and learning to hail it as an ensign of deliverance, some of the shrewder slaves, coming in contact with their masters and overhearing their conversations, invented a phraseology to convey in the most unsuspected manner news to each other from the battle-field. Fragile women and helpless children were left on the plantations while their natural protectors were at the front, and yet these bondmen refrained from violence. Freedom was coming in the wake of the Union army, and while numbers deserted to join their forces, others remained at home, slept in their cabins by night and attended to their work by day;

but under this apparently careless exterior there was an undercurrent of thought which escaped the cognizance of their masters. In conveying tidings of the war, if they wished to announce a victory of the Union army, they said the butter was fresh, or that the fish and eggs were in good condition. If defeat befell them, then the butter and other produce were rancid or stale.

Entering his home, Robert set his basket down. In one arm he held a bundle of papers which he had obtained from the train to sell to the boarders, who were all anxious to hear from the seat of battle. He slipped one copy out and, looking cautiously around, said to Linda, the cook, in a low voice:—

"Splendid news in the papers. Secesh routed. Yankees whipped 'em out of their boots. Papers full of it. I tell you the eggs and the butter's mighty fresh this morning."

"Oh, sho, chile," said Linda, "I can't read de newspapers, but ole Missus' face is newspaper nuff for me. I looks at her ebery mornin' wen she comes inter dis kitchen. Ef her face is long an' she walks kine o' droopy den I thinks things is gwine wrong for dem. But ef she comes out yere looking mighty pleased, an' larffin all ober her face, an' steppin' so frisky, den I knows de Secesh is gittin' de bes' ob de Yankees. Robby, honey, does you really b'lieve for good and righty dat dem Yankees is got horns?"

"Of course not."

"Well, I yered so."

"Well, you heard a mighty big whopper."

"Anyhow, Bobby, things goes mighty contrary in dis house. Ole Miss is in de parlor prayin' for de Secesh to gain de day, and we's prayin' in de cabins and kitchens for de Yankees to get de bes' ob it. But wasn't Miss Nancy glad wen dem Yankees run'd away at Bull's Run. It was nuffin but Bull's Run an' run away Yankees. How she did larff and skip 'bout de house. An' den me thinks to myself you'd better not holler till you gits out ob de woods. I specs 'fore dem Yankees gits froo you'll be larffin tother side ob your mouf. While you was gone to market ole Miss com'd out yere, her face looking as long as my arm, tellin' us all 'bout de war and saying dem Yankees whipped our folks all to pieces. And she was 'fraid dey'd all be down yere soon. I thought they couldn't come too soon for we. But I didn't tell her so."

"No, I don't expect you did."

"No, I didn't; ef you buys me for a fool you loses your money shore. She said when dey com'd down yere she wanted all de men to hide, for dey'd kill all de men, but dey wouldn't tech de women."

"It's no such thing. She's put it all wrong. Why them Yankees are our best friends."

"Dat's jis' what I thinks. Ole Miss was jis' tryin to skeer a body. An' when she war done she jis' set down and sniffled an' cried, an' I war so glad I didn't know what to do. But I had to hole in. An' I made out I war orful sorry. An' Jinny said, 'O Miss Nancy, I hope dey won't come yere.' An' she said, 'I'se jis' 'fraid dey will come down yere and gobble up eberything dey can lay dere hands on.' An' she jis' looked as ef her heart war mos' broke, an' den she went inter de house. An' when she war gone, we jis' broke loose. Jake turned somersets, and said he warnt 'fraid ob dem Yankees; he know'd which side his brad was buttered on. Dat Jake is a cuter. When he goes down ter git de letters he cuts up all kines ob shines and capers. An' to look at him skylarking dere while de folks is waitin' for dere letters, an' talkin' 'bout de war, yer wouldn't think dat boy had a thimbleful of sense. But Jake's listenin' all de time wid his eyes and his mouf wide open, an' ketchin' eberything he kin, an' a heap ob news he gits dat way. As to Jinny, she jis' capered and danced all ober de flore. An' I jis' had to put my han' ober her mouf to keep ole Miss from yereing her. Oh, but we did hab a good time. Boy, yer oughter been yere."

"And, Aunt Linda, what did you do?"

"Oh, honey, I war jis' ready to crack my sides larffin, jis' to see what a long face Jinny puts on wen ole Miss is talkin', an' den to see dat face wen missus' back is turned, why it's good as a circus. It's nuff to make a horse larff."

"Why, Aunt Linda, you never saw a circus?"

"No, but I'se hearn tell ob dem, and I thinks dey mus' be mighty funny. An' I know it's orful funny to see how straight Jinny's face looks wen she's almos' ready to bust, while ole Miss is frettin' and fumin' 'bout dem Yankees an' de war. But, somehow, Robby, I ralely b'lieves dat we cullud folks is mixed up in dis fight. I seed it all in a vision. An' soon as dey fired on dat fort, Uncle Dan'el says to me: 'Linda, we's gwine to git our freedom.' An' I says: 'Wat makes you think so?' An' he says: 'Dey've fired on Fort Sumter, an' de Norf is boun' to whip.' "

"I hope so," said Robert. "I think that we have a heap of friends up there."

"Well, I'm jis' gwine to keep on prayin' an' b'lievin'. "

Just then the bell rang, and Robert, answering, found Mrs. Johnson suffering from a severe headache, which he thought was occasioned by her worrying over the late defeat of the Confederates. She sent him on an errand, which he executed with his usual dispatch, and returned to some work which he had to do in the kitchen. Robert was quite a favorite with Aunt Linda, and they often had confidential chats together.

"Bobby," she said, when he returned, "I thinks we ort ter hab a prayer-meetin' putty soon."

"I am in for that. Where will you have it?"

"Lem me see. Las' Sunday we had it in Gibson's woods; Sunday 'fore las', in de old cypress swamp; an' nex' Sunday we'el hab one in McCullough's woods. Las' Sunday we had a good time. I war jis' chock full an' runnin' ober. Aunt Milly's daughter's bin monin all summer, an' she's jis' come throo. We had a powerful time. Eberythin' on dat groun' was jis' alive. I tell yer, dere was a shout in de camp."

"Well, you had better look out, and not shout too much, and pray and sing too loud, because, 'fore you know, the patrollers will be on your track and break up your meetin' in a mighty big hurry, before you can say 'Jack Robinson.' "

"Oh, we looks out for dat. We's got a nice big pot, dat got cracked las' winter, but it will hole a lot o' water, an' we puts it whar we can tell it eberything. We has our own good times. An' I want you to come Sunday night an' tell all 'bout the good eggs, fish, and butter. Mark my words, Bobby, we's all gwine to git free. I seed it all in a vision, as plain as de nose on yer face."

"Well, I hope your vision will come out all right, and that the eggs will keep and the butter be fresh till we have our next meetin'."

"Now, Bob, you sen' word to Uncle Dan'el, Tom Anderson, an' de rest ob dem, to come to McCullough's woods nex' Sunday night. I want to hab a sin-killin' an' debil-dribin' time. But, boy, you'd better git out er yere. Ole Miss'll be down on yer like a scratch cat."

Although the slaves were denied unrestricted travel, and the holding of meetings without the surveillance of a white man, yet they contrived to meet by stealth and hold gatherings where they could mingle their prayers and tears, and lay plans for escaping to the Union army. Outwitting the vigilance of the patrollers and home guards, they established these meetings miles apart, extending into several States.

Sometimes their hope of deliverance was cruelly blighted by hearing of some adventurous soul who, having escaped to the Union army, had been pursued and returned again to bondage. Yet hope survived all these disasters which gathered around the fate of their unfortunate brethren, who were remanded to slavery through the undiscerning folly of those who were strengthening the hands which were dealing their deadliest blows at the heart of the Nation. But slavery had cast such a glamour over the Nation, and so warped the consciences of men, that they failed to read aright the legible transcript of Divine retribution which was written upon the shuddering earth, where the blood of God's poor children had been as water freely spilled.

CHAPTER II

Contraband of War

prayer ptg

A few evenings after this conversation between Robert and Linda, a prayer-meeting was held. Under the cover of night a few dusky figures met by stealth in McCullough's woods.

"Howdy," said Robert, approaching Uncle Daniel, the leader of the prayer-meeting, who had preceded him but a few minutes.

"Thanks and praise; I'se all right. How is you, chile?"

"Oh, I'm all right," said Robert, smiling, and grasping Uncle Daniel's hand.

"What's de news?" exclaimed several, as they turned their faces eagerly towards Robert.

"I hear," said Robert, "that they are done sending the runaways back to their masters."

"Is dat so?" said a half dozen earnest voices. "How did you yere it?"

"I read it in the papers. And Tom told me he heard them talking about it last night, at his house. How did you hear it, Tom? Come, tell us all about it."

Tom Anderson hesitated a moment, and then said:—

"Now, boys, I'll tell you all 'bout it. But you's got to be mighty mum 'bout it. It won't do to let de cat outer de bag."

"Dat's so! But tell us wat you yered. We ain't gwine to say nuffin to nobody."

"Well," said Tom, "las' night ole Marster had company. Two big ginerals, and dey was hoppin' mad. One ob dem looked like a turkey gobbler, his face war so red. An' he sed one ob dem Yankee ginerals, I thinks dey called him Beas' Butler, sed dat de slaves dat runned away war some big name—I don't know what he called it. But it meant dat all ob we who com'd to de Yankees should be free."

"Contraband of war," said Robert, who enjoyed the distinction of being a good reader, and was pretty well posted about the war. Mrs. Johnson had taught him to read on the same principle she would have taught a pet animal amusing tricks. She had never imagined the time would come when he would use the machinery she had put in his hands to help overthrow the institution to which she was so ardently attached.

"What does it mean? Is it somethin' good for us?"

"I think," said Robert, a little vain of his superior knowledge, "it is the best kind of good. It means if two armies are fighting and the horses of one run away, the other has a right to take them. And it is just the same if a slave runs away from the Secesh to the Union lines. He is called a contraband, just the same as if he were an ox or a horse. They wouldn't send the horses back, and they won't send us back."

"Is dat so?" said Uncle Daniel, a dear old father, with a look of saintly patience on his face. "Well, chillen, what do you mean to do?"

"Go, jis' as soon as we kin git to de army," said Tom Anderson.

"What else did the generals say? And how did you come to hear them, Tom?" asked Robert Johnson.

"Well, yer see, Marster's too ole and feeble to go to de war, but his heart's in it. An' it makes him feel good all ober when dem big ginerals comes an' tells him all 'bout it. Well, I war laying out on de porch fas' asleep an' snorin' drefful hard. Oh, I war so soun' asleep dat wen Marster wanted some ice-water he had to shake me drefful hard to wake me up. An' all de time I war wide 'wake as he war."

"What did they say?" asked Robert, who was always on the lookout for news from the battle-field.

"One ob dem said, dem Yankees war talkin' of puttin' guns in our han's and settin' us all free. An' de oder said, 'Oh, sho! ef dey puts guns in dere hands dey'll soon be in our'n; and ef dey sets em free dey wouldn't know how to take keer ob demselves.' "

"Only let 'em try it," chorused a half dozen voices, "an' dey'll soon see who'll git de bes' ob de guns; an' as to taking keer ob ourselves, I specs we kin take keer ob ourselves as well as take keer ob dem."

"Yes," said Tom, "who plants de cotton and raises all de crops?"

> " 'They eat the meat and give us the bones,
>   Eat the cherries and give us the stones,'

And I'm getting tired of the whole business," said Robert.

"But, Bob," said Uncle Daniel, "you've got a good owner. You don't hab to run away from bad times and wuss a comin'."

"It isn't so good, but it might be better. I ain't got nothing 'gainst my ole Miss, except she sold my mother from me. And a boy ain't nothin' without his mother. I forgive her, but I never forget her, and never expect to. But if she were the best woman on earth I would rather have my freedom than belong to her. Well, boys, here's a chance for us just as soon as the Union army gets in sight. What will you do?"

"I'se a goin," said Tom Anderson, "jis' as soon as dem Linkum soldiers gits in sight."

"An' I'se a gwine wid you, Tom," said another. "I specs my ole Marster'll feel right smart lonesome when I'se gone, but I don't keer 'bout stayin' for company's sake."

"My ole Marster's room's a heap better'n his company," said Tom Anderson, "an' I'se a goner too. Dis yer freedom's too good to be lef' behind, wen you's got a chance to git it. I won't stop to bid ole Marse good bye."

"What do you think," said Robert, turning to Uncle Daniel; "won't you go with us?"

"No, chillen, I don't blame you for gwine; but I'se gwine to stay. Slavery's done got all de marrow out ob dese poor ole bones. Ef freedom comes it won't do me much good; we ole one's will die out, but it will set you youngsters all up."

"But, Uncle Daniel, you're not too old to want your freedom?"

"I knows dat. I lubs de bery name of freedom. I'se been praying and hoping for it dese many years. An' ef I warn't boun', I would go wid you ter-morrer. I won't put a straw in your way. You boys go, and my prayers will go wid you. I can't go, it's no use. I'se gwine to stay on de ole place till Marse Robert comes back, or is brought back."

"But, Uncle Daniel," said Robert, "what's the use of praying for a thing if, when it comes, you won't take it? As much as you have been praying and talking about freedom, I thought that when the chance came you would have been one of the first to take it. Now, do tell us why you won't go with us. Ain't you willing?"

"Why, Robbie, my whole heart is wid you. But when Marse Robert went to de war, he called me into his room and said to me, 'Uncle Dan'el, I'se gwine to de war, an' I want you to look arter my wife an' chillen, an' see dat eberything goes right on de place. An' I promised him I'd do it, an' I mus' be as good as my word. 'Cept de overseer, dere isn't a white man on de plantation, an' I hear he has to report ter-morrer or be treated as a deserter. An' der's nobody here to look arter Miss Mary an' de chillen, but myself, an' to see dat eberything goes right. I promised Marse Robert I would do it, an' I mus' be as good as my word."

"Well, what should you keer?" said Tom Anderson. "Who

looked arter you when you war sole from your farder and mudder, an' neber seed dem any more, and wouldn't know dem to-day ef you met dem in your dish?"

"Well, dats neither yere nor dere. Marse Robert couldn't help what his father did. He war an orful mean man. But he's dead now, and gone to see 'bout it. But his wife war the nicest, sweetest lady dat eber I did see. She war no more like him dan chalk's like cheese. She used to visit de cabins, an' listen to de pore women when de overseer used to cruelize dem so bad, an' drive dem to work late and early. An' she used to sen' dem nice things when they war sick, and hab der cabins whitewashed an' lookin' like new pins, an' look arter dere chillen. Sometimes she'd try to git ole Marse to take dere part when de oberseer got too mean. But she might as well a sung hymns to a dead horse. All her putty talk war like porin water on a goose's back. He'd jis' bluff her off, an' tell her she didn't run dat plantation, and not for her to bring him any nigger news. I never thought ole Marster war good to her. I often ketched her crying, an' she'd say she had de headache, but I thought it war de heartache. 'Fore ole Marster died, she got so thin an' peaked I war 'fraid she war gwine to die; but she seed him out. He war killed by a tree fallin' on him, an' ef eber de debil got his own he got him. I seed him in a vision arter he war gone. He war hangin' up in a pit, sayin' 'Oh! oh!' wid no close on. He war allers blusterin', cussin', and swearin' at somebody. Marse Robert ain't a bit like him. He takes right arter his mother. Bad as ole Marster war, I think she jis' lob'd de groun' he walked on. Well, women's mighty curious kind of folks anyhow. I sometimes thinks de wuss you treats dem de better dey likes you."

"Well," said Tom, a little impatiently, "what's yer gwine to do? Is yer gwine wid us, ef yer gits a chance?"

"Now, jes' you hole on till I gits a chance to tell yer why I'se gwine to stay."

"Well, Uncle Daniel, let's hear it," said Robert.

"I was jes' gwine to tell yer when Tom put me out. Ole

Marster died when Marse Robert war two years ole, and his pore mother when he war four. When he died, Miss Anna used to keep me 'bout her jes' like I war her shadder. I used to nuss Marse Robert jes' de same as ef I were his own fadder. I used to fix his milk, rock him to sleep, ride him on my back, an' nothin' pleased him better'n fer Uncle Dan'el to ride him piggy-back."

"Well, Uncle Daniel," said Robert, "what has that got to do with your going with us and getting your freedom?"

"Now, jes' wait a bit, and don't frustrate my mine. I seed day arter day Miss Anna war gettin' weaker and thinner, an' she looked so sweet and talked so putty, I thinks to myself, 'you ain't long for dis worl'.' And she said to me one day, 'Uncle Dan'el, when I'se gone, I want you to be good to your Marster Robert.' An' she looked so pale and weak I war almost ready to cry. I couldn't help it. She hed allers bin mighty good to me. An' I beliebs in praisin' de bridge dat carries me ober. She said, 'Uncle Dan'el, I wish you war free. Ef I had my way you shouldn't serve any one when I'm gone; but Mr. Thurston had eberything in his power when he made his will. I war tied hand and foot, and I couldn't help it.' In a little while she war gone—jis' faded away like a flower. I belieb ef dere's a saint in glory, Miss Anna's dere."

"Oh, I don't take much stock in white folks' religion," said Robert, laughing carelessly.

"The way," said Tom Anderson, "dat some of dese folks cut their cards yere, I think dey'll be as sceece in hebben as hen's teeth. I think wen some of dem preachers brings de Bible 'round an' tells us 'bout mindin our marsters and not stealin' dere tings, dat dey preach to please de white folks, an' dey frows coleness ober de meetin'."

"An' I," said Aunt Linda, "neber did belieb in dem Bible preachers. I yered one ob dem sayin' wen he war dyin', it war all dark wid him. An' de way he treated his house-girl, pore thing, I don't wonder dat it war dark wid him."

"O, I guess," said Robert, "that the Bible is all right, but some of these church folks don't get the right hang of it."

241

"May be dat's so," said Aunt Linda. "But I allers wanted to learn how to read. I once had a book, and tried to make out what war in it, but ebery time my mistus caught me wid a book in my hand, she used to whip my fingers. An' I couldn't see ef it war good for white folks, why it warn't good for cullud folks."

"Well," said Tom Anderson, "I belieb in de good ole-time religion. But arter dese white folks is done fussin' and beatin' de cullud folks, I don't want 'em to come talking religion to me. We used to hab on our place a real Guinea man, an' once he made ole Marse mad, an' he had him whipped. Old Marse war trying to break him in, but dat fellow war spunk to de backbone, an' when he 'gin talkin' to him 'bout savin' his soul an' gittin' to hebbin, he tole him ef he went to hebbin an' foun' he war dare, he wouldn't go in. He wouldn't stay wid any such rascal as he war."

"What became of him?" asked Robert.

"Oh, he died. But he had some quare notions 'bout religion. He thought dat when he died he would go back to his ole country. He allers kep' his ole Guinea name."

"What was it?"

"Potobombra. Do you know what he wanted Marster to do 'fore he died?" continued Anderson.

"No."

"He wanted him to gib him his free papers."

"Did he do it?"

"Ob course he did. As de poor fellow war dying an' he couldn't sell him in de oder world, he jis' wrote him de papers to yumor him. He didn't want to go back to Africa a slave. He thought if he did, his people would look down on him, an' he wanted to go back a free man. He war orful weak when Marster brought him de free papers. He jis' ris up in de bed, clutched dem in his han's, smiled, an' gasped out, 'I'se free at las'; an' fell back on de pillar, an' he war gone. Oh, but he war spunky. De oberseers, arter dey foun' out who he war, gin'rally gabe him a wide birth. I specs his father war some ole Guinea king."

"Well, chillen," said Uncle Daniel, "we's kept up dis meeting long enough. We'd better go home, and not all go one way, cause de patrollers might git us all inter trouble, an' we must try to slip home by hook or crook."

"An' when we meet again, Uncle Daniel can finish his story, an' be ready to go with us," said Robert.

"I wish," said Tom Anderson, "he would go wid us, de wuss kind."

CHAPTER III

Uncle Daniel's Story

The Union had snapped asunder because it lacked the cohesion of justice, and the Nation was destined to pass through the crucible of disaster and defeat, till she was ready to clasp hands with the negro and march abreast with him to freedom and victory.

The Union army was encamping a few miles from C——, in North Carolina. Robert, being well posted on the condition of affairs, had stealthily contrived to call a meeting in Uncle Daniel's cabin. Uncle Daniel's wife had gone to bed as a sick sister, and they held a prayer-meeting by her bedside. It was a little risky, but as Mr. Thurston did not encourage the visits of the patrollers, and heartily detested having them prying into his cabins, there was not much danger of molestation.

"Well, Uncle Daniel, we want to hear your story, and see if you have made up your mind to go with us," said Robert, after he had been seated a few minutes in Uncle Daniel's cabin.

"No, chillen, I've no objection to finishin' my story, but I ain't made up my mind to leave the place till Marse Robert gits back."

"You were telling us about Marse Robert's mother. How did you get along after she died?"

"Arter she war gone, ole Marster's folks come to look arter things. But eberything war lef' to Marse Robert, an' he wouldn't do widout me. Dat chile war allers at my heels. I

couldn't stir widout him, an' when he missed me, he'd fret
an' cry so I had ter stay wid him; an' wen he went to school,
I had ter carry him in de mornin' and bring him home in de
ebenin'. An' I learned him to hunt squirrels, an' rabbits, an'
ketch fish, an' set traps for birds. I beliebs he lob'd me better
dan any ob his kin'. An' he showed me how to read."

"Well," said Tom, "ef he lob'd you so much, why didn't
he set you free?"

"Marse Robert tole me, ef he died fust he war gwine ter
leave me free—dat I should neber sarve any one else."

"Oh, sho!" said Tom, "promises, like pie crusts, is made
to be broken. I don't trust none ob dem. I'se been yere dese
fifteen years, an' I'se neber foun' any troof in dem. An' I'se
gwine wid dem North men soon's I gits a chance. An' ef you
knowed what's good fer you, you'd go, too."

"No, Tom; I can't go. When Marster Robert went to de
front, he called me to him an' said: 'Uncle Daniel,' an' he
was drefful pale when he said it, 'I are gwine to de war, an'
I want yer to take keer of my wife an' chillen, jis' like yer
used to take keer of me wen yer called me your little boy.'
Well, dat jis' got to me, an' I couldn't help cryin', to save
my life."

"I specs," said Tom, "your tear bags must lie mighty close
to your eyes. I wouldn't cry ef dem Yankees would make
ebery one of dem go to de front, an' stay dere foreber. Dey'd
only be gittin' back what dey's been a doin' to us."

"Marster Robert war nebber bad to me. An' I beliebs in
stannin' by dem dat stans by you. Arter Miss Anna died, I
had great 'sponsibilities on my shoulders; but I war orful
lonesome, an' thought I'd like to git a wife. But dere warn't
a gal on de plantation, an' nowhere's roun', dat filled de bill.
So I jis' waited, an' 'tended to Marse Robert till he war ole
'nough to go to college. Wen he went, he allers 'membered
me in de letters he used to write his grandma. Wen he war
gone, I war lonesomer dan eber. But, one day, I jis' seed de
gal dat took de rag off de bush. Gundover had jis' brought
her from de up-country. She war putty as a picture!" he ex-

claimed, looking fondly at his wife, who still bore traces of great beauty. "She had putty hair, putty eyes, putty mouth. She war putty all over; an' she know'd how to put on style."

"O, Daniel," said Aunt Katie, half chidingly, "how you do talk."

"Why, it's true. I 'member when you war de puttiest gal in dese diggins; when nobody could top your cotton."

"I don't," said Aunt Katie.

"Well, I do. Now, let me go on wid my story. De fust time I seed her, I sez to myself, 'Dat's de gal for me, an' I means to hab her ef I kin git her.' So I scraped 'quaintance wid her, and axed her ef she would hab me ef our marsters would let us. I warn't 'fraid 'bout Marse Robert, but I warn't quite shore 'bout Gundover. So when Marse Robert com'd home, I axed him, an' he larf'd an' said, 'All right,' an' dat he would speak to ole Gundover 'bout it. He didn't relish it bery much, but he didn't like to 'fuse Marse Robert. He wouldn't sell her, for she tended his dairy, an' war mighty handy 'bout de house. He said, I mought marry her an' come to see her wheneber Marse Robert would gib me a pass. I wanted him to sell her, but he wouldn't hear to it, so I had to put up wid what I could git. Marse Robert war mighty good to me, but ole Gundover's wife war de meanest woman dat I eber did see. She used to go out on de plantation an' boss things like a man. Arter I war married, I had a baby. It war de dearest, cutest little thing you eber did see; but, pore thing, it got sick and died. It died 'bout three o'clock; and in de mornin', Katie, habbin her cows to milk, lef' her dead baby in de cabin. When she com'd back from milkin' her thirty cows, an' went to look for her pore little baby, some one had been to her cabin an' took'd de pore chile away an' put it in de groun'. Pore Katie, she didn't eben hab a chance to kiss her baby 'fore it war buried. Ole Gundover's wife has been dead thirty years, an' she didn't die a day too soon. An' my little baby has gone to glory, an' is wingin' wid the angels an' a lookin' out for us. One ob de las' things ole Gundover's wife did 'fore she died war to order a woman whipped 'cause she com'd to de field a little late when her husband war sick, an' she had stopped to tend him. Dat mornin' she war taken sick wid de fever, an' in a few days she war gone out like de snuff ob a candle. She lef' several sons, an' I specs she would almos' turn ober in her grave ef she know'd she had ten culled granchillen somewhar down in de lower kentry."

"Isn't it funny," said Robert, "how these white folks look down on colored people, an' then mix up with them?"

"Marster war away when Miss 'Liza treated my Katie so mean, an' when I tole him 'bout it, he war tearin' mad, an' went ober an' saw ole Gundover, an' foun' out he war hard up for money, an' he bought Katie and brought her home to lib wid me, and we's been a libin in clover eber sence. Marster Robert has been mighty good to me. He stood by me in my troubles, an' now his trouble's come, I'm a gwine to stan' by him. I used to think Gundover's wife war jealous ob my Katie. She war so much puttier. Gundover's wife couldn't tech my Katie wid a ten foot pole."

"But, Aunt Katie, you have had your trials," said Robert, now that Daniel had finished his story; "don't you feel bitter towards these people who are fighting to keep you in slavery?"

Aunt Katie turned her face towards the speaker. It was a thoughtful, intelligent face, saintly and calm. A face which expressed the idea of a soul which had been fearfully tempest tossed, but had passed through suffering into peace. Very touching was the look of resignation and hope which over-spread her features as she replied, with the simple child-like faith which she had learned in the darkest hour, "The Lord says, we must forgive." And with her that thought, as coming from the lips of Divine Love, was enough to settle the whole question of forgiveness of injuries and love to enemies.

"Well," said Thomas Anderson, turning to Uncle Daniel, "we can't count on yer to go wid us?"

"Boys," said Uncle Daniel, and there was grief in his voice, "I'se mighty glad you hab a chance for your freedom;

but, ez I tole yer, I promised Marse Robert I would stay, an'
I mus' be as good as my word. Don't you youngsters stay for
an ole stager like me. I'm ole an' mos' worn out. Freedom
wouldn't do much for me, but I want you all to be as free as
the birds; so, you chillen, take your freedom when you kin
get it."

"But, Uncle Dan'el, you won't say nothin' 'bout our going, will you?" said the youngest of the company.

Uncle Daniel slowly arose. There was a mournful flash in
his eye, a tremor of emotion in his voice, as he said, "Look
yere, boys, de boy dat axed dat question war a new comer
on dis plantation, but some ob you's bin here all ob your
lives; did you eber know ob Uncle Dan'el gittin' any ob you
inter trouble?"

"No, no," exclaimed a chorus of voices, "but many's de
time you've held off de blows wen de oberseer got too mean,
an' cruelized us too much, wen Marse Robert war away. An'
wen he got back, you made him settle de oberseer's hash."

"Well, boys," said Uncle Daniel, with an air of mournful
dignity, "I'se de same Uncle Dan'el I eber war. Ef any ob
you wants to go, I habben't a word to say agin it. I specs
dem Yankees be all right, but I knows Marse Robert, an' I
don't know dem, an' I ain't a gwine ter throw away dirty
water 'til I gits clean."

"Well, Uncle Ben," said Robert, addressing a stalwart man
whose towering form and darkly flashing eye told that slavery
had failed to put the crouch in his shoulders or general ab-
jectness into his demeanor, "you will go with us, for sure,
won't you?"

"Yes," spoke up Tom Anderson, " 'cause de trader's done
took your wife, an' got her for his'n now."

As Ben Tunnel looked at the speaker, a spasm of agony
and anger darkened his face and distorted his features, as if
the blood of some strong race were stirring with sudden vigor
through his veins. He clutched his hands together, as if he
were struggling with an invisible foe, and for a moment he
remained silent. Then suddenly raising his head, he ex-

claimed, "Boys, there's not one of you loves freedom more than I do, but——"

"But what?" said Tom. "Do you think white folks is your bes' friends?"

"I'll think so when I lose my senses."

"Well, now, I don't belieb you're 'fraid, not de way I yeard you talkin' to de oberseer wen he war threatnin' to hit your mudder. He saw you meant business, an' he let her alone. But, what's to hinder you from gwine wid us?"

"My mother," he replied, in a low, firm voice. "That is the only thing that keeps me from going. If it had not been for her, I would have gone long ago. She's all I've got, an' I'm all she's got."

It was touching to see the sorrow on the strong face, to detect the pathos and indignation in his voice, as he said, "I used to love Mirandy as I love my life. I thought the sun rose and set in her. I never saw a handsomer woman than she was. But she fooled me all over the face and eyes, and took up with that hell-hound of a trader, Lukens; an' he gave her a chance to live easy, to wear fine clothes, an' be waited on like a lady. I thought at first I would go crazy, but my poor mammy did all she could to comfort me. She would tell me there were as good fish in the sea as were ever caught out of it. Many a time I've laid my poor head on her lap, when it seemed as if my brain was on fire and my heart was almost ready to burst. But in course of time I got over the worst of it; an' Mirandy is the first an' last woman that ever fooled me. But that dear old mammy of mine, I mean to stick by her as long as there is a piece of her. I can't go over to the army an' leave her behind, for if I did, an' anything should happen, I would never forgive myself."

"But couldn't you take her with you," said Robert, "the soldiers said we could bring our women."

"It isn't that. The Union army is several miles from here, an' my poor mammy is so skeery that, if I were trying to get her away and any of them Secesh would overtake us, an' begin to question us, she would get skeered almost to death, an' break down an' begin to cry, an' then the fat would be in the fire. So, while I love freedom more than a child loves its mother's milk, I've made up my mind to stay on the plantation. I wish, from the bottom of my heart, I could go. But I can't take her along with me, an' I don't want to be free and leave her behind in slavery. I was only five years old when my master and, as I believe, father, sold us both here to this lower country, an' we've been here ever since. It's no use talking, I won't leave her to be run over by everybody."

A few evenings after this interview, the Union soldiers entered the town of C——, and established their headquarters near the home of Thomas Anderson.

Out of the little company, almost every one deserted to the Union army, leaving Uncle Daniel faithful to his trust, and Ben Tunnel hushing his heart's deep aspirations for freedom in a passionate devotion to his timid and affectionate mother.

CHAPTER IV

Arrival of the Union Army

A few evenings before the stampede of Robert and his friends to the army, and as he sat alone in his room reading the latest news from the paper he had secreted, he heard a cautious tread and a low tap at his window. He opened the door quietly and whispered:—

"Anything new, Tom?"

"Yes."

"What is it? Come in."

"Well, I'se done bin seen dem Yankees, an' dere ain't a bit of troof in dem stories I'se bin yerin 'bout 'em."

"Where did you see 'em?"

"Down in de woods whar Marster tole us to hide. Yesterday ole Marse sent for me to come in de settin'-room. An' what do you think? Instead ob makin' me stan' wid my hat in my han' while he went froo a whole rigamarole, he axed me to sit down, an' he tole me he 'spected de Yankees would want us to go inter de army, an' dey would put us in front whar we'd all git killed; an' I tole him I didn't want to go, I didn't want to git all momached up. An' den he said we'd better go down in de woods an' hide. Massa Tom and Frank said we'd better go as quick as eber we could. Dey said dem Yankees would put us in dere wagons and make us haul like we war mules. Marse Tom ain't libin' at de great house jis' now. He's keepin' bachellar's hall."

"Didn't he go to the battle?"

"No; he foun' a pore white man who war hard up for money, an' he got him to go."

"But, Tom, you didn't believe these stories about the Yankees. Tom and Frank can lie as fast as horses can trot. They wanted to scare you, and keep you from going to the Union army."

"I knows dat now, but I didn't 'spect so den."

"Well, when did you see the soldiers? Where are they? And what did they say to you?"

"Dey's right down in Gundover's woods. An' de Gineral's got his headquarters almos' next door to our house."

"That near? Oh, you don't say so!"

"Yes, I do. An', oh, golly, ain't I so glad! I jis' stole yere to told you all 'bout it. Yesterday mornin' I war splittin' some wood to git my breakfas', an' I met one ob dem Yankee sogers. Well, I war so skeered, my heart flew right up in my mouf, but I made my manners to him and said, 'Good mornin', Massa.' He said, 'Good mornin'; but don't call me "massa." ' Dat war de fust white man I eber seed dat didn't want ter be called 'massa,' eben ef he war as pore as Job's turkey. Den I begin to feel right sheepish, an' he axed me ef my marster war at home, an' ef he war a Reb. I tole him he hadn't gone to de war, but he war Secesh all froo, inside and outside. He war too ole to go to de war, but dat he war all de time gruntin' an' groanin', an' I 'spected he'd grunt hisself to death."

"What did he say?"

"He said he specs he'll grunt worser dan dat fore dey get froo wid him. Den he axed me ef I would hab some breakfas,' an' I said, 'No, t'ank you, sir.' An' I war jis' as hungry as a dorg, but I war 'feared to eat. I war 'feared he war gwine to pizen me."

"Poison you! don't you know the Yankees are our best friends?"

"Well, ef dat's so, I'se mighty glad, cause de woods is full ob dem."

"Now, Tom, I thought you had cut your eye-teeth long

enough not to let them Anderson boys fool you. Tom, you must not think because a white man says a thing, it must be so, and that a colored man's word is no account 'longside of his. Tom, if ever we get our freedom, we've got to learn to trust each other and stick together if we would be a people. Somebody else can read the papers as well as Marse Tom and Frank. My ole Miss knows I can read the papers, an' she never tries to scare me with big whoppers 'bout the Yankees. She knows she can't catch ole birds with chaff, so she is just as sweet as a peach to her Bobby. But as soon as I get a chance I will play her a trick the devil never did."

"What's that?"

"I'll leave her. I ain't forgot how she sold my mother from me. Many a night I have cried myself to sleep, thinking about her, and when I get free I mean to hunt her up."

"Well, I ain't tole you all. De gemman said he war 'cruiting for de army; dat Massa Linkum hab set us all free, an' dat he wanted some more sogers to put down dem Secesh; dat we should all hab our freedom, our wages, an' some kind ob money. I couldn't call it like he did."

"Bounty money," said Robert.

"Yes, dat's jis' what he called it, bounty money. An' I said dat I war in for dat, teeth and toe-nails."

Robert Johnson's heart gave a great bound. Was that so? Had that army, with freedom emblazoned on its banners, come at last to offer them deliverance if they would accept it? Was it a bright, beautiful dream, or a blessed reality soon to be grasped by his willing hands? His heart grew buoyant with hope; the lightness of his heart gave elasticity to his step and sent the blood rejoicingly through his veins. Freedom was almost in his grasp, and the future was growing rose-tinted and rainbow-hued. All the ties which bound him to his home were as ropes of sand, now that freedom had come so near.

When the army was afar off, he had appeared to be light-hearted and content with his lot. If asked if he desired his freedom, he would have answered, very naively, that he was

eating his white bread and believed in letting well enough
alone; he had no intention of jumping from the frying-pan
into the fire. But in the depths of his soul the love of freedom
was an all-absorbing passion; only danger had taught him
caution. He had heard of terrible vengeance being heaped
upon the heads of some who had sought their freedom and
failed in the attempt. Robert knew that he might abandon
hope if he incurred the wrath of men whose overthrow was
only a question of time. It would have been madness and
folly for him to have attempted an insurrection against slavery, with the words of McClellan ringing in his ears: "If you
rise I shall put you down with an iron hand," and with the
home guards ready to quench his aspirations for freedom with
bayonets and blood. What could a set of unarmed and undisciplined men do against the fearful odds which beset their
path?

Robert waited eagerly and hopefully his chance to join the
Union army; and was ready and willing to do anything required of him by which he could earn his freedom and prove
his manhood. He conducted his plans with the greatest secrecy. A few faithful and trusted friends stood ready to desert
with him when the Union army came within hailing distance. When it came, there was a stampede to its ranks of
men ready to serve in any capacity, to labor in the tents,
fight on the fields, or act as scouts. It was a strange sight to
see these black men rallying around the Stars and Stripes,
when white men were trampling them under foot and rid-
dling them with bullets.

CHAPTER V

The Release of Iola Leroy

"Well, boys," said Robert to his trusted friends, as they gathered together at a meeting in Gundover's woods, almost under the shadow of the Union army, "how many of you are ready to join the army and fight for your freedom."

"All ob us."

"The soldiers," continued Robert, "are camped right at the edge of the town. The General has his headquarters in the heart of the town, and one of the officers told me yesterday that the President had set us all free, and that as many as wanted to join the army could come along to the camp. So I thought, boys, that I would come and tell you. Now, you can take your bag and baggage, and get out of here as soon as you choose."

"We'll be ready by daylight," said Tom. "It won't take me long to pack up," looking down at his seedy clothes, with a laugh. "I specs ole Marse'll be real lonesome when I'm gone. An' won't he be hoppin' mad when he finds I'm a goner? I specs he'll hate it like pizen."

"O, well," said Robert, "the best of friends must part. Don't let it grieve you."

"I'se gwine to take my wife an' chillen," said one of the company.

"I'se got nobody but myself," said Tom; "but dere's a mighty putty young gal dere at Marse Tom's. I wish I could git her away. Dey tells me dey's been sellin' her all ober de kentry; but dat she's a reg'lar spitfire; dey can't lead nor dribe her."

"Do you think she would go with us?" said Robert.

"I think she's jis' dying to go. Dey say dey can't do nuffin wid her. Marse Tom's got his match dis time, and I'se glad ob it. I jis' glories in her spunk."

"How did she come there?"

"Oh, Marse bought her ob de trader to keep house for him. But ef you seed dem putty white han's ob hern you'd never tink she kept her own house, let 'lone anybody else's."

"Do you think you can get her away?"

"I don't know; 'cause Marse Tom keeps her mighty close. My! but she's putty. Beautiful long hair comes way down her back; putty blue eyes, an' jis' ez white ez anybody's in dis place. I'd jis' wish you could see her yoresef. I heerd Marse Tom talkin' 'bout her las' night to his brudder; tellin' him she war mighty airish, but he meant to break her in."

An angry curse rose to the lips of Robert, but he repressed it and muttered to himself, "Graceless scamp, he ought to have his neck stretched." Then turning to Tom, said:—

"Get her, if you possibly can, but you must be mighty mum about it."

"Trus' me for dat," said Tom.

Tom was very anxious to get word to the beautiful but intractable girl who was held in durance vile by her reckless and selfish master, who had tried in vain to drag her down to his own low level of sin and shame. But all Tom's efforts were in vain. Finally he applied to the Commander of the post, who immediately gave orders for her release. The next day Tom had the satisfaction of knowing that Iola Leroy had been taken as a trembling dove from the gory vulture's nest and given a place of security. She was taken immediately to the General's headquarters. The General was much impressed by her modest demeanor, and surprised to see the refinement and beauty she possessed. Could it be possible that this young and beautiful girl had been a chattel, with no power to protect herself from the highest insults that law-

IOLA LEROY, OR SHADOWS UPLIFTED

less brutality could inflict upon innocent and defenseless womanhood? Could he ever again glory in his American citizenship, when any white man, no matter how coarse, cruel, or brutal, could buy or sell her for the basest purposes? Was it not true that the cause of a hapless people had become entangled with the lightnings of heaven, and dragged down retribution upon the land?

The field hospital was needing gentle, womanly ministrations, and Iola Leroy, released from the hands of her tormentors, was given a place as nurse; a position to which she adapted herself with a deep sense of relief. Tom was doubly gratified at the success of his endeavors, which had resulted in the rescue of the beautiful young girl and the discomfiture of his young master who, in the words of Tom, "was mad enough to bite his head off" (a rather difficult physical feat).

Iola, freed from her master's clutches, applied herself readily to her appointed tasks. The beautiful, girlish face was full of tender earnestness. The fresh, young voice was strangely sympathetic, as if some great sorrow had bound her heart in loving compassion to every sufferer who needed her gentle ministrations.

Tom Anderson was a man of herculean strength and remarkable courage. But, on account of physical defects, instead of enlisting as a soldier, he was forced to remain a servant, although he felt as if every nerve in his right arm was tingling to strike a blow for freedom. He was well versed in the lay of the country, having often driven his master's cotton to market when he was a field hand. After he became a coachman, he had become acquainted with the different roads and localities of the country. Besides, he had often accompanied his young masters on their hunting and fishing expeditions. Although he could not fight in the army, he proved an invaluable helper. When tents were to be pitched, none were more ready to help than he. When burdens were to be borne, none were more willing to bend beneath them than Thomas Anderson. When the battle-field was to be searched for the wounded and dying, no hand was more tender in its ministrations of kindness than his. As a general factotum in the army, he was ever ready and willing to serve anywhere and at any time, and to gather information from every possible source which could be of any service to the Union army. As a Pagan might worship a distant star and wish to call it his own, so he loved Iola. And he never thought he could do too much for the soldiers who had rescued her and were bringing deliverance to his race.

"What do you think of Miss Iola?" Robert asked him one day, as they were talking together.

"I jis' think dat she's splendid. Las' week I had to take some of our pore boys to de hospital, an' she war dere, lookin' sweet an' putty ez an angel, a nussin' dem pore boys, an' ez good to one ez de oder. It looks to me ez ef dey ralely lob'd her shadder. She sits by 'em so patient, an' writes 'em sech nice letters to der frens, an' yit she looks so heart-broke an' pitiful, it jis' gits to me, an' makes me mos' ready to cry. I'm so glad dat Marse Tom had to gib her up. He war too mean to eat good victuals."

"He ought," said Robert, "to be made to live on herrings' heads and cold potatoes. It makes my blood boil just to think that he was going to have that lovely looking young girl whipped for his devilment. He ought to be ashamed to hold up his head among respectable people."

"I tell you, Bob, de debil will neber git his own till he gits him. When I seed how he war treating her I neber rested till I got her away. He buyed her, he said, for his housekeeper; as many gals as dere war on de plantation, why didn't he git one ob dem to keep house, an' not dat nice lookin' young lady? Her han's look ez ef she neber did a day's work in her life. One day when he com'd down to breakfas,' he chucked her under de chin, an' tried to put his arm roun' her waist. But she jis' frew it off like a chunk ob fire. She looked like a snake had bit her. Her eyes fairly spit fire. Her face got red ez blood, an' den she turned so pale I thought she war gwine to faint, but she didn't, an' I yered her say, 'I'll die fust.' I war mad 'nough to stan' on my head. I could hab tore'd him all to pieces wen he said he'd hab her whipped."

"Did he do it?"

"I don't know. But he's mean 'nough to do enythin'. Why, dey say she war sole seben times in six weeks, 'cause she's so putty, but dat she war game to de las'."

"Well, Tom," said Robert, "getting that girl away was one of the best things you ever did in your life."

"I think so, too. Not dat I specs enythin' ob it. I don't spose she would think ob an ugly chap like me; but it does me good to know dat Marse Tom ain't got her."

CHAPTER VI

Robert Johnson's Promotion and Religion

Robert Johnson, being able to meet the army requirements, was enlisted as a substitute to help fill out the quota of a Northern regiment. With his intelligence, courage, and prompt obedience, he rose from the ranks and became lieutenant of a colored company. He was daring, without being rash; prompt, but not thoughtless; firm, without being harsh. Kind and devoted to the company he drilled, he soon won the respect of his superior officers and the love of his comrades.

"Johnson," said a young officer, Captain Sybil, of Maine, who had become attached to Robert, "what is the use of your saying you're a colored man, when you are as white as I am, and as brave a man as there is among us. Why not quit this company, and take your place in the army just the same as a white man? I know your chances for promotion would be better."

"Captain, you may doubt my word, but to-day I would rather be a lieutenant in my company than a captain in yours."

"I don't understand you."

"Well, Captain, when a man's been colored all his life it comes a little hard for him to get white all at once. Were I to try it, I would feel like a cat in a strange garret. Captain, I think my place is where I am most needed. You do not need me in your ranks, and my company does. They are excellent fighters, but they need a leader. To silence a battery, to capture a flag, to take a fortification, they will rush into the jaws of death."

"Yes, I have often wondered at their bravery."

"Captain, these battles put them on their mettle. They have been so long taught that they are nothing and nobody, that they seem glad to prove they are something and somebody."

"But, Johnson, you do not look like them, you do not talk like them. It is a burning shame to have held such a man as you in slavery."

"I don't think it was any worse to have held me in slavery than the blackest man in the South."

"You are right, Johnson. The color of a man's skin has nothing to do with the possession of his rights."

"Now, there is Tom Anderson," said Robert," he is just as black as black can be. He has been bought and sold like a beast, and yet there is not a braver man in all the company. I know him well. He is a noble-hearted fellow. True as steel. I love him like a brother. And I believe Tom would risk his life for me any day. He don't know anything about his father or mother. He was sold from them before he could remember. He can read a little. He used to take lessons from a white gardener in Virginia. He would go between the hours of 9 P. M. and 4 A. M. He got a book of his own, tore it up, greased the pages, and hid them in his hat. Then if his master had ever knocked his hat off he would have thought them greasy papers, and not that Tom was carrying his library on his head. I had another friend who lived near us. When he was nineteen years old he did not know how many letters there were in the A B C's. One night, when his work was done, his boss came into his cabin and saw him with a book in his hand. He threatened to give him five hundred lashes if he caught him again with a book, and said he hadn't work enough to do. He was getting out logs, and his task was ten logs a day. His employer threatened to increase it to twelve.

He said it just harassed him; it set him on fire. He thought there must be something good in that book if the white man didn't want him to learn. One day he had an errand in the kitchen, and he heard one of the colored girls going over the A B C's. Here was the key to the forbidden knowledge. She had heard the white children saying them, and picked them up by heart, but did not know them by sight. He was not content with that, but sold his cap for a book and wore a cloth on his head instead. He got the sounds of the letters by heart, then cut off the bark of a tree, carved the letters on the smooth inside, and learned them. He wanted to learn how to write. He had charge of a warehouse where he had a chance to see the size and form of letters. He made the beach of the river his copybook, and thus he learned to write. Tom never got very far with his learning, but I used to get the papers and tell him all I knew about the war."

"How did you get the papers?"

"I used to have very good privileges for a slave. All of our owners were not alike. Some of them were quite clever, and others were worse than git out. I used to get the morning papers to sell to the boarders and others, and when I got them I would contrive to hide a paper, and let some of the fellow-servants know how things were going on. And our owners thought we cared nothing about what was going on."

"How was that? I thought you were not allowed to hold meetings unless a white man were present."

"That was so. But we contrived to hold secret meetings in spite of their caution. We knew whom we could trust. My ole Miss wasn't mean like some of them. She never wanted the patrollers around prowling in our cabins, and poking their noses into our business. Her husband was an awful drunkard. He ran through every cent he could lay his hands on, and she was forced to do something to keep the wolf from the door, so she set up a boarding-house. But she didn't take in Tom, Dick, and Harry. Nobody but the big bugs stopped with her. She taught me to read and write, and to cast up accounts. It was so handy for her to have some one who could figure up her accounts, and read or write a note, if she were from home and wanted the like done. She once told her cousin how I could write and figure up. And what do you think her cousin said?"

" 'Pleased,' I suppose, 'to hear it.' "

"Not a bit of it. She said, if I belonged to her, she would cut off my thumbs; her husband said, 'Oh, then he couldn't pick cotton.' As to my poor thumbs, it did not seem to be taken into account what it would cost me to lose them. My ole Miss used to have a lot of books. She would let me read any one of them except a novel. She wanted to take care of my soul, but she wasn't taking care of her own."

"Wasn't she religious?"

"She went for it. I suppose she was as good as most of them. She said her prayers and went to church, but I don't know that that made her any better. I never did take much stock in white folks' religion."

"Why, Robert, I'm afraid you are something of an infidel."

"No, Captain, I believe in the real, genuine religion. I ain't got much myself, but I respect them that have. We had on our place a dear, old saint, named Aunt Kizzy. She was a happy soul. She had seen hard times, but was what I call a living epistle. I've heard her tell how her only child had been sold from her, when the man who bought herself did not want to buy her child. Poor little fellow! he was only two years old. I asked her one day how she felt when her child was taken away. 'I felt,' she said, 'as if I was going to my grave. But I knew if I couldn't get justice here, I could get it in another world.' "

"That was faith," said Captain Sybil, as if speaking to himself, "a patient waiting for death to redress the wrongs of life."

"Many a time," continued Robert, "have I heard her humming to herself in the kitchen and saying, 'I has my trials, ups and downs, but it won't allers be so. I specs one day to wing and wing wid de angels, Hallelujah! Den I specs to hear a voice sayin', "Poor ole Kizzy, she's done de bes' she kin. Go down, Gabriel, an' tote her in." Den I specs to put on my golden slippers, my long white robe, an' my starry crown, an' walk dem golden streets, Hallelujah!' I've known that dear, old soul to travel going on two miles, after her work was done, to have some one read to her. Her favorite chapter began with, 'Let not your heart be troubled, ye believe in God, believe also in Me.' "

"I have been deeply impressed," said Captain Sybil, "with the child-like faith of some of these people. I do not mean to say that they are consistent Christians, but I do think that this faith has in a measure underlain the life of the race. It has been a golden thread woven amid the sombre tissues of their lives. A ray of light shimmering amid the gloom of their condition. And what would they have been without it?"

"I don't know. But I know what she was with it. And I believe if there are any saints in glory, Aunt Kizzy is one of them."

"She is dead, then?"

"Yes, went all right, singing and rejoicing until the last, 'Troubles over, troubles over, and den my troubles will be over. We'll walk de golden streets all 'roun' in de New Jerusalem.' Now, Captain, that's the kind of religion that I want. Not that kind which could ride to church on Sundays, and talk so solemn with the minister about heaven and good things, then come home and light down on the servants like a thousand of bricks. I have no use for it. I don't believe in it. I never did and I never will. If any man wants to save my soul he ain't got to beat my body. That ain't the kind of religion I'm looking for. I ain't got a bit of use for it. Now, Captain, ain't I right?"

"Well, yes, Robert, I think you are more than half right. You ought to know my dear, old mother who lives in Maine. We have had colored company at our house, and I never saw her show the least difference between her colored and white guests. She is a Quaker preacher, and don't believe in war, but when the rest of the young men went to the front, I wanted to go also. So I thought it all over, and there seemed to be no way out of slavery except through the war. I had been taught to hate war and detest slavery. Now the time had come when I could not help the war, but I could strike a blow for freedom. So I told my mother I was going to the front, that I expected to be killed, but I went to free the slave. It went hard with her. But I thought that I ought to come, and I believe my mother's prayers are following me."

"Captain," said Robert, rising, "I am glad that I have heard your story. I think that some of these Northern soldiers do two things—hate slavery and hate niggers."

"I am afraid that is so with some of them. They would rather be whipped by Rebels than conquer with negroes. Oh, I heard a soldier," said Captain Sybil, "say, when the colored men were being enlisted, that he would break his sword and resign. But he didn't do either. After Colonel Shaw led his charge at Fort Wagner, and died in the conflict, he got bravely over his prejudices. The conduct of the colored troops there and elsewhere has done much to turn public opinion in their favor. I suppose any white soldier would rather have his black substitute receive the bullets than himself."

CHAPTER VII

Tom Anderson's Death

"Where is Tom?" asked Captain Sybil; "I have not seen him for several hours."

"He's gone down the sound with some of the soldiers," replied Robert. "They wanted Tom to row them."

"I am afraid those boys will get into trouble, and the Rebs will pick them off," responded Sybil.

"O, I hope not," answered Robert.

"I hope not, too; but those boys are too venturesome."

"Tom knows the lay of the land better than any of us," said Robert. "He is the most wide-awake and gamiest man I know. I reckon when the war is over Tom will be a preacher. Did you ever hear him pray?"

"No; is he good at that?"

"First-rate," continued Robert. "It would do you good to hear him. He don't allow any cursing and swearing when he's around. And what he says is law and gospel with the boys. But he's *so* good-natured; and they *can't* get mad at him."

"Yes, Robert, there is not a man in our regiment I would sooner trust than Tom. Last night, when he brought in that wounded scout, he couldn't have been more tender if he had been a woman. How gratefully the poor fellow looked in Tom's face as he laid him down so carefully and staunched the blood which had been spurting out of him. Tom seemed to know it was an artery which had been cut, and he did just the right thing to stop the bleeding. He knew there wasn't a moment to be lost. He wasn't going to wait for the doctor. I have often heard that colored people are ungrateful, but I don't think Tom's worst enemy would say that about him."

"Captain," said Robert, with a tone of bitterness in his voice, "what had we to be grateful for? For ages of poverty, ignorance, and slavery? I think if anybody should be grateful, it is the people who have enslaved us and lived off our labor for generations. Captain, I used to know a poor old woman who couldn't bear to hear any one play on the piano."

"Is that so? Why, I always heard that colored people were a musical race."

"So we are; but that poor woman's daughter was sold, and her mistress took the money to buy a piano. Her mother could never bear to hear a sound from it."

"Poor woman!" exclaimed Captain Sybil, sympathetically; "I suppose it seemed as if the wail of her daughter was blending with the tones of the instrument. I think, Robert, there is a great deal more in the colored people than we give them credit for. Did you know Captain Sellers?"

"The officer who escaped from prison and got back to our lines?" asked Robert.

"Yes. Well, he had quite an experience in trying to escape. He came to an aged couple, who hid him in their cabin and shared their humble food with him. They gave him some corn-bread, bacon, and coffee which he thought was made of scorched bran. But he said that he never ate a meal that he relished more than the one he took with them. Just before he went they knelt down and prayed with him. It seemed as if his very hair stood on his head, their prayer was so solemn. As he was going away the man took some shingles and nailed them on his shoes to throw the bloodhounds off his track. I don't think he will ever cease to feel kindly towards colored people. I do wonder what has become of the boys? What can keep them so long?"

Just as Captain Sybil and Robert were wondering at the delay of Tom and the soldiers they heard the measured tread of men who were slowly bearing a burden. They were carrying Tom Anderson to the hospital, fearfully wounded, and nigh to death. His face was distorted, and the blood was streaming from his wounds. His respiration was faint, his pulse hurried, as if life were trembling on its frailest cords.

Robert and Captain Sybil hastened at once towards the wounded man. On Robert's face was a look of intense anguish, as he bent pityingly over his friend.

"O, this is dreadful! How did it happen?" cried Robert.

Captain Sybil, pressing anxiously forward, repeated Robert's question.

"Captain," said one of the young soldiers, advancing and saluting his superior officer, "we were all in the boat when it struck against a mud bank, and there was not strength enough among us to shove her back into the water. Just then the Rebels opened fire upon us. For awhile we lay down in the boat, but still they kept firing. Tom took in the whole situation, and said: 'Some one must die to get us out of this. I mought's well be him as any. You are soldiers and can fight. If they kill me, it is nuthin'.' So Tom leaped out to shove the boat into the water. Just then the Rebel bullets began to rain around him. He received seven or eight of them, and I'm afraid there is no hope for him."

"O, Tom, I wish you hadn't gone. O, Tom! Tom!" cried Robert, in tones of agony.

A gleam of grateful recognition passed over the drawn features of Tom, as the wail of his friend fell on his ear. He attempted to speak, but the words died upon his lips, and he became unconscious.

"Well," said Captain Sybil, "put him in one of the best wards. Give him into Miss Leroy's care. If good nursing can win him back to life, he shall not want for any care or pains that she can bestow. Send immediately for Dr. Gresham."

Robert followed his friend into the hospital, tenderly and carefully helped to lay him down, and remained awhile, gazing in silent grief upon the sufferer. Then he turned to go, leaving him in the hands of Iola, but hoping against hope that his wounds would not be fatal.

With tender devotion Iola watched her faithful friend. He recognized her when restored to consciousness, and her presence was as balm to his wounds. He smiled faintly, took her hand in his, stroked it tenderly, looked wistfully into her face, and said, "Miss Iola, I ain't long fer dis! I'se 'most home!"

"Oh, no," said Iola, "I hope that you will soon get over this trouble, and live many long and happy days."

"No, Miss Iola, it's all ober wid me. I'se gwine to glory; gwine to glory; gwine to ring dem charmin' bells. Tell all de boys to meet me in heben; dat dey mus' 'list in de hebenly war."

"O, Mr. Tom," said Iola, tenderly, "do not talk of leaving me. You are the best friend I have had since I was torn from my mother. I should be so lonely without you."

"Dere's a frien' dat sticks closer dan a brudder. He will be wid yer in de sixt' trial, an' in de sebbent' he'll not fo'sake yer."

"Yes," answered Iola, "I know that. He is all our dependence. But I can't help grieving when I see you suffering so. But, dear friend, be quiet, and try to go to sleep."

"I'll do enythin' fer yer, Miss Iola."

Tom closed his eyes and lay quiet. Tenderly and anxiously Iola watched over him as the hours waned away. The doctor came, shook his head gravely, and, turning to Iola, said, "There is no hope, but do what you can to alleviate his sufferings."

As Iola gazed upon the kind but homely features of Tom, she saw his eyes open and an unexpressed desire upon his face.

Tenderly and sadly bending over him, with tears in her dark, luminous eyes, she said, "Is there anything I can do for you?"

"Yes," said Tom, with laboring breath; "let me hole yore han', an' sing 'Ober Jordan inter glory' an' 'We'll anchor bye and bye.' "

Iola laid her hand gently in the rough palm of the dying man, and, with a tremulous voice, sang the parting hymns.

Tenderly she wiped the death damps from his dusky brow, and imprinted upon it a farewell kiss. Gratitude and affection lit up the dying eye, which seemed to be gazing into the eternities. Just then Robert entered the room, and, seating himself quietly by Tom's bedside, read the death signs in his face.

"Good-bye, Robert," said Tom, "meet me in de kingdom." Suddenly a look of recognition and rapture lit up his face, and he murmured, "Angels, bright angels, all's well, all's well!"

Slowly his hand released its pressure, a peaceful calm overspread his countenance, and without a sigh or murmur Thomas Anderson, Iola's faithful and devoted friend, passed away, leaving the world so much poorer for her than it was before. Just then Dr. Gresham, the hospital physician, came to the bedside, felt for the pulse which would never throb again, and sat down in silence by the cot.

"What do you think, Doctor," said Iola, "has he fainted?"

"No," said the doctor, "poor fellow! he is dead."

Iola bowed her head in silent sorrow, and then relieved the anguish of her heart by a flood of tears. Robert rose, and sorrowfully left the room.

Iola, with tearful eyes and aching heart, clasped the cold hands over the still breast, closed the waxen lid over the eye which had once beamed with kindness or flashed with courage, and then went back, after the burial, to her daily round of duties, feeling the sad missing of something from her life.

CHAPTER VIII

The Mystified Doctor

"Colonel," said Dr. Gresham to Col. Robinson, the commander of the post, "I am perfectly mystified by Miss Leroy."

"What is the matter with her?" asked Col. Robinson. "Is she not faithful to her duties and obedient to your directions?"

"Faithful is not the word to express her tireless energy and devotion to her work," responded Dr. Gresham. "She must have been a born nurse to put such enthusiasm into her work."

"Why, Doctor, what is the matter with you? You talk like a lover."

A faint flush rose to the cheek of Dr. Gresham as he smiled, and said, "Oh! come now, Colonel, can't a man praise a woman without being in love with her?"

"Of course he can," said Col. Robinson; "but I know where such admiration is apt to lead. I've been there myself. But, Doctor, had you not better defer your love-making till you're out of the woods?"

"I assure you, Colonel, I am not thinking of love or courtship. That is the business of the drawing-room, and not of the camp. But she did mystify me last night."

"How so?" asked Col. Robinson.

"When Tom was dying," responded the doctor, "I saw that beautiful and refined young lady bend over and kiss him. When she found that he was dead, she just cried as if her heart was breaking. Well, that was a new thing to me. I can eat with colored people, walk, talk, and fight with them, but kissing them is something I don't hanker after."

"And yet you saw Miss Leroy do it?"

"Yes; and that puzzles me. She is one of the most refined and lady-like women I ever saw. I hear she is a refugee, but she does not look like the other refugees who have come to our camp. Her accent is slightly Southern, but her manner is Northern. She is self-respecting without being supercilious; quiet, without being dull. Her voice is low and sweet, yet at times there are tones of such passionate tenderness in it that you would think some great sorrow has darkened and over-shadowed her life. Without being the least gloomy, her face at times is pervaded by an air of inexpressible sadness. I sometimes watch her when she is not aware that I am look-ing at her, and it seems as if a whole volume was depicted on her countenance. When she smiles, there is a longing in her eyes which is never satisfied. I cannot understand how a Southern lady, whose education and manners stamp her as a woman of fine culture and good breeding, could consent to occupy the position she so faithfully holds. It is a mystery I cannot solve. Can you?"

"I think I can," answered Col. Robinson.

"Will you tell me?" queried the doctor.

"Yes, on one condition."

"What is it?"

"Everlasting silence."

"I promise," said the doctor. "The secret between us shall be as deep as the sea."

"She has not requested secrecy, but at present, for her sake, I do not wish the secret revealed. Miss Leroy was a slave."

"Oh, no," said Dr. Gresham, starting to his feet, "it can't be so! A woman as white as she a slave?"

"Yes, it is so," continued the colonel. "In these States the child follows the condition of its mother. This beautiful and accomplished girl was held by one of the worst Rebels in town. Tom told me of it and I issued orders for her release."

"Well, well! Is that so?" said Dr. Gresham, thoughtfully stroking his beard. "Wonders will never cease. Why, I was just beginning to think seriously of her."

"What's to hinder your continuing to think?" asked Col. Robinson.

"What you tell me changes the whole complexion of affairs," replied the doctor.

"If that be so I am glad I told you before you got head over heels in love."

"Yes," said Dr. Gresham, absently.

Dr. Gresham was a member of a wealthy and aristocratic family, proud of its lineage, which it could trace through generations of good blood to its ancestral isle. He had become deeply interested in Iola before he had heard her story, but after it had been revealed to him he tried to banish her from his mind; but his constant observation of her only increased his interest and admiration. The deep pathos of her story, the tenderness of her ministrations, bestowed alike on black and white, and the sad loneliness of her condition, awakened within him a desire to defend and protect her all through her future life. The fierce clashing of war had not taken all the romance out of his nature. In Iola he saw realized his ideal of the woman whom he was willing to marry. A woman, tender, strong, and courageous, and rescued only by the strong arm of his Government from a fate worse than death. She was young in years, but old in sorrow; one whom a sad destiny had changed from a light-hearted girl to a heroic woman. As he observed her, he detected an undertone of sorrow in her most cheerful words, and observed a quick flushing and sudden paling of her cheek, as if she were living over scenes that were thrilling her soul with indignation or chilling her heart with horror. As nurse and physician, Iola and Dr. Gresham were constantly thrown together. His friends sent him magazines and books, which he gladly shared with her. The hospital was a sad place. Mangled forms, stricken down in the flush of their prime and energy; pale young corpses, sacrificed on the altar of slavery, constantly drained on her sympathies. Dr. Gresham was glad to have some reading matter which might divert her mind from the memories of her mournful past, and also furnish them both with interesting themes of conversation in their moments of relaxation from the harrowing scenes through which they were constantly passing. Without any effort or consciousness on her part, his friendship ripened into love. To him her presence was a pleasure, her absence a privation; and her loneliness drew deeply upon his sympathy. He would have merited his own self-contempt if, by word or deed, he had done anything to take advantage of her situation. All the manhood and chivalry of his nature rose in her behalf, and, after carefully revolving the matter, he resolved to win her for his bride, bury her secret in his Northern home, and hide from his aristocratic relations all knowledge of her mournful past. One day he said to Iola:—

"This hospital life is telling on you. Your strength is failing, and although you possess a wonderful amount of physical endurance, you must not forget that saints have bodies and dwell in tabernacles of clay, just the same as we common mortals."

"Compliments aside," she said, smiling; "what are you driving at, Doctor?"

"I mean," he replied, "that you are running down, and if you do not quit and take some rest you will be our patient instead of our nurse. You'd better take a furlough, go North, and return after the first frost."

"Doctor, if that is your only remedy," replied Iola, "I am afraid that I am destined to die at my post. I have no special friends in the North, and no home but this in the South. I am homeless and alone."

There was something so sad, almost despairing in her tones, in the drooping of her head, and the quivering of her lip, that they stirred Dr. Gresham's heart with sudden pity, and, drawing nearer to her, he said, "Miss Leroy, you need not be all alone. Let me claim the privilege of making your life bright and happy. Iola, I have loved you ever since I have seen your devotion to our poor, sick boys. How faithfully you, a young and gracious girl, have stood at your post and performed your duties. And now I ask, will you not permit me to clasp hands with you for life? I do not ask for a hasty reply. Give yourself time to think over what I have proposed."

CHAPTER IX

Eugene Leroy and
Alfred Lorraine

Nearly twenty years before the war, two young men, of French and Spanish descent, sat conversing on a large verandah which surrounded an ancient home on the Mississippi River. It was French in its style of architecture, large and rambling, with no hint of modern improvements.

The owner of the house was the only heir of a Creole planter. He had come into possession of an inheritance consisting of vast baronial estates, bank stock, and a large number of slaves. Eugene Leroy, being deprived of his parents, was left, at an early age, to the care of a distant relative, who had sent him to school and college, and who occasionally invited him to spend his vacations at his home. But Eugene generally declined his invitations, as he preferred spending his vacations at the watering places in the North, with their fashionable and not always innocent gayeties. Young, vivacious, impulsive, and undisciplined, without the restraining influence of a mother's love or the guidance of a father's hand, Leroy found himself, when his college days were over, in the dangerous position of a young man with vast possessions, abundant leisure, unsettled principles, and uncontrolled desires. He had no other object than to extract from life its most seductive draughts of ease and pleasure. His companion, who sat opposite him on the verandah, quietly smoking a cigar, was a remote cousin, a few years older than himself, the warmth of whose Southern temperament had been modified by an infusion of Northern blood.

Eugene was careless, liberal, and impatient of details, while his companion and cousin, Alfred Lorraine, was selfish, eager, keen, and alert; also hard, cold, methodical, and ever ready to grasp the main chance. Yet, notwithstanding the difference between them, they had formed a warm friendship for each other.

"Alfred," said Eugene, "I am going to be married."

Lorraine opened his eyes with sudden wonder, and exclaimed: "Well, that's the latest thing out! Who is the fortunate lady who has bound you with her silken fetters? Is it one of those beautiful Creole girls who were visiting Augustine's plantation last winter? I watched you during our visit there and thought that you could not be proof against their attractions. Which is your choice? It would puzzle me to judge between the two. They had splendid eyes, dark, luminous, and languishing; lovely complexions and magnificent hair. Both were delightful in their manners, refined and cultured, with an air of vivacity mingled with their repose of manner which was perfectly charming. As the law only allows us one, which is your choice? Miss Annette has more force than her sister, and if I could afford the luxury of a wife she would be my choice."

"Ah, Alf," said Eugene, "I see that you are a practical business man. In marrying you want a wife to assist you as an efficient plantation mistress. One who would tolerate no waste in the kitchen and no disorder in the parlor."

"Exactly so," responded Lorraine; "I am too poor to marry a mere parlor ornament. You can afford to do it; I cannot."

"Nonsense, if I were as poor as a church mouse I would marry the woman I love."

"Very fine sentiments," said Lorraine, "and were I as rich as you I would indulge in them also. You know, when my father died I had great expectations. We had always lived in good style, and I never thought for a moment he was not a rich man, but when his estate was settled I found it was greatly involved, and I was forced to face an uncertain future, with scarcely a dollar to call my own. Land, negroes, cattle, and horses all went under the hammer. The only thing I retained was the education I received at the North; that was my father's best investment, and all my stock in trade. With that only as an outfit, it would be madness for me to think of marrying one of those lovely girls. They remind me of beautiful canary birds, charming and pretty, but not fitted for the wear and tear of plantation life. Well, which is your choice?"

"Neither," replied Eugene.

"Then, is it that magnificent looking widow from New Orleans, whom we met before you had that terrible spell of sickness and to whom you appeared so devoted?"

"Not at all. I have not heard from her since that summer. She was fascinating and handsome, but fearfully high strung."

"Were you afraid of her?"

"No; but I valued my happiness too much to trust it in her hands."

"Sour grapes!" said Lorraine.

"No! but I think that slavery and the lack of outside interests are beginning to tell on the lives of our women. They lean too much on their slaves, have too much irresponsible power in their hands, are narrowed and compressed by the routine of plantation life and the lack of intellectual stimulus."

"Yes, Eugene, when I see what other women are doing in the fields of literature and art, I cannot help thinking an amount of brain power has been held in check among us. Yet I cannot abide those Northern women, with their suffrage views and abolition cant. They just shock me."

"But your mother was a Northern woman," said Eugene.

"Yes; but she got bravely over her Northern ideas. As I remember her, she was just as much a Southerner as if she had been to the manor born. She came here as a schoolteacher, but soon after she came she married my father. He was easy and indulgent with his servants, and held them with a very loose rein. But my mother was firm and energetic. She made the niggers move around. No shirking nor dawdling with her. When my father died, she took matters in hand, but she only outlived him a few months. If she had lived I believe that she would have retrieved our fortune. I know that she had more executive ability than my father. He was very squeamish about selling his servants, but she would have put every one of them in her pocket before permitting them to eat her out of house and home. But whom *are* you going to marry?"

"A young lady who graduates from a Northern seminary next week," responded Eugene.

"I think you are very selfish," said Lorraine. "You might have invited a fellow to go with you to be your best man."

"The wedding is to be strictly private. The lady whom I am to marry has negro blood in her veins."

"The devil she has!" exclaimed Lorraine, starting to his feet, and looking incredulously on the face of Leroy. "Are you in earnest? Surely you must be jesting."

"I am certainly in earnest," answered Eugene Leroy. "I mean every word I say."

"Oh, it can't be possible! Are you mad?" exclaimed Lorraine.

"Never was saner in my life."

"What under heaven could have possessed you to do such a foolish thing? Where did she come from."

"Right here, on this plantation. But I have educated and manumitted her, and I intend marrying her."

"Why, Eugene, it is impossible that you can have an idea of marrying one of your slaves. Why, man, she is your property, to have and to hold to all intents and purposes. Are you not satisfied with the power and possession the law gives you?"

"No. Although the law makes her helpless in my hands, to me her defenselessness is her best defense."

"Eugene, we have known each other all of our lives, and, although I have always regarded you as eccentric, I never saw you so completely off your balance before. The idea of you, with your proud family name, your vast wealth in land and negroes, intending to marry one of them, is a mystery I cannot solve. Do explain to me why you are going to take this extremely strange and foolish step."

"You never saw Marie?"

"No; and I don't want to."

"She is very beautiful. In the North no one would suspect that she has one drop of negro blood in her veins, but here, where I am known, to marry her is to lose caste. I could live with her, and not incur much if any social opprobrium. Society would wink at the transgression, even if after she had become the mother of my children I should cast her off and send her and them to the auction block."

"Men," replied Lorraine, "would merely shrug their shoulders; women would say you had been sowing your wild oats. Your money, like charity, would cover a multitude of faults."

"But if I make her my lawful wife and recognize her children as my legitimate heirs, I subject myself to social ostracism and a senseless persecution. We Americans boast of freedom, and yet here is a woman whom I love as I never loved any other human being, but both law and public opinion debar me from following the inclination of my heart. She is beautiful, faithful, and pure, and yet all that society will tolerate is what I would scorn to do."

"But has not society the right to guard the purity of its blood by the rigid exclusion of an alien race?"

"Excluding it! How?" asked Eugene.

"By debarring it from social intercourse."

"Perhaps it has," continued Eugene, "but should not society have a greater ban for those who, by consorting with an alien race, rob their offspring of a right to their names and to an inheritance in their property, and who fix their social status among an enslaved and outcast race? Don't eye me so curiously; I am not losing my senses."

"I think you have done that already," said Lorraine.

"Don't you know that if she is as fair as a lily, beautiful as a houri, and chaste as ice, that still she is a negro?"

"Oh, come now; she isn't much of a negro."

"It doesn't matter, however. One drop of negro blood in her veins curses all the rest."

"I know it," said Eugene, sadly, "but I have weighed the consequences, and am prepared to take them."

"Well, Eugene, your course is *so* singular! I do wish that you would tell me why you take this unprecedented step?"

Eugene laid aside his cigar, looked thoughtfully at Lorraine, and said, "Well, Alfred, as we are kinsmen and life-long friends, I will not resent your asking my reason for doing that which seems to you the climax of absurdity, and if you will have the patience to listen I will tell you."

"Proceed, I am all attention."

"My father died," said Eugene, "as you know, when I was too young to know his loss or feel his care and, being an only child, I was petted and spoiled. I grew up to be wayward, self-indulgent, proud, and imperious. I went from home and made many friends both at college and in foreign lands. I was well supplied with money and, never having been forced to earn it, was ignorant of its value and careless of its use. My lavish expenditures and liberal benefactions attracted to me a number of parasites, and men older than myself led me into the paths of vice, and taught me how to gather the flowers of sin which blossom around the borders of hell. In a word, I left my home unwarned and unarmed against the seductions of vice. I returned an initiated devotee to debasing pleasures. Years of my life were passed in foreign lands; years in which my soul slumbered and seemed pervaded with a moral paralysis; years, the memory of which fills my soul with sorrow and shame. I went to the capitals of the old world to see life, but in seeing life I became acquainted with death, the death of true manliness and self-respect. You look astonished; but I tell you, Alf, there is many a poor clod-hopper, on whom are the dust and grime of unremitting toil,

who feels more self-respect and true manliness than many of
us with our family prestige, social position, and proud ancestral halls. After I had lived abroad for years, I returned a
broken-down young man, prematurely old, my constitution
a perfect wreck. A life of folly and dissipation was telling
fearfully upon me. My friends shrank from me in dismay. I
was sick nigh unto death, and had it not been for Marie's
care I am certain that I should have died. She followed me
down to the borders of the grave, and won me back to life
and health. I was slow in recovering and, during the time, I
had ample space for reflection, and the past unrolled itself
before me. I resolved, over the wreck and ruin of my past
life, to build a better and brighter future. Marie had a voice
of remarkable sweetness, although it lacked culture. Often
when I was nervous and restless I would have her sing some
of those weird and plaintive melodies which she had learned
from the plantation negroes. Sometimes I encouraged her to
talk, and I was surprised at the native vigor of her intellect.
By degrees I became acquainted with her history. She was
all alone in the world. She had no recollection of her father,
but remembered being torn from her mother while clinging
to her dress. The trader who bought her mother did not wish
to buy her. She remembered having a brother, with whom
she used to play, but she had been separated from him also,
and since then had lost all trace of them. After she was sold
from her mother she became the property of an excellent old
lady, who seems to have been very careful to imbue her mind
with good principles; a woman who loved purity, not only
for her own daughters, but also for the defenseless girls in
her home. I believe it was the lady's intention to have freed
Marie at her death, but she died suddenly, and, the estate
being involved, she was sold with it and fell into the hands
of my agent. I became deeply interested in her when I heard
her story, and began to pity her."

"And I suppose love sprang from pity."

"I not only pitied her, but I learned to respect her. I had
met with beautiful women in the halls of wealth and fashion,

both at home and abroad, but there was something in her different from all my experience of womanhood."

"I should think so," said Lorraine, with a sneer; "but I should like to know what it was."

"It was something such as I have seen in old cathedrals, lighting up the beauty of a saintly face. A light which the poet tells was never seen on land or sea. I thought of this beautiful and defenseless girl adrift in the power of a reckless man, who, with all the advantages of wealth and education, had trailed his manhood in the dust, and she, with simple, childlike faith in the Unseen, seemed to be so good and pure that she commanded my respect and won my heart. In her presence every base and unholy passion died, subdued by the supremacy of her virtue."

"Why, Eugene, what has come over you? Talking of the virtue of these quadroon girls! You have lived so long in the North and abroad, that you seem to have lost the cue of our Southern life. Don't you know that these beautiful girls have been the curse of our homes? You have no idea of the hearts which are wrung by their presence."

"But, Alfred, suppose it is so. Are they to blame for it? What can any woman do when she is placed in the hands of an irresponsible master; when she knows that resistance is vain? Yes, Alfred, I agree with you, these women are the bane of our Southern civilization; but they are the victims and we are the criminals."

"I think from the airs that some of them put on when they get a chance, that they are very willing victims."

"So much the worse for our institution. If it is cruel to debase a hapless victim, it is an increase of cruelty to make her contented with her degradation. Let me tell you, Alf, you cannot wrong or degrade a woman without wronging or degrading yourself."

"What is the matter with you, Eugene? Are you thinking of taking priest's orders?"

"No, Alf," said Eugene, rising and rapidly pacing the floor, "you may defend the system as much as you please, but you cannot deny that the circumstances it creates, and the temptation it affords, are sapping our strength and undermining our character."

"That may be true," said Lorraine, somewhat irritably, "but you had better be careful how you air your Northern notions in public."

"Why so?"

"Because public opinion is too sensitive to tolerate any such discussions."

"And is not that a proof that we are at fault with respect to our institutions?"

"I don't know. I only know we are living in the midst of a magazine of powder, and it is not safe to enter it with a lighted candle."

"Let me proceed with my story," continued Eugene. "During the long months in which I was convalescing, I was left almost entirely to the companionship of Marie. In my library I found a Bible, which I began to read from curiosity, but my curiosity deepened into interest when I saw the rapt expression on Marie's face. I saw in it a loving response to sentiments to which I was a stranger. In the meantime my conscience was awakened, and I scorned to take advantage of her defenselessness. I felt that I owed my life to her faithful care, and I resolved to take her North, manumit, educate, and marry her. I sent her to a Northern academy, but as soon as some of the pupils found that she was colored, objections were raised, and the principal was compelled to dismiss her. During my search for a school I heard of one where three girls of mixed blood were pursuing their studies, every one of whom would have been ignominiously dismissed had their connection with the negro race been known. But I determined to run no risks. I found a school where her connection with the negro race would be no bar to her advancement. She graduates next week, and I intend to marry her before I return home. She was faithful when others were faithless, stood by me when others deserted me to die in loneliness and neglect, and now I am about to reward her care with all the love and devotion it is in my power to bestow. That is why I am about to marry my faithful and devoted nurse, who snatched me from the jaws of death. Now that I have told you my story, what say you?"

"Madness and folly inconceivable!" exclaimed Lorraine.

"What to you is madness and folly is perfect sanity with me. After all, Alf, is there not an amount of unreason in our prejudices?"

"That may be true; but I wasn't reasoned into it, and I do not expect to be reasoned out of it."

"Will you accompany me North?"

"No; except to put you in an insane asylum. You are the greatest crank out," said Lorraine, thoroughly disgusted.

"No, thank you; I'm all right. I expect to start North to-morrow. You had better come and go."

"I would rather follow you to your grave," replied Lorraine, hotly, while an expression of ineffable scorn passed over his cold, proud face.

CHAPTER X

Shadows in the Home

On the next morning after this conversation Leroy left for the North, to attend the commencement and witness the graduation of his ward. Arriving in Ohio, he immediately repaired to the academy and inquired for the principal. He was shown into the reception-room, and in a few moments the principal entered.

"Good morning," said Leroy, rising and advancing towards him; "how is my ward this morning?"

"She is well, and has been expecting you. I am glad you came in time for the commencement. She stands among the foremost in her class."

"I am glad to hear it. Will you send her this?" said Leroy, handing the principal a card. The principal took the card and immediately left the room.

Very soon Leroy heard a light step, and looking up he saw a radiantly beautiful woman approaching him.

"Good morning, Marie," he said, greeting her cordially, and gazing upon her with unfeigned admiration. "You are looking very handsome this morning."

"Do you think so?" she asked, smiling and blushing. "I am glad you are not disappointed; that you do not feel your money has been spent in vain."

"Oh, no, what I have spent on your education has been the best investment I ever made."

"I hope," said Marie, "you may always find it so. But Mas——"

"Hush!" said Leroy, laying his hand playfully on her lips; "you are free. I don't want the dialect of slavery to linger on your lips. You must not call me that name again."

"Why not?"

"Because I have a nearer and dearer one by which I wish to be called."

Leroy drew her nearer, and whispered in her ear a single word. She started, trembled with emotion, grew pale, and blushed painfully. An awkward silence ensued, when Leroy, pressing her hand, exclaimed: "This is the hand that plucked me from the grave, and I am going to retain it as mine; mine to guard with my care until death us do part."

Leroy looked earnestly into her eyes, which fell beneath his ardent gaze. With admirable self-control, while a great joy was thrilling her heart, she bowed her beautiful head and softly repeated, "Until death us do part."

Leroy knew Southern society too well to expect it to condone his offense against its social customs, or give the least recognition to his wife, however cultured, refined, and charming she might be, if it were known that she had the least infusion of negro blood in her veins. But he was brave enough to face the consequences of his alliance, and marry the woman who was the choice of his heart, and on whom his affections were centred.

After Leroy had left the room, Marie sat awhile thinking of the wonderful change that had come over her. Instead of being a lonely slave girl, with the fatal dower of beauty, liable to be bought and sold, exchanged, and bartered, she was to be the wife of a wealthy planter; a man in whose honor she could confide, and on whose love she could lean.

Very interesting and pleasant were the commencement exercises in which Marie bore an important part. To enlist sympathy for her enslaved race, and appear to advantage before Leroy, had aroused all of her energies. The stimulus of hope, the manly love which was environing her life, brightened her eye and lit up the wonderful beauty of her countenance. During her stay in the North she had constantly been brought in contact with anti-slavery people. She was not aware that there was so much kindness among the white people of the country until she had tested it in the North. From the anti-slavery people in private life she had learned some of the noblest lessons of freedom and justice, and had become imbued with their sentiments. Her theme was "American Civilization, its Lights and Shadows."

Graphically she portrayed the lights, faithfully she showed the shadows of our American civilization. Earnestly and feelingly she spoke of the blind Sampson in our land, who might yet shake the pillars of our great Commonwealth. Leroy listened attentively. At times a shadow of annoyance would overspread his face, but it was soon lost in the admiration her earnestness and zeal inspired. Like Esther pleading for the lives of her people in the Oriental courts of a despotic king, she stood before the audience, pleading for those whose lips were sealed, but whose condition appealed to the mercy and justice of the Nation. Strong men wiped the moisture from their eyes, and women's hearts throbbed in unison with the strong, brave words that were uttered in behalf of freedom for all and chains for none. Generous applause was freely bestowed, and beautiful bouquets were showered upon her. When it was known that she was to be the wife of her guardian, warm congratulations were given, and earnest hopes expressed for the welfare of the lonely girl, who, nearly all her life, had been deprived of a parent's love and care. On the eve of starting South Leroy procured a license, and united his destiny with the young lady whose devotion in the darkest hour had won his love and gratitude.

In a few days Marie returned as mistress to the plantation from which she had gone as a slave. But as unholy alliances were common in those days between masters and slaves, no one took especial notice that Marie shared Leroy's life as mistress of his home, and that the family silver and jewelry were in her possession. But Leroy, happy in his choice, attended to the interests of his plantation, and found companionship in his books and in the society of his wife. A few male companions visited him occasionally, admired the magnificent beauty of his wife, shook their heads, and spoke of him as being very eccentric, but thought his marriage the great mistake of his life. But none of his female friends ever entered his doors, when it became known that Marie held the position of mistress of his mansion, and presided at his table. But she, sheltered in the warm clasp of loving arms, found her life like a joyous dream.

Into that quiet and beautiful home three children were born, unconscious of the doom suspended over their heads.

"Oh, how glad I am," Marie would often say, "that these children are free. I could never understand how a cultured white man could have his own children enslaved. I can understand how savages, fighting with each other, could doom their vanquished foes to slavery, but it has always been a puzzle to me how a civilized man could drag his own children, bone of his bone, flesh of his flesh, down to the position of social outcasts, abject slaves, and political pariahs."

"But, Marie," said Eugene, "all men do not treat their illegitimate children in the manner you describe. The last time I was in New Orleans I met Henri Augustine at the depot, with two beautiful young girls. At first I thought that they were his own children, they resembled him so closely. But afterwards I noticed that they addressed him as 'Mister.' Before we parted he told me that his wife had taken such a dislike to their mother that she could not bear to see them on the place. At last, weary of her dissatisfaction, he had promised to bring them to New Orleans and sell them. Instead, he was going to Ohio to give them their freedom, and make provision for their future."

"What a wrong!" said Marie.

"Who was wronged?" said Leroy, in astonishment.

"Everyone in the whole transaction," answered Marie. "Your friend wronged himself by sinning against his own soul. He wronged his wife by arousing her hatred and jealousy through his unfaithfulness. He wronged those children by giving them the *status* of slaves and outcasts. He wronged their mother by imposing upon her the burdens and cares of maternity without the rights and privileges of a wife. He made her crown of motherhood a circlet of shame. Under other circumstances she might have been an honored wife and happy mother. And I do think such men wrong their own legitimate children by transmitting to them a weakened moral fibre."

"Oh, Marie, you have such an uncomfortable way of putting things. You make me feel that we have done those things which we ought not to have done, and have left undone those things which we ought to have done."

"If it annoys you," said Marie, "I will stop talking."

"Oh, no, go on," said Leroy, carelessly; and then he continued more thoughtfully, "I know a number of men who have sent such children North, and manumitted, educated, and left them valuable legacies. We are all liable to err, and, having done wrong, all we can do is to make reparation."

"My dear husband, this is a wrong where reparation is impossible. Neither wealth nor education can repair the wrong of a dishonored birth. There are a number of slaves in this section who are servants to their own brothers and sisters; whose fathers have robbed them not simply of liberty but of the right of being well born. Do you think these things will last forever?"

"I suppose not. There are some prophets of evil who tell us that the Union is going to dissolve. But I know it would puzzle their brains to tell where the crack will begin. I reckon we'll continue to jog along as usual. 'Cotton fights, and cotton conquers for American slavery.' "

Even while Leroy dreamed of safety the earthquake was cradling its fire; the ground was growing hollow beneath his tread; but his ear was too dull to catch the sound; his vision too blurred to read the signs of the times.

"Marie," said Leroy, taking up the thread of the discourse, "slavery is a sword that cuts both ways. If it wrongs the negro, it also curses the white man. But we are in it, and what can we do?"

"Get out of it as quickly as possible."

"That is easier said than done. I would willingly free every slave on my plantation if I could do so without expatriating them. Some of them have wives and children on other plantations, and to free them is to separate them from their kith and kin. To let them remain here as a free people is out of the question. My hands are tied by law and custom."

"Who tied them?" asked Marie.

"A public opinion, whose meshes I cannot break. If the negro is the thrall of his master, we are just as much the thralls of public opinion."

"Why do you not battle against public opinion, if you think it is wrong?"

"Because I have neither the courage of a martyr, nor the faith of a saint; and so I drift along, trying to make the condition of our slaves as comfortable as I possibly can. I believe there are slaves on this plantation whom the most flattering offers of freedom would not entice away."

"I do not think," said Marie, "that some of you planters understand your own slaves. Lying is said to be the vice of slaves. The more intelligent of them have so learned to veil their feelings that you do not see the undercurrent of discontent beneath their apparent good humor and jollity. The more discontented they are, the more I respect them. To me a contented slave is an abject creature. I hope that I shall see the day when there will not be a slave in the land. I hate the whole thing from the bottom of my heart."

"Marie, your Northern education has unfitted you for Southern life. You are free, yourself, and so are our children. Why not let well enough alone?"

"Because I love liberty, not only for myself but for every human being. Think how dear these children are to me; and then for the thought to be forever haunting me, that if you were dead they could be turned out of doors and divided among your relatives. I sometimes lie awake at night thinking of how there might be a screw loose somewhere, and, after all, the children and I might be reduced to slavery."

"Marie, what in the world is the matter with you? Have you had a presentiment of my death, or, as Uncle Jack says, 'hab you seed it in a vision?' "

"No, but I have had such sad forebodings that they almost set me wild. One night I dreamt that you were dead; that the lawyers entered the house, seized our property, and remanded us to slavery. I never can be satisfied in the South with such a possibility hanging over my head."

"Marie, dear, you are growing nervous. Your imagination is too active. You are left too much alone on this plantation. I hope that for your own and the children's sake I will be enabled to arrange our affairs so as to find a home for you where you will not be doomed to the social isolation and ostracism that surround you here."

"I don't mind the isolation for myself, but the children. You have enjoyed silence on me with respect to their connection with the negro race, but I do not think we can conceal it from them very long. It will not be long before Iola will notice the offishness of girls of her own age, and the scornful glances which, even now, I think, are leveled at her. Yesterday Harry came crying to me, and told me that one of the neighbor's boys had called him 'nigger.' "

A shadow flitted over Leroy's face, as he answered, somewhat soberly, "Oh, Marie, do not meet trouble half way. I have manumitted you, and the children will follow your condition. I have made you all legatees of my will. Except my cousin, Alfred Lorraine, I have only distant relatives, whom I scarcely know and who hardly know me."

"Your cousin Lorraine? Are you sure our interests would be safe in his hands?"

"I think so; I don't think Alfred would do anything dishonorable."

"He might not with his equals. But how many men would be bound by a sense of honor where the rights of a colored woman are in question? Your cousin was bitterly opposed to our marriage, and I would not trust any important interests in his hands. I do hope that in providing for our future you will make assurance doubly sure."

"I certainly will, and all that human foresight can do shall be done for you and our children."

"Oh," said Marie, pressing to her heart a beautiful child of six summers, "I think it would almost make me turn over in my grave to know that every grace and charm which this child possesses would only be so much added to her value as an article of merchandise."

As Marie released the child from her arms she looked wonderingly into her mother's face and clung closely to her, as if to find refuge from some unseen evil. Leroy noticed this, and sighed unconsciously, as an expression of pain flitted over his face.

"Now, Marie," he continued, "stop tormenting yourself with useless fears. Although, with all her faults, I still love the South, I will make arrangements either to live North or go to France. There life will be brighter for us all. Now, Marie, seat yourself at the piano and sing:—

'Sing me the songs that to me were so dear,
    Long, long ago.
Sing me the songs I delighted to hear,
    Long, long ago.' "

As Marie sang the anxiety faded from her face, a sense of security stole over her, and she sat among her loved ones a happy wife and mother. What if no one recognized her on that lonely plantation! Her world was, nevertheless, there. The love and devotion of her husband brightened every avenue of her life, while her children filled her home with music, mirth, and sunshine.

Marie had undertaken their education, but she could not give them the culture which comes from the attrition of thought, and from contact with the ideas of others. Since her school-days she had read extensively and thought much, and in solitude her thoughts had ripened. But for her children there were no companions except the young slaves of the plantation, and she dreaded the effect of such intercourse upon their lives and characters.

Leroy had always been especially careful to conceal from his children the knowledge of their connection with the negro race. To Marie this silence was oppressive.

One day she said to him, "I see no other way of finishing the education of these children than by sending them to some Northern school."

"I have come," said Leroy, "to the same conclusion. We had better take Iola and Harry North and make arrangements for them to spend several years in being educated. Riches take wings to themselves and fly away, but a good education is an investment on which the law can place no attachment. As there is a possibility of their origin being discovered, I will find a teacher to whom I can confide our story, and upon whom I can enjoin secrecy. I want them well fitted for any emergency in life. When I discover for what they have the most aptitude I will give them especial training in that direction."

A troubled look passed over the face of Marie, as she hesitatingly said: "I am so afraid that you will regret our marriage when you fully realize the complications it brings."

"No, no," said Leroy, tenderly, "it is not that I regret our marriage, or feel the least disdain for our children on account of the blood in their veins; but I do not wish them to grow up under the contracting influence of this race prejudice. I do not wish them to feel that they have been born under a proscription from which no valor can redeem them, nor that any social advancement or individual development can wipe off the ban which clings to them. No, Marie, let them go North, learn all they can, aspire all they may. The painful knowledge will come all too soon. Do not forestall it. I want them simply to grow up as other children; not being patronized by friends nor disdained by foes."

"My dear husband, you may be perfectly right, but are you not preparing our children for a fearful awakening? Are you not acting on the plan, 'After me the deluge?' "

"Not at all, Marie. I want our children to grow up without having their self-respect crushed in the bud. You know that the North is not free from racial prejudice."

"I know it," said Marie, sadly, "and I think one of the great mistakes of our civilization is that which makes color, and not character, a social test."

"I think so, too," said Leroy. "The strongest men and women of a down-trodden race may bare their bosoms to an adverse fate and develop courage in the midst of opposition, but we have no right to subject our children to such crucial tests before their characters are formed. For years, when I lived abroad, I had an opportunity to see and hear of men of African descent who had distinguished themselves and obtained a recognition in European circles, which they never could have gained in this country. I now recall the name of Ira Aldridge, a colored man from New York City, who was covered with princely honors as a successful tragedian. Alexander Dumas was not forced to conceal his origin to succeed as a novelist. When I was in St. Petersburg I was shown the works of Alexander Sergevitch, a Russian poet, who was spoken of as the Byron of Russian literature, and reckoned one of the finest poets that Russia has produced in this century. He was also a prominent figure in fashionable society, and yet he was of African lineage. One of his paternal ancestors was a negro who had been ennobled by Peter the Great. I can't help contrasting the recognition which these men had received with the treatment which has been given to Frederick Douglass and other intelligent colored men in this country. With me the wonder is not that they have achieved so little, but that they have accomplished so much. No, Marie, we will have our children educated without being subjected to the depressing influences of caste feeling. Perhaps by the time their education is finished I will be ready to wind up my affairs and take them abroad, where merit and ability will give them entrance into the best circles of art, literature, and science."

After this conversation Leroy and his wife went North, and succeeded in finding a good school for their children. In a private interview he confided to the principal the story of the cross in their blood, and, finding him apparently free from racial prejudice, he gladly left the children in his care. Gracie, the youngest child, remained at home, and her mother spared no pains to fit her for the seminary against the time her sister should have finished her education.

CHAPTER XI

The Plague and the Law

Years passed, bringing no special change to the life of Leroy and his wife. Shut out from the busy world, its social cares and anxieties, Marie's life flowed peacefully on. Although removed by the protecting care of Leroy from the condition of servitude, she still retained a deep sympathy for the enslaved, and was ever ready to devise plans to ameliorate their condition.

Leroy, although in the midst of slavery, did not believe in the rightfulness of the institution. He was in favor of gradual emancipation, which would prepare both master and slave for a moral adaptation to the new conditions of freedom. While he was willing to have the old rivets taken out of slavery, politicians and planters were devising plans to put in new screws. He was desirous of having it ended in the States; they were clamorous to have it established in the Territories.

But so strong was the force of habit, combined with the feebleness of his moral resistance and the nature of his environment, that instead of being an athlete, armed for a glorious strife, he had learned to drift where he should have steered, to float with the current instead of nobly breasting the tide. He conducted his plantation with as much lenity as it was possible to infuse into a system darkened with the shadow of a million crimes.

Leroy had always been especially careful not to allow his

children to spend their vacations at home. He and Marie generally spent that time with them at some summer resort.

"I would like," said Marie, one day, "to have our children spend their vacations at home. Those summer resorts are pleasant, yet, after all, there is no place like home. But," and her voice became tremulous, "our children would now notice their social isolation and inquire the cause." A faint sigh arose to the lips of Leroy, as she added: "Man is a social being; I've known it to my sorrow."

There was a tone of sadness in Leroy's voice, as he replied: "Yes, Marie, let them stay North. We seem to be entering on a period fraught with great danger. I cannot help thinking and fearing that we are on the eve of a civil war."

"A civil war!" exclaimed Marie, with an air of astonishment. "A civil war about what?"

"Why, Marie, the thing looks to me so wild and foolish I hardly know how to explain. But some of our leading men have come to the conclusion that North and South had better separate, and instead of having one to have two independent governments. The spirit of secession is rampant in the land. I do not know what the result will be, and I fear it will bode no good to the country. Between the fire-eating Southerners and the meddling Abolitionists we are about to be plunged into a great deal of trouble. I fear there are breakers ahead. The South is dissatisfied with the state of public opinion in the North. We are realizing that we are two peoples in the midst of one nation. William H. Seward has proclaimed that the conflict between freedom and slavery is irrepressible, and that the country cannot remain half free and half slave."

"How will *you* go?" asked Marie.

"My heart is with the Union. I don't believe in secession. There has been no cause sufficient to justify a rupture. The North has met us time and again in the spirit of concession and compromise. When we wanted the continuance of the African slave trade the North conceded that we should have twenty years of slave-trading for the benefit of our plantations. When we wanted more territory she conceded to our desires and gave us land enough to carve out four States, and there yet remains enough for four more. When we wanted power to recapture our slaves when they fled North for refuge, Daniel Webster told Northerners to conquer their prejudices, and they gave us the whole Northern States as a hunting ground for our slaves. The Presidential chair has been filled the greater number of years by Southerners, and the majority of offices has been shared by our men. We wanted representation in Congress on a basis which would include our slaves, and the North, whose suffrage represents only men, gave us a three-fifths representation for our slaves, whom we count as property. I think the step will be suicidal. There are extremists in both sections, but I hope, between them both, wise counsels and measures will prevail."

Just then Alfred Lorraine was ushered into the room. Occasionally he visited Leroy, but he always came alone. His wife was the only daughter of an enterprising slavetrader, who had left her a large amount of property. Her social training was deficient, her education limited, but she was too proud of being a pure white woman to enter the home of Leroy, with Marie as its presiding genius. Lorraine tolerated Marie's presence as a necessary evil, while to her he always seemed like a presentiment of trouble. With his coming a shadow fell upon her home, hushing its music and darkening its sunshine. A sense of dread oppressed her. There came into her soul an intuitive feeling that somehow his coming was fraught with danger. When not peering around she would often catch his eyes bent on her with a baleful expression.

Leroy and his cousin immediately fell into a discussion on the condition of the country. Lorraine was a rank Secessionist, ready to adopt the most extreme measures of the leaders of the movement, even to the reopening of the slave trade. Leroy thought a dissolution of the Union would involve a fearful expenditure of blood and treasure for which, before the eyes of the world, there could be no justification. The debate lasted late into the night, leaving both Lorraine and

Leroy just as set in their opinions as they were before they began. Marie listened attentively awhile, then excused herself and withdrew.

After Lorraine had gone Marie said: "There is something about your cousin that fills me with nameless dread. I always feel when he enters the room as if some one were walking over my grave. I do wish he would stay at home."

"I wish so, too, since he disturbs you. But, Marie, you are growing nervous. How cold your hands are. Don't you feel well?"

"Oh, yes; I am only a little faint. I wish he would never come. But, as he does, I must make the best of it."

"Yes, Marie, treat him well for my sake. He is the only relative I have who ever darkens our doors."

"I have no faith in his friendship for either myself or my children. I feel that while he makes himself agreeable to you he hates me from the bottom of his heart, and would do anything to get me out of the way. Oh, I am so glad I am your lawful wife, and that you married me before you brought me back to this State! I believe that if you were gone he wouldn't have the least scruple against trying to prove our marriage invalid and remanding us to slavery."

Leroy looked anxiously and soberly at his wife, and said: "Marie, I do not think so. Your life is too lonely here. Write your orders to New Orleans, get what you need for the journey, and let us spend the summer somewhere in the North."

Just then Marie's attention was drawn to some household matters, and it was a short time before she returned.

"Tom," continued Leroy, "has just brought the mail, and here is a letter from Iola."

Marie noticed that he looked quite sober as he read, and that an expression of vexation was lingering on his lips.

"What is the matter?" asked Marie.

"Nothing much; only a tempest in a teapot. The presence of a colored girl in Mr. Galen's school has caused a breeze of excitement. You know Mr. Galen is quite an Abolitionist, and, being true to his principles, he could not consistently refuse when a colored woman applied for her daughter's admission. Of course, when he took her he was compelled to treat her as any other pupil. In so doing he has given mortal offense to the mother of two Southern boys. She has threatened to take them away if the colored girl remains."

"What will he do about it?" asked Marie, thoughtfully.

"Oh, it is a bitter pill, but I think he will have to swallow it. He is between two fires. He cannot dismiss her from the school and be true to his Abolition principles; yet if he retains her he will lose his Southern customers, and I know he cannot afford to do that."

"What does Iola say?"

"He has found another boarding place for her, but she is to remain in the school. He had to throw that sop to the whale."

"Does she take sides against the girl?"

"No, I don't think she does. She says she feels sorry for her, and that she would hate to be colored. 'It is so hard to be looked down on for what one can't help.' "

"Poor child! I wish we could leave the country. I never would consent to her marrying any one without first revealing to him her connection with the negro race. This is a subject on which I am not willing to run any risks."

"My dear Marie, when you shall have read Iola's letter you will see it is more than a figment of my imagination that has made me so loth to have our children know the paralyzing power of caste."

Leroy, always liberal with his wife and children, spared neither pains nor expense to have them prepared for their summer outing. Iola was to graduate in a few days. Harry was attending a school in the State of Maine, and his father had written to him, apprising him of his intention to come North that season. In a few days Leroy and his wife started North, but before they reached Vicksburg they were met by the intelligence that the yellow fever was spreading in the Delta, and that pestilence was breathing its bane upon the morning air and distilling its poison upon the midnight dews.

"Let us return home," said Marie.

"It is useless," answered Leroy. "It is nearly two days since we left home. The fever is spreading south of us with fearful rapidity. To return home is to walk into the jaws of death. It was my intention to have stopped at Vicksburg, but now I will go on as soon as I can make the connections."

Early next morning Leroy and his wife started again on their journey. The cars were filled with terror-stricken people who were fleeing from death, when death was everywhere. They fled from the city only to meet the dreaded apparition in the country. As they journeyed on Leroy grew restless and feverish. He tried to brace himself against the infection which was creeping slowly but insidiously into his life, dulling his brain, fevering his blood, and prostrating his strength. But vain were all his efforts. He had no armor strong enough to repel the invasion of death. They stopped at a small town on the way and obtained the best medical skill and most careful nursing, but neither skill nor art availed. On the third day death claimed Leroy as a victim, and Marie wept in hopeless agony over the grave of her devoted husband, whose sad lot it was to die from home and be buried among strangers.

But before he died he placed his will in Marie's hands, saying: "I have left you well provided for. Kiss the children for me and bid them good-bye."

He tried to say a parting word to Gracie, but his voice failed, and he fainted into the stillness of death. A mortal paleness overspread his countenance, on which had already gathered the shadows that never deceive. In speechless agony Marie held his hand until it released its pressure in death, and then she stood alone beside her dead, with all the bright sunshine of her life fading into the shadows of the grave. Heart-broken and full of fearful forebodings, Marie left her cherished dead in the quiet village of H—— and returned to her death-darkened home.

It was a lovely day in June, birds were singing their sweetest songs, flowers were breathing their fragrance on the air, when

Mam Liza, sitting at her cabin-door, talking with some of the house servants, saw a carriage approaching, and wondered who was coming.

"I wonder," she said, excitedly, "whose comin' to de house when de folks is done gone."

But her surprise was soon changed to painful amazement, when she saw Marie, robed in black, alighting from the carriage, and holding Gracie by the hand. She caught sight of the drooping head and grief-stricken face, and rushed to her, exclaiming:—

"Whar's Marse Eugene?"

"Dead," said Marie, falling into Mammy Liza's arms, sobbing out, "dead! *he died* of yellow fever."

A wild burst of sorrow came from the lips of the servants, who had drawn near.

"Where is he?" said Mam Liza, speaking like one suddenly bewildered.

"He is buried in H——. I could not bring him home," said Marie.

"My pore baby," said Mam Liza, with broken sobs. "I'se drefful sorry. My heart's most broke into two." Then, controlling herself, she dismissed the servants who stood around, weeping, and led Marie to her room.

"Come, honey, lie down an' lem'me git yer a cup ob tea."

"Oh, no; I don't want anything," said Marie, wringing her hands in bitter agony.

"Oh, honey," said Mam Liza, "yer mustn't gib up. Yer knows whar to put yer trus'. Yer can't lean on de arm of flesh in dis tryin' time." Kneeling by the side of her mistress she breathed out a prayer full of tenderness, hope, and trust.

Marie grew calmer. It seemed as if that earnest, trustful prayer had breathed into her soul a feeling of resignation.

Gracie stood wonderingly by, vainly trying to comprehend the great sorrow which was overwhelming the life of her mother.

After the first great burst of sorrow was over, Marie sat down to her desk and wrote a letter to Iola, informing her

of her father's death. By the time she had finished it she
grew dizzy and faint, and fell into a swoon. Mammy Liza
tenderly laid her on the bed, and helped restore her to
consciousness.

Lorraine, having heard of his cousin's death, came immediately to see Marie. She was too ill to have an interview
with him, but he picked up the letter she had written and
obtained Iola's address.

Lorraine made a careful investigation of the case, to ascertain whether Marie's marriage was valid. To his delight
he found there was a flaw in the marriage and an informal-
ity in the manumission. He then determined to invalidate
Marie's claim, and divide the inheritance among Leroy's
white relations. In a short time strangers, distant relatives of
her husband, became frequent visitors at the plantation, and
made themselves offensively familiar. At length the dreadful
storm burst.

Alfred Lorraine entered suit for his cousin's estate, and for
the remanding of his wife and children to slavery. In a
short time he came armed with legal authority, and said to
Marie:—

"I have come to take possession of these premises."

"By what authority?" she gasped, turning deathly pale. He
hesitated a moment, as if his words were arrested by a sense
of shame.

"By what authority?" she again demanded.

"By the authority of the law," answered Lorraine, "which
has decided that Leroy's legal heirs are his white blood relations, and that your marriage is null and void."

"But," exclaimed Marie, "I have our marriage certificate.
I was Leroy's lawful wife."

"Your marriage certificate is not worth the paper it is written on."

"Oh, you must be jesting, cruelly jesting. It can't be so."

"Yes; it is so. Judge Starkins has decided that your manumission is unlawful; your marriage a bad precedent, and

inimical to the welfare of society; and that you and your children are remanded to slavery."

Marie stood as one petrified. She seemed a statue of fear and despair. She tried to speak, reached out her hand as if she were groping in the dark, turned pale as death as if all the blood in her veins had receded to her heart, and, with one heart-rending cry of bitter agony, she fell senseless to the floor. Her servants, to whom she had been so kind in her days of prosperity, bent pityingly over her, chafed her cold hands, and did what they could to restore her to consciousness. For awhile she was stricken with brain fever, and her life seemed trembling on its frailest cord.

Gracie was like one perfectly dazed. When not watching by her mother's bedside she wandered aimlessly about the house, growing thinner day by day. A slow fever was consuming her life. Faithfully and carefully Mammy Liza watched over her, and did all she could to bring smiles to her lips and light to her fading eyes, but all in vain. Her only interest in life was to sit where she could watch her mother as she tossed to and fro in delirium, and to wonder what had brought the change in her once happy home. Finally she, too, was stricken with brain fever, which intervened as a mercy between her and the great sorrow that was overshadowing her young life. Tears would fill the servants' eyes as they saw the dear child drifting from them like a lovely vision, too bright for earth's dull cares and weary, wasting pain.

CHAPTER XII

School-Girl Notions

During Iola's stay in the North she found a strong tide of opposition against slavery. Arguments against the institution had entered the Church and made legislative halls the arenas of fierce debate. The subject had become part of the social converse of the fireside, and had enlisted the best brain and heart of the country. Anti-slavery discussions were pervading the strongest literature and claiming a place on the most popular platforms.

Iola, being a Southern girl and a slave-holder's daughter, always defended slavery when it was under discussion.

"Slavery can't be wrong," she would say, "for my father is a slave-holder, and my mother is as good to our servants as she can be. My father often tells her that she spoils them, and lets them run over her. I never saw my father strike one of them. I love my mammy as much as I do my own mother, and I believe she loves us just as if we were her own children. When we are sick I am sure that she could not do anything more for us than she does."

"But, Iola," responded one of her school friends, "after all, they are not free. Would you be satisfied to have the most beautiful home, the costliest jewels, or the most elegant wardrobe if you were a slave?"

"Oh, the cases are not parallel. Our slaves do not want their freedom. They would not take it if we gave it to them."

"That is not the case with them all. My father has seen men who have encountered almost incredible hardships to get their freedom. Iola, did you ever attend an anti-slavery meeting?"

"No; I don't think these Abolitionists have any right to meddle in our affairs. I believe they are prejudiced against us, and want to get our property. I read about them in the papers when I was at home. I don't want to hear my part of the country run down. My father says the slaves would be very well contented if no one put wrong notions in their heads."

"I don't know," was the response of her friend, "but I do not think that that slave mother who took her four children, crossed the Ohio River on the ice, killed one of the children and attempted the lives of the other two, was a contented slave. And that other one, who, running away and finding herself pursued, threw herself over the Long Bridge into the Potomac, was evidently not satisfied. I do not think the numbers who are coming North on the Underground Railroad can be very contented. It is not natural for people to run away from happiness, and if they are so happy and contented, why did Congress pass the Fugitive Slave Bill?"

"Well, I don't think," answered Iola, "any of our slaves would run away. I know mamma don't like slavery very much. I have often heard her say that she hoped the time would come when there would not be a slave in the land. My father does not think as she does. He thinks slavery is not wrong if you treat them well and don't sell them from their families. I intend, after I have graduated, to persuade pa to buy a house in New Orleans, and spend the winter there. You know this will be my first season out, and I hope that you will come and spend the winter with me. We will have such gay times, and you will so fall in love with our sunny South that you will never want to come back to shiver amid the snows and cold of the North. I think one winter in the South would cure you of your Abolitionism."

"Have you seen her yet?"

This question was asked by Louis Bastine, an attorney who had come North in the interests of Lorraine. The scene was the New England village where Mr. Galen's academy was located, and which Iola was attending. This question was addressed to Camille Lecroix, Bastine's intimate friend, who had lately come North. He was the son of a planter who lived near Leroy's plantation, and was familiar with Iola's family history. Since his arrival North, Bastine had met him and communicated to him his intentions.

"Yes; just caught a glimpse of her this morning as she was going down the street," was Camille's reply.

"She is a most beautiful creature," said Louis Bastine. "She has the proud poise of Leroy, the most splendid eyes I ever saw in a woman's head, lovely complexion, and a glorious wealth of hair. She would bring $2000 any day in a New Orleans market."

"I always feel sorry," said Camille, "when I see one of those Creole girls brought to the auction block. I have known fathers who were deeply devoted to their daughters, but who through some reverse of fortune were forced to part with them, and I always think the blow has been equally terrible on both sides. I had a friend who had two beautiful daughters whom he had educated in the North. They were cultured, and really belles in society. They were entirely ignorant of their lineage, but when their father died it was discovered that their mother had been a slave. It was a fearful blow. They would have faced poverty, but the knowledge of their tainted blood was more than they could bear."

"What became of them?"

"They both died, poor girls. I believe they were as much killed by the blow as if they had been shot. To tell you the truth, Bastine, I feel sorry for this girl. I don't believe she has the least idea of her negro blood."

"No, Leroy has been careful to conceal it from her," replied Bastine.

"Is that so?" queried Camille. "Then he has made a great mistake."

"I can't help that," said Bastine; "business is business."

"How can you get her away?" asked Camille. "You will

have to be very cautious, because if these pesky Abolitionists get an inkling of what you're doing they will balk your game double quick. And when you come to look at it, isn't it a shame to attempt to reduce that girl to slavery? She is just as white as we are, as good as any girl in the land, and better educated than thousands of white girls. A girl with her apparent refinement and magnificent beauty, were it not for the cross in her blood, I would be proud to introduce to our set. She would be the sensation of the season. I believe today it would be easier for me to go to the slums and take a young girl from there, and have her introduced as my wife, then to have society condone the offense if I married that lovely girl. There is not a social circle in the South that would not take it as a gross insult to have her introduced into it."

"Well," said Bastine, "my plan is settled. Leroy has never allowed her to spend her vacations at home. I understand she is now very anxious to get home, and, as Lorraine's attorney, I have come on his account to take her home."

"How will you do it?"

"I shall tell her her father is dangerously ill, and desires her to come as quickly as possible."

"And what then?"

"Have her inventoried with the rest of the property."

"Don't she know that her father is dead?"

"I think not," said Bastine. "She is not in mourning, but appeared very light-hearted this morning, laughing and talking with two other girls. I was struck with her great beauty, and asked a gentleman who she was. He said, 'Miss Leroy, of Mississippi.' I think Lorraine has managed the affair so as to keep her in perfect ignorance of her father's death. I don't like the job, but I never let sentiment interfere with my work."

Poor Iola! When she said slavery was not a bad thing, little did she think that she was destined to drink to its bitter dregs the cup she was so ready to press to the lips of others.

"How do you think she will take to her situation?" asked Camille.

"O, I guess," said Bastine, "she will sulk and take it pretty hard at first; but if she is managed right she will soon get over it. Give her plenty of jewelry, fine clothes, and an easy time."

"All this business must be conducted with the utmost secrecy and speed. Her mother could not have written to her, for she has been suffering with brain fever and nervous prostration since Leroy's death. Lorraine knows her market value too well, and is too shrewd to let so much property pass out of his hands without making an effort to retain it."

"Has she any brothers or sisters?"

"Yes, a brother," replied Bastine; "but he is at another school, and I have no orders from Lorraine in reference to him. If I can get the girl I am willing to let well enough alone. I dread the interview with the principal more than anything else. I am afraid he will hem and haw, and have his doubts. Perhaps, when he sees my letters and hears my story, I can pull the wool over his eyes."

"But, Louis, this is a pitiful piece of business. I should hate to be engaged in it."

A deep flush of shame overspread for a moment the face of Lorraine's attorney, as he replied: "I don't like the job, but I have undertaken it, and must go through with it."

"I see no '*must*' about it. Were I in your place I would wash my hands of the whole business."

"I can't afford it," was Bastine's hard, business-like reply. On the next morning after this conversation between these two young men, Louis Bastine presented himself to the principal of the academy, with the request that Iola be permitted to leave immediately to attend the sick-bed of her father, who was dangerously ill. The principal hesitated, but while he was deliberating, a telegram, purporting to come from Iola's mother, summoned Iola to her father's bedside without delay. The principal, set at rest in regard to the truthfulness of the dispatch, not only permitted but expedited her departure.

Iola and Bastine took the earliest train, and traveled without pausing until they reached a large hotel in a Southern city. There they were obliged to wait a few hours until they could resume their journey, the train having failed to make connection. Iola sat in a large, lonely parlor, waiting for the servant to show her to a private room. She had never known a great sorrow. Never before had the shadows of death mingled with the sunshine of her life.

Anxious, travel-worn, and heavy-hearted, she sat in an easy chair, with nothing to divert her from the grief and anxiety which rendered every delay a source of painful anxiety.

"Oh, I hope that he will be alive and growing better!" was the thought which kept constantly revolving in her mind, until she fell asleep. In her dreams she was at home, encircled in the warm clasp of her father's arms, feeling her mother's kisses lingering on her lips, and hearing the joyous greetings of the servants and Mammy Liza's glad welcome as she folded her to her heart. From this dream of bliss she was awakened by a burning kiss pressed on her lips, and a strong arm encircling her. Gazing around and taking in the whole situation, she sprang from her seat, her eyes flashing with rage and scorn, her face flushed to the roots of her hair, her voice shaken with excitement, and every nerve trembling with angry emotion.

"How dare you do such a thing! Don't you know if my father were here he would crush you to the earth?"

"Not so fast, my lovely tigress," said Bastine, "your father knew what he was doing when he placed you in my charge."

"My father made a great mistake, if he thought he had put me in charge of a gentleman."

"I am your guardian for the present," replied Bastine. "I am to see you safe home, and then my commission ends."

"I wish it were ended now," she exclaimed, trembling

with anger and mortification. Her voice was choked by emotion, and broken by smothered sobs. Louis Bastine thought to himself, "she is a real spitfire, but beautiful even in her wrath."

During the rest of her journey Iola preserved a most freezing reserve towards Bastine. At length the journey was ended. Pale and anxious she rode up the avenue which led to her home.

A strange silence pervaded the place. The servants moved sadly from place to place, and spoke in subdued tones. The windows were heavily draped with crape, and a funeral air pervaded the house.

Mammy Liza met her at the door, and, with streaming eyes and convulsive sobs, folded her to her heart, as Iola exclaimed, in tones of hopeless anguish:—

"Oh, papa's dead!"

"Oh, my pore baby!" said mammy, "ain't you hearn tell 'bout it? Yore par's dead, an' your mar's bin drefful sick. She's better now."

Mam Liza stepped lightly into Mrs. Leroy's room, and gently apprised her of Iola's arrival. In a darkened room lay the stricken mother, almost distracted by her late bereavement.

"Oh, Iola," she exclaimed, as her daughter entered, "is this you? I am so sorry you came."

Then, burying her head in Iola's bosom, she wept convulsively. "Much as I love you," she continued, between her sobs, "and much as I longed to see you, I am sorry you came."

"Why, mother," replied Iola, astonished, "I received your telegram last Wednesday, and I took the earliest train I could get."

"My dear child, I never sent you a telegram. It was a trick to bring you down South and reduce you to slavery."

Iola eyed her mother curiously. What did she mean? Had grief dethroned her reason? Yet her eye was clear, her manner perfectly rational.

Marie saw the astounded look on Iola's face, and nerving

herself to the task, said: "Iola, I must tell you what your father always enjoined me to be silent about. I did not think it was the wisest thing, but I yielded to his desires. I have negro blood in my veins. I was your father's slave before I married him. His relatives have set aside his will. The courts have declared our marriage null and void and my manumission illegal, and we are all to be remanded to slavery."

An expression of horror and anguish swept over Iola's face, and, turning deathly pale, she exclaimed, "Oh, mother, it can't be so! you must be dreaming!"

"No, my child; it is a terrible reality."

Almost wild with agony, Iola paced the floor, as the fearful truth broke in crushing anguish upon her mind. Then bursting into a paroxysm of tears succeeded by peals of hysterical laughter, said:—

"I used to say that slavery is right. I didn't know what I was talking about." Then growing calmer, she said, "Mother, who is at the bottom of this downright robbery?"

"Alfred Lorraine; I have always dreaded that man, and what I feared has come to pass. Your father had faith in him; I never had."

"But, mother, could we not contest his claim. You have your marriage certificate and papa's will."

"Yes, my dear child, but Judge Starkins has decided that we have no standing in the court, and no testimony according to law."

"Oh, mother, what can I do?"

"Nothing, my child, unless you can escape to the North."

"And leave you?"

"Yes."

"Mother, I will never desert you in your hour of trial. But can nothing be done? Had father no friends who would assist us?"

"None that I know of. I do not think he had an acquaintance who approved of our marriage. The neighboring planters have stood so aloof from me that I do not know where to turn for either help or sympathy. I believe it was Lorraine who sent the telegram. I wrote to you as soon as I could after your father's death, but fainted just as I finished directing the letter. I do not think he knows where your brother is, and, if possible, he must not know. If you can by any means, *do* send a letter to Harry and warn him not to attempt to come home. I don't know how you will succeed, for Lorraine has us all under surveillance. But it is according to law.''

"What law, mother?"

"The law of the strong against the weak.''

"Oh, mother, it seems like a dreadful dream, a fearful nightmare! But I cannot shake it off. Where is Gracie?"

"The dear child has been running down ever since her papa's death. She clung to me night and day while I had the brain fever, and could not be persuaded to leave me. She hardly ate anything for more than a week. She has been dangerously ill for several days, and the doctor says she cannot live. The fever has exhausted all her rallying power, and yet, dear as she is to me, I would rather consign her to the deepest grave than see her forced to be a slave.''

"So would I. I wish I could die myself.''

"Oh, Iola, do not talk so. Strive to be a Christian, to have faith in the darkest hour. Were it not for my hope of heaven I couldn't stand all this trouble.''

"Mother, are these people Christians who made these laws which are robbing us of our inheritance and reducing us to slavery? If this is Christianity I hate and despise it. Would the most cruel heathen do worse?"

"My dear child, I have not learned my Christianity from them. I have learned it at the foot of the cross, and from this book,'' she said, placing a New Testament in Iola's hands. "Some of the most beautiful lessons of faith and trust I have ever learned were from among our lowly people in their humble cabins.''

"Mamma!'' called a faint voice from the adjoining room. Marie immediately arose and went to the bedside of her sick child, where Mammy Liza was holding her faithful vigils. The child had just awakened from a fitful sleep.

"I thought," she said, "that I heard Iola's voice. Has she come?"

"Yes, darling; do you want to see her?"

"Oh, yes," she said, as a bright smile broke over her dying features.

Iola passed quickly into the room. Gracie reached out her thin, bloodless hand, clasped Iola's palm in hers, and said: "I am so glad you have come. Dear Iola, stand by mother. You and Harry are all she has. It is not hard to die. You and mother and Harry must meet me in heaven."

Swiftly the tidings went through the house that Gracie was dying. The servants gathered around her with tearful eyes, as she bade them all good-bye. When she had finished, and Mammy had lowered the pillow, an unwonted radiance lit up her eye, and an expression of ineffable gladness overspread her face, as she murmured: "It is beautiful, so beautiful!" Fainter and fainter grew her voice, until, without a struggle or sigh, she passed away beyond the power of oppression and prejudice.

CHAPTER XIII

A Rejected Suitor

Very unexpected was Dr. Gresham's proposal to Iola. She had heartily enjoyed his society and highly valued his friendship, but he had never been associated in her mind with either love or marriage. As he held her hand in his a tell-tale flush rose to her cheek, a look of grateful surprise beamed from her eye, but it was almost immediately succeeded by an air of inexpressible sadness, a drooping of her eyelids, and an increasing pallor of her cheek. She withdrew her hand from his, shook her head sadly, and said:—

"No, Doctor; that can never be. I am very grateful to you for your kindness. I value your friendship, but neither gratitude nor friendship is love, and I have nothing more than those to give."

"Not at present," said Dr. Gresham; "but may I not hope your friendship will ripen into love?"

"Doctor, I could not promise. I do not think that I should. There are barriers between us that I cannot pass. Were you to know them I think you would say the same."

Just then the ambulance brought in a wounded scout, and Iola found relief from the wounds of her own heart in attending to his.

Dr. Gresham knew the barrier that lay between them. It was one which his love had surmounted. But he was too noble and generous to take advantage of her loneliness to press his suit. He had lived in a part of the country where he had scarcely ever seen a colored person, and around the race their misfortunes had thrown a halo of romance. To him the negro was a picturesque being, over whose woes he had wept when a child, and whose wrongs he was ready to redress when a man. But when he saw the lovely girl who had been rescued by the commander of the post from the clutches of slavery, all the manhood and chivalry in his nature arose in her behalf, and he was ready to lay on the altar of her heart his first grand and overmastering love. Not discouraged by her refusal, but determined to overcome her objections, Dr. Gresham resolved that he would abide his time.

Iola was not indifferent to Dr. Gresham. She admired his manliness and respected his character. He was tall and handsome, a fine specimen of the best brain and heart of New England. He had been nurtured under grand and ennobling influences. His father was a devoted Abolitionist. His mother was kindhearted, but somewhat exclusive and aristocratic. She would have looked upon his marriage with Iola as a mistake and feared that such an alliance would hurt the prospects of her daughters.

During Iola's stay in the North, she had learned enough of the racial feeling to influence her decision in reference to Dr. Gresham's offer. Iola, like other girls, had had her beautiful day-dreams before she was rudely awakened by the fate which had dragged her into the depths of slavery. In the chambers of her imagery were pictures of noble deeds; of high, heroic men, knightly, tender, true, and brave. In Dr. Gresham she saw the ideal of her soul exemplified. But in her lonely condition, with all its background of terrible sorrow and deep abasement, she had never for a moment thought of giving or receiving love from one of that race who had been so lately associated in her mind with horror, aversion, and disgust. His kindness to her had been a new experience. His companionship was an unexpected pleasure. She had learned to enjoy his presence and to miss him when absent, and when she began to question her heart she found that unconsciously it was entwining around him.

"Yes," she said to herself, "I do like him; but I can never

marry him. To the man I marry my heart must be as open as the flowers to the sun. I could not accept his hand and hide from him the secret of my birth; and I could not consent to choose the happiest lot on earth without first finding my poor heart-stricken and desolate mother. Perhaps some day I may have the courage to tell him my sad story, and then make my heart the sepulchre in which to bury all the love which might have gladdened and brightened my whole life."

During the sad and weary months which ensued while the war dragged its slow length along, Dr. Gresham and Iola often met by the bedsides of the wounded and dying, and sometimes he would drop a few words at which her heart would beat quicker and her cheek flush more vividly. But he was so kind, tender, and respectful, that Iola had no idea he knew her race affiliations. She knew from unmistakable signs that Dr. Gresham had learned to love her, and that he had power to call forth the warmest affection of her soul; but she fought with her own heart and repressed its rising love. She felt that it was best for his sake that they should not marry. When she saw the evidences of his increasing love she regretted that she had not informed him at the first of the barrier that lay between them; it might have saved him unnecessary suffering. Thinking thus, Iola resolved, at whatever cost of pain it might be to herself, to explain to Dr. Gresham what she meant by the insurmountable barrier. Iola, after a continuous strain upon her nervous system for months, began to suffer from general debility and nervous depression. Dr. Gresham saw the increasing pallor on Iola's cheek and the loss of buoyancy in her step. One morning, as she turned from the bed of a young soldier for whom she had just written a letter to his mother, there was such a look of pity and sorrow on her face that Dr. Gresham's whole heart went out in sympathy for her, and he resolved to break the silence he had imposed upon himself.

"Iola," he said, and there was a depth of passionate tenderness in his voice, a volume of unexpressed affection in his face, "you are wronging yourself. You are sinking beneath burdens too heavy for you to bear. It seems to me that besides the constant drain upon your sympathies there is some great sorrow preying upon your life; some burden that ought to be shared." He gazed upon her so ardently that each cord of her heart seemed to vibrate, and unbidden tears sprang to her lustrous eyes, as she said, sadly:—

"Doctor, you are right."

"Iola, my heart is longing to lift those burdens from your life. Love, like faith, laughs at impossibilities. I can conceive of no barrier too high for my love to surmount. Consent to be mine, as nothing else on earth is mine."

"Doctor, you know not what you ask," replied Iola. "Instead of coming into this hospital a self-sacrificing woman, laying her every gift and advantage upon the altar of her country, I came as a rescued slave, glad to find a refuge from a fate more cruel than death; a fate from which I was rescued by the intervention of my dear dead friend, Thomas Anderson. I was born on a lonely plantation on the Mississippi River, where the white population was very sparse. We had no neighbors who ever visited us; no young white girls with whom I ever played in my childhood; but, never having enjoyed such companionship, I was unconscious of any sense of privation. Our parents spared no pains to make the lives of their children (we were three) as bright and pleasant as they could. Our home was so happy. We had a large number of servants, who were devoted to us. I never had the faintest suspicion that there was any wrongfulness in slavery, and I never dreamed of the dreadful fate which broke in a storm of fearful anguish over our devoted heads. Papa used to take us to New Orleans to see the Mardi Gras, and while there we visited the theatres and other places of amusement and interest. At home we had books, papers, and magazines to beguile our time. Perfectly ignorant of my racial connection, I was sent to a Northern academy, and soon made many friends among my fellow-students. Companionship with girls of my own age was a new experience, which I thoroughly enjoyed. I spent several years in New England, and was busily preparing for my commencement exercises when my father was snatched away—died of yellow fever on his way North to witness my graduation. Through a stratagem, I was brought hurriedly from the North, and found that my father was dead; that his nearest kinsman had taken possession of our property; that my mother's marriage had been declared illegal, because of an imperceptible infusion of negro blood in her veins; and that she and her children had been remanded to slavery. I was torn from my mother, sold as a slave, and subjected to cruel indignities, from which I was rescued and a place given to me in this hospital. Doctor, I did not choose my lot in life, but I have no other alternative than to accept it. The intense horror and agony I felt when I was first told the story are over. Thoughts and purposes have come to me in the shadow I should never have learned in the sunshine. I am constantly rousing myself up to suffer and be strong. I intend, when this conflict is over, to cast my lot with the freed people as a helper, teacher, and friend. I have passed through a fiery ordeal, but this ministry of suffering will not be in vain. I feel that my mind has matured beyond my years. I am a wonder to myself. It seems as if years had been compressed into a few short months. In telling you this, do you not, can you not, see that there is an insurmountable barrier between us?"

"No, I do not," replied Dr. Gresham. "I love you for your own sake. And with this the disadvantages of birth have nothing to do."

"You say so now, and I believe that you are perfectly sincere. To-day your friendship springs from compassion, but, when that subsides, might you not look on me as an inferior?"

"Iola, you do not understand me. You think too meanly of me. You must not judge me by the worst of my race. Surely our country has produced a higher type of manhood than the men by whom you were tried and tempted."

"Tried, but not tempted," said Iola, as a deep flush overspread her face; "I was never tempted. I was sold from State to State as an article of merchandise. I had outrages heaped on me which might well crimson the cheek of honest womanhood with shame, but I never fell into the clutches of an owner for whom I did not feel the utmost loathing and intensest horror. I have heard men talk glibly of the degradation of the negro, but there is a vast difference between abasement of condition and degradation of character. I was abased, but the men who trampled on me were the degraded ones."

"But, Iola, you must not blame all for what a few have done."

"A few have done? Did not the whole nation consent to our abasement?" asked Iola, bitterly.

"No, Miss Iola, we did not all consent to it. Slavery drew a line of cleavage in this country. Although we were under one government we were farther apart in our sentiments than if we had been divided by lofty mountains and separated by wide seas. And had not Northern sentiment been brought to bear against the institution, slavery would have been intact until to-day."

"But, Doctor, the negro is under a social ban both North and South. Our enemies have the ear of the world, and they can depict us just as they please."

"That is true; but the negro has no other alternative than to make friends of his calamities. Other men have plead his cause, but out of the race must come its own defenders. With them the pen must be mightier than the sword. It is the weapon of civilization, and they must use it in their own defense. We cannot tell what is in them until they express themselves."

"Yes, and I think there is a large amount of latent and undeveloped ability in the race, which they will learn to use for their own benefit. This my hospital experience has taught me."

"But," said Dr. Gresham, "they must learn to struggle, labor, and achieve. By facts, not theories, they will be judged in the future. The Anglo-Saxon race is proud, domineering, aggressive, and impatient of a rival, and, as I think, has more capacity for dragging down a weaker race than uplifting it. They have been a conquering and achieving people, marvelous in their triumphs of mind over matter. They have manifested the traits of character which are developed by success and victory."

"And yet," said Iola, earnestly, "I believe the time will come when the civilization of the negro will assume a better phase than you Anglo-Saxons possess. You will prove unworthy of your high vantage ground if you only use your superior ability to victimize feebler races and minister to a selfish greed of gold and a love of domination."

"But, Iola," said Dr. Gresham, a little impatiently, "what has all this to do with our marriage? Your complexion is as fair as mine. What is to hinder you from sharing my Northern home, from having my mother to be your mother?" The tones of his voice grew tender, as he raised his eyes to Iola's face and anxiously awaited her reply.

"Dr. Gresham," said Iola, sadly, "should the story of my life be revealed to your family, would they be willing to ignore all the traditions of my blood, forget all the terrible humiliations through which I have passed? I have too much self-respect to enter your home under a veil of concealment. I have lived in New England. I love the sunshine of her homes and the freedom of her institutions. But New England is not free from racial prejudice, and I would never enter a family where I would be an unwelcome member."

"Iola, dear, you have nothing to fear in that direction."

"Doctor," she said, and a faint flush rose to her cheek, "suppose we should marry, and little children in after years should nestle in our arms, and one of them show unmistakable signs of color, would you be satisfied?"

She looked steadfastly into his eyes, which fell beneath her truth-seeking gaze. His face flushed as if the question had suddenly perplexed him. Iola saw the irresolution on his face, and framed her answer accordingly.

"Ah, I see," she said, "that you are puzzled. You had not taken into account what might result from such a marriage. I will relieve you from all embarrassment by simply saying I cannot be your wife. When the war is over I intend to search the country for my mother. Doctor, were you to give me a palace-like home, with velvet carpets to hush my tread, and magnificence to surround my way, I should miss her voice amid all other tones, her presence amid every scene. Oh, you do not know how hungry my heart is for my mother! Were I to marry you I would carry an aching heart into your home and dim its brightness. I have resolved never to marry until I have found my mother. The hope of finding her has colored all my life since I regained my freedom. It has helped sustain me in the hour of fearful trial. When I see her I want to have the proud consciousness that I bring her back a heart just as loving, faithful, and devoted as the last hour we parted."

"And is this your final answer?"

"It is. I have pledged my life to that resolve, and I believe time and patience will reward me."

There was a deep shadow of sorrow and disappointment on the face of Dr. Gresham as he rose to leave. For a moment he held her hand as it lay limp in his own. If she wavered in her determination it was only for a moment. No quivering of her lip or paling of her cheek betrayed any struggle of her heart. Her resolve was made, and his words were powerless to swerve her from the purpose of her soul.

After Dr. Gresham had gone Iola went to her room and sat buried in thought. It seemed as if the fate of Tantalus was hers, without his crimes. Here she was lonely and heart-stricken, and unto her was presented the offer of love, home, happiness, and social position; the heart and hand of a man too noble and generous to refuse her companionship for life on account of the blood in her veins. Why should she refuse these desirable boons? But, mingling with these beautiful visions of manly love and protecting care she saw the anguish of her heart-stricken mother and the pale, sweet face of her dying sister, as with her latest breath she had said, "Iola, stand by mamma!"

"No, no," she said to herself; "I was right to refuse Dr. Gresham. How dare I dream of happiness when my poor mamma's heart may be slowly breaking? I should be ashamed to live and ashamed to die were I to choose a happy lot for myself and leave poor mamma to struggle alone. I will never be satisfied till I get tidings of her. And when I have found her I will do all I can to cheer and brighten the remnant of her life."

CHAPTER XIV

Harry Leroy

It was several weeks after Iola had written to her brother that her letter reached him. The trusty servant to whom she delivered it watched his opportunity to mail it. At last he succeeded in slipping it into Lorraine's mail and dropping them all into the postoffice together. Harry was studying at a boys' academy in Maine. His father had given that State the preference because, while on a visit there, he had been favorably impressed with the kindness and hospitality of the people. He had sent his son a large sum of money, and given him permission to spend awhile with some school-chums till he was ready to bring the family North, where they could all spend the summer together. Harry had returned from his visit, and was looking for letters and remittances from home, when a letter, all crumpled, was handed him by the principal of the academy. He recognized his sister's handwriting and eagerly opened the letter. As he read, he turned very pale; then a deep flush overspread his face and an angry light flashed from his eyes. As he read on, his face became still paler; he gasped for breath and fell into a swoon. Appalled at the sudden change which had swept over him like a deadly sirocco, the principal rushed to the fallen boy, picked up the missive that lay beside him, and immediately rang for help and dispatched for the doctor. The doctor came at once and was greatly puzzled. Less than an hour before, he had seen him with a crowd of merry, laughter-loving boys, apparently as light-hearted and joyous as any of them; now he lay with features drawn and pinched, his face deadly pale, as if some terrible suffering had sent all the blood in his veins to stagnate around his heart. Harry opened his eyes, shuddered, and relapsed into silence. The doctor, all at sea in regard to the cause of the sudden attack, did all that he could to restore him to consciousness and quiet the perturbation of his spirit. He succeeded, but found he was strangely silent. A terrible shock had sent a tremor through every nerve, and the doctor watched with painful apprehension its effect upon his reason. Giving him an opiate and enjoining that he should be kept perfectly quiet, the doctor left the room, sought the principal, and said:—

"Mr. Bascom, here is a case that baffles my skill. I saw that boy pass by my window not more than half an hour ago, full of animation, and now he lies hovering between life and death. I have great apprehension for his reason. Can you throw any light on the subject?"

Mr. Bascom hesitated.

"I am not asking you as a matter of idle curiosity, but as a physician. I must have all the light I can get in making my diagnosis of the case."

The principal arose, went to his desk, took out the letter which he had picked up from the floor, and laid it in the physician's hand. As the doctor read, a look of indignant horror swept over his face. Then he said: "Can it be possible! I never suspected such a thing. It must be a cruel, senseless hoax."

"Doctor," said Mr. Bascom, "I have been a life-long Abolitionist and have often read of the cruelties and crimes of American slavery, but never before did I realize the low moral tone of the social life under which such shameless cruelties could be practiced on a defenseless widow and her orphaned children. Let me read the letter again. Just look at it, all tear-blotted and written with a trembling hand:—

'DEAR BROTHER:—I have dreadful news for you and I hardly know how to tell it. Papa and Gracie are both dead. He died of yellow fever. Mamma is almost distracted. Papa's cousin has taken possession of our property, and instead of heirs we are chattels. Mamma has explained the whole situation to me. She was papa's slave before she married. He loved her, manumitted, educated, and married her. When he died Mr. Lorraine entered suit for his property and Judge Starkins has decided in his favor. The decree of the court has made their marriage invalid, robbed us of our inheritance, and remanded us all to slavery. Mamma is too wretched to attempt to write herself, but told me to entreat you not to attempt to come home. You can do us no good, and that mean, cruel Lorraine may do you much harm. Don't attempt, I beseech you, to come home. Show this letter to Mr. Bascom and let him advise you what to do. But don't, for our sake, attempt to come home.

'Your heart-broken sister,
'IOLA LEROY.' "

"This," said the doctor, "is a very awkward affair. The boy is too ill to be removed. It is doubtful if the nerves which have trembled with such fearful excitement will ever recover their normal condition. It is simply a work of mercy to watch over him with the tenderest care."

Fortunately for Harry he had fallen into good hands, and the most tender care and nursing were bestowed upon him. For awhile Harry was strangely silent, never referring to the terrible misfortune which had so suddenly overshadowed his life. It seemed as if the past were suddenly blotted out of his memory. But he was young and of an excellent constitution, and in a few months he was slowly recovering.

"Doctor," said he one day, as the physician sat at his bedside, "I seem to have had a dreadful dream, and to have dreamt that my father was dead, and my mother and sister were in terrible trouble, but I could not help them. Doctor, was it a dream, or was it a reality? It could not have been a dream, for when I fell asleep the grass was green and the birds were singing, but now the winds are howling and the frost is on the ground. Doctor, tell me how it is? How long have I been here?"

Sitting by his bedside, and taking his emaciated hand in his, the doctor said, in a kind, fatherly tone: "My dear boy, you have been very ill, and everything depends on your keeping quiet, very quiet."

As soon as he was strong enough the principal gave him his letter to read.

"But, Mr. Bascom," Harry said, "I do not understand this. It says my mother and father were legally married. How could her marriage be set aside and her children robbed of their inheritance? This is not a heathen country. I hardly think barbarians would have done any worse; yet this is called a Christian country."

"Christian in name," answered the principal. "When your father left you in my care, knowing that I was an Abolitionist, he confided his secret to me. He said that life was full of vicissitudes, and he wished you to have a good education. He wanted you and your sister to be prepared for any emergency. He did not wish you to know that you had negro blood in your veins. He knew that the spirit of caste pervaded the nation, North and South, and he was very anxious to have his children freed from its depressing influences. He did not intend to stay South after you had finished your education."

"But," said Harry, "I cannot understand. If my mother was lawfully married, how could they deprive her of her marital rights?"

"When Lorraine," continued Mr. Bascom, "knew your father was dead, all he had to do was to find a flaw in her manumission, and, of course, the marriage became illegal. She could not then inherit property nor maintain her freedom; and her children followed her condition."

Harry listened attentively. Things which had puzzled him once now became perfectly clear. He sighed heavily, and, turning to the principal, said: "I see things in a new light.

Now I remember that none of the planters' wives ever visited my mother; and we never went to church except when my father took us to the Cathedral in New Orleans. My father was a Catholic, but I don't think mamma is."

"Now, Harry," said the principal, "life is before you. If you wish to stay North, I will interest friends in your behalf, and try to get you a situation. Going South is out of the question. It is probable that by this time your mother and sister are removed from their home. You are powerless to fight against the law that enslaved them. Should you fall into the clutches of Lorraine, he might give you a great deal of trouble. You would be pressed into the Confederate service to help them throw up barricades, dig trenches, and add to the strength of those who enslaved your mother and sister."

"Never! never!" cried Harry. "I would rather die than do it! I should despise myself forever if I did."

"Numbers of our young men," said Mr. Bascom, "have gone to the war which is now raging between North and South. You have been sick for several months, and much has taken place of which you are unaware. Would you like to enlist?"

"I certainly would; not so much for the sake of fighting for the Government, as with the hope of finding my mother and sister, and avenging their wrongs. I should like to meet Lorraine on the battle-field."

"What kind of a regiment would you prefer, white or colored?"

Harry winced when the question was asked. He felt the reality of his situation as he had not done before. It was as if two paths had suddenly opened before him, and he was forced to choose between them. On one side were strength, courage, enterprise, power of achievement, and memories of a wonderful past. On the other side were weakness, ignorance, poverty, and the proud world's social scorn. He knew nothing of colored people except as slaves, and his whole soul shrank from equalizing himself with them. He was fair enough to pass unchallenged among the fairest in the land,

and yet a Christless prejudice had decreed that he should be a social pariah. He sat, thoughtful and undecided, as if a great struggle were going on in his mind. Finally the principal said, "I do not think that you should be assigned to a colored regiment because of the blood in your veins, but you will have, in such a regiment, better facilities for finding your mother and sister."

"You are right, Mr. Bascom. To find my mother and sister I call no task too heavy, no sacrifice too great."

Since Harry had come North he had learned to feel profound pity for the slave. But there is a difference between looking on a man as an object of pity and protecting him as such, and being identified with him and forced to share his lot. To take his place with them on the arena of life was the test of his life, but love was stronger than pride.

His father was dead. His mother and sister were enslaved by a mockery of justice. It was more than a matter of choice where he should stand on the racial question. He felt that he must stand where he could strike the most effective blow for their freedom. With that thought strong in his mind, and as soon as he recovered, he went westward to find a colored regiment. He told the recruiting officer that he wished to be assigned to a colored regiment.

"Why do you wish that," said the officer, looking at Harry with an air of astonishment."

"Because I am a colored man."

The officer look puzzled. It was a new experience. He had seen colored men with fair complexions anxious to lose their identity with the colored race and pose as white men, but here was a man in the flush of his early manhood, to whom could come dreams of promotion from a simple private to a successful general, deliberately turning his back upon every gilded hope and dazzling opportunity, to cast his lot with the despised and hated negro.

"I do not understand you," said the officer. "Surely you are a white man, and, as such, I will enlist you in a white regiment."

"No," said Harry, firmly, "I am a colored man, and unless I can be assigned to a colored regiment I am not willing to enter the army."

"Well," said the officer, "you are the d—d'st fool I ever saw—a man as white as you are turning his back upon his chances of promotion! But you can take your choice."

So Harry was permitted to enter the army. By his promptness and valor he soon won the hearts of his superior officers, and was made drill sergeant. Having nearly all of his life been used to colored people, and being taught by his mother to be kind and respectful to them, he was soon able to gain their esteem. He continued in the regiment until Grant began the task of opening the Mississippi. After weeks of fruitless effort, Grant marched his army down the west side of the river, while the gunboats undertook the perilous task of running the batteries. Men were found for the hour. The volunteers offered themselves in such numbers that lots were cast to determine who should have the opportunity to enlist in an enterprise so fraught with danger. Harry was one on whom the lot fell.

Grant crossed the river below, coiled his forces around Vicksburg like a boa-constrictor, and held it in his grasp. After forty-seven days of endurance the city surrendered to him. Port Hudson, after the surrender of Vicksburg, gave up the unequal contest, and the Mississippi was open to the Gulf.

CHAPTER XV

Robert and His Company

"Good morning, gentlemen," said Robert Johnson, as he approached Colonel Robinson, the commander of the post, who was standing at the door of his tent, talking with Captain Sybil.

"Good morning," responded Colonel Robinson, "I am glad you have come. I was just about to send for you. How is your company getting on?"

"First rate, sir," replied Robert.

"In good health?"

"Excellent. They are all in good health and spirits. Our boys are used to hardship and exposure, and the hope of getting their freedom puts new snap into them."

"I am glad of it," said Colonel Robinson. "They make good fighters and very useful allies. Last night we received very valuable intelligence from some fugitives who had escaped through the Rebel lines. I do not think many of the Northern people realize the service they have been to us in bringing information and helping our boys when escaping from Rebel prisons. I never knew a full-blooded negro to betray us. A month ago, when we were encamped near the Rebel lines, a colored woman managed admirably to keep us posted as to the intended movements of the enemy. She was engaged in laundry work, and by means of hanging her sheets in different ways gave us the right signals."

"I hope," said Captain Sybil, "that the time will come when some faithful historian will chronicle all the deeds of daring and service these people have performed during this struggle, and give them due credit therefor."

"Our great mistake," said Colonel Robinson, "was our long delay in granting them their freedom, and even what we have done is only partial. The border States still retain their slaves. We ought to have made a clean sweep of the whole affair. Slavery is a serpent which we nourished in its weakness, and now it is stinging us in its strength."

"I think so, too," said Captain Sybil. "But in making his proclamation of freedom, perhaps Mr. Lincoln went as far as he thought public opinion would let him."

"It is remarkable," said Colonel Robinson, "how these Secesh hold out. It surprises me to see how poor white men, who, like the negroes, are victims of slavery, rally around the Stripes and Bars. These men, I believe, have been looked down on by the aristocratic slave-holders, and despised by the well-fed and comfortable slaves, yet they follow their leaders into the very jaws of death; face hunger, cold, disease, and danger; and all for what? What, under heaven, are they fighting for? Now, the negro, ignorant as he is, has learned to regard our flag as a banner of freedom, and to look forward to his deliverance as a consequence of the overthrow of the Rebellion."

"I think," said Captain Sybil "that these ignorant white men have been awfully deceived. They have had presented to their imaginations utterly false ideas of the results of Secession, and have been taught that its success would bring them advantages which they had never enjoyed in the Union."

"And I think," said Colonel Robinson, "that the women and ministers have largely fed and fanned the fires of this Rebellion, and have helped to create a public opinion which has swept numbers of benighted men into the conflict. Well might one of their own men say, 'This is a rich man's war and a poor man's fight.' They were led into it through their ignorance, and held in it by their fears."

"I think," said Captain Sybil, "that if the public school

333

had been common through the South this war would never have occurred. Now things have reached such a pass that able-bodied men must report at headquarters, or be treated as deserters. Their leaders are desperate men, of whom it has been said: 'They have robbed the cradle and the grave.' "

"They are fighting against fearful odds," said Colonel Robinson, "and their defeat is only a question of time."

"As soon," said Robert, "as they fired on Fort Sumter, Uncle Daniel, a dear old father who had been praying and hoping for freedom, said to me: 'Dey's fire on Fort Sumter, an' mark my words, Bob, de Norf boun' ter whip.' "

"Had we freed the slaves at the outset," said Captain Sybil, "we wouldn't have given the Rebels so much opportunity to strengthen themselves by means of slave labor in raising their crops, throwing up their entrenchments, and building their fortifications. Slavery was deadly cancer eating into the life of the nation; but somehow, it had cast such a glamour over us that we have acted somewhat as if our national safety were better preserved by sparing the cancer than by cutting it out."

"Political and racial questions have sadly complicated this matter," said Colonel Robinson. "The North is not wholly made up of anti-slavery people. At the beginning of this war we were not permeated with justice, and so were not ripe for victory. The battle of Bull Run inaugurated the war by a failure. Instead of glory we gathered shame, and defeat in place of victory."

"We have been slow," said Captain Sybil, "to see our danger and to do our duty. Our delay has cost us thousands of lives and millions of dollars. Yet it may be it is all for the best. Our national wound was too deep to be lightly healed. When the President issued his Emancipation Proclamation my heart overflowed with joy, and I said: 'This is the first bright rift in the war cloud.' "

"And did you really think that they would accept the terms of freedom and lay down their arms?" asked Robert.

"I hardly thought they would," continued Captain Sybil.

"I did not think that their leaders would permit it. I believe the rank and file of their army are largely composed of a mass of ignorance, led, manipulated, and moulded by educated and ambitious wickedness. In attempting to overthrow the Union, a despotism and reign of terror were created which encompassed them as fetters of iron, and they will not accept the conditions until they have reached the last extremity. I hardly think they are yet willing to confess that such extremity has been reached."

"Captain," said Robert, as they left Colonel Robinson's tent, "I have lived all my life where I have had a chance to hear the 'Secesh' talk, and when they left their papers around I used to read everything I could lay my hands on. It seemed to me that the big white men not only ruled over the poor whites and made laws for them, but over the whole nation."

"That was so," replied Captain Sybil. "The North was strong but forbearing. It was busy in trade and commerce, and permitted them to make the Northern States hunting-grounds for their slaves. When we sent back Simms and Burns from beneath the shadow of Bunker Hill Monument and Faneuil Hall, they mistook us; looked upon us as a lot of money-grabbers, who would be willing to purchase peace at any price. I do not believe when they fired on the 'Star of the West' that they had the least apprehension of the fearful results which were to follow their madness and folly."

"Well, Captain," asked Robert, "if the free North would submit to be called on to help them catch their slaves, what could be expected of us, who all our lives had known no other condition than that of slavery? How much braver would you have been, if your first recollections had been those of seeing your mother maltreated, your father cruelly beaten, or your fellow-servants brutally murdered? I wonder why they never enslaved the Indians!"

"You are mistaken, Robert, if you think the Indians were never enslaved. I have read that the Spaniards who visited the coasts of America kidnapped thousands of Indians, whom they sent to Europe and the West Indies as slaves. Columbus himself, we are informed, captured five hundred natives, and sent them to Spain. The Indian had the lesser power of endurance, and Las Cassas suggested the enslavement of the negro, because he seemed to possess greater breadth of physical organization and stronger power of endurance. Slavery was an old world's crime which, I have heard, the Indians never practiced among themselves. Perhaps it would have been harder to reduce them to slavery and hold them in bondage when they had a vast continent before them, where they could hide in the fastnesses of its mountains or the seclusion of its forests, than it was for white men to visit the coasts of Africa and, with their superior knowledge, obtain cargoes of slaves, bring them across the ocean, hem them in on the plantations, and surround them with a pall of dense ignorance."

"I remember," said Robert, "in reading a history I once came across at our house, that when the Africans first came to this country they did not all speak one language. Some had only met as mutual enemies. They were not all one color, their complexions ranging from tawny yellow to deep black."

"Yes," said Captain Sybil, "and in dealing with the negro we wanted his labor; in dealing with the Indian we wanted his lands. For one we had weapons of war; for the other we had real and invisible chains, the coercion of force, and the terror of the unseen world."

"That's exactly so, Captain! When I was a boy I used to hear the old folks tell what would happen to bad people in another world; about the devil pouring hot lead down people's throats and stirring them up with a pitch-fork; and I used to get so scared that I would be afraid to go to bed at night. I don't suppose the Indians ever heard of such things, or, if they had, I never heard of them being willing to give away all their lands on earth, and quietly wait for a home in heaven."

"But, surely, Robert, you do not think religion has degraded the negro?"

"Oh, I wouldn't say that. But a man is in a tight fix when he takes his part, like Nat Turner or Denmark Veasy, and is made to fear that he will be hanged in this world and be burned in the next. And, since I come to think of it, we colored folks used to get mightily mixed up about our religion. Mr. Gundover had on his plantation a real smart man. He was religious, but he would steal."

"Oh, Robert," queried Sybil, "how could he be religious and steal?"

"He didn't think," retorted Robert, "it was any harm to steal from his master. I guess he thought it was right to get from his master all he could. He would have thought it wrong to steal from his fellow-servants. He thought that downright mean, but I wouldn't have insured the lives of Gundover's pigs and chickens, if Uncle Jack got them in a tight place. One day there was a minister stopping with Mr. Gundover. As a matter of course, in speaking of his servants, he gave Jack's sins an airing. He would much rather confess Jack's sins than his own. Now Gundover wanted to do two things, save his pigs and poultry, and save Jack's soul. He told the minister that Jack was a liar and a thief, and gave the minister a chance to talk with Uncle Jack about the state of his soul. Uncle Jack listened very quietly, and when taxed with stealing his master's wheat he was ready with an answer. 'Now Massa Parker,' said Jack, 'lem'me tell yer jis' how it war 'bout dat wheat. Wen ole Jack com'd down yere, dis place war all growed up in woods. He go ter work, clared up de groun' an' plowed, an' planted, an' riz a crap, an' den wen it war all done, he hadn't a dollar to buy his ole woman a gown; an' he jis' took a bag ob wheat.' "

"What did Mr. Parker say?" asked Sybil.

"I don't know, though I reckon he didn't think it was a bad steal after all, but I don't suppose he told Jack so. When he came to the next point, about Jack's lying, I suppose he thought he had a clear case; but Jack was equal to the occasion."

"How did he clear up that charge?" interrogated Captain Sybil.

"Finely. I think if he had been educated he would have made a first-rate lawyer. He said, 'Marse Parker, dere's old Joe. His wife don't lib on dis plantation. Old Joe go ober ter see her, but he stayed too long, an' didn't git back in time fer his work. Massa's oberseer kotched him an' cut him all up. When de oberseer went inter de house, pore old Joe war all tired an' beat up, an' so he lay down by de fence corner and go ter sleep. Bimeby Massa oberseer com'd an' axed, "all bin a workin' libely?" I say "Yes, Massa." ' Then said Mr. Parker, 'You were lying, Joe had been sleeping, not working.' 'I know's dat, but ef I tole on Joe, Massa oberseer cut him all up again, and Massa Jesus says, "Blessed am de Peace-maker." ' I heard," continued Robert, "that Mr. Parker said to Gundover, 'You seem to me like a man standing in a stream where the blood of Jesus can reach you, but you are standing between it and your slaves. How will you answer that in the Day of Judgment?' "

"What did Gundover say?" asked Captain Sybil.

"He turned pale, and said, 'For God's sake don't speak of the Day of Judgment in connection with slavery.' "

Just then a messenger brought a communication to Captain Sybil. He read it attentively, and, turning to Robert, said, "Here are orders for an engagement at Five Forks to-morrow. Oh, this wasting of life and scattering of treasure might have been saved had we only been wiser. But the time is passing. Look after your company, and see that everything is in readiness as soon as possible."

Carefully Robert superintended the arrangements for the coming battle of a strife which for years had thrown its crimson shadows over the land. The Rebels fought with a valor worthy of a better cause. The disaster of Bull Run had been retrieved. Sherman had made his famous march to the sea. Fighting Joe Hooker had scaled the stronghold of the storm king and won a victory in the palace chamber of the clouds; the Union soldiers had captured Columbia, replanted the Stars and Stripes in Charleston, and changed that old sepulchre of slavery into the cradle of a new-born freedom. Farragut had been as triumphant on water as the other generals had been victorious on land, and New Orleans had been wrenched from the hands of the Confederacy. The Rebel leaders were obstinate. Misguided hordes had followed them to defeat and death. Grant was firm and determined to fight it out if it took all summer. The closing battles were fought with desperate courage and firm resistance, but at last the South was forced to succumb. On the ninth day of April, 1865, General Lee surrendered to General Grant. The lost cause went down in blood and tears, and on the brows of a ransomed people God poured the chrism of a new era, and they stood a race newly anointed with freedom.

CHAPTER XVI

After the Battle

Very sad and heart-rending were the scenes with which Iola
came in constant contact. Well may Christian men and
women labor and pray for the time when nations shall learn
war no more; when, instead of bloody conflicts, there shall
be peaceful arbitration. The battle in which Robert fought,
after his last conversation with Captain Sybil, was one of the
decisive struggles of the closing conflict. The mills of doom
and fate had ground out a fearful grist of agony and death,

> "And lives of men and souls of States
> Were thrown like chaff beyond the gates."

Numbers were taken prisoners. Pale, young corpses strewed
the earth; manhood was stricken down in the flush of its
energy and prime. The ambulances brought in the wounded
and dying. Captain Sybil laid down his life on the altar of
freedom. His prediction was fulfilled. Robert was brought into
the hospital, wounded, but not dangerously. Iola remembered him as being the friend of Tom Anderson, and her
heart was drawn instinctively towards him. For awhile he was
delirious, but her presence had a soothing effect upon him.
He sometimes imagined that she was his mother, and he
would tell her how he had missed her; and then at times he
would call her sister. Iola, tender and compassionate, humored his fancies, and would sing to him in low, sweet tones

some of the hymns she had learned in her old home in Mississippi. One day she sang a few verses of the hymn beginning with the words—

> "Drooping souls no longer grieve,
>   Heaven is propitious;
> If on Christ you do believe,
>   You will find Him precious."

"That," said he, looking earnestly into Iola's face, "was my mother's hymn. I have not heard it for years. Where did you learn it?"

Iola gazed inquiringly upon the face of her patient, and saw, by his clear gaze and the expression of his face, that his reason had returned.

"In my home, in Mississippi, from my own dear mother," was Iola's reply.

"Do you know where she learned it?" asked Robert.

"When she was a little girl she heard her mother sing it. Years after, a Methodist preacher came to our house, sang this hymn, and left the book behind him. My father was a Catholic, but my mother never went to any church. I did not understand it then, but I do now. We used to sing together, and read the Bible when we were alone."

"Do you remember where she came from, and who was her mother?" asked Robert, anxiously.

"My dear friend, you must be quiet. The fever has left you, but I will not answer for the consequences if you get excited."

Robert lay quiet and thoughtful for awhile and, seeing he was wakeful, Iola said, "Have you any friends to whom you would like to send a letter?"

A pathetic expression flitted over his face, as he sadly replied, "I haven't, to my knowledge, a single relation in the world. When I was about ten years old my mother and sister were sold from me. It is more than twenty years since I have heard from them. But that hymn which you were singing reminded me so much of my mother! She used to sing it when I was a child. Please sing it again."

Iola's voice rose soft and clear by his bedside, till he fell into a quiet slumber. She remembered that her mother had spoken of her brother before they had parted, and her interest and curiosity were awakened by Robert's story. While he slept, she closely scrutinized Robert's features, and detected a striking resemblance between him and her mother.

"Oh, I *do* wonder if he can be my mother's brother, from whom she has been separated so many years!"

Anxious as she was to ascertain if there was any relationship between Robert and her mother, she forebore to question him on the subject which lay so near her heart. But one day, when he was so far recovered as to be able to walk around, he met Iola on the hospital grounds, and said to her:—

"Miss Iola, you remind me so much of my mother and sister that I cannot help wondering if you are the daughter of my long-lost sister."

"Do you think," asked Iola, "if you saw the likeness of your sister you would recognize her?"

"I am afraid not. But there is one thing I can remember about her: she used to have a mole on her check, which mother used to tell her was her beauty spot."

"Look at this," said Iola, handing him a locket which contained her mother's picture.

Robert grasped the locket eagerly, scanned the features attentively, then, handing it back, said: "I have only a faint remembrance of my sister's features; but I never could recognize in that beautiful woman the dear little sister with whom I used to play. Oh, the cruelty of slavery! How it wrenched and tore us apart! Where is *your* mother now?"

"Oh, I cannot tell," answered Iola. "I left her in Mississippi. My father was a wealthy Creole planter, who fell in love with my mother. She was his slave, but he educated her in the North, freed, and married her. My father was very careful to have the fact of our negro blood concealed from us. I had not the slightest suspicion of it. When he was dead the secret was revealed. His white relations set aside my father's will, had his marriage declared invalid, and my mother and her children were remanded to slavery." Iola shuddered as she pronounced the horrid word, and grew deadly pale; but, regaining her self-possession, continued: "Now, that freedom has come, I intend to search for my mother until I find her."

"I do not wonder," said Robert, "that we had this war. The nation had sinned enough to suffer."

"Yes," said Iola, "if national sins bring down national judgments, then the nation is only reaping what it sowed."

"What are your plans for the future, or have you any?" asked Robert.

"I intend offering myself as a teacher in one of the schools which are being opened in different parts of the country," replied Iola. "As soon as I am able I will begin my search for my dear mother. I will advertise for her in the papers, hunt for her in the churches, and use all the means in my power to get some tidings of her and my brother Harry. What a cruel thing it was to separate us!"

CHAPTER XVII

Flames in the School-room

"Good morning," said Dr. Gresham, approaching Robert and Iola. "How are you both? You have mended rapidly," turning to Robert, "but then it was only a flesh wound. Your general health being good, and your blood in excellent condition, it was not hard for you to rally."

"Where have you been, Doctor? I have a faint recollection of having seen you on the morning I was brought in from the field, but not since."

"I have been on a furlough. I was running down through exhaustion and overwork, and I was compelled to go home for a few weeks' rest. But now, as they are about to close the hospital, I shall be permanently relieved. I am glad that this cruel strife is over. It seemed as if I had lived through ages during these last few years. In the early part of the war I lost my arm by a stray shot, and my armless sleeve is one of the mementos of battle I shall carry with me through life. Miss Leroy," he continued, turning respectfully to Iola, "would you permit me to ask you, as I would have some one ask my sister under the same circumstances, if you have matured any plans for the future, or if I can be of the least service to you? If so, I would be pleased to render you any service in my power."

"My purpose," replied Iola, "is to hunt for my mother, and to find her if she is alive. I am willing to go anywhere and do anything to find her. But I will need a standpoint from whence I can send out lines of inquiry. It must take time, in the disordered state of affairs, even to get a clue by which I may discover her whereabouts."

"How would you like to teach?" asked the Doctor. "Schools are being opened all around us. Numbers of excellent and superior women are coming from the North to engage as teachers of the freed people. Would you be willing to take a school among these people? I think it will be uphill work. I believe it will take generations to get over the duncery of slavery. Some of these poor fellows who came into our camp did not know their right hands from their left, nor their ages, nor even the days of the month. It took me some time, in a number of cases, to understand their language. It saddened my heart to see such ignorance. One day I asked one a question, and he answered, "I no shum'.""

"What did he mean?" asked Iola.

"That he did not see it," replied the doctor. "Of course, this does not apply to all of them. Some of them are wide-awake and sharp as steel traps. I think some of that class may be used in helping others."

"I should be very glad to have an opportunity to teach," said Iola. "I used to be a great favorite among the colored children on my father's plantation."

In a few days after this conversation the hospital was closed. The sick and convalescent were removed, and Iola obtained a position as a teacher. Very soon Iola realized that while she was heartily appreciated by the freedmen, she was an object of suspicion and dislike to their former owners. The North had conquered by the supremacy of the sword, and the South had bowed to the inevitable. But here was a new army that had come with an invasion of ideas, that had come to supplant ignorance with knowledge, and it was natural that its members should be unwelcome to those who had made it a crime to teach their slaves to read the name of the ever blessed Christ. But Iola had found her work, and the freedmen their friend.

When Iola opened her school she took pains to get acquainted with the parents of the children, and she gained their confidence and co-operation. Her face was a passport to their hearts. Ignorant of books, human faces were the scrolls from which they had been reading for ages. They had been the sunshine and shadow of their lives.

Iola had found a school-room in the basement of a colored church, where the doors were willingly opened to her. Her pupils came from miles around, ready and anxious to get some "book larnin'." Some of the old folks were eager to learn, and it was touching to see the eyes which had grown dim under the shadows of slavery, donning spectacles and trying to make out the words. As Iola had nearly all of her life been accustomed to colored children she had no physical repulsions to overcome, no prejudices to conquer in dealing with parents and children. In their simple childish fashion they would bring her fruits and flowers, and gladden her lonely heart with little tokens of affection.

One day a gentleman came to the school and wished to address the children. Iola suspended the regular order of the school, and the gentleman essayed to talk to them on the achievements of the white race, such as building steamboats and carrying on business. Finally, he asked how they did it?

"They've got money," chorused the children.

"But how did they get it?"

"They took it from us," chimed the youngsters. Iola smiled, and the gentleman was nonplussed; but he could not deny that one of the powers of knowledge is the power of the strong to oppress the weak.

The school was soon overcrowded with applicants, and Iola was forced to refuse numbers, because their quarters were too cramped. The school was beginning to lift up the home, for Iola was not satisfied to teach her children only the rudiments of knowledge. She had tried to lay the foundation of good character. But the elements of evil burst upon her loved and cherished work. One night the heavens were lighted with lurid flames, and Iola beheld the school, the pride and joy of her pupils and their parents, a smouldering ruin. Iola gazed with sorrowful dismay on what seemed the cruel work of an incendiary's torch. While she sat, mourn-fully contemplating the work of destruction, her children formed a procession, and, passing by the wreck of their school, sang:—

> "Oh, do not be discouraged,
> For Jesus is your friend."

As they sang, the tears sprang to Iola's eyes, and she said to herself, "I am not despondent of the future of my people; there is too much elasticity in their spirits, too much hope in their hearts, to be crushed out by unreasoning malice."

347

CHAPTER XVIII

Searching for Lost Ones

To bind anew the ties which slavery had broken and gather together the remnants of his scattered family became the earnest purpose of Robert's life. Iola, hopeful that in Robert she had found her mother's brother, was glad to know she was not alone in *her* search. Having sent out lines of inquiry in different directions, she was led to hope, from some of the replies she had received, that her mother was living somewhere in Georgia.

Hearing that a Methodist conference was to convene in that State, and being acquainted with the bishop of that district, she made arrangements to accompany him thither. She hoped to gather some tidings of her mother through the ministers gathered from different parts of that State.

From her brother she had heard nothing since her father's death. On his way to the conference, the bishop had an engagement to dedicate a church, near the city of C——, in North Carolina. Iola was quite willing to stop there a few days, hoping to hear something of Robert Johnson's mother. Soon after she had seated herself in the cars she was approached by a gentleman, who reached out his hand to her, and greeted her with great cordiality. Iola looked up, and recognized him immediately as one of her last patients at the hospital. It was none other than Robert Johnson.

"I am so glad to meet you," he said. "I am on my way to C——in search of my mother. I want to see the person who

348

sold her last, and, if possible, get some clew to the direction in which she went."

"And I," said Iola, "am in search of my mother. I am convinced that when we find those for whom we are searching they will prove to be very nearly related. Mamma said, before we were parted, that her brother had a red spot on his temple. If I could see that spot I should rest assured that my mother is your sister."

"Then," said Robert, "I can give you that assurance," and smilingly he lifted his hair from his temple, on which was a large, red spot.

"I am satisfied," exclaimed Iola, fixing her eyes, beaming with hope and confidence, on Robert. "Oh, I am so glad that I can, without the least hesitation, accept your services to join with me in the further search. What are your plans?"

"To stop for awhile in C——," said Robert, "and gather all the information possible from those who sold and bought my mother. I intend to leave no stone unturned in searching for her."

"Oh, I do hope that you will succeed. I expect to stop over there a few days, and I shall be so glad if, before I leave, I hear your search has been crowned with success, or, at least, that you have been put on the right track. Although I was born and raised in the midst of slavery, I had not the least idea of its barbarous selfishness till I was forced to pass through it. But we lived so much alone I had no opportunity to study it, except on our own plantation. My father and mother were very kind to their slaves. But it was slavery, all the same, and I hate it, root and branch."

Just then the conductor called out the station.

"We stop here," said Robert. "I am going to see Mrs. Johnson, and hunt up some of my old acquaintances. Where do you stop?"

"I don't know," replied Iola. "I expect that friends will be here to meet us. Bishop B——, permit me to introduce you to Mr. Robert Johnson, whom I have every reason to believe is my mother's brother. Like myself, he is engaged in hunting up his lost relatives."

"And I," said Robert, "am very much pleased to know that we are not without favorable clues."

"Bishop," said Iola, "Mr. Johnson wishes to know where I am to stop. He is going on an exploring expedition, and wishes to let me know the result."

"We stop at Mrs. Allston's, 313 New Street," said the bishop. "If I can be of any use to you, I am at your service."

"Thank you," said Robert, lifting his hat, as he left them to pursue his inquiries about his long-lost mother.

Quickly he trod the old familiar streets which led to his former home. He found Mrs. Johnson, but she had aged very fast since the war. She was no longer the lithe, active woman, with her proud manner and resolute bearing. Her eye had lost its brightness, her step its elasticity, and her whole appearance indicated that she was slowly sinking beneath a weight of sorrow which was heavier far than her weight of years. When she heard that Robert had called to see her she was going to receive him in the hall, as she would have done any of her former slaves, but her mind immediately changed when she saw him. He was not the light-hearted, careless, mischief-loving Robby of former days, but a handsome man, with heavy moustache, dark, earnest eyes, and proud military bearing. He smiled, and reached out his hand to her. She hardly knew how to address him. To her colored people were either boys and girls, or "aunties and uncles." She had never in her life addressed a colored person as "Mr. or Mrs." To do so now was to violate the social customs of the place. It would be like learning a new language in her old age. Robert immediately set her at ease by addressing her under the old familiar name of "Miss Nancy." This immediately relieved her of all embarrassment. She invited him into the sitting-room, and gave him a warm welcome.

"Well, Robby," she said, "I once thought that you would have been the last one to leave me. You know I never ill-treated you, and I gave you everything you needed. People said that I was spoiling you. I thought you were as happy as the days were long. When I heard of other people's servants leaving them I used to say to myself, 'I can trust my Bobby; he will stick to me to the last.' But I fooled myself that time. Soon as the Yankee soldiers got in sight you left me without saying a word. That morning I came down into the kitchen and asked Linda, 'Where's Robert? Why hasn't he set the table?' She said 'she hadn't seen you since the night before.' I thought maybe you were sick, and I went to see, but you were not in your room. I couldn't believe at first that you were gone. Wasn't I always good to you?"

"Oh, Miss Nancy," replied Robert; "you were good, but freedom was better."

"Yes," she said, musingly, "I suppose I would have done the same. But, Robby, it did go hard with me at first. However, I soon found out that my neighbors had been going through the same thing. But it's all over now. Let by-gones be by-gones. What are you doing now, and where are you living?"

"I am living in the city of P——. I have opened a hardware store there. But just now I am in search of my mother and sister."

"I hope that you may find them."

"How long," asked Robert, "do you think it has been since they left here?"

"Let me see; it must have been nearly thirty years. You got my letter?"

"Yes, ma'am; thank you."

"There have been great changes since you left here," Mrs. Johnson said. "Gundover died, and a number of colored men have banded together, bought his plantation, and divided it among themselves. And I hear they have a very nice settlement out there. I hope, since the Government has set them free, that they will succeed."

After Robert's interview with Mrs. Johnson he thought he would visit the settlement and hunt up his old friends. He easily found the place. It was on a clearing in Gundover's woods, where Robert and Uncle Daniel had held their last prayer-meeting. Now the gloomy silence of those woods was broken by the hum of industry, the murmur of cheerful voices, and the merry laughter of happy children. Where they had trodden with fear and misgiving, freedmen walked with light and bounding hearts. The school-house had taken the place of the slave-pen and auction-block.

"How is yer, ole boy?" asked one laborer of another.

"Everything is lobly," replied the other. The blue sky arching overhead and the beauty of the scenery justified the expression.

Gundover had died soon after the surrender. Frank Anderson had grown reckless and drank himself to death. His brother Tom had been killed in battle. Their mother, who was Gundover's daughter, had died insane. Their father had also passed away. The defeat of the Confederates, the loss of his sons, and the emancipation of his slaves, were blows from which he never recovered. As Robert passed leisurely along, delighted with the evidences of thrift and industry which constantly met his eye, he stopped to admire a garden filled with beautiful flowers, clambering vines, and rustic adornments.

On the porch sat an elderly woman, darning stockings, the very embodiment of content and good humor. Robert looked inquiringly at her. On seeing him, she almost immediately exclaimed, "Shore as I'se born, dat's Robert! Look yere, honey, whar did yer come from? I'll gib my head fer a choppin' block ef dat ain't Miss Nancy's Bob. Ain't yer our Bobby? Shore yer is."

"Of course I am," responded Robert. "It isn't anybody else. How did you know me?"

"How did I knew yer? By dem mischeebous eyes, ob course. I'd a knowed yer if I had seed yer in Europe."

"In Europe, Aunt Linda? Where's that?"

"I don't know. I specs it's some big city, somewhar. But yer looks jis' splendid. Yer looks good 'nuff ter kiss."

"Oh, Aunt Linda, don't say that. You make me blush."

"Oh you go 'long wid yer. I specs yer's got a nice little wife up dar whar yer comes from, dat kisses yer ebery day, an' Sunday, too."

"Is that the way your old man does you?"

"Oh, no, not a bit. He isn't one ob de kissin' kine. But sit down," she said, handing Robert a chair. "Won't yer hab a glass ob milk? Boy, I'se a libin' in clover. Neber 'spected ter see sich good times in all my born days."

"Well, Aunt Linda," said Robert, seating himself near her, and drinking the glass of milk which she had handed him, "how goes the battle? How have you been getting on since freedom?"

"Oh, fust rate, fust rate! Wen freedom com'd I jist lit out ob Miss Johnson's kitchen soon as I could. I wanted ter re'lize I war free, an' I couldn't, tell I got out er de sight and soun' ob ole Miss. When de war war ober an' de sogers war still stoppin' yere, I made pies an' cakes, sole em to de sogers, an' jist made money han' ober fist. An' I kep' on a workin' an' a savin' till my ole man got back from de war wid his wages and his bounty money. I felt right set up an' mighty big wen we counted all dat money. We had neber seen so much money in our lives befo', let alone hab it fer ourselbs. An' I sez, 'John, you take dis money an' git a nice place wid it.' An' he sez, 'Dere's no use tryin', kase dey don't want ter sell us any lan'.' Ole Gundover said, 'fore he died, dat he would let de lan' grow up in trees 'fore he'd sell it to us. An' dere war Mr. Brayton; he buyed some lan' and sole it to some cullud folks, an' his ole frien's got so mad wid him dat dey wouldn't speak ter him, an' he war borned down yere. I tole ole Miss Anderson's daughter dat we wanted ter git some homes ob our ownselbs. She sez, 'Den you won't want ter work for us?' Jis' de same as ef we could eat an' drink our houses. I tell yer, Robby, dese white folks don't know eberything."

"That's a fact, Aunt Linda."

"Den I sez ter John, 'wen one door shuts anoder opens.' An' shore 'nough, ole Gundover died, an' his place war all in debt, an' had to be sole. Some Jews bought it, but dey didn't want to farm it, so dey gib us a chance to buy it. Dem Jews hez been right helpful to cullud people wen dey hab lan' to sell. I reckon dey don't keer who buys it so long as dey gits de money. Well, John didn't gib in at fust; didn't want to let on his wife knowed more dan he did, an' dat he war ruled ober by a woman. Yer know he is an' ole Firginian, an' some ob dem ole Firginians to do lub to rule a woman. But I kep' naggin at him, till I specs he got tired of my tongue, an' he went and buyed dis piece ob lan'. Dis house war on it, an' war all gwine to wrack. It used to belong to John's ole marster. His wife died right in dis house, an' arter dat her husband went right to de dorgs; an' now he's in de pore-house. My! but ain't dem tables turned. When we knowed it war our own, warn't my ole man proud! I seed it in him, but he wouldn't let on. Ain't you men powerful 'ceitful?"

"Oh, Aunt Linda, don't put me in with the rest!"

"I don't know 'bout dat. Put you all in de bag for 'ceitfulness, an' I don't know which would git out fust."

"Well, Aunt Linda, I suppose by this time you know how to read and write?"

"No, chile, sence freedom's com'd I'se bin scratchin' too hard to get a libin' to put my head down to de book."

"But, Aunt Linda, it would be such company when your husband is away, to take a book. Do you never get lonesome?"

"Chile, I ain't got no time ter get lonesome. Ef you had eber so many chickens to feed, an' pigs squealin' fer somethin' ter eat, an' yore ducks an' geese squakin' 'roun' yer, yer wouldn't hab time ter git lonesome."

"But, Aunt Linda, you might be sick for months, and think what a comfort it would be if you could read your Bible."

"Oh, I could hab prayin' and singin'. Dese people is mighty good 'bout prayin' by de sick. Why, Robby, I think it would gib me de hysterics ef I war to try to git book larnin' froo my pore ole head. How long is yer gwine to stay? An' whar is yer stoppin?"

"I got here to-day," said Robert, "but I expect to stay several days."

"Well, I wants yer to meet my ole man, an' talk 'bout ole times. Couldn't yer come an' stop wid me, or isn't my house sniptious 'nuff?"

"Yes, thank you; but there is a young lady in town whom I think is my niece, my sister's daughter, and I want to be with her all I can."

"Your niece! Whar did you git any niece from?"

"Don't you remember," asked Robert, "that my mother had a little daughter, when Mrs. Johnson sold her? Well, I believe this young lady is that daughter's child."

"Laws a marcy!" exclaimed Aunt Linda, "yer don't tell me so! Whar did yer ketch up wid her?"

"I met her first," said Robert, "at the hospital here, when our poor Tom was dying; and when I was wounded at Five Forks she attended me in the field hospital there. She was just as good as gold."

"Well, did I eber! You jis' fotch dat chile to see me, ef she ain't too fine. I'se pore, but I'se clean, an' I ain't forgot how ter git up good dinners. Now, I wants ter hab a good talk 'bout our feller-servants."

"Yes, and I," said Robert, "want to hear all about Uncle Daniel, and Jennie, and Uncle Ben Tunnel."

"Well, I'se got lots an' gobs ter tell yer. I'se kep' track ob dem all. Aunt Katie died an' went ter hebben in a blaze ob glory. Uncle Dan'el stayed on de place till Marse Robert com'd back. When de war war ober he war smashed all ter pieces. I did pity him from de bottom ob my heart. When he went ter de war he looked so brave an' han'some; an' wen he com'd back he looked orful. 'Fore he went he gib Uncle Dan'el a bag full ob money ter take kere ob. 'An wen he com'd back Uncle Dan'el gibed him ebery cent ob it. It warn't ebery white pusson he could hab trusted wid it. 'Cause yer know, Bobby, money's a mighty temptin' thing. Dey tells me dat Marster Robert los' a heap ob property by de war; but Marse Robert war always mighty good ter Uncle Dan'el and Aunt Katie. He war wid her wen she war dyin' an' she got holt his han' an' made him promise dat he would meet her in glory. I neber seed anybody so happy in my life. She singed an' prayed ter de last. I tell you dis ole time religion is good 'nuff fer me. Mr. Robert didn't stay yere long arter her, but I beliebs he went all right. But 'fore he went he looked out fer Uncle Dan'el. Did you see dat nice little cabin down dere wid de green shutters an' nice little garden in front? Well, 'fore Marse Robert died he gib Uncle Dan'el dat place, an' Miss Mary and de chillen looks arter him yet; an' he libs jis' as snug as a bug in a rug. I'se gwine ter axe him ter take supper wid you. He'll be powerful glad ter see you."

"Do you ever go to see old Miss?" asked Robert.

"Oh, yes; I goes ebery now and den. But she's jis' fell froo. Ole Johnson jis' drunk hisself to death. He war de biggest guzzler I eber seed in my life. Why, dat man he drunk up ebery thing he could lay his han's on. Sometimes he would go 'roun' tryin' to borrer money from pore cullud folks. 'Twas rale drefful de way dat pore feller did frow hisself away. But drink did it all. I tell you, Bobby, dat drink's a drefful thing wen it gits de upper han' ob you. You'd better steer clar ob it."

"That's so," assented Robert.

"I know'd Miss Nancy's fadder and mudder. Dey war mighty rich. Some ob de real big bugs. Marse Jim used to know dem, an' come ober ter de plantation, an' eat an' drink wen he got ready, an' stay as long as he choose. Ole Cousins used to have wine at dere table ebery day, an' Marse Jim war mighty fon' ob dat wine, an' sometimes he would drink till he got quite boozy. Ole Cousins liked him bery well, till he foun' out he wanted his darter, an' den he didn't want him fer rags nor patches. But Miss Nancy war mighty headstrong, an' allers liked to hab her own way; an' dis time she got it. But didn't she step her foot inter it? Ole Johnson war mighty han'some, but when dat war said all war said. She run'd off an' got married, but wen she got down she war too spunkey to axe her pa for anything. Wen you war wid her, yer know she only took big bugs. But wen de war com'd 'roun' it tore her all ter pieces, an' now she's as pore as Job's turkey. I feel's right sorry fer her. Well, Robby, things is turned 'roun' mighty quare. Ole Mistus war up den, an' I war down; now, she's down, an I'se up. But I pities her, 'cause she warn't so bad arter all. De wuss thing she eber did war to sell your mudder, an' she wouldn't hab done dat but she snatched de whip out ob her han' an gib her a lickin'. Now I belieb in my heart she war 'fraid ob your mudder arter dat. But we women had ter keep 'em from whippin' us, er dey'd all de time been libin' on our bones. She had no man ter whip us 'cept dat ole drunken husband ob hern, an' he war allers too drunk ter whip hisself. He jis' wandered off, an' I reckon he died in somebody's pore-house. He warn't no 'count nohow you fix it. Weneber I goes to town I carries her some garden sass, er a little milk an' butter. An' she's mighty glad ter git it. I ain't got nothin' agin her. She neber struck me a lick in her life, an' I belieb in praising de bridge dat carries me ober. Dem Yankees set me free, an' I thinks a powerful heap ob dem. But it does rile me ter see dese mean white men comin' down yere an' settin' up dere grog-shops, tryin' to fedder dere nests sellin' licker to pore culled people. Deys de bery kine ob men dat used ter keep dorgs to ketch de runaways. I'd be chokin' fer a drink 'fore I'd eber spen' a cent wid dem, a spreadin' dere traps to git de black folks' money. You jis' go down town 'fore sun up to-morrer mornin' an' you see ef dey don't hab dem bars open to sell dere drams to dem hard workin' culled people 'fore dey goes ter work. I thinks some niggers is mighty big fools."

"Oh, Aunt Linda, don't run down your race. Leave that for the white people."

"I ain't runnin' down my people. But a fool's a fool, wether he's white or black. An' I think de nigger who will spen' his hard-earned money in dese yere new grog-shops is de biggest kine ob a fool, an' I sticks ter dat. You know we didn't hab all dese low places in slave times. An' what is dey fer, but to get the people's money. An' it's a shame how dey do sling de licker 'bout 'lection times."

"But don't the temperance people want the colored people to vote the temperance ticket?"

"Yes, but some ob de culled people gits mighty skittish ef dey tries to get em to vote dare ticket 'lection time, an' keeps dem at a proper distance wen de 'lection's ober. Some ob dem say dere's a trick behine it, an' don't want to tech it. Dese white folks could do a heap wid de culled folks ef dey'd only treat em right."

"When our people say there is a trick behind it," said Robert, "I only wish they could see the trick before it—the trick of worse than wasting their money, and of keeping themselves and families poorer and more ignorant than there is any need for them to be."

"Well, Bobby, I beliebs we might be a people ef it warn't for dat mizzable drink. An' Robby, I jis' tells yer what I wants; I wants some libe man to come down yere an' splain things ter dese people. I don't mean a politic man, but a man who'll larn dese people how to bring up dere chillen, to keep our gals straight, an' our boys from runnin' in de saloons an' gamblin' dens."

"Don't your preachers do that?" asked Robert.

"Well, some ob dem does, an' some ob dem doesn't. An' wen dey preaches, I want dem to practice wat dey preach. Some ob dem says dey's called, but I jis' thinks laziness called some ob dem. An' I thinks since freedom come deres some mighty pore sticks set up for preachers. Now dere's John Anderson, Tom's brudder; you 'member Tom."

"Yes; as brave a fellow and as honest as ever stepped in shoe leather."

"Well, his brudder war mighty diff'rent. He war down in de lower kentry wen de war war ober. He war mighty smart, an' had a good head-piece, an' a orful glib tongue. He set up store an' sole whisky, an' made a lot ob money. Den he wanted ter go to de legislatur. Now what should he do but make out he'd got 'ligion, an' war called to preach. He had no more 'ligion dan my ole dorg. But he had money an' built a meetin' house, whar he could hole meeting, an' hab funerals; an' you know cullud folks is mighty great on funerals. Well dat jis' tuck wid de people, an' he got 'lected to de legislatur. Den he got a fine house, an' his ole wife warn't good 'nuff for him. Den dere war a young school-teacher, an' he begun cuttin' his eyes at her. But she war as deep in de mud as he war in de mire, an' he jis' gib up his ole wife and married her, a fusty thing. He war a mean ole hypocrit, an' I wouldn't sen' fer him to bury my cat. Robby, I'se down on dese kine ob preachers like a thousand bricks."

"Well, Aunt Linda, all the preachers are not like him."

"No; I knows dat; not by a jug full. We's got some mighty good men down yere, an' we's glad when dey comes, an' orful sorry when dey goes 'way. De las preacher we had war a mighty good man. He didn't like too much hollerin'."

"Perhaps," said Robert, "he thought it were best for only one to speak at a time."

"I specs so. His wife war de nicest and sweetest lady dat eber I did see. None ob yer airish, stuck up folks, like a tarrapin carryin' eberything on its back. She used ter hab meetins fer de mudders, an' larn us how to raise our chillen, an' talk so putty to de chillen. I sartinly did lub dat woman."

"Where is she now?" asked Robert.

"De Conference moved dem 'bout thirty miles from yere. Deys gwine to hab a big meetin' ober dere next Sunday. Don't you 'member dem meetins we used to hab in de woods? We don't hab to hide like we did den. But it don't seem as ef de people had de same good 'ligion we had den. 'Pears like folks is took up wid makin' money an' politics."

"Well, Aunt Linda, don't you wish those good old days would come back?"

"No, chile; neber! neber! Wat fer you take me? I'd ruther lib in a corn-crib. Freedom needn't keep me outer heben;

an' ef I'se sich a fool as ter lose my 'ligion cause I'se free, I oughtn' ter git dere."

"But, Aunt Linda, if old Miss were able to take care of you, wouldn't you just as leave be back again?"

There was a faint quiver of indignation in Aunt Linda's voice, as she replied:—

"Don't yer want yer freedom? Well I wants ter pat my free foot. Halleluyah! But, Robby, I wants yer ter go ter dat big meetin' de wuss kine."

"How will I get there?" asked Robert.

"Oh, dat's all right. My ole man's got two ob de nicest mules you eber set yer eyes on. It'll jis' do yer good ter look at dem. I 'spect you'll see some ob yer ole frens dere. Dere's a nice settlemen' of cullud folks ober dere, an' I wants yer to come an' bring dat young lady. I wants dem folks to see wat nice folks I kin bring to de meetin'. I hope's yer didn't lose all your 'ligion in de army."

"Oh, I hope not," replied Robert.

"Oh, chile, yer mus' be shore 'bout dat. I don't want yer to ride hope's hoss down to torment. Now be shore an' come to-morrer an' bring dat young lady, an' take supper wid me. I'se all on nettles to see dat chile."

CHAPTER XIX

Striking Contrasts

The next day, Robert, accompanied by Iola, went to the settlement to take supper with Aunt Linda, and a very luscious affair it was. Her fingers had not lost their skill since she had tasted the sweets of freedom. Her biscuits were just as light and flaky as ever. Her jelly was as bright as amber, and her preserves were perfectly delicious. After she had set the table she stood looking in silent admiration, chuckling to herself: "Ole Mistus can't set sich a table as dat. She ought'er be yere to see it. Specs 'twould make her mouf water. Well, I mus' let bygones be bygones. But dis yere freedom's mighty good."

Aunt Linda had invited Uncle Daniel, and, wishing to give him a pleasant surprise, she had refrained from telling him that Robert Johnson was the one she wished him to meet.

"Do you know dis gemmen?" said Aunt Linda to Uncle Daniel, when the latter arrived.

"Well, I can't say's I do. My eyes is gittin dim, an' I disremembers him."

"Now jis' you look right good at him. Don't yer 'member him?"

Uncle Daniel looked puzzled and, slowly scanning Robert's features, said: "He do look like somebody I used ter know, but I can't make him out ter save my life. I don't know whar to place him. Who is de gemmen, ennyhow?"

"Why, Uncle Dan'el," replied Aunt Linda, "dis is Robby;

Miss Nancy's bad, mischeebous Robby, dat war allers playin' tricks on me."

"Well, shore's I'se born, ef dis ain't our ole Bobby!" exclaimed Uncle Daniel, delightedly. "Why, chile, whar did yer come from? Thought you war dead an' buried long 'go."

"Why, Uncle Daniel, did you send anybody to kill me?" asked Robert, laughingly.

"Oh, no'n 'deed, chile! but I yeard dat you war killed in de battle, an' I never 'spected ter see you agin."

"Well, here I am," replied Robert, "large as life, and just as natural. And this young lady, Uncle Daniel, I believe is my niece." As he spoke he turned to Iola. "Do you remember my mother?"

"Oh, yes," said Uncle Daniel, looking intently at Iola as she stepped forward and cordially gave him her hand.

"Well, I firmly believe," continued Robert, "that this is the daughter of the little girl whom Miss Nancy sold away with my mother."

"Well, I'se rale glad ter see her. She puts me mighty much in mine ob dem days wen we war all young togedder; wen Miss Nancy sed, 'Harriet war too high fer her.' It jis' seems like yisterday wen I yeard Miss Nancy say, 'No house could flourish whar dere war two mistresses.' Well, Mr. Robert——"

"Oh, no, no, Uncle Daniel," interrupted Robert, "don't say that! Call me Robby or Bob, just as you used to."

"Well, Bobby, I'se glad klar from de bottom of my heart ter see yer."

"Even if you wouldn't go with us when we left?"

"Oh, Bobby, dem war mighty tryin' times. You boys didn't know it, but Marster Robert hab giben me a bag ob money ter take keer ob, an' I promised him I'd do it an' I had ter be ez good ez my word."

"Oh, Uncle Daniel, why didn't you tell us boys all about it? We could have helped you take care of it."

"Now, wouldn't dat hab bin smart ter let on ter you chaps,

an' hab you huntin' fer it from Dan ter Barsheba? I specs some ob you would bin a rootin' fer it yit!"

"Well, Uncle Daniel, we were young then; I can't tell what we would have done if we had found it. But we are older now."

"Yes, yer older, but I wouldn't put it pas' yer eben now, ef yer foun' out whar it war."

"Yes," said Iola, laughing, "they say 'caution is the parent of safety.' "

"Money's a mighty tempting thing," said Robert, smiling.

"But, Robby, dere's nothin' like a klar conscience; a klar conscience, Robby!"

Just then Aunt Linda, who had been completing the preparations for her supper, entered the room with her husband, and said, "Salters, let me interdoos you ter my fren', Mr. Robert Johnson, an' his niece, Miss Leroy."

"Why, is it possible," exclaimed Robert, rising, and shaking hands, "that you are Aunt Linda's husband?"

"Dat's what de parson sed," replied Salters.

"I thought," pursued Robert, "that your name was John Andrews. It was such when you were in my company."

"All de use I'se got fer dat name is ter git my money wid it; an' wen dat's done, all's done. Got 'nuff ob my ole Marster in slave times, widout wearin' his name in freedom. Wen I got done wid him, I got done wid his name. Wen I 'listed, I war John Andrews; and wen I gits my pension, I'se John Andrews; but now Salters is my name, an' I likes it better."

"But how came you to be Aunt Linda's husband? Did you get married since the war?"

"Lindy an' me war married long 'fore de war. But my ole Marster sole me away from her an' our little gal, an' den sole her chile ter somebody else. Arter freedom, I hunted up our little gal, an' foun' her. She war a big woman den. Den I com'd right back ter dis place an' foun' Lindy. She hedn't married agin, nuther hed I; so we jis' let de parson marry us out er de book; an' we war mighty glad ter git togedder agin, an' feel hitched togedder fer life."

"Well, Uncle Daniel," said Robert, turning the conversation toward him, "you and Uncle Ben wouldn't go with us, but you came out all right at last."

"Yes, indeed," said Aunt Linda, "Ben got inter a stream of luck. Arter freedom com'd, de people had a heap of fath in Ben; an' wen dey wanted some one to go ter Congress dey jist voted for Ben ter go. An' he went, too. An' wen Salters went to Washin'ton to git his pension, who should he see dere wid dem big men but our Ben, lookin' jist as big as any ob dem."

"An' it did my ole eyes good jist ter see it," broke in Salters; "if I couldn't go dere myself, I war mighty glad to see some one ob my people dat could. I felt like de boy who, wen somebody said he war gwine to slap off his face, said, 'Yer kin slap off my face, but I'se got a big brudder, an' you can't slap off his face.' I went to see him 'fore I lef', and he war jist de same as he war wen we war boys togedder. He hadn't got de big head a bit."

"I reckon Mirandy war mighty sorry she didn't stay wid him. I know I should be," said Aunt Linda.

"Uncle Daniel," asked Robert, "are you still preaching?"

"Yes, chile, I'se still firing off de Gospel gun."

"I hear some of the Northern folks are down here teaching theology, that is, teaching young men how to preach. Why don't you study theology?"

"Look a yere, boy, I'se been a preachin' dese thirty years, an' you come yere a tellin' me 'bout studying yore ologies. I larn'd my 'ology at de foot ob de cross. You bin dar?"

"Dear Uncle Daniel," said Iola, "the moral aspect of the nation would be changed if it would learn at the same cross to subordinate the spirit of caste to the spirit of Christ."

"Does yer 'member Miss Nancy's Harriet," asked Aunt Linda, "dat she sole away kase she wouldn't let her whip her? Well, we think dis is Harriet's gran'chile. She war sole away from her mar, an' now she's a lookin' fer her."

"Well, I hopes she may fine her," replied Salters. "I war sole 'way from my mammy wen I war eighteen mont's ole, an' I wouldn't know her now from a bunch ob turnips."

"I," said Iola, "am on my way South seeking for my mother, and I shall not give up until I find her."

"Come," said Aunt Linda, "we mustn't stan' yer talkin', or de grub'll git cole. Come, frens, sit down, an' eat some ob my pore supper."

Aunt Linda sat at the table in such a flutter of excitement that she could hardly eat, but she gazed with intense satisfaction on her guests. Robert sat on her right hand, contrasting Aunt Linda's pleasant situation with the old days in Mrs. Johnson's kitchen, where he had played his pranks upon her, and told her the news of the war.

Over Iola there stole a spirit of restfulness. There was something so motherly in Aunt Linda's manner that it seemed to recall the bright, sunshiny days when she used to nestle in Mam Liza's arms, in her own happy home. The conversation was full of army reminiscences and recollections of the days of slavery. Uncle Daniel was much interested, and, as they rose from the table, exclaimed:—

"Robby, seein' yer an' hearin' yer talk, almos' puts new springs inter me. I feel 'mos' like I war gittin' younger."

After the supper, Salters and his guests returned to the front room, which Aunt Linda regarded with so much pride, and on which she bestowed so much care.

"Well, Captin," said Salters, "I neber 'spected ter see you agin. Do you know de las' time I seed yer? Well, you war on a stretcher, an' four ob us war carryin' you ter de hospital. War you much hurt?"

"No," replied Robert, "it was only a flesh wound; and this young lady nursed me so carefully that I soon got over it."

"Is dat de way you foun' her?"

"Yes, Andrews,"——

"Salters, ef you please," interrupted Salters. "I'se only Andrews wen I gits my money."

"Well, Salters," continued Robert, "our freedom was a

costly thing. Did you know that Captain Sybil was killed in one of the last battles of the war? These young chaps, who are taking it so easy, don't know the hardships through which we older ones passed. But all the battles are not fought, nor all the victories won. The colored man has escaped from one slavery, and I don't want him to fall into another. I want the young folks to keep their brains clear, and their right arms strong, to fight the battles of life manfully, and take their places alongside of every other people in this country. And I cannot see what is to hinder them if they get a chance."

"I don't nuther," said Salters. "I don't see dat dey drinks any more dan anybody else, nor dat dere is any meanness or debilment dat a black man kin do dat a white man can't keep step wid him."

"Yes," assented Robert, "but while a white man is stealing a thousand dollars, a black man is getting into trouble taking a few chickens."

"All that may be true," said Iola, "but there are some things a white man can do that we cannot afford to do."

"I beliebs eberybody, Norf and Souf, is lookin' at us; an' some ob dem ain't got no good blood fer us, nohow you fix it," said Salters.

"I specs cullud folks mus' hab done somethin'," interposed Aunt Linda.

"O, nonsense," said Robert. "I don't think they are any worse than the white people. I don't believe, if we had the power, we would do any more lynching, burning, and murdering than they do."

"Dat's so," said Aunt Linda, "it's ralely orful how our folks hab been murdered sence de war. But I don't think dese young folks is goin' ter take things as we's allers done."

"We war cowed down from the beginnin'," said Uncle Daniel, "but dese young folks ain't comin' up dat way."

"No," said Salters, "fer one night arter some ob our pore people had been killed, an' some ob our women had run'd away 'bout seventeen miles, my gran'son, looking me squar in de face, said: 'Ain't you got five fingers? Can't you pull a trigger as well as a white man?' I tell yer, Cap, dat jis' got to me, an' I made up my mine dat my boy should neber call me a coward."

"It is not to be expected," said Robert, "that these young people are going to put up with things as we did, when we weren't permitted to hold a meeting by ourselves, or to own a club or learn to read."

"I tried," said Salters, "to git a little out'er de book wen I war in de army. On Sundays I sometimes takes a book an' tries to make out de words, but my eyes is gittin' dim an' de letters all run togedder, an' I gits sleepy, an' ef yer wants to put me to sleep jis' put a book in my han'. But wen it comes to gittin' out a stan' ob cotton, an' plantin' corn, I'se dere all de time. But dat gran'son ob mine is smart as a steel trap. I specs he'll be a preacher."

Salters looked admiringly at his grandson, who sat grinning in the corner, munching a pear he had brought from the table.

"Yes," said Aunt Linda, "his fadder war killed by the Secesh, one night, comin' home from a politic meetin', an' his pore mudder died a few weeks arter, an' we mean to make a man ob him."

"He's got to larn to work fust," said Salters, "an' den ef he's right smart I'se gwine ter sen' him ter college. An' ef he can't get a libin' one way, he kin de oder."

"Yes," said Iola, "I hope he will turn out an excellent young man, for the greatest need of the race is noble, earnest men, and true women."

"Job," said Salters, turning to his grandson, "tell Jake ter hitch up de mules, an' you stay dere an' help him. We's all gwine ter de big meetin'. Yore grandma hab set her heart on goin', an' it'll be de same as a spell ob sickness ef she don't hab a chance to show her bes' bib an' tucker. That ole gal's as proud as a peacock."

"Now, John Salters," exclaimed Aunt Linda, "ain't you 'shamed ob yourself? Allers tryin' to poke fun at yer pore wife. Never mine; wait till I'se gone, an' you'll miss me."

"Ef I war single," said Salters, "I could git a putty young gal, but it wouldn't be so easy wid you."

"Why not?" said Iola, smiling.

" 'Cause young men don't want ole hens, an' old men want young pullets," was Salter's reply.

"Robby, honey," said Aunt Linda, "when you gits a wife, don't treat her like dat man treats me."

"Oh, his head's level," answered Robert; "at least it was in the army."

"Dat's jis' de way; you see dat, Miss Iola? One man takin' up for de oder. But I'll be eben wid you bof. I must go now an' git ready."

Iola laughed. The homely enjoyment of that evening was very welcome to her after the trying scenes through which she had passed. Further conversation was interrupted by the appearance of the wagon, drawn by two fine mules. John Salters stopped joking his wife to admire his mules.

"Jis' look at dem," he said. "Ain't dey beauties? I bought 'em out ob my bounty-money. Arter de war war ober I had a little money, an' I war gwine ter rent a plantation on sheers an' git out a good stan' ob cotton. Cotton war bringin' orful high prices den, but Lindy said to me, 'Now, John, you'se got a lot ob money, an' you'd better salt it down. I'd ruther lib on a little piece ob lan' ob my own dan a big piece ob somebody else's. Well, I says to Lindy, I dun know nuthin' 'bout buyin' lan', an' I'se 'fraid arter I'se done buyed it an' put all de marrer ob dese bones in it, dat somebody's far-off cousin will come an' say de title ain't good, an' I'll lose it all."

"You're right thar, John," said Uncle Daniel. "White man's so unsartin, black man's nebber safe."

"But somehow," continued Salters, "Lindy warn't satisfied wid rentin', so I buyed a piece ob lan', an' I'se glad now I'se got it. Lindy's got a lot ob gumption; knows most as much as a man. She ain't got dat long head fer nuffin. She's got lots ob sense, but I don't like to tell her so."

"Why not?" asked Iola. "Do you think it would make her feel too happy?"

"Well, it don't do ter tell you women how much we thinks ob you. It sets you up too much. Ole Gundover's overseer war my marster, an' he used ter lib in dis bery house. I'se fixed it up sence I'se got it. Now I'se better off dan he is, 'cause he tuck to drink, an' all his frens is gone, an' he's in de pore-house."

Just then Linda came to the door with her baskets.

"Now, Lindy, ain't you ready yet? Do hurry up."

"Yes, I'se ready, but things wouldn't go right ef you didn't hurry me."

"Well, put your chicken fixins an' cake right in yere. Captin, you'll ride wid me, an' de young lady an' my ole woman'll take de back seat. Uncle Dan'el, dere's room for you ef you'll go."

"No, I thank you. It's time fer ole folks to go to bed. Good night! An', Bobby, I hopes to see you agin'."

CHAPTER XX

A Revelation

It was a lovely evening for the journey. The air was soft and balmy. The fields and hedges were redolent with flowers. Not a single cloud obscured the brightness of the moon or the splendor of the stars. The ancient trees were festooned with moss, which hung like graceful draperies. Ever and anon a startled hare glided over the path, and whip-poor-wills and crickets broke the restful silence of the night. Robert rode quietly along, quaffing the beauty of the scene and thinking of his boyish days, when he gathered nuts and wild plums in those woods; he also indulged pleasant reminiscences of later years, when, with Uncle Daniel and Tom Anderson, he attended the secret prayer-meetings. Iola rode along, conversing with Aunt Linda, amused and interested at the quaintness of her speech and the shrewdness of her intellect. To her the ride was delightful.

"Does yer know dis place, Robby," asked Aunt Linda, as they passed an old resort.

"I should think I did," replied Robert. "It is the place where we held our last prayer-meeting."

"An' dere's dat ole broken pot we used, ter tell 'bout de war. But warn't ole Miss hoppin' wen she foun' out you war goin' to de war! I thought she'd go almos' wile. Now, own up, Robby, didn't you feel kine ob mean to go off widout eben biddin' her good bye? An' I ralely think ole Miss war fon' ob yer. Now, own up, honey, didn't yer feel a little down in de mouf wen yer lef' her."

"Not much," responded Robert. "I only thought she was getting paid back for selling my mother."

"Dat's so, Robby! yore mudder war a likely gal, wid long black hair, an' kine ob ginger-bread color. An' you neber hearn tell ob her sence dey sole her to Georgia?"

"Never," replied Robert, "but I would give everything I have on earth to see her once more. I *do* hope, if she is living, that I may meet her before I die."

"You's right, boy, cause she lub'd you as she lub'd her own life. Many a time hes she set in my ole cabin an' cried 'bout yer wen you war fas' asleep. It's all ober now, but I'se gwine to hole up fer dem Yankees dat gib me my freedom, an' sent dem nice ladies from de Norf to gib us some sense. Some ob dese folks calls em nigger teachers, an' won't hab nuffin to do wid 'em, but I jis' thinks dey's splendid. But dere's some triflin' niggers down yere who'll sell der votes for almost nuffin. Does you 'member Jake Williams an' Gundover's Tom? Well dem two niggers is de las' ob pea-time. Dey's mighty small pertaters an' few in a hill."

"Oh, Aunt Linda," said Robert, "don't call them niggers. They are our own people."

"Dey ain't my kine ob people. I jis' calls em niggers, an' niggers I means; an' de bigges' kine ob niggers. An' if my John war sich a nigger I'd whip him an' leave him."

"An' what would I be a doin'," queried John, suddenly rousing up at the mention of his name.

"Standing still and taking it, I suppose," said Iola, who had been quietly listening to and enjoying the conversation.

"Yes, an' I'd ketch myself stan'in' still an' takin' it," was John's plucky response.

"Well, you oughter, ef you's mean enough to wote dat ticket ter put me back inter slavery," was Aunt Linda's parting shot. "Robby," she continued, "you 'member Miss Nancy's Jinnie?"

"Of course I do," said Robert.

"She married Mr. Gundover's Dick. Well, dere warn't much git up an' go 'bout him. So, wen 'lection time com'd, de man he war workin' fer tole him ef he woted de radical ticket he'd turn him off. Well, Jinnie war so 'fraid he'd do it, dat she jis' follered him fer days."

"Poor fellow!" exclaimed Robert. "How did he come out?"

"He certainly was between two fires," interposed Iola.

"Oh, Jinnie gained de day. She jis' got her back up, and said, 'Now ef yer wote dat ticket ter put me back inter slavery, you take yore rags an' go.' An' Dick jis' woted de radical ticket. Jake Williams went on de Secesh side, woted whar he thought he'd git his taters, but he got fooled es slick es greese."

"How was that?" asked Robert.

"Some ob dem folks, dat I 'spects buyed his wote, sent him some flour an' sugar. So one night his wife hab company ter tea. Dey made a big spread, an' put a lot ob sugar on de table fer supper, an' Tom jis' went fer dat sugar. He put a lot in his tea. But somehow it didn't tase right, an' wen dey come ter fine out what war de matter, dey hab sent him a barrel ob san' wid some sugar on top, an' wen de sugar war all gone de san' war dare. Wen I yeard it, I jis' split my sides a larfin. It war too good to keep; an' wen it got roun', Jake war as mad as a March hare. But it sarved him right."

"Well, Aunt Linda, you mustn't be too hard on Uncle Jake; you know he's getting old."

"Well he ain't too ole ter do right. He aint' no older dan Uncle Dan'el. An' I yered dey offered him $500 ef he'd go on dere side. An' Uncle Dan'el wouldn't tech it. An' dere's Uncle Job's wife; why didn't she go dat way? She war down on Job's meanness."

"What did she do?"

"Wen 'lection time 'rived, he com'd home bringing some flour an' meat; an' he says her Aunt Polly, 'Ole woman, I got dis fer de wote.' She jis' picked up dat meat an' flour an' sent it sailin' outer doors, an' den com'd back an' gib him a good tongue-lashin'. 'Oder people,' she said, 'a wotin' ter lib good, an' you a sellin' yore wote! Ain't you got 'nuff ob ole

Marster, an' ole Marster bin cuttin' you up? It shan't stay yere.' An' so she wouldn't let de things stay in de house."

"What did Uncle Job do?"

"He jis' stood dere an' cried."

"And didn't you feel sorry for him?" asked Iola.

"Not a bit! he hedn't no business ter be so shabby."

"But, Aunt Linda," pursued Iola, "if it were shabby for an ignorant colored man to sell his vote, wasn't it shabbier for an intelligent white man to buy it?"

"You see," added Robert, "all the shabbiness is not on our side."

"I knows dat," said Aunt Linda, "but I can't help it. I wants my people to wote right, an' to think somethin' ob demselves."

"Well, Aunt Linda, they say in every flock of sheep there will be one that's scabby," observed Iola.

"Dats so! But I ain't got no use fer scabby sheep."

"Lindy," cried John, "we's most dar! Don't you yere dat singin'? Dey's begun a'ready."

"Neber mine," said Aunt Linda, "sometimes de las' ob de wine is de bes'."

Thus discoursing they had beguiled the long hours of the night and made their long journey appear short.

Very soon they reached the church, a neat, commodious, frame building, with a blue ceiling, white walls within and without, and large windows with mahogany-colored facings. It was a sight full of pathetic interest to see that group which gathered from miles around. They had come to break bread with each other, relate their experiences, and tell of their hopes of heaven. In that meeting were remnants of broken families—mothers who had been separated from their children before the war, husbands who had not met their wives for years. After the bread had been distributed and the hand-shaking was nearly over, Robert raised the hymn which Iola had sung for him when he was recovering from his wounds, and Iola, with her clear, sweet tones, caught up the words and joined him in the strain. When the hymn was finished a dear old mother rose from her seat. Her voice was quite strong. With still a lingering light and fire in her eye, she said:—

"I rise, bredren an' sisters, to say I'm on my solemn march to glory."

"Amen!" "Glory!" came from a number of voices.

"I'se had my trials an' temptations, my ups an' downs; but I feels I'll soon be in one ob de many mansions. If it hadn't been for dat hope I 'spects I would have broken down long ago. I'se bin through de deep waters, but dey didn't overflow me; I'se bin in de fire, but de smell ob it isn't on my garments. Bredren an' sisters, it war a drefful time when I war tored away from my pore little chillen."

"Dat's so!" exclaimed a chorus of voices. Some of her hearers moaned, others rocked to and fro, as thoughts of similar scenes in their own lives arose before them.

"When my little girl," continued the speaker, "took hole ob my dress an' begged me ter let her go wid me, an' I couldn't do it, it mos' broke my heart. I had a little boy, an' wen my mistus sole me she kep' him. She carried on a boardin' house. Many's the time I hab stole out at night an' seen dat chile an' sleep'd wid him in my arms tell mos' day. Bimeby de people I libed wid got hard up fer money, an' dey sole me one way an' my pore little gal de oder; an' I neber laid my eyes on my pore chillen sence den. But, honeys, let de wind blow high or low, I 'spects to outwedder de storm an' anchor by'm bye in bright glory. But I'se bin a prayin' fer one thing, an' I beliebs I'll git it; an' dat is dat I may see my chillen 'fore I die. Pray fer me dat I may hole out an' hole on, an' neber make a shipwrack ob faith, an' at las' fine my way from earth to glory."

Having finished her speech, she sat down and wiped away the tears that flowed all the more copiously as she remembered her lost children. When she rose to speak her voice and manner instantly arrested Robert's attention. He found his mind reverting to the scenes of his childhood. As she proceeded his attention became riveted on her. Unbidden tears filled his eyes and great sobs shook his frame. He trembled in every limb. Could it be possible that after years of patient search through churches, papers, and inquiring friends, he had accidentally stumbled on his mother—the mother who, long years ago, had pillowed his head upon her bosom and left her parting kiss upon his lips? How should he reveal himself to her? Might not sudden joy do what years of sorrow had failed to accomplish? Controlling his feelings as best he could, he rose to tell his experience. He referred to the days when they used to hold their meetings in the lonely woods and gloomy swamps. How they had prayed for freedom and plotted to desert to the Union army; and continuing, he said: "Since then, brethren and sisters, I have had my crosses and trials, but I try to look at the mercies. Just think what it was then and what it is now! How many of us, since freedom has come, have been looking up our scattered relatives. I have just been over to visit my old mistress, Nancy Johnson, and to see if I could get some clue to my long-lost mother, who was sold from me nearly thirty years ago."

Again there was a chorus of moans.

On resuming, Robert's voice was still fuller of pathos.

"When," he said, "I heard that dear old mother tell her experience it seemed as if some one had risen from the dead. She made me think of my own dear mother, who used to steal out at night to see me, fold me in her arms, and then steal back again to her work. After she was sold away I never saw her face again by daylight. I have been looking for her ever since the war, and I think at last I have got on the right track. If Mrs. Johnson, who kept the boarding-house in C——, is the one who sold that dear old mother from her son, then she is the one I am looking for, and I am the son she has been praying for."

The dear old mother raised her eyes. They were clear and tearless. An expression of wonder, hope, and love flitted over her face. It seemed as if her youth were suddenly renewed

375

and, bounding from her seat, she rushed to the speaker in a paroxysm of joy. "Oh, Robby! Robby! is dis you? Is dat my pore, dear boy I'se been prayin' 'bout all dese years? Oh, glory! glory!" And overflowing with joyous excitement she threw her arms around him, looking the very impersonation of rapturous content. It was a happy time. Mothers whose children had been torn from them in the days of slavery knew how to rejoice in her joy. The young people caught the infection of the general happiness and rejoiced with them that rejoiced. There were songs of rejoicing and shouts of praise. The undertone of sadness which had so often mingled with their songs gave place to strains of exultation; and tears of tender sympathy flowed from eyes which had often been blurred by anguish. The child of many prayers and tears was restored to his mother.

Iola stood by the mother's side, smiling, and weeping tears of joy. When Robert's mother observed Iola, she said to Robert, "Is dis yore wife?"

"Oh, no," replied Robert, "but I believe she is your grandchild, the daughter of the little girl who was sold away from you so long ago. She is on her way to the farther South in search of her mother."

"Is she? Dear chile! I hope she'll fine her! She puts me in mine ob my pore little Marie. Well, I'se got one chile, an' I means to keep on prayin' tell I fine my daughter. I'm so happy! I feel's like a new woman!"

"My dear mother," said Robert, "now that I have found you, I mean to hold you fast just as long as you live. Ever since the war I have been trying to find out if you were living, but all efforts failed. At last, I thought I would come and hunt you myself and, now that I have found you, I am going to take you home to live with me, and to be as happy as the days are long. I am living in the North, and doing a good business there. I want you to see joy according to all the days wherein you have seen sorrow. I do hope this young lady will find *her* ma and that, when found, she will prove to be your daughter!"

"Yes, pore, dear chile! I specs her mudder's heart's mighty hungry fer her. I does hope she's my gran'chile."

Tenderly and caressingly Iola bent over the happy mother, with her heart filled with mournful memories of her own mother.

Aunt Linda was induced to stay until the next morning, and then gladly assisted Robert's mother in arranging for her journey northward. The friends who had given her a shelter in their hospitable home, learned to value her so much that it was with great reluctance they resigned her to the care of her son. Aunt Linda was full of bustling activity, and her spirits overflowed with good humor.

"Now, Harriet," she said, as they rode along on their return journey, "you mus' jis' thank me fer finin' yore chile, 'cause I got him to come to dat big meetin' wid me."

"Oh, Lindy," she cried, "I'se glad from de bottom ob my heart ter see you's all. I com'd out dere ter git a blessin', an' I'se got a double po'tion. De frens I war libin' wid war mighty good ter me. Dey lib'd wid me in de lower kentry, an' arter de war war ober I stopped wid 'em and helped take keer ob de chillen; an' when dey com'd up yere dey brought me wid 'em. I'se com'd a way I didn't know, but I'se mighty glad I'se com'd."

"Does you know dis place?" asked Aunt Linda, as they approached the settlement.

"No'n 'deed I don't. It's all new ter me."

"Well, dis is whar I libs. Ain't you mighty tired? I feels a little stiffish. Dese bones is gittin' ole."

"Dat's so! But I'se mighty glad I'se lib'd to see my boy 'fore I crossed ober de riber. An' now I feel like ole Simeon."

"But, mother," said Robert, "if you are ready to go, I am not willing to let you. I want you to stay ever so long where I can see you."

A bright smile overspread her face. Robert's words reassured and gladdened her heart. She was well satisfied to have a pleasant aftermath from life on this side of the river.

After arriving home Linda's first thought was to prepare

dinner for her guests. But, before she began her work of preparation, she went to the cupboard to get a cup of home-made
wine.

"Here," she said, filling three glasses, "is some wine I made
myself from dat grape-vine out dere. Don't it look nice and
clar? Jist taste it. It's fus'-rate."

"No, thank you," said Robert. "I'm a temperance man,
and never take anything which has alcohol in it."

"Oh, dis ain't got a bit ob alcohol in it. I made it
myself."

"But, Aunt Linda, you didn't make the law which fer-
ments grape-juice and makes it alcohol."

"But, Robby, ef alcohol's so bad, w'at made de Lord put
it here?"

"Aunt Lindy," said Iola, "I heard a lady say that there
were two things the Lord didn't make. One is sin, and the
other alcohol."

"Why, Aunt Linda," said Robert, "there are numbers of
things the Lord has made that I wouldn't touch with a pair
of tongs."

"What are they?"

"Rattlesnakes, scorpions, and moccasins."

"Oh, sho!"

"Aunt Linda," said Iola, "the Bible says that the wine at
last will bite like a serpent and sting like an adder."

"And, Aunt Linda," added Robert, "as I wouldn't wind
a serpent around my throat, I don't want to put something
inside of it which will bite like a serpent and sting as an
adder."

"I reckon Robby's right," said his mother, setting down
her glass and leaving the wine unfinished. "You young folks
knows a heap more dan we ole folks."

"Well," declared Aunt Linda, "you all is temp'rence to
de backbone. But what could I do wid my wine ef we didn't
drink it?"

"Let it turn to vinegar, and sign the temperance pledge,"
replied Robert.

"I don't keer 'bout it myself, but I don't 'spect John would be willin' ter let it go, 'cause he likes it a heap."

"Then you must give it up for his sake and Job's," said Robert. "They may learn to like it too well."

"You know, Aunt Linda," said Iola, "people don't get to be drunkards all at once. And you wouldn't like to feel, if Job should learn to drink, that you helped form his appetite."

"Dat's so! I beliebs I'll let dis turn to winegar, an' not make any more."

"That's right, Aunt Linda. I hope you'll hold to it," said Robert, encouragingly.

Very soon Aunt Linda had an excellent dinner prepared. After it was over Robert went with Iola to C——, where her friend, the bishop, was awaiting her return. She told him the wonderful story of Robert's finding his mother, and of her sweet, childlike faith.

The bishop, a kind, fatherly man, said, "Miss Iola, I hope that such happiness is in store for you. My dear child, still continue to pray and trust. I am old-fashioned enough to believe in prayer. I knew an old lady living in Illinois, who was a slave. Her son got a chance to come North and beg money to buy his mother. The mother was badly treated, and made up her mind to run away. But before she started she thought she would kneel down to pray. And something, she said, reasoned within her, and whispered, 'Stand still and see what I am going to do for you.' So real was it to her that she unpacked her bundle and desisted from her flight. Strange as it may appear to you, her son returned, bringing with him money enough to purchase her freedom, and she was redeemed from bondage. Had she persisted in running away she might have been lost in the woods and have died, exhausted by starvation. But she believed, she trusted, and was delivered. Her son took her North, where she could find a resting place for the soles of her feet."

That night Iola and the bishop left for the South.

CHAPTER XXI

A Home for Mother

After Iola had left the settlement, accompanied by Robert as far as the town, it was a pleasant satisfaction for the two old friends to settle themselves down, and talk of times past, departed friends, and long-forgotten scenes.

"What," said Mrs. Johnson, as we shall call Robert's mother, "hab become ob Miss Nancy's husband? Is he still a libin'?"

"Oh, he drunk hisself to death," responded Aunt Linda.

"He used ter be mighty handsome."

"Yes, but drink war his ruination."

"An' how's Miss Nancy?"

"Oh, she's com'd down migh'ly. She's pore as a church mouse. I thought 'twould com'd home ter her wen she sole yer 'way from yore chillen. Dere's nuffin goes ober de debil's back dat don't come under his belly. Do yo 'member Miss Nancy's fardder?"

"Ob course I does!"

"Well," said Aunt Linda, "he war a nice ole gemmen. Wen he died, I said de las' gemmen's dead, an' dere's noboddy ter step in his shoes."

"Pore Miss Nancy!" exclaimed Robert's mother. "I ain't nothin' agin her. But I wouldn't swap places wid her, 'cause I'se got my son; an' I beliebs he'll do a good part by me."

"Mother," said Robert, as he entered the room, "I've

brought an old friend to see you. Do you remember Uncle Daniel?"

Uncle Daniel threw back his head, reached out his hand, and manifested his joy with "Well, Haryet! is dis you? I neber 'spected to see you in dese lower grouns! How does yer do? an' whar hab you bin all dis time?"

"O, I'se been tossin' roun' 'bout; but it's all com'd right at las'. I'se lib'd to see my boy 'fore I died."

"My wife an' boys is in glory," said Uncle Daniel. "But I 'spects to see 'em 'fore long. 'Cause I'se tryin' to dig deep, build sure, an' make my way from earth ter glory."

"Dat's de right kine ob talk, Dan'el. We ole folks ain't got long ter stay yere."

They chatted together until Job and Salters came home for supper. After they had eaten, Uncle Daniel said:—

"We'll hab a word ob prayer."

There, in that peaceful habitation, they knelt down, and mingled their prayers together, as they had done in bygone days, when they had met by stealth in lonely swamps or silent forests.

The next morning Robert and his mother started northward. They were well supplied with a bountiful luncheon by Aunt Linda, who had so thoroughly enjoyed their sojourn with her. On the next day he arrived in the city of P——, and took his mother to his boarding-house, until he could find a suitable home into which to install her. He soon came across one which just suited his taste, but when the agent discovered that Robert's mother was colored, he told him that the house had been previously engaged. In company with his mother he looked at several other houses in desirable neighborhoods, but they were constantly met with the answer, "The house is engaged," or, "We do not rent to colored people."

At length Robert went alone, and, finding a desirable house, engaged it, and moved into it. In a short time it was discovered that he was colored, and, at the behest of the local sentiment of the place, the landlord used his utmost endeavors to oust him, simply because he belonged to an unfashionable and unpopular race. At last he came across a landlord who was broad enough to rent him a good house, and he found a quiet resting place among a set of well-to-do and well-disposed people.

CHAPTER XXII

Further Lifting of the Veil

In one of those fearful conflicts by which the Mississippi was freed from Rebel intrusion and opened to commerce Harry was severely wounded, and forced to leave his place in the ranks for a bed in the hospital.

One day, as he lay in his bed, thinking of his former home in Mississippi and wondering if the chances of war would ever restore him to his loved ones, he fell into a quiet slumber. When he awoke he found a lady bending over him, holding in her hands some fruit and flowers. As she tenderly bent over Harry's bed their eyes met, and with a thrill of gladness they recognized each other.

"Oh, my son, my son!" cried Marie, trying to repress her emotion, as she took his wasted hand in hers, and kissed the pale cheeks that sickness and suffering had blanched. Harry was very weak, but her presence was a call to life. He returned the pressure of her hand, kissed it, and his eyes grew full of sudden light, as he murmured faintly, but joyfully:—

"Mamma; oh, mamma! have I found you at last?"

The effort was too much, and he immediately became unconscious.

Anxious, yet hopeful, Marie sat by the bedside of her son till consciousness was restored. Caressingly she bent over his couch, murmuring in her happiness the tenderest, sweetest words of motherly love. In Harry's veins flowed new life and vigor, calming the restlessness of his nerves.

As soon as possible Harry was carried to his mother's

home; a home brought into the light of freedom by the victories of General Grant. Nursed by his mother's tender, loving care, he rapidly recovered, but, being too disabled to re-enter the army, he was honorably discharged.

Lorraine had taken Marie to Vicksburg, and there allowed her to engage in confectionery and preserving for the wealthy ladies of the city. He had at first attempted to refugee with her in Texas, but, being foiled in the attempt, he was compelled to enlist in the Confederate Army, and met his fate by being killed just before the surrender of Vicksburg.

"My dear son," Marie would say, as she bent fondly over him, "I am deeply sorry that you are wounded, but I am glad that the fortunes of war have brought us together. Poor Iola! I *do* wonder what has become of her? Just as soon as this war is over I want you to search the country all over. Poor child! How my heart has ached for her!"

Time passed on. Harry and his mother searched and inquired for Iola, but no tidings of her reached them.

Having fully recovered his health, and seeing the great need of education for the colored people, Harry turned his attention toward them, and joined the new army of Northern teachers.

He still continued his inquiries for his sister, not knowing whether or not she had succumbed to the cruel change in her life. He thought she might have passed into the white basis for the sake of bettering her fortunes. Hope deferred, which had sickened his mother's heart, had only roused him to renewed diligence.

A school was offered him in Georgia, and thither he repaired, taking his mother with him. They were soon established in the city of A——. In hope of finding Iola he visited all the conferences of the Methodist Church, but for a long time his search was in vain.

"Mamma," said Harry, one day during his vacation, "there is to be a Methodist Conference in this State in the city of S——, about one hundred and fifty miles from here. I intend to go and renew my search for Iola."

"Poor child!" burst out Marie, as the tears gathered in her eyes, "I wonder if she is living."

"I think so," said Harry, kissing the pale cheek of his mother; "I don't feel that Iola is dead. I believe we will find her before long."

"It seems to me my heart would burst with joy to see my dear child just once more. I am glad that you are going. When will you leave?"

"To-morrow morning."

"Well, my son, go, and my prayers will go with you," was Marie's tender parting wish.

Early next morning Harry started for the conference, and reached the church before the morning session was over. Near him sat two ladies, one fair, the other considerably darker. There was something in the fairer one that reminded him forcibly of his sister, but she was much older and graver than he imagined his sister to be. Instantly he dismissed the thought that had forced itself into his mind, and began to listen attentively to the proceedings of the conference.

When the regular business of the morning session was over the bishop arose and said:—

"I have an interesting duty to perform. I wish to introduce a young lady to the conference, who was the daughter of a Mississippi planter. She is now in search of her mother and brother, from whom she was sold a few months before the war. Her father married her mother in Ohio, where he had taken her to be educated. After his death they were robbed of their inheritance and enslaved by a distant relative named Lorraine. Miss Iola Leroy is the young lady's name. If any one can give the least information respecting the objects of her search it will be thankfully received."

"I can," exclaimed a young man, rising in the midst of the audience, and pressing eagerly, almost impetuously, forward. "I am her brother, and I came here to look for her."

Iola raised her eyes to his face, so flushed and bright with the glow of recognition, rushed to him, threw her arms around his neck, kissed him again and again, crying: "O, Harry!" Then she fainted from excitement. The women gathered around her with expressions of tender sympathy, and gave her all the care she needed. They called her the "dear child," for without any effort on her part she had slidden into their hearts and found a ready welcome in each sympathizing bosom.

Harry at once telegraphed the glad tidings to his mother, who waited their coming with joyful anticipation. Long before the cars reached the city, Mrs. Leroy was at the depot, restlessly walking the platform or eagerly peering into the darkness to catch the first glimpse of the train which was bearing her treasures.

At length the cars arrived, and, as Harry and Iola alighted, Marie rushed forward, clasped Iola in her arms and sobbed out her joy in broken words.

Very happy was the little family that sat together around the supper-table for the first time for years. They partook of that supper with thankful hearts and with eyes overflowing with tears of joy. Very touching were the prayers the mother uttered, when she knelt with her children that night to return thanks for their happy reunion, and to seek protection through the slumbers of the night.

The next morning, as they sat at the breakfast-table, Marie said:—

"My dear child, you are so changed I do not think I would have known you if I had met you in the street!"

"And I," said Harry, "can hardly realize that you are our own Iola, whom I recognized as sister a half dozen years ago."

"Am I so changed?" asked Iola, as a faint sigh escaped her lips.

"Why, Iola," said Harry, "you used to be the most harum-scarum girl I ever knew—laughing, dancing, and singing from morning until night."

"Yes, I remember," said Iola. "It all comes back to me

like a dream. Oh, mamma! I have passed through a fiery ordeal of suffering since then. But it is useless," and as she continued her face assumed a brighter look, "to brood over the past. Let us be happy in the present. Let me tell you something which will please you. Do you remember telling me about your mother and brother?"

"Yes," said Marie, in a questioning tone.

"Well," continued Iola, with eyes full of gladness, "I think I have found them."

"Can it be possible!" exclaimed Marie, in astonishment. "It is more than thirty years since we parted. I fear you are mistaken."

"No, mamma; I have drawn my conclusions from good circumstantial evidence. After I was taken from you, I passed through a fearful siege of suffering, which would only harrow up your soul to hear. I often shudder at the remembrance. The last man in whose clutches I found myself was mean, brutal, and cruel. I was in his power when the Union army came into C——, where I was living. A number of colored men stampeded to the Union ranks, with a gentleman as a leader, whom I think is your brother. A friend of his reported my case to the commander of the post, who instantly gave orders for my release. A place was given me as nurse in the hospital. I attended that friend in his last illness. Poor fellow! he was the best friend I had in all the time I have been tossing about. The gentleman whom I think is your brother appeared to be very anxious about his friend's recovery, and was deeply affected by his death. In one of the last terrible battles of the war, that of Five Forks, he was wounded and put into the hospital ward where I was an attendant. For awhile he was delirious, and in his delirium he would sometimes think that I was his mother and at other times his sister. I humored his fancies, would often sing to him when he was restless, and my voice almost invariably soothed him to sleep. One day I sang to him that old hymn we used to sing on the plantation:—

'Drooping souls no longer grieve,
    Heaven is propitious;
If on Christ you do believe,
    You will find Him precious.' "

"I remember," said Marie, with a sigh, as memories of the past swept over her.

"After I had finished the hymn," continued Iola, "he looked earnestly and inquiringly into my face, and asked, 'Where did you learn that hymn? I have heard my mother sing it when I was a boy, but I have never heard it since.' I think, mamma, the words, 'I was lost but now I'm found; glory! glory! glory!' had imprinted themselves on his memory, and that his mind was assuming a higher state of intellectuality. He asked me to sing it again, which I did, until he fell asleep. Then I noticed a marked resemblance between him and Harry, and I thought, 'Suppose he should prove to be your long-lost brother?' During his convalescence we found that we had a common ground of sympathy. We were anxious to be reunited to our severed relations. We had both been separated from our mothers. He told me of his little sister, with whom he used to play. She had a mole on her cheek which he called her beauty spot. He had the red spot on his forehead which you told me of."

CHAPTER XXIII

Delightful Reunions

Very bright and happy was the home where Marie and her children were gathered under one roof. Mrs. Leroy's neighbors said she looked ten years younger. Into that peaceful home came no fearful forebodings of cruel separations. Harry and Iola were passionately devoted to their mother, and did all they could to flood her life with sunshine.

"Iola, dear," said Harry, one morning at the breakfast-table, "I have a new pleasure in store for you."

"What is it, brother mine?" asked Iola, assuming an air of interest.

"There is a young lady living in this city to whom I wish to introduce you. She is one of the most remarkable women I have ever met."

"Do tell me all about her," said Iola. "Is she young and handsome, brilliant and witty?"

"She," replied Harry, "is more than handsome, she is lovely; more than witty, she is wise; more than brilliant, she is excellent."

"Well, Harry," said Mrs. Leroy, smiling, "if you keep on that way I shall begin to fear that I shall soon be supplanted by a new daughter."

"Oh, no, mamma," replied Harry, looking slightly confused, "I did not mean that."

"Well, Harry," said Iola, amused, "go on with your description; I am becoming interested. Tax your powers of description to give me her likeness."

"Well, in the first place," continued Harry, "I suppose she is about twenty-five years old."

"Oh, the idea," interrupted Iola, "of a gentleman talking of a lady's age. That is a tabooed subject."

"Why, Iola, that adds to the interest of my picture. It is her combination of earnestness and youthfulness which enhances her in my estimation."

"Pardon the interruption," said Iola; "I am anxious to hear more about her."

"Well, she is of medium height, somewhat slender, and well formed, with dark, expressive eyes, full of thought and feeling. Neither hair nor complexion show the least hint of blood admixture."

"I am glad of it," said Iola. "Every person of unmixed blood who succeeds in any department of literature, art, or science is a living argument for the capability which is in the race."

"Yes," responded Harry, "for it is not the white blood which is on trial before the world. Well, I will bring her around this evening."

In the evening Harry brought Miss Delany to call on his sister and mother. They were much pleased with their visitor. Her manner was a combination of suavity and dignity. During the course of the evening they learned that she was a graduate of the University of A——. One day she saw in the newspapers that colored women were becoming unfit to be servants for white people. She then thought that if they are not fit to be servants for white people, they are unfit to be mothers to their own children, and she conceived the idea of opening a school to train future wives and mothers. She began on a small scale, in a humble building and her work was soon crowned with gratifying success. She had enlarged her quarters, increased her teaching force, and had erected a large and commodious school-house through her own exertions and the help of others.

Marie cordially invited her to call again, saying, as she rose to go: "I am very glad to have met you. Young women like you always fill my heart with hope for the future of our race. In you I see reflected some of the blessed possibilities which lie within us."

"Thank you," said Miss Delany, "I want to be classed among those of whom it is said, 'She has done what she could.'"

Very pleasant was the acquaintance which sprang up between Miss Delany and Iola. Although she was older than Iola, their tastes were so congenial, their views of life and duty in such unison, that their acquaintance soon ripened into strong and lasting friendship. There were no foolish rivalries and jealousies between them. Their lives were too full of zeal and earnestness for them to waste in selfishness their power to be moral and spiritual forces among a people who so much needed their helping hands. Miss Delany gave Iola a situation in her school; but before the term was quite over she was forced to resign, her health having been so undermined by the fearful strain through which she had passed, that she was quite unequal to the task. She remained at home, and did what her strength would allow in assisting her mother in the work of canning and preserving fruits.

In the meantime, Iola had been corresponding with Robert. She had told him of her success in finding her mother and brother, and had received an answer congratulating her on the glad fruition of her hopes. He also said that his business was flourishing, that his mother was keeping house for him, and, to use her own expression, was as happy as the days are long. She was firmly persuaded that Marie was her daughter, and she wanted to see her before she died.

"There is one thing," continued the letter, "that your mother may remember her by. It was a little handkerchief on which were a number of cats' heads. She gave one to each of us."

"I remember it well," said Marie, "she must, indeed, be my mother. Now, all that is needed to complete my happiness is her presence, and my brother's. And I intend, if I live long enough, to see them both."

Iola wrote Robert that her mother remembered the incident of the handkerchief, and was anxious to see them.

In the early fall Robert started for the South in order to clear up all doubts with respect to their relationship. He found Iola, Harry, and their mother living cosily together. Harry was teaching and was a leader among the rising young men of the State. His Northern education and later experience had done much toward adapting him to the work of the new era which had dawned upon the South.

Marie was very glad to welcome Robert to her home, but it was almost impossible to recognize her brother in that tall, handsome man, with dark-brown eyes and wealth of chestnut-colored hair, which he readily lifted to show the crimson spot which lay beneath it.

But as they sat together, and recalled the long-forgotten scenes of their childhood, they concluded that they were brother and sister.

"Marie," said Robert, "how would you like to leave the South?"

"I should like to go North, but I hate to leave Harry. He's a splendid young fellow, although I say it myself. He is so fearless and outspoken that I am constantly anxious about him, especially at election time."

Harry then entered the room, and, being introduced to Robert, gave him a cordial welcome. He had just returned from school.

"We were talking of you, my son," said Marie.

"What were you saying? Nothing of the absent but good?" asked Harry.

"I was telling your uncle, who wants me to come North, that I would go, but I am afraid that you will get into trouble and be murdered, as many others have been."

"Oh, well, mother, I shall not die till my time comes. And if I die helping the poor and needy, I shall die at my post. Could a man choose a better place to die?"

"Were you aware of the virulence of caste prejudice and the disabilities which surround the colored people when you cast your lot with them?" asked Robert.

"Not fully," replied Harry; "but after I found out that I was colored, I consulted the principal of the school, where I was studying, in reference to the future. He said that if I stayed in the North, he had friends whom he believed would give me any situation I could fill, and I could simply take my place in the rank of workers, the same as any other man. Then he told me of the army, and I made up my mind to enter it, actuated by a desire to find my mother and sister; and at any rate I wanted to avenge their wrongs. I do not feel so now. Since I have seen the fearful ravages of war, I have learned to pity and forgive. The principal said he thought I would be more apt to find my family if I joined a colored regiment in the West than if I joined one of the Maine companies. I confess at first I felt a shrinking from taking the step, but love for my mother overcame all repugnance on my part. Now that I have linked my fortunes to the race I intend to do all I can for its elevation."

As he spoke Robert gazed admiringly on the young face, lit up by noble purposes and lofty enthusiasm.

"You are right, Harry. I think it would be treason, not only to the race, but to humanity, to have you ignoring your kindred and masquerading as a white man."

"I think so, too," said Marie.

"But, sister, I am anxious for you all to come North. If Harry feels that the place of danger is the post of duty, let him stay, and he can spend his vacations with us. I think both you and Iola need rest and change. Mother longs to see you before she dies. She feels that we have been the children of many prayers and tears, and I want to make her last days as happy as possible. The South has not been a paradise to you all the time, and I should think you would be willing to leave it."

"Yes, that is so. Iola needs rest and change, and she would be such a comfort to mother. I suppose, for her sake,

I will consent to have her go back with you, at least for while."

In a few days, with many prayers and tears, Marie, half reluctantly, permitted Iola to start for the North in company with Robert Johnson, intending to follow as soon as she could settle her business and see Harry in a good boarding place.

Very joyful was the greeting of the dear grandmother. Iola soon nestled in her heart and lent additional sunshine to her once checkered life, and Robert, who had so long been robbed of kith and kin, was delighted with the new accession to his home life.

CHAPTER XXIV

Northern Experience

"Uncle Robert," said Iola, after she had been North several weeks, "I have a theory that every woman ought to know how to earn her own living. I believe that a great amount of sin and misery springs from the weakness and inefficiency of women."

"Perhaps that's so, but what are you going to do about it?"

"I am going to join the great rank of bread-winners. Mr. Waterman has advertised for a number of saleswomen, and I intend to make application."

"When he advertises for help he means white women," said Robert.

"He said nothing about color," responded Iola.

"I don't suppose he did. He doesn't expect any colored girl to apply."

"Well, I think I could fill the place. At least I should like to try. And I do not think when I apply that I am in duty bound to tell him my great-grandmother was a negro."

"Well, child, there is no necessity for you to go out to work. You are perfectly welcome here, and I hope that you feel so."

"Oh, I certainly do. But still I would rather earn my own living."

That morning Iola applied for the situation, and, being prepossessing in her appearance, she obtained it.

For awhile everything went as pleasantly as a marriage

bell. But one day a young colored lady, well-dressed and well-bred in her manner, entered the store. It was an acquaintance which Iola had formed in the colored church which she attended. Iola gave her a few words of cordial greeting, and spent a few moments chatting with her. The attention of the girls who sold at the same counter was attracted, and their suspicion awakened. Iola was a stranger in that city. Who was she, and who were her people? At last it was decided that one of the girls should act as a spy, and bring what information she could concerning Iola.

The spy was successful. She found out that Iola was living in a good neighborhood, but that none of the neighbors knew her. The man of the house was very fair, but there was an old woman whom Iola called "Grandma," and she was unmistakably colored. The story was sufficient. If that were true, Iola must be colored, and she should be treated accordingly.

Without knowing the cause, Iola noticed a chill in the social atmosphere of the store, which communicated itself to the cash-boys, and they treated her so insolently that her situation became very uncomfortable. She saw the proprietor, resigned her position, and asked for and obtained a letter of recommendation to another merchant who had advertised for a saleswoman.

In applying for the place, she took the precaution to inform her employer that she was colored. It made no difference to him; but he said:—

"Don't say anything about it to the girls. They might not be willing to work with you."

Iola smiled, did not promise, and accepted the situation. She entered upon her duties, and proved quite acceptable as a saleswoman.

One day, during an interval in business, the girls began to talk of their respective churches, and the question was put to Iola:—

"Where do you go to church?"

"I go," she replied, "to Rev. River's church, corner of Eighth and L Streets."

"Oh, no; you must be mistaken. There is no church there except a colored one."

"That is where I go."

"Why do you go there?"

"Because I liked it when I came here, and joined it."

"A member of a colored church? What under heaven possessed you to do such a thing?"

"Because I wished to be with my own people."

Here the interrogator stopped, and looked surprised and pained, and almost instinctively moved a little farther from her. After the store was closed, the girls had an animated discussion, which resulted in the information being sent to Mr. Cohen that Iola was a colored girl, and that they protested against her being continued in his employ. Mr. Cohen yielded to the pressure, and informed Iola that her services were no longer needed.

When Robert came home in the evening, he found that Iola had lost her situation, and was looking somewhat discouraged.

"Well, uncle," she said, "I feel out of heart. It seems as if the prejudice pursues us through every avenue of life, and assigns us the lowest places."

"That is so," replied Robert, thoughtfully.

"And yet I am determined," said Iola, "to win for myself a place in the fields of labor. I have heard of a place in New England, and I mean to try for it, even if I only stay a few months."

"Well, if you *will* go, say nothing about your color."

"Uncle Robert, I see no necessity for proclaiming that fact on the house-top. Yet I am resolved that nothing shall tempt me to deny it. The best blood in my veins is African blood, and I am not ashamed of it."

"Hurrah for you!" exclaimed Robert, laughing heartily.

As Iola wished to try the world for herself, and so be prepared for any emergency, her uncle and grandmother were content to have her go to New England. The town to which she journeyed was only a few hours' ride from the city of

P——, and Robert, knowing that there is no teacher like experience, was willing that Iola should have the benefit of her teaching.

Iola, on arriving in H——, sought the firm, and was informed that her services were needed. She found it a pleasant and lucrative position. There was only one drawback—her boarding place was too far from her work. There was an institution conducted by professed Christian women, which was for the special use of respectable young working girls. This was in such a desirable location that she called at the house to engage board.

The matron conducted her over the house, and grew so friendly in the interview that she put her arm around her, and seemed to look upon Iola as a desirable accession to the home. But, just as Iola was leaving, she said to the matron: "I must be honest with you; I am a colored woman."

Swift as light a change passed over the face of the matron. She withdrew her arm from Iola, and said: "I must see the board of managers about it."

When the board met, Iola's case was put before them, but they decided not to receive her. And these women, professors of a religion which taught, "If ye have respect to persons ye commit sin," virtually shut the door in her face because of the outcast blood in her veins.

Considerable feeling was aroused by the action of these women, who, to say the least, had not put their religion in the most favorable light.

Iola continued to work for the firm until she received letters from her mother and uncle, which informed her that her mother, having arranged her affairs in the South, was ready to come North. She then resolved to return to the city of P——, to be ready to welcome her mother on her arrival.

Iola arrived in time to see that everything was in order for her mother's reception. Her room was furnished neatly, but with those touches of beauty that womanly hands are such adepts in giving. A few charming pictures adorned the walls, and an easy chair stood waiting to receive the travel-worn mother. Robert and Iola met her at the depot; and grandma was on her feet at the first sound of the bell, opened the door, clasped Marie to her heart, and nearly fainted for joy.

"Can it be possible dat dis is my little Marie?" she exclaimed.

It did seem almost impossible to realize that this faded woman, with pale cheeks and prematurely whitened hair, was the rosy-cheeked child from whom she had been parted more than thirty years.

"Well," said Robert, after the first joyous greeting was over, "love is a very good thing, but Marie has had a long journey and needs something that will stick by the ribs. How about dinner, mother?"

"It's all ready," said Mrs. Johnson.

After Marie had gone to her room and changed her dress, she came down and partook of the delicious repast which her mother and Iola had prepared for her.

In a few days Marie was settled in the home, and was well pleased with the change. The only drawback to her happiness was the absence of her son, and she expected him to come North after the closing of his school.

"Uncle Robert," said Iola, after her mother had been with them several weeks, "I am tired of being idle."

"What's the matter now?" asked Robert. "You are surely not going East again, and leave your mother?"

"Oh, I hope not," said Marie, anxiously. "I have been so long without you."

"No, mamma, I am not going East. I can get suitable employment here in the city of P——."

"But, Iola," said Robert, "you have tried, and been defeated. Why subject yourself to the same experience again?"

"Uncle Robert, I think that every woman should have some skill or art which would insure her at least a comfortable support. I believe there would be less unhappy marriages if labor were more honored among women."

"Well, Iola," said her mother, "what is your skill?"

"Nursing. I was very young when I went into the hospital,

but I succeeded so well that the doctor said I must have been a born nurse. Now, I see by the papers, that a gentleman who has an invalid daughter wants some one who can be a nurse and companion for her, and I mean to apply for the situation. I do not think, if I do my part well in that position, that the blood in my veins will be any bar to my success."

A troubled look stole over Marie's face. She sighed faintly, but made no remonstrance. And so it was decided that Iola should apply for the situation.

Iola made application, and was readily accepted. Her patient was a frail girl of fifteen summers, who was ill with a low fever. Iola nursed her carefully, and soon had the satisfaction of seeing her restored to health. During her stay, Mr. Cloten, the father of the invalid, had learned some of the particulars of Iola's Northern experience as a bread-winner, and he resolved to give her employment in his store when her services were no longer needed in the house. As soon as a vacancy occurred he gave Iola a place in his store.

The morning she entered on her work he called his employés together, and told them that Miss Iola had colored blood in her veins, but that he was going to employ her and give her a desk. If any one objected to working with her, he or she could step to the cashier's desk and receive what was due. Not a man remonstrated, not a woman demurred; and Iola at last found a place in the great army of bread-winners, which the traditions of her blood could not affect.

"How did you succeed?" asked Mrs. Cloten of her husband, when he returned to dinner.

"Admirably! 'Everything is lovely and the goose hangs high.' I gave my employés to understand that they could leave if they did not wish to work with Miss Leroy. Not one of them left, or showed any disposition to rebel."

"I am very glad," said Mrs. Cloten. "I am ashamed of the way she has been treated in our city, when seeking to do her share in the world's work. I am glad that you were brave enough to face this cruel prejudice, and give her a situation."

"Well, my dear, do not make me a hero for a single act.

I am grateful for the care Miss Leroy gave our Daisy. Money can buy services, but it cannot purchase tender, loving sympathy. I was also determined to let my employés know that I, not they, commanded my business. So, do not crown me a hero until I have won a niche in the temple of fame. In dealing with Southern prejudice against the negro, we Northerners could do it with better grace if we divested ourselves of our own. We irritate the South by our criticisms, and, while I confess that there is much that is reprehensible in their treatment of colored people, yet if our Northern civilization is higher than theirs we should 'criticise by creation.' We should stamp ourselves on the South, and not let the South stamp itself on us. When we have learned to treat men according to the complexion of their souls, and not the color of their skins, we will have given our best contribution towards the solution of the negro problem."

"I feel, my dear," said Mrs. Cloten, "that what you have done is a right step in the right direction, and I hope that other merchants will do the same. We have numbers of business men, rich enough to afford themselves the luxury of a good conscience."

CHAPTER XXV

An Old Friend

"Good-morning, Miss Leroy," said a cheery voice in tones of glad surprise, and, intercepting her path, Dr. Gresham stood before Iola, smiling, and reaching out his hand.

"Why, Dr. Gresham, is this you?" said Iola, lifting her eyes to that well-remembered face. "It has been several years since we met. How have you been all this time, and where?"

"I have been sick, and am just now recovering from malaria and nervous prostration. I am attending a medical convention in this city, and hope that I shall have the pleasure of seeing you again."

Iola hesitated, and then replied: "I should be pleased to have you call."

"It would give me great pleasure. Where shall I call?"

"My home is 1006 South Street, but I am only at home in the evenings."

They walked together a short distance till they reached Mr. Cloten's store; then, bidding the doctor good morning, Iola left him repeating to himself the words of his favorite poet:—

> "Thou art too lovely and precious a gem
>   To be bound to their burdens and sullied by them."

No one noticed the deep flush on Iola's face as she entered the store, nor the subdued, quiet manner with which she

402

applied herself to her tasks. She was living over again the past, with its tender, sad, and thrilling reminiscences.

In the evening Dr. Gresham called on Iola. She met him with a pleasant welcome. Dr. Gresham gazed upon her with unfeigned admiration, and thought that the years, instead of detracting from, had only intensified, her loveliness. He had thought her very beautiful in the hospital, in her gray dress and white collar, with her glorious wealth of hair drawn over her ears. But now, when he saw her with that hair artistically arranged, and her finely-proportioned form arrayed in a dark crimson dress, relieved by a shimmer of lace and a bow of white ribbon at her throat, he thought her superbly handsome. The lines which care had written upon her young face had faded away. There was no undertone of sorrow in her voice as she stood up before him in the calm loveliness of her ripened womanhood, radiant in beauty and gifted in intellect. Time and failing health had left their traces upon Dr. Gresham. His step was less bounding, his cheek a trifle paler, his manner somewhat graver than it was when he had parted from Iola in the hospital, but his meeting with her had thrilled his heart with unexpected pleasure. Hopes and sentiments which long had slept awoke at the touch of her hand and the tones of her voice, and Dr. Gresham found himself turning to the past, with its sad memories and disappointed hopes. No other face had displaced her image in his mind; no other love had woven itself around every tendril of his soul. His heart and hand were just as free as they were the hour they had parted.

"To see you again," said Dr. Gresham, "is a great and unexpected pleasure."

"You had not forgotten me, then?" said Iola, smiling.

"Forget you! I would just as soon forget my own existence. I do not think that time will ever efface the impressions of those days in which we met so often. When last we met you were intending to search for your mother. Have you been successful?"

"More than successful," said Iola, with a joyous ring in

her voice. "I have found my mother, brother, grandmother, and uncle, and, except my brother, we are all living together, and we are so happy. Excuse me a few minutes," she said, and left the room. Iola soon returned, bringing with her her mother and grandmother.

"These," said Iola, introducing her mother and grandmother, "are the once-severed branches of our family; and this gentleman you have seen before," continued Iola, as Robert entered the room.

Dr. Gresham looked scrutinizingly at him and said: "Your face looks familiar, but I saw so many faces at the hospital that I cannot just now recall your name."

"Doctor," said Robert Johnson, "I was one of your last patients, and I was with Tom Anderson when he died."

"Oh, yes," replied Dr. Gresham; "it all comes back to me. You were wounded at the battle of Five Forks, were you not?"

"Yes," said Robert.

"I saw you when you were recovering. You told me that you thought you had a clue to your lost relatives, from whom you had been so long separated. How have you succeeded?"

"Admirably! I have been fortunate in finding my mother, my sister, and her children."

"Ah, indeed! I am delighted to hear it. Where are they?"

"They are right here. This is my mother," said Robert, bending fondly over her, as she returned his recognition with an expression of intense satisfaction; "and this," he continued, "is my sister, and Miss Leroy is my niece."

"Is it possible! I am very glad to hear it. It has been said that every cloud has its silver lining, and the silver lining of our war cloud is the redemption of a race and the reunion of severed hearts. War is a dreadful thing; but worse than the war was the slavery which preceded it."

"Slavery," said Iola, "was a fearful cancer eating into the nation's heart, sapping its vitality, and undermining its life."

"And war," said Dr. Gresham, "was the dreadful surgery by which the disease was eradicated. The cancer has been removed, but for years to come I fear that we will have to deal with the effects of the disease. But I believe that we have vitality enough to outgrow those effects."

"I think, Doctor," said Iola, "that there is but one remedy by which our nation can recover from the evil entailed upon her by slavery."

"What is that?" asked Robert.

"A fuller comprehension of the claims of the Gospel of Jesus Christ, and their application to our national life."

Gospel

"Yes," said Robert; "while politicians are stumbling on the barren mountains of fretful controversy, and asking what shall we do with the negro, I hold that Jesus answered that question nearly two thousand years ago, when he said, 'Whatsoever ye would that men should do to you, do ye even so to them.' "

"Yes," said Dr. Gresham; "the application of that rule in dealing with the negro would solve the whole problem."

"Slavery," said Mrs. Leroy, "is dead, but the spirit which animated it still lives; and I think that a reckless disregard for human life is more the outgrowth of slavery than any actual hatred of the negro."

"The problem of the nation," continued Dr. Gresham, "is not what men will do with the negro, but what will they do with the reckless, lawless white men who murder, lynch, and burn their fellow-citizens. To me these lynchings and burn-ings are perfectly alarming. Both races have reacted on each other—men fettered the slave, and cramped their own souls; denied him knowledge, and darkened their spiritual insight; subdued him to the pliancy of submission, and in their turn became the thralls of public opinion. The negro came here from the heathenism of Africa; but the young colonies could not take into their early civilization a stream of barbaric blood without being affected by its influence, and the negro, poor and despised as he is, has laid his hands on our Southern civilization and helped mould its character."

"Yes," said Mrs. Leroy; "the colored nurse could not nes-tle her master's child in her arms, hold up his baby footsteps on their floors, and walk with him through the impressible and formative period of his young life without leaving upon him the impress of her hand."

"I am glad," said Robert, "for the whole nation's sake, that slavery has been destroyed."

"And our work," said Dr. Gresham, "is to build over the desolations of the past a better and brighter future. The great distinction between savagery and civilization is the creation and maintenance of law. A people cannot habitually trample on law and justice without retrograding toward barbarism. But I am hopeful that time will bring us changes for the better; that, as we get farther away from the war, we will outgrow the animosities and prejudices engendered by slavery. The short-sightedness of our fathers linked the negro's destiny to ours. We are feeling the friction of the ligatures which bind us together, but I hope that the time will speedily come when the best members of both races will unite for the maintenance of law and order and the progress and prosperity of the country, and that the intelligence and virtue of the South will be strong to grapple effectually with its ignorance and vice."

"I hope that time will speedily come," said Marie. "My son is in the South, and I am always anxious for his safety. He is not only a teacher, but a leading young man in the community where he lives."

"Yes," said Robert, "and when I see the splendid work he is doing in the South, I am glad that, instead of trying to pass for a white man, he has cast his lot with us."

"But," answered Dr. Gresham, "he would possess advantages as a white man which he could not if he were known to be colored."

"Doctor," said Iola, decidedly, "he has greater advantages as a colored man."

"I do not understand you," said Dr. Gresham, looking somewhat puzzled.

"Doctor," continued Iola, "I do not think life's highest advantages are those that we can see with our eyes or grasp with our hands. To whom to-day is the world most indebted—to its millionaires or to its martyrs?"

"Taking it from the ideal standpoint," replied the doctor, "I should say its martyrs."

"To be," continued Iola, "the leader of a race to higher planes of thought and action, to teach men clearer views of life and duty, and to inspire their souls with loftier aims, is a far greater privilege than it is to open the gates of material prosperity and fill every home with sensuous enjoyment."

"And I," said Mrs. Leroy, her face aglow with fervid feeling, "would rather—ten thousand times rather—see Harry the friend and helper of the poor and ignorant than the companion of men who, under the cover of night, mask their faces and ride the country on lawless raids."

"Dr. Gresham," said Robert, "we ought to be the leading nation of the earth, whose influence and example should give light to the world."

"Not simply," said Iola, "a nation building up a great material prosperity, founding magnificent cities, grasping the commerce of the world, or excelling in literature, art, and science, but a nation wearing sobriety as a crown and righteousness as the girdle of her loins."

Dr. Gresham gazed admiringly upon Iola. A glow of enthusiasm overspread her beautiful, expressive face. There was a rapt and far-off look in her eye, as if she were looking beyond the present pain to a brighter future for the race with which she was identified, and felt the grandeur of a divine commission to labor for its uplifting.

As Dr. Gresham was parting with Robert, he said: "This meeting has been a very unexpected pleasure. I have spent a delightful evening. I only regret that I had not others to share it with me. A doctor from the South, a regular Bourbon, is stopping at the hotel. I wish he could have been here to-night. Come down to the Concordia, Mr. Johnson, to-morrow night. If you know any colored man who is a strong champion of equal rights, bring him along. Good-night. I shall look for you," said the doctor, as he left the door.

When Robert returned to the parlor he said to Iola: "Dr. Gresham has invited me to come to his hotel to-morrow night, and to bring some wide-awake colored man with me. There is a Southerner whom he wishes me to meet. I suppose he wants to discuss the negro problem, as they call it. He wants some one who can do justice to the subject. I wonder whom I can take with me?"

"I will tell you who, I think, will be a capital one to take with you, and I believe he would go," said Iola.

"Who?" asked Robert.

"Rev. Carmicle, your pastor."

"He is just the one," said Robert, "courteous in his manner and very scholarly in his attainments. He is a man whom if everybody hated him no one could despise him."

CHAPTER XXVI

Open Questions

In the evening Robert and Rev. Carmicle called on Dr. Gresham, and found Dr. Latrobe, the Southerner, and a young doctor by the name of Latimer, already there. Dr. Gresham introduced Dr. Latrobe, but it was a new experience to receive colored men socially. His wits, however, did not forsake him, and he received the introduction and survived it.

"Permit me, now," said Dr. Gresham, "to introduce you to my friend, Dr. Latimer, who is attending our convention. He expects to go South and labor among the colored people. Don't you think that there is a large field of usefulness before him?"

"Yes," replied Dr. Latrobe, "if he will let politics alone."

"And why let politics alone?" asked Dr. Gresham.

"Because," replied Dr. Latrobe, "we Southerners will never submit to negro supremacy. We will never abandon our Caucasian civilization to an inferior race."

"Have you any reason," inquired Rev. Carmicle, "to dread that a race which has behind it the heathenism of Africa and the slavery of America, with its inheritance of ignorance and poverty, will be able, in less than one generation, to domineer over a race which has behind it ages of dominion, freedom, education, and Christianity?"

A slight shade of vexation and astonishment passed over the face of Dr. Latrobe. He hesitated a moment, then replied:—

"I am not afraid of the negro as he stands alone, but what I dread is that in some closely-contested election ambitious men will use him to hold the balance of power and make him an element of danger. He is ignorant, poor, and clannish, and they may impact him as their policy would direct."

"Any more," asked Robert, "than the leaders of the Rebellion did the ignorant, poor whites during our late conflict?"

"Ignorance, poverty, and clannishness," said Dr. Gresham, "are more social than racial conditions, which may be outgrown."

"And I think," said Rev. Carmicle, "that we are outgrowing them as fast as any other people would have done under the same conditions."

"The negro," replied Dr. Latrobe, "always has been and always will be an element of discord in our country."

"What, then, is your remedy?" asked Dr. Gresham.

"I would eliminate him from the politics of the country."

"As disfranchisement is a punishment for crime, is it just to punish a man before he transgresses the law?" asked Dr. Gresham.

"If," said Dr. Latimer, "the negro is ignorant, poor, and clannish, let us remember that in part of our land it was once a crime to teach him to read. If he is poor, for ages he was forced to bend to unrequited toil. If he is clannish, society has segregated him to himself."

"And even," said Robert, "has given him a negro pew in your churches and a negro seat at your communion table."

"Wisely, or unwisely," said Dr. Gresham, "the Government has put the ballot in his hands. It is better to teach him to use that ballot aright than to intimidate him by violence or vitiate his vote by fraud."

"To-day," said Dr. Latimer, "the negro is not plotting in beer-saloons against the peace and order of society. His fingers are not dripping with dynamite, neither is he spitting upon your flag, nor flaunting the red banner of anarchy in your face."

"Power," said Dr. Gresham, "naturally gravitates into the strongest hands. The class who have the best brain and most wealth can strike with the heaviest hand. I have too much faith in the inherent power of the white race to dread the competition of any other people under heaven."

"I think you Northerners fail to do us justice," said Dr. Latrobe. "The men into whose hands you put the ballot were our slaves, and we would rather die than submit to them. Look at the carpet-bag governments the wicked policy of the Government inflicted upon us. It was only done to humiliate us."

"Oh, no!" said Dr. Gresham, flushing, and rising to his feet. "We had no other alternative than putting the ballot in their hands."

"I will not deny," said Rev. Carmicle, "that we have made woeful mistakes, but with our antecedents it would have been miraculous if we had never committed any mistakes or made any blunders."

"They were allies in war," continued Dr. Gresham, "and I am sorry that we have not done more to protect them in peace."

"Protect them in peace!" said Robert, bitterly. "What protection does the colored man receive from the hands of the Government? I know of no civilized country outside of America where men are still burned for real or supposed crimes."

"Johnson," said Dr. Gresham, compassionately, "it is impossible to have a policeman at the back of each colored man's chair, and a squad of soldiers at each cross-road, to detect with certainty, and punish with celerity, each invasion of his rights. We tried provisional governments and found them a failure. It seemed like leaving our former allies to be mocked with the name of freedom and tortured with the essence of slavery. The ballot is our weapon of defense, and we gave it to them for theirs."

"And there," said Dr. Latrobe, emphatically, "is where

you signally failed. We are numerically stronger in Congress to-day than when we went out. You made the law, but the administration of it is in our hands, and we are a unit."

"But, Doctor," said Rev. Carmicle, "you cannot willfully deprive the negro of a single right as a citizen without sending demoralization through your own ranks."

"I think," said Dr. Latrobe, "that we are right in suppressing the negro's vote. This is a white man's government, and a white man's country. We own nineteen-twentieths of the land, and have about the same ratio of intelligence. I am a white man, and, right or wrong, I go with my race."

"But, Doctor," said Rev. Carmicle, "there are rights more sacred than the rights of property and superior intelligence."

"What are they?" asked Dr. Latrobe.

"The rights of life and liberty," replied Rev. Carmicle.

"That is true," said Dr. Gresham; "and your Southern civilization will be inferior until you shall have placed protection to those rights at its base, not in theory but in fact."

"But, Dr. Gresham, we have to live with these people, and the North is constantly irritating us by its criticisms."

"The world," said Dr. Gresham, "is fast becoming a vast whispering gallery, and lips once sealed can now state their own grievances and appeal to the conscience of the nation, and, as long as a sense of justice and mercy retains a hold upon the heart of our nation, you cannot practice violence and injustice without rousing a spirit of remonstrance. And if it were not so I would be ashamed of my country and of my race."

"You speak," said Dr. Latrobe, "as if we had wronged the negro by enslaving him and being unwilling to share citizenship with him. I think that slavery has been of incalculable value to the negro. It has lifted him out of barbarism and fetich worship, given him a language of civilization, and introduced him to the world's best religion. Think what he was in Africa and what he is in America!"

"The negro," said Dr. Gresham, thoughtfully, "is not the only branch of the human race which has been low down in the scale of civilization and freedom, and which has out-grown the measure of his chains. Slavery, polygamy, and human sacrifices have been practiced among Europeans in bygone days; and when Tyndall tells us that out of savages unable to count to the number of their fingers and speaking only a language of nouns and verbs, arise at length our Newtons and Shakspeares, I do not see that the negro could not have learned our language and received our religion without the intervention of ages of slavery."

"If," said Rev. Carmicle, "Mohammedanism, with its imperfect creed, is successful in gathering large numbers of negroes beneath the Crescent, could not a legitimate commerce and the teachings of a pure Christianity have done as much to plant the standard of the Cross over the ramparts of sin and idolatry in Africa? Surely we cannot concede that the light of the Crescent is greater than the glory of the Cross, that there is less constraining power in the Christ of Calvary than in the Prophet of Arabia? I do not think that I underrate the difficulties in your way when I say that you young men are holding in your hands golden opportunities which it would be madness and folly to throw away. It is your grand opportunity to help build up a new South, not on the shifting sands of policy and expediency, but on the broad basis of equal justice and universal freedom. Do this and you will be blessed, and will make your life a blessing."

After Robert and Rev. Carmicle had left the hotel, Drs. Latimer, Gresham, and Latrobe sat silent and thoughtful awhile, when Dr. Gresham broke the silence by asking Dr. Latrobe how he had enjoyed the evening.

"Very pleasantly," he replied. "I was quite interested in that parson. Where was he educated?"

"In Oxford, I believe. I was pleased to hear him say that he had no white blood in his veins."

"I should think not," replied Dr. Latrobe, "from his looks. But one swallow does not make a summer. It is the exceptions which prove the rule."

"Don't you think," asked Dr. Gresham, "that we have been too hasty in our judgment of the negro? He has come handicapped into life, and is now on trial before the world. But it is not fair to subject him to the same tests that you would a white man. I believe that there are possibilities of growth in the race which we have never comprehended."

"The negro," said Dr. Latrobe, "is perfectly comprehensible to me. The only way to get along with him is to let him know his place, and make him keep it."

"I think," replied Dr. Gresham, "every man's place is the one he is best fitted for."

"Why," asked Dr. Latimer, "should any place be assigned to the negro more than to the French, Irish, or German?"

"Oh," replied Dr. Latrobe, "they are all Caucasians."

"Well," said Dr. Gresham, "is all excellence summed up in that branch of the human race?"

"I think," said Dr. Latrobe, proudly, "that we belong to the highest race on earth and the negro to the lowest."

"And yet," said Dr. Latimer, "you have consorted with them till you have bleached their faces to the whiteness of your own. Your children nestle in their bosoms; they are around you as body servants, and yet if one of them should attempt to associate with you your bitterest scorn and indignation would be visited upon them."

"I think," said Dr. Latrobe, "that feeling grows out of our Anglo-Saxon regard for the marriage relation. These white negroes are of illegitimate origin, and we would scorn to share our social life with them. Their blood is tainted."

"Who tainted it?" asked Dr. Latimer, bitterly. "You give absolution to the fathers, and visit the misfortunes of the mothers upon the children."

"But, Doctor, what kind of society would we have if we put down the bars and admitted everybody to social equality?"

"This idea of social equality," said Dr. Latimer, "is only a bugbear which frightens well-meaning people from dealing justly with the negro. I know of no place on earth where there is perfect social equality, and I doubt if there is such a thing in heaven. The sinner who repents on his death-bed cannot be the equal of St. Paul or the Beloved Disciple."

"Doctor," said Dr. Gresham, "I sometimes think that the final solution of this question will be the absorption of the negro into our race."

"Never! never!" exclaimed Dr. Latrobe, vehemently. "It would be a death blow to American civilization."

"Why, Doctor," said Dr. Latimer, "you Southerners began this absorption before the war. I understand that in one decade the mixed bloods rose from one-ninth to one-eighth of the population, and that as early as 1663 a law was passed in Maryland to prevent English women from intermarrying with slaves; and, even now, your laws against miscegenation presuppose that you apprehend danger from that source."

"Doctor, it is no use talking," replied Dr. Latrobe, wearily. "There are niggers who are as white as I am, but the taint of blood is there and we always exclude it."

"How do you know it is there?" asked Dr. Gresham.

"Oh, there are tricks of blood which always betray them. My eyes are more practiced than yours. I can always tell them. Now, that Johnson is as white as any man; but I knew he was a nigger the moment I saw him. I saw it in his eye."

Dr. Latimer smiled at Dr. Latrobe's assertion, but did not attempt to refute it; and bade him good-night.

"I think," said Dr. Latrobe, "that our war was the great mistake of the nineteenth century. It has left us very serious complications. We cannot amalgamate with the negroes. We cannot expatriate them. Now, what are we to do with them?"

"Deal justly with them," said Dr. Gresham, "and let them alone. Try to create a moral sentiment in the nation, which will consider a wrong done to the weakest of them as a wrong done to the whole community. Whenever you find ministers too righteous to be faithless, cowardly, and time serving; women too Christly to be scornful; and public men too noble to be tricky and too honest to pander to the prejudices of the people, stand by them and give them your moral support."

"Doctor," said Latrobe, "with your views you ought to be a preacher striving to usher in the millennium."

"It can't come too soon," replied Dr. Gresham.

CHAPTER XXVII

Diverging Paths

On the eve of his departure from the city of P——, Dr. Gresham called on Iola, and found her alone. They talked awhile of reminiscences of the war and hospital life, when Dr. Gresham, approaching Iola, said:—

"Miss Leroy, I am glad the great object of your life is accomplished, and that you have found all your relatives. Years have passed since we parted, years in which I have vainly tried to get a trace of you and have been baffled, but I have found you at last!" Clasping her hand in his, he continued, "I would it were so that I should never lose you again! Iola, will you not grant me the privilege of holding this hand as mine all through the future of our lives? Your search for your mother is ended. She is well cared for. Are you not free at last to share with me my Northern home, free to be mine as nothing else on earth is mine." Dr. Gresham looked eagerly on Iola's face, and tried to read its varying expression. "Iola, I learned to love you in the hospital. I have tried to forget you, but it has been all in vain. Your image is just as deeply engraven on my heart as it was the day we parted."

"Doctor," she replied, sadly, but firmly, as she withdrew her hand from his, "I feel now as I felt then, that there is an insurmountable barrier between us."

"What is it, Iola?" asked Dr. Gresham, anxiously.

"It is the public opinion which assigns me a place with the colored people."

"But what right has public opinion to interfere with our marriage relations? Why should we yield to its behests?"

"Because it is stronger than we are, and we cannot run counter to it without suffering its penalties."

"And what are they, Iola? Shadows that you merely dread?"

"No! no! the penalties of social ostracism North and South, except here and there some grand and noble exceptions. I do not think that you fully realize how much prejudice against colored people permeates society, lowers the tone of our religion, and reacts upon the life of the nation. After freedom came, mamma was living in the city of A——, and wanted to unite with a Christian church there. She made application for membership. She passed her examination as a candidate, and was received as a church member. When she was about to make her first communion, she unintentionally took her seat at the head of the column. The elder who was administering the communion gave her the bread in the order in which she sat, but before he gave her the wine some one touched him on the shoulder and whispered a word in his ear. He then passed mamma by, gave the cup to others, and then returned to her. From that rite connected with the holiest memories of earth, my poor mother returned humiliated and depressed."

"What a shame!" exclaimed Dr. Gresham, indignantly.

"I have seen," continued Iola, "the same spirit manifested in the North. Mamma once attempted to do missionary work in this city. One day she found an outcast colored girl, whom she wished to rescue. She took her to an asylum for fallen women and made an application for her, but was refused. Colored girls were not received there. Soon after mamma found among the colored people an outcast white girl. Mamma's sympathies, unfettered by class distinction, were aroused in her behalf, and, in company with two white ladies, she went with the girl to that same refuge. For her the door was freely opened and admittance readily granted. It was as if two women were sinking in the quicksands, and on the solid land stood other women with life-lines in their hands, seeing the deadly sands slowly creeping up around the hapless victims. To one they readily threw the lines of deliverance, but for the other there was not one strand of salvation. Sometime since, to the same asylum, came a poor fallen girl who had escaped from the clutches of a wicked woman. For her the door would have been opened, had not the vile woman from whom she was escaping followed her to that place of refuge and revealed the fact that she belonged to the colored race. That fact was enough to close the door upon her, and to send her back to sin and to suffer, and perhaps to die as a wretched outcast. And yet in this city where a number of charities are advertised, I do not think there is one of them which, in appealing to the public, talks more religion than the managers of this asylum. This prejudice against the colored race environs our lives and mocks our aspirations."

"Iola, I see no use in your persisting that you are colored when your eyes are as blue and complexion as white as mine."

"Doctor, were I your wife, are there not people who would caress me as a white woman who would shrink from me in scorn if they knew I had one drop of negro blood in my veins? When mistaken for a white woman I should hear things alleged against the race at which my blood would boil. No, Doctor, I am not willing to live under a shadow of concealment which I thoroughly hate as if the blood in my veins were an undetected crime of my soul."

"Iola, dear, surely you paint the picture too darkly."

"Doctor, I have painted it with my heart's blood. It is easier to outgrow the dishonor of crime than the disabilities of color. You have created in this country an aristocracy of color wide enough to include the South with its treason and Utah with its abominations, but too narrow to include the best and bravest colored man who bared his breast to the bullets of the enemy during your fratricidal strife. Is not the most arrant Rebel to-day more acceptable to you than the most faithful colored man?"

"No! no!" exclaimed Dr. Gresham, vehemently. "You are wrong. I belong to the Grand Army of the Republic. We have no separate State Posts for the colored people, and, were such a thing proposed, the majority of our members, I believe, would be against it. In Congress colored men have the same seats as white men, and the color line is slowly fading out in our public institutions."

"But how is it in the Church?" asked Iola.

"The Church is naturally conservative. It preserves old truths, even if it is somewhat slow in embracing new ideas. It has its social as well as its spiritual side. Society is woman's realm. The majority of church members are women, who are said to be the aristocratic element of our country. I fear that one of the last strongholds of this racial prejudice will be found beneath the shadow of some of our churches. I think, on account of this social question, that large bodies of Christian temperance women and other reformers, in trying to reach the colored people even for their own good, will be quicker to form separate associations than our National Grand Army, whose ranks are open to black and white, liberals and conservatives, saints and agnostics. But, Iola, we have drifted far away from the question. No one has a right to interfere with our marriage if we do not infringe on the rights of others."

"Doctor," she replied, gently, "I feel that our paths must diverge. My life-work is planned. I intend spending my future among the colored people of the South."

"My dear friend," he replied, anxiously, "I am afraid that you are destined to sad disappointment. When the novelty wears off you will be disillusioned, and, I fear, when the time comes that you can no longer serve them they will forget your services and remember only your failings."

"But, Doctor, they need me; and I am sure when I taught among them they were very grateful for my services."

"I think," he replied, "these people are more thankful than grateful."

"I do not think so; and if I did it would not hinder me from doing all in my power to help them. I do not expect all the finest traits of character to spring from the hot-beds of slavery and caste. What matters it if they do forget the singer, so they don't forget the song? No, Doctor, I don't think that I could best serve my race by forsaking them and marrying you."

"Iola," he exclaimed, passionately, "if you love your race, as you call it, work for it, live for it, suffer for it, and, if need be, die for it; but don't marry for it. Your education has unfitted you for social life among them."

"It was," replied Iola, "through their unrequited toil that I was educated, while they were compelled to live in ignorance. I am indebted to them for the power I have to serve them. I wish other Southern women felt as I do. I think they could do so much to help the colored people at their doors if they would look at their opportunities in the light of the face of Jesus Christ. Nor am I wholly unselfish in allying myself with the colored people. All the rest of my family have done so. My dear grandmother is one of the excellent of the earth, and we all love her too much to ignore our relationship with her. I did not chose my lot in life, and the simplest thing I can do is to accept the situation and do the best I can."

"And is this your settled purpose?" he asked, sadly.

"It is, Doctor," she replied, tenderly but firmly. "I see no other. I must serve the race which needs me most."

"Perhaps you are right," he replied; "but I cannot help feeling sad that our paths, which met so pleasantly, should diverge so painfully. And yet, not only the freedmen, but the whole country, need such helpful self-sacrificing teachers as you will prove; and if earnest prayers and holy wishes can brighten your path, your lines will fall in the pleasantest places."

As he rose to go, sympathy, love, and admiration were blended in the parting look he gave her; but he felt it was useless to attempt to divert her from her purpose. He knew that for the true reconstruction of the country something more was needed than bayonets and bullets, or the schemes of selfish politicians or plotting demagogues. He knew that the South needed the surrender of the best brain and heart of the country to build, above the wastes of war, more stately temples of thought and action.

CHAPTER XXVIII

Dr. Latrobe's Mistake

On the morning previous to their departure for their respective homes, Dr. Gresham met Dr. Latrobe in the parlor of the Concordia.

"How," asked Dr. Gresham, "did you like Dr. Latimer's paper?"

"Very much, indeed. It was excellent. He is a very talented young man. He sits next to me at lunch and I have conversed with him several times. He is very genial and attractive, only he seems to be rather cranky on the negro question. I hope if he comes South that he will not make the mistake of mixing up with the negroes. It would be throwing away his influence and ruining his prospects. He seems to be well versed in science and literature and would make a very delightful accession to our social life."

"I think," replied Dr. Gresham, "that he is an honor to our profession. He is one of the finest specimens of our young manhood."

Just then Dr. Latimer entered the room. Dr. Latrobe arose and, greeting him cordially, said: "I was delighted with your paper; it was full of thought and suggestion."

"Thank you," answered Dr. Latimer, "it was my aim to make it so."

"And you succeeded admirably," replied Dr. Latrobe. "I could not help thinking how much we owe to heredity and environment."

"Yes," said Dr. Gresham. "Contir
sends to our shores subjects to be dev
Emancipation has given us millions of
them our influence and example should
a curse."

"Well," said Dr. Latimer, "I intend to go south, and
help those who so much need helpers from their own
ranks."

"I hope," answered Dr. Latrobe, "that if you go
South you will only sustain business relations with the negroes, and not commit the folly of equalizing yourself with
them."

"Why not?" asked Dr. Latimer, steadily looking him in
the eye.

"Because in equalizing yourself with them you drag us
down; and our social customs must be kept intact."

"You have been associating with me at the convention for
several days; I do not see that the contact has dragged you
down, has it?"

"You! What has that got to do with associating with niggers?" asked Dr. Latrobe, curtly.

"The blood of that race is coursing through my veins. I
am one of them," replied Dr. Latimer, proudly raising his
head.

"You!" exclaimed Dr. Latrobe, with an air of profound
astonishment and crimsoning face.

"Yes;" interposed Dr. Gresham, laughing heartily at Dr.
Latrobe's discomfiture. "He belongs to that negro race both
by blood and choice. His father's mother made overtures to
receive him as her grandson and heir, but he has nobly refused to forsake his mother's people and has cast his lot with
them."

"And I," said Dr. Latimer, "would have despised myself
if I had done otherwise."

"Well, well," said Dr. Latrobe, rising, "I was never so
deceived before. Good morning!"

Dr. Latrobe had thought he was clear-sighted enough to detect the presence of negro blood when all physical traces had disappeared. But he had associated with Dr. Latimer for several days, and admired his talent, without suspecting for one moment his racial connection. He could not help feeling a sense of vexation at the signal mistake he had made.

Dr. Frank Latimer was the natural grandson of a Southern lady, in whose family his mother had been a slave. The blood of a proud aristocratic ancestry was flowing through his veins, and generations of blood admixture had effaced all trace of his negro lineage. His complexion was blonde, his eye bright and piercing, his lips firm and well moulded; his manner very affable; his intellect active and well stored with information. He was a man capable of winning in life through his rich gifts of inheritance and acquirements. When freedom came, his mother, like Hagar of old, went out into the wide world to seek a living for herself and child. Through years of poverty she labored to educate her child, and saw the glad fruition of her hopes when her son graduated as an M.D. from the University of P——.

After his graduation he met his father's mother, who recognized him by his resemblance to her dear, departed son. All the mother love in her lonely heart awoke, and she was willing to overlook "the missing link of matrimony," and adopt him as her heir, if he would ignore his identity with the colored race.

Before him loomed all the possibilities which only birth and blood can give a white man in our Democratic country. But he was a man of too much sterling worth of character to be willing to forsake his mother's race for the richest advantages his grandmother could bestow.

Dr. Gresham had met Dr. Latimer at the beginning of the convention, and had been attracted to him by his frank and genial manner. One morning, when conversing with him, Dr. Gresham had learned some of the salient points of his history, which, instead of repelling him, had only deepened his admiration for the young doctor. He was much amused when he saw the pleasant acquaintanceship between him and Dr. Latrobe, but they agreed to be silent about his racial connection until the time came when they were ready to divulge it; and they were hugely delighted at his signal blunder.

CHAPTER XXIX

Visitors from the South

"Mamma is not well," said Iola to Robert. "I spoke to her about sending for a doctor, but she objected and I did not insist."

"I will ask Dr. Latimer, whom I met at the Concordia, to step in. He is a splendid young fellow. I wish we had thousands like him."

In the evening the doctor called. Without appearing to make a professional visit he engaged Marie in conversation, watched her carefully, and came to the conclusion that her failing health proceeded more from mental than physical causes.

"I am so uneasy about Harry," said Mrs. Leroy. "He is so fearless and outspoken. I do wish the attention of the whole nation could be turned to the cruel barbarisms which are a national disgrace. I think the term 'bloody shirt' is one of the most heartless phrases ever invented to divert attention from cruel wrongs and dreadful outrages."

Just then Iola came in and was introduced by her uncle to Dr. Latimer, to whom the introduction was a sudden and unexpected pleasure.

After an interchange of courtesies, Marie resumed the conversation, saying: "Harry wrote me only last week that a young friend of his had lost his situation because he refused to have his pupils strew flowers on the streets through which Jefferson Davis was to pass."

"I think," said Dr. Latimer, indignantly, "that the Israelites had just as much right to scatter flowers over the bodies of the Egyptians, when the waves threw back their corpses on the shores of the Red Sea, as these children had to strew the path of Jefferson Davis with flowers. We want our boys to grow up manly citizens, and not cringing sycophants. When do you expect your son, Mrs. Leroy?"

"Some time next week," answered Marie.

"And his presence will do you more good than all the medicine in my chest."

"I hope, Doctor," said Mrs. Leroy, "that we will not lose sight of you, now that your professional visit is ended; for I believe your visit was the result of a conspiracy between Iola and her uncle."

Dr. Latimer laughed, as he answered, "Ah, Mrs. Leroy, I see you have found us all out."

"Oh, Doctor," exclaimed Iola, with pleasing excitement, "there is a young lady coming here to visit me next week. Her name is Miss Lucille Delany, and she is my ideal woman. She is grand, brave, intellectual, and religious."

"Is that so? She would make some man an excellent wife," replied Dr. Latimer.

"Now isn't that perfectly manlike," answered Iola, smiling. "Mamma, what do you think of that? Did any of you gentlemen ever see a young woman of much ability that you did not look upon as a flotsam all adrift until some man had appropriated her?"

"I think, Miss Leroy, that the world's work, if shared, is better done than when it is performed alone. Don't you think your life-work will be better done if some one shares it with you?" asked Dr. Latimer, slowly, and with a smile in his eyes.

"That would depend on the person who shared it," said Iola, faintly blushing.

"Here," said Robert, a few evenings after this conversation, as he handed Iola a couple of letters, "is something which will please you."

Iola took the letters, and, after reading one of them, said:

"Miss Delany and Harry will be here on Wednesday; and this one is an invitation which also adds to my enjoyment."

"What is it?" asked Marie; "an invitation to a hop or a german?"

"No; but something which I value far more. We are all invited to Mr. Stillman's to a *conversazione*."

"What is the object?"

"His object is to gather some of the thinkers and leaders of the race to consult on subjects of vital interest to our welfare. He has invited Dr. Latimer, Professor Gradnor, of North Carolina, Mr. Forest, of New York, Hon. Dugdale, Revs. Carmicle, Cantnor, Tunster, Professor Langhorne, of Georgia, and a few ladies, Mrs. Watson, Miss Brown, and others."

"I am glad that it is neither a hop nor a german," said Iola, "but something for which I have been longing."

"Why, Iola," said Robert, "don't you believe in young people having a good time?"

"Oh, yes," answered Iola, seriously, "I believe in young people having amusements and recreations; but the times are too serious for us to attempt to make our lives a long holiday."

"Well, Iola," answered Robert, "this is the first holiday we have had in two hundred and fifty years, and you shouldn't be too exacting."

"Yes," replied Marie, "human beings naturally crave enjoyment, and if not furnished with good amusements they are apt to gravitate to low pleasures."

"Some one," said Robert, "has said that the Indian belongs to an old race and looks gloomily back to the past, and that the negro belongs to a young race and looks hopefully towards the future."

"If that be so," replied Marie, "our race-life corresponds more to the follies of youth than the faults of maturer years."

On Dr. Latimer's next visit he was much pleased to see a great change in Marie's appearance. Her eye had grown brighter, her step more elastic, and the anxiety had faded from her face. Harry had arrived, and with him came Miss Delany.

"Good evening, Dr. Latimer," said Iola, cheerily, as she entered the room with Miss Lucille Delany. "This is my friend, Miss Delany, from Georgia. Were she not present I would say she is one of the grandest women in America."

"I am very much pleased to meet you," said Dr. Latimer, cordially; "I have heard Miss Leroy speak of you. We were expecting you," he added, with a smile.

Just then Harry entered the room, and Iola presented him to Dr. Latimer, saying, "This is my brother, about whom mamma was so anxious."

"Had you a pleasant journey?" asked Dr. Latimer, after the first greetings were over.

"Not especially," answered Miss Delany. "Southern roads are not always very pleasant to travel. When Mr. Leroy entered the cars at A——, where he was known, had he taken his seat among the white people he would have been remanded to the colored car."

"But after awhile," said Harry, "as Miss Delany and myself were sitting together, laughing and chatting, a colored man entered the car, and, mistaking me for a white man, asked the conductor to have me removed, and I had to insist that I was colored in order to be permitted to remain. It would be ludicrous, if it were not vexatious, to be too white to be black, and too black to be white."

"Caste plays such fantastic tricks in this country," said Dr. Latimer.

"I tell Mr. Leroy," said Miss Delany, "that when he returns he must put a label on himself, saying, 'I am a colored man,' to prevent annoyance."

CHAPTER XXX

Friends in Council

On the following Friday evening, Mr. Stillman's pleasant, spacious parlors were filled to overflowing with a select company of earnest men and women deeply interested in the welfare of the race.

Bishop Tunster had prepared a paper on "Negro Emigration." Dr. Latimer opened the discussion by speaking favorably of some of the salient points, but said:—

"I do not believe self-exilement is the true remedy for the wrongs of the negro. Where should he go if he left this country?"

"Go to Africa," replied Bishop Tunster, in his bluff, hearty tones. "I believe that Africa is to be redeemed to civilization, and that the negro is to be gathered into the family of nations and recognized as a man and a brother."

"Go to Africa?" repeated Professor Langhorne, of Georgia. "Does the United States own one foot of African soil? And have we not been investing our blood in the country for ages?"

"I am in favor of missionary efforts," said Professor Gradnor, of North Carolina, "for the redemption of Africa, but I see no reason for expatriating ourselves because some persons do not admire the color of our skins."

"I do not believe," said Mr. Stillman, "in emptying on the shores of Africa a horde of ignorant, poverty-stricken people, as missionaries of civilization or Christianity. And while I am in favor of missionary efforts, there is need here for the best heart and brain to work in unison for justice and righteousness."

"America," said Miss Delany, "is the best field for human development. God has not heaped up our mountains with such grandeur, flooded our rivers with such majesty, crowned our valleys with such fertility, enriched our mines with such wealth, that they should only minister to grasping greed and sensuous enjoyment."

"Climate, soil, and physical environments," said Professor Gradnor, "have much to do with shaping national characteristics. If in Africa, under a tropical sun, the negro has lagged behind other races in the march of civilization, at least for once in his history he has, in this country, the privilege of using climatic advantages and developing under new conditions."

"Yes," replied Dr. Latimer, "and I do not wish our people to become restless and unsettled before they have tried one generation of freedom."

"I am always glad," said Mr. Forest, a tall, distinguished-looking gentleman from New York, "when I hear of people who are ill treated in one section of the country emigrating to another. Men who are deaf to the claims of mercy, and oblivious to the demands of justice, can feel when money is slipping from their pockets."

"The negro," said Hon. Dugdale, "does not present to my mind the picture of an effete and exhausted people, destined to die out before a stronger race. Gilbert Haven once saw a statue which suggested this thought, 'I am black, but comely; the sun has looked down upon me, but I will teach you who despise me to feel that I am your superior.' The men who are acquiring property and building up homes in the South show us what energy and determination may do even in that part of the country. I believe such men can do more to conquer prejudice than if they spent all their lives in shouting for their rights and ignoring their duties. No! as there are millions of us in this country, I think it best to settle down and work out our own salvation here."

"How many of us to-day," asked Professor Langhorne, "would be teaching in the South, if every field of labor in the North was as accessible to us as to the whites? It has been estimated that a million young white men have left the South since the war, and, had our chances been equal to theirs, would we have been any more willing to stay in the South with those who need us than they? But this prejudice, by impacting us together, gives us a common cause and brings our intellect in contact with the less favored of our race."

"I do not believe," said Miss Delany, "that the Southern white people themselves desire any wholesale exodus of the colored from their labor fields. It would be suicidal to attempt their expatriation."

"History," said Professor Langhorne, "tells that Spain was once the place where barbarian Europe came to light her lamp. Seven hundred years before there was a public lamp in London you might have gone through the streets of Cordova amid ten miles of lighted lamps, and stood there on solidly paved land, when hundreds of years afterwards, in Paris, on a rainy day you would have sunk to your ankles in the mud. But she who bore the name of the 'Terror of Nations,' and the 'Queen of the Ocean,' was not strong enough to dash herself against God's law of retribution and escape unscathed. She inaugurated a crusade of horror against a million of her best laborers and artisans. Vainly she expected the blessing of God to crown her work of violence. Instead of seeing the fruition of her hopes in the increased prosperity of her land, depression and paralysis settled on her trade and business. A fearful blow was struck at her agriculture; decay settled on her manufactories; money became too scarce to pay the necessary expenses of the king's exchequer; and that once mighty empire became a fallen kingdom, pierced by her crimes and dragged down by her transgressions."

"We did not," said Iola, "place the bounds of our habitation. And I believe we are to be fixtures in this country. But beyond the shadows I see the coruscation of a brighter day; and we can help usher it in, not by answering hate with hate, or giving scorn for scorn, but by striving to be more generous, noble, and just. It seems as if all creation travels to respond to the song of the Herald angels, 'Peace on earth, good-will toward men.' "

The next paper was on "Patriotism," by Rev. Cantnor. It was a paper in which the white man was extolled as the master race, and spoke as if it were a privilege for the colored man to be linked to his destiny and to live beneath the shadow of his power. He asserted that the white race of this country is the broadest, most Christian, and humane of that branch of the human family.

Dr. Latimer took exception to his position. "Law," he said, "is the pivot on which the whole universe turns; and obedience to law is the gauge by which a nation's strength or weakness is tried. We have had two evils by which our obedience to law has been tested—slavery and the liquor traffic. How have we dealt with them both? We have been weighed in the balance and found wanting. Millions of slaves and serfs have been liberated during this century, but not even in semi-barbaric Russia, heathen Japan, or Catholic Spain has slavery been abolished through such a fearful conflict as it was in the United States. The liquor traffic still sends its floods of ruin and shame to the habitations of men, and no political party has been found with enough moral power and numerical strength to stay the tide of death."

"I think," said Professor Gradnor, "that what our country needs is truth more than flattery. I do not think that our moral life keeps pace with our mental development and material progress. I know of no civilized country on the globe, Catholic, Protestant, or Mohammedan, where life is less secure than it is in the South. Nearly eighteen hundred years ago the life of a Roman citizen in Palestine was in danger from mob violence. That pagan government threw around him a wall of living clay, consisting of four hundred and seventy men, when more than forty Jews had bound themselves with an oath that they would neither eat nor drink until they had taken the life of the Apostle Paul. Does not true patriotism demand that citizenship should be as much protected in Christian America as it was in heathen Rome?"

"I would have our people," said Miss Delany, "more interested in politics. Instead of forgetting the past, I would have them hold in everlasting remembrance our great deliverance. Hitherto we have never had a country with tender, precious memories to fill our eyes with tears, or glad reminiscences to thrill our hearts with pride and joy. We have been aliens and outcasts in the land of our birth. But I want my pupils to do all in their power to make this country worthy of their deepest devotion and loftiest patriotism. I want them to feel that its glory is their glory, its dishonor their shame."

"Our esteemed friend, Mrs. Watson," said Iola, "sends regrets that she cannot come, but has kindly favored us with a poem, called the "Rallying Cry." In her letter she says that, although she is no longer young, she feels that in the conflict for the right there's room for young as well as old. She hopes that we will here unite the enthusiasm of youth with the experience of age, and that we will have a pleasant and profitable conference. Is it your pleasure that the poem be read at this stage of our proceedings, or later on?"

"Let us have it now," answered Harry, "and I move that Miss Delany be chosen to lend to the poem the charm of her voice."

"I second the motion," said Iola, smiling, and handing the poem to Miss Delany.

Miss Delany took the poem and read it with fine effect. The spirit of the poem had entered her soul.

A RALLYING CRY

Oh, children of the tropics,
Amid our pain and wrong

Have you no other mission
   Than music, dance, and song?

When through the weary ages
   Our dripping tears still fall,
Is this a time to dally
   With pleasure's silken thrall?

Go, muffle all your viols;
   As heroes learn to stand,
With faith in God's great justice
   Nerve every heart and hand.

Dream not of ease nor pleasure,
   Nor honor, wealth, nor fame,
Till from the dust you've lifted
   Our long-dishonored name;

And crowned that name with glory
   By deeds of holy worth,
To shine with light emblazoned,
   The noblest name on earth.

Count life a dismal failure,
   Unblessing and unblest,
That seeks 'mid ease inglorious
   For pleasure or for rest.

With courage, strength, and valor
   Your lives and actions brace;
Shrink not from toil or hardship,
   And dangers bravely face.

Engrave upon your banners,
   In words of golden light,
That honor, truth, and justice
   Are more than godless might.

Above earth's pain and sorrow
   Christ's dying face I see;

I hear the cry of anguish:—
  "Why hast thou forsaken me?"

In the pallor of that anguish
  I see the only light,
To flood with peace and gladness
  Earth's sorrow, pain, and night.

Arrayed in Christly armor
  'Gainst error, crime, and sin,
The victory can't be doubtful,
  For God is sure to win.

The next paper was by Miss Iola Leroy, on the "Education of Mothers."

"I agree," said Rev. Eustace, of St. Mary's parish, "with the paper. The great need of the race is enlightened mothers."

"And enlightened fathers, too," added Miss Delany, quickly. "If there is anything I chafe to see it is a strong, hearty man shirking his burdens, putting them on the shoulders of his wife, and taking life easy for himself."

"I always pity such mothers," interposed Iola, tenderly.

"I think," said Miss Delany, with a flash in her eye and a ring of decision in her voice, "that such men ought to be drummed out of town!" As she spoke, there was an expression which seemed to say, "And I would like to help do it!"

Harry smiled, and gave her a quick glance of admiration.

"I do not think," said Mrs. Stillman, "that we can begin too early to teach our boys to be manly and self-respecting, and our girls to be useful and self-reliant."

"You know," said Mrs. Leroy, "that after the war we were thrown upon the nation a homeless race to be gathered into homes, and a legally unmarried race to be taught the sacredness of the marriage relation. We must instill into our young people that the true strength of a race means purity in women and uprightness in men; who can say, with Sir Galahad:—

'My strength is the strength of ten,
Because my heart is pure.'

And where this is wanting neither wealth nor culture can make up the deficiency."

"There is a field of Christian endeavor which lies between the school-house and the pulpit, which needs the hand of a woman more in private than in public," said Miss Delany.

"Yes, I have often felt the need of such work in my own parish. We need a union of women with the warmest hearts and clearest brains to help in the moral education of the race," said Rev. Eustace.

"Yes," said Iola, "if we would have the prisons empty we must make the homes more attractive."

"In civilized society," replied Dr. Latimer, "there must be restraint either within or without. If parents fail to teach restraint within, society has her check-reins without in the form of chain-gangs, prisons, and the gallows."

The closing paper was on the "Moral Progress of the Race," by Hon. Dugdale. He said: "The moral progress of the race was not all he could desire, yet he could not help feeling that, compared with other races, the outlook was not hopeless. I am so sorry to see, however, that in some States there is an undue proportion of colored people in prisons."

"I think," answered Professor Langhorne, of Georgia, "that this is owing to a partial administration of law in meting out punishment to colored offenders. I know red-handed murderers who walk in this Republic unwhipped of justice, and I have seen a colored woman sentenced to prison for weeks for stealing twenty-five cents. I knew a colored girl who was executed for murder when only a child in years. And it was through the intervention of a friend of mine, one of the bravest young men of the South, that a boy of fifteen was saved from the gallows."

"When I look," said Mr. Forest, "at the slow growth of modern civilization—the ages which have been consumed in reaching our present altitude, and see how we have outgrown slavery, feudalism, and religious persecutions, I cannot despair of the future of the race."

"Just now," said Dr. Latimer, "we have the fearful grinding and friction which comes in the course of an adjustment of the new machinery of freedom in the old ruts of slavery. But I am optimistic enough to believe that there will yet be a far higher and better Christian civilization than our country has ever known."

"And in that civilization I believe the negro is to be an important factor," said Rev. Cantnor.

"I believe it also," said Miss Delany, hopefully, "and this thought has been a blessed inspiration to my life. When I come in contact with Christless prejudices, I feel that my life is too much a part of the Divine plan, and invested with too much intrinsic worth, for me to be the least humiliated by indignities that beggarly souls can inflict. I feel more pitiful than resentful to those who do not know how much they miss by living mean, ignoble lives."

"My heart," said Iola, "is full of hope for the future. Pain and suffering are the crucibles out of which come gold more fine than the pavements of heaven, and gems more precious than the foundations of the Holy City."

"If," said Mrs. Leroy, "pain and suffering are factors in human development, surely we have not been counted too worthless to suffer."

"And is there," continued Iola, "a path which we have trodden in this country, unless it be the path of sin, into which Jesus Christ has not put His feet and left it luminous with the light of His steps? Has the negro been poor and homeless? The birds of the air had nests and the foxes had holes, but the Son of man had not where to lay His head. Has our name been a synonym for contempt? 'He shall be called a Nazarene.' Have we been despised and trodden under foot? Christ was despised and rejected of men. Have we been ignorant and unlearned? It was said of Jesus Christ, 'How knoweth this man letters, never having learned?' Have we been beaten and bruised in the prison-house of bondage?

'They took Jesus and scourged Him.' Have we been slaughtered, our bones scattered at the graves' mouth? He was spit upon by the mob, smitten and mocked by the rabble, and died as died Rome's meanest criminal slave. To-day that cross of shame is a throne of power. Those robes of scorn have changed to habiliments of light, and that crown of mockery to a diadem of glory. And never, while the agony of Gethsemane and the sufferings of Calvary have their hold upon my heart, will I recognize any religion as His which despises the least of His brethren."

As Iola finished, there was a ring of triumph in her voice, as if she were reviewing a path she had trodden with bleeding feet, and seen it change to lines of living light. Her soul seemed to be flashing through the rare loveliness of her face and etherealizing its beauty.

Every one was spell-bound. Dr. Latimer was entranced, and, turning to Hon. Dugdale, said, in a low voice and with deep-drawn breath, "She is angelic!"

Hon. Dugdale turned, gave a questioning look, then replied, "She is strangely beautiful! Do you know her?"

"Yes; I have met her several times. I accompanied her here to-night. The tones of her voice are like benedictions of peace; her words a call to higher service and nobler life."

Just then Rev. Carmicle was announced. He had been on a Southern tour, and had just returned.

"Oh, Doctor," exclaimed Mrs. Stillman, "I am delighted to see you. We were about to adjourn, but we will postpone action to hear from you."

"Thank you," replied Rev. Carmicle. "I have not the cue to the meeting, and will listen while I take breath."

"Pardon me," answered Mrs. Stillman. "I should have been more thoughtful than to press so welcome a guest into service before I had given him time for rest and refreshment; but if the courtesy failed on my lips it did not fail in my heart. I wanted our young folks to see one of our thinkers who had won distinction before the war."

"My dear friend," said Rev. Carmicle, smiling, "some of

these young folks will look on me as a back number. You know the cry has already gone forth, 'Young men to the front.' "

"But we need old men for counsel," interposed Mr. Forest, of New York.

"Of course," said Rev. Carmicle, "we older men would rather retire gracefully than be relegated or hustled to a back seat. But I am pleased to see doors open to you which were closed to us, and opportunities which were denied us embraced by you."

"How," asked Hon. Dugdale, "do you feel in reference to our people's condition in the South?"

"Very hopeful, although at times I cannot help feeling anxious about their future. I was delighted with my visits to various institutions of learning, and surprised at the desire manifested among the young people to obtain an education. Where toil-worn mothers bent beneath their heavy burdens their more favored daughters are enjoying the privileges of education. Young people are making recitations in Greek and Latin where it was once a crime to teach their parents to read. I also became acquainted with colored professors and presidents of colleges. Saw young ladies who had graduated as doctors. Comfortable homes have succeeded old cabins of slavery. Vast crops have been raised by free labor. I read with interest and pleasure a number of papers edited by colored men. I saw it estimated that two millions of our people had learned to read, and I feel deeply grateful to the people who have supplied us with teachers who have stood their ground so nobly among our people."

"But," asked Mr. Forest, "you expressed fears about the future of our race. From whence do your fears arise?"

"From the unfortunate conditions which slavery has entailed upon that section of our country. I dread the results of that racial feeling which ever and anon breaks out into restlessness and crime. Also, I am concerned about the lack of home training for those for whom the discipline of the plantation has been exchanged for the penalties of prisons and chain-gangs. I am sorry to see numbers of our young men growing away from the influence of the church and drifting into prisons. I also fear that in some sections, as colored men increase in wealth and intelligence, there will be an increase of race rivalry and jealousy. It is said that savages, by putting their ears to the ground, can hear a far-off tread. So, to-day, I fear that there are savage elements in our civilization which hear the advancing tread of the negro and would retard his coming. It is the incarnation of these elements that I dread. It is their elimination I do so earnestly desire. Whether it be outgrown or not is our unsolved problem. Time alone will tell whether or not the virus of slavery and injustice has too fully permeated our Southern civilization for a complete recovery. Nations, honey-combed by vice, have fallen beneath the weight of their iniquities. Justice is always uncompromising in its claims and inexorable in its demands. The laws of the universe are never repealed to accommodate our follies."

"Surely," said Bishop Tunster, "the negro has a higher mission than that of aimlessly drifting through life and patiently waiting for death."

"We may not," answered Rev. Carmicle, "have the same dash, courage, and aggressiveness of other races, accustomed to struggle, achievement, and dominion, but surely the world needs something better than the results of arrogance, aggressiveness, and indomitable power. For the evils of society there are no solvents as potent as love and justice, and our greatest need is not more wealth and learning, but a religion replete with life and glowing with love. Let this be the impelling force in the race and it cannot fail to rise in the scale of character and condition."

"And," said Dr. Latimer," instead of narrowing our sympathies to mere racial questions, let us broaden them to humanity's wider issues."

"Let us," replied Rev. Carmicle, "pass it along the lines, that to be willfully ignorant is to be shamefully criminal. Let us teach our people not to love pleasure or to fear death, but

to learn the true value of life, and to do their part to eliminate the paganism of caste from our holy religion and the
lawlessness of savagery from our civilization."

"How did you enjoy the evening, Marie?" asked Robert,
as they walked homeward.

"I was interested and deeply pleased," answered Marie.

"I," said Robert, "was thinking of the wonderful changes
that have come to us since the war. When I sat in those
well-lighted, beautifully-furnished rooms, I was thinking of
the meetings we used to have in by-gone days. How we used
to go by stealth into lonely woods and gloomy swamps, to
tell of our hopes and fears, sorrows and trials. I hope that we
will have many more of these gatherings. Let us have the
next one here."

"I am sure," said Marie, "I would gladly welcome such a
conference at any time. I think such meetings would be so
helpful to our young people."

CHAPTER XXXI

Dawning Affections

"Doctor," said Iola, as they walked home from the *conversazione*, "I wish I could do something more for our people than I am doing. I taught in the South till failing health compelled me to change my employment. But, now that I am well and strong, I would like to do something of lasting service for the race."

"Why not," asked Dr. Latimer, "write a good, strong book which would be helpful to them? I think there is an amount of dormant talent among us, and a large field from which to gather materials for such a book."

"I would do it, willingly, if I could; but one needs both leisure and money to make a successful book. There is material among us for the broadest comedies and the deepest tragedies, but, besides money and leisure, it needs patience, perseverance, courage, and the hand of an artist to weave it into the literature of the country."

"Miss Leroy, you have a large and rich experience; you possess a vivid imagination and glowing fancy. Write, out of the fullness of your heart, a book to inspire men and women with a deeper sense of justice and humanity."

"Doctor," replied Iola, "I would do it if I could, not for the money it might bring, but for the good it might do. But who believes any good can come out of the black Nazareth?"

"Miss Leroy, out of the race must come its own thinkers and writers. Authors belonging to the white race have written good racial books, for which I am deeply grateful, but it seems to be almost impossible for a white man to put himself completely in our place. No man can feel the iron which enters another man's soul."

"Well, Doctor, when I write a book I shall take you for the hero of my story."

"Why, what have I done," asked Dr. Latimer, in a surprised tone, "that you should impale me on your pen?"

"You have done nobly," answered Iola, "in refusing your grandmother's offer."

"I only did my duty," he modestly replied.

"But," said Iola, "when others are trying to slip out from the race and pass into the white basis, I cannot help admiring one who acts as if he felt that the weaker the race is the closer he would cling to it."

"My mother," replied Dr. Latimer, "faithful and true, belongs to that race. Where else should I be? But I know a young lady who could have cast her lot with the favored race, yet chose to take her place with the freed people, as their teacher, friend, and adviser. This young lady was alone in the world. She had been fearfully wronged, and to her stricken heart came a brilliant offer of love, home, and social position. But she bound her heart to the mast of duty, closed her ears to the syren song, and could not be lured from her purpose."

A startled look stole over Iola's face, and, lifting her eyes to his, she faltered:—

"Do you know her?"

"Yes, I know her and admire her; and she ought to be made the subject of a soul-inspiring story. Do you know of whom I speak?"

"How should I, Doctor? I am sure you have not made me your confidante," she responded, demurely; then she quickly turned and tripped up the steps of her home, which she had just reached.

After this conversation Dr. Latimer became a frequent visitor at Iola's home, and a firm friend of her brother. Harry was at that age when, for the young and inexperienced, vice puts on her fairest guise and most seductive smiles. Dr. Latimer's wider knowledge and larger experience made his friendship for Harry very valuable, and the service he rendered him made him a favorite and ever-welcome guest in the family.

"Are you all alone," asked Robert, one night, as he entered the cosy little parlor where Iola sat reading. "Where are the rest of the folks?"

"Mamma and grandma have gone to bed," answered Iola. "Harry and Lucille are at the concert. They are passionately fond of music, and find facilities here that they do not have in the South. They wouldn't go to hear a seraph where they must take a negro seat. I was too tired to go. Besides, 'two's company and three's a crowd,' " she added, significantly.

"I reckon you struck the nail on the head that time," said Robert, laughing. "But you have not been alone all the time. Just as I reached the corner I saw Dr. Latimer leaving the door. I see he still continues his visits. Who is his patient now?"

"Oh, Uncle Robert," said Iola, smiling and flushing, "he is out with Harry and Lucille part of the time, and drops in now and then to see us all."

"Well," said Robert, "I suppose the case is now an affair of the heart. But I cannot blame him for it," he added, looking fondly on the beautiful face of his niece, which sorrow had touched only to chisel into more loveliness. "How do you like him?"

"I must have within me," answered Iola, with unaffected truthfulness, "a large amount of hero worship. The characters of the Old Testament I most admire are Moses and Nehemiah. They were willing to put aside their own advantages for their race and country. Dr. Latimer comes up to my ideal of a high, heroic manhood."

"I think," answered Robert, smiling archly, "he would be delighted to hear your opinion of him."

"I tell him," continued Iola, "that he belongs to the days

446

of chivalry. But he smiles and says, 'he only belongs to the days of hard-pan service.' "

"Some one," said Robert, "was saying to-day that he stood in his own light when he refused his grandmother's offer to receive him as her son."

"I think," said Iola, "it was the grandest hour of his life when he made that decision. I have admired him ever since I heard his story."

"But, Iola, think of the advantages he set aside. It was no sacrifice for me to remain colored, with my lack of education and race sympathies, but Dr. Latimer had doors open to him as a white man which are forever closed to a colored man. To be born white in this country is to be born to an inheritance of privileges, to hold in your hands the keys that open before you the doors of every occupation, advantage, opportunity, and achievement."

"I know that, uncle," answered Iola; "but even these advantages are too dearly bought if they mean loss of honor, true manliness, and self respect. He could not have retained these had he ignored his mother and lived under a veil of concealment, constantly haunted by a dread of detection. The gain would not have been worth the cost. It were better that he should walk the ruggedest paths of life a true man than tread the softest carpets a moral cripple."

"I am afraid," said Robert, laying his hand caressingly upon her head, "that we are destined to lose the light of our home."

"Oh, uncle, how you talk! I never dreamed of what you are thinking," answered Iola, half reproachfully.

"And how," asked Robert, "do you know what I am thinking about?"

"My dear uncle, I'm not blind."

"Neither am I," replied Robert, significantly, as he left the room.

Iola's admiration for Dr. Latimer was not a one-sided affair. Day after day she was filling a larger place in his heart.

The touch of her hand thrilled him with emotion. Her lightest words were an entrancing melody to his ear. Her noblest sentiments found a response in his heart. In their desire to help the race their hearts beat in loving unison. One grand and noble purpose was giving tone and color to their lives and strengthening the bonds of affection between them.

CHAPTER XXXII

Wooing and Wedding

Harry's vacation had been very pleasant. Miss Delany, with her fine conversational powers and ready wit, had added much to his enjoyment. Robert had given his mother the pleasantest room in the house, and in the evening the family would gather around her, tell her the news of the day, read to her from the Bible, join with her in thanksgiving for mercies received and in prayer for protection through the night. Harry was very grateful to Dr. Latimer for the kindly interest he had shown in accompanying Miss Delany and himself to places of interest and amusement. He was grateful, too, that in the city of P—— doors were open to them which were barred against them in the South.

The bright, beautiful days of summer were gliding into autumn, with its glorious wealth of foliage, and the time was approaching for the departure of Harry and Miss Delany to their respective schools, when Dr. Latimer received several letters from North Carolina, urging him to come South, as physicians were greatly needed there. Although his practice was lucrative in the city of P——, he resolved he would go where his services were most needed.

A few evenings before he started he called at the house, and made an engagement to drive Iola to the park.

At the time appointed he drove up to the door in his fine equipage. Iola stepped gracefully in and sat quietly by his side to enjoy the loveliness of the scenery and the gorgeous grandeur of the setting sun.

"I expect to go South," said Dr. Latimer, as he drove slowly along.

"Ah, indeed," said Iola, assuming an air of interest, while a shadow flitted over her face. "Where do you expect to pitch your tent?"

"In the city of C——, North Carolina," he answered.

"Oh, I wish," she exclaimed, "that you were going to Georgia, where you could take care of that high-spirited brother of mine."

"I suppose if he were to hear you he would laugh, and say that he could take care of himself. But I know a better plan than that."

"What is it?" asked Iola, innocently.

"That you will commit yourself, instead of your brother, to my care."

"Oh, dear," replied Iola, drawing a long breath. "What would mamma say?"

"That she would willingly resign you, I hope."

"And what would grandma and Uncle Robert say?" again asked Iola.

"That they would cheerfully acquiesce. Now, what would I say if they all consent?"

"I don't know," modestly responded Iola.

"Well," replied Dr. Latimer, "I would say:—

'Could deeds my love discover,
   Could valor gain thy charms,
To prove myself thy lover
   I'd face a world in arms.' "

"And prove a good soldier," added Iola, smiling, "when there is no battle to fight."

"Iola, I am in earnest," said Dr. Latimer, passionately. "In the work to which I am devoted every burden will be lighter, every path smoother, if brightened and blessed with your companionship."

A sober expression swept over Iola's face, and, dropping her eyes, she said: "I must have time to think."

Quietly they rode along the river bank until Dr. Latimer broke the silence by saying:—

"Miss Iola, I think that you brood too much over the condition of our people."

"Perhaps I do," she replied, "but they never burn a man in the South that they do not kindle a fire around my soul."

"I am afraid," replied Dr. Latimer, "that you will grow morbid and nervous. Most of our people take life easily—why shouldn't you?"

"Because," she answered, "I can see breakers ahead which they do not."

"Oh, give yourself no uneasiness. They will catch the fret and fever of the nineteenth century soon enough. I have heard several of our ministers say that it is chiefly men of disreputable characters who are made the subjects of violence and lynch-law."

"Suppose it is so," responded Iola, feelingly. "If these men believe in eternal punishment they ought to feel a greater concern for the wretched sinner who is hurried out of time with all his sins upon his head, than for the godly man who passes through violence to endless rest."

"That is true; and I am not counseling you to be selfish; but, Miss Iola, had you not better look out for yourself?"

"Thank you, Doctor, I am feeling quite well."

"I know it, but your devotion to study and work is too intense," he replied.

"I am preparing to teach, and must spend my leisure time in study. Mr. Cloten is an excellent employer, and treats his employés as if they had hearts as well as hands. But to be an expert accountant is not the best use to which I can put my life."

"As a teacher you will need strong health and calm nerves. You had better let me prescribe for you. You need," he added, with a merry twinkle in his eyes, "change of air, change of scene, and change of name."

"Well, Doctor," said Iola, laughing, "that is the newest nostrum out. Had you not better apply for a patent?"

"Oh," replied Dr. Latimer, with affected gravity, "you know you must have unlimited faith in your physician."

"So you wish me to try the faith cure?" asked Iola, laughing.

"Yes, faith in me," responded Dr. Latimer, seriously.

"Oh, here we are at home!" exclaimed Iola. "This has been a glorious evening, Doctor. I am indebted to you for a great pleasure. I am extremely grateful."

"You are perfectly welcome," replied Dr. Latimer. "The pleasure has been mutual, I assure you."

"Will you not come in?" asked Iola.

Tying his horse, he accompanied Iola into the parlor. Seating himself near her, he poured into her ears words eloquent with love and tenderness.

"Iola," he said, "I am not an adept in courtly phrases. I am a plain man, who believes in love and truth. In asking you to share my lot, I am not inviting you to a life of ease and luxury, for year after year I may have to struggle to keep the wolf from the door, but your presence would make my home one of the brightest spots on earth, and one of the fairest types of heaven. Am I presumptuous in hoping that your love will become the crowning joy of my life?"

His words were more than a tender strain wooing her to love and happiness, they were a clarion call to a life of high and holy worth, a call which found a response in her heart. Her hand lay limp in his. She did not withdraw it, but, raising her lustrous eyes to his, she softly answered: "Frank, I love you."

After he had gone, Iola sat by the window, gazing at the splendid stars, her heart quietly throbbing with a delicious sense of joy and love. She had admired Dr. Gresham and, had there been no barrier in her way, she might have learned to love him; but Dr. Latimer had grown irresistibly upon her heart. There were depths in her nature that Dr. Gresham had never fathomed; aspirations in her soul with which he had never mingled. But as the waves leap up to the strand, so her soul went out to Dr. Latimer. Between their lives were no impeding barriers, no inclination impelling one way and duty compelling another. Kindred hopes and tastes had knit their hearts; grand and noble purposes were lighting up their lives; and they esteemed it a blessed privilege to stand on the threshold of a new era and labor for those who had passed from the old oligarchy of slavery into the new commonwealth of freedom.

On the next evening, Dr. Latimer rang the bell and was answered by Harry, who ushered him into the parlor, and then came back to the sitting-room, saying, "Iola, Dr. Latimer has called to see you."

"Has he?" answered Iola, a glad light coming into her eyes. "Come, Lucille, let us go into the parlor."

"Oh, no," interposed Harry, shrugging his shoulders and catching Lucille's hand. "He didn't ask for you. When we went to the concert, we were told three's a crowd. And I say one good turn deserves another."

"Oh, Harry, you are so full of nonsense. Let Lucille go!" said Iola.

"Indeed I will not. I want to have a good time as well as you," said Harry.

"Oh, you're the most nonsensical man I know," interposed Miss Delany. Yet she stayed with Harry.

"You're looking very bright and happy," said Dr. Latimer to Iola, as she entered.

"My ride in the park was so refreshing! I enjoyed it so much! The day was so lovely, the air delicious, the birds sang so sweetly, and the sunset was so magnificent."

"I am glad of it. Why, Iola, your home is so happy your heart should be as light as a school-girl's."

"Doctor," she replied, "I must be prematurely old. I have scarcely known what it is to be light-hearted since my father's death."

"I know it, darling," he answered, seating himself beside her, and drawing her to him. "You have been tried in the fire, but are you not better for the crucial test?"

"Doctor," she replied, "as we rode along yesterday, mingling with the sunshine of the present came the shadows of the past. I was thinking of the bright, joyous days of my girlhood, when I defended slavery, and of how the cup that I would have pressed to the lips of others was forced to my own. Yet, in looking over the mournful past, I would not change the Iola of then for the Iola of now."

"Yes," responded Dr. Latimer, musingly,

> " 'Darkness shows us worlds of light
> We never saw by day.' "

"Oh, Doctor, you cannot conceive what it must have been to be hurled from a home of love and light into the dark abyss of slavery; to be compelled to take your place among a people you have learned to look upon as inferiors and social outcasts; to be in the power of men whose presence would fill you with horror and loathing, and to know that there is no earthly power to protect you from the highest insults which brutal cowardice could shower upon you. I am so glad that no other woman of my race will suffer as I have done."

The flush deepened on her face, a mournful splendor beamed from her beautiful eyes, into which the tears had slowly gathered.

"Darling," he said, his voice vibrating with mingled feelings of tenderness and resentment, "you must forget the sad past. You are like a tender lamb snatched from the jaws of a hungry wolf, but who still needs protecting, loving care. But it must have been terrible," he added, in a painful tone.

"It was indeed! For awhile I was like one dazed. I tried to pray, but the heavens seemed brass over my head. I was wild with agony, and had I not been placed under conditions which roused all the resistance of my soul, I would have lost my reason."

"Was it not a mistake to have kept you ignorant of your colored blood?"

"It was the great mistake of my father's life, but dear papa knew something of the cruel, crushing power of caste; and he tried to shield us from it."

"Yes, yes," replied Dr. Latimer, thoughtfully, "in trying to shield you from pain he plunged you into deeper suffering."

"I never blame him, because I know he did it for the best. Had he lived he would have taken us to France, where I should have had a life of careless ease and pleasure. But now my life has a much grander significance than it would have had under such conditions. Fearful as the awakening was, it was better than to have slept through life."

"Best for you and best for me," said Dr. Latimer. "There are souls that never awaken; but if they miss the deepest pain they also lose the highest joy."

Dr. Latimer went South, after his engagement, and through his medical skill and agreeable manners became very successful in his practice. In the following summer, he built a cosy home for the reception of his bride, and came North, where, with Harry and Miss Delany as attendants, he was married to Iola, amid a pleasant gathering of friends, by Rev. Carmicle.

CHAPTER XXXIII

Conclusion

It was late in the summer when Dr. Latimer and his bride reached their home in North Carolina. Over the cottage porch were morning-glories to greet the first flushes of the rising day, and roses and jasmines to distill their fragrance on the evening air. Aunt Linda, who had been apprised of their coming, was patiently awaiting their arrival, and Uncle Daniel was pleased to know that "dat sweet young lady who had sich putty manners war comin' to lib wid dem."

As soon as they arrived, Aunt Linda rushed up to Iola, folded her in her arms, and joyfully exclaimed: "How'dy, honey! Ise so glad you's come. I seed it in a vision dat somebody fair war comin' to help us. An' wen I yered it war you, I larffed and jist rolled ober, and larffed and jist gib up."

"But, Aunt Linda, I am not very fair," replied Mrs. Latimer.

"Well, chile, you's fair to me. How's all yore folks in de up kentry?"

"All well. I expect them down soon to live here."

"What, Har'yet, and Robby, an' yer ma? Oh, dat is too good. I allers said Robby had san' in his craw, and war born for good luck. He war a mighty nice boy. Har'yet's in clover now. Well, ebery dorg has its day, and de cat has Sunday. I allers tole Har'yet ter keep a stiff upper lip; dat it war a long road dat had no turn."

Dr. Latimer was much gratified by the tender care Aunt Linda bestowed on Iola.

"I ain't goin' to let her do nuffin till she gits seasoned. She looks as sweet as a peach. I allers wanted some nice lady to come down yere and larn our gals some sense. I can't read myself, but I likes ter yere dem dat can."

"Well, Aunt Linda, I am going to teach in the Sunday-school, help in the church, hold mothers' meetings to help these boys and girls to grow up to be good men and women. Won't you get a pair of spectacles and learn to read?"

"Oh, yer can't git dat book froo my head, no way you fix it. I knows nuff to git to hebben, and dats all I wants to know." Aunt Linda was kind and obliging, but there was one place where she drew the line, and that was at learning to read.

Harry and Miss Delany accompanied Iola as far as her new home, and remained several days. The evening before their departure, Harry took Miss Delany a drive of several miles through the pine barrens.

"This thing is getting very monotonous," Harry broke out, when they had gone some distance.

"Oh, I enjoy it!" replied Miss Delany. "These stately pines look so grand and solemn, they remind me of a procession of hooded monks."

"What in the world are you talking about, Lucille?" asked Harry, looking puzzled.

"About those pine-trees," replied Miss Delany, in a tone of surprise.

"Pshaw, I wasn't thinking about them. I'm thinking about Iola and Frank."

"What about them?" asked Lucille.

"Why, when I was in P——, Dr. Latimer used to be first-rate company, but now it is nothing but what Iola wants, and what Iola says, and what Iola likes. I don't believe that there is a subject I could name to him, from spinning a top to circumnavigating the globe, that he wouldn't somehow contrive to bring Iola in. And I don't believe you could talk ten minutes to Iola on any subject, from dressing a doll to the latest discovery in science, that she wouldn't manage to lug in Frank."

"Oh, you absurd creature!" responded Lucille, "this is their honeymoon, and they are deeply in love with each other. Wait till you get in love with some one."

"I am in love now," replied Harry, with a serious air.

"With whom?" asked Lucille, archly.

"With you," answered Harry, trying to take her hand.

"Oh, Harry!" she exclaimed, playfully resisting. "Don't be so nonsensical! Don't you think the bride looked lovely, with that dress of spotless white and with those orange blossoms in her hair?"

"Yes, she did; that's a fact," responded Harry. "But, Lucille, I think there is a great deal of misplaced sentiment at weddings," he added, more seriously.

"How so?"

"Oh, here are a couple just married, and who are as happy as happy can be; and people will crowd around them wishing them much joy; but who thinks of wishing joy to the forlorn old bachelors and restless old maids?"

"Well, Harry, if you want people to wish you much happiness, why don't you do as the doctor has done, get yourself a wife?"

"I will," he replied, soberly, "when you say so."

"Oh, Harry, don't be so absurd."

"Indeed there isn't a bit of absurdity about what I say. I am in earnest." There was something in the expression of Harry's face and the tone of his voice which arrested the banter on Lucille's lips.

"I think it was Charles Lamb," replied Lucille, "who once said that school-teachers are uncomfortable people, and, Harry, I would not like to make you uncomfortable by marrying you."

"You will make me uncomfortable by not marrying me."

"But," replied Lucille, "your mother may not prefer me for a daughter. You know, Harry, complexional prejudices are not confined to white people."

"My mother," replied Harry, with an air of confidence, "is too noble to indulge in such sentiments."

"And Iola, would she be satisfied?"

"Why, it would add to her satisfaction. She is not one who can't be white and won't be black."

"Well, then," replied Lucille, "I will take the question of your comfort into consideration."

The above promise was thoughtfully remembered by Lucille till a bridal ring and happy marriage were the result.

Soon after Iola had settled in C—— she quietly took her place in the Sunday-school as a teacher, and in the church as a helper. She was welcomed by the young pastor, who found in her a strong and faithful ally. Together they planned meetings for the especial benefit of mothers and children. When the dens of vice are spreading their snares for the feet of the tempted and inexperienced her doors are freely opened for the instruction of the children before their feet have wandered and gone far astray. She has no carpets too fine for the tread of their little feet. She thinks it is better to have stains on her carpet than stains on their souls through any neglect of hers. In lowly homes and windowless cabins her visits are always welcome. Little children love her. Old age turns to her for comfort, young girls for guidance, and mothers for counsel. Her life is full of blessedness.

Doctor Latimer by his kindness and skill has won the name of the "Good Doctor." But he is more than a successful doctor; he is a true patriot and a good citizen. Honest, just, and discriminating, he endeavors by precept and example to instill into the minds of others sentiments of good citizenship. He is a leader in every reform movement for the benefit of the community; but his patriotism is not confined to race lines. "The world is his country, and mankind his countrymen." While he abhors their deeds of violence, he pities the short-sighted and besotted men who seem madly intent upon laying magazines of powder under the cradles of unborn generations. He has great faith in the possibilities of the negro, and believes that, enlightened and Christianized, he will sink the old animosities of slavery into the new community of interests arising from freedom; and that his influence upon the South will be as the influence of the sun upon the earth. As when the sun passes from Capricorn to Cancer, beauty, greenness, and harmony spring up in his path, so he hopes that the future career of the negro will be a greater influence for freedom and social advancement than it was in the days of yore for slavery and its inferior civilization.

Harry and Lucille are at the head of a large and flourishing school. Lucille gives her ripening experience to her chosen work, to which she was too devoted to resign. And through the school they are lifting up the homes of the people. Some have pitied, others blamed, Harry for casting his lot with the colored people, but he knows that life's highest and best advantages do not depend on the color of the skin or texture of the hair. He has his reward in the improved condition of his pupils and the superb manhood and noble life which he has developed in his much needed work.

Uncle Daniel still lingers on the shores of time, a cheery, lovable old man, loved and respected by all; a welcome guest in every home. Soon after Iola's marriage, Robert sold out his business and moved with his mother and sister to North Carolina. He bought a large plantation near C——, which he divided into small homesteads, and sold to poor but thrifty laborers, and his heart has been gladdened by their increased prosperity and progress. He has seen the one-roomed cabins change to comfortable cottages, in which cleanliness and order have supplanted the prolific causes of disease and death. Kind and generous, he often remembers Mrs. Johnson and sends her timely aid.

Marie's pale, spiritual face still bears traces of the beauty which was her youthful dower, but its bloom has been succeeded by an air of sweetness and dignity. Though frail in health, she is always ready to lend a helping hand wherever and whenever she can.

Grandmother Johnson was glad to return South and spend the remnant of her days with the remaining friends of her early life. Although feeble, she is in full sympathy with her children for the uplifting of the race. Marie and her mother are enjoying their aftermath of life, one by rendering to others all the service in her power, while the other, with her face turned toward the celestial city, is

> "Only waiting till the angels
> Open wide the mystic gate."

The shadows have been lifted from all their lives; and peace, like bright dew, has descended upon their paths. Blessed themselves, their lives are a blessing to others.

Note

From threads of fact and fiction I have woven a story whose
mission will not be in vain if it awaken in the hearts of our
countrymen a stronger sense of justice and a more Christlike
humanity in behalf of those whom the fortunes of war threw,
homeless, ignorant and poor, upon the threshold of a new
era. Nor will it be in vain if it inspire the children of those
upon whose brows God has poured the chrism of that new
era to determine that they will embrace every opportunity,
develop every faculty, and use every power God has given
them to rise in the scale of character and condition, and to
add their quota of good citizenship to the best welfare of the
nation. There are scattered among us materials for mournful
tragedies and mirth-provoking comedies, which some hand
may yet bring into the literature of the country, glowing with
the fervor of the tropics and enriched by the luxuriance of
the Orient, and thus add to the solution of our unsolved
American problem.

The race has not had very long to straighten its hand from
the hoe, to grasp the pen and wield it as a power for good,
and to erect above the ruined auction-block and slave-pen
institutions of learning, but

> There is light beyond the darkness,
> Joy beyond the present pain;

There is hope in God's great justice
  And the negro's rising brain.
Though the morning seems to linger
  O'er the hill-tops far away,
Yet the shadows bear the promise
  Of a brighter coming day.

THE MARROW OF
TRADITION

BY

CHARLES W. CHESNUTT

I like you and your book, ingenious Hone!
In whose capacious all-embracing leaves
The very marrow of tradition's shown.
                              CHARLES LAMB,
                        To the Editor of the
                          Every-Day Book.

CHAPTER I

At Break of Day

"Stay here beside her, major. I shall not be needed for an hour yet. Meanwhile I'll go downstairs and snatch a bit of sleep, or talk to old Jane."

The night was hot and sultry. Though the windows of the chamber were wide open, and the muslin curtains looped back, not a breath of air was stirring. Only the shrill chirp of the cicada and the muffled croaking of the frogs in some distant marsh broke the night silence. The heavy scent of magnolias, overpowering even the strong smell of drugs in the sickroom, suggested death and funeral wreaths, sorrow and tears, the long home, the last sleep. The major shivered with apprehension as the slender hand which he held in his own contracted nervously and in a spasm of pain clutched his fingers with a viselike grip.

Major Carteret, though dressed in brown linen, had thrown off his coat for greater comfort. The stifling heat, in spite of the palm-leaf fan which he plied mechanically, was scarcely less oppressive than his own thoughts. Long ago, while yet a mere boy in years, he had come back from Appomattox to find his family, one of the oldest and proudest in the state, hopelessly impoverished by the war,—even their ancestral home swallowed up in the common ruin. His elder brother had sacrificed his life on the bloody altar of the lost cause, and his father, broken and chagrined, died not many years later, leaving the major the last of his line. He had tried in various pursuits to gain a foothold in the new life, but with indifferent success until he won the hand of Olivia Merkell, whom he had seen grow from a small girl to glorious womanhood. With her money he had founded the Morning Chronicle, which he had made the leading organ of his party and the most influential paper in the State. The fine old house in which they lived was hers. In this very room she had first drawn the breath of life; it had been their nuptial chamber; and here, too, within a few hours, she might die, for it seemed impossible that one could long endure such frightful agony and live.

One cloud alone had marred the otherwise perfect serenity of their happiness. Olivia was childless. To have children to perpetuate the name of which he was so proud, to write it still higher on the roll of honor, had been his dearest hope. His disappointment had been proportionately keen. A few months ago this dead hope had revived, and altered the whole aspect of their lives. But as time went on, his wife's age had begun to tell upon her, until even Dr. Price, the most cheerful and optimistic of physicians, had warned him, while hoping for the best, to be prepared for the worst. To add to the danger, Mrs. Carteret had only this day suffered from a nervous shock, which, it was feared, had hastened by several weeks the expected event.

Dr. Price went downstairs to the library, where a dim light was burning. An old black woman, dressed in a gingham frock, with a red bandana handkerchief coiled around her head by way of turban, was seated by an open window. She rose and curtsied as the doctor entered and dropped into a willow rocking-chair near her own.

"How did this happen, Jane?" he asked in a subdued voice, adding, with assumed severity, "You ought to have taken better care of your mistress."

"Now look a-hyuh, Doctuh Price," returned the old woman in an unctuous whisper, "you don' wanter come talkin' none er yo' foolishness 'bout my not takin' keer er Mis' 'Livy. She never would 'a' said sech a thing! Seven er eight mont's ago, w'en she sent fer me, I says ter her, says I:—

" 'Lawd, Lawd, honey! You don' tell me dat after all dese long w'ary years er waitin' de good Lawd is done heared yo' prayer an' is gwine ter sen' you de chile you be'n wantin' so long an' so bad? Bless his holy name! Will I come an' nuss yo' baby? Why, honey, I nussed you, an' nussed yo' mammy thoo her las' sickness, an' laid her out w'en she died. I would n' *let* nobody e'se nuss yo' baby; an' mo'over, I'm gwine ter come an' nuss you too. You're young side er me, Mis' 'Livy, but you're ove'ly ole ter be havin' yo' fus' baby, an' you'll need somebody roun', honey, w'at knows all 'bout de fam'ly, an' deir ways an' deir weaknesses, an' I don' know who dat'd be ef it wa'n't me.'

" ' 'Deed, Mammy Jane,' says she, 'dere ain' nobody e'se I'd have but you. You kin come ez soon ez you wanter an' stay ez long ez you mineter.'

"An hyuh I is, an' hyuh I'm gwine ter stay. Fer Mis' 'Livy is my ole mist'ess's daughter, an' my ole mist'ess wuz good ter me, an' dey ain' none er her folks gwine ter suffer ef ole Jane kin he'p it."

"Your loyalty does you credit, Jane," observed the doctor; "but you have n't told me yet what happened to Mrs. Carteret to-day. Did the horse run away, or did she see something that frightened her?"

"No, suh, de hoss did n' git skeered at nothin', but Mis' 'Livy did see somethin', er somebody; an' it wa'n't no fault er mine ner her'n neither,—it goes fu'ther back, suh, fu'ther dan dis day er dis year. Does you 'member de time w'en my ole mist'ess, Mis' 'Livy upstairs's mammy, died? No? Well, you wuz prob'ly 'way ter school den, studyin' ter be a doctuh. But I'll tell you all erbout it.

"W'en my ole mist'ess, Mis' 'Liz'beth Merkell,—an' a good mist'ess she wuz,—tuck sick fer de las' time, her sister Polly— ole Mis' Polly Ochiltree w'at is now—come ter de house ter he'p nuss her. Mis' 'Livy upstairs yander wuz erbout six years ole den, de sweetes' little angel you ever laid eyes on; an' on her dyin' bed Mis' 'Liz'beth ax' Mis' Polly fer ter stay hyuh an' take keer er her chile, an' Mis' Polly she promise'. She wuz a widder fer de secon' time, an' did n' have no child'en, an' could jes' as well come as not.

"But dere wuz trouble after de fune'al, an' it happen' right hyuh in dis lib'ary. Mars Sam wuz settin' by de table, w'en Mis' Polly come downstairs, slow an' solemn, an' stood dere in de middle er de flo', all in black, till Mars Sam sot a cheer fer her.

" 'Well, Samuel,' says she, 'now dat we've done all we can fer po' 'Liz'beth, it only 'mains fer us ter consider Olivia's future.'

"Mars Sam nodded his head, but did n' say nothin'.

" 'I don' need ter tell you,' says she, 'dat I am willin' ter carry out de wishes er my dead sister, an' sac'ifice my own comfo't, an' make myse'f yo' housekeeper an' yo' child's nuss, fer my dear sister's sake. It wuz her dyin' wish, an' on it I will ac', ef it is also yo'n.'

"Mars Sam did n' want Mis' Polly ter come, suh; fur he did n' like Mis' Polly. He wuz skeered er Miss Polly."

"I don't wonder," yawned the doctor, "if she was anything like she is now."

"Wuss, suh, fer she wuz younger, an' stronger. She always would have her say, no matter 'bout what, an' her own way, no matter who 'posed her. She had already be'n in de house fer a week, an' Mars Sam knowed ef she once come ter stay, she'd be de mist'ess of eve'ybody in it an' him too. But w'at could he do but say yas?

" 'Den it is unde'stood, is it,' says Mis' Polly, w'en he had spoke, 'dat I am ter take cha'ge er de house?'

" 'All right, Polly,' says Mars Sam, wid a deep sigh.

"Mis' Polly 'lowed he wuz sighin' fer my po' dead mist'ess, fer she did n' have no idee er his feelin's to'ds her,—she alluz did 'low dat all de gent'emen wuz in love wid 'er.

" 'You won' fin' much ter do,' Mars Sam went on, 'fer Julia is a good housekeeper, an' kin ten' ter mos' eve'ything, under yo' d'rections.'

"Mis' Polly stiffen' up like a ramrod. 'It mus' be unde'stood, Samuel,' says she, 'dat w'en I 'sumes cha'ge er yo' house, dere ain' gwine ter be no 'vided 'sponsibility; an' as fer dis Julia, me an' her could n' git 'long tergether nohow. Ef I stays, Julia goes.'

"W'en Mars Sam heard dat, he felt better, an' 'mence' ter pick up his courage. Mis' Polly had showed her han' too plain. My mist'ess had n' got col' yit, an' Mis' Polly, who'd be'n a widder fer two years dis las' time, wuz already fig'rin' on takin' her place fer good, an' she did n' want no other woman roun' de house dat Mars Sam might take a' in- trus' in.

" 'My dear Polly,' says Mars Sam, quite determine', 'I could n' possibly sen' Julia 'way. Fac' is, I could n' git 'long widout Julia. She 'd be'n runnin' dis house like clockwo'k befo' you come, an' I likes her ways. My dear, dead 'Liz'beth sot a heap er sto' by Julia, an' I'm gwine ter keep her here fer 'Liz'beth's sake.'

"Mis' Polly's eyes flash' fire.

" 'Ah,' says she, 'I see—I see! You perfers her housekeep- in' ter mine, indeed! Dat is a fine way ter talk ter a lady! An' a heap er rispec' you is got fer de mem'ry er my po' dead sister!'

"Mars Sam knowed w'at she 'lowed she seed wa'n't so; but he did n' let on, fer it only made him de safer. He wuz willin' fer her ter 'magine w'at she please', jes' so long ez she kep' out er his house an' let him alone.

" 'No, Polly,' says he, gittin' bolder ez she got madder, 'dere ain' no use talkin'. Nothin' in de worl' would make me part wid Julia.'

"Mis' Polly she r'ared an' she pitch', but Mars Sam helt on like grim death. Mis' Polly would n' give in neither, an' so she fin'lly went away. Dey made some kind er 'rangement afterwa'ds, an' Miss Polly tuck Mis' 'Livy ter her own house. Mars Sam paid her bo'd an' 'lowed Mis' Polly somethin' fer takin' keer er her."

"And Julia stayed?"

"Julia stayed, suh, an' a couple er years later her chile wuz bawn, right here in dis house."

"But you said," observed the doctor, "that Mrs. Ochiltree was in error about Julia."

"Yas, suh, so she wuz, w'en my ole mist'ess died. But dis wuz two years after,—an' w'at has ter be has ter be. Julia had a easy time; she had a black gal ter wait on her, a buggy to ride in, an' eve'ything she wanted. Eve'ybody s'posed Mars Sam would give her a house an' lot, er leave her somethin' in his will. But he died suddenly, and did n' leave no will, an' Mis' Polly got herse'f 'pinted gyardeen ter young Mis' 'Livy, an' driv Julia an' her young un out er de house, an' lived here in dis house wid Mis' 'Livy till Mis' 'Livy ma'ied Majah Carteret."

"And what became of Julia?" asked Dr. Price.

Such relations, the doctor knew very well, had been all too common in the old slavery days, and not a few of them had been projected into the new era. Sins, like snakes, die hard. The habits and customs of a people were not to be changed in a day, nor by the stroke of a pen. As family physician, and father confessor by brevet, Dr. Price had looked upon more than one hidden skeleton; and no one in town had had better opportunities than old Jane for learning the undercurrents in the lives of the old families.

"Well," resumed Jane, "eve'ybody s'posed, after w'at had happen', dat Julia 'd keep on livin' easy, fer she wuz young an' good-lookin'. But she did n'. She tried ter make a livin' sewin', but Mis' Polly would n' let de bes' w'ite folks hire her. Den she tuck up washin', but did n' do no better at dat; an' bimeby she got so discourage' dat she ma'ied a shif'less yaller man, an' died er consumption soon after,—an' wuz 'bout ez well off, fer dis man could n' hardly feed her nohow."

"And the child?"

"One er de No'the'n w'ite lady teachers at de mission school tuck a likin' ter little Janet, an' put her thoo school, an' den sent her off ter de No'th fer ter study ter be a school

472

teacher. W'en she come back, 'stead er teachin' she ma'ied ole Adam Miller's son."

"The rich stevedore's son, Dr. Miller?"

"Yas, suh, dat's de man,—you knows 'im. Dis yer boy wuz jes' gwine 'way fer ter study ter be a doctuh, an' he ma'ied dis Janet, an' tuck her 'way wid 'im. Dey went off ter Europe, er Irope, er Orope, er somewhere er 'nother, 'way off yander, an' come back here las' year an' sta'ted dis yer horspital an' school fer ter train de black gals fer nusses."

"He's a very good doctor, Jane, and is doing a useful work. Your chapter of family history is quite interesting,—I knew part of it before, in a general way; but you have n't yet told me what brought on Mrs. Carteret's trouble."

"I'm jes' comin' ter dat dis minute, suh,—w'at I be'n tellin' you is all a part of it. Dis yer Janet, w'at's Mis' 'Livy's half-sister, is ez much like her ez ef dey wuz twins. Folks sometimes takes 'em fer one ernudder,—I s'pose it tickles Janet mos' ter death, but it do make Mis' 'Livy rippin'. An' den 'way back yander jes' after de wah, w'en de ole Carteret mansion had ter be sol', Adam Miller bought it, an' dis yer Janet an' her husban' is be'n livin' in it ever sence ole Adam died, 'bout a year ago; an' dat makes de majah mad, 'ca'se he don' wanter see cullud folks livin' in de ole fam'ly mansion w'at he wuz bawn in. An' mo'over, an' dat 's de wust of all, w'iles Mis' 'Livy ain' had no child'en, befo', dis yer sister er her'n is got a fine-lookin' little yaller boy, w'at favors de fam'ly so dat ef Mis' 'Livy 'd see de chile anywhere, it 'd mos' break her heart fer ter think 'bout her not havin' no child'en herse'f. So ter-day, w'en Mis' 'Livy wuz out ridin' an' met dis yer Janet wid her boy, an' w'en Mis' 'Livy got ter studyin' 'bout her own chances, an' how she mought not come thoo safe, she jes' had a fit er hysterics right dere in de buggy. She wuz mos' home, an' William got her here, an' you knows de res'."

Major Carteret, from the head of the stairs, called the doctor anxiously.

"You had better come along up now, Jane," said the doctor.

For two long hours they fought back the grim spectre that stood by the bedside. The child was born at dawn. Both mother and child, the doctor said, would live.

"Bless its 'ittle hea't!" exclaimed Mammy Jane, as she held up the tiny mite, which bore as much resemblance to mature humanity as might be expected of an infant which had for only a few minutes drawn the breath of life. "Bless its 'ittle hea't! it's de ve'y spit an' image er its pappy!"

The doctor smiled. The major laughed aloud. Jane's unconscious witticism, or conscious flattery, whichever it might be, was a welcome diversion from the tense strain of the last few hours.

"Be that as it may," said Dr. Price cheerfully, "and I'll not dispute it, the child is a very fine boy,—a very fine boy, indeed! Take care of it, major," he added with a touch of solemnity, "for your wife can never bear another."

With the child's first cry a refreshing breeze from the distant ocean cooled the hot air of the chamber; the heavy odor of the magnolias, with its mortuary suggestiveness, gave place to the scent of rose and lilac and honeysuckle. The birds in the garden were singing lustily.

All these sweet and pleasant things found an echo in the major's heart. He stood by the window, and looking toward the rising sun, breathed a silent prayer of thanksgiving. All nature seemed to rejoice in sympathy with his happiness at the fruition of this long-deferred hope, and to predict for this wonderful child a bright and glorious future.

Old Mammy Jane, however, was not entirely at ease concerning the child. She had discovered, under its left ear, a small mole, which led her to fear that the child was born for bad luck. Had the baby been black, or yellow, or poor-white, Jane would unhesitatingly have named, as his ultimate fate, a not uncommon form of taking off, usually resultant upon the infraction of certain laws, or, in these swift modern days, upon too violent a departure from established social customs.

It was manifestly impossible that a child of such high quality as the grandson of her old mistress should die by judicial strangulation; but nevertheless the warning was a serious thing, and not to be lightly disregarded.

Not wishing to be considered as a prophet of evil omen, Jane kept her own counsel in regard to this significant discovery. But later, after the child was several days old, she filled a small vial with water in which the infant had been washed, and took it to a certain wise old black woman, who lived on the farther edge of the town and was well known to be versed in witchcraft and conjuration. The conjure woman added to the contents of the bottle a bit of calamus root, and one of the cervical vertebrae from the skeleton of a black cat, with several other mysterious ingredients, the nature of which she did not disclose. Following instructions given her, Aunt Jane buried the bottle in Carteret's back yard, one night during the full moon, as a good-luck charm to ward off evil from the little grandson of her dear mistress, so long since dead and gone to heaven.

CHAPTER II

The Christening Party

They named the Carteret baby Theodore Felix. Theodore was a family name, and had been borne by the eldest son for several generations, the major himself being a second son. Having thus given the child two beautiful names, replete with religious and sentimental significance, they called him—"Dodie."

The baby was christened some six weeks after its birth, by which time Mrs. Carteret was able to be out. Old Mammy Jane, who had been brought up in the church, but who, like some better informed people in all ages, found religion not inconsistent with a strong vein of superstition, felt her fears for the baby's future much relieved when the rector had made the sign of the cross and sprinkled little Dodie with the water from the carved marble font, which had come from England in the reign of King Charles the Martyr, as the ill-fated son of James I. was known to St. Andrew's. Upon this special occasion Mammy Jane had been provided with a seat downstairs among the white people, to her own intense satisfaction, and to the secret envy of a small colored attendance in the gallery, to whom she was ostentatiously pointed out by her grandson Jerry, porter at the Morning Chronicle office, who sat among them in the front row.

On the following Monday evening the major gave a christening party in honor of this important event. Owing to Mrs. Carteret's still delicate health, only a small number of intimate friends and family connections were invited to attend.

These were the rector of St. Andrew's; old Mrs. Polly Ochil-tree, the godmother; old Mr. Delamere, a distant relative and also one of the sponsors; and his grandson, Tom Delamere. The major had also invited Lee Ellis, his young city editor, for whom he had a great liking apart from his business value, and who was a frequent visitor at the house. These, with the family itself, which consisted of the major, his wife, and his half-sister, Clara Pemberton, a young woman of about eigh-teen, made up the eight persons for whom covers were laid.

Ellis was the first to arrive, a tall, loose-limbed young man, with a slightly freckled face, hair verging on auburn, a firm chin, and honest gray eyes. He had come half an hour early, and was left alone for a few minutes in the parlor, a spacious, high-ceilinged room, with large windows, and fitted up in excellent taste, with stately reminiscences of a past genera-tion. The walls were hung with figured paper. The ceiling was whitewashed, and decorated in the middle with a plaster centre-piece, from which hung a massive chandelier spar-kling with prismatic rays from a hundred crystal pendants. There was a handsome mantel, set with terra-cotta tiles, on which fauns and satyrs, nymphs and dryads, disported them-selves in idyllic abandon. The furniture was old, and in keep-ing with the room.

At seven o'clock a carriage drove up, from which alighted an elderly gentleman, with white hair and mustache, and bowed somewhat with years. Short of breath and painfully weak in the legs, he was assisted from the carriage by a col-ored man, apparently about forty years old, to whom short side-whiskers and spectacles imparted an air of sobriety. This attendant gave his arm respectfully to the old gentleman, who leaned upon it heavily, but with as little appearance of dependence as possible. The servant, assuming a similar un-consciousness of the weight resting upon his arm, assisted the old gentleman carefully up the steps.

"I'm all right now, Sandy," whispered the gentleman as soon as his feet were planted firmly on the piazza. "You may come back for me at nine o'clock."

Having taken his hand from his servant's arm, he advanced to meet a lady who stood in the door awaiting him, a tall, elderly woman, gaunt and angular of frame, with a mottled face, and high cheekbones partially covered by bands of hair entirely too black and abundant for a person of her age, if one might judge from the lines of her mouth, which are rarely deceptive in such matters.

"Perhaps you'd better not send your man away, Mr. Delamere," observed the lady, in a high shrill voice, which grated upon the old gentleman's ears. He was slightly hard of hearing, but, like most deaf people, resented being screamed at. "You might need him before nine o'clock. One never knows what may happen after one has had the second stroke. And moreover, our butler has fallen down the back steps—negroes are so careless!—and sprained his ankle so that he can't stand. I'd like to have Sandy stay and wait on the table in Peter's place, if you don't mind."

"I thank you, Mrs. Ochiltree, for your solicitude," replied Mr. Delamere, with a shade of annoyance in his voice, "but my health is very good just at present, and I do not anticipate any catastrophe which will require my servant's presence before I am ready to go home. But I have no doubt, madam," he continued, with a courteous inclination, "that Sandy will be pleased to serve you, if you desire it, to the best of his poor knowledge."

"I shill be honored, ma'am," assented Sandy, with a bow even deeper than his master's, "only I'm 'feared I ain't rightly dressed fer ter wait on table. I wuz only goin' ter pra'r-meetin', an' so I did n' put on my bes' clo's. Ef Mis' Ochiltree ain' gwine ter need me fer de nex' fifteen minutes, I kin ride back home in de ca'ige an' dress myse'f suitable for de occasion, suh."

"If you think you'll wait on the table any better," said Mrs. Ochiltree, "you may go along and change your clothes; but hurry back, for it is seven now, and dinner will soon be served."

Sandy retired with a bow. While descending the steps to

the carriage, which had waited for him, he came face to face with a young man just entering the house.

"Am I in time for dinner, Sandy?" asked the newcomer.

"Yas, Mistuh Tom, you're in plenty er time. Dinner won't be ready till *I* git back, which won' be fer fifteen minutes er so yit."

Throwing away the cigarette which he held between his fingers, the young man crossed the piazza with a light step, and after a preliminary knock, for an answer to which he did not wait, entered the house with the air of one thoroughly at home. The lights in the parlor had been lit, and Ellis, who sat talking to Major Carteret when the newcomer entered, covered him with a jealous glance.

Slender and of medium height, with a small head of almost perfect contour, a symmetrical face, dark almost to swarthiness, black eyes, which moved somewhat restlessly, curly hair of raven tint, a slight mustache, small hands and feet, and fashionable attire, Tom Delamere, the grandson of the old gentleman who had already arrived, was easily the handsomest young man in Wellington. But no discriminating observer would have characterized his beauty as manly. It conveyed no impression of strength, but did possess a certain element, feline rather than feminine, which subtly negatived the idea of manliness.

He gave his hand to the major, nodded curtly to Ellis, saluted his grandfather respectfully, and inquired for the ladies.

"Olivia is dressing for dinner," replied the major; "Mrs. Ochiltree is in the kitchen, struggling with the servants. Clara—Ah, here she comes now!"

Ellis, whose senses were preternaturally acute where Clara was concerned, was already looking toward the hall and was the first to see her. Clad in an evening gown of simple white, to the close-fitting corsage of which she had fastened a bunch of pink roses, she was to Ellis a dazzling apparition. To him her erect and well-moulded form was the embodiment of symmetry, her voice sweet music, her movements the perfection of grace; and it scarcely needed a lover's imagination to read in her fair countenance a pure heart and a high spirit,—the truthfulness that scorns a lie, the pride which is not haughtiness. There were suggestive depths of tenderness, too, in the curl of her lip, the droop of her long lashes, the glance of her blue eyes,—depths that Ellis had long since divined, though he had never yet explored them. She gave Ellis a friendly nod as she came in, but for the smile with which she greeted Delamere, Ellis would have given all that he possessed,—not a great deal, it is true, but what could a man do more?

"You are the last one, Tom," she said reproachfully. "Mr. Ellis has been here half an hour."

Delamere threw a glance at Ellis which was not exactly friendly. Why should this fellow always be on hand to emphasize his own shortcomings?

"The rector is not here," answered Tom triumphantly. "You see I am not the last."

"The rector," replied Clara, "was called out of town at six o'clock this evening, to visit a dying man, and so cannot be here. You are the last, Tom, and Mr. Ellis was the first."

Ellis was ruefully aware that this comparison in his favor was the only visible advantage that he had gained from his early arrival. He had not seen Miss Pemberton a moment sooner by reason of it. There had been a certain satisfaction in being in the same house with her, but Delamere had arrived in time to share or, more correctly, to monopolize, the sunshine of her presence.

Delamere gave a plausible excuse which won Clara's pardon and another enchanting smile, which pierced Ellis like a dagger. He knew very well that Delamere's excuse was a lie. Ellis himself had been ready as early as six o'clock, but judging this to be too early, had stopped in at the Clarendon Club for half an hour, to look over the magazines. While coming out he had glanced into the card-room, where he had seen his rival deep in a game of cards, from which Delamere had evidently not been able to tear himself until the last moment. He had accounted for his lateness by a story quite inconsistent with these facts.

The two young people walked over to a window on the opposite side of the large room, where they stood talking to one another in low tones. The major had left the room for a moment. Old Mr. Delamere, who was watching his grandson and Clara with an indulgent smile, proceeded to rub salt into Ellis's wounds.

"They make a handsome couple," he observed. "I remember well when her mother, in her youth an ideally beautiful woman, of an excellent family, married Daniel Pemberton, who was not of so good a family, but had made money. The major, who was only a very young man then, disapproved of the match; he considered that his mother, although a widow and nearly forty, was marrying beneath her. But he has been a good brother to Clara, and a careful guardian of her estate. Ah, young gentleman, you cannot appreciate, except in imagination, what it means, to one standing on the brink of eternity, to feel sure that he will live on in his children and his children's children!"

Ellis was appreciating at that moment what it meant, in cold blood, with no effort of the imagination, to see the girl whom he loved absorbed completely in another man. She had looked at him only once since Tom Delamere had entered the room, and then merely to use him as a spur with which to prick his favored rival.

"Yes, sir," he returned mechanically, "Miss Clara is a beautiful young lady."

"And Tom is a good boy—a fine boy," returned the old gentleman. "I am very well pleased with Tom, and shall be entirely happy when I see them married."

Ellis could not echo this sentiment. The very thought of this marriage made him miserable. He had always understood that the engagement was merely tentative, a sort of family understanding, subject to confirmation after Delamere should have attained his majority, which was still a year off, and when the major should think Clara old enough to marry.

Ellis saw Delamere with the eye of a jealous rival, and judged him mercilessly,—whether correctly or not the sequel will show. He did not at all believe that Tom Delamere would make a fit husband for Clara Pemberton; but his opinion would have had no weight,—he could hardly have expressed it without showing his own interest. Moreover, there was no element of the sneak in Lee Ellis's make-up. The very fact that he might profit by the other's discomfiture left Delamere secure, so far as he could be affected by anything that Ellis might say. But Ellis did not shrink from a fair fight, and though in this one the odds were heavily against him, yet so long as this engagement remained indefinite, so long, indeed, as the object of his love was still unwed, he would not cease to hope. Such a sacrifice as this marriage clearly belonged in the catalogue of impossibilities. Ellis had not lived long enough to learn that impossibilities are merely things of which we have not learned, or which we do not wish to happen.

Sandy returned at the end of a quarter of an hour, and dinner was announced. Mr. Delamere led the way to the dining-room with Mrs. Ochiltree. Tom followed with Clara. The major went to the head of the stairs and came down with Mrs. Carteret upon his arm, her beauty rendered more delicate by the pallor of her countenance and more complete by the happiness with which it glowed. Ellis went in alone. In the rector's absence it was practically a family party which sat down, with the exception of Ellis, who, as we have seen, would willingly have placed himself in the same category.

The table was tastefully decorated with flowers, which grew about the house in lavish profusion. In warm climates nature adorns herself with true feminine vanity.

"What a beautiful table!" exclaimed Tom, before they were seated.

"The decorations are mine," said Clara proudly. "I cut the flowers and arranged them all myself."

"Which accounts for the admirable effect," rejoined Tom with a bow, before Ellis, to whom the same thought had occurred, was able to express himself. He had always counted himself the least envious of men, but for this occasion he coveted Tom Delamere's readiness.

"The beauty of the flowers," observed old Mr. Delamere, with sententious gallantry, "is reflected upon all around them. It is a handsome company."

Mrs. Ochiltree beamed upon the table with a dry smile.

"I don't perceive any effect that it has upon you or me," she said. "And as for the young people, 'Handsome is as handsome does.' If Tom here, for instance, were as good as he looks"—

"You flatter me, Aunt Polly," Tom broke in hastily, anticipating the crack of the whip; he was familiar with his aunt's conversational idiosyncrasies.

"If you are as good as you look," continued the old lady, with a cunning but indulgent smile, "some one has been slandering you."

"Thanks, Aunt Polly! Now you don't flatter me."

"There is Mr. Ellis," Mrs. Ochiltree went on, "who is not half so good-looking, but is steady as a clock, I dare say."

"Now, Aunt Polly," interposed Mrs. Carteret, "let the gentlemen alone."

"She does n't mean half what she says," continued Mrs. Carteret apologetically, "and only talks that way to people whom she likes."

Tom threw Mrs. Carteret a grateful glance. He had been apprehensive, with the sensitiveness of youth, lest his old great-aunt should make a fool of him before Clara's family. Nor had he relished the comparison with Ellis, who was out of place, anyway, in this family party. He had never liked the fellow, who was too much of a plodder and a prig to make a suitable associate for a whole-souled, generous-hearted young gentleman. He tolerated him as a visitor at Carteret's and as a member of the Clarendon Club, but that was all.

"Mrs. Ochiltree has a characteristic way of disguising her feelings," observed old Mr. Delamere, with a touch of sarcasm.

Ellis had merely flushed and felt uncomfortable at the reference to himself. The compliment to his character hardly offset the reflection upon his looks. He knew he was not exactly handsome, but it was not pleasant to have the fact emphasized in the presence of the girl he loved; he would like at least fair play, and judgment upon the subject left to the young lady.

Mrs. Ochiltree was quietly enjoying herself. In early life she had been accustomed to impale fools on epigrams, like flies on pins, to see them wriggle. But with advancing years she had lost in some measure the faculty of nice discrimination,—it was pleasant to see her victims squirm, whether they were fools or friends. Even one's friends, she argued, were not always wise, and were sometimes the better for being told the truth. At her niece's table she felt at liberty to speak her mind, which she invariably did, with a frankness that sometimes bordered on brutality. She had long ago outgrown the period where ambition or passion, or its partners, envy and hatred, were springs of action in her life, and simply retained a mild enjoyment in the exercise of an old habit, with no active malice whatever. The ruling passion merely grew stronger as the restraining faculties decreased in vigor.

A diversion was created at this point by the appearance of old Mammy Jane, dressed in a calico frock, with clean white neckerchief and apron, carrying the wonderful baby in honor of whose naming this feast had been given. Though only six weeks old, the little Theodore had grown rapidly, and Mammy Jane declared was already quite large for his age, and displayed signs of an unusually precocious intelligence. He was passed around the table and duly admired. Clara thought his hair was fine. Ellis inquired about his teeth. Tom put his finger in the baby's fist to test his grip. Old Mr. Delamere was unable to decide as yet whether he favored most his father or his mother. The object of these attentions endured them patiently for several minutes, and then protested with a vocal vigor which led to his being taken promptly back upstairs. Whatever fate might be in store for him, he manifested no sign of weak lungs.

"Sandy," said Mrs. Carteret when the baby had retired, "pass that tray standing upon the side table, so that we may all see the presents."

Mr. Delamere had brought a silver spoon, and Tom a napkin ring. Ellis had sent a silver watch; it was a little premature, he admitted, but the boy would grow to it, and could use it to play with in the mean time. It had a glass back, so that he might see the wheels go round. Mrs. Ochiltree's present was an old and yellow ivory rattle, with a handle which the child could bite while teething, and a knob screwed on at the end to prevent the handle from slipping through the baby's hand.

"I saw that in your cedar chest, Aunt Polly," said Clara, "when I was a little girl, and you used to pull the chest out from under your bed to get me a dime."

"You kept the rattle in the right-hand corner of the chest," said Tom, "in the box with the red silk purse, from which you took the gold piece you gave me every Christmas."

A smile shone on Mrs. Ochiltree's severe features at this appreciation, like a ray of sunlight on a snowbank.

"Aunt Polly's chest is like the widow's cruse," said Mrs. Carteret, "which was never empty."

"Or Fortunatus's purse, which was always full," added old Mr. Delamere, who read the Latin poets, and whose allusions were apt to be classical rather than scriptural.

"It will last me while I live," said Mrs. Ochiltree, adding cautiously, "but there 'll not be a great deal left. It won't take much to support an old woman for twenty years."

Mr. Delamere's man Sandy had been waiting upon the table with the decorum of a trained butler, and a gravity all his own. He had changed his suit of plain gray for a long blue coat with brass buttons, which dated back to the fashion of a former generation, with which he wore a pair of plaid trousers of strikingly modern cut and pattern. With his whiskers, his spectacles, and his solemn air of responsibility, he would have presented, to one unfamiliar with the negro type, an amusingly impressive appearance. But there was nothing incongruous about Sandy to this company, except perhaps to Tom Delamere, who possessed a keen eye for contrasts and always regarded Sandy, in that particular rig, as a very comical darkey.

"Is it quite prudent, Mrs. Ochiltree," suggested the major at a moment when Sandy, having set down the tray, had left the room for a little while, "to mention, in the presence of the servants, that you keep money in the house?"

"I beg your pardon, major," observed old Mr. Delamere, with a touch of stiffness. "The only servant in hearing of the conversation has been my own; and Sandy is as honest as any man in Wellington."

"You mean, sir," replied Carteret, with a smile, "as honest as any *negro* in Wellington."

"I make no exceptions, major," returned the old gentleman, with emphasis. "I would trust Sandy with my life,—he saved it once at the risk of his own."

"No doubt," mused the major, "the negro is capable of a certain doglike fidelity,—I make the comparison in a kindly sense,—a certain personal devotion which is admirable in itself, and fits him eminently for a servile career. I should imagine, however, that one could more safely trust his life with a negro than his portable property."

"Very clever, major! I read your paper, and know that your feeling is hostile toward the negro, but"—

The major made a gesture of dissent, but remained courteously silent until Mr. Delamere had finished.

"For my part," the old gentleman went on, "I think they have done very well, considering what they started from, and their limited opportunities. There was Adam Miller, for instance, who left a comfortable estate. His son George carries on the business, and the younger boy, William, is a good doctor and stands well with his profession. His hospital is a good thing, and if my estate were clear, I should like to do something for it."

"You are mistaken, sir, in imagining me hostile to the negro," explained Carteret. "On the contrary, I am friendly to his best interests. I give him employment; I pay taxes for schools to educate him, and for court-houses and jails to keep him in order. I merely object to being governed by an inferior and servile race."

Mrs. Carteret's face wore a tired expression. This question was her husband's hobby, and therefore her own nightmare. Moreover, she had her personal grievance against the negro race, and the names mentioned by old Mr. Delamere had brought it vividly before her mind. She had no desire to mar the harmony of the occasion by the discussion of a distasteful subject.

Mr. Delamere, glancing at his hostess, read something of this thought, and refused the challenge to further argument.

"I do not believe, major," he said, "that Olivia relishes the topic. I merely wish to say that Sandy is an exception to any rule which you may formulate in derogation of the negro. Sandy is a gentleman in ebony!"

Tom could scarcely preserve his gravity at this characterization of old Sandy, with his ridiculous air of importance, his long blue coat, and his loud plaid trousers. That suit would make a great costume for a masquerade. He would borrow it some time,—there was nothing in the world like it.

"Well, Mr. Delamere," returned the major good-humoredly, "no doubt Sandy is an exceptionally good negro,—he might well be, for he has had the benefit of your example all his life,—and we know that he is a faithful servant. But nevertheless, if I were Mrs. Ochiltree, I should put my money in the bank. Not all negroes are as honest as Sandy, and an elderly lady might not prove a match for a burly black burglar."

"Thank you, major," retorted Mrs. Ochiltree, with spirit,

"I'm not yet too old to take care of myself. That cedar chest has been my bank for forty years, and I shall not change my habits at my age."

At this moment Sandy reëntered the room. Carteret made a warning gesture, which Mrs. Ochiltree chose not to notice.

"I've proved a match for two husbands, and am not afraid of any man that walks the earth, black or white, by day or night. I have a revolver, and know how to use it. Whoever attempts to rob me will do so at his peril."

After dinner Clara played the piano and sang duets with Tom Delamere. At nine o'clock Mr. Delamere's carriage came for him, and he went away accompanied by Sandy. Under cover of the darkness the old gentleman leaned on his servant's arm with frank dependence, and Sandy lifted him into the carriage with every mark of devotion.

Ellis had already excused himself to go to the office and look over the late proofs for the morning paper. Tom remained a few minutes longer than his grandfather, and upon taking his leave went round to the Clarendon Club, where he spent an hour or two in the card-room with a couple of congenial friends. Luck seemed to favor him, and he went home at midnight with a comfortable balance of winnings. He was fond of excitement, and found a great deal of it in cards. To lose was only less exciting than to win. Of late he had developed into a very successful player,—so successful, indeed, that several members of the club generally found excuses to avoid participating in a game where he made one.

CHAPTER III

The Editor at Work

To go back a little, for several days after his child's birth Major Carteret's chief interest in life had been confined to the four walls of the chamber where his pale wife lay upon her bed of pain, and those of the adjoining room where an old black woman crooned lovingly over a little white infant. A new element had been added to the major's consciousness, broadening the scope and deepening the strength of his affections. He did not love Olivia the less, for maternity had crowned her wifehood with an added glory; but side by side with this old and tried attachment was a new passion, stirring up dormant hopes and kindling new desires. His regret had been more than personal at the thought that with himself an old name should be lost to the State; and now all the old pride of race, class, and family welled up anew, and swelled and quickened the current of his life.

Upon the major's first appearance at the office, which took place the second day after the child's birth, he opened a box of cigars in honor of the event. The word had been passed around by Ellis, and the whole office force, including reporters, compositors, and pressmen, came in to congratulate the major and smoke at his expense. Even Jerry, the colored porter,—Mammy Jane's grandson and therefore a protégé of the family,—presented himself among the rest, or rather, after the rest. The major shook hands with them all except Jerry, though he acknowledged the porter's congratulations with a kind nod and put a good cigar into his outstretched palm, for which Jerry thanked him without manifesting any consciousness of the omission. He was quite aware that under ordinary circumstances the major would not have shaken hands with white workingmen, to say nothing of negroes; and he had merely hoped that in the pleasurable distraction of the moment the major might also overlook the distinction of color. Jerry's hope had been shattered, though not rudely; for the major had spoken pleasantly and the cigar was a good one. Mr. Ellis had once shaken hands with Jerry,—but Mr. Ellis was a young man, whose Quaker father had never owned any slaves, and he could not be expected to have as much pride as one of the best "quality," whose families had possessed land and negroes for time out of mind. On the whole, Jerry preferred the careless nod of the editor-in-chief to the more familiar greeting of the subaltern.

Having finished this pleasant ceremony, which left him with a comfortable sense of his new dignity, the major turned to his desk. It had been much neglected during the week, and more than one matter claimed his attention; but as typical of the new trend of his thoughts, the first subject he took up was one bearing upon the future of his son. Quite obviously the career of a Carteret must not be left to chance,—it must be planned and worked out with a due sense of the value of good blood.

There lay upon his desk a letter from a well-known promoter, offering the major an investment which promised large returns, though several years must elapse before the enterprise could be put upon a paying basis. The element of time, however, was not immediately important. The Morning Chronicle provided him an ample income. The money available for this investment was part of his wife's patrimony. It was invested in a local cotton mill, which was paying ten per cent., but this was a beggarly return compared with the immense profits promised by the offered investment,—profits which would enable his son, upon reaching manhood, to take a place in the world commensurate with the dignity of his ancestors, one of whom, only a few generations removed, had owned an estate of ninety thousand acres of land and six thousand slaves.

This letter having been disposed of by an answer accepting the offer, the major took up his pen to write an editorial. Public affairs in the state were not going to his satisfaction. At the last state election his own party, after an almost unbroken rule of twenty years, had been defeated by the so-called "Fusion" ticket, a combination of Republicans and Populists. A clean sweep had been made of the offices in the state, which were now filled by new men. Many of the smaller places had gone to colored men, their people having voted almost solidly for the Fusion ticket. In spite of the fact that the population of Wellington was two thirds colored, this state of things was gall and wormwood to the defeated party, of which the Morning Chronicle was the acknowledged organ. Major Carteret shared this feeling. Only this very morning, while passing the city hall, on his way to the office, he had seen the steps of that noble building disfigured by a fringe of job-hunting negroes, for all the world—to use a local simile—like a string of buzzards sitting on a rail, awaiting their opportunity to batten upon the helpless corpse of a moribund city.

Taking for his theme the unfitness of the negro to participate in government,—an unfitness due to his limited education, his lack of experience, his criminal tendencies, and more especially to his hopeless mental and physical inferiority to the white race,—the major had demonstrated, it seemed to him clearly enough, that the ballot in the hands of the negro was a menace to the commonwealth. He had argued, with entire conviction, that the white and black races could never attain social and political harmony by commingling their blood; he had proved by several historical parallels that no two unassimilable races could ever live together except in the relation of superior and inferior; and he was just dipping his gold pen into the ink to indite his conclusions from the premises thus established, when Jerry, the porter, announced two visitors.

491

"Gin'l Belmont an' Cap'n McBane would like ter see you, suh."

"Show them in, Jerry."

The man who entered first upon this invitation was a dapper little gentleman with light-blue eyes and a Vandyke beard. He wore a frock coat, patent leather shoes, and a Panama hat. There were crow's-feet about his eyes, which twinkled with a hard and, at times, humorous shrewdness. He had sloping shoulders, small hands and feet, and walked with the leisurely step characteristic of those who have been reared under hot suns.

Carteret gave his hand cordially to the gentleman thus described.

"How do you do, Captain McBane," he said, turning to the second visitor.

The individual thus addressed was strikingly different in appearance from his companion. His broad shoulders, burly form, square jaw, and heavy chin betokened strength, energy, and unscrupulousness. With the exception of a small, bristling mustache, his face was clean shaven, with here and there a speck of dried blood due to a carelessly or unskillfully handled razor. A single deep-set gray eye was shadowed by a beetling brow, over which a crop of coarse black hair, slightly streaked with gray, fell almost low enough to mingle with his black, bushy eyebrows. His coat had not been brushed for several days, if one might judge from the accumulation of dandruff upon the collar, and his shirt-front, in the middle of which blazed a showy diamond, was plentifully stained with tobacco juice. He wore a large slouch hat, which, upon entering the office, he removed and held in his hand.

Having greeted this person with an unconscious but quite perceptible diminution of the warmth with which he had welcomed the other, the major looked around the room for seats for his visitors, and perceiving only one chair, piled with exchanges, and a broken stool propped against the wall, pushed a button, which rang a bell in the hall, summoning the colored porter to his presence.

"Jerry," said the editor when his servant appeared, "bring a couple of chairs for these gentlemen."

While they stood waiting, the visitors congratulated the major on the birth of his child, which had been announced in the Morning Chronicle, and which the prominence of the family made in some degree a matter of public interest.

"And now that you have a son, major," remarked the gentleman first described, as he lit one of the major's cigars, "you 'll be all the more interested in doing something to make this town fit to live in, which is what we came up to talk about. Things are in an awful condition! A negro justice of the peace has opened an office on Market Street, and only yesterday summoned a white man to appear before him. Negro lawyers get most of the business in the criminal court. Last evening a group of young white ladies, going quietly along the street arm-in-arm, were forced off the sidewalk by a crowd of negro girls. Coming down the street just now, I saw a spectacle of social equality and negro domination that made my blood boil with indignation,—a white and a black convict, chained together, crossing the city in charge of a negro officer! We cannot stand that sort of thing, Carteret,— it is the last straw! Something must be done, and that quickly!"

The major thrilled with responsive emotion. There was something prophetic in this opportune visit. The matter was not only in his own thoughts, but in the air; it was the spontaneous revulsion of white men against the rule of an inferior race. These were the very men, above all others in the town, to join him in a movement to change these degrading conditions.

General Belmont, the smaller of the two, was a man of good family, a lawyer by profession, and took an active part in state and local politics. Aristocratic by birth and instinct, and a former owner of slaves, his conception of the obligations and rights of his caste was nevertheless somewhat lower than that of the narrower but more sincere Carteret. In serious affairs Carteret desired the approval of his conscience, even if he had to trick that docile organ into acquiescence. This was not difficult to do in politics, for he believed in the divine right of white men and gentlemen, as his ancestors had believed in and died for the divine right of kings. General Belmont was not without a gentleman's distaste for meanness, but he permitted no fine scruples to stand in the way of success. He had once been minister, under a Democratic administration, to a small Central American state. Political rivals had characterized him as a tricky demagogue, which may of course have been a libel. He had an amiable disposition, possessed the gift of eloquence, and was a prime social favorite.

Captain George McBane had sprung from the poor-white class, to which, even more than to the slaves, the abolition of slavery had opened the door of opportunity. No longer overshadowed by a slaveholding caste, some of this class had rapidly pushed themselves forward. Some had made honorable records. Others, foremost in negro-baiting and election frauds, had done the dirty work of politics, as their fathers had done that of slavery, seeking their reward at first in minor offices,—for which men of gentler breeding did not care,—until their ambition began to reach out for higher honors.

Of this class McBane—whose captaincy, by the way, was merely a polite fiction—had been one of the most successful. He had held, until recently, as the reward of questionable political services, a contract with the State for its convict labor, from which in a few years he had realized a fortune. But the methods which made his contract profitable had not commended themselves to humane people, and charges of cruelty and worse had been preferred against him. He was rich enough to escape serious consequences from the investigation which followed, but when the Fusion ticket carried the state he lost his contract, and the system of convict labor was abolished. Since then McBane had devoted himself to politics: he was ambitious for greater wealth, for office, and for social recognition. A man of few words and self-engrossed, he seldom spoke of his aspirations except where speech might favor them, preferring to seek his ends by secret "deals" and combinations rather than to challenge criticism and provoke rivalry by more open methods.

At sight, therefore, of these two men, with whose careers and characters he was entirely familiar, Carteret felt sweep over his mind the conviction that now was the time and these the instruments with which to undertake the redemption of the state from the evil fate which had befallen it.

Jerry, the porter, who had gone downstairs to the counting-room to find two whole chairs, now entered with one in each hand. He set a chair for the general, who gave him an amiable nod, to which Jerry responded with a bow and a scrape. Captain McBane made no acknowledgment, but fixed Jerry so fiercely with his single eye that upon placing the chair Jerry made his escape from the room as rapidly as possible.

"I don' like dat Cap'n McBane," he muttered, upon reaching the hall. "Dey says he got dat eye knock' out tryin' ter whip a cullud 'oman, when he wuz a boy, an' dat he ain' never had no use fer niggers sence,—'cep'n' fer what he could make outen 'em wid his convic' labor contrac's. His daddy wuz a' overseer befo' 'im, an' it come nachul fer him ter be a nigger-driver. I don' want dat one eye er his'n restin' on me no longer 'n I kin he'p, an' I don' know how I'm gwine ter like dis job ef he 's gwine ter be comin' roun' here. He ain' nothin' but po' w'ite trash nohow; but Lawd! Lawd! look at de money he's got,—livin' at de hotel, wearin' di'mon's, an' colloguin' wid de bes' quality er dis town! 'Pears ter me de bottom rail is gittin' mighty close ter de top. Well, I s'pose it all comes f'm bein' w'ite. I wush ter Gawd I wuz w'ite!"

After this fervent aspiration, having nothing else to do for the time being, except to remain within call, and having caught a few words of the conversation as he went in with the chairs, Jerry, who possessed a certain amount of curiosity, placed close to the wall the broken stool upon which he sat while waiting in the hall, and applied his ear to a hole in the plastering of the hallway. There was a similar defect in the inner wall, between the same two pieces of studding, and while this inner opening was not exactly opposite the outer, Jerry was enabled, through the two, to catch in a more or less fragmentary way what was going on within.

He could hear the major, now and then, use the word "negro," and McBane's deep voice was quite audible when he referred, it seemed to Jerry with alarming frequency, to "the damned niggers," while the general's suave tones now and then pronounced the word "niggro,"—a sort of compromise between ethnology and the vernacular. That the gentlemen were talking politics seemed quite likely, for gentlemen generally talked politics when they met at the Chronicle office. Jerry could hear the words "vote," "franchise," "eliminate," "constitution," and other expressions which marked the general tenor of the talk, though he could not follow it all,—partly because he could not hear everything distinctly, and partly because of certain limitations which nature had placed in the way of Jerry's understanding anything very difficult or abstruse.

He had gathered enough, however, to realize, in a vague way, that something serious was on foot, involving his own race, when a bell sounded over his head, at which he sprang up hastily and entered the room where the gentlemen were talking.

"Jerry," said the major, "wait on Captain McBane."

"Yas, suh," responded Jerry, turning toward the captain, whose eye he carefully avoided meeting directly.

"Take that half a dollar, boy," ordered McBane, "an' go 'cross the street to Mr. Sykes's, and tell him to send me three whiskies. Bring back the change, and make has'e."

The captain tossed the half dollar at Jerry, who, looking to one side, of course missed it. He picked the money up, however, and backed out of the room. Jerry did not like Captain McBane, to begin with, and it was clear that the captain was no gentleman, or he would not have thrown the money at him. Considering the source, Jerry might have overlooked this discourtesy had it not been coupled with the remark about the change, which seemed to him in very poor taste.

Returning in a few minutes with three glasses on a tray, he passed them round, handed Captain McBane his change, and retired to the hall.

"Gentlemen," exclaimed the captain, lifting his glass, "I propose a toast: 'No nigger domination.'"

"Amen!" said the others, and three glasses were solemnly drained.

"Major," observed the general, smacking his lips. "*I* should like to use Jerry for a moment, if you will permit me."

Jerry appeared promptly at the sound of the bell. He had remained conveniently near,—calls of this sort were apt to come in sequence.

"Jerry," said the general, handing Jerry half a dollar, "go over to Mr. Brown's,—I get my liquor there,—and tell them to send me three glasses of my special mixture. And, Jerry,— you may keep the change!"

"Thank y', gin'l, thank y', marster," replied Jerry, with unctuous gratitude, bending almost double as he backed out of the room.

"Dat's a gent'eman, a rale ole-time gent'eman," he said to himself when he had closed the door."But dere 's somethin' gwine on in dere,—dere sho' is! 'No nigger damnation!' Dat soun's all right,—I'm sho' dere ain' no nigger I knows w'at wants damnation, do' dere 's lots of 'em w'at deserves it; but ef dat one-eyed Cap'n McBane got anything ter do wid it, w'atever it is, it don' mean no good fer de niggers,— damnation 'd be better fer 'em dan dat Cap'n McBane! He looks at a nigger lack he could jes' eat 'im alive."

"This mixture, gentlemen," observed the general when Jerry had returned with the glasses, "was originally compounded by no less a person than the great John C. Calhoun himself, who confided the recipe to my father over the convivial board. In this nectar of the gods, gentlemen, I drink with you to 'White Supremacy!'"

"White Supremacy everywhere!" added McBane with fervor.

"Now and forever!" concluded Carteret solemnly.

When the visitors, half an hour later, had taken their departure, Carteret, inspired by the theme, and in less degree by the famous mixture of the immortal Calhoun, turned to his desk and finished, at a white heat, his famous editorial in which he sounded the tocsin of a new crusade.

At noon, when the editor, having laid down his pen, was leaving the office, he passed Jerry in the hall without a word or a nod. The major wore a rapt look, which Jerry observed with a vague uneasiness.

"He looks jes' lack he wuz walkin' in his sleep," muttered Jerry uneasily. "Dere's somethin' up, sho 's you bawn! 'No nigger damnation!' Anybody 'd 'low dey wuz all gwine ter heaven; but I knows better! W'en a passel er w'ite folks gits ter talkin' 'bout de niggers lack dem in yander, it's mo' lackly dey 're gwine ter ketch somethin' e'se dan heaven! I got ter keep my eyes open an' keep up wid w'at's happenin'. Ef dere's gwine ter be anudder flood 'roun' here, I wants ter git in de ark wid de w'ite folks,—I may haf ter be anudder Ham, an' sta't de cullud race all over ag'in."

CHAPTER IV

Theodore Felix

The young heir of the Carterets had thriven apace, and at six months old was, according to Mammy Jane, whose experience qualified her to speak with authority, the largest, finest, smartest, and altogether most remarkable baby that had ever lived in Wellington. Mammy Jane had recently suffered from an attack of inflammatory rheumatism, as the result of which she had returned to her own home. She nevertheless came now and then to see Mrs. Carteret. A younger nurse had been procured to take her place, but it was understood that Jane would come whenever she might be needed.

"You really mean that about Dodie, do you, Mammy Jane?" asked the delighted mother, who never tired of hearing her own opinion confirmed concerning this wonderful child, which had come to her like an angel from heaven.

"Does I mean it!" exclaimed Mammy Jane, with a tone and an expression which spoke volumes of reproach. "Now, Mis' 'Livy, what is I ever uttered er said er spoke er done dat would make you s'pose I could tell you a lie 'bout yo' own chile?"

"No, Mammy Jane, I'm sure you would n't."

" 'Deed, ma'am, I'm tellin' you de Lawd's truf. I don' haf ter tell no lies ner strain no p'ints 'bout my ole mist'ess's gran'chile. Dis yer boy is de ve'y spit an' image er yo' brother, young Mars Alick, w'at died w'en he wuz 'bout eight mont's ole, w'iles I wuz laid off havin' a baby er my own, an' could n' be roun' ter look after 'im. An' dis chile is a rale quality chile, he is,—I never seed a baby wid sech fine hair fer his age, ner sech blue eyes, ner sech a grip, ner sech a heft. W'y, dat chile mus' weigh 'bout twenty-fo' poun's, an' he not but six mont's ole. Does dat gal w'at does de nussin' w'iles I'm gone ten' ter dis chile right, Mis' 'Livy?"

"She does fairly well, Mammy Jane, but I could hardly expect her to love the baby as you do. There's no one like you, Mammy Jane."

" 'Deed dere ain't honey; you is talkin' de gospel truf now! None er dese yer young folks ain' got de trainin' my ole mist'ess give me. Dese yer newfangle' schools don' l'arn 'em nothin' ter compare wid it. I 'm jes' gwine ter give dat gal a piece er my min', befo' I go, so she'll ten' ter dis chile right."

The nurse came in shortly afterwards, a neat-looking brown girl, dressed in a clean calico gown, with a nurse's cap and apron.

"Look a-here, gal," said Mammy Jane sternly, "I wants you ter understan' dat you got ter take good keer er dis chile; fer I nussed his mammy dere, an' his gran'mammy befo' 'im, an' you is got a priv'lege dat mos' lackly you don' 'preciate. I wants you to 'member, in yo' incomin's an' outgoin's, dat I got my eye on you, an' am gwine ter see dat you does yo' wo'k right."

"Do you need me for anything, ma'am?" asked the young nurse, who had stood before Mrs. Carteret, giving Mammy Jane a mere passing glance, and listening impassively to her harangue. The nurse belonged to the younger generation of colored people. She had graduated from the mission school, and had received some instruction in Dr. Miller's class for nurses. Standing, like most young people of her race, on the border line between two irreconcilable states of life, she had neither the picturesqueness of the slave, nor the unconscious dignity of those of whom freedom has been the immemorial birthright; she was in what might be called the chip-on-the-shoulder stage, through which races as well as individuals must pass in climbing the ladder of life,—not an interesting, at least not an agreeable stage, but an inevitable one, and for that reason entitled to a paragraph in a story of Southern life, which, with its as yet imperfect blending of old with new, of race with race, of slavery with freedom, is like no other life under the sun.

Had this old woman, who had no authority over her, been a little more polite, or a little less offensive, the nurse might have returned her a pleasant answer. These old-time negroes, she said to herself, made her sick with their slavering over the white folks, who, she supposed, favored them and made much of them because they had once belonged to them,— much the same reason why they fondled their cats and dogs. For her own part, they gave her nothing but her wages, and small wages at that, and she owed them nothing more than equivalent service. It was purely a matter of business; she sold her time for their money. There was no question of love between them.

Receiving a negative answer from Mrs. Carteret, she left the room without a word, ignoring Mammy Jane completely, and leaving that venerable relic of ante-bellum times gasping in helpless astonishment.

"Well, I nevuh!" she ejaculated, as soon as she could get her breath, "ef dat ain' de beatinis' pe'fo'mance I ever seed er heared of! Dese yer young niggers ain' got de manners dey wuz bawned wid! I don' know w'at dey 're comin' to, w'en dey ain' got no mo' rispec' fer ole age—I don' know—I don' know!"

"Now what are you croaking about, Jane?" asked Major Carteret, who came into the room and took the child into his arms.

Mammy Jane hobbled to her feet and bobbed a curtsy. She was never lacking in respect to white people of proper quality; but Major Carteret, the quintessence of aristocracy, called out all her reserves of deference. The major was always kind and considerate to these old family retainers, brought up in the feudal atmosphere now so rapidly passing away. Mammy Jane loved Mrs. Carteret; toward the major she entertained a feeling bordering upon awe.

"Well, Jane," returned the major sadly, when the old nurse had related her grievance, "the old times have vanished, the old ties have been ruptured. The old relations of dependence and loyal obedience on the part of the colored people, the responsibility of protection and kindness upon that of the whites, have passed away forever. The young negroes are too self-assertive. Education is spoiling them, Jane; they have been badly taught. They are not content with their station in life. Some time they will overstep the mark. The white people are patient, but there is a limit to their endurance."

"Dat's w'at I tells dese young niggers," groaned Mammy Jane, with a portentous shake of her turbaned head, "w'en I hears 'em gwine on wid deir foolishniss; but dey don' min' me. Dey 'lows dey knows mo' d'n I does, 'ca'se dey be'n l'arnt ter look in a book. But, pshuh! my ole mist'ess showed me mo' d'n dem niggers 'll l'arn in a thousan' years! I 's fetch' my gran'son' Jerry up ter be 'umble, an' keep in 'is place. An' I tells dese other niggers dat ef dey 'd do de same, an' not crowd de w'ite folks, dey 'd git ernuff ter eat, an' live out deir days in peace an' comfo't. But dey don' min' me—dey don' min' me!"

"If all the colored people were like you and Jerry, Jane," rejoined the major kindly, "there would never be any trouble. You have friends upon whom, in time of need, you can rely implicitly for protection and succor. You served your mistress faithfully before the war; you remained by her when the other negroes were running hither and thither like sheep without a shepherd; and you have transferred your allegiance to my wife and her child. We think a great deal of you, Jane."

"Yes, indeed, Mammy Jane," assented Mrs. Carteret, with sincere affection, glancing with moist eyes from the child in her husband's arms to the old nurse, whose dark face was glowing with happiness at these expressions of appreciation, "you shall never want so long as we have anything. We would share our last crust with you."

"Thank y', Mis' 'Livy," said Jane with reciprocal emotion,

"I knows who my frien's is, an' I ain' gwine ter let nothin' worry me. But fer de Lawd's sake, Mars Philip, gimme dat chile, an' lemme pat 'im on de back, er he 'll choke hisse'f ter death!"

The old nurse had been the first to observe that little Dodie, for some reason, was gasping for breath. Catching the child from the major's arms, she patted it on the back, and shook it gently. After a moment of this treatment, the child ceased to gasp, but still breathed heavily, with a strange, whistling noise.

"Oh, my child!" exclaimed the mother, in great alarm, taking the baby in her own arms, "what can be the matter with him, Mammy Jane?"

"Fer de Lawd's sake, ma'am, I don' know, 'less he 's swallered somethin'; an' he ain' had nothin' in his han's but de rattle Mis' Polly give 'im."

Mrs. Carteret caught up the ivory rattle, which hung suspended by a ribbon from the baby's neck.

"He has swallowed the little piece of the end of the handle," she cried, turning pale with fear, "and it has lodged in his throat. Telephone Dr. Price to come immediately, Philip, before my baby chokes to death! Oh, my baby, my precious baby!"

An anxious half hour passed, during which the child lay quiet, except for its labored breathing. The suspense was relieved by the arrival of Dr. Price, who examined the child carefully.

"It's a curious accident," he announced at the close of his inspection. "So far as I can discover, the piece of ivory has been drawn into the trachea, or windpipe, and has lodged in the mouth of the right bronchus. I'll try to get it out without an operation, but I can't guarantee the result."

At the end of another half hour Dr. Price announced his inability to remove the obstruction without resorting to more serious measures.

"I do not see," he declared, "how an operation can be avoided."

"Will it be dangerous?" inquired the major anxiously, while Mrs. Carteret shivered at the thought.

"It will be necessary to cut into his throat from the outside. All such operations are more or less dangerous, especially on small children. If this were some other child, I might undertake the operation unassisted; but I know how you value this one, major, and I should prefer to share the responsibility with a specialist."

"Is there one in town?" asked the major.

"No, but we can get one from out of town."

"Send for the best one in the country," said the major, "who can be got here in time. Spare no expense, Dr. Price. We value this child above any earthly thing."

"The best is the safest," replied Dr. Price. "I will send for Dr. Burns, of Philadelphia, the best surgeon in that line in America. If he can start at once, he can reach here in sixteen or eighteen hours, and the case can wait even longer, if inflammation does not set in."

The message was dispatched forthwith. By rare good fortune the eminent specialist was able to start within an hour or two after the receipt of Dr. Price's telegram. Meanwhile the baby remained restless and uneasy, the doctor spending most of his time by its side. Mrs. Carteret, who had never been quite strong since the child's birth, was a prey to the most agonizing apprehensions.

Mammy Jane, while not presuming to question the opinion of Dr. Price, and not wishing to add to her mistress's distress, was secretly oppressed by forebodings which she was unable to shake off. The child was born for bad luck. The mole under its ear, just at the point where the hangman's knot would strike, had foreshadowed dire misfortune. She had already observed several little things which had rendered her vaguely anxious.

For instance, upon one occasion, on entering the room where the baby had been left alone, asleep in his crib, she had met a strange cat hurrying from the nursery, and, upon examining closely the pillow upon which the child lay, had *ē Jane's narrator thought*

found a depression which had undoubtedly been due to the weight of the cat's body. The child was restless and uneasy, and Jane had ever since believed that the cat had been sucking little Dodie's breath, with what might have been fatal results had she not appeared just in the nick of time.

This untimely accident of the rattle, a fatality for which no one could be held responsible, had confirmed the unlucky omen. Jane's duties in the nursery did not permit her to visit her friend the conjure woman; but she did find time to go out in the back yard at dusk, and to dig up the charm which she had planted there. It had protected the child so far; but perhaps its potency had become exhausted. She picked up the bottle, shook it vigorously, and then laid it back, with the other side up. Refilling the hole, she made a cross over the top with the thumb of her left hand, and walked three times around it.

What this strange symbolism meant, or whence it derived its origin, Aunt Jane did not know. The cross was there, and the Trinity, though Jane was scarcely conscious of these, at this moment, as religious emblems. But she hoped, on general principles, that this performance would strengthen the charm and restore little Dodie's luck. It certainly had its moral effect upon Jane's own mind, for she was able to sleep better, and contrived to impress Mrs. Carteret with her own hopefulness.

CHAPTER V

A Journey Southward

As the south-bound train was leaving the station at Philadelphia, a gentleman took his seat in the single sleeping-car attached to the train, and proceeded to make himself comfortable. He hung up his hat and opened his newspaper, in which he remained absorbed for a quarter of an hour. When the train had left the city behind, he threw the paper aside, and looked around at the other occupants of the car. One of these, who had been on the car since it had left New York, rose from his seat upon perceiving the other's glance, and came down the aisle.

"How do you do, Dr. Burns?" he said, stopping beside the seat of the Philadelphia passenger.

The gentleman looked up at the speaker with an air of surprise, which, after the first keen, incisive glance, gave place to an expression of cordial recognition.

"Why, it's Miller!" he exclaimed, rising and giving the other his hand, "William Miller—Dr. Miller, of course. Sit down, Miller, and tell me all about yourself,—what you're doing, where you've been, and where you're going. I'm delighted to meet you, and to see you looking so well—and so prosperous."

"I deserve no credit for either, sir," returned the other, as he took the proffered seat, "for I inherited both health and prosperity. It is a fortunate chance that permits me to meet you."

The two acquaintances, thus opportunely thrown together

so that they might while away in conversation the tedium of their journey, represented very different and yet very similar types of manhood. A celebrated traveler, after many years spent in barbarous or savage lands, has said that among all varieties of mankind the similarities are vastly more important and fundamental than the differences. Looking at these two men with the American eye, the differences would perhaps be the more striking, or at least the more immediately apparent, for the first was white and the second black, or, more correctly speaking, brown; it was even a light brown, but both his swarthy complexion and his curly hair revealed what has been described in the laws of some of our states as a "visible admixture" of African blood.

Having disposed of this difference, and having observed that the white man was perhaps fifty years of age and the other not more than thirty, it may be said that they were both tall and sturdy, both well dressed, the white man with perhaps a little more distinction; both seemed from their faces and their manners to be men of culture and accustomed to the society of cultivated people. They were both handsome men, the elder representing a fine type of Anglo-Saxon, as the term is used in speaking of our composite white population; while the mulatto's erect form, broad shoulders, clear eyes, fine teeth, and pleasingly moulded features showed nowhere any sign of that degeneration which the pessimist so sadly maintains is the inevitable heritage of mixed races.

As to their personal relations, it has already appeared that they were members of the same profession. In past years they had been teacher and pupil. Dr. Alvin Burns was professor in the famous medical college where Miller had attended lectures. The professor had taken an interest in his only colored pupil, to whom he had been attracted by his earnestness of purpose, his evident talent, and his excellent manners and fine physique. It was in part due to Dr. Burns's friendship that Miller had won a scholarship which had enabled him, without drawing too heavily upon his father's resources, to spend in Europe, studying in the hospitals of Paris and Vi-

enna, the two most delightful years of his life. The same
influence had strengthened his natural inclination toward
operative surgery, in which Dr. Burns was a distinguished
specialist of national reputation.

Miller's father, Adam Miller, had been a thrifty colored
man, the son of a slave, who, in the olden time, had bought
himself with money which he had earned and saved, over
and above what he had paid his master for his time. Adam
Miller had inherited his father's thrift, as well as his trade,
which was that of a stevedore, or contractor for the loading
and unloading of vessels at the port of Wellington. In the
flush turpentine days following a few years after the civil war,
he had made money. His savings, shrewdly invested, had by
constant accessions become a competence. He had brought
up his eldest son to the trade; the other he had given a
professional education, in the proud hope that his children
or his grandchildren might be gentlemen in the town where
their ancestors had once been slaves.

Upon his father's death, shortly after Dr. Miller's return
from Europe, and a year or two before the date at which this
story opens, he had promptly spent part of his inheritance
in founding a hospital, to which was to be added a training
school for nurses, and in time perhaps a medical college and
a school of pharmacy. He had been strongly tempted to leave
the South, and seek a home for his family and a career for
himself in the freer North, where race antagonism was less
keen, or at least less oppressive, or in Europe, where he had
never found his color work to his disadvantage. But his people had needed him, and he had wished to help them, and
had sought by means of this institution to contribute to their
uplifting. As he now informed Dr. Burns, he was returning
from New York, where he had been in order to purchase
equipment for his new hospital, which would soon be ready
for the reception of patients.

"How much I can accomplish I do not know," said Miller,
"but I'll do what I can. There are eight or nine million of

us, and it will take a great deal of learning of all kinds to leaven that lump."

"It is a great problem, Miller, the future of your race," returned the other, "a tremendously interesting problem. It is a serial story which we are all reading, and which grows in vital interest with each successive installment. It is not only your problem, but ours. Your race must come up or drag ours down."

"We shall come up," declared Miller; "slowly and painfully, perhaps, but we shall win our way. If our race had made as much progress everywhere as they have made in Wellington, the problem would be well on the way toward solution."

"Wellington?" exclaimed Dr. Burns. "That's where I'm going. A Dr. Price, of Wellington, has sent for me to perform an operation on a child's throat. Do you know Dr. Price?"

"Quite well," replied Miller, "he is a friend of mine."

"So much the better. I shall want you to assist me. I read in the Medical Gazette, the other day, an account of a very interesting operation of yours. I felt proud to number you among my pupils. It was a remarkable case—a rare case. I must certainly have you with me in this one."

"I shall be delighted, sir," returned Miller, "if it is agreeable to all concerned."

Several hours were passed in pleasant conversation while the train sped rapidly southward. They were already far down in Virginia, and had stopped at a station beyond Richmond, when the conductor entered the car.

"All passengers," he announced, "will please transfer to the day coaches ahead. The sleeper has a hot box, and must be switched off here."

Dr. Burns and Miller obeyed the order, the former leading the way into the coach immediately in front of the sleeping-car.

"Let's sit here, Miller," he said, having selected a seat near the rear of the car and deposited his suitcase in a rack. "It's on the shady side."

Miller stood a moment hesitatingly, but finally took the seat indicated, and a few minutes later the journey was again resumed.

When the train conductor made his round after leaving the station, he paused at the seat occupied by the two doctors, glanced interrogatively at Miller, and then spoke to Dr. Burns, who sat in the end of the seat nearest the aisle.

"This man is with you?" he asked, indicating Miller with a slight side movement of his head, and a keen glance in his direction.

"Certainly," replied Dr. Burns curtly, and with some surprise. "Don't you see that he is?"

The conductor passed on. Miller paid no apparent attention to this little interlude, though no syllable had escaped him. He resumed the conversation where it had been broken off, but nevertheless followed with his eyes the conductor, who stopped at a seat near the forward end of the car, and engaged in conversation with a man whom Miller had not hitherto noticed.

As this passenger turned his head and looked back toward Miller, the latter saw a broad-shouldered, burly white man, and recognized in his square-cut jaw, his coarse, firm mouth, and the single gray eye with which he swept Miller for an instant with a scornful glance, a well-known character of Wellington, with whom the reader has already made acquaintance in these pages. Captain McBane wore a frock coat and a slouch hat; several buttons of his vest were unbuttoned, and his solitaire diamond blazed in his soiled shirt-front like the headlight of a locomotive.

The conductor in his turn looked back at Miller, and retraced his steps. Miller braced himself for what he feared was coming, though he had hoped, on account of his friend's presence, that it might be avoided.

"Excuse me, sir," said the conductor, addressing Dr. Burns, "but did I understand you to say that this man was your servant?"

"No, indeed!" replied Dr. Burns indignantly. "The gentleman is not my servant, nor anybody's servant, but is my friend. But, by the way, since we are on the subject, may I ask what affair it is of yours?"

"It's very much my affair," returned the conductor, somewhat nettled at this questioning of his authority. "I'm sorry to part *friends*, but the law of Virginia does not permit colored passengers to ride in the white cars. You'll have to go forward to the next coach," he added, addressing Miller this time.

"I have paid my fare on the sleeping-car, where the separate-car law does not apply," remonstrated Miller.

"I can't help that. You can doubtless get your money back from the sleeping-car company. But this is a day coach, and is distinctly marked 'White,' as you must have seen before you sat down here. The sign is put there for that purpose."

He indicated a large card neatly framed and hung at the end of the car, containing the legend, "White," in letters about a foot long, painted in white upon a dark background, typical, one might suppose, of the distinction thereby indicated.

"You shall not stir a step, Miller," exclaimed Dr. Burns wrathfully. "This is an outrage upon a citizen of a free country. You shall stay right here."

"I'm sorry to discommode you," returned the conductor, "but there's no use kicking. It's the law of Virginia, and I am bound by it as well as you. I have already come near losing my place because of not enforcing it, and I can take no more such chances, since I have a family to support."

"And my friend has his rights to maintain," returned Dr. Burns with determination. "There is a vital principle at stake in the matter."

"Really, sir," argued the conductor, who was a man of peace and not fond of controversy, "there's no use talking— he absolutely cannot ride in this car."

"How can you prevent it?" asked Dr. Burns, lapsing into the argumentative stage.

"The law gives me the right to remove him by force. I

can call on the train crew to assist me, or on the other passengers. If I should choose to put him off the train entirely, in the middle of a swamp, he would have no redress—the law so provides. If I did not wish to use force, I could simply switch this car off at the next siding, transfer the white passengers to another, and leave you and your friend in possession until you were arrested and fined or imprisoned."

"What he says is absolutely true, doctor," interposed Miller at this point. "It is the law, and we are powerless to resist it. If we made any trouble, it would merely delay your journey and imperil a life at the other end. I'll go into the other car."

"You shall not go alone," said Dr. Burns stoutly, rising in his turn. "A place that is too good for you is not good enough for me. I will sit wherever you do."

"I'm sorry again," said the conductor, who had quite recovered his equanimity, and calmly conscious of his power, could scarcely restrain an amused smile; "I dislike to interfere, but white passengers are not permitted to ride in the colored car."

"This is an outrage," declared Dr. Burns, "a d——d outrage! You are curtailing the rights, not only of colored people, but of white men as well. I shall sit where I please!"

"I warn you, sir," rejoined the conductor, hardening again, "that the law will be enforced. The beauty of the system lies in its strict impartiality—it applies to both races alike."

"And is equally infamous in both cases," declared Dr. Burns. "I shall immediately take steps"—

"Never mind, doctor," interrupted Miller, soothingly, "it's only for a little while. I'll reach my destination just as surely in the other car, and we can't help it, anyway. I'll see you again at Wellington."

Dr. Burns, finding resistance futile, at length acquiesced and made way for Miller to pass him.

The colored doctor took up his valise and crossed the platform to the car ahead. It was an old car, with faded upholstery, from which the stuffing projected here and there through torn places. Apparently the floor had not been swept for several days. The dust lay thick upon the window sills, and the watercooler, from which he essayed to get a drink, was filled with stale water which had made no recent acquaintance with ice. There was no other passenger in the car, and Miller occupied himself in making a rough calculation of what it would cost the Southern railroads to haul a whole car for every colored passenger. It was expensive, to say the least; it would be cheaper, and quite as considerate of their feelings, to make the negroes walk.

The car was conspicuously labeled at either end with large cards, similar to those in the other car, except that they bore the word "Colored" in black letters upon a white background. The author of this piece of legislation had contrived, with an ingenuity worthy of a better cause, that not merely should the passengers be separated by the color line, but that the reason for this division should be kept constantly in mind. Lest a white man should forget that he was white,—not a very likely contingency,—these cards would keep him constantly admonished of the fact; should a colored person endeavor, for a moment, to lose sight of his disability, these staring signs would remind him continually that between him and the rest of mankind not of his own color, there was by law a great gulf fixed.

Having composed himself, Miller had opened a newspaper, and was deep in an editorial which set forth in glowing language the inestimable advantages which would follow to certain recently acquired islands by the introduction of American liberty, when the rear door of the car opened to give entrance to Captain George McBane, who took a seat near the door and lit a cigar. Miller knew him quite well by sight and by reputation, and detested him as heartily. He represented the aggressive, offensive element among the white people of the New South, who made it hard for a negro to maintain his self-respect or to enjoy even the rights conceded to colored men by Southern laws. McBane had undoubtedly identified him to the conductor in the other car. Miller had no desire to thrust himself upon the society of white people, which, indeed, to one who had traveled so much and so far, was no novelty; but he very naturally resented being at this late day—the law had been in operation only a few months—branded and tagged and set apart from the rest of mankind upon the public highways, like an unclean thing. Nevertheless, he preferred even this to the exclusive society of Captain George McBane.

"Porter," he demanded of the colored train attaché who passed through the car a moment later, "is this a smoking car for white men?"

"No, suh," replied the porter, "but they comes in here sometimes, when they ain' no cullud ladies on the kyar."

"Well, I have paid first-class fare, and I object to that man's smoking in here. You tell him to go out."

"I'll tell the conductor, suh," returned the porter in a low tone. "I'd jus' as soon talk ter the devil as ter that man."

The white man had spread himself over two seats, and was smoking vigorously, from time to time spitting carelessly in the aisle, when the conductor entered the compartment.

"Captain," said Miller, "this car is plainly marked 'Colored.' I have paid first-class fare, and I object to riding in a smoking car."

"All right," returned the conductor, frowning irritably. "I'll speak to him."

He walked over to the white passenger, with whom he was evidently acquainted, since he addressed him by name.

"Captain McBane," he said, "it's against the law for you to ride in the nigger car."

"Who are you talkin' to?" returned the other. "I'll ride where I damn please."

"Yes, sir, but the colored passenger objects. I'm afraid I'll have to ask you to go into the smoking-car."

"The hell you say!" rejoined McBane. "I'll leave this car when I get good and ready, and that won't be till I've finished this cigar. See?"

He was as good as his word. The conductor escaped from the car before Miller had time for further expostulation. Finally McBane, having thrown the stump of his cigar into the aisle and added to the floor a finishing touch in the way of expectoration, rose and went back into the white car.

Left alone in his questionable glory, Miller buried himself again in his newspaper, from which he did not look up until the engine stopped at a tank station to take water.

As the train came to a standstill, a huge negro, covered thickly with dust, crawled off one of the rear trucks unobserved, and ran round the rear end of the car to a watering-trough by a neighboring well. Moved either by extreme thirst or by the fear that his time might be too short to permit him to draw a bucket of water, he threw himself down by the trough, drank long and deep, and plunging his head into the water, shook himself like a wet dog, and crept furtively back to his dangerous perch.

Miller, who had seen this man from the car window, had noticed a very singular thing. As the dusty tramp passed the rear coach, he cast toward it a glance of intense ferocity. Up to that moment the man's face, which Miller had recognized under its grimy coating, had been that of an ordinarily good-natured, somewhat reckless, pleasure-loving negro, at present rather the worse for wear. The change that now came over it suggested a concentrated hatred almost uncanny in its murderousness. With awakened curiosity Miller followed the direction of the negro's glance, and saw that it rested upon a window where Captain McBane sat looking out. When Miller looked back, the negro had disappeared.

At the next station a Chinaman, of the ordinary laundry type, boarded the train, and took his seat in the white car without objection. At another point a colored nurse found a place with her mistress.

"White people," said Miller to himself, who had seen these passengers from the window, "do not object to the negro as a servant. As the traditional negro,—the servant,—he is welcomed; as an equal, he is repudiated."

Miller was something of a philosopher. He had long ago had the conclusion forced upon him that an educated man of his race, in order to live comfortably in the United States, must be either a philosopher or a fool; and since he wished to be happy, and was not exactly a fool, he had cultivated philosophy. By and by he saw a white man, with a dog, enter the rear coach. Miller wondered whether the dog would be allowed to ride with his master, and if not, what disposition would be made of him. He was a handsome dog, and Miller, who was fond of animals, would not have objected to the company of a dog, as a dog. He was nevertheless conscious of a queer sensation when he saw the porter take the dog by the collar and start in his own direction, and felt consciously relieved when the canine passenger was taken on past him into the baggage-car ahead. Miller's hand was hanging over the arm of his seat, and the dog, an intelligent shepherd, licked it as he passed. Miller was not entirely sure that he would not have liked the porter to leave the dog there; he was a friendly dog, and seemed inclined to be sociable.

Toward evening the train drew up at a station where quite a party of farm laborers, fresh from their daily toil, swarmed out from the conspicuously labeled colored waiting-room, and into the car with Miller. They were a jolly, good-natured crowd, and, free from the embarrassing presence of white people, proceeded to enjoy themselves after their own fashion. Here an amorous fellow sat with his arm around a buxom girl's waist. A musically inclined individual—his talents did not go far beyond inclination—produced a mouth-organ and struck up a tune, to which a limber-legged boy danced in the aisle. They were noisy, loquacious, happy, dirty, and malodorous. For a while Miller was amused and pleased. They were his people, and he felt a certain expansive warmth toward them in spite of their obvious shortcomings. By and by, however, the air became too close, and he went out upon the platform. For the sake of the democratic ideal, which meant so much to his race, he might have endured the affliction. He could easily imagine that people of refinement, with the power in their hands, might be tempted to strain the democratic ideal in order to avoid such contact; but personally, and apart from the mere matter of racial sympathy, these people were just as offensive to him as to the whites in the other end of the train. Surely, if a classification of passengers on trains was at all desirable, it might be made upon some more logical and considerate basis than a mere arbitrary, tactless, and, by the very nature of things, brutal drawing of a color line. It was a veritable bed of Procrustes, this standard which the whites had set for the negroes. Those who grew above it must have their heads cut off, figuratively speaking,—must be forced back to the level assigned to their race; those who fell beneath the standard set had their necks stretched, literally enough, as the ghastly record in the daily papers gave conclusive evidence.

Miller breathed more freely when the lively crowd got off at the next station, after a short ride. Moreover, he had a light heart, a conscience void of offense, and was only thirty years old. His philosophy had become somewhat jaded on this journey, but he pulled it together for a final effort. Was it not, after all, a wise provision of nature that had given to a race, destined to a long servitude and a slow emergence therefrom, a cheerfulness of spirit which enabled them to catch pleasure on the wing, and endure with equanimity the ills that seemed inevitable? The ability to live and thrive under adverse circumstances is the surest guaranty of the future. The race which at the last shall inherit the earth—the residuary legatee of civilization—will be the race which remains longest upon it. The negro was here before the Anglo-Saxon was evolved, and his thick lips and heavy-lidded eyes looked out from the inscrutable face of the Sphinx across the sands of Egypt while yet the ancestors of those who now oppress him were living in caves, practicing human sacrifice, and painting themselves with woad—and the negro is here yet.

" 'Blessed are the meek,' " quoted Miller at the end of these consoling reflections, " 'for they shall inherit the earth.' If this be true, the negro may yet come into his estate, for meekness seems to be set apart as his portion."

The journey came to an end just as the sun had sunk into the west.

Simultaneously with Miller's exit from the train, a great black figure crawled off the trucks of the rear car, on the side opposite the station platform. Stretching and shaking himself with a free gesture, the black man, seeing himself unobserved, moved somewhat stiffly round the end of the car to the station platform.

" 'Fo de Lawd!" he muttered, "ef I had n' had a cha'm' life, I'd 'a' never got here on dat ticket, an' dat's a fac'—it sho' am! I kind er 'lowed I wuz gone a dozen times, ez it wuz. But I got my job ter do in dis worl', an' I knows I ain' gwine ter die 'tel I've 'complished it. I jes' want one mo' look at dat man, an' den I'll haf ter git somethin' ter eat; fer two raw turnips in twelve hours is slim pickin's fer a man er my size!"

CHAPTER VI

Janet

As the train drew up at the station platform, Dr. Price came forward from the white waiting-room, and stood expectantly by the door of the white coach. Miller, having left his car, came down the platform in time to intercept Burns as he left the train, and to introduce him to Dr. Price.

"My carriage is in waiting," said Dr. Price. "I should have liked to have you at my own house, but my wife is out of town. We have a good hotel, however, and you will doubtless find it more convenient."

"You are very kind, Dr. Price. Miller, won't you come up and dine with me?"

"Thank you, no," said Miller, "I am expected at home. My wife and child are waiting for me in the buggy yonder by the platform."

"Oh, very well; of course you must go; but don't forget our appointment. Let's see, Dr. Price, I can eat and get ready in half an hour—that will make it"—

"I have asked several of the local physicians to be present at eight o'clock," said Dr. Price. "The case can safely wait until then."

"Very well, Miller, be on hand at eight. I shall expect you without fail. Where shall he come, Dr. Price?"

"To the residence of Major Philip Carteret, on Vine Street."

"I have invited Dr. Miller to be present and assist in the operation," Dr. Burns continued, as they drove toward the hotel. "He was a favorite pupil of mine, and is a credit to the profession. I presume you saw his article in the Medical Gazette?"

"Yes, and I assisted him in the case," returned Dr. Price. "It was a colored lad, one of his patients, and he called me in to help him. He is a capable man, and very much liked by the white physicians."

Miller's wife and child were waiting for him in fluttering anticipation. He kissed them both as he climbed into the buggy.

"We came at four o'clock," said Mrs. Miller, a handsome young woman, who might be anywhere between twenty-five and thirty, and whose complexion, in the twilight, was not distinguishable from that of a white person, "but the train was late two hours, they said. We came back at six, and have been waiting ever since."

"Yes, papa," piped the child, a little boy of six or seven, who sat between them, "and I am very hungry."

Miller felt very much elated as he drove homeward through the twilight. By his side sat the two persons whom he loved best in all the world. His affairs were prosperous. Upon opening his office in the city, he had been received by the members of his own profession with a cordiality generally frank, and in no case much reserved. The colored population of the city was large, but in the main poor, and the white physicians were not unwilling to share this unprofitable practice with a colored doctor worthy of confidence. In the intervals of the work upon his hospital, he had built up a considerable practice among his own people; but except in the case of some poor unfortunate whose pride had been lost in poverty or sin, no white patient had ever called upon him for treatment. He knew very well the measure of his powers,—a liberal education had given him opportunity to compare himself with other men,—and was secretly conscious that in point of skill and knowledge he did not suffer by comparison with any other physician in the town. He liked to believe that the race antagonism which hampered his progress and that of his people was a mere temporary thing; the outcome of former conditions, and bound to disappear in time, and that when a colored man should demonstrate to the community in which he lived that he possessed character and power, that community would find a way in which to enlist his services for the public good.

He had already made himself useful, and had received many kind words and other marks of appreciation. He was now offered a further confirmation of his theory: having recognized his skill, the white people were now ready to take advantage of it. Any lurking doubt he may have felt when first invited by Dr. Burns to participate in the operation, had been dispelled by Dr. Price's prompt acquiescence.

On the way homeward Miller told his wife of this appointment. She was greatly interested; she was herself a mother, with an only child. Moreover, there was a stronger impulse than mere humanity to draw her toward the stricken mother. Janet had a tender heart, and could have loved this white sister, her sole living relative of whom she knew. All her life long she had yearned for a kind word, a nod, a smile, the least thing that imagination might have twisted into a recognition of the tie between them. But it had never come.

And yet Janet was not angry. She was of a forgiving temper; she could never bear malice. She was educated, had read many books, and appreciated to the full the social forces arrayed against any such recognition as she had dreamed of. Of the two barriers between them a man might have forgiven the one; a woman would not be likely to overlook either the bar sinister or the difference of race, even to the slight extent of a silent recognition. Blood is thicker than water, but, if it flow too far from conventional channels, may turn to gall and wormwood. Nevertheless, when the heart speaks, reason falls into the background, and Janet would have worshiped this sister, even afar off, had she received even the slightest encouragement. So strong was this weakness that she had been angry with herself for her lack of pride, or even of a decent self-respect. It was, she sometimes thought, the heritage of her mother's race, and she was ashamed of it as part of the taint of slavery. She had never acknowledged, even to her husband, from whom she concealed nothing else, her secret thoughts upon this lifelong sorrow. This silent grief was nature's penalty, or society's revenge, for whatever heritage of beauty or intellect or personal charm had come to her with her father's blood. For she had received no other inheritance. Her sister was rich by right of her birth; if Janet had been fortunate, her good fortune had not been due to any provision made for her by her white father.

She knew quite well how passionately, for many years, her proud sister had longed and prayed in vain for the child which had at length brought joy into her household, and she could feel, by sympathy, all the sickening suspense with which the child's parents must await the result of this dangerous operation.

"O Will," she adjured her husband anxiously, when he had told her of the engagement, "you must be very careful. Think of the child's poor mother! Think of our own dear child, and what it would mean to lose him!"

CHAPTER VII

The Operation

Dr. Price was not entirely at ease in his mind as the two doctors drove rapidly from the hotel to Major Carteret's. Himself a liberal man, from his point of view, he saw no reason why a colored doctor might not operate upon a white male child,—there are fine distinctions in the application of the color line,—but several other physicians had been invited, some of whom were men of old-fashioned notions, who might not relish such an innovation.

This, however, was but a small difficulty compared with what might be feared from Major Carteret himself. For he knew Carteret's unrelenting hostility to anything that savored of recognition of the negro as the equal of white men. It was traditional in Wellington that no colored person had ever entered the front door of the Carteret residence, and that the luckless individual who once presented himself there upon alleged business and resented being ordered to the back door had been unceremoniously thrown over the piazza railing into a rather thorny clump of rosebushes below. If Miller were going as a servant, to hold a basin or a sponge, there would be no difficulty; but as a surgeon—well, he would n't borrow trouble. Under the circumstances the major might yield a point.

But as they neared the house the major's unyielding disposition loomed up formidably. Perhaps if the matter were properly presented to Dr. Burns, he might consent to withdraw the invitation. It was not yet too late to send Miller a note.

"By the way, Dr. Burns," he said, "I'm very friendly to Dr. Miller, and should personally like to have him with us to-night. But—I ought to have told you this before, but I could n't very well do so, on such short notice, in Miller's presence—we are a conservative people, and our local customs are not very flexible. We jog along in much the same old way our fathers did. I 'm not at all sure that Major Carteret or the other gentlemen would consent to the presence of a negro doctor."

"I think you misjudge your own people," returned Dr. Burns, "they are broader than you think. We have our prejudices against the negro at the North, but we do not let them stand in the way of anything that *we* want. At any rate, it is too late now, and I will accept the responsibility. If the question is raised, I will attend to it. When I am performing an operation I must be *aut Caesar, aut nullus.*"

Dr. Price was not reassured, but he had done his duty and felt the reward of virtue. If there should be trouble, he would not be responsible. Moreover, there was a large fee at stake, and Dr. Burns was not likely to prove too obdurate.

They were soon at Carteret's, where they found assembled the several physicians invited by Dr. Price. These were successively introduced as Drs. Dudley, Hooper, and Ashe, all of whom were gentlemen of good standing, socially and in their profession, and considered it a high privilege to witness so delicate an operation at the hands of so eminent a member of their profession.

Major Carteret entered the room and was duly presented to the famous specialist. Carteret's anxious look lightened somewhat at sight of the array of talent present. It suggested, of course, the gravity of the impending event, but gave assurance of all the skill and care which science could afford.

Dr. Burns was shown to the nursery, from which he returned in five minutes.

"The case is ready," he announced. "Are the gentlemen all present?"

"I believe so," answered Dr. Price quickly.

Miller had not yet arrived. Perhaps, thought Dr. Price, a happy accident, or some imperative call, had detained him. This would be fortunate indeed. Dr. Burns's square jaw had a very determined look. It would be a pity if any acrimonious discussion should arise on the eve of a delicate operation. If the clock on the mantel would only move faster, the question might never come up.

"I don't see Dr. Miller," observed Dr. Burns, looking around the room. "I asked him to come at eight. There are ten minutes yet."

Major Carteret looked up with a sudden frown.

"May I ask to whom you refer?" he inquired, in an ominous tone.

The other gentlemen showed signs of interest, not to say emotion. Dr. Price smiled quizzically.

"Dr. Miller, of your city. He was one of my favorite pupils. He is also a graduate of the Vienna hospitals, and a surgeon of unusual skill. I have asked him to assist in the operation."

Every eye was turned toward Carteret, whose crimsoned face had set in a look of grim determination.

"The person to whom you refer is a negro, I believe?" he said.

"He is a colored man, certainly," returned Dr. Burns, "though one would never think of his color after knowing him well."

"I do not know, sir," returned Carteret, with an effort at self-control, "what the customs of Philadelphia or Vienna may be; but in the South we do not call negro doctors to attend white patients. I could not permit a negro to enter my house upon such an errand."

"I am here, sir," replied Dr. Burns with spirit, "to perform a certain operation. Since I assume the responsibility, the case must be under my entire control. Otherwise I cannot operate."

"Gentlemen," interposed Dr. Price, smoothly, "I beg of you both—this is a matter for calm discussion, and any asperity is to be deplored. The life at stake here should not be imperiled by any consideration of minor importance."

"Your humanity does you credit, sir," retorted Dr. Burns. "But other matters, too, are important. I have invited this gentleman here. My professional honor is involved, and I merely invoke my rights to maintain it. It is a matter of principle, which ought not to give way to a mere prejudice."

"That also states the case for Major Carteret," rejoined Dr. Price, suavely. "He has certain principles,—call them prejudices, if you like,—certain inflexible rules of conduct by which he regulates his life. One of these, which he shares with us all in some degree, forbids the recognition of the negro as a social equal."

"I do not know what Miller's social value may be," replied Dr. Burns, stoutly, "or whether you gain or lose by your attitude toward him. I have invited him here in a strictly professional capacity, with which his color is not at all concerned."

"Dr. Burns does not quite appreciate Major Carteret's point of view," said Dr. Price. "This is not with him an unimportant matter, or a mere question of prejudice, or even of personal taste. It is a sacred principle, lying at the very root of our social order, involving the purity and prestige of our race. You Northern gentlemen do not quite appreciate our situation; if you lived here a year or two you would act as we do. Of course," he added, diplomatically, "if there were no alternative—if Dr. Burns were willing to put Dr. Miller's presence on the ground of imperative necessity"—

"I do nothing of the kind, sir," retorted Dr. Burns with some heat. "I have not come all the way from Philadelphia to undertake an operation which I cannot perform without the aid of some particular physician. I merely stand upon my professional rights."

Carteret was deeply agitated. The operation must not be deferred; his child's life might be endangered by delay. If the negro's presence were indispensable he would even submit to it, though in order to avoid so painful a necessity, he would rather humble himself to the Northern doctor. The latter course involved merely a personal sacrifice—the former a vital principle. Perhaps there was another way of escape. Miller's presence could not but be distasteful to Mrs. Carteret for other reasons. Miller's wife was the living evidence of a painful episode in Mrs. Carteret's family, which the doctor's presence would inevitably recall. Once before, Mrs. Carteret's life had been endangered by encountering, at a time of great nervous strain, this ill-born sister and her child. She was even now upon the verge of collapse at the prospect of her child's suffering, and should be protected from the intrusion of any idea which might add to her distress.

"Dr. Burns," he said, with the suave courtesy which was part of his inheritance, "I beg your pardon for my heat, and throw myself upon your magnanimity, as between white men"—

"I am a gentleman, sir, before I am a white man," interposed Dr. Burns, slightly mollified, however, by Carteret's change of manner.

"The terms should be synonymous," Carteret could not refrain from saying. "As between white men, and gentlemen, I say to you, frankly, that there are vital, personal reasons, apart from Dr. Miller's color, why his presence in this house would be distasteful. With this statement, sir, I throw myself upon your mercy. My child's life is worth more to me than any earthly thing, and I must be governed by your decision."

Dr. Burns was plainly wavering. The clock moved with provoking slowness. Miller would be there in five minutes.

"May I speak with you privately a moment, doctor?" asked Dr. Price.

They withdrew from the room and were engaged in conversation for a few moments. Dr. Burns finally yielded.

"I shall nevertheless feel humiliated when I meet Miller again," he said, "but of course if there is a personal question involved, that alters the situation. Had it been merely a matter of color, I should have maintained my position. As things stand, I wash my hands of the whole affair, so far as Miller is concerned, like Pontius Pilate—yes, indeed, sir, I feel very much like that individual."

"I'll explain the matter to Miller," returned Dr. Price, amiably, "and make it all right with him. We Southern people understand the negroes better than you do, sir. Why should we not? They have been constantly under our interested observation for several hundred years. You feel this vastly more than Miller will. He knows the feeling of the white people, and is accustomed to it. He wishes to live and do business here, and is quite too shrewd to antagonize his neighbors or come where he is not wanted. He is in fact too much of a gentleman to do so."

"I shall leave the explanation to you entirely," rejoined Dr. Burns, as they reëntered the other room.

Carteret led the way to the nursery, where the operation was to take place. Dr. Price lingered for a moment. Miller was not likely to be behind the hour, if he came at all, and it would be well to head him off before the operation began.

Scarcely had the rest left the room when the doorbell sounded, and a servant announced Dr. Miller.

Dr. Price stepped into the hall and met Miller face to face.

He had meant to state the situation to Miller frankly, but now that the moment had come he wavered. He was a fine physician, but he shrank from strenuous responsibilities. It had been easy to theorize about the negro; it was more difficult to look this man in the eyes—whom at this moment he felt to be as essentially a gentleman as himself—and tell him the humiliating truth.

As a physician his method was to ease pain—he would rather take the risk of losing a patient from the use of an anaesthetic than from the shock of an operation. He liked Miller, wished him well, and would not wittingly wound his feelings. He really thought him too much of a gentleman for the town, in view of the restrictions with which he must inevitably be hampered. There was something melancholy, to a cultivated mind, about a sensitive, educated man who happened to be off color. Such a person was a sort of social misfit, an odd quantity, educated out of his own class, with no possible hope of entrance into that above it. He felt quite sure that if he had been in Miller's place, he would never have settled in the South—he would have moved to Europe, or to the West Indies, or some Central or South American state where questions of color were not regarded as vitally important.

Dr. Price did not like to lie, even to a negro. To a man of his own caste, his word was his bond. If it were painful to lie, it would be humiliating to be found out. The principle of *noblesse oblige* was also involved in the matter. His claim of superiority to the colored doctor rested fundamentally upon the fact that he was white and Miller was not; and yet this superiority, for which he could claim no credit, since he had not made himself, was the very breath of his nostrils,— he would not have changed places with the other for wealth untold; and as a gentleman, he would not care to have another gentleman, even a colored man, catch him in a lie. Of this, however, there was scarcely any danger. A word to the other surgeons would insure their corroboration of whatever he might tell Miller. No one of them would willingly wound Dr. Miller or embarrass Dr. Price; indeed, they need not know that Miller had come in time for the operation.

"I'm sorry, Miller," he said with apparent regret, "but we were here ahead of time, and the case took a turn which would admit of no delay, so the gentlemen went in. Dr. Burns is with the patient now, and asked me to explain why we did not wait for you."

"I'm sorry too," returned Miller, regretfully, but nothing doubting. He was well aware that in such cases danger might attend upon delay. He had lost his chance, through no fault of his own or of any one else.

"I hope that all is well?" he said, hesitatingly, not sure whether he would be asked to remain.

"All is well, so far. Step round to my office in the morn-

529

ing, Miller, or come in when you're passing, and I'll tell you the details."

This was tantamount to a dismissal, so Miller took his leave. Descending the doorsteps, he stood for a moment, undecided whether to return home or to go to the hotel and await the return of Dr. Burns, when he heard his name called from the house in a low tone.

"Oh, doctuh!"

He stepped back toward the door, outside of which stood the colored servant who had just let him out.

"Dat's all a lie, doctuh," he whispered, " 'bout de operation bein' already pe'fo'med. Dey-all had jes' gone in de minute befo' you come—Doctuh Price had n' even got out 'n de room. Dey be'n quollin' 'bout you fer de las ha'f hour. Majah Ca'te'et say he would n' have you, an' de No'then doctuh say he would n't do nothin' widout you, an' Doctuh Price he j'ined in on bofe sides, an' dey had it hot an' heavy, nip an' tuck, till bimeby Majah Ca'te'et up an' say it wa'n't altogether yo' color he objected to, an' wid dat de No'then doctuh give in. He's a fine man, suh, but dey wuz too much fer 'im!"

"Thank you, Sam, I'm much obliged," returned Miller mechanically. "One likes to know the truth."

Truth, it has been said, is mighty, and must prevail; but it sometimes leaves a bad taste in the mouth. In the ordinary course of events Miller would not have anticipated such an invitation, and for that reason had appreciated it all the more. The rebuff came with a corresponding shock. He had the heart of a man, the sensibilities of a cultivated gentleman; the one was sore, the other deeply wounded. He was not altogether sure, upon reflection, whether he blamed Dr. Price very much for the amiable lie, which had been meant to spare his feelings, or thanked Sam a great deal for the unpalatable truth.

Janet met him at the door. "How is the baby?" she asked excitedly.

about Prejudice & scruples [handwritten annotation]

"Dr. Price says he is doing well."

"What is the matter, Will, and why are you back so soon?"

He would have spared her the story, but she was a woman, and would have it. He was wounded, too, and wanted sympathy, of which Janet was an exhaustless fountain. So he told her what had happened. She comforted him after the manner of a loving woman, and felt righteously indignant toward her sister's husband, who had thus been instrumental in the humiliation of her own. Her anger did not embrace her sister, and yet she felt obscurely that their unacknowledged relationship had been the malignant force which had given her husband pain, and defeated his honorable ambition.

When Dr. Price entered the nursery, Dr. Burns was leaning attentively over the operating table. The implements needed for the operation were all in readiness—the knives, the basin, the sponge, the materials for dressing the wound—all the ghastly paraphernalia of vivisection.

Mrs. Carteret had been banished to another room, where Clara vainly attempted to soothe her. Old Mammy Jane, still burdened by her fears, fervently prayed the good Lord to spare the life of the sweet little grandson of her dear old mistress.

Dr. Burns had placed his ear to the child's chest, which had been bared for the incision. Dr. Price stood ready to administer the anæsthetic. Little Dodie looked up with a faint expression of wonder, as if dimly conscious of some unusual event. The major shivered at the thought of what the child must undergo.

"There's a change in his breathing," said Dr. Burns, lifting his head. "The whistling noise is less pronounced, and he breathes easier. The obstruction seems to have shifted."

Applying his ear again to the child's throat, he listened for a moment intently, and then picking the baby up from the table, gave it a couple of sharp claps between the shoulders. Simultaneously a small object shot out from the child's mouth, struck Dr. Price in the neighborhood of his waist-band, and then rattled lightly against the floor. Whereupon the baby, as though conscious of his narrow escape, smiled and gurgled, and reaching upward clutched the doctor's whiskers with his little hand, which, according to old Jane, had a stronger grip than any other infant's in Wellington.

CHAPTER VIII

The Campaign Drags

The campaign for white supremacy was dragging. Carteret had set out, in the columns of the Morning Chronicle, all the reasons why this movement, inaugurated by the three men who had met, six months before, at the office of the Chronicle, should be supported by the white public. Negro citizenship was a grotesque farce—Sambo and Dinah raised from the kitchen to the cabinet were a spectacle to make the gods laugh. The laws by which it had been sought to put the negroes on a level with the whites must be swept away in theory, as they had failed in fact. If it were impossible, without a further education of public opinion, to secure the repeal of the fifteenth amendment, it was at least the solemn duty of the state to endeavor, through its own constitution, to escape from the domination of a weak and incompetent electorate and confine the negro to that inferior condition for which nature had evidently designed him.

In spite of the force and intelligence with which Carteret had expressed these and similar views, they had not met the immediate response anticipated. There were thoughtful men, willing to let well enough alone, who saw no necessity for such a movement. They believed that peace, prosperity, and popular education offered a surer remedy for social ills than the reopening of issues supposed to have been settled. There were timid men who shrank from civic strife. There were busy men, who had something else to do. There were a few fair men, prepared to admit, privately, that a class constituting half to two thirds of the population were fairly entitled to some representation in the law-making bodies. Perhaps there might have been found, somewhere in the state, a single white man ready to concede that all men were entitled to equal rights before the law.

That there were some white men who had learned little and forgotten nothing goes without saying, for knowledge and wisdom are not impartially distributed among even the most favored race. There were ignorant and vicious negroes, and they had a monopoly of neither ignorance nor crime, for there were prosperous negroes and poverty-stricken whites. Until Carteret and his committee began their baleful campaign the people of the state were living in peace and harmony. The anti-negro legislation in more southern states, with large negro majorities, had awakened scarcely an echo in this state, with a population two thirds white. Even the triumph of the Fusion party had not been regarded as a race issue. It remained for Carteret and his friends to discover, with inspiration from whatever supernatural source the discriminating reader may elect, that the darker race, docile by instinct, humble by training, patiently waiting upon its as yet uncertain destiny, was an incubus, a corpse chained to the body politic, and that the negro vote was a source of danger to the state, no matter how cast or by whom directed.

To discuss means for counteracting this apathy, a meeting of the "Big Three," as they began to designate themselves jocularly, was held at the office of the "Morning Chronicle," on the next day but one after little Dodie's fortunate escape from the knife.

"It seems," said General Belmont, opening the discussion, "as though we had undertaken more than we can carry through. It is clear that we must reckon on opposition, both at home and abroad. If we are to hope for success, we must extend the lines of our campaign. The North, as well as our own people, must be convinced that we have right upon our side. We are conscious of the purity of our motives, but we should avoid even the appearance of evil."

McBane was tapping the floor impatiently with his foot during this harangue.

"I don't see the use," he interrupted, "of so much beating about the bush. We may as well be honest about this thing. We are going to put the niggers down because we want to, and think we can; so why waste our time in mere pretense? I'm no hypocrite myself,—if I want a thing I take it, provided I'm strong enough."

[margin note: McBane's one good value is honesty — very ironic!]

"My dear captain," resumed the general, with biting suavity, "your frankness does your credit,—'an honest man's the noblest work of God,'—but we cannot carry on politics in these degenerate times without a certain amount of diplomacy. In the good old days when your father was alive, and perhaps nowadays in the discipline of convicts, direct and simple methods might be safely resorted to; but this is a modern age, and in dealing with so fundamental a right as the suffrage we must profess a decent regard for the opinions of even that misguided portion of mankind which may not agree with us. This is the age of crowds, and we must have the crowd with us."

[margin note: Dvhsen]

The captain flushed at the allusion to his father's calling, at which he took more offense than at the mention of his own. He knew perfectly well that these old aristocrats, while reaping the profits of slavery, had despised the instruments by which they were attained—the poor-white overseer only less than the black slave. McBane was rich; he lived in Wellington, but he had never been invited to the home of either General Belmont or Major Carteret, nor asked to join the club of which they were members. His face, therefore, wore a distinct scowl, and his single eye glowed ominously. He would help these fellows carry the state for white supremacy, and then he would have his innings,—he would have more to say than they dreamed, as to who should fill the offices under the new deal. Men of no better birth or breeding than he had represented Southern states in Congress since the war. Why should he not run for governor, representative, whatever he chose? He had money enough to buy out half a dozen of these broken-down aristocrats, and money was all-powerful.

"You see, captain," the general went on, looking McBane smilingly and unflinchingly in the eye, "we need white immigration—we need Northern capital. 'A good name is better than great riches,' and we must prove our cause a righteous one."

"We must be armed at all points," added Carteret, "and prepared for defense as well as for attack,—we must make our campaign a national one."

"For instance," resumed the general, "you, Carteret, represent the Associated Press. Through your hands passes all the news of the state. What more powerful medium for the propagation of an idea? The man who would govern a nation by writing its songs was a blethering idiot beside the fellow who can edit its news dispatches. The negroes are playing into our hands,—every crime that one of them commits is reported by us. With the latitude they have had in this state they are growing more impudent and self-assertive every day. A yellow demagogue in New York made a speech only a few days ago, in which he deliberately, and in cold blood, advised negroes to defend themselves to the death when attacked by white people! I remember well the time when it was death for a negro to strike a white man."

"It's death now, if he strikes the right one," interjected McBane, restored to better humor by this mention of a congenial subject.

The general smiled a fine smile. He had heard the story of how McBane had lost his other eye.

"The local negro paper is quite outspoken, too," continued the general, "if not impudent. We must keep track of that; it may furnish us some good campaign material."

"Yes," returned Carteret, "we must see to that. I threw a copy into the waste-basket this morning, without looking at it. Here it is now!"

CHAPTER IX

A White Man's "Nigger"

Carteret fished from the depths of the wastebasket and handed to the general an eighteen by twenty-four sheet, poorly printed on cheap paper, with a "patent" inside, a number of advertisements of proprietary medicines, quack doctors, and fortune-tellers, and two or three columns of editorial and local news. Candor compels the admission that it was not an impressive sheet in any respect, except when regarded as the first local effort of a struggling people to make public expression of their life and aspirations. From this point of view it did not speak at all badly for a class to whom, a generation before, newspapers, books, and learning had been forbidden fruit.

"It's an elegant specimen of journalism, is n't it?" laughed the general, airily. "Listen to this 'ad':—

" 'Kinky, curly hair made straight by one application of our specific. Our face bleach will turn the skin of a black or brown person four or five shades lighter, and of a mulatto perfectly white. When you get the color you wish, stop using the preparation.'

"Just look at those heads!—'Before using' and 'After using.' We'd better hurry, or there'll be no negroes to disfranchise! If they don't stop till they get the color they desire, and the stuff works according to contract, they'll all be white. Ah! what have we here? This looks as though it might be serious."

Opening the sheet the general read aloud an editorial ar-

537

ticle, to which Carteret listened intently, his indignation increasing in strength from the first word to the last, while McBane's face grew darkly purple with anger.

The article was a frank and somewhat bold discussion of lynching and its causes. It denied that most lynchings were for the offense most generally charged as their justification, and declared that, even of those seemingly traced to this cause, many were not for crimes at all, but for voluntary acts which might naturally be expected to follow from the miscegenation laws by which it was sought, in all the Southern States, to destroy liberty of contract, and, for the purpose of maintaining a fanciful purity of race, to make crimes of marriages to which neither nature nor religion nor the laws of other states interposed any insurmountable barrier. Such an article in a Northern newspaper would have attracted no special attention, and might merely have furnished food to an occasional reader for serious thought upon a subject not exactly agreeable; but coming from a colored man, in a Southern city, it was an indictment of the laws and social system of the South that could not fail of creating a profound sensation.

"Infamous—infamous!" exclaimed Carteret, his voice trembling with emotion. "The paper should be suppressed immediately."

"The impudent nigger ought to be horsewhipped and run out of town," growled McBane.

"Gentlemen," said the general soothingly, after the first burst of indignation had subsided, "I believe we can find a more effective use for this article, which, by the way, will not bear too close analysis,—there's some truth in it, at least there's an argument."

"That is not the point," interrupted Carteret.

"No," interjected McBane with an oath, "that ain't at all the point. Truth or not, no damn nigger has any right to say it."

"This article," said Carteret, "violates an unwritten law of the South. If we are to tolerate this race of weaklings

among us, until they are eliminated by the stress of competition, it must be upon terms which we lay down. One of
our conditions is violated by this article, in which our wisdom is assailed, and our women made the subject of offensive
comment. We must make known our disapproval."

"I say lynch the nigger, break up the press, and burn down
the newspaper office," McBane responded promptly.

"Gentlemen," interposed the general, "would you mind
suspending the discussion for a moment, while I send Jerry
across the street? I think I can then suggest a better plan."

Carteret rang the bell for Jerry, who answered promptly.
He had been expecting such a call ever since the gentlemen
had gone in.

"Jerry," said the general, "step across to Brown's and tell
him to send me three Calhoun cocktails. Wait for them,—
here's the money."

"Yas, suh," replied Jerry, taking the proffered coin.

"And make has'e, charcoal," added McBane, "for we're
gettin' damn dry."

A momentary cloud of annoyance darkened Carteret's
brow. McBane had always grated upon his aristocratic susceptibilities. The captain was an upstart, a product of the
democratic idea operating upon the poor white man, the
descendant of the indentured bondservant and the socially
unfit. He had wealth and energy, however, and it was necessary to make use of him; but the example of such men was
a strong incentive to Carteret in his campaign against the
negro. It was distasteful enough to rub elbows with an illiterate and vulgar white man of no ancestry,—the risk of similar contact with negroes was to be avoided at any cost. He
could hardly expect McBane to be a gentleman, but when
among men of that class he might at least try to imitate their
manners. A gentleman did not order his own servants around
offensively, to say nothing of another's.

The general had observed Carteret's annoyance, and remarked pleasantly while they waited for the servant's return:—

"Jerry, now, is a very good negro. He's not one of your new negroes, who think themselves as good as white men, and want to run the government. Jerry knows his place,—he is respectful, humble, obedient, and content with the face and place assigned to him by nature."

"Yes, he's one of the best of 'em," sneered McBane. "He'll call any man 'master' for a quarter, or 'God' for half a dollar; for a dollar he'll grovel at your feet, and for a cast-off coat you can buy an option on his immortal soul,—if he has one! I've handled niggers for ten years, and I know 'em from the ground up. They're all alike,—they're a scrub race, an affliction to the country, and the quicker we're rid of 'em all the better."

Carteret had nothing to say by way of dissent. McBane's sentiments, in their last analysis, were much the same as his, though he would have expressed them less brutally.

"The negro," observed the general, daintily flicking the ash from his cigar, "is all right in his place and very useful to the community. We lived on his labor for quite a long time, and lived very well. Nevertheless we are better off without slavery, for we can get more out of the free negro, and with less responsibility. I really do not see how we could get along without the negroes. If they were all like Jerry, we'd have no trouble with them."

Having procured the drinks, Jerry, the momentary subject of the race discussion which goes on eternally in the South, was making his way back across the street, somewhat disturbed in mind.

"O Lawd!" he groaned, "I never troubles trouble till trouble troubles me; but w'en I got dem drinks befo', Gin'l Belmont gimme half a dollar an' tol' me ter keep de change. Dis time he did n' say nothin' 'bout de change. I s'pose he jes' fergot erbout it, but w'at is a po' nigger gwine ter do w'en he has ter conten' wid w'ite folks's fergitfulniss? I don' see no way but ter do some fergittin' myse'f. I'll jes' stan' outside de do' here till dey gits so wrop' up in deir talk dat dey won' 'member nothin' e'se, an' den at de right minute I'll han' de glasses 'round, an' mos' lackly de gin'l fergit all 'bout de change."

While Jerry stood outside, the conversation within was plainly audible, and some inkling of its purport filtered through his mind.

"Now, gentlemen," the general was saying, "here's my plan. That editorial in the negro newspaper is good campaign matter, but we should reserve it until it will be most effective. Suppose we just stick it in a pigeon-hole, and let the editor,—what's his name?"

"The nigger's name is Barber," replied McBane. "I'd like to have him under me for a month or two; he'd write no more editorials."

"Let Barber have all the rope he wants," resumed the general, "and he'll be sure to hang himself. In the mean time we will continue to work up public opinion,—we can use this letter privately for that purpose,—and when the state campaign opens we'll print the editorial, with suitable comment, scatter it broadcast through the state, fire the Southern heart, organize the white people on the color line, have a little demonstration with red shirts and shotguns, scare the negroes into fits, win the state for white supremacy, and teach our colored fellow citizens that we are tired of negro domination and have put an end to it forever. The Afro-American Banner will doubtless die about the same time."

"And so will the editor!" exclaimed McBane ferociously; "I'll see to that. But I wonder where that nigger is with them cocktails? I'm so thirsty I could swallow blue blazes."

"Here's yo' drinks, gin'l," announced Jerry, entering with the glasses on a tray.

The gentlemen exchanged compliments and imbibed— McBane at a gulp, Carteret with more deliberation, leaving about half the contents of his glass.

The general drank slowly, with every sign of appreciation. "If the illustrious statesman," he observed, "whose name this mixture bears, had done nothing more than invent it, his fame would still deserve to go thundering down the endless ages."

"It ain't bad liquor," assented McBane, smacking his lips.

Jerry received the empty glasses on the tray and left the room. He had scarcely gained the hall when the general called him back.

"O Lawd!" groaned Jerry, "he's gwine ter ax me fer de change. Yas, suh, yas, suh; comin' gin'l, comin', suh!"

"You may keep the change, Jerry," said the general.

Jerry's face grew radiant at this announcement. "Yas, suh, gin'l; thank y', suh; much obleedzed, suh. I wuz jus' gwine ter fetch it in, suh, w'en I had put de tray down. Thank y', suh, truly, suh!"

Jerry backed and bowed himself out into the hall.

"Dat wuz a close shave," he muttered, as he swallowed the remaining contents of Major Carteret's glass. "I 'lowed dem twenty cents wuz gone dat time,—an' whar I wuz gwine ter git de money ter take my gal ter de chu'ch festibal ternight, de Lawd only knows!—'less'n I borried it off'n Mr. Ellis, an' I owes him sixty cents a'ready. But I wonduh w'at dem w'ite folks in dere is up ter? Dere's one thing sho',—dey're gwine ter git after de niggers some way er 'nuther, an' w'en dey does, whar is Jerry gwine ter be? Dat's de mos' impo'tantes' question. I'm gwine ter look at dat newspaper dey be'n talkin' 'bout, an' 'less'n my min' changes might'ly, I'm gwine ter keep my mouf shet an' stan' in wid de Angry-Saxon race,—ez dey calls deyse'ves nowadays,—an' keep on de right side er my bread an' meat. W'at nigger ever give me twenty cents in all my bawn days?"

"By the way, major," said the general, who lingered behind McBane as they were leaving, "is Miss Clara's marriage definitely settled upon?"

"Well, general, not exactly; but it's the understanding that they will marry when they are old enough."

"I was merely thinking," the general went on, "that if I were you I'd speak to Tom about cards and liquor. He gives more time to both than a young man can afford. I'm speaking in his interest and in Miss Clara's,—we of the old families ought to stand together."

"Thank you, general, for the hint. I'll act upon it."

This political conference was fruitful in results. Acting upon the plans there laid out, McBane traveled extensively through the state, working up sentiment in favor of the new movement. He possessed a certain forceful eloquence; and white supremacy was so obviously the divine intention that he had merely to affirm the doctrine in order to secure adherents.

General Belmont, whose business required him to spend most of the winter in Washington and New York, lost no opportunity to get the ear of lawmakers, editors, and other leaders of national opinion, and to impress upon them, with persuasive eloquence, the impossibility of maintaining existing conditions, and the tremendous blunder which had been made in conferring the franchise upon the emancipated race.

Carteret conducted the press campaign, and held out to the Republicans of the North the glittering hope that, with the elimination of the negro vote, and a proper deference to Southern feeling, a strong white Republican party might be built up in the New South. How well the bait took is a matter of history,—but the promised result is still in the future. The disfranchisement of the negro has merely changed the form of the same old problem. The negro had no vote before the rebellion, and few other rights, and yet the negro question was, for a century, the pivot of American politics. It plunged the nation into a bloody war, and it will trouble the American government and the American conscience until a sustained attempt is made to settle it upon principles of justice and equity.

The personal ambitions entertained by the leaders of this movement are but slightly involved in this story. McBane's aims have been touched upon elsewhere. The general would have accepted the nomination for governor of the state, with a vision of a senatorship in the future. Carteret hoped to vindicate the supremacy of his race, and make the state fit for his son to live in, and, incidentally, he would not refuse any office, worthy of his dignity, which a grateful people might thrust upon him.

So powerful a combination of bigot, self-seeking demagogue, and astute politician was fraught with grave menace to the peace of the state and the liberties of the people,—by which is meant the whole people, and not any one class, sought to be built up at the expense of another.

CHAPTER X

Delamere Plays a Trump

Carteret did not forget what General Belmont had said in regard to Tom. The major himself had been young, not so very long ago, and was inclined toward indulgence for the foibles of youth. A young gentleman should have a certain knowledge of life,—but there were limits. Clara's future happiness must not be imperiled.

The opportunity to carry out this purpose was not long delayed. Old Mr. Delamere wished to sell some timber which had been cut at Belleview, and sent Tom down to the Chronicle office to leave an advertisement. The major saw him at the desk, invited him into his sanctum, and delivered him a mild lecture. The major was kind, and talked in a fatherly way about the danger of extremes, the beauty of moderation, and the value of discretion as a rule of conduct. He mentioned collaterally the unblemished honor of a fine old family, its contemplated alliance with his own, and dwelt upon the sweet simplicity of Clara's character. The major was a man of feeling and of tact, and could not have put the subject in a way less calculated to wound the *amour propre* of a very young man.

Delamere had turned red with anger while the major was speaking. He was impulsive, and an effort was required to keep back the retort that sprang once or twice to his lips; but his conscience was not clear, and he could not afford hard words with Clara's guardian and his grandfather's friend. Clara was rich, and the most beautiful girl in town; they were engaged; he loved her as well as he could love anything of which he seemed sure; and he did not mean that anyone else should have her. The major's mild censure disturbed slightly his sense of security; and while the major's manner did not indicate that he knew anything definite against him, it would be best to let well enough alone.

"Thank you, major," he said, with well-simulated frankness. "I realize that I may have been a little careless, more from thoughtless than anything else; but my heart is all right, sir, and I am glad that my conduct has been brought to your attention, for what you have said enables me to see it in a different light. I will be more careful of my company hereafter; for I love Clara, and mean to try to be worthy of her. Do you know whether she will be at home this evening?"

"I have heard nothing to the contrary," replied the major warmly. "Call her up by telephone and ask—or come up and see. You're always welcome, my boy."

Upon leaving the office, which was on the second floor, Tom met Ellis coming up the stairs. It had several times of late occurred to Tom that Ellis had a sneaking fondness for Clara. Panoplied in his own engagement, Tom had heretofore rather enjoyed the idea of a hopeless rival. Ellis was such a solemn prig, and took life so seriously, that it was a pleasure to see him sit around sighing for the unattainable. That he should be giving pain to Ellis added a certain zest to his own enjoyment.

But this interview with the major had so disquieted him that upon meeting Ellis upon the stairs he was struck by a sudden suspicion. He knew that Major Carteret seldom went to the Clarendon Club, and that he must have got his information from some one else. Ellis was a member of the club, and a frequent visitor. Who more likely than he to try to poison Clara's mind, or the minds of her friends, against her accepted lover? Tom did not think that the world was using him well of late; bad luck had pursued him, in cards and other things, and despite his assumption of humility, Carteret's lecture had left him in an ugly mood. He nodded curtly

546

to Ellis without relaxing the scowl that disfigured his handsome features.

"That's the damned sneak who's been giving me away," he muttered. "I'll get even with him yet for this."

Delamere's suspicions with regard to Ellis's feelings were not, as we have seen, entirely without foundation. Indeed, he had underestimated the strength of this rivalry and its chances of success. Ellis had been watching Delamere for a year. There had been nothing surreptitious about it, but his interest in Clara had led him to note things about his favored rival which might have escaped the attention of others less concerned.

Ellis was an excellent judge of character, and had formed a very decided opinion of Tom Delamere. To Ellis, unbiased by ancestral traditions, biased perhaps by jealousy, Tom Delamere was a type of the degenerate aristocrat. If, as he had often heard, it took three or four generations to make a gentleman, and as many more to complete the curve and return to the base from which it started, Tom Delamere belonged somewhere on the downward slant, with large possibilities of further decline. Old Mr. Delamere, who might be taken as the apex of an ideal aristocratic development, had been distinguished, during his active life, as Ellis had learned, for courage and strength of will, courtliness of bearing, deference to his superiors, of whom there had been few, courtesy to his equals, kindness and consideration for those less highly favored, and above all, a scrupulous sense of honor; his grandson Tom was merely the shadow without the substance, the empty husk without the grain. Of grace he had plenty. In manners he could be perfect, when he so chose. Courage and strength he had none. Ellis had seen this fellow, who boasted of his descent from a line of cavaliers, turn pale with fright and spring from a buggy to which was harnessed a fractious horse, which a negro stable-boy drove fearlessly. A valiant carpet-knight, skilled in all parlor exercises, great at whist or euchre, a dream of a dancer, unexcelled in cakewalk or "coon" impersonations, for which he was in large social demand, Ellis had seen him kick an inoffensive negro out of his path and treat a poor-white man with scant courtesy. He suspected Delamere of cheating at cards, and knew that others entertained the same suspicion. For while regular in his own habits,—his poverty would not have permitted him any considerable extravagance,—Ellis's position as a newspaper man kept him in touch with what was going on about town. He was a member, proposed by Carteret, of the Clarendon Club, where cards were indulged in within reasonable limits, and a certain set were known to bet dollars in terms of dimes.

Delamere was careless, too, about money matters. He had a habit of borrowing, right and left, small sums which might be conveniently forgotten by the borrower, and for which the lender would dislike to ask. Ellis had a strain of thrift, derived from a Scotch ancestry, and a tenacious memory for financial details. Indeed, he had never had so much money that he could lose track of it. He never saw Delamere without being distinctly conscious that Delamere owed him four dollars, which he had lent at a time when he could ill afford to spare it. It was a prerogative of aristocracy, Ellis reflected, to live upon others, and the last privilege which aristocracy in decay would willingly relinquish. Neither did the aristocratic memory seem able to retain the sordid details of a small pecuniary transaction.

No doubt the knowledge that Delamere was the favored lover of Miss Pemberton lent a touch of bitterness to Ellis's reflections upon his rival. Ellis had no grievance against the "aristocracy" of Wellington. The "best people" had received him cordially, though his father had not been of their caste; but Ellis hated a hypocrite, and despised a coward, and he felt sure that Delamere was both. Otherwise he would have struggled against his love for Clara Pemberton. His passion for her had grown with his appreciation of Delamere's unworthiness. As a friend of the family, he knew the nature and terms of the engagement, and that if the marriage took place at all, it would not be for at least a year. This was a long time,—many things might happen in a year, especially to a man like Tom Delamere. If for any reason Delamere lost his chance, Ellis meant to be next in the field. He had not made love to Clara, but he had missed no opportunity of meeting her and making himself quietly and unobtrusively agreeable.

On the day after this encounter with Delamere on the stairs of the Chronicle office, Ellis, while walking down Vine Street, met old Mrs. Ochiltree. She was seated in her own buggy, which was of ancient build and pattern, driven by her colored coachman and man of all work.

"Mr. Ellis," she called in a shrill voice, having directed her coachman to draw up at the curb as she saw the young man approaching, "come here. I want to speak to you."

Ellis came up to the buggy and stood uncovered beside it.

"People are saying," said Mrs. Ochiltree, "that Tom Delamere is drinking hard, and has to be carried home intoxicated, two or three times a week, by old Mr. Delamere's man Sandy. Is there any truth in the story?"

"My dear Mrs. Ochiltree, I am not Tom Delamere's keeper. Sandy could tell you better than I."

"You are dodging my question, Mr. Ellis. Sandy would n't tell me the truth, and I know that you would n't lie,—you don't look like a liar. They say Tom is gambling scandalously. What do you know about that?"

"You must excuse me, Mrs. Ochiltree. A great deal of what we hear is mere idle gossip, and the truth is often grossly exaggerated. I'm a member of the same club with Delamere, and gentlemen who belong to the same club are not in the habit of talking about one another. As long as a man retains his club membership, he's presumed to be a gentleman. I would n't say anything against Delamere if I could."

"You don't need to," replied the old lady, shaking her finger at him with a cunning smile. "You are a very open young man, Mr. Ellis, and I can read you like a book. You are much smarter than you look, but you can't fool me. Good-morning."

Mrs. Ochiltree drove immediately to her niece's, where

she found Mrs. Carteret and Clara at home. Clara was very fond of the baby, and was holding him in her arms. He was a fine baby, and bade fair to realize the bright hopes built upon him.

"You hold a baby very naturally, Clara," chuckled the old lady. "I suppose you are in training. But you ought to talk to Tom. I have just learned from Mr. Ellis that Tom is carried home drunk two or three times a week, and that he is gambling in the most reckless manner imaginable."

Clara's eyes flashed indignantly. Ere she could speak, Mrs. Carteret exclaimed:—

"Why, Aunt Polly! did Mr. Ellis say that?"

"I got it from Dinah," she replied, "who heard it from her husband, who learned it from a waiter at the club. And"—

"Pshaw!" said Mrs. Carteret, "mere servants' gossip."

"No, it isn't, Olivia. I met Mr. Ellis on the street, and asked him point blank, and he did n't deny it. He's a member of the club, and ought to know."

"Well, Aunt Polly, it can't be true. Tom is here every other night, and how could he carry on so without showing the signs of it? and where would he get the money? You know he has only a moderate allowance."

"He may win it at cards,—it's better to be born lucky than rich," returned Mrs. Ochiltree. "Then he has expectations, and can get credit. There's not doubt that Tom is going on shamefully."

Clara's indignation had not yet found vent in speech; Olivia had said all that was necessary, but she had been thinking rapidly. Even if all this had been true, why should Mr. Ellis have said it? Or, if he had not stated it directly, he had left the inference to be drawn. It seemed a most unfair and ungentlemanly thing. What motive could Ellis have for such an act?

She was not long in reaching a conclusion which was not flattering to Ellis. Mr. Ellis came often to the house, and she had enjoyed his society in a friendly way. That he had found her pleasant company had been very evident. She had never taken his attentions seriously, however, or regarded his visits as made especially to her, nor had the rest of the family treated them from that point of view. Her engagement to Tom Delamere, though not yet formally ratified, was so well understood by the world of Wellington that Mr. Ellis would scarcely have presumed to think of her as anything more than a friend.

This revelation of her aunt's, however, put a different face upon his conduct. Certain looks and sighs and enigmatical remarks of Ellis, to which she had paid but casual attention and attached no particular significance, now recurred to her memory with a new meaning. He had now evidently tried, in a roundabout way, to besmirch Tom's character and undermine him in her regard. While loving Tom, she had liked Ellis well enough, as a friend; but he had abused the privileges of friendship, and she would teach him a needed lesson.

Nevertheless, Mrs. Ochiltree's story had given Clara food for thought. She was uneasily conscious, after all, that there might be a grain of truth in what had been said, enough, at least, to justify her in warning Tom to be careful, lest his enemies should distort some amiable weakness into a serious crime.

She put this view of the case to Tom at their next meeting, assuring him, at the same time, of her unbounded faith and confidence. She did not mention Ellis's name, lest Tom, in righteous indignation, might do something rash, which he might thereafter regret. If any subtler or more obscure motive kept her silent as to Ellis, she was not aware of it; for Clara's views of life were still in the objective stage, and she had not yet fathomed the deepest recesses of her own consciousness.

Delamere had the cunning of weakness. He knew, too, better than any one else could know, how much truth there was in the rumors concerning him, and whether or not they could be verified too easily for him to make an indignant denial. After a little rapid reflection, he decided upon a different course.

"Clara," he said with a sigh, taking the hand which she generously yielded to soften any suggestion of reproach which he may have read into her solicitude, "you are my guardian angel. I do not know, of course, who has told you this pack of lies,—for I can see that you have heard more than you have told me,—but I think I could guess the man they came from. I am not perfect, Clara, though I have done nothing of which a gentleman should be ashamed. There is one sure way to stop the tongue of calumny. My home life is not ideal,—grandfather is an old, weak man, and the house needs the refining and softening influence of a lady's presence. I do not love club life; its ideals are not elevating. With you by my side, dearest, I should be preserved from every influence except the purest and the best. Don't you think, dearest, that the major might be induced to shorten our weary term of waiting?"

"Oh, Tom," she demurred blushingly, "I shall be young enough at eighteen; and you are barely twenty-one."

But Tom proved an eloquent pleader, and love a still more persuasive advocate. Clara spoke to the major the same evening, who looked grave at the suggestion, and said he would think about it. They were both very young; but where both parties were of good family, in good health and good circumstances, an early marriage might not be undesirable. Tom was perhaps a little unsettled, but blood would tell in the long run, and marriage always exercised a steadying influence.

The only return, therefore, which Ellis received for his well-meant effort to ward off Mrs. Ochiltree's embarrassing inquiries was that he did not see Clara upon his next visit, which was made one afternoon while he was on night duty at the office. In conversation with Mrs. Carteret he learned that Clara's marriage had been definitely agreed upon, and the date fixed,—it was to take place in about six months.

Meeting Miss Pemberton on the street the following day, he received the slightest of nods. When he called again at the house, after a week of misery, she treated him with a sarcastic coolness which chilled his heart.

"How have I offended you, Miss Clara?" he demanded desperately, when they were left alone for a moment.

"Offended me?" she replied, lifting her eyebrows with an air of puzzled surprise. "Why, Mr. Ellis! What could have put such a notion into your head? Oh dear, I think I hear Dodie,—I know you'll excuse me, Mr. Ellis, won't you? Sister Olivia will be back in a moment; and we're expecting Aunt Polly this afternoon,—if you'll stay awhile she'll be glad to talk to you! You can tell her all the interesting news about your friends!"

CHAPTER XI

The Baby and the Bird

When Ellis, after this rebuff, had disconsolately taken his leave, Clara, much elated at the righteous punishment she had inflicted upon the slanderer, ran upstairs to the nursery, and snatching Dodie from Mammy Jane's arms, began dancing gayly with him round the room.

"Look a-hyuh, honey," said Mammy Jane, "you better be keerful wid dat chile, an' don' drap 'im on de flo'. You might let him fall on his head an' break his neck. My, my! but you two does make a pretty pictur'! You'll be wantin' ole Jane ter come an' nuss yo' child'en some er dese days," she chuckled unctuously.

Mammy Jane had been very much disturbed by the recent dangers through which little Dodie had passed; and his escape from strangulation, in the first place, and then from the knife had impressed her as little less than miraculous. She was not certain whether this result had been brought about by her manipulation of the buried charm, or by the prayers which had been offered for the child, but was inclined to believe that both had cooperated to avert the threatened calamity. The favorable outcome of this particular incident had not, however, altered the general situation. Prayers and charms, after all, were merely temporary things, which must be constantly renewed, and might be forgotten or overlooked; while the mole, on the contrary, neither faded nor went away. If its malign influence might for a time seem to disappear, it was merely lying dormant, like the germs of some deadly disease, awaiting its opportunity to strike at an unguarded spot.

Clara and the baby were laughing in great glee, when a mockingbird, perched on the topmost bough of a small tree opposite the nursery window, burst suddenly into song, with many a trill and quaver. Clara, with the child in her arms, sprang to the open window.

"Sister Olivia," she cried, turning her face toward Mrs. Carteret, who at that moment entered the room, "come and look at Dodie."

The baby was listening intently to the music, meanwhile gurgling with delight, and reaching his chubby hands toward the source of this pleasing sound. It seemed as though the mockingbird were aware of his appreciative audience, for he ran through the songs of a dozen different birds, selecting, with the discrimination of a connoisseur and entire confidence in his own powers, those which were most difficult and most alluring.

Mrs. Carteret approached the window, followed by Mammy Jane, who waddled over to join the admiring party. So absorbed were the three women in the baby and the bird that neither one of them observed a neat top buggy, drawn by a sleek sorrel pony, passing slowly along the street before the house. In the buggy was seated a lady, and beside her a little boy, dressed in a child's sailor suit and a straw hat. The lady, with a wistful expression, was looking toward the party grouped in the open window.

Mrs. Carteret, chancing to lower her eyes for an instant, caught the other woman's look directed toward her and her child. With a glance of cold aversion she turned away from the window.

Old Mammy Jane had observed this movement, and had divined the reason for it. She stood beside Clara, watching the retreating buggy.

"Uhhuh!" she said to herself, "it's huh sister Janet! She ma'ied a doctuh, an' all dat, an' she lives in a big house, an' she's be'n roun' de worl' an de Lawd knows where e'se; but

Mis' 'Livy don' like de sight er her, an' never will, ez long ez de sun rises an' sets. Dey ce't'nly does favor one anudder,—anybody mought 'low dey wuz twins, ef dey did n' know better. Well, well! Fo'ty yeahs ago who'd 'a' ever expected ter see a nigger gal ridin' in her own buggy? My, my! but I don' know,—I don' know! It don' look right, an' it ain' gwine ter las'!—you can't make me b'lieve!''

Meantime Janet, stung by Mrs. Carteret's look,—the nearest approach she had ever made to a recognition of her sister's existence,—had turned away with hardening face. She had struck her pony sharply with the whip, much to the gentle creature's surprise, when the little boy, who was still looking back, caught his mother's sleeve and exclaimed excitedly:—

"Look, look, mamma! The baby,—the baby!"

Janet turned instantly, and with a mother's instinct gave an involuntary cry of alarm.

At the moment when Mrs. Carteret had turned away from the window, and while Mammy Jane was watching Janet, Clara had taken a step forward, and was leaning against the window-sill. The baby, convulsed with delight, had given a spasmodic spring and slipped from Clara's arms. Instinctively the young woman gripped the long skirt as it slipped through her hands, and held it tenaciously, though too frightened for an instant to do more. Mammy Jane, ashen with sudden dread, uttered an inarticulate scream, but retained self-possession enough to reach down and draw up the child, which hung dangerously suspended, head downward, over the brick pavement below.

"Oh, Clara, Clara, how could you!" exclaimed Mrs. Carteret reproachfully; "you might have killed my child!"

She had snatched the child from Jane's arms, and was holding him closely to her own breast. Struck by a sudden thought, she drew near the window and looked out. Twice within a few weeks her child had been in serious danger, and upon each occasion a member of the Miller family had been involved, for she had heard of Dr. Miller's presumption in trying to force himself where he must have known he would be unwelcome.

Janet was just turning her head away as the buggy moved slowly off. Olivia felt a violent wave of antipathy sweep over her toward this baseborn sister who had thus thrust herself beneath her eyes. If she had not cast her brazen glance toward the window, she herself would not have turned away and lost sight of her child. To this shameless intrusion, linked with Clara's carelessness, had been due the catastrophe, so narrowly averted, which might have darkened her own life forever. She took to her bed for several days, and for a long time was cold toward Clara, and did not permit her to touch the child.

Mammy Jane entertained a theory of her own about the accident, by which the blame was placed, in another way, exactly where Mrs. Carteret had laid it. Julia's daughter, Janet, had been looking intently toward the window just before little Dodie had sprung from Clara's arms. Might she not have cast the evil eye upon the baby, and sought thereby to draw him out of the window? One would not ordinarily expect so young a woman to possess such a power, but she might have acquired it, for this very purpose, from some more experienced person. By the same reasoning, the mockingbird might have been a familiar of the witch, and the two might have conspired to lure the infant to destruction. Whether this were so or not, the transaction at least wore a peculiar look. There was no use telling Mis' 'Livy about it, for she did n't believe, or pretended not to believe, in witchcraft and conjuration. But one could not be too careful. The child was certainly born to be exposed to great dangers,—the mole behind the left ear was an unfailing sign,—and no precaution should be omitted to counteract its baleful influence.

While adjusting the baby's crib, a few days later, Mrs. Carteret found fastened under one of the slats a small bag of cotton cloth, about half an inch long and tied with a black thread, upon opening which she found a few small roots or fibres and a pinch of dried and crumpled herbs. It was a good-luck charm which Mammy Jane had placed there to ward off the threatened evil from the grandchild of her dear old mistress. Mrs. Carteret's first impulse was to throw the bag into the fire, but on second thoughts she let it remain. To remove it would give unnecessary pain to the old nurse. Of course these old negro superstitions were absurd,—but if the charm did no good, it at least would do no harm.

CHAPTER XII

Another Southern Product

One morning shortly after the opening of the hospital, while Dr. Miller was making his early rounds, a new patient walked in with a smile on his face and a broken arm hanging limply by his side. Miller recognized in him a black giant by the name of Josh Green, who for many years had worked on the docks for Miller's father,—and simultaneously identified him as the dust-begrimed negro who had stolen a ride to Wellington on the trucks of a passenger car.

"Well, Josh," asked the doctor, as he examined the fracture, "how did you get this? Been fighting again?"

"No, suh, I don' s'pose you could ha'dly call it a fight. One er dem dagoes off'n a Souf American boat gimme some er his jaw, an' I give 'im a back answer, an' here I is wid a broken arm. He got holt er a belayin'-pin befo' I could hit 'im."

"What became of the other man?" demanded Miller suspiciously. He perceived, from the indifference with which Josh bore the manipulation of the fractured limb, that such an accident need not have interfered seriously with the use of the remaining arm, and he knew that Josh had a reputation for absolute fearlessness.

"Lemme see," said Josh reflectively, "ef I kin 'member w'at *did* become er him! Oh, yes, I 'member now! Dey tuck him ter de Marine Horspittle in de amberlance, 'cause his leg wuz broke, an' I reckon somethin' must 'a' accident'ly hit 'im in de jaw, fer he wuz scatt'rin' teeth all de way 'long

559

de street. I did n' wan' ter kill de man, fer he might have somebody dependin' on 'im, an' I knows how dat'd be ter dem. But no man kin call me a damn' low-down nigger and keep on enjoyin' good health right along.''

"It was considerate of you to spare his life,'' said Miller dryly, ''but you'll hit the wrong man some day. These are bad times for bad negroes. You'll get into a quarrel with a white man, and at the end of it there'll be a lynching, or a funeral. You'd better be peaceable and endure a little injustice, rather than run the risk of a sudden and violent death.''

"I expec's ter die a vi'lent death in a quarrel wid a w'ite man,'' replied Josh, in a matter-of-fact tone, ''an' fu'thermo', he's gwine ter die at the same time, er a little befo'. I be'n takin' my own time 'bout killin' 'im; I ain' be'n crowdin' de man, but I'll be ready after a w'ile, an' den he kin look out!''

"And I suppose you're merely keeping in practice on these other fellows who come your way. When I get your arm dressed, you'd better leave town till that fellow's boat sails; it may save you the expense of a trial and three months in the chain-gang. But this talk about killing a man is all nonsense. What has any man in this town done to you, that you should thirst for his blood?''

"No, suh, it ain' nonsense,—it's straight, solem' fac'. I'm gwine ter kill dat man as sho' as I'm settin' in dis cheer; an' dey ain' nobody kin say I ain' got a right ter kill 'im. Does you 'member de Ku-Klux?''

"Yes, but I was a child at the time, and recollect very little about them. It is a page of history which most people are glad to forget.''

"Yas, suh; I was a chile, too, but I wuz right in it, an' so I 'members mo' erbout it 'n you does. My mammy an' daddy lived 'bout ten miles f'm here, up de river. One night a crowd er w'ite men come ter ou' house an' tuck my daddy out an' shot 'im ter death, an' skeered my mammy so she ain' be'n herse'f f'm dat day ter dis. I wa'n't mo' 'n ten years ole at de time, an' w'en my mammy seed de w'ite men comin', she tol' me ter run. I hid in de bushes an' seen de whole thing, an' it wuz branded on my mem'ry, suh, like a red-hot iron bran's de skin. De w'ite folks had masks on, but one of 'em fell off,—he wuz de boss, he wuz de head man, an' tol' de res' w'at ter do,—an' I seen his face. It wuz a easy face ter 'member; an' I swo' den, 'way down deep in my hea't, little ez I wuz, dat some day er 'nother I'd kill dat man. I ain't never had no doubt erbout it; it's jus' w'at I'm livin' fer, an' I know I ain' gwine ter die till I've done it. Some lives fer one thing an' some fer another, but dat's my job. I ain' be'n in no has'e, fer I'm not ole yit, an' dat man is in good health. I'd like ter see a little er de worl' befo' I takes chances on leavin' it sudden; an', mo'over, somebody's got ter take keer er de ole 'oman. But her time'll come some er dese days, an den *his* time'll be come—an' prob'ly mine. But I ain' keerin' 'bout myse'f: w'en I git thoo wid him, it won' make no diff'ence 'bout me."

Josh was evidently in dead earnest. Miller recalled, very vividly, the expression he had seen twice on his patient's face, during the journey to Wellington. He had often seen Josh's mother, old Aunt Milly,—"Silly Milly," the children called her,—wandering aimlessly about the street, muttering to herself incoherently. He had felt a certain childish awe at the sight of one of God's creatures who had lost the light of reason, and he had always vaguely understood that she was the victim of human cruelty, though he had dated it farther back into the past. This was his first knowledge of the real facts of the case.

He realized, too, for a moment, the continuity of life, how inseparably the present is woven with the past, how certainly the future will be but the outcome of the present. He had supposed this old wound healed. The negroes were not a vindictive people. If, swayed by passion or emotion, they sometimes gave way to gusts of rage, these were of brief duration. Absorbed in the contemplation of their doubtful present and their uncertain future, they gave little thought to the past,—it was a dark story, which they would willingly forget. He knew the timeworn explanation that the Ku-Klux movement, in the main, was merely an ebullition of boyish spirits, begun to amuse young white men by playing upon the fears and superstitions of ignorant negroes. Here, however, was its tragic side,—the old wound still bleeding, the fruit of one tragedy, the seed of another. He could not approve of Josh's application of the Mosaic law of revenge, and yet the incident was not without significance. Here was a negro who could remember an injury, who could shape his life to a definite purpose, if not a high or holy one. When his race reached the point where they would resent a wrong, there was hope that they might soon attain the stage where they would try, and, if need be, die, to defend a right. This man, too, had a purpose in life, and was willing to die that he might accomplish it. Miller was willing to give up his life to a cause. Would he be equally willing, he asked himself, to die for it? Miller had no prophetic instinct to tell him how soon he would have the opportunity to answer his own question. But he could not encourage Josh to carry out this dark and revengeful purpose. Every worthy consideration required him to dissuade his patient from such a desperate course.

"You had better put away these murderous fancies, Josh," he said seriously. "The Bible says that we should 'forgive our enemies, bless them that curse us, and do good to them that despitefully use us.' "

"Yas, suh, I've l'arnt all dat in Sunday-school, an' I've heared de preachers say it time an' time ag'in. But it 'pears ter me dat dis fergitfulniss an' fergivniss is mighty one-sided. De w'ite folks don' fergive nothin' de niggers does. Dey got up de Ku-Klux, dey said, on 'count er de kyarpit-baggers. Dey be'n talkin' 'bout de kyarpit-baggers ever sence, an' dey 'pears ter fergot all 'bout de Ku-Klux. But I ain' fergot. De niggers is be'n train' ter fergiveniss; an' fer fear dey might fergit how ter fergive, de w'ite folks gives 'em somethin' new ev'y now an' den, ter practice on. A w'ite man kin do w'at he wants ter a nigger, but de minute de nigger gits back at 'im, up

goes de nigger, an' don' come down tell somebody cuts 'im
down. If a nigger gits a' office, er de race 'pears ter be pros-
perin' too much, de w'ite folks up an' kills a few, so dat de
res' kin keep on fergivin' an' bein' thankful dat dey're lef'
alive. Don' talk ter me 'bout dese w'ite folks,—I knows 'em,
I does! Ef a nigger wants ter git down on his marrow-bones,
an' eat dirt, an' call 'em 'marster,' *he's* a good nigger, dere's
room fer *him*. But I ain' no w'ite folks' nigger, I ain'. I don'
call no man 'marster.' I don' wan' nothin' but w'at I wo'k
fer, but I wants all er dat. I never moles's no w'ite man,
'less'n he moles's me fus'. But w'en de ole 'oman dies, doctuh, an' I gits a good chance at dat w'ite man,—dere ain' no
use talkin', suh!—dere's gwine ter be a mix-up, an' a fune'al,
er two fune'als—er may be mo', ef anybody is keerliss enough
to git in de way."

"Josh," said the doctor, laying a cool hand on the other's
brow, "you're feverish, and don't know what you're talking
about. I should n't let my mind dwell on such things, and
you must keep quiet until this arm is well, or you may never
be able to hit any one with it again."

Miller determined that when Josh got better he would talk
to him seriously and dissuade him from this dangerous design. He had not asked the name of Josh's enemy, but the
look of murderous hate which the dust-begrimed tramp of
the railway journey had cast at Captain George McBane rendered any such question superfluous. McBane was probably
deserving of any evil fate which might befall him; but such
a revenge would do no good, would right no wrong; while
every such crime, committed by a colored man, would be
imputed to the race, which was already staggering under a
load of obloquy because, in the eyes of a prejudiced and
undiscriminating public, it must answer as a whole for the
offenses of each separate individual. To die in defense of the
right was heroic. To kill another for revenge was pitifully
human and weak: "Vengeance is mine, I will repay," saith
the Lord.

CHAPTER XIII

The Cakewalk

Old Mr. Delamere's servant, Sandy Campbell, was in deep trouble.

A party of Northern visitors had been staying for several days at the St. James Hotel. The gentlemen of the party were concerned in a projected cotton mill, while the ladies were much interested in the study of social conditions, and especially in the negro problem. As soon as their desire for information became known, they were taken courteously under the wing of prominent citizens and their wives, who gave them, at elaborate luncheons, the Southern white man's views of the negro, sighing sentimentally over the disappearance of the good old negro of before the war, and gravely deploring the degeneracy of his descendants. They enlarged upon the amount of money the Southern whites had spent for the education of the negro, and shook their heads over the inadequate results accruing from this unexampled generosity. It was sad, they said, to witness this spectacle of a dying race, unable to withstand the competition of a superior type. The severe reprisals taken by white people for certain crimes committed by negroes were of course not the acts of the best people, who deplored them; but still a certain charity should be extended towards those who in the intense and righteous anger of the moment should take the law into their own hands and deal out rough but still substantial justice; for no negro was ever lynched without incontestable proof of his guilt. In order to be perfectly fair, and give their visitors an opportunity to see both sides of the question, they accompanied the Northern visitors to a colored church where they might hear a colored preacher, who had won a jocular popularity throughout the whole country by an oft-repeated sermon intended to demonstrate that the earth was flat like a pancake. This celebrated divine could always draw a white audience, except on the days when his no less distinguished white rival in the field of sensationalism preached his equally famous sermon to prove that hell was exactly one half mile, linear measure, from the city limits of Wellington. Whether accidentally or not, the Northern visitors had no opportunity to meet or talk alone with any colored person in the city except the servants at the hotel. When one of the party suggested a visit to the colored mission school, a Southern friend kindly volunteered to accompany them.

The visitors were naturally much impressed by what they learned from their courteous hosts, and felt inclined to sympathize with the Southern people, for the negro is not counted as a Southerner, except to fix the basis of congressional representation. There might of course be things to criticise here and there, certain customs for which they did not exactly see the necessity, and which seemed in conflict with the highest ideals of liberty: but surely these courteous, soft-spoken ladies and gentlemen, entirely familiar with local conditions, who descanted so earnestly and at times pathetically upon the grave problems confronting them, must know more about it than people in the distant North, without their means of information. The negroes who waited on them at the hotel seemed happy enough, and the teachers whom they had met at the mission school had been well-dressed, well-mannered, and apparently content with their position in life. Surely a people who made no complaints could not be very much oppressed.

In order to give the visitors, ere they left Wellington, a pleasing impression of Southern customs, and particularly of the joyous, happy-go-lucky disposition of the Southern darky and his entire contentment with existing conditions, it was decided by the hotel management to treat them, on the last night of their visit, to a little diversion, in the shape of a genuine negro cakewalk.

On the afternoon of this same day Tom Delamere strolled into the hotel, and soon gravitated to the bar, where he was a frequent visitor. Young men of leisure spent much of their time around the hotel, and no small part of it in the bar. Delamere had been to the club, but had avoided the card-room. Time hanging heavy on his hands, he had sought the hotel in the hope that some form of distraction might present itself.

"Have you heard the latest, Mr. Delamere?" asked the bartender, as he mixed a cocktail for his customer.

"No, Billy; what is it?"

There 's to be a big cakewalk upstairs to-night. The No'the'n gentlemen an' ladies who are down here to see about the new cotton fact'ry want to study the nigger some more, and the boss has got up a cakewalk for 'em, 'mongst the waiters and chambermaids, with a little outside talent."

"Is it to be public?" asked Delamere.

"Oh, no, not generally, but friends of the house won't be barred out. The clerk 'll fix it for you. Ransom, the head waiter, will be floor manager."

Delamere was struck with a brilliant idea. The more he considered it, the brighter it seemed. Another cocktail imparted additional brilliancy to the conception. He had been trying, after a feeble fashion, to keep his promise to Clara, and was really suffering from lack of excitement.

He left the bar-room, found the head waiter, held with him a short conversation, and left in his intelligent and itching palm a piece of money.

The cakewalk was a great success. The most brilliant performer was a late arrival, who made his appearance just as the performance was about to commence. The newcomer was dressed strikingly, the conspicuous features of his attire being a long blue coat with brass buttons and a pair of plaid trousers. He was older, too, than the other participants, which made his agility the more remarkable. His partner was a new chambermaid, who had just come to town, and whom the head waiter introduced to the newcomer upon his arrival. The cake was awarded to this couple by a unanimous vote. The man presented it to his partner with a grandiloquent flourish, and returned thanks in a speech which sent the Northern visitors into spasms of delight at the quaintness of the darky dialect and the darky wit. To cap the climax, the winner danced a buck dance with a skill and agility that brought a shower of complimentary silver, which he gathered up and passed to the head waiter.

Ellis was off duty for the evening. Not having ventured to put in an appearance at Carteret's since his last rebuff, he found himself burdened with a superfluity of leisure, from which he essayed to find relief by dropping into the hotel office at about nine o'clock. He was invited up to see the cakewalk, which he rather enjoyed, for there was some graceful dancing and posturing. But the grotesque contortions of one participant had struck him as somewhat overdone, even for the comical type of negro. He recognized the fellow, after a few minutes' scrutiny, as the body-servant of old Mr. Delamere. The man's present occupation, or choice of diversion, seemed out of keeping with his employment as attendant upon an invalid old gentleman, and strangely inconsistent with the gravity and decorum which had been so noticeable when this agile cakewalker had served as butler at Major Carteret's table, upon the occasion of the christening dinner. There was a vague suggestion of unreality about this performance, too, which Ellis did not attempt to analyze, but which recurred vividly to his memory upon a subsequent occasion.

Ellis had never pretended to that intimate knowledge of negro thought and character by which some of his acquaintances claimed the ability to fathom every motive of a negro's conduct, and predict in advance what any one of the darker race would do under a given set of circumstances. He would not have believed that a white man could possess two so widely varying phases of character; but as to negroes, they were as yet a crude and undeveloped race, and it was not safe to make predictions concerning them. No one could tell at what moment the thin veneer of civilization might peel off and reveal the underlying savage.

The champion cakewalker, much to the surprise of his sable companions, who were about equally swayed by admiration and jealousy, disappeared immediately after the close of the performance. Any one watching him on his way home through the quiet streets to old Mr. Delamere's would have seen him now and then shaking with laughter. It had been excellent fun. Nevertheless, as he neared home, a certain aspect of the affair, hitherto unconsidered, occurred to him, and it was in a rather serious frame of mind that he cautiously entered the house and sought his own room.

The cakewalk had results which to Sandy were very serious. The following week he was summoned before the disciplinary committee of his church and charged with unchristian conduct, in the following particulars, to wit: dancing, and participating in a sinful diversion called a cakewalk, which was calculated to bring the church into disrepute and make it the mockery of sinners.

Sandy protested his innocence vehemently, but in vain. The proof was overwhelming. He was positively identified by Sister 'Manda Patterson, the hotel cook, who had watched the whole performance from the hotel corridor for the sole, single, solitary, and only purpose, she averred, of seeing how far human wickedness could be carried by a professing Christian. The whole thing had been shocking and offensive to her, and only a stern sense of duty had sustained her in looking on, that she might be qualified to bear witness against the offender. She had recognized his face, his clothes, his voice, his walk—there could be no shadow of doubt that it was Brother Sandy. This testimony was confirmed by one of the deacons, whose son, a waiter at the hotel, had also seen Sandy at the cakewalk.

Sandy stoutly insisted that he was at home the whole evening; that he had not been near the hotel for three months; and that he had never in his life taken part in a cakewalk, and that he did not know how to dance. It was replied that wickedness, like everything else, must have a beginning; that dancing was an art that could be acquired in secret, and came natural to some people. In the face of positive proof, Sandy's protestations were of no avail; he was found guilty, and suspended from church fellowship until he should have repented and made full confession.

Sturdily refusing to confess a fault of which he claimed to be innocent, Sandy remained in contumacy, thereby falling somewhat into disrepute among the members of his church, the largest in the city. The effect of a bad reputation being subjective as well as objective, and poor human nature arguing that one may as well have the game as the name, Sandy insensibly glided into habits of which the church would not have approved, though he took care that they should not interfere with his duties to Mr. Delamere. The consolation thus afforded, however, followed as it was by remorse of conscience, did not compensate him for the loss of standing in the church, which to him was a social club as well as a religious temple. At times, in conversation with young Delamere, he would lament his hard fate.

Tom laughed until he cried at the comical idea which Sandy's plaint always brought up, of half-a-dozen negro preachers sitting in solemn judgment upon that cakewalk,—it had certainly been a good cakewalk!—and sending poor Sandy to spiritual Coventry.

"Cheer up, Sandy, cheer up!" he would say when Sandy seemed most depressed. "Go into my room and get yourself

a good drink of liquor. The devil's church has a bigger congregation than theirs, and we have the consolation of knowing that when we die, we'll meet all our friends on the other
side. Brace up, Sandy, and be a man, or, if you can't be a
man, be as near a man as you can!"

Hoping to revive his drooping spirits, Sandy too often accepted the proffered remedy.

CHAPTER XIV

The Maunderings
of Old Mrs. Ochiltree

When Mrs. Carteret had fully recovered from the shock attendant upon the accident at the window, where little Dodie had so narrowly escaped death or serious injury, she ordered her carriage one afternoon and directed the coachman to drive her to Mrs. Ochiltree's.

Mrs. Carteret had discharged her young nurse only the day before, and had sent for Mammy Jane, who was now recovered from her rheumatism, to stay until she could find another girl. The nurse had been ordered not to take the child to negroes' houses. Yesterday, in driving past the old homestead of her husband's family, now occupied by Dr. Miller and his family, Mrs. Carteret had seen her own baby's carriage standing in the yard.

When the nurse returned home, she was immediately discharged. She offered some sort of explanation, to the effect that her sister worked for Mrs. Miller, and that some family matter had rendered it necessary for her to see her sister. The explanation only aggravated the offense: if Mrs. Carteret could have overlooked the disobedience, she would by no means have retained in her employment a servant whose sister worked for the Miller woman.

Old Mrs. Ochiltree had within a few months begun to show signs of breaking up. She was over seventy years old, and had been of late, by various afflictions, confined to the house much of the time. More than once within the year, Mrs. Carteret had asked her aunt to come and live with her; but Mrs. Ochiltree, who would have regarded such a step as an acknowledgment of weakness, preferred her lonely independence. She resided in a small, old-fashioned house, standing back in the middle of a garden on a quiet street. Two old servants made up her modest household.

This refusal to live with her niece had been lightly borne, for Mrs. Ochiltree was a woman of strong individuality, whose comments upon her acquaintance, present or absent, were marked by a frankness at times no less than startling. This characteristic caused her to be more or less avoided. Mrs. Ochiltree was aware of this sentiment on the part of her acquaintance, and rather exulted in it. She hated fools. Only fools ran away from her, and that because they were afraid she would expose their folly. If most people were fools, it was no fault of hers, and she was not obliged to indulge them by pretending to believe that they knew anything. She had once owned considerable property, but was reticent about her affairs, and told no one how much she was worth, though it was supposed that she had considerable ready money, besides her house and some other real estate. Mrs. Carteret was her nearest living relative, though her grand-nephew Tom Delamere had been a great favorite with her. If she did not spare him her tongue-lashings, it was nevertheless expected in the family that she would leave him something handsome in her will.

Mrs. Ochiltree had shared in the general rejoicing upon the advent of the Carteret baby. She had been one of his godmothers, and had hinted at certain intentions held by her concerning him. During Mammy Jane's administration she had tried the old nurse's patience more or less by her dictatorial interference. Since her partial confinement to the house, she had gone, when her health and the weather would permit, to see the child, and at other times had insisted that it be sent to her in charge of the nurse at least every other day.

Mrs. Ochiltree's faculties had shared insensibly in the decline of her health. This weakness manifested itself by fits of absent-mindedness, in which she would seemingly lose connection with the present, and live over again, in imagination, the earlier years of her life. She had buried two husbands, had tried in vain to secure a third, and had never borne any children. Long ago she had petrified into a character which nothing under heaven could change, and which, if death is to take us as it finds us, and the future life to keep us as it takes us, promised anything but eternal felicity to those with whom she might associate after this life. Tom Delamere had been heard to say, profanely, that if his Aunt Polly went to heaven, he would let his mansion in the skies on a long lease, at a low figure.

When the carriage drove up with Mrs. Carteret, her aunt was seated on the little front piazza, with her wrinkled hands folded in her lap, dozing the afternoon away in fitful slumber.

"Tie the horse, William," said Mrs. Carteret, "and then go in and wake Aunt Polly, and tell her I want her to come and drive with me."

Mrs. Ochiltree had not observed her niece's approach, nor did she look up when William drew near. Her eyes were closed, and she would let her head sink slowly forward, recovering it now and then with a spasmodic jerk.

"Colonel Ochiltree," she muttered, "was shot at the battle of Culpepper Court House, and left me a widow for the second time. But I would not have married any man on earth after him."

"Mis' Ochiltree!" cried William, raising his voice, "oh, Mis' Ochiltree!"

"If I had found a man,—a real man,—I might have married again. I did not care for weaklings. I could have married John Delamere if I had wanted him. But pshaw! I could have wound him round"—

"Go round to the kitchen, William," interrupted Mrs. Carteret impatiently, "and tell Aunt Dinah to come and wake her up."

William returned in a few moments with a fat, comfortable looking black woman, who curtsied to Mrs. Carteret at the gate, and then going up to her mistress seized her by the shoulder and shook her vigorously.

"Wake up dere, Mis' Polly," she screamed, as harshly as her mellow voice would permit. "Mis' 'Livy wants you ter go drivin' wid 'er!"

"Dinah," exclaimed the old lady, sitting suddenly upright with a defiant assumption of wakefulness, "why do you take so long to come when I call? Bring me my bonnet and shawl. Don't you see my niece waiting for me at the gate?"

"Hyuh dey is, hyuh dey is!" returned Dinah, producing the bonnet and shawl, and assisting Mrs. Ochiltree to put them on.

Leaning on William's arm, the old lady went slowly down the walk, and was handed to the rear seat with Mrs. Carteret.

"How's the baby to-day, Olivia, and why did n't you bring him?"

"He has a cold to-day, and is a little hoarse," replied Mrs. Carteret, "so I thought it best not to bring him out. Drive out the Weldon road, William, and back by Pine Street."

The drive led past an eminence crowned by a handsome brick building of modern construction, evidently an institution of some kind, surrounded on three sides by a grove of venerable oaks.

"Hugh Poindexter," Mrs. Ochiltree exclaimed explosively, after a considerable silence, "has been building a new house, in place of the old family mansion burned after the war."

"It is n't Mr. Poindexter's house, Aunt Polly. That is the new colored hospital built by the colored doctor."

"The new colored hospital, indeed, and the colored doctor! Before the war the negroes were all healthy, and when they got sick we took care of them ourselves! Hugh Poindexter has sold the graves of his ancestors to a negro,—I should have starved first!"

"He had his grandfather's grave opened, and there was

nothing to remove, except a few bits of heart-pine from the coffin. All the rest had crumbled into dust."

"And he sold the dust to a negro! The world is upside down."

"He had the tombstone transferred to the white cemetery, Aunt Polly, and he has moved away."

"Esau sold his birthright for a mess of pottage. When I die, if you outlive me, Olivia, which is not likely, I shall leave my house and land to this child! He is a Carteret,—he would never sell them to a negro. I can't trust Tom Delamere, I'm afraid."

The carriage had skirted the hill, passing to the rear of the new building.

"Turn to the right, William," ordered Mrs. Carteret, addressing the coachman, "and come back past the other side of the hospital."

A turn to the right into another road soon brought them to the front of the building, which stood slightly back from the street, with no intervening fence or inclosure. A sorrel pony in a light buggy was fastened to a hitching-post near the entrance. As they drove past, a lady came out of the front door and descended the steps, holding by the hand a very pretty child about six years old.

"Who is that woman, Olivia?" asked Mrs. Ochiltree abruptly, with signs of agitation.

The lady coming down the steps darted at the approaching carriage a look which lingered involuntarily.

Mrs. Carteret, perceiving this glance, turned away coldly.

With a sudden hardening of her own features the other woman lifted the little boy into the buggy and drove sharply away in the direction opposite to that taken by Mrs. Carteret's carriage.

"Who is that woman, Olivia?" repeated Mrs. Ochiltree, with marked emotion.

"I have not the honor of her acquaintance," returned Mrs. Carteret sharply. "Drive faster, William."

"I want to know who that woman is," persisted Mrs.

Ochiltree querulously. "William," she cried shrilly, poking the coachman in the back with the end of her cane, "who is that woman?"

"Dat's Mis' Miller, ma'am," returned the coachman, touching his hat; "Doctuh Miller's wife."

"What was her mother's name?"

"Her mother's name wuz Julia Brown. She's be'n dead dese twenty years er mo'. Why, you knowed Julia, Mis' Polly!—she used ter b'long ter yo' own father befo' de wah; an' after de wah she kep' house fer"—

"Look to your horses, William!" exclaimed Mrs. Carteret sharply.

"It's that hussy's child," said Mrs. Ochiltree, turning to her niece with great excitement. "When your father died, I turned the mother and the child out into the street. The mother died and went to—the place provided for such as she. If I had n't been just in time, Olivia, they would have turned you out. I saved the property for you and your son! You can thank me for it all!"

"Hush, Aunt Polly, for goodness' sake! William will hear you. Tell me about it when you get home."

Mrs. Ochiltree was silent, except for a few incoherent mumblings. What she might say, what distressing family secret she might repeat in William's hearing, should she take another talkative turn, was beyond conjecture.

Olivia looked anxiously around for something to distract her aunt's attention, and caught sight of a colored man, dressed in sober gray, who was coming toward the carriage.

"There's Mr. Delamere's Sandy!" exclaimed Mrs. Carteret, touching her aunt on the arm. "I wonder how his master is? Sandy, oh, Sandy!"

Sandy approached the carriage, lifting his hat with a slight exaggeration of Chesterfieldian elegance. Sandy, no less than his master, was a survival of an interesting type. He had inherited the feudal deference for his superiors in position, joined to a certain self-respect which saved him from sycophancy. His manners had been formed upon those of old Mr.

Delamere, and were not a bad imitation; for in the man, as in the master, they were the harmonious reflection of a mental state.

"How is Mr. Delamere, Sandy?" asked Mrs. Carteret, acknowledging Sandy's salutation with a nod and a smile.

"He ain't ez peart ez he has be'n, ma'am," replied Sandy, "but he's doin' tol'able well. De doctuh say he's good fer a dozen years yet, ef he'll jes' take good keer of hisse'f an' keep f'm gittin' excited; fer sence dat secon' stroke, excitement is dange'ous fer 'im."

"I'm sure you take the best care of him," returned Mrs. Carteret kindly.

"You can't do anything for him, Sandy," interposed old Mrs. Ochiltree, shaking her head slowly to emphasize her dissent. "All the doctors in creation could n't keep him alive another year. I shall outlive him by twenty years, though we are not far from the same age."

"Lawd, ma'am!" exclaimed Sandy, lifting his hands in affected amazement,—his study of gentle manners had been more than superficial,—"whoever would 'a' s'picion' dat you an' Mars John wuz nigh de same age? I'd 'a' 'lowed you wuz ten years younger 'n him, easy, ef you wuz a day!"

"Give my compliments to the poor old gentleman," returned Mrs. Ochiltree, with a simper of senile vanity, though her back was weakening under the strain of the effort to sit erect that she might maintain this illusion of comparative youthfulness. "Bring him to see me some day when he is able to walk."

"Yas'm, I will," rejoined Sandy. "He's gwine out ter Belleview nex' week, fer ter stay a mont' er so, but I'll fetch him 'roun' w'en he comes back. I'll tell 'im dat you ladies 'quired fer 'im."

Sandy made another deep bow, and held his hat in his hand until the carriage had moved away. He had not condescended to notice the coachman at all, who was one of the young negroes of the new generation; while Sandy regarded himself as belonging to the quality, and seldom stooped to notice those beneath him. It would not have been becoming in him, either, while conversing with white ladies, to have noticed a colored servant. Moreover, the coachman was a Baptist, while Sandy was a Methodist, though under a cloud, and considered a Methodist in poor standing as better than a Baptist of any degree of sanctity.

"Lawd, Lawd!" chuckled Sandy, after the carriage had departed, "I never seed nothin' lack de way dat ole lady do keep up her temper! Wid one foot in de grave, an' de other hov'rin' on de edge, she talks 'bout my ole marster lack he wuz in his secon' chil'hood. But I'm jes' willin' ter bet dat he'll outlas' her! She ain't half de woman she wuz dat night I waited on de table at de christenin' pa'ty, w'en she 'lowed she wuz n' feared er no man livin'."

CHAPTER XV

Mrs. Carteret
Seeks an Explanation

As a stone dropped into a pool of water sets in motion a series of concentric circles which disturb the whole mass in varying degree, so Mrs. Ochiltree's enigmatical remark had started in her niece's mind a disturbing train of thought. Had her words, Mrs. Carteret asked herself, any serious meaning, or were they the mere empty babblings of a clouded intellect?

"William," she said to the coachman when they reached Mrs. Ochiltree's house, "you may tie the horse and help us out. I shall be here a little while."

William helped the ladies down, assisted Mrs. Ochiltree into the house, and then went round to the kitchen. Dinah was an excellent hand at potato-pone and other culinary delicacies dear to the Southern heart, and William was a welcome visitor in her domain.

"Now, Aunt Polly," said Mrs. Carteret resolutely, as soon as they were alone, "I want to know what you meant by what you said about my father and Julia, and this—this child of hers?"

The old woman smiled cunningly, but her expression soon changed to one more grave.

"Why do you want to know?" she asked suspiciously. "You've got the land, the houses, and the money. You've nothing to complain of. Enjoy yourself, and be thankful!"

"I'm thankful to God," returned Olivia, "for all his good

579

gifts,—and He has blessed me abundantly,—but why should I be thankful to *you* for the property my father left me?"

"Why should you be thankful to me?" rejoined Mrs. Ochiltree with querulous indignation. "You'd better ask why *should n't* you be thankful to me. What have I not done for you?"

"Yes, Aunt Polly, I know you've done a great deal. You reared me in your own house when I had been cast out of my father's; you have been a second mother to me, and I am very grateful,—you can never say that I have not shown my gratitude. But if you have done anything else for me, I wish to know it. Why should I thank you for my inheritance?"

"Why should you thank me? Well, because I drove that woman and her brat away."

"But she had no right to stay, Aunt Polly, after father died. Of course she had no moral right before, but it was his house, and he could keep her there if he chose. But after his death she surely had no right."

"Perhaps not so surely as you think,—if she had not been a negro. Had she been white, there might have been a difference. When I told her to go, she said"—

"What did she say, Aunt Polly," demanded Olivia eagerly.

It seemed for a moment as though Mrs. Ochiltree would speak no further: but her once strong will, now weakened by her bodily infirmities, yielded to the influence of her niece's imperious demand.

"I'll tell you the whole story," she said, "and then you'll know what I did for you and yours."

Mrs. Ochiltree's eyes assumed an introspective expression, and her story, as it advanced, became as keenly dramatic as though memory had thrown aside the veil of intervening years and carried her back directly to the events which she now described.

"Your father," she said, "while living with that woman,

left home one morning the picture of health. Five minutes later he tottered into the house groaning with pain, stricken unto death by the hand of a just God, as a punishment for his sins."

Olivia gave a start of indignation, but restrained herself.

"I was at once informed of what had happened, for I had means of knowing all that took place in the household. Old Jane—she was younger then—had come with you to my house; but her daughter remained, and through her I learned all that went on.

"I hastened immediately to the house, entered without knocking, and approached Mr. Merkell's bedroom, which was on the lower floor and opened into the hall. The door was ajar, and as I stood there for a moment I heard your father's voice.

" 'Listen, Julia,' he was saying. 'I shall not live until the doctor comes. But I wish you to know, *dear* Julia!'—he called her 'dear Julia!'—'before I die, that I have kept my promise. You did me one great service, Julia,—you saved me from Polly Ochiltree!' Yes, Olivia, that is what he said! 'You have served me faithfully and well, and I owe you a great deal, which I have tried to pay.'

" 'Oh, Mr. Merkell, dear Mr. Merkell,' cried the hypocritical hussy, falling to her knees by his bedside, and shedding her crocodile tears, 'you owe me nothing. You have done more for me than I could ever repay. You will not die and leave me,—no, no, it cannot be!'

" 'Yes, I am going to die,—I am dying now, Julia. But listen,—compose yourself and listen, for this is a more important matter. Take the keys from under my pillow, open the desk in the next room, look in the second drawer on the right, and you will find an envelope containing three papers: one of them is yours, one is the paper I promised to make, and the third is a letter which I wrote last night. As soon as the breath has left my body, deliver the envelope to the address indorsed upon it. Do not delay one moment, or you may live to regret it. Say nothing until you have delivered the package, and then be guided by the advice which you receive,—it will come from a friend of mine who will not see you wronged.'

"I slipped away from the door without making my presence known and entered, by a door from the hall, the room adjoining the one where Mr. Merkell lay. A moment later there was a loud scream. Returning quickly to the hall, I entered Mr. Merkell's room as though just arrived.

" 'How is Mr. Merkell?' I demanded, as I crossed the threshold.

" 'He is dead,' sobbed the woman, without lifting her head,—she had fallen on her knees by the bedside. She had good cause to weep, for my time had come.

" 'Get up,' I said. 'You have no right here. You pollute Mr. Merkell's dead body by your touch. Leave the house immediately,—your day is over!'

" 'I will not!' she cried, rising to her feet and facing me with brazen-faced impudence. 'I have a right to stay,—he has given me the right!'

" 'Ha, ha!' I laughed. 'Mr. Merkell is dead, and I am mistress here henceforth. Go, and go at once,—do you hear?'

" 'I hear, but I shall not heed. I can prove my rights! I shall not leave!'

" 'Very well,' I replied, 'we shall see. The law will decide.'

"I left the room, but did not leave the house. On the contrary, I concealed myself where I could see what took place in the room adjoining the deathchamber.

"She entered the room a moment later, with her child on one arm and the keys in the other hand. Placing the child on the floor, she put the key in the lock, and seemed surprised to find the desk already unfastened. She opened the desk, picked up a roll of money and a ladies' watch, which first caught her eye, and was reaching toward the drawer upon the right, when I interrupted her:—

" 'Well, thief, are you trying to strip the house before you leave it?'

"She gave an involuntary cry, clasped one hand to her bosom and with the other caught up her child, and stood like a wild beast at bay.

" 'I am not a thief,' she panted. 'The things are mine!'

" 'You lie,' I replied. 'You have no right to them,—no more right than you have to remain in this house!'

" 'I have a right,' she persisted, 'and I can prove it!'

"She turned toward the desk, seized the drawer, and drew it open. Never shall I forget her look,—never shall I forget that moment; it was the happiest of my life. The drawer was empty!

"Pale as death she turned and faced me.

" 'The papers!' she shrieked, 'the papers! *You* have stolen them!'

" 'Papers?' I laughed, 'what papers? Do you take me for a thief, like yourself?'

" 'There were papers here,' she cried, 'only a minute since. They are mine,—give them back to me!'

" 'Listen, woman,' I said sternly, 'you are lying—or dreaming. My brother-in-law's papers are doubtless in his safe at his office, where they ought to be. As for the rest,—you are a thief.'

" 'I am not,' she screamed; 'I am his wife. He married me, and the papers that were in the desk will prove it.'

" 'Listen,' I exclaimed, when she had finished,—'listen carefully, and take heed to what I say. You are a liar. You have no proofs,—there never were any proofs of what you say, because it never happened,—it is absurd upon the face of it. Not one person in Wellington would believe it. Why should he marry you? He did not need to! You are merely lying,—you are not even self-deceived. If he had really married you, you would have made it known long ago. That you did not is proof that your story is false.'

"She was hit so hard that she trembled and sank into a chair. But I had no mercy—she had saved your father from *me*—'dear Julia,' indeed!

" 'Stand up,' I ordered. 'Do not dare to sit down in my presence. I have you on the hip, my lady, and will teach you your place.'

"She struggled to her feet, and stood supporting herself with one hand on the chair. I could have killed her, Olivia! She had been my father's slave; if it had been before the war, I would have had her whipped to death.

" 'You are a thief,' I said, 'and of that there *are* proofs. I have caught you in the act. The watch in your bosom is my own, the money belongs to Mr. Merkell's estate, which belongs to my niece, his daughter Olivia. I saw you steal them. My word is worth a hundred times over, for I am a lady, and you are—what? And now hear me: if ever you breathe to a living soul one word of this preposterous story, I will charge you with the theft, and have you sent to the penitentiary. Your child will be taken from you, and you shall never see it again. I will give you now just ten minutes to take your brat and your rags out of this house forever. But before you go, put down your plunder there upon the desk!'

"She laid down the money and the watch, and a few minutes later left the house with the child in her arms.

"And now, Olivia, you know how I saved your estate, and why you should be grateful to me."

Olivia had listened to her aunt's story with intense interest. Having perceived the old woman's mood, and fearful lest any interruption might break the flow of her narrative, she had with an effort kept back the one question which had been hovering upon her lips, but which could now no longer be withheld.

"What became of the papers, Aunt Polly?"

"Ha, ha!" chuckled Mrs. Ochiltree with a cunning look, "did I not tell you that she found no papers?"

A change had come over Mrs. Ochiltree's face, marking the reaction from her burst of energy. Her eyes were half closed, and she was muttering incoherently. Olivia made some slight effort to arouse her, but in vain, and realizing the futility of any further attempt to extract information from her aunt at this time, she called William and drove homeward.

CHAPTER XVI

Ellis Takes a Trick

Late one afternoon a handsome trap, drawn by two spirited bays, drove up to Carteret's gate. Three places were taken by Mrs. Carteret, Clara, and the major, leaving the fourth seat vacant.

"I've asked Ellis to drive out with us," said the major, as he took the lines from the colored man who had the trap in charge. "We'll go by the office and pick him up."

Clara frowned, but perceiving Mrs. Carteret's eye fixed upon her, restrained any further expression of annoyance.

The major's liking for Ellis had increased within the year. The young man was not only a good journalist, but possessed sufficient cleverness and tact to make him excellent company. The major was fond of argument, but extremely tenacious of his own opinions. Ellis handled the foils of discussion with just the requisite skill to draw out the major, permitting himself to be vanquished, not too easily, but, as it were, inevitably, by the major's incontrovertible arguments.

Olivia had long suspected Ellis of feeling a more than friendly interest in Clara. Herself partial to Tom, she had more than once thought it hardly fair to Delamere, or even to Clara, who was young and impressionable, to have another young man constantly about the house. True, there had seemed to be no great danger, for Ellis had neither the family nor the means to make him a suitable match for the major's sister; nor had Clara made any secret of her dislike for Ellis, or of her resentment for his supposed depreciation

586

of Delamere. Mrs. Carteret was inclined to a more just and reasonable view of Ellis's conduct in this matter, but nevertheless did not deem it wise to undeceive Clara. Dislike was a stout barrier, which remorse might have broken down. The major, absorbed in schemes of empire and dreams of his child's future, had not become cognizant of the affair. His wife, out of friendship for Tom, had refrained from mentioning it; while the major, with a delicate regard for Clara's feelings, had said nothing at home in regard to his interview with her lover.

At the Chronicle office Ellis took the front seat beside the major. After leaving the city pavements, they bowled along merrily over an excellent toll-road, built of oyster shells from the neighboring sound, stopping at intervals to pay toll to the gate-keepers, most of whom were white women with tallow complexions and snuff-stained lips,—the traditional "poor-white." For part of the way the road was bordered with a growth of scrub oak and pine, interspersed with stretches of cleared land, white with the opening cotton or yellow with ripening corn. To the right, along the distant river-bank, were visible here and there groups of turpentine pines, though most of this growth had for some years been exhausted. Twenty years before, Wellington had been the world's greatest shipping port for naval stores. But as the turpentine industry had moved southward, leaving a trail of devastated forests in its rear, the city had fallen to a poor fifth or sixth place in this trade, relying now almost entirely upon cotton for its export business.

Occasionally our party passed a person, or a group of persons,—mostly negroes approximating the pure type, for those of lighter color grew noticeably scarcer as the town was left behind. Now and then one of these would salute the party respectfully, while others glanced at them indifferently or turned away. There would have seemed, to a stranger, a lack of spontaneous friendliness between the people of these two races, as though each felt that it had no part or lot in the other's life. At one point the carriage drew near a party of colored folks who were laughing and jesting among themselves with great glee. Paying no attention to the white people, they continued to laugh and shout boisterously as the carriage swept by.

Major Carteret's countenance wore an angry look.

"The negroes around this town are becoming absolutely insufferable," he averred. "They are sadly in need of a lesson in manners."

Half an hour later they neared another group, who were also making merry. As the carriage approached, they became mute and silent as the grave until the major's party had passed.

"The negroes are a sullen race," remarked the major thoughtfully. "They will learn their lesson in a rude school, and perhaps much sooner than they dream. By the way," he added, turning to the ladies, "what was the arrangement with Tom? Was he to come out this evening?"

"He came out early in the afternoon," replied Clara, "to go a-fishing. He is to join us at the hotel."

After an hour's drive they reached the hotel, in front of which stretched the beach, white and inviting, along the shallow sound. Mrs. Carteret and Clara found seats on the veranda. Having turned the trap over to a hostler, the major joined a group of gentlemen, among whom was General Belmont, and was soon deep in the discussion of the standing problem of how best to keep the negroes down.

Ellis remained by the ladies. Clara seemed restless and ill at ease. Half an hour elapsed and Delamere had not appeared.

"I wonder where Tom is," said Mrs. Carteret.

"I guess he has n't come in yet from fishing," said Clara. "I wish he would come. It's lonesome here. Mr. Ellis, would you mind looking about the hotel and seeing if there's any one here that we know?"

For Ellis the party was already one too large. He had accepted this invitation eagerly, hoping to make friends with

Clara during the evening. He had never been able to learn definitely the reason of her coldness, but had dated it from his meeting with old Mrs. Ochiltree, with which he felt it was obscurely connected. He had noticed Delamere's scowling look, too, at their last meeting. Clara's injustice, whatever its cause, he felt keenly. To Delamere's scowl he had paid little attention,—he despised Tom so much that, but for his engagement to Clara, he would have held his opinions in utter contempt.

He had even wished that Clara might make some charge against him,—he would have preferred that to her attitude of studied indifference, the only redeeming feature about which was that it *was* studied, showing that she, at least, had him in mind. The next best thing, he reasoned, to having a woman love you, is to have her dislike you violently,—the main point is that you should be kept in mind, and made the subject of strong emotions. He thought of the story of Hall Caine's, where the woman, after years of persecution at the hands of an unwelcome suitor, is on the point of yielding, out of sheer irresistible admiration for the man's strength and persistency, when the lover, unaware of his victory and despairing of success, seizes her in his arms and, springing into the sea, finds a watery grave for both. The analogy of this case with his own was, of course, not strong. He did not anticipate any tragedy in their relations; but he was glad to be thought of upon almost any terms. He would not have done a mean thing to make her think of him; but if she did so because of a misconception, which he was given no opportunity to clear up, while at the same time his conscience absolved him from evil and gave him the compensating glow of martyrdom, it was at least better than nothing.

He would, of course, have preferred to be upon a different footing. It had been a pleasure to have her speak to him during the drive,—they had exchanged a few trivial remarks in the general conversation. It was a greater pleasure to have her ask a favor of him—a pleasure which, in this instance, was partly offset when he interpreted her request to mean that he was to look for Tom Delamere. He accepted the situation gracefully, however, and left the ladies alone.

Knowing Delamere's habits, he first went directly to the bar-room,—the atmosphere would be congenial, even if he were not drinking. Delamere was not there. Stepping next into the office, he asked the clerk if young Mr. Delamere had been at the hotel.

"Yes, sir," returned the man at the desk, "he was here at luncheon, and then went out fishing in a boat with several other gentlemen. I think they came back about three o'clock. I'll find out for you."

He rang the bell, to which a colored boy responded.

"Front," said the clerk, "see if young Mr. Delamere's upstairs. Look in 255 or 256, and let me know at once."

The bell-boy returned in a moment.

"Yas, suh," he reported, with a suppressed grin, "he's in 256, suh. De do' was open, an' I seed 'im from de hall, suh."

"I wish you'd go up and tell him," said Ellis, "that— What are you grinning about?" he asked suddenly, noticing the waiter's expression.

"Nothin', suh, nothin' at all, suh," responded the negro, lapsing into the stolidity of a wooden Indian. "What shall I tell Mr. Delamere, suh?"

"Tell him," resumed Ellis, still watching the boy suspiciously,—"no, I'll tell him myself."

He ascended the broad stair to the second floor. There was an upper balcony and a parlor, with a piano for the musically inclined. To reach these one had to pass along the hall upon which the room mentioned by the bell-boy opened. Ellis was quite familiar with the hotel. He could imagine circumstances under which he would not care to speak to Delamere; he would merely pass through the hall and glance into the room casually, as any one else might do, and see what the darky downstairs might have meant by his impudence.

It required but a moment to reach the room. The door

was not wide open, but far enough ajar for him to see what was going on within.

Two young men, members of the fast set at the Clarendon Club, were playing cards at a small table, near which stood another, decorated with an array of empty bottles and glasses. Sprawling on a lounge, with flushed face and disheveled hair, his collar unfastened, his vest buttoned awry, lay Tom Delamere, breathing stertorously, in what seemed a drunken sleep. Lest there should be any doubt of the cause of his condition, the fingers of his right hand had remained clasped mechanically around the neck of a bottle which lay across his bosom.

Ellis turned away in disgust, and went slowly back to the ladies.

"There seems to be no one here yet," he reported. "We came a little early for the evening crowd. The clerk says Tom Delamere was here to luncheon, but he has n't seen him for several hours."

"He 's not a very gallant cavalier," said Mrs. Carteret severely. "He ought to have been waiting for us."

Clara was clearly disappointed, and made no effort to conceal her displeasure, leaving Ellis in doubt as to whether or not he were its object. Perhaps she suspected him of not having made a very thorough search. Her next remark might have borne such a construction.

"Sister Olivia," she said pettishly, "let's go up to the parlor. I can play the piano anyway, if there's no one to talk to."

"I find it very comfortable here, Clara," replied her sister placidly. "Mr. Ellis will go with you. You'll probably find some one in the parlor, or they'll come when you begin to play."

Clara's expression was not cordial, but she rose as if to go. Ellis was in a quandary. If she went through the hall, the chances were at least even that she would see Delamere. He did not care a rap for Delamere,—if he chose to make a public exhibition of himself, it was his own affair; but to see him would surely spoil Miss Pemberton's evening, and, in her frame of mind, might lead to the suspicion that Ellis had prearranged the exposure. Even if she should not harbor this unjust thought, she would not love the witness of her discomfiture. We had rather not meet the persons who have seen, even though they never mention, the skeletons in our closets. Delamere had disposed of himself for the evening. Ellis would have a fairer field with Delamere out of sight and unaccounted for, than with Delamere in evidence in his present condition.

"Would n't you rather take a stroll on the beach, Miss Clara?" he asked, in the hope of creating a diversion.

"No, I'm going to the parlor. *You* need n't come, Mr. Ellis, if you'd rather go down to the beach. I can quite as well go alone."

"I'd rather go with you," he said meekly.

They were moving toward the door opening into the hall, from which the broad staircase ascended. Ellis, whose thoughts did not always respond quickly to a sudden emergency, was puzzling his brain as to how he should save her from any risk of seeing Delamere. Through the side door leading from the hall into the office, he saw the bell-boy to whom he had spoken seated on the bench provided for the servants.

"Won't you wait for me just a moment, Miss Clara, while I step into the office? I'll be with you in an instant."

Clara hesitated.

"Oh, certainly," she replied nonchalantly.

Ellis went direct to the bell-boy. "Sit right where you are," he said, "and don't move a hair. What is the lady in the hall doing?"

"She's got her back tu'ned this way, suh. I 'spec' she's lookin' at the picture on the opposite wall, suh."

"All right," whispered Ellis, pressing a coin into the servant's hand. "I'm going up to the parlor with the lady. You go up ahead of us, and keep in front of us along the hall. Don't dare to look back. I shall keep on talking to the lady, so that you can tell by my voice where we are. When you get to room 256, go in and shut the door behind you: pretend that you were called,—ask the gentlemen what they want,— tell any kind of a lie you like;—but keep the door shut until you're sure we've got by. Do you hear?"

"Yes, suh," replied the negro intelligently.

The plan worked without a hitch. Ellis talked steadily, about the hotel, the furnishings, all sorts of irrelevant subjects, to which Miss Pemberton paid little attention. She was angry with Delamere, and took no pains to conceal her feelings. The bell-boy entered room 256 just before they reached the door. Ellis had heard loud talking as they approached, and as they were passing there was a crash of broken glass, as though some object had been thrown at the door.

"What is the matter there?" exclaimed Clara, quickening her footsteps and instinctively drawing closer to Ellis.

"Some one dropped a glass, I presume," replied Ellis calmly.

Miss Pemberton glanced at him suspiciously. She was in a decidedly perverse mood. Seating herself at the piano, she played brilliantly for a quarter of an hour. Quite a number of couples strolled up to the parlor, but Delamere was not among them.

"Oh dear!" exclaimed Miss Pemberton, as she let her fingers fall upon the keys with a discordant crash, after the last note, "I don't see why we came out here to-night. Let's go back downstairs."

Ellis felt despondent. He had done his utmost to serve and to please Miss Pemberton, but was not likely, he foresaw, to derive much benefit from his opportunity. Delamere was evidently as much or more in her thoughts by reason of his absence than if he had been present. If the door should have been opened, and she should see him from the hall upon their return, Ellis could not help it. He took the side next to the door, however, meaning to hurry past the room so that she might not recognize Delamere.

Fortunately the door was closed and all quiet within the

room. On the stairway they met the bellboy, rubbing his head with one hand and holding a bottle of seltzer upon a tray in the other. The boy was well enough trained to give no sign of recognition, though Ellis guessed the destination of the bottle.

Ellis hardly knew whether to feel pleased or disappointed at the success of his manoeuvers. He had spared Miss Pemberton some mortification, but he had saved Tom Delamere from merited exposure. Clara ought to know the truth, for her own sake.

On the beach, a few rods away, fires were burning, around which several merry groups had gathered. The smoke went mostly to one side, but a slight whiff came now and then to where Mrs. Carteret sat awaiting them.

"They're roasting oysters," said Mrs. Carteret. "I wish you'd bring me some, Mr. Ellis."

Ellis strolled down to the beach. A large iron plate, with a turned-up rim like a great baking-pan, supported by legs which held it off the ground, was set over a fire built upon the sand. This primitive oven was heaped with small oysters in the shell, taken from the neighboring sound, and hauled up to the hotel by a negro whose pony cart stood near by. A wet coffee-sack of burlaps was spread over the oysters, which, when steamed sufficiently, were opened by a colored man and served gratis to all who cared for them.

Ellis secured a couple of plates of oysters, which he brought to Mrs. Carteret and Clara; they were small, but finely flavored.

Meanwhile Delamere, who possessed a remarkable faculty of recuperation from the effects of drink, had waked from his sleep, and remembering his engagement, had exerted himself to overcome the ravages of the afternoon's debauch. A dash of cold water braced him up somewhat. A bottle of seltzer and a big cup of strong coffee still further strengthened his nerves.

When Ellis returned to the veranda, after having taken

away the plates, Delamere had joined the ladies and was explaining the cause of his absence.

He had been overcome by the heat, he said, while out fishing, and had been lying down ever since. Perhaps he ought to have sent for a doctor, but the fellows had looked after him. He had n't sent word to his friends because he had n't wished to spoil their evening.

"That was very considerate of you, Tom," said Mrs. Carteret dryly, "but you ought to have let us know. We have been worrying about you very much. Clara has found the evening dreadfully dull."

"Indeed, no, sister Olivia," said the young lady cheerfully, "I've been having a lovely time. Mr. Ellis and I have been up in the parlor; I played the piano; and we've been eating oysters and having a most delightful time. Won': you take me down there to the beach, Mr. Ellis? I want to see the fires. Come on."

"Can't I go?" asked Tom jealously.

"No, indeed, you must n't stir a foot! You must not over-tax yourself too soon; it might do you serious injury. Stay here with sister Olivia."

She took Ellis's arm with exaggerated cordiality. Delamere glared after them angrily. Ellis did not stop to question her motives, but took the goods the gods provided. With no very great apparent effort, Miss Pemberton became quite friendly, and they strolled along the beach, in sight of the hotel, for nearly half an hour. As they were coming up she asked him abruptly,—

"Mr. Ellis, did you know Tom was in the hotel?"

Ellis was looking across the sound, at the lights of a distant steamer which was making her way toward the harbor.

"I wonder," he said musingly, as though he had not heard her question, "if that is the Ocean Belle?"

"And was he really sick?" she demanded.

"She's later than usual this trip," continued Ellis, pursuing his thought. "She was due about five o'clock."

Miss Pemberton, under cover of the darkness, smiled a fine smile, which foreboded ill for some one. When they joined the party on the piazza, the major had come up and was saying that it was time to go. He had been engaged in conversation, for most of the evening, with General Belmont and several other gentlemen.

"Here comes the general now. Let me see. There are five of us. The general has offered me a seat in his buggy, and Tom can go with you-all."

The general came and spoke to the ladies. Tom murmured his thanks; it would enable him to make up a part of the delightful evening he had missed.

When Mrs. Carteret had taken the rear seat, Clara promptly took the place beside her. Ellis and Delamere sat in front. When Delamere, who had offered to drive, took the reins, Ellis saw that his hands were shaking.

"Give me the lines," he whispered. "Your nerves are unsteady and the road is not well lighted."

Delamere prudently yielded the reins. He did not like Ellis's tone, which seemed sneering rather than expressive of sympathy with one who had been suffering. He wondered if the beggar knew anything about his illness. Clara had been acting strangely. It would have been just like Ellis to have slandered him. The upstart had no business with Clara anyway. He would cheerfully have strangled Ellis, if he could have done so with safety to himself and no chance of discovery.

The drive homeward through the night was almost a silent journey. Mrs. Carteret was anxious about her baby. Clara did not speak, except now and then to Ellis with reference to some object in or near the road. Occasionally they passed a vehicle in the darkness, sometimes barely avoiding a collision. Far to the north the sky was lit up with the glow of a forest fire. The breeze from the Sound was deliciously cool. Soon the last toll-gate was passed and the lights of the town appeared.

Ellis threw the lines to William, who was waiting, and hastened to help the ladies out.

"Good-night, Mr. Ellis," said Clara sweetly, as she gave Ellis her hand. "Thank you for a very pleasant evening. Come up and see us soon."

She ran into the house without a word to Tom.

CHAPTER XVII

The Social Aspirations
of Captain McBane

It was only eleven o'clock, and Delamere, not being at all sleepy, and feeling somewhat out of sorts as the combined results of his afternoon's debauch and the snubbing he had received at Clara's hands, directed the major's coachman, who had taken charge of the trap upon its arrival, to drive him to the St. James Hotel before returning the horses to the stable. First, however, the coachman left Ellis at his boardinghouse, which was near by. The two young men parted with as scant courtesy as was possible without an open rupture.

Delamere hoped to find at the hotel some form of distraction to fill in an hour or two before going home. Ill fortune favored him by placing in his way the burly form of Captain George McBane, who was sitting in an armchair alone, smoking a midnight cigar, under the hotel balcony. Upon Delamere's making known his desire for amusement, the captain proposed a small game of poker in his own room.

McBane had been waiting for some such convenient opportunity. We have already seen that the captain was desirous of social recognition, which he had not yet obtained beyond the superficial acquaintance acquired by association with men about town. He had determined to assault society in its citadel by seeking membership in the Clarendon Club, of which most gentlemen of the best families of the city were members.

The Clarendon Club was a historic institution, and its membership a social cult, the temple of which was located just off the main street of the city, in a dignified old colonial mansion which had housed it for the nearly one hundred years during which it had maintained its existence unbroken. There had grown up around it many traditions and special usages. Membership in the Clarendon was the *sine qua non* of high social standing, and was conditional upon two of three things,—birth, wealth, and breeding. Breeding was the prime essential, but, with rare exceptions, must be backed by either birth or money.

Having decided, therefore, to seek admission into this social arcanum, the captain, who had either not quite appreciated the standard of the Clarendon's membership, or had failed to see that he fell beneath it, looked about for an intermediary through whom to approach the object of his desire. He had already thought of Tom Delamere in this connection, having with him such an acquaintance as one forms around a hotel, and having long ago discovered that Delamere was a young man of superficially amiable disposition, vicious instincts, lax principles, and a weak will, and, which was quite as much to the purpose, a member of the Clarendon Club. Possessing mental characteristics almost entirely opposite, Delamere and the captain had certain tastes in common, and had smoked, drunk, and played cards together more than once.

Still more to his purpose, McBane had detected Delamere trying to cheat him at cards. He had said nothing about this discovery, but had merely noted it as something which at some future time might prove useful. The captain had not suffered by Delamere's deviation from the straight line of honor, for while Tom was as clever with the cards as might be expected of a young man who had devoted most of his leisure for several years to handling them, McBane was past master in their manipulation. During a stormy career he had touched more or less pitch, and had escaped few sorts of defilement.

The appearance of Delamere at a late hour, unaccompanied, and wearing upon his countenance an expression in which the captain read aright the craving for mental and physical excitement, gave him the opportunity for which he had been looking. McBane was not the man to lose an opportunity, nor did Delamere require a second invitation. Neither was it necessary, during the progress of the game, for the captain to press upon his guest the contents of the decanter which stood upon the table within convenient reach.

The captain permitted Delamere to win from him several small amounts, after which he gradually increased the stakes and turned the tables.

Delamere, with every instinct of a gamester, was no more a match for McBane in self-control than in skill. When the young man had lost all his money, the captain expressed his entire willingness to accept notes of hand, for which he happened to have convenient blanks in his apartment.

When Delamere, flushed with excitement and wine, rose from the gaming table at two o'clock, he was vaguely conscious that he owed McBane a considerable sum, but could not have stated how much. His opponent, who was entirely cool and collected, ran his eye carelessly over the bits of paper to which Delamere had attached his signature.

"Just one thousand dollars even," he remarked.

The announcement of this total had as sobering an effect upon Delamere as though he had been suddenly deluged with a shower of cold water. For a moment he caught his breath. He had not a dollar in the world with which to pay this sum. His only source of income was an allowance from his grandfather, the monthly installment of which, drawn that very day, he had just lost to McBane, before starting in upon the notes of hand.

"I'll give you your revenge another time," said McBane, as they rose. "Luck is against you to-night, and I'm unwilling to take advantage of a clever young fellow like you. Meantime," he added, tossing the notes of hand carelessly on a bureau, "don't worry about these bits of paper. Such small matters should n't cut any figure between friends; but if you are around the hotel to-morrow, I should like to speak to you upon another subject."

"Very well, captain," returned Tom somewhat ungraciously.

Delamere had been completely beaten with his own weapons. He had tried desperately to cheat McBane. He knew perfectly well that McBane had discovered his efforts and had cheated him in turn, for the captain's play had clearly been gauged to meet his own. The biter had been bit, and could not complain of the outcome.

The following afternoon McBane met Delamere at the hotel, and bluntly requested the latter to propose him for membership in the Clarendon Club.

Delamere was annoyed at this request. His aristocratic gorge rose at the presumption of this son of an overseer and ex-driver of convicts. McBane was good enough to win money from, or even to lose money to, but not good enough to be recognized as a social equal. He would instinctively have blackballed McBane had he been proposed by some one else; with what grace could he put himself forward as the sponsor for this impossible social aspirant? Moreover, it was clearly a vulgar, cold-blooded attempt on McBane's part to use his power over him for a personal advantage.

"Well, now, Captain McBane," returned Delamere diplomatically, "I've never put any one up yet, and it's not regarded as good form for so young a member as myself to propose candidates. I'd much rather you'd ask some older man."

"Oh, well," replied McBane, "just as you say, only I thought you had cut your eye teeth."

Delamere was not pleased with McBane's tone. His remark was not acquiescent, though couched in terms of assent. There was a sneering savagery about it, too, that left Delamere uneasy. He was, in a measure, in McBane's power. He could not pay the thousand dollars, unless it fell from heaven, or he could win it from some one else. He would not dare go to his grandfather for help. Mr. Delamere did not even know that his grandson gambled. He might not have objected, perhaps, to a gentleman's game, with moderate stakes, but he would certainly, Tom knew very well, have looked upon a thousand dollars as a preposterous sum to be lost at cards by a man who had nothing with which to pay it. It was part of Mr. Delamere's creed that a gentleman should not make debts that he was not reasonably able to pay.

There was still another difficulty. If he had lost the money to a gentleman, and it had been his first serious departure from Mr. Delamere's perfectly well understood standard of honor, Tom might have risked a confession and thrown himself on his grandfather's mercy; but he owed other sums here and there, which, to his just now much disturbed imagination, loomed up in alarming number and amount. He had recently observed signs of coldness, too, on the part of certain members of the club. Moreover, like most men with one commanding vice, he was addicted to several subsidiary forms of iniquity, which in case of a scandal were more than likely to come to light. He was clearly and most disagreeably caught in the net of his own hypocrisy. His grandfather believed him a model of integrity, a pattern of honor; he could not afford to have his grandfather undeceived.

He thought of old Mrs. Ochiltree. If she were a liberal soul, she could give him a thousand dollars now, when he needed it, instead of making him wait until she died, which might not be for ten years or more, for a legacy which was steadily growing less and might be entirely exhausted if she lived long enough,—some old people were very tenacious of life! She was a careless old woman, too, he reflected, and very foolishly kept her money in the house. Latterly she had been growing weak and childish. Some day she might be robbed, and then his prospective inheritance from that source would vanish into thin air!

With regard to this debt to McBane, if he could not pay it, he could at least gain a long respite by proposing the captain at the club. True, he would undoubtedly be black-balled, but before this inevitable event his name must remain posted for several weeks, during which interval McBane would be conciliatory. On the other hand, to propose Mc-Bane would arouse suspicion of his own motives; it might reach his grandfather's ears, and lead to a demand for an explanation, which it would be difficult to make. Clearly, the better plan would be to temporize with McBane, with the hope that something might intervene to remove this cursed obligation.

"Suppose, captain," he said affably, "we leave the matter open for a few days. This is a thing that can't be rushed. I'll feel the pulse of my friends and yours, and when we get the lay of the land, the affair can be accomplished much more easily."

"Well, that's better," returned McBane, somewhat mollified,—"*if* you'll do that."

"To be sure I will," replied Tom easily, too much relieved to resent, if not too preoccupied to perceive, the implied doubt of his veracity.

McBane ordered and paid for more drinks, and they parted on amicable terms.

"We'll let these notes stand for the time being, Tom," said McBane, with significant emphasis, when they separated.

Delamere winced at the familiarity. He had reached that degree of moral deterioration where, while principles were of little moment, the externals of social intercourse possessed an exaggerated importance. McBane had never before been so personal. He had addressed the young aristocrat first as "Mr. Delamere," then, as their acquaintance advanced, as "Delamere." He had now reached the abbreviated Christian name stage of familiarity. There was no lower depth to which Tom could sink, unless McBane should invent a nickname by which to address him.

He did not like McBane's manner,—it was characterized by a veiled insolence which was exceedingly offensive. He would go over to the club and try his luck with some honest player,—perhaps something might turn up to relieve him from his embarrassment.

He put his hand in his pocket mechanically,—and found it empty! In the present state of his credit, he could hardly play without money.

A thought struck him. Leaving the hotel, he hastened home, where he found Sandy dusting his famous suit of clothes on the back piazza. Mr. Delamere was not at home, having departed for Belleview about two o'clock, leaving Sandy to follow him in the morning.

"Hello, Sandy," exclaimed Tom, with an assumed jocularity which he was very far from feeling, "what are you doing with those gorgeous garments?"

"I'm a-dustin' of 'em, Mistuh Tom, dat's w'at I'm a-doin'. Dere 's somethin' wrong 'bout dese clo's er mine—I don' never seem ter be able ter keep 'em clean no mo'. Ef I b'lieved in dem ole-timey sayin's, I'd 'low dere wuz a witch come here eve'y night an' tuk 'em out an' wo' 'em, er tuk me out an' rid me in 'em. Dere wuz somethin' wrong 'bout dat cakewalk business, too, dat I ain' never unde'stood and' don' know how ter 'count fer, 'less dere wuz some kin' er dev'lishness goin' on dat don' show on de su'face."

"Sandy," asked Tom irrelevantly, "have you any money in the house?"

"Yas, suh, I got de money Mars John give me ter git dem things ter take out ter Belleview in de mawnin'."

"I mean money of your own."

"I got a qua'ter ter buy terbacker wid," returned Sandy cautiously.

"Is that all? Haven't you some saved up?"

"Well, yas, Mistuh Tom," returned Sandy, with evident reluctance, "dere's a few dollahs put away in my bureau drawer fer a rainy day,—not much, suh."

"I'm a little short this afternoon, Sandy, and need some money right away. Grandfather is n't here, so I can't get any from him. Let me take what you have for a day or two, Sandy, and I'll return it with good interest."

"Now, Mistuh Tom," said Sandy seriously, "I don't min' lettin' you take my money, but I hopes you ain' gwine ter use it fer none er dem rakehelly gwines-on er yo'n,—gamblin' an' bettin' an' so fo'th. Yo' grandaddy'll fin' out 'bout you yit, ef you don' min' yo' P's an' Q's. I does my bes' ter keep yo' misdoin's f'm 'im, an' sense I b'en tu'ned out er de chu'ch—thoo no fault er my own, God knows!—I've tol' lies 'nuff 'bout you ter sink a ship. But it ain't right, Mistuh Tom, it ain't right! an' I only does it fer de sake er de fam'ly honuh, dat Mars John sets so much sto' by, an' ter save his feelin's; fer de doctuh says he mus' n' git ixcited 'bout nothin', er it mought bring on another stroke."

"That's right, Sandy," replied Tom approvingly; "but the family honor is as safe in my hands as in grandfather's own, and I'm going to use the money for an excellent purpose, in fact to relieve a case of genuine distress; and I'll hand it back to you in a day or two,—perhaps to-morrow. Fetch me the money, Sandy,—that's a good darky!"

"All right, Mistuh Tom, you shill have de money; but I wants ter tell you, suh, dat in all de yeahs I has wo'ked fer yo' gran'daddy, he has never called me a 'darky' ter my face, suh. Co'se I knows dere's w'ite folks an' black folks,—but dere's manners, suh, dere's manners, an' gent'emen oughter be de ones ter use 'em, suh, ef dey ain't ter be fergot enti'ely!"

"There, there, Sandy," returned Tom in a conciliatory tone, "I beg your pardon! I've been associating with some Northern white folks at the hotel, and picked up the word from them. You're a high-toned colored gentleman, Sandy,— the finest one on the footstool."

Still muttering to himself, Sandy retired to his own room, which was in the house, so that he might be always near his master. He soon returned with a time-stained leather pocket-book and a coarse-knit cotton sock, from which two receptacles he painfully extracted a number of bills and coins.

"You count dat, Mistuh Tom, so I'll know how much I'm lettin' you have."

"This is n't worth anything," said Tom, pushing aside one roll of bills. "It's Confederate money."

"So it is, suh. It ain't wuth nothin' now; but it has be'n money, an' who kin tell but what it mought be money agin? De rest er dem bills is greenbacks,—dey'll pass all right, I reckon."

The good money amounted to about fifty dollars, which Delamere thrust eagerly into his pocket.

"You won't say anything to grandfather about this, will you, Sandy," he said, as he turned away.

"No, suh, co'se I won't! Does I ever tell 'im 'bout yo' gwines-on? Ef I did," he added to himself, as the young man disappeared down the street, "I wouldn' have time ter do nothin' e'se ha'dly. I don' know whether I'll ever see dat money agin er no, do' I 'magine de ole gent'eman would n' lemme lose it ef he knowed. But I ain' gwine ter tell him, whether I git my money back er no, fer he is jes' so wrop' up in dat boy dat I b'lieve it'd jes' break his hea't ter fin' out how he's be'n gwine on. Doctuh Price has tol' me not ter let de ole gent'eman git ixcited, er e'se dere 's no tellin' w'at mought happen. He's be'n good ter me, he has, an' I'm gwine ter take keer er him,—dat's w'at I is, ez long ez I has de chance."

Delamere went directly to the club, and soon lounged into the card-room, where several of the members were engaged in play. He sauntered here and there, too much absorbed in his own thoughts to notice that the greetings he received were less cordial than those usually exchanged between the members of a small and select social club. Finally, when Augustus, commonly and more appropriately called "Gus," Davidson came into the room, Tom stepped toward him.

"Will you take a hand in a game, Gus?"

"Don't care if I do," said the other. "Let's sit over here."

Davidson led the way to a table near the fireplace, near which stood a tall screen, which at times occupied various places in the room. Davidson took the seat opposite the fireplace, leaving Delamere with his back to the screen.

Delamere staked half of Sandy's money, and lost. He staked the rest, and determined to win, because he could not afford to lose. He had just reached out his hand to gather in the stakes, when he was charged with cheating at cards, of which two members, who had quietly entered the room and posted themselves behind the screen, had secured specific proof.

A meeting of the membership committee was hastily summoned, it being an hour at which most of them might be found at the club. To avoid a scandal, and to save the feelings of a prominent family, Delamere was given an opportunity to resign quietly from the club, on condition that he paid all his gambling debts within three days, and took an oath never to play cards again for money. This latter condition was made at the suggestion of an elderly member, who apparently believed that a man who would cheat at cards would stick at perjury.

Delamere acquiesced very promptly. The taking of the oath was easy. The payment of some fifteen hundred dollars of debts was a different matter. He went away from the club thoughtfully, and it may be said, in full justice to a past which was far from immaculate, that in his present thoughts he touched a depth of scoundrelism far beyond anything of which he had as yet deemed himself capable. When a man of good position, of whom much is expected, takes to evil courses, his progress is apt to resemble that of a well-bred woman who has started on the downward path,—the pace is all the swifter because of the distance which must be traversed to reach the bottom. Delamere had made rapid headway; having hitherto played with sin, his servant had now become his master, and held him in an iron grip.

CHAPTER XVIII

Sandy Sees His Own Ha'nt

Having finished cleaning his clothes, Sandy went out to the kitchen for supper, after which he found himself with nothing to do. Mr. Delamere's absence relieved him from attendance at the house during the evening. He might have smoked his pipe tranquilly in the kitchen until bedtime, had not the cook intimated, rather pointedly, that she expected other company. To a man of Sandy's tact a word was sufficient, and he resigned himself to seeking companionship elsewhere.

Under normal circumstances, Sandy would have attended prayer-meeting on this particular evening of the week; but being still in contumacy, and cherishing what he considered the just resentment of a man falsely accused, he stifled the inclination which by long habit led him toward the church, and set out for the house of a friend with whom it occurred to him that he might spend the evening pleasantly. Unfortunately, his friend proved to be not at home, so Sandy turned his footsteps toward the lower part of the town, where the streets were well lighted, and on pleasant evenings quite animated. On the way he met Josh Green, whom he had known for many years, though their paths did not often cross. In his loneliness Sandy accepted an invitation to go with Josh and have a drink,—a single drink.

When Sandy was going home about eleven o'clock, three sheets in the wind, such was the potent effect of the single drink and those which had followed it, he was scared almost into soberness by a remarkable apparition. As it seemed to Sandy, he saw himself hurrying along in front of himself toward the house. Possibly the muddled condition of Sandy's intellect had so affected his judgment as to vitiate any conclusion he might draw, but Sandy was quite sober enough to perceive that the figure ahead of him wore his best clothes and looked exactly like him, but seemed to be in something more of a hurry, a discrepancy which Sandy at once corrected by quickening his own pace so as to maintain as nearly as possible an equal distance between himself and his double. The situation was certainly an incomprehensible one, and savored of the supernatural.

"Ef dat's me gwine 'long in front," mused Sandy, in vinous perplexity, "den who is dis behin' here? Dere ain' but one er me, an' my ha'nt would n' leave my body 'tel I wuz dead. Ef dat's me in front, den I mus' be my own ha'nt; an' whichever one of us is de ha'nt, de yuther must be dead an' don' know it. I don' know what ter make er no sech gwineson, I don't. Maybe it ain' me after all, but it certainly do look lack me."

When the apparition disappeared in the house by the side door, Sandy stood in the yard for several minutes, under the shade of an elm-tree, before he could make up his mind to enter the house. He took courage, however, upon the reflection that perhaps, after all, it was only the bad liquor he had drunk. Bad liquor often made people see double.

He entered the house. It was dark, except for a light in Tom Delamere's room. Sandy tapped softly at the door.

"Who's there?" came Delamere's voice, in a somewhat startled tone, after a momentary silence.

"It's me, suh; Sandy."

They both spoke softly. It was the rule of the house when Mr. Delamere had retired, and though he was not at home, habit held its wonted sway.

"Just a moment, Sandy."

Sandy waited patiently in the hall until the door was opened. If the room showed any signs of haste or disorder,

Sandy was too full of his own thoughts—and other things—to notice them.

"What do you want, Sandy," asked Tom.

"Mistuh Tom," asked Sandy solemnly, "ef I wuz in yo' place, an' you wuz in my place, an' we wuz bofe in de same place, whar would I be?"

Tom looked at Sandy keenly, with a touch of apprehension. Did Sandy mean anything in particular by this enigmatical inquiry, and if so, what? But Sandy's face clearly indicated a state of mind in which consecutive thought was improbable; and after a brief glance Delamere breathed more freely.

"I give it up, Sandy," he responded lightly. "That's too deep for me."

" 'Scuse me, Mistuh Tom, but is you heared er seed anybody er anything come in de house fer de las' ten minutes?"

"Why, no, Sandy, I have n't heard any one. I came from the club an hour ago. I had forgotten my key, and Sally got up and let me in, and then went back to bed. I've been sitting here reading ever since. I should have heard any one who came in."

"Mistuh Tom," inquired Sandy anxiously, "would you 'low dat I'd be'n drinkin' too much?"

"No, Sandy, I should say you were sober enough, though of course you may have had a few drinks. Perhaps you'd like another? I've got something good here."

"No, suh, Mistuh Tom, no, suh! No mo' liquor fer me, suh, never! When liquor kin make a man see his own ha'nt, it's 'bout time fer dat man ter quit drinkin', it sho' is! Goodnight, Mistuh Tom."

As Sandy turned to go, Delamere was struck by a sudden and daring thought. The creature of impulse, he acted upon it immediately.

"By the way, Sandy," he exclaimed carelessly, "I can pay you back that money you were good enough to lend me this afternoon. I think I'll sleep better if I have the debt off my mind, and I shouldn't wonder if you would. You don't mind having it in gold, do you?"

"No, indeed, suh," replied Sandy. "I ain' seen no gol' fer so long dat de sight er it'd be good fer my eyes."

Tom counted out ten five-dollar gold pieces upon the table at his elbow.

"And here's another, Sandy," he said, adding an eleventh, "as interest for the use of it."

"Thank y', Mistuh Tom. I did n't spec' no intrus', but I don' never 'fuse gol' w'en I kin git it."

"And here," added Delamere, reaching carelessly into a bureau drawer, "is a little old silk purse that I've had since I was a boy. I'll put the gold in it, Sandy; it will hold it very nicely."

"Thank y', Mistuh Tom. You're a gentleman, suh, an' wo'thy er de fam'ly name. Good-night, suh, an' I hope yo' dreams'll be pleasanter 'n' mine. Ef it wa'n't fer dis gol' kinder takin' my min' off'n dat ha'nt, I don' s'pose I'd be able to do much sleepin' ter-night. Good-night, suh."

"Good-night, Sandy."

Whether or not Delamere slept soundly, or was troubled by dreams, pleasant or unpleasant, it is nevertheless true that he locked his door, and sat up an hour later, looking through the drawers of his bureau, and burning several articles in the little iron stove which constituted part of the bedroom furniture.

It is also true that he rose very early, before the household was stirring. The cook slept in a room off the kitchen, which was in an outhouse in the back yard. She was just stretching herself, preparatory to getting up, when Tom came to her window and said that he was going off fishing, to be gone all day, and that he would not wait for breakfast.

CHAPTER XIX

A Midnight Walk

Ellis left the office of the Morning Chronicle about eleven o'clock the same evening and set out to walk home. His boarding-house was only a short distance beyond old Mr. Delamere's residence, and while he might have saved time and labor by a slightly shorter route, he generally selected this one because it led also by Major Carteret's house. Sometimes there would be a ray of light from Clara's room, which was on one of the front corners; and at any rate he would have the pleasure of gazing at the outside of the casket that enshrined the jewel of his heart. It was true that this purely sentimental pleasure was sometimes dashed with bitterness at the thought of his rival; but one in love must take the bitter with the sweet, and who would say that a spice of jealousy does not add a certain zest to love? On this particular evening, however, he was in a hopeful mood. At the Clarendon Club, where he had gone, a couple of hours before, to verify a certain news item for the morning paper, he had heard a story about Tom Delamere which, he imagined, would spike that gentleman's guns for all time, so far as Miss Pemberton was concerned. So grave an affair as cheating at cards could never be kept secret,—it was certain to reach her ears; and Ellis was morally certain that Clara would never marry a man who had been proved dishonorable. In all probability there would be no great sensation about the matter. Delamere was too well connected; too many prominent people would be involved,—even Clara, and the editor himself, of whom Delamere was a distant cousin. The reputation of the club was also to be considered. Ellis was not the man to feel a malicious delight in the misfortunes of another, nor was he a pessimist who welcomed scandal and disgrace with open arms, as confirming a gloomy theory of human life. But, with the best intentions in the world, it was no more than human nature that he should feel a certain elation in the thought that his rival had been brought about merely by the unmasking of a hypocrite, who had held him at an unfair disadvantage in the race for Clara's favor.

The night was quiet, except for the faint sound of distant music now and then, or the mellow laughter of some group of revelers. Ellis met but few pedestrians, but as he neared old Mr. Delamere's, he saw two men walking in the same direction as his own, on the opposite side of the street. He had observed that they kept at about an equal distance apart, and that the second, from the stealthy manner in which he was making his way, was anxious to keep the first in sight, without disclosing his own presence. This aroused Ellis's curiosity, which was satisfied in some degree when the man in advance stopped beneath a lamp-post and stood for a moment looking across the street, with his face plainly visible in the yellow circle of light. It was a dark face, and Ellis recognized it instantly as that of old Mr. Delamere's body servant, whose personal appearance had been very vividly impressed upon Ellis at the christening dinner at Major Carteret's. He had seen Sandy once since, too, at the hotel cakewalk. The negro had a small bundle in his hand, the nature of which Ellis could not make out.

When Sandy had stopped beneath the lamp-post, the man who was following him had dodged behind a tree-trunk. When Sandy moved on, Ellis, who had stopped in turn, saw the man in hiding come out and follow Sandy. When this second man came in range of the light, Ellis wondered that there should be two men so much alike. The first of the two had undoubtedly been Sandy. Ellis had recognized the peculiar, old-fashioned coat that Sandy had worn upon the two occasions when he had noticed him. Barring this difference, and the somewhat unsteady gait of the second man, the two were as much alike as twin brothers.

When they had entered Mr. Delamere's house, one after the other,—in the stillness of the night Ellis could perceive that each of them tried to make as little noise as possible,—Ellis supposed that they were probably relatives, both employed as servants, or that some younger negro, taking Sandy for a model, was trying to pattern himself after his superior. Why all this mystery, of course he could not imagine, unless the younger man had been out without permission and was trying to avoid the accusing eye of Sandy. Ellis was vaguely conscious that he had seen the other negro somewhere, but he could not for the moment place him,—there were so many negroes, nearly three negroes to one white man in the city of Wellington!

The subject, however, while curious, was not important as compared with the thoughts of his sweetheart which drove it from his mind. Clara had been kind to him the night before,—whatever her motive, she had been kind, and could not consistently return to her attitude of coldness. With Delamere hopelessly discredited, Ellis hoped to have at least fair play,—with fair play, he would take his chances of the outcome.

CHAPTER XX

A Shocking Crime

On Friday morning, when old Mrs. Ochiltree's cook Dinah went to wake her mistress, she was confronted with a sight that well-nigh blanched her ebony cheek and caused her eyes almost to start from her head with horror. As soon as she could command her trembling limbs sufficiently to make them carry her, she rushed out of the house and down the street, bareheaded, covering in an incredibly short time the few blocks that separated Mrs. Ochiltree's residence from that of her niece.

She hastened around the house, and finding the back door open and the servants stirring, ran into the house and up the stairs with the familiarity of an old servant, not stopping until she reached the door of Mrs. Carteret's chamber, at which she knocked in great agitation.

Entering in response to Mrs. Carteret's invitation, she found the lady, dressed in a simple wrapper, superintending the morning toilet of little Dodie, who was a wakeful child, and insisted upon rising with the birds, for whose music he still showed a great fondness, in spite of his narrow escape while listening to the mockingbird.

"What is it, Dinah?" asked Mrs. Carteret, alarmed at the frightened face of her aunt's old servitor.

"O my Lawd, Mis' 'Livy, my Lawd, my Lawd! My legs is trim'lin' so dat I can't ha'dly hol' my han's stiddy 'nough ter say w'at I got ter say! O Lawd have mussy on us po' sinners! W'atever is gwine ter happen in dis worl' er sin an' sorrer!"

"What in the world is the matter, Dinah?" demanded Mrs. Carteret, whose own excitement had increased with the length of this preamble. "Has anything happened to Aunt Polly?"

"Somebody done broke in de house las' night, Mis' 'Livy, an' kill' Mis' Polly, an' lef' her layin' dead on de flo', in her own blood, wid her cedar chis' broke' open, an' eve'thing scattered roun' de flo'! O my Lawd, my Lawd, my Lawd, my Lawd!"

Mrs. Carteret was shocked beyond expression. Perhaps the spectacle of Dinah's unrestrained terror aided her to retain a greater measure of self-control than she might otherwise have been capable of. Giving the nurse some directions in regard to the child, she hastily descended the stairs, and seizing a hat and jacket from the rack in the hall, ran immediately with Dinah to the scene of the tragedy. Before the thought of this violent death all her aunt's faults faded into insignificance, and only her good qualities were remembered. She had reared Olivia; she had stood up for the memory of Olivia's mother when others had seemed to forget what was due to it. To her niece she had been a second mother, and had never been lacking in affection.

More than one motive, however, lent wings to Mrs. Carteret's feet. Her aunt's incomplete disclosures on the day of the drive past the hospital had been weighing upon Mrs. Carteret's mind, and she had intended to make another effort this very day, to get an answer to her question about the papers which the woman had claimed were in existence. Suppose her aunt had really found such papers,—papers which would seem to prove the preposterous claim made by her father's mulatto mistress? Suppose that, with the fatuity which generally leads human beings to keep compromising documents, her aunt had preserved these papers? If they should be found there in the house, there might be a scandal, if nothing worse, and this was to be avoided at all hazards.

Guided by some fortunate instinct, Dinah had as yet informed no one but Mrs. Carteret of her discovery. If they could reach the house before the murder became known to any third person, she might be the first to secure access to the remaining contents of the cedar chest, which would be likely to be held as evidence in case the officers of the law forestalled her own arrival.

They found the house wrapped in the silence of death. Mrs. Carteret entered the chamber of the dead woman. Upon the floor, where it had fallen, lay the body in a pool of blood, the strongly marked countenance scarcely more grim in the rigidity of death than it had been in life. A gaping wound in the head accounted easily for the death. The cedar chest stood open, its strong fastenings having been broken by a steel bar which still lay beside it. Near it were scattered pieces of old lace, antiquated jewelry, tarnished silverware,—the various mute souvenirs of the joys and sorrows of a long and active life.

Kneeling by the open chest, Mrs. Carteret glanced hurriedly through its contents. There were no papers there except a few old deeds and letters. She had risen with a sigh of relief, when she perceived the end of a paper projecting from beneath the edge of a rug which had been carelessly rumpled, probably by the burglar in his hasty search for plunder. This paper, or sealed envelope as it proved to be, which evidently contained some inclosure, she seized, and at the sound of approaching footsteps thrust hastily into her own bosom.

The sight of two agitated women rushing through the quiet streets at so early an hour in the morning had attracted attention and aroused curiosity, and the story of the murder, having once become known, spread with the customary rapidity of bad news. Very soon a policeman, and a little later a sheriff's officer, arrived at the house and took charge of the remains to await the arrival of the coroner.

By nine o'clock a coroner's jury had been summoned, who, after brief deliberation, returned a verdict of willful murder at the hands of some person or persons unknown, while engaged in the commission of a burglary.

No sooner was the verdict announced than the community, or at least the white third of it, resolved itself spontaneously into a committee of the whole to discover the perpetrator of this dastardly crime, which, at this stage of the affair, seemed merely one of robbery and murder.

Suspicion was at once directed toward the negroes, as it always is when a unexplained crime is committed in a Southern community. The suspicion was not entirely an illogical one. Having been, for generations, trained up to thriftlessness, theft, and immorality, against which only thirty years of very limited opportunity can be offset, during which brief period they have been denied in large measure the healthful social stimulus and sympathy which holds most men in the path of rectitude, colored people might reasonably be expected to commit at least a share of crime proportionate to their numbers. The population of the town was at least two thirds colored. The chances were, therefore, in the absence of evidence, at least two to one that a man of color had committed the crime. The Southern tendency to charge the negroes with all the crime and immorality of that region, unjust and exaggerated as the claim may be, was therefore not without a logical basis to the extent above indicated.

It must not be imagined that any logic was needed, or any reasoning consciously worked out. The mere suggestion that the crime had been committed by a negro was equivalent to proof against any negro that might be suspected and could not prove his innocence. A committee of white men was hastily formed. Acting independently of the police force, which was practically ignored as likely to favor the negroes, this committee set to work to discover the murderer.

The spontaneous activity of the whites was accompanied by a visible shrinkage of the colored population. This could not be taken as any indication of guilt, but was merely a recognition of the palpable fact that the American habit of lynching had so whetted the thirst for black blood that a negro suspected of crime had to face at least the possibility of a short shrift and a long rope, not to mention more gruesome horrors, without the intervention of judge or jury. Since to have a black face at such a time was to challenge suspicion, and since there was neither the martyr's glory nor the saint's renown in being killed for some one else's crime, and very little hope of successful resistance in case of an attempt at lynching, it was obviously the part of prudence for those thus marked to seek immunity in a temporary disappearance from public view.

CHAPTER XXI

The Necessity
of an Example

About ten o'clock on the morning of the discovery of the murder, Captain McBane and General Belmont, as though moved by a common impulse, found themselves at the office of the Morning Chronicle. Carteret was expecting them, though there had been no appointment made. These three resourceful and energetic minds, representing no organized body, and clothed with no legal authority, had so completely arrogated to themselves the leadership of white public sentiment as to come together instinctively when an event happened which concerned the public, and, as this murder presumably did, involved the matter of race.

"Well, gentlemen," demanded McBane impatiently, "what are we going to do with the scoundrel when we catch him?"

"They've got the murderer," announced a reporter, entering the room.

"Who is he?" they demanded in a breath.

"A nigger by the name of Sandy Campbell, a servant of old Mr. Delamere."

"How did they catch him?"

"Our Jerry saw him last night, going toward Mrs. Ochiltree's house, and a white man saw him coming away, half an hour later."

"Has he confessed?"

"No, but he might as well. When the posse went to arrest him, they found him cleaning the clothes he had worn last night, and discovered in his room a part of the plunder. He denies it strenuously, but it seems a clear case."

"There can be no doubt," said Ellis, who had come into the room behind the reporter. "I saw the negro last night, at twelve o'clock, going into Mr. Delamere's yard, with a bundle in his hand."

Ellis sees "Sandy" or Delamere

"He is the last negro I should have suspected," said Carteret. "Mr. Delamere had implicit confidence in him."

"All niggers are alike," remarked McBane sententiously. "The only way to keep them from stealing is not to give them the chance. A nigger will steal a cent off a dead man's eye. He has assaulted and murdered a white woman,—an example should be made of him."

Carteret recalled very distinctly the presence of this negro at his own residence on the occasion of little Theodore's christening dinner. He remembered having questioned the prudence of letting a servant know that Mrs. Ochiltree kept money in the house. Mr. Delamere had insisted strenuously upon the honesty of this particular negro. The whole race, in the major's opinion, was morally undeveloped, and only held within bounds by the restraining influence of the white people. Under Mr. Delamere's thumb this Sandy had been a model servant,—faithful, docile, respectful, and self-respecting; but Mr. Delamere had grown old, and had probably lost in a measure his moral influence over his servant. Left to his own degraded ancestral instincts, Sandy had begun to deteriorate, and a rapid decline had culminated in this robbery and murder,—and who knew what other horror? The criminal was a negro, the victim a white woman;—it was only reasonable to expect the worst.

major's assumption

"He'll swing for it," observed the general.

Ellis went into another room, where his duty called him.

"He should burn for it," averred McBane. "I say, burn the nigger."

Bilmont alludes to lynching

"This," said Carteret, "is something more than an ordi-

[handwritten margin notes: "more talk of lynching"; "lynching takes many forms"; "idea that wrong person/victim for fear + intimidation"; "logic of KKK like thinking"]

nary crime, to be dealt with by the ordinary processes of law. It is a murderous and fatal assault upon a woman of our race,—upon our race in the person of its womanhood, its crown and flower. If such crimes are not punished with swift and terrible directness, the whole white womanhood of the South is in danger."

"Burn the nigger," repeated McBane automatically.

"Neither is this a mere sporadic crime," Carteret went on. "It is symptomatic; it is the logical and inevitable result of the conditions which have prevailed in this town for the past year. It is the last straw."

"Burn the nigger," reiterated McBane. "We seem to have the right nigger, but whether we have or not, burn *a* nigger. It is an assault upon the white race, in the person of old Mrs. Ochiltree, committed by the black race, in the person of some nigger. It would justify the white people in burning *any* nigger. The example would be all the more powerful if we got the wrong one. It would serve notice on the niggers that we shall hold the whole race responsible for the misdeeds of each individual."

"In ancient Rome," said the general, "when a master was killed by a slave, all his slaves were put to the sword."

"We couldn't afford that before the war," said McBane, "but the niggers don't belong to anybody now, and there's nothing to prevent our doing as we please with them. A dead nigger is no loss to any white man. I say, burn the nigger."

"I do not believe," said Carteret, who had gone to the window and was looking out,—"I do not believe that we need trouble ourselves personally about his punishment. I should judge, from the commotion in the street, that the public will take the matter into its own hands. I, for one, would prefer that any violence, however justifiable, should take place without my active intervention."

"It won't take place without mine, if I know it," exclaimed McBane, starting for the door.

"Hold on a minute, captain," exclaimed Carteret. "There's more at stake in this matter than the life of a black

scoundrel. Wellington is in the hands of negroes and scala-
wags. What better time to rescue it?"

"It's a trifle premature," replied the general. "I should
have preferred to have this take place, if it was to happen,
say three months hence, on the eve of the election,—but
discussion always provokes thirst with me; I wonder if I could
get Jerry to bring us some drinks?"

Carteret summoned the porter. Jerry's usual manner had
taken on an element of self-importance, resulting in what
one might describe as a sort of condescending obsequious-
ness. Though still a porter, he was also a hero, and wore his
aureole.

"Jerry," said the general kindly, "the white people are
very much pleased with the assistance you have given them
in apprehending this scoundrel Campbell. You have rendered a great public service, Jerry, and we wish you to know
that it is appreciated."

"Thank y', gin'l, thank y', suh! I alluz tries ter do my
duty, suh, an' stan' by dem dat stan's by me. Dat low-down
nigger oughter be lynch', suh, don't you think, er e'se bu'nt?
Dere ain' nothin' too bad ter happen ter 'im."

"No doubt he will be punished as he deserves, Jerry,"
returned the general, "and we will see that you are suitably
rewarded. Go across the street and get me three Calhoun
cocktails. I seem to have nothing less than a two-dollar bill,
but you may keep the change, Jerry,—all the change."

Jerry was very happy. He had distinguished himself in the
public view, for to Jerry, as to the white people themselves,
the white people were the public. He had won the goodwill
of the best people, and had already begun to reap a tangible
reward. It is true that several strange white men looked at
him with lowering brows as he crossed the street, which was
curiously empty of colored people; but he nevertheless went
firmly forward, panoplied in the consciousness of his own
rectitude, and serenely confident of the protection of the
major and the major's friends.

"Jerry is about the only negro I have seen since nine

623

o'clock," observed the general when the porter had gone. "If this were election day, where would the negro vote be?"

"In hiding, where most of the negro population is to-day," answered McBane. "It's a pity, if old Mrs. Ochiltree had to go this way, that it could n't have been deferred a month or six weeks."

Carteret frowned at this remark, which, coming from McBane, seemed lacking in human feeling, as well as in respect to his wife's dead relative.

"But," resumed the general, "if this negro is lynched, as he well deserves to be, it will not be without its effect. We still have in reserve for the election a weapon which this affair will only render more effective. What became of the piece in the negro paper?"

"I have it here," answered Carteret. "I was just about to use it as the text for an editorial."

"Save it awhile longer," responded the general. "This crime itself will give you text enough for a four-volume work."

When this conference ended, Carteret immediately put into press an extra edition of the Morning Chronicle, which was soon upon the streets, giving details of the crime, which was characterized as an atrocious assault upon a defenseless old lady, whose age and sex would have protected her from harm at the hands of any one but a brute in the lowest human form. This event, the Chronicle suggested, had only confirmed the opinion, which had been of the late growing upon the white people, that drastic efforts were necessary to protect the white women of the South against brutal, lascivious, and murderous assaults at the hands of negro men. It was only another significant example of the results which might have been foreseen from the application of a false and pernicious political theory, by which ignorance, clothed in a little brief authority, was sought to be exalted over knowledge, vice over virtue, an inferior and degraded race above the heaven-crowned Anglo-Saxon. If an outraged people, justly infuriated, and impatient of the slow processes of the courts, should assert their inherent sovereignty, which the law after all was merely intended to embody, and should choose, in obedience to the higher law, to set aside, temporarily, the ordinary judicial procedure, it would serve as a warning and an example to the vicious elements of the community, of the swift and terrible punishment which would fall, like the judgment of God, upon any one who laid sacrilegious hands upon white womanhood.

CHAPTER XXII

How Not to Prevent
a Lynching

Dr. Miller, who had sat up late the night before with a difficult case at the hospital, was roused, about eleven o'clock, from a deep and dreamless sleep. Struggling back into consciousness, he was informed by his wife, who stood by his bedside, that Mr. Watson, the colored lawyer, wished to see him upon a matter of great importance.

"Nothing but a matter of life and death would make me get up just now," he said with a portentous yawn.

"This *is* a matter of life and death," replied Janet. "Old Mrs. Polly Ochiltree was robbed and murdered last night, and Sandy Campbell has been arrested for the crime,—and they are going to lynch him!"

"Tell Watson to come right up," exclaimed Miller, springing out of bed. "We can talk while I'm dressing."

While Miller made a hasty toilet Watson explained the situation. Campbell had been arrested on the charge of murder. He had been seen, during the night, in the neighborhood of the scene of the crime, by two different persons, a negro and a white man, and had been identified later while entering Mr. Delamere's house, where he lived, and where damning proofs of his guilt had been discovered; the most important item of which was an old-fashioned knit silk purse, recognized as Mrs. Ochiltree's, and several gold pieces of early coinage, of which the murdered woman was known to have a number. Watson brought with him one of the first copies procurable of the extra edition of the Chronicle, which contained these facts and further information.

They were still talking when Mrs. Miller, knocking at the door, announced that big Josh Green wished to see the doctor about Sandy Campbell. Miller took his collar and necktie in his hand and went downstairs, where Josh sat waiting.

"Doctuh," said Green, "de w'ite folks is talkin' 'bout lynchin' Sandy Campbell fer killin' ole Mis' Ochiltree. He never done it, an' dey ought n' ter be 'lowed ter lynch 'im."

"They ought not to lynch him, even if he committed the crime," returned Miller, "but still less if he did n't. What do you know about it?"

"I know he was wid me, suh, las' night, at de time when dey say ole Mis' Ochiltree wuz killed. We wuz down ter Sam Taylor's place, havin' a little game of kyards an' a little liquor. Den we lef dere an' went up ez fur ez de corner er Main an' Vine Streets, where we pa'ted, an' Sandy went 'long to'ds home. Mo'over, dey say he had on check' britches an' a blue coat. When Sandy wuz wid me he had on gray clo's, an' when we sep'rated he wa'n't in no shape ter be changin' his clo's, let 'lone robbin' er killin' anybody."

"Your testimony ought to prove an alibi for him," declared Miller.

"Dere ain' gwine ter be no chance ter prove nothin', 'less'n we kin do it mighty quick! Dey say dey 're gwine ter lynch 'im ter-night,—some on 'em is talkin' 'bout burnin' 'im. My idee is ter hunt up de niggers an' git 'em ter stan' tergether an' gyard de jail."

"Why should n't we go to the principal white people of the town and tell them Josh's story, and appeal to them to stop this thing until Campbell can have a hearing?"

"It would n't do any good," said Watson despondently; "their blood is up. It seems that some colored man attacked Mrs. Ochiltree,—and he was a murderous villain, whoever he may be. To quote Josh would destroy the effect of his story,—we know he never harmed any one but himself"—

"An' a few keerliss people w'at got in my way," corrected Josh.

"He has been in court several times for fighting,—and that's against him. To have been at Sam Taylor's place is against Sandy, too, rather than in his favor. No, Josh, the white people would believe that you were trying to shield Sandy, and you would probably be arrested as an accomplice."

"But look a-here, Mr. Watson,—Dr. Miller, is we-all jes' got ter set down here, widout openin' ou' mouths, an' let dese w'ite folks hang er bu'n a man w'at we *know* ain' guilty? Dat ain't no law, ner jestice, ner nothin'! Ef you-all won't he'p, I'll do somethin' myse'f! Dere's two niggers ter one white man in dis town, an' I'm sho' I kin fin' fifty of 'em w'at'll fight, ef dey kin fin' anybody ter lead 'em."

"Now hold on, Josh," argued Miller; "what is to be gained by fighting? Suppose you got your crowd together and surrounded the jail,—what then?"

"There'd be a clash," declared Watson, "and instead of one dead negro there'd be fifty. The white people are claiming now that Campbell did n't stop with robbery and murder. A special edition of the Morning Chronicle, just out, suggests a further purpose, and has all the old shopworn cant about race purity and supremacy and imperative necessity, which always comes to the front whenever it is sought to justify some outrage on the colored folks. The blood of the whites is up, I tell you!"

"Is there anything to that suggestion?" asked Miller incredulously.

"It doesn't matter whether there is or not," returned Watson. "Merely to suggest it proves it. Nothing was said about this feature until the paper came out,—and even its statement is vague and indefinite,—but now the claim is in every mouth. I met only black looks as I came down the street. White men with whom I have long been on friendly terms passed me without a word. A negro has been arrested on suspicion,—the entire race is condemned on general principles."

"The whole thing is profoundly discouraging," said Miller sadly. "Try as we may to build up the race in the essentials of good citizenship and win the good opinion of the best people, some black scoundrel comes along, and by a single criminal act, committed in the twinkling of an eye, neutralizes the effect of a whole year's work."

"It's mighty easy neut'alize', er whatever you call it," said Josh sullenly. "De w'ite folks don' want too good an opinion er de niggers,—ef dey had a good opinion of 'em, dey would n' have no excuse fer 'busin' an' hangin' an' burnin' em. But ef dey can't keep from doin' it, let 'em git de right man! Dis way er pickin' up de fus' nigger dey comes across, an' stringin' 'im up rega'dliss, ought ter be stop', an' stop' right now!"

"Yes, that's the worst of lynch law," said Watson; "but we are wasting valuable time,—it's hardly worth while for us to discuss a subject we are all agreed upon. One of our race, accused of certain acts, is about to be put to death without judge or jury, ostensibly because he committed a crime,— really because he is a negro, for if he were white he would not be lynched. It is thus made a race issue, on the one side as well as on the other. What can we do to protect him?"

"We kin fight, ef we haf ter," replied Josh resolutely.

"Well, now, let us see. Suppose the colored people armed themselves? Messages would at once be sent to every town and county in the neighborhood. White men from all over the state, armed to the teeth, would at the slightest word pour into town on every railroad train, and extras would be run for their benefit."

"They're already coming in," said Watson.

"We might go to the sheriff," suggested Miller, "and demand that he telegraph the governor to call out the militia."

"I spoke to the sheriff an hour ago," replied Watson. "He has a white face and a whiter liver. He does not dare call out the militia to protect a negro charged with such a brutal crime;—and if he did, the militia are white men, and who can say that their efforts would not be directed to keeping the negroes out of the way, in order that the white devils might do their worst? The whole machinery of the state is in the hands of white men, elected partly by our votes. When the color line is drawn, if they choose to stand together with the rest of their race against us, or to remain passive and let the others work their will, we are helpless,—our cause is hopeless."

"We might call on the general government," said Miller. "Surely the President would intervene."

"Such a demand would be of no avail," returned Watson. "The government can only intervene under certain conditions, of which it must be informed through designated channels. It never sees anything that is not officially called to its attention. The whole negro population of the South might be slaughtered before the necessary red tape could be spun out to inform the President that a state of anarchy prevailed. There's no hope there."

"Den w'at we gwine ter do?" demanded Josh indignantly; "jes' set here an' let 'em hang Sandy, er bu'n 'im?"

"God knows!" exclaimed Miller. "The outlook is dark, but we should at least try to do something. There must be *some* white men in the town who would stand for law and order,—there's no possible chance for Sandy to escape hanging by due process of law, if he is guilty. We might at least try half a dozen gentlemen."

"We'd better leave Josh here," said Watson. "He's too truculent. If he went on the street he'd make trouble, and if he accompanied us he'd do more harm than good. Wait for us here, Josh, until we've seen what we can do. We'll be back in half an hour."

In half an hour they had both returned.

"It's no use," reported Watson gloomily. "I called at the mayor's office and found it locked. He is doubtless afraid on his own account, and would not dream of asserting his authority. I then looked up Judge Everton, who has always seemed to be fair. My reception was cold. He admitted that lynching was, as a rule, unjustifiable, but maintained that there were exceptions to all rules,—that laws were made, after all, to express the will of the people in regard to the ordinary administration of justice, but that in an emergency the sovereign people might assert itself and take the law into its own hands,—the creature was not greater than the creator. He laughed at my suggestion that Sandy was innocent. 'If he is innocent,' he said, 'then produce the real criminal. You negroes are standing in your own light when you try to protect such dastardly scoundrels as this Campbell, who is an enemy of society and not fit to live. I shall not move in the matter. If a negro wants the protection of the law, let him obey the law.' A wise judge,—a second Daniel come to judgment! If this were the law, there would be no need of judges or juries."

"I called on Dr. Price," said Miller, "my good friend Dr. Price, who would rather lie than hurt my feelings. 'Miller,' he declared, 'this is no affair of mine, or yours. I have too much respect for myself and my profession to interfere in such a matter, and you will accomplish nothing, and only lessen your own influence, by having anything to say.' 'But the man may be innocent,' I replied; 'there is every reason to believe that he is.' He shook his head pityingly. 'You are self-deceived, Miller; your prejudice has warped your judgment. The proof is overwhelming that he robbed this old lady, laid violent hands upon her, and left her dead. If he did no more, he has violated the written and unwritten law of the Southern States. I could not save him if I would, Miller, and frankly, I would not if I could. If he is innocent, his people can console themselves with the reflection that Mrs. Ochiltree was also innocent, and balance one crime against the other, the white against the black. Of course I shall take no part in whatever may be done,—but it is not my affair, nor yours. Take my advice, Miller, and keep out of it.'

"That is the situation," added Miller, summing up. "Their friendship for us, a slender stream at the best, dries up entirely when it strikes their prejudices. There is seemingly not one white man in Wellington who will speak a word for law, order, decency, or humanity. Those who do not participate will stand idly by and see an untried man deliberately and brutally murdered. Race prejudice is the devil unchained."

"Well, den, suh," said Josh, "where does we stan' now? W'at is we gwine ter do? I would n' min' fightin', fer my time ain't come yit,—I feels dat in my bones. W'at we gwine ter do, dat's w'at I wanter know."

"What does old Mr. Delamere have to say about the matter?" asked Miller suddenly. "Why have n't we thought of him before? Has he been seen?"

"No," replied Watson gloomily, "and for a good reason,— he is not in town. I came by the house just now, and learned that he went out to his country place yesterday afternoon to remain a week. Sandy was to have followed him out there this morning,—it's a pity he did n't go yesterday. The old gentleman has probably heard nothing about the matter."

"How about young Delamere?"

"He went away early this morning, down the river, to fish. He'll probably not hear of it before night, and he's only a boy anyway, and could very likely do nothing," said Watson.

Miller looked at his watch.

"Belleview is ten miles away," he said. "It is now eleven o'clock. I can drive out there in an hour and a half at the farthest. I'll go and see Mr. Delamere,—he can do more than any living man, if he is able to do anything at all. There's never been a lynching here, and one good white man, if he choose, may stem the flood long enough to give justice a chance. Keep track of the white people while I'm gone, Watson; and you, Josh, learn what the colored folks are saying, and do nothing rash until I return. In the meantime, do all that you can to find out who did commit this most atrocious murder."

CHAPTER XXIII

Belleview

Miller did not reach his destination without interruption. At some point a considerable stretch of the road was under repair, which made it necessary for him to travel slowly. His horse cast a shoe, and threatened to go lame; but in the course of time he arrived at the entrance gate of Belleview, entering which he struck into a private road, bordered by massive oaks, whose multitudinous branches, hung with long streamers of trailing moss, formed for much of the way a thick canopy above his head. It took him only a few minutes to traverse the quarter of a mile that lay between the entrance gate and the house itself.

This old colonial plantation, rich in legendary lore and replete with historic distinction, had been in the Delamere family for nearly two hundred years. Along the bank of the river which skirted its domain the famous pirate Blackbeard had held high carnival, and was reputed to have buried much treasure, vague traditions of which still lingered among the negroes and poor-whites of the country roundabout. The beautiful residence, rising white and stately in a grove of ancient oaks, dated from 1750, and was built of brick which had been brought from England. Enlarged and improved from generation to generation, it stood, like a baronial castle, upon a slight eminence from which could be surveyed the large demesne still belonging to the estate, which had shrunk greatly from its colonial dimensions. While still embracing several thousand acres, part forest and part cleared land, it had not of late years been profitable; in spite of which Mr. Delamere, with the conservatism of his age and caste, had never been able to make up his mind to part with any considerable portion of it. His grandson, he imagined, could make the estate pay and yet preserve it in its integrity. Here, in pleasant weather, surrounded by the scenes which he loved, old Mr. Delamere spent much of the time during his declining years.

Dr. Miller had once passed a day at Belleview, upon Mr. Delamere's invitation. For this old-fashioned gentleman, whose ideals not even slavery had been able to spoil, regarded himself as a trustee for the great public, which ought, in his opinion, to take as much pride as he in the contemplation of this historic landmark. In earlier years Mr. Delamere had been a practicing lawyer, and had numbered Miller's father among his clients. He had always been regarded as friendly to the colored people, and, until age and ill health had driven him from active life, had taken a lively interest in their advancement since the abolition of slavery. Upon the public opening of Miller's new hospital, he had made an effort to be present, and had made a little speech of approval and encouragement which had manifested his kindliness and given Miller much pleasure.

It was with the consciousness, therefore, that he was approaching a friend, as well as Sandy's master, that Miller's mind was chiefly occupied as his tired horse, scenting the end of his efforts, bore him with a final burst of speed along the last few rods of the journey; for the urgency of Miller's errand, involving as it did the issues of life and death, did not permit him to enjoy the charm of mossy oak or forest reaches, or even to appreciate the noble front of Belleview House when it at last loomed up before him.

"Well, William," said Mr. Delamere, as he gave his hand to Miller from the armchair in which he was seated under the broad and stately portico, "I did n't expect to see you out here. You'll excuse my not rising,—I'm none too firm on my legs. Did you see anything of my man Sandy back there on the road? He ought to have been here by nine o'clock, and it's now one. Sandy is punctuality itself, and I don't know how to account for his delay."

Clearly there need be no time wasted in preliminaries. Mr. Delamere had gone directly to the subject in hand.

"He will not be here to-day, sir," replied Miller. "I have come to you on his account."

In a few words Miller stated the situation.

"Preposterous!" exclaimed the old gentleman, with more vigor than Miller had supposed him to possess. "Sandy is absolutely incapable of such a crime as robbery, to say nothing of murder; and as for the rest, that is absurd upon the face of it! And so the poor old woman is dead! Well, well, well! she could not have lived much longer anyway; but Sandy did not kill her,—it's simply impossible! Why, I raised that boy! He was born on my place. I'd as soon believe such a thing of my own grandson as of Sandy! No negro raised by a Delamere would ever commit such a crime. I really believe, William, that Sandy has the family honor of the Delameres quite as much at heart as I have. Just tell them I say Sandy is innocent, and it will be all right."

"I'm afraid, sir," rejoined Miller, who kept his voice up so that the old gentleman could understand without having it suggested that Miller knew he was hard of hearing, "that you don't quite appreciate the situation. *I* believe Sandy innocent; *you* believe him innocent; but there are suspicious circumstances which do not explain themselves, and the white people of the city believe him guilty, and are going to lynch him before he has a chance to clear himself."

"Why does n't he explain the suspicious circumstances?" asked Mr. Delamere. "Sandy is truthful and can be believed. I would take Sandy's word as quickly as another man's oath."

"He has no chance to explain," said Miller. "The case is prejudged. A crime has been committed. Sandy is charged with it. He is black, and therefore he is guilty. No colored lawyer would be allowed in the jail, if one should dare to go there. No white lawyer will intervene. He'll be lynched to-night, without judge, jury, or preacher, unless we can stave the thing off for a day or two."

"Have you seen my grandson?" asked the old gentleman. "Is he not looking after Sandy?"

"No, sir. It seems he went down the river this morning to fish, before the murder was discovered; no one knows just where he has gone, or at what hour he will return."

"Well, then," said Mr. Delamere, rising from his chair with surprising vigor, "I shall have to go myself. No faithful servant of mine shall be hanged for a crime he did n't commit, so long as I have a voice to speak or a dollar to spend. There'll be no trouble after I get there, William. The people are naturally wrought up at such a crime. A fine old woman,—she had some detestable traits, and I was always afraid she wanted to marry me, but she was of an excellent family and had many good points,—an old woman of one of the best families, struck down by the hand of a murderer! You must remember, William, that blood is thicker than water, and that the provocation is extreme, and that a few hotheads might easily lose sight of the great principles involved and seek immediate vengeance, without too much discrimination. But they are good people, William, and when I have spoken, and they have an opportunity for a sober second thought, they will do nothing rashly, but will wait for the operation of the law, which will, of course, clear Sandy."

"I'm sure I hope so," returned Miller. "Shall I try to drive you back, sir, or will you order your own carriage?"

"My horses are fresher, William, and I'll have them brought around. You can take the reins, if you will,—I'm rather old to drive,—and my man will come behind with your buggy."

In a few minutes they set out along the sandy road. Having two fresh horses, they made better headway than Miller had made coming out, and reached Wellington easily by three o'clock.

"I think, William," said Mr. Delamere, as they drove into

the town, "that I had first better talk with Sandy. He may be able to explain away the things that seem to connect him with this atrocious affair; and that will put me in a better position to talk to other people about it."

Miller drove directly to the county jail. Thirty or forty white men, who seemed to be casually gathered near the door, closed up when the carriage approached. The sheriff, who had seen them from the inside, came to the outer door and spoke to the visitor through a grated wicket.

"Mr. Wemyss," said Mr. Delamere, when he had made his way to the entrance with the aid of his cane, "I wish to see my servant, Sandy Campbell, who is said to be in your custody."

The sheriff hesitated. Meantime there was some parleying in low tones among the crowd outside. No one interfered, however, and in a moment the door opened sufficiently to give entrance to the old gentleman, after which it closed quickly and clangorously behind him.

Feeling no desire to linger in the locality, Miller, having seen his companion enter the jail, drove the carriage round to Mr. Delamere's house, and leaving it in charge of a servant with instructions to return for his master in a quarter of an hour, hastened to his own home to meet Watson and Josh and report the result of his efforts.

CHAPTER XXIV

Two Southern Gentlemen

The iron bolt rattled in the lock, the door of a cell swung open, and when Mr. Delamere had entered was quickly closed again.

"Well, Sandy!"

"Oh, Mars John! Is you fell from hebben ter he'p me out er here? I prayed de Lawd ter sen' you, an' He answered my prayer, an' here you is, Mars John,—here you is! Oh, Mars John, git me out er dis place!"

"Tut, tut, Sandy!" answered his master; "of course I'll get you out. That's what I've come for. How in the world did such a mistake ever happen? You would no more commit such a crime than I would!"

"No, suh, 'deed I would n', an' you know I would n'! I would n' want ter bring no disgrace on de fam'ly dat raise' me, ner ter make no trouble fer you, suh; but here I is, suh, lock' up in jail, an' folks talkin' 'bout hangin' me for somethin' dat never entered my min', suh. I swea' ter God I never thought er such a thing!"

"Of course you did n't, Sandy," returned Mr. Delamere soothingly; "and now the next thing, and the simplest thing, is to get you out of this. I'll speak to the officers, and at the preliminary hearing to-morrow I'll tell them all about you, and they will let you go. You won't mind spending one night in jail for your sins."

"No, suh, ef I wuz, sho' I'd be 'lowed ter spen' it here.

But dey say dey 're gwine ter lynch me ter-night,—I kin hear 'em talkin' f'm de winders er de cell, suh."

"Well, I say, Sandy, that they shall do no such thing! Lynch a man brought up by a Delamere, for a crime of which he is innocent? Preposterous! I'll speak to the authorities and see that you are properly protected until this mystery is unraveled. If Tom had been here, he would have had you out before now, Sandy. My grandson is a genuine Delamere, is he not, Sandy?"

"Yas, suh, yas, suh," returned Sandy, with a lack of enthusiasm which he tried to conceal from his master. "An' I s'pose ef he had n' gone fishin' so soon dis mawnin', he'd 'a' be'n lookin' after me, suh."

"It has been my love for him and your care of me, Sandy," said the old gentleman tremulously, "that have kept me alive so long; but now explain to me everything concerning this distressing matter, and I shall then be able to state your case to better advantage."

"Well, suh," returned Sandy, "I mought's well tell de whole tale an' not hol' nothin' back. I wuz kind er lonesome las' night, an' sence I be'n tu'ned outen de chu'ch on account er dat cakewalk I did n' go ter, so he'p me God! I did n' feel like gwine ter prayer-meetin', so I went roun' ter see Solomon Williams, an' he wa'n't home, an' den I walk' down street an' met Josh Green, an' he ax' me inter Sam Taylor's place, an' I sot roun' dere wid Josh till 'bout 'leven o'clock, w'en I sta'ted back home. I went straight ter de house, suh, an' went ter bed an' ter sleep widout sayin' a wo'd ter a single soul excep' Mistuh Tom, who wuz settin' up readin' a book w'en I come in. I wish I may drap dead in my tracks, suh, ef dat ain't de God's truf, suh, eve'y wo'd of it!"

"I believe every word of it, Sandy; now tell me about the clothes that you are said to have been found cleaning, and the suspicious articles that were found in your room?"

"Dat's w'at beats me, Mars John," replied Sandy, shaking his head mournfully. "W'en I lef' home las' night after supper, my clo's wuz all put erway in de closet in my room, folded up on de she'f ter keep de moths out. Dey wuz my good clo's,—de blue coat dat you wo' ter de weddin' fo'ty years ago, an' dem dere plaid pants I gun Mistuh Cohen fo' dollars fer three years ago; an' w'en I looked in my closet dis mawnin', suh, befo' I got ready ter sta't fer Belleview, dere wuz my clo's layin' on de flo', all muddy an' crumple' up, des lack somebody had wo' 'em in a fight! Somebody e'se had wo' my clo's,—er e'se dere'd be'n some witchcraf', er some sort er devilment gwine on dat I can't make out, suh, ter save my soul!"

"There was no witchcraft, Sandy, but that there was some deviltry might well be. Now, what other negro, who might have been mistaken for you, could have taken your clothes? Surely no one about the house?"

"No, suh, no, suh. It could n't 'a' be'n Jeff, fer he wuz at Belleview wid you; an' it could n't 'a' be'n Billy, fer he wuz too little ter wear my clo's; an' it could n't 'a' be'n Sally, fer she's a 'oman. It's a myst'ry ter me, suh!"

"Have you no enemies? Is there any one in Wellington whom you imagine would like to do you an injury?"

"Not a livin' soul dat I knows of, suh. I've be'n tu'ned out'n de chu'ch, but I don' know who my enemy is dere, er ef it wuz all a mistake, like dis yer jailin' is; but de Debbil is in dis somewhar, Mars John,—an' I got my reasons fer sayin' so."

"What do you mean, Sandy?"

Sandy related his experience of the preceding evening; how he had seen the apparition preceding him to the house, and how he had questioned Tom upon the subject.

"There 's some mystery here, Sandy," said Mr. Delamere reflectively. "Have you told me all, now, upon your honor? I am trying to save your life, Sandy, and I must be able to trust your word implicitly. You must tell me every circumstance; a very little and seemingly unimportant bit of evidence may sometimes determine the issue of a great lawsuit. There is one thing especially, Sandy: where did you get the gold which was found in your trunk?"

Sandy's face lit up with hopefulness.

"Why, Mars John, I kin 'splain dat part easy. Dat wuz money I had lent out, an' I got back f'm—But no, suh, I promise' not ter tell."

"Circumstances absolve you from your promise, Sandy. Your life is of more value to you than any other thing. If you will explain where you got the gold, and the silk purse that contained it, which is said to be Mrs. Ochiltree's, you will be back home before tonight."

Old Mr. Delamere's faculties, which had been waning somewhat in sympathy with his health, were stirred to unusual acuteness by his servant's danger. He was watching Sandy with all the awakened instincts of the trial lawyer. He could see clearly enough that, in beginning to account for the possession of the gold, Sandy had started off with his explanation in all sincerity. At the mention of the silk purse, however, his face had blanched to an ashen gray, and the words had frozen upon his lips.

A less discerning observer might have taken these things as signs of guilt, but not so Mr. Delamere.

"Well, Sandy," said his master encouragingly, "go on. You got the gold from"—

Sandy remained silent. He had had a great shock, and had taken a great resolution.

"Mars John," he asked dreamily, "you don' b'lieve dat I done dis thing?"

"Certainly not, Sandy, else why should I be here?"

"An' nothin' would n' make you b'lieve it, suh?"

"No, Sandy,—I could not believe it of you. I've known you too long and too well."

"An' you would n' b'lieve it, not even ef I would n' say one wo'd mo' about it?"

"No, Sandy, I believe you no more capable of this crime than I would be,—or my grandson, Tom. I wish Tom were here, that he might help me overcome your stubbornness; but you'll not be so foolish, so absurdly foolish, Sandy, as to keep silent and risk your life merely to shield some one else, when by speaking you might clear up this mystery and be restored at once to liberty. Just tell me where you got the gold," added the old gentleman persuasively. "Come, now, Sandy, that's a good fellow!"

"Mars John," asked Sandy softly, "w'en my daddy, 'way back yander befo' de wah, wuz about ter be sol' away f'm his wife an' child'en you bought him an' dem, an' kep' us all on yo' place tergether, did n't you, suh?"

"Yes, Sandy, and he was a faithful servant, and proved worthy of all I did for him."

"An w'en he had wo'ked fer you ten years, suh, you sot 'im free?"

"Yes, Sandy, he had earned his freedom."

"An' w'en de wah broke out, an' my folks wuz scattered, an' I did n' have nothin' ter do ner nowhar ter go, you kep' me on yo' place, and tuck me ter wait on you, suh, did n't you?"

"Yes, Sandy, and you have been a good servant and a good friend; but tell me now about this gold, and I'll go and get you out of this, right away, for I need you, Sandy, and you'll not be of any use to me shut up here!"

"Jes' hol' on a minute befo' you go, Mars John; fer ef dem people outside should git holt er me befo' you *does* git me out er here, I may never see you no mo', suh, in dis worl'. W'en Mars Billy McLean shot me by mistake, w'ile we wuz out huntin' dat day, who wuz it boun' up my woun's an' kep' me from bleedin' ter def, an' kyar'ed me two miles on his own shoulders ter a doctuh?"

"Yes, Sandy, and when black Sally ran away with your young mistress and Tom, when Tom was a baby, who stopped the runaway, and saved their lives at the risk of his own?"

"Dat wa'n't nothin', suh; anybody could 'a' done dat, w'at wuz strong ernuff an' swif' ernuff. You is be'n good ter me, suh, all dese years, an' I've tried ter do my duty by you, suh, an' by Mistuh Tom, who wuz yo' own gran'son, an' de las' one er de fam'ly."

"Yes, you have, Sandy, and when I am gone, which will

not be very long, Tom will take care of you, and see that you never want. But we are wasting valuable time, Sandy, in these old reminiscences. Let us get back to the present. Tell me about the gold, now, so that I may at once look after your safety. It may not even be necessary for you to remain here all night."

"Jes' one wo'd mo', Mars John, befo' you go! I know you're gwine ter do de bes' you kin fer me, an' I'm sorry I can't he'p you no mo' wid it; but ef dere should be any accident, er ef you *can't* git me out er here, don' bother yo' min' 'bout it no mo', suh, an' don' git yo'se'f ixcited, fer you know de doctuh says, suh, dat you can't stan' ixcitement; but jes' leave me in de han's er de Lawd, suh,—He'll look after me, here er hereafter. I know I've fell f'm grace mo'd'n once, but I've done made my peace wid Him in dis here jail-house, suh, an' I ain't 'feared ter die—ef I haf ter. I ain' got no wife ner child'n ter mo'n fer me, an' I'll die knowin' dat I've done my duty ter dem dat hi'ed me, an' trusted me, an' had claims on me. Fer I wuz raise' by a Delamere, suh, an' all de ole Delameres wuz gent'emen, an' deir principles spread ter de niggers 'round 'em, suh; an' ef I has ter die fer some-thin' I did n' do,—I kin die, suh, like a gent'eman! But ez fer dat gol', suh, I ain' gwine ter say one wo'd mo' 'bout it ter nobody in dis worl'!"

Nothing could shake Sandy's determination. Mr. Dela-mere argued, expostulated, but all in vain. Sandy would not speak.

More and more confident of some mystery, which would come out in time, if properly investigated, Mr. Delamere, strangely beset by a vague sense of discomfort over and be-yond that occasioned by his servant's danger, hurried away upon his errand of mercy. He felt less confident of the out-come than when he had entered the jail, but was quite as much resolved that no effort should be spared to secure pro-tection for Sandy until there had been full opportunity for the truth to become known.

"Take good care of your prisoner, sheriff," he said sternly, as he was conducted to the door. "He will not be long in your custody, and I shall see that you are held strictly accountable for his safety."

"I'll do what I can, sir," replied the sheriff in an even tone and seemingly not greatly impressed by this warning. "If the prisoner is taken from me, it will be because the force that comes for him is too strong for resistance."

"There should be no force too strong for an honest man in your position to resist,—whether successfully or not is beyond the question. The officer who is intimidated by threats, or by his own fears, is recreant to his duty, and no better than the mob which threatens him. But you will have no such test, Mr. Wemyss! I shall see to it myself that there is no violence!"

CHAPTER XXV

The Honor of a Family

Mr. Delamere's coachman, who, in accordance with instructions left by Miller, had brought the carriage around to the jail and was waiting anxiously at the nearest corner, drove up with some trepidation as he saw his master emerge from the prison. The old gentleman entered the carriage and gave the order to be driven to the office of the Morning Chronicle. According to Jerry, the porter, whom he encountered at the door, Carteret was in his office, and Mr. Delamere, with the aid of his servant, climbed the stairs painfully and found the editor as his desk.

"Carteret," exclaimed Mr. Delamere, "what is all this talk about lynching my man for murder and robbery and criminal assault? It's perfectly absurd! The man was raised by me; he has lived in my house forty years. He has been honest, faithful, and trustworthy. He would no more be capable of this crime than you would, or my grandson Tom. Sandy has too much respect for the family to do anything that would reflect disgrace upon it."

"My dear Mr. Delamere," asked Carteret, with an indulgent smile, "how could a negro possibly reflect discredit upon a white family? I should really like to know."

"How, sir? A white family raised him. Like all the negroes, he has been clay in the hands of the white people. They are what we have made them, or permitted them to become."

"We are not God, Mr. Delamere! We do not claim to have created these—masterpieces."

"No; but we thought to overrule God's laws, and we enslaved these people for our greed, and sought to escape the manstealer's curse by laying to our souls the flattering unction that we are making of barbarous negroes civilized and Christian men. If we did not, if instead of making them Christians we have made some of them brutes, we have only ourselves to blame, and if these prey upon society, it is our just punishment! But my negroes, Carteret, were well raised and well behaved. This man is innocent of this offense, I solemnly affirm, and I want your aid to secure his safety until a fair trial can be had."

"On your bare word, sir?" asked Carteret, not at all moved by this outburst.

Old Mr. Delamere trembled with anger, and his withered cheek flushed darkly, but he restrained his feelings, and answered with an attempt at calmness:—

"Time was, sir, when the word of a Delamere was held as good as his bond, and those who questioned it were forced to maintain their skepticism upon the field of honor. Time was, sir, when the law was enforced in this state in a manner to command the respect of the world! Our lawyers, our judges, our courts, were a credit to humanity and civilization. I fear I have outlasted my epoch,—I have lived to hear of white men, the most favored of races, the heirs of civilization, the conservators of liberty, howling like red Indians around a human being slowly roasting at the stake."

"My dear sir," said Carteret soothingly, "you should undeceive yourself. This man is no longer your property. The negroes are no longer under our control, and with their emancipation ceased our responsibility. Their insolence and disregard for law have reached a point where they must be sternly rebuked."

"The law," retorted Mr. Delamere, "furnishes a sufficient penalty for any crime, however heinous, and our code is by no means lenient. To my old-fashioned notions, death would seem an adequate punishment for any crime, and torture has been abolished in civilized countries for a hundred years. It would be better to let a crime go entirely unpunished, than to use it as a pretext for turning the whole white population into a mob of primitive savages, dancing in hellish glee around the mangled body of a man who has never been tried for a crime. All this, however, is apart from my errand, which is to secure your assistance in heading off this mob until Sandy can have a fair hearing and an opportunity to prove his innocence."

"How can I do that, Mr. Delamere?"

"You are editor of the Morning Chronicle. The Chronicle is the leading newspaper of the city. This morning's issue practically suggested the mob; the same means will stop it. I will pay the expense of an extra edition, calling off the mob, on the ground that newly discovered evidence has shown the prisoner's innocence."

"But where is the evidence?" asked Carteret.

Again Mr. Delamere flushed and trembled. "My evidence, sir! I say the negro was morally incapable of the crime. A man of forty-five does not change his nature over-night. He is no more capable of a disgraceful deed than my grandson would be!"

Carteret smiled sadly.

"I am sorry, Mr. Delamere," he said, "that you should permit yourself to be so exercised about a worthless scoundrel who has forfeited his right to live. The proof against him is overwhelming. As to his capability of crime, we will apply your own test. You have been kept in the dark too long, Mr. Delamere,—indeed, we all have,—about others as well as this negro. Listen, sir: last night, at the Clarendon Club, Tom Delamere was caught cheating outrageously at cards. He had been suspected for some time; a trap was laid for him, and he fell into it. Out of regard for you and for my family, he has been permitted to resign quietly, with the understanding that he first pay off his debts, which are considerable."

Mr. Delamere's face, which had taken on some color in the excitement of the interview, had gradually paled to a chalky white while Carteret was speaking. His head sunk forward; already an old man, he seemed to have aged ten years in but little more than as many seconds.

"Can this be true?" he demanded in a hoarse whisper. "Is it—entirely authentic?"

"True as gospel; true as it is that Mrs. Ochiltree has been murdered, and that this negro killed her. Ellis was at the club a few minutes after the affair happened, and learned the facts from one of the participants. Tom made no attempt at denial. We have kept the matter out of the other papers, and I would have spared your feelings,—I surely would not wish to wound them,—but the temptation proved too strong for me, and it seemed the only way to convince you: it was your own test. If a gentleman of a distinguished name and an honorably ancestry, with all the restraining forces of social position surrounding him, to hold him in check, can stoop to dishonor, what is the improbability of an illiterate negro's being at least *capable* of crime?"

"Enough, sir," said the old gentleman. "You have proved enough. My grandson may be a scoundrel,—I can see, in the light of this revelation, how he might be; and he seems not to have denied it. I maintain, nevertheless, that my man Sandy is innocent of the charge against him. He *has* denied it, and it has not been proved. Carteret, I owe that negro my life; he, and his father before him, have served me and mine faithfully and well. I cannot see him killed like a dog, without judge or jury,—no, not even if he were guilty, which I do not believe!"

Carteret felt a twinge of remorse for the pain he had inflicted upon the fine old man, this ideal gentleman of the ideal past,—the past which he himself so much admired and regretted. He would like to spare his old friend any further agitation; he was in a state of health where too great excitement might prove fatal. But how could he? The negro was guilty, and sure to die sooner or later. He had not meant to interfere, and his intervention might be fruitless.

"Mr. Delamere," he said gently, "there is but one way to gain time. You say the negro is innocent. Appearances are against him. The only way to clear him is to produce the real criminal, or prove an alibi. If you, or some other white man of equal standing, could swear that the negro was in your presence last night at any hour when this crime could have taken place, it might be barely possible to prevent the lynching for the present; and when he is tried, which will probably be not later than next week, he will have every opportunity to defend himself, with you to see that he gets no less than justice. I think it can be managed, though there is still a doubt. I will do my best, for your sake, Mr. Delamere,—solely for your sake, be it understood, and not for that of the negro, in whom you are entirely deceived."

"I shall not examine your motives, Carteret," replied the other, "if you can bring about what I desire."

"Whatever is done," added Carteret, "must be done quickly. It is now four o'clock; no one can answer for what may happen after seven. If he can prove an alibi, there may yet be time to save him. White men might lynch a negro on suspicion; they would not kill a man who was proven, by the word of white men, to be entirely innocent."

"I do not know," returned Mr. Delamere, shaking his head sadly. "After what you have told me, it is no longer safe to assume what white men will or will not do;—what I have learned here has shaken my faith in humanity. I am going away, but shall return in a short time. Shall I find you here?"

"I will await your return," said Carteret.

He watched Mr. Delamere pityingly as the old man moved away on the arm of the coachman waiting in the hall. He did not believe that Mr. Delamere could prove an alibi for his servant, and without some positive proof the negro would surely die,—as he well deserved to die.

CHAPTER XXVI

The Discomfort of Ellis

Mr. Ellis was vaguely uncomfortable. In the first excitement following the discovery of the crime, he had given his bit of evidence, and had shared the universal indignation against the murderer. When public feeling took definite shape in the intention to lynch the prisoner, Ellis felt a sudden sense of responsibility growing upon himself. When he learned, an hour later, that it was proposed to burn the negro, his part in the affair assumed a still graver aspect; for his had been the final word to fix the prisoner's guilt.

Ellis did not believe in lynch law. He had argued against it, more than once, in private conversation, and had written several editorials against the practice, while in charge of the Morning Chronicle during Major Carteret's absence. A young man, however, and merely representing another, he had not set up as a reformer, taking rather the view that this summary method of punishing crime, with all its possibilities of error, to say nothing of the resulting disrespect of the law and contempt for the time-honored methods of establishing guilt, was a mere temporary symptom of the unrest caused by the unsettled relations of the two races at the South. There had never before been any special need for any vigorous opposition to lynch law, so far as the community was concerned, for there had not been a lynching in Wellington since Ellis had come there, eight years before, from a smaller town, to seek a place for himself in the world of action. Twenty years before, indeed, there had been wild doings, during the brief Ku-Klux outbreak, but that was before Ellis's time,—or at least when he was but a child. He had come of a Quaker family,—the modified Quakers of the South,—and while sharing in a general way the Southern prejudice against the negro, his prejudices had been tempered by the peaceful tenets of his father's sect. His father had been a Whig, and a non-slaveholder; and while he had gone with the South in the civil war so far as a man of peace could go, he had not done so for love of slavery.

As the day wore on, Ellis's personal responsibility for the intended *auto-da-fé* bore more heavily upon him. Suppose he had been wrong? He had seen the accused negro; he had recognized him by his clothes, his whiskers, his spectacles, and his walk; but he had also seen another man, who resembled Sandy so closely that but for the difference in their clothes, he was forced to acknowledge, he could not have told them apart. Had he not seen the first man, he would have sworn with even greater confidence that the second was Sandy. There had been, he recalled, about one of the men— he had not been then nor was he now able to tell which— something vaguely familiar, and yet seemingly discordant to whichever of the two it was, or, as it seemed to him now, to any man of that race. His mind reverted to the place where he had last seen Sandy, and then a sudden wave of illumi- nation swept over him, and filled him with a thrill of horror. The cakewalk,—the dancing,—the speech,—they were not Sandy's at all, nor any negro's! It was a white man who had stood in the light of the street lamp, so that the casual passer- by might see and recognize in him old Mr. Delamere's ser- vant. The scheme was a dastardly one, and worthy of a heart that was something worse than weak and vicious.

Ellis resolved that the negro should not, if he could pre- vent it, die for another's crime; but what proof had he him- self to offer in support of his theory? Then again, if he denounced Tom Delamere as the murderer, it would involve, in all probability, the destruction of his own hopes with re- gard to Clara. Of course she could not marry Delamere after

the disclosure,—the disgraceful episode at the club would
have been enough to make that reasonably certain; it had
put a nail in Delamere's coffin, but this crime had driven it
in to the head and clinched it. On the other hand, would
Miss Pemberton ever speak again to the man who had been
the instrument of bringing disgrace upon the family? Spies,
detectives, police officers, may be useful citizens, but they are
rarely pleasant company for other people. We fee the exe-
cutioner, but we do not touch his bloody hand. We might
feel a certain tragic admiration for Brutus condemning his
sons to death, but we would scarcely invite Brutus to dinner
after the event. It would harrow our feelings too much.

Perhaps, thought Ellis, there might be a way out of the
dilemma. It might be possible to save this innocent negro
without, for the time being, involving Delamere. He believed that murder will out, but it need not be through his
initiative. He determined to go to the jail and interview the
prisoner, who might give such an account of himself as would
establish his innocence beyond a doubt. If so, Ellis would
exert himself to stem the tide of popular fury. If, as a last
resort, he could save Sandy only by denouncing Delamere,
he would do his duty, let it cost him what it might.

The gravity of this errand was not lessened by what he
saw and heard on the way to the jail. The anger of the people
was at a white heat. A white woman had been assaulted and
murdered by a brutal negro. Neither advanced age, nor high
social standing, had been able to protect her from the ferocity of a black savage. Her sex, which should have been her
shield and buckler, had made her an easy mark for the vil-
lainy of a black brute. To take the time to try him would be
a criminal waste of public money. To hang him would be
too slight a punishment for so dastardly a crime. An example
must be made.

Already the preparations were under way for the impending execution. A T-rail from the railroad yard had been procured, and men were burying it in the square before the jail.
Others were bringing chains, and a load of pine wood was

piled in convenient proximity. Some enterprising individual had begun the erection of seats from which, for a pecuniary consideration, the spectacle might be the more easily and comfortably viewed.

Ellis was stopped once or twice by persons of his acquaintance. From one he learned that the railroads would run excursions from the neighboring towns in order to bring spectators to the scene; from another that the burning was to take place early in the evening, so that the children might not be kept up beyond their usual bedtime. In one group that he passed he heard several young men discussing the question of which portions of the negro's body they would prefer for souvenirs. Ellis shuddered and hastened forward. Whatever was to be done must be done quickly, or it would be too late. He saw that already it would require a strong case in favor of the accused to overcome the popular verdict.

Going up the steps of the jail, he met Mr. Delamere, who was just coming out, after a fruitless interview with Sandy.

"Mr. Ellis," said the old gentleman, who seemed greatly agitated, "this is monstrous!"

"It is indeed, sir!" returned the younger man. "I mean to stop it if I can. The negro did not kill Mrs. Ochiltree."

Mr. Delamere looked at Ellis keenly, and, as Ellis recalled afterwards, there was death in his eyes. Unable to draw a syllable from Sandy, he had found his servant's silence more eloquent than words. Ellis felt a presentiment that this affair, however it might terminate, would be fatal to this fine old man, whom the city could ill spare, in spite of his age and infirmities.

"Mr. Ellis," asked Mr. Delamere, in a voice which trembled with ill-suppressed emotion, "do you know who killed her?"

Ellis felt a surging pity for his old friend; but every step that he had taken toward the jail had confirmed and strengthened his own resolution that this contemplated crime, which he dimly felt to be far more atrocious than that of which Sandy was accused, in that it involved a whole community rather than one vicious man, should be stopped at any cost. Deplorable enough had the negro been guilty, it became, in view of his certain innocence, an unspeakable horror, which for all time would cover the city with infamy.

"Mr. Delamere," he replied, looking the elder man squarely in the eyes, "I think I do,—and I am very sorry."

"And who was it, Mr. Ellis?"

He put the question hopelessly, as though the answer were a foregone conclusion.

"I do not wish to say at present," replied Ellis, with a remorseful pang, "unless it becomes absolutely necessary, to save the negro's life. Accusations are dangerous,—as this case proves,—unless the proof be certain."

For a moment it seemed as though Mr. Delamere would collapse upon the spot. Rallying almost instantly, however, he took the arm which Ellis involuntarily offered, and said with an effort:—

"Mr Ellis, you are a gentleman whom it is an honor to know. If you have time, I wish you would go with me to my house,—I can hardly trust myself alone,—and thence to the Chronicle office. This thing shall be stopped, and you will help me stop it."

It required but a few minutes to cover the half mile that lay between the prison and Mr. Delamere's residence.

CHAPTER XXVII

The Vagaries
of the Higher Law

Mr. Delamere went immediately to his grandson's room, which he entered alone, closing and locking the door behind him. He had requested Ellis to wait in the carriage.

The bed had been made, and the room was apparently in perfect order. There was a bureau in the room, through which Mr. Delamere proceeded to look thoroughly. Finding one of the drawers locked, he tried it with a key of his own, and being unable to unlock it, took a poker from beside the stove and broke it ruthlessly open.

The contents served to confirm what he had heard concerning his grandson's character. Thrown together in disorderly confusion were bottles of wine and whiskey; soiled packs of cards; a dice-box with dice; a box of poker chips, several revolvers, and a number of photographs and paper-covered books at which the old gentleman merely glanced to ascertain their nature.

So far, while his suspicion had been strengthened, he had found nothing to confirm it. He searched the room more carefully, and found, in the wood-box by the small heating-stove which stood in the room, a torn and crumpled bit of paper. Stooping to pick this up, his eye caught a gleam of something yellow beneath the bureau, which lay directly in his line of vision.

First he smoothed out the paper. It was apparently the

True Tom discovered by Mr D

lower half of a label, or part of the cover of a small box, torn diagonally from corner to corner. From the business card at the bottom, which gave the name of a firm of manufacturers of theatrical supplies in a Northern city, and from the letters remaining upon the upper and narrower half, the bit of paper had plainly formed part of the wrapper of a package of burnt cork.

Closing his fingers spasmodically over this damning piece of evidence, Mr. Delamere knelt painfully, and with the aid of his cane drew out from under the bureau the yellow object which had attracted his attention. It was a five-dollar gold piece of a date back toward the beginning of the century.

To make assurance doubly sure, Mr. Delamere summoned the cook from the kitchen in the back yard. In answer to her master's questions, Sally averred that Mr. Tom had got up very early, had knocked at her window,—she slept in a room off the kitchen in the yard,—and had told her that she need not bother about breakfast for him, as he had had a cold bite from the pantry; that he was going hunting and fishing, and would be gone all day. According to Sally, Mr. Tom had come in about ten o'clock the night before. He had forgotten his night-key, Sandy was out, and she had admitted him with her own key. He had said that he was very tired and was going immediately to bed.

Mr. Delamere seemed perplexed; the crime had been committed later in the evening than ten o'clock. The cook cleared up the mystery.

"I reckon he must 'a' be'n dead ti'ed, suh, fer I went back ter his room fifteen or twenty minutes later after he come in fer ter fin' out w'at he wanted fer breakfus'; an' I knock' two or three times, rale ha'd, an' Mistuh Tom did n' wake up no mo' d'n de dead. He sho'ly had a good sleep, er he'd never 'a' got up so ea'ly."

"Thank you, Sally," said Mr. Delamere, when the woman had finished, "that will do."

"Will you be home ter suppah, suh?" asked the cook.

"Yes."

It was a matter of the supremest indifference to Mr. Delamere whether he should ever eat again, but he would not betray his feelings to a servant. In a few minutes he was driving rapidly with Ellis toward the office of the Morning Chronicle. Ellis could see that Mr. Delamere had discovered something of tragic import. Neither spoke. Ellis gave all his attention to the horses, and Mr. Delamere remained wrapped in his own sombre reflections.

When they reached the office, they were informed by Jerry that Major Carteret was engaged with General Belmont and Captain McBane. Mr. Delamere knocked peremptorily at the door of the inner office, which was opened by Carteret in person.

"Oh, it is you, Mr. Delamere."

"Carteret," exclaimed Mr. Delamere, "I must speak to you immediately, and alone."

"Excuse me a moment, gentlemen," said Carteret, turning to those within the room. "I'll be back in a moment—don't go away."

Ellis had left the room, closing the door behind him. Mr. Delamere and Carteret were quite alone.

"Carteret," declared the old gentleman, "this murder must not take place."

" 'Murder' is a hard word," replied the editor, frowning slightly.

"It is the right word," rejoined Mr. Delamere, decidedly. "It would be a foul and most unnatural murder, for Sandy did not kill Mrs. Ochiltree."

Carteret with difficulty restrained a smile of pity. His old friend was very much excited, as the tremor in his voice gave proof. The criminal was his trusted servant, who had proved unworthy of confidence. No one could question Mr. Delamere's motives; but he was old, his judgment was no longer to be relied upon. It was a great pity that he should so excite and overstrain himself about a worthless negro, who had forfeited his life for a dastardly crime. Mr. Delamere had had two paralytic strokes, and a third might prove fatal. He must be dealt with gently.

"Mr. Delamere," he said, with patient tolerance, "I think you are deceived. There is but one sure way to stop this execution. If your servant is innocent, you must produce the real criminal. If the negro, with such overwhelming proofs against him, is not guilty, who is?"

"I will tell you who is," replied Mr. Delamere. "The murderer is,"—the words came with a note of anguish, as though torn from his very heart,—"the murderer is Tom Delamere, my own grandson!"

"Impossible, sir!" exclaimed Carteret, starting back involuntarily. "That could not be! The man was seen leaving the house, and he was black!"

"All cats are gray in the dark, Carteret; and, moreover, nothing is easier than for a white man to black his face. God alone knows how many crimes have been done in this guise! Tom Delamere, to get the money to pay his gambling debts, committed this foul murder, and then tried to fasten it upon as honest and faithful a soul as ever trod the earth."

Carteret, though at first overwhelmed by this announcement, perceived with quick intuition that it might easily be true. It was but a step from fraud to crime, and in Delamere's need of money there lay a palpable motive for robbery,—the murder may have been an afterthought. Delamere knew as much about the cedar chest as the negro could have known, and more.

But a white man must not be condemned without proof positive.

"What foundation is there, sir," he asked, "for this astounding charge?"

Mr. Delamere related all that had taken place since he had left Belleview a couple of hours before, and as he proceeded, step by step, every word carried a conviction to Carteret. Tom Delamere's skill as a mimic and a negro impersonator was well known; he had himself laughed at more than one of his performances. There had been a powerful motive, and Mr. Delamere's discoveries had made clear the means. Tom's unusual departure, before breakfast, on a fishing expedition was a suspicious circumstance. There was a certain devilish ingenuity about the affair which he would hardly have expected of Tom Delamere, but for which the reason was clear enough. One might have thought that Tom would have been satisfied with merely blacking his face, and leaving to chance the identification of the negro who might be apprehended. He would hardly have implicated, out of pure malignity, his grandfather's old servant, who had been his own care-taker for many years. Here, however, Carteret could see where Tom's own desperate position operated to furnish a probable motive for the crime. The surest way to head off suspicion from himself was to direct it strongly toward some particular person, and this he had been able to do conclusively by his access to Sandy's clothes, his skill in making up to resemble him, and by the episode of the silk purse. By placing himself beyond reach during the next day, he would not be called upon to corroborate or deny any inculpating statements which Sandy might make, and in the very probable case that the crime should be summarily avenged, any such statements on Sandy's part would be regarded as mere desperate subterfuges of the murderer to save his own life. It was a bad affair.

"The case seems clear," said Carteret reluctantly but conclusively. "And now, what shall we do about it?"

"I want you to print the handbill," said Mr. Delamere, "and circulate it through the town, stating that Sandy Campbell is innocent and Tom Delamere guilty of this crime. If this is not done, I will go myself and declare it to all who will listen, and I will publicly disown the villain who is no more grandson of mine. There is no deeper sink of iniquity into which he could fall."

Carteret's thoughts were chasing one another tumultuously. There could be no doubt that the negro was innocent, from the present aspect of affairs, and he must not be lynched; but in what sort of position would the white people be placed, if Mr. Delamere carried out his Spartan purpose of making the true facts known? The white people of the city had raised the issue of their own superior morality, and had themselves made this crime a race question. The success of the impending "revolution," for which he and his *confrères* had labored so long, depended in large measure upon the maintenance of their race prestige, which would be injured in the eyes of the world by such a fiasco. While they might yet win by sheer force, their cause would suffer in the court of morals, where they might stand convicted as pirates, instead of being applauded as patriots. Even the negroes would have the laugh on them,—the people whom they hoped to make approve and justify their own despoilment. To be laughed at by the negroes was a calamity only less terrible than failure or death.

Such an outcome of an event which had already been heralded to the four corners of the earth would throw a cloud of suspicion upon the stories of outrage which had gone up from the South for so many years, and had done so much to win the sympathy of the North for the white South and to alienate it from the colored people. The reputation of the race was threatened. They must not lynch the negro, and yet, for the credit of the town, its aristocracy, and the race, the truth of this ghastly story must not see the light,—at least not yet.

"Mr. Delamere," he exclaimed, "I am shocked and humiliated. The negro must be saved, of course, but—consider the family honor."

"Tom is no longer a member of my family. I disown him. He has covered the family name—my name, sir—with infamy. We have no longer a family honor. I wish never to hear his name spoken again!"

For several minutes Carteret argued with his old friend. Then he went into the other room and consulted with General Belmont.

As a result of these conferences, and of certain urgent

messages sent out, within half an hour thirty or forty of the leading citizens of Wellington were gathered in the Morning Chronicle office. Several other curious persons, observing that there was something in the wind, and supposing correctly that it referred to the projected event of the evening, crowded in with those who had been invited.

Carteret was in another room, still arguing with Mr. Delamere. "It's a mere formality, sir," he was saying suavely, "accompanied by a mental reservation. We know the facts; but this must be done to justify us, in the eyes of the mob, in calling them off before they accomplish their purpose."

"Carteret," said the old man, in a voice eloquent of the struggle through which he had passed, "I would not perjure myself to prolong my own miserable existence another day, but God will forgive a sin committed to save another's life. Upon your head be it, Carteret, and not on mine!"

"Gentlemen," said Carteret, entering with Mr. Delamere the room where the men were gathered, and raising his hand for silence, "the people of Wellington were on the point of wreaking vengeance upon a negro who was supposed to have been guilty of a terrible crime. The white men of this city, impelled by the highest and holiest sentiments, were about to take steps to defend their hearthstones and maintain the purity and ascendency of their race. Your purpose sprung from hearts wounded in their tenderest susceptibilities."

" 'Rah, 'rah!" shouted a tipsy sailor, who had edged in with the crowd.

"But this same sense of justice," continued Carteret oratorically, "which would lead you to visit swift and terrible punishment upon the guilty, would not permit you to slay an innocent man. Even a negro, as long as he behaves himself and keeps in his place, is entitled to the protection of the law. We may be stern and unbending in the punishment of crime, as befits our masterful race, but we hold the scales of justice with even and impartial hand."

" 'Rah f' 'mpa'tial han'!" cried the tipsy sailor, who was immediately ejected with slight ceremony.

lie to preserve & control Delamere

Correption to the last

"We have discovered, beyond a doubt, that the negro Sandy Campbell, now in custody, did not commit this robbery and murder, but that it was perpetrated by some unknown man, who has fled from the city. Our venerable and distinguished fellow townsman, Mr. Delamere, in whose employment this Campbell has been for many years, will vouch for his character, and states, furthermore, that Campbell was with him all last night, covering any hour at which this crime could have been committed."

"If Mr. Delamere will swear to that," said some one in the crowd, "the negro should not be lynched."

There were murmurs of dissent. The preparations had all been made. There would be great disappointment if the lynching did not occur.

"Let Mr. Delamere swear, if he wants to save the nigger," came again from the crowd.

"Certainly," assented Carteret. "Mr. Delamere can have no possible objection to taking the oath. Is there a notary public present, or a justice of the peace?"

A man stepped forward. "I am a justice of the peace," he announced.

"Very well, Mr. Smith," said Carteret, recognizing the speaker. "With your permission, I will formulate the oath, and Mr. Delamere may repeat it after me, if he will. I solemnly swear,"—

"I solemnly swear,"—

Mr. Delamere's voice might have come from the tomb, so hollow and unnatural did it sound.

"So help me God,"—

"So help me God,"—

"That the negro Sandy Campbell, now in jail on the charge of murder, robbery, and assault, was in my presence last night between the hours of eight and two o'clock."

Mr. Delamere repeated this statement in a firm voice; but to Ellis, who was in the secret, his words fell upon the ear like clods dropping upon the coffin in an open grave.

"I wish to add," said General Belmont, stepping forward,

"that it is not our intention to interfere, by anything which may be done at this meeting, with the orderly process of the law, or to advise the prisoner's immediate release. The prisoner will remain in custody, Mr. Delamere, Major Carteret, and I guaranteeing that he will be proved entirely innocent at the preliminary hearing to-morrow morning."

Several of those present looked relieved; others were plainly disappointed; but when the meeting ended, the news went out that the lynching had been given up. Carteret immediately wrote and had struck off a handbill giving a brief statement of the proceedings, and sent out a dozen boys to distribute copies among the people in the streets. That no precaution might be omitted, a call was issued to the Wellington Grays, the crack independent military company of the city, who in an incredibly short time were on guard at the jail.

Thus a slight change in the point of view had demonstrated the entire ability of the leading citizens to maintain the dignified and orderly processes of the law whenever they saw fit to do so.

The night passed without disorder, beyond the somewhat rough handling of two or three careless negroes that came in the way of small parties of the disappointed who had sought alcoholic consolation.

At ten o'clock the next morning, a preliminary hearing of the charge against Campbell was had before a magistrate. Mr. Delamere, perceptibly older and more wizened than he had seemed the day before, and leaning heavily on the arm of a servant, repeated his statement of the evening before. Only one or two witnesses were called, among whom was Mr. Ellis, who swore positively that in his opinion the prisoner was not the man whom he had seen and at first supposed to be Campbell. The most sensational piece of testimony was that of Dr. Price, who had examined the body, and who swore that the wound in the head was not necessarily fatal, and might have been due to a fall,—that she had more than likely died of shock attendant upon the robbery, she being of advanced age and feeble health. There was no evidence, he said, of any other personal violence.

Sandy was not even bound over to the grand jury, but was discharged upon the ground that there was not sufficient evidence upon which to hold him. Upon his release he received the congratulations of many present, some of whom would cheerfully have done him to death a few hours before. With the childish fickleness of a mob, they now experienced a satisfaction almost as great as, though less exciting than, that attendant upon taking life. We speak of the mysteries of inanimate nature. The workings of the human heart are the profoundest mystery of the universe. One moment they make us despair our kind, and the next we see in them the reflection of the divine image. Sandy, having thus escaped from the Mr. Hyde of the mob, now received the benediction of its Dr. Jekyll. Being no cynical philosopher, and realizing how nearly the jaws of death had closed upon him, he was profoundly grateful for his escape, and felt not the slightest desire to investigate or criticise any man's motives.

With the testimony of Dr. Price, the worst feature of the affair came to an end. The murder eliminated or rendered doubtful, the crime became a mere vulgar robbery, the extent of which no one could estimate, since no living soul knew how much money Mrs. Ochiltree had had in the cedar chest. The absurdity of the remaining charge became more fully apparent in the light of the reaction from the excitement of the day before.

Nothing further was ever done about the case; but though the crime went unpunished, it carried evil in its train. As we have seen, the charge against Campbell had been made against the whole colored race. All over the United States the Associated Press had flashed the report of another dastardly outrage by a burly black brute,—all black brutes it seems are burly,—and of the impending lynching with its prospective horrors. This news, being highly sensational in its character, had been displayed in large black type on the front pages of the daily papers. The dispatch that followed, to the effect that the accused had been found innocent and the lynching frustrated, received slight attention, if any, in a fine-print paragraph on an inside page. The facts of the case never came out at all. The family honor of the Delameres was preserved, and the prestige of the white race in Wellington was not seriously impaired.

Upon leaving the preliminary hearing, old Mr. Delamere had requested General Belmont to call at his house during the day upon professional business. This the general did in the course of the afternoon.

"Belmont," said Mr. Delamere, "I wish to make my will. I should have drawn it with my own hand; but you know my motives, and can testify to my soundness of mind and memory."

He thereupon dictated a will, by the terms of which he left to his servant, Sandy Campbell, three thousand dollars, as a mark of the testator's appreciation of services rendered and sufferings endured by Sandy on behalf of his master. After some minor dispositions, the whole remainder of the estate was devised to Dr. William Miller, in trust for the uses of his hospital and training-school for nurses, on condition that the institution be incorporated and placed under the management of competent trustees. Tom Delamere was not mentioned in the will.

"There, Belmont," he said, "that load is off my mind. Now, if you will call in some witnesses,—most of my people can write,—I shall feel entirely at ease."

The will was signed by Mr. Delamere, and witnessed by Jeff and Billy, two servants in the house, neither of whom received any information as to its contents, beyond the statement that they were witnessing their master's will.

"I wish to leave that with you for safe keeping, Belmont," said Mr. Delamere, after the witnesses had retired. "Lock it up in your safe until I die, which will not be very long, since I have no further desire to live."

An hour later Mr. Delamere suffered a third paralytic stroke, from which he died two days afterwards, without having in the meantime recovered the power of speech.

The will was never produced. The servants stated, and General Belmont admitted, that Mr. Delamere had made a will a few days before his death; but since it was not discoverable, it seemed probable that the testator had destroyed it. This was all the more likely, the general was inclined to think, because the will had been of a most unusual character. What the contents of the will were, he of course did not state, it having been made under the seal of professional secrecy.

This suppression was justified by the usual race argument: Miller's hospital was already well established, and, like most negro institutions, could no doubt rely upon Northern philanthropy for any further support it might need. Mr. Delamere's property belonged of right to the white race, and by the higher law should remain in the possession of white people. Loyalty to one's race was a more sacred principle than deference to a weak old man's whims.

Having reached this conclusion, General Belmont's first impulse was to destroy the will; on second thoughts he locked it carefully away in his safe. He would hold it awhile. It might some time be advisable to talk the matter over with young Delamere, who was of a fickle disposition and might wish to change his legal adviser.

CHAPTER XXVIII

In Season and Out

Wellington soon resumed its wonted calm, and in a few weeks the intended lynching was only a memory. The robbery and assault, however, still remained a mystery to all but a chosen few. The affair had been dropped as absolutely as though it had never occurred. No colored man ever learned the reasons of this sudden change of front, and Sandy Campbell's loyalty to his old employer's memory kept him silent. Tom Delamere did not offer to retain Sandy in his service, though he presented him with most of the old gentleman's wardrobe. It is only justice to Tom to state that up to this time he had not been informed of the contents of his grandfather's latest will. Major Carteret gave Sandy employment as butler, thus making a sort of vicarious atonement, on the part of the white race, of which the major felt himself in a way the embodiment, for the risk to which Sandy had been subjected.

Shortly after these events Sandy was restored to the bosom of the church, and, enfolded by its sheltering arms, was no longer tempted to stray from the path of rectitude, but became even a more rigid Methodist than before his recent troubles.

Tom Delamere did not call upon Clara again in the character of a lover. Of course they could not help meeting, from time to time, but he never dared presume upon their former relations. Indeed, the social atmosphere of Wellington remained so frigid toward Delamere that he left town, and did not return for several months.

Ellis was aware that Delamere had been thrown over, but a certain delicacy restrained him from following up immediately the advantage which the absence of his former rival gave him. It seemed to him, with the quixotry of a clean, pure mind, that Clara would pass through a period of mourning for her lost illusion, and that it would be indelicate, for the time being, to approach her with a lover's attentions. The work of the office had been unusually heavy of late. The major, deeply absorbed in politics, left the detail work of the paper to Ellis. Into the intimate counsels of the revolutionary committee Ellis had not been admitted, nor would he have desired to be. He knew, of course, in a general way, the results that it was sought to achieve; and while he did not see their necessity, he deferred to the views of older men, and was satisfied to remain in ignorance of anything which he might disapprove. Moreover, his own personal affairs occupied his mind to an extent that made politics or any other subject a matter of minor importance.

As for Dr. Miller, he never learned of Mr. Delamere's good intentions toward his institution, but regretted the old gentleman's death as the loss of a sincere friend and well-wisher of his race in their unequal struggle.

Despite the untiring zeal of Carteret and his associates, the campaign for the restriction of the suffrage, which was to form the basis of a permanent white supremacy, had seemed to languish for a while after the Ochiltree affair. The lull, however, was only temporary, and more apparent than real, for the forces adverse to the negro were merely gathering strength for a more vigorous assault. While little was said in Wellington, public sentiment all over the country became every day more favorable to the views of the conspirators. The nation was rushing forward with giant strides toward colossal wealth and world-dominion, before the exigencies of which mere abstract ethical theories must not be permitted to stand. The same argument that justified the conquest of an inferior nation could not be denied to those who sought the suppression of an inferior race. In the South, an obscure jealousy of the negro's progress, an obscure fear of the very equality so contemptuously denied, furnished a rich soil for successful agitation. Statistics of crime, ingeniously manipulated, were made to present a fearful showing against the negro. Vital statistics were made to prove that he had degenerated from an imaginary standard of physical excellence which had existed under the benign influence of slavery. Constant lynchings emphasized his impotence, and bred everywhere a growing contempt for his rights.

At the North, a new Pharaoh had risen, who knew not Israel,—a new generation, who knew little of the fierce passions which had played around the negro in a past epoch, and derived their opinions of him from the "coon song" and the police reports. Those of his old friends who survived were disappointed that he had not flown with clipped wings; that he had not in one generation of limited opportunity attained the level of the whites. The whole race question seemed to have reached a sort of *impasse*, a blind alley, of which no one could see the outlet. The negro had become a target at which any one might try a shot. Schoolboys gravely debated the question as to whether or not the negro should exercise the franchise. The pessimist gave him up in despair; while the optimist, smilingly confident that everything would come out all right in the end, also turned aside and went his buoyant way to more pleasing themes.

For a time there were white men in the state who opposed any reactionary step unless it were of general application. They were conscientious men, who had learned the ten commandments and wished to do right; but this class was a small minority, and their objections were soon silenced by the all-powerful race argument. Selfishness is the most constant of human motives. Patriotism, humanity, or the love of God may lead to sporadic outbursts which sweep away the heaped-up wrongs of centuries; but they languish at times, while the love of self works on ceaselessly, unwearyingly, burrowing always at the very roots of life, and heaping up fresh wrongs for other centuries to sweep away. The state was at the mercy of venal and self-seeking politicians, bent upon regaining their ascendency at any cost, stultifying their own minds by vague sophistries and high-sounding phrases, which deceived none but those who wished to be deceived, and these but imperfectly; and dulling the public conscience by a loud clamor in which the calm voice of truth was for the moment silenced. So the cause went on.

Carteret, as spokesman of the campaign, and sincerest of all its leaders, performed prodigies of labor. The Morning Chronicle proclaimed, in season and out, the doctrine of "White Supremacy." Leaving the paper in charge of Ellis, the major made a tour of the state, rousing the white people of the better class to an appreciation of the terrible danger which confronted them in the possibility that a few negroes might hold a few offices or dictate the terms upon which white men should fill them. Difficulties were explained away. The provisions of the Federal Constitution, it was maintained, must yield to the "higher law," and if the Constitution could neither be altered nor bent to this end, means must be found to circumvent it.

The device finally hit upon for disfranchising the colored people in this particular state was the notorious "grandfather clause." After providing various restrictions of the suffrage, based upon education, character, and property, which it was deemed would in effect disfranchise the colored race, an exception was made in favor of all citizens whose fathers or grandfathers had been entitled to vote prior to 1867. Since none but white men could vote prior to 1867, this exception obviously took in the poor and ignorant whites, while the same class of negroes were excluded.

It was ingenious, but it was not fair. In due time a constitutional convention was called, in which the above scheme was adopted and submitted to a vote of the people for ratification. The campaign was fought on the color line. Many white Republicans, deluded with the hope that by elimination of the negro vote their party might receive accessions from the Democratic ranks, went over to the white party. By fraud in one place, by terrorism in another, and everywhere by the resistless moral force of the united whites, the negroes were reduced to the apathy of despair, their few white allies demoralized, and the amendment adopted by a large majority. The negroes were taught that this is a white man's country, and that the sooner they made up their minds to this fact, the better for all concerned. The white people would be good to them so long as they behaved themselves and kept their place. As theoretical equals,—practical equality being forever out of the question, either by nature or by law,—there could have been nothing but strife between them, in which the weaker party would invariably have suffered most.

Some colored men accepted the situation thus outlined, if not as desirable, at least as inevitable. Most of them, however, had little faith in this condescending friendliness which was to take the place of constitutional rights. They knew they had been treated unfairly; that their enemies had prevailed against them; that their whilom friends had stood passively by and seen them undone. Many of the most enterprising and progressive left the state, and those who remain still labor under a sense of wrong and outrage which renders them distinctly less valuable as citizens.

The great steal was made, but the thieves did not turn honest,—the scheme still shows the mark of the burglar's tools. Sins, like chickens, come home to roost. The South paid a fearful price for the wrong of negro slavery; in some form or other it will doubtless reap the fruits of this later iniquity.

Drastic as were these "reforms," the results of which we have anticipated somewhat, since the new Constitution was not to take effect immediately, they moved all too slowly for the little coterie of Wellington conspirators, whose ambitions and needs urged them to prompt action. Under the new Constitution it would be two full years before the "nigger amendment" became effective, and meanwhile the Wellington district would remain hopelessly Republican. The committee decided, about two months before the fall election, that an active local campaign must be carried on, with a view to discourage the negroes from attending the polls on election day.

The question came up for discussion one forenoon in a meeting at the office of the Morning Chronicle, at which all of the "Big Three" were present.

"Something must be done," declared McBane, "and that damn quick. Too many white people are saying that it will be better to wait until the amendment goes into effect. That would mean to leave the niggers in charge of this town for two years after the state has declared for white supremacy! I'm opposed to leaving it in their hands one hour,—them's my sentiments!"

This proved to be the general opinion, and the discussion turned to the subject of ways and means.

"What became of that editorial in the nigger paper?" inquired the general in his blandest tones, cleverly directing a smoke ring toward the ceiling. "It lost some of its point back there, when we came near lynching that nigger; but now that that has blown over, why would n't it be a good thing to bring into play at the present juncture? Let's read it over again."

Carteret extracted the paper from the pigeon-hole where he had placed it some months before. The article was read aloud with emphasis and discussed phrase by phrase. Of its wording there could be little criticism,—it was temperately and even cautiously phrased. As suggested by the general, the Ochiltree affair had proved that it was not devoid of truth. Its great offensiveness lay in its boldness: that a negro should publish in a newspaper what white people would scarcely acknowledge to themselves in secret was much as though a Russian *moujik* or a German peasant should rush into print to question the divine right of the Lord's

Anointed. The article was racial *lèse-majesté* in the most aggravated form. A peg was needed upon which to hang a *coup d'état*, and this editorial offered the requisite opportunity. It was unanimously decided to republish the obnoxious article, with comment adapted to fire the inflammable Southern heart and rouse it against any further self-assertion of the negroes in politics or elsewhere.

"The time is ripe!" exclaimed McBane. "In a month we can have the niggers so scared that they won't dare stick their heads out of doors on 'lection day."

"I wonder," observed the general thoughtfully, after this conclusion had been reached, "if we could n't have Jerry fetch us some liquor?"

Jerry appeared in response to the usual summons. The general gave him the money, and ordered three Calhoun cocktails. When Jerry returned with the glasses on a tray, the general observed him with pointed curiosity.

"What in h—ll is the matter with you, Jerry? Your black face is splotched with brown and yellow patches, and your hair shines as though you had fallen head-foremost into a firkin of butter. What's the matter with you?"

Jerry seemed much embarrassed by this inquiry.

"Nothin', suh, nothin', " he stammered, "It's—it's jes' somethin' I be'n puttin' on my hair, suh, ter improve de quality, suh."

"Jerry," returned the general, bending a solemn look upon the porter, "you have been playing with edged tools, and your days are numbered. You have been reading the Afro-American Banner."

He shook open the paper, which he had retained in his hand, and read from one of the advertisements:—

" 'Kinky, curly hair made straight in two applications. Dark skins lightened two shades; mulattoes turned perfectly white.'

"This stuff is rank poison, Jerry," continued the general with a mock solemnity which did not impose upon Jerry, who nevertheless listened with an air of great alarm. He suspected that the general was making fun of him; but he also knew that the general would like to think that Jerry believed him in earnest; and to please the white folks was Jerry's consistent aim in life. "I can see the signs of decay in your face, and your hair will all fall out in a week or two at the latest,—mark my words!"

McBane had listened to this pleasantry with a sardonic sneer. It was a waste of valuable time. To Carteret it seemed in doubtful taste. These grotesque advertisements had their tragic side. They were proof that the negroes had read the handwriting on the wall. These pitiful attempts to change their physical characteristics were an acknowledgment, on their own part, that the negro was doomed, and that the white man was to inherit the earth and hold all other races under his heel. For, as the months passed, Carteret's thoughts, centering more and more upon the negro, had led him farther and farther, until now he was firmly convinced that there was no permanent place for the negro in the United States, if indeed anywhere in the world, except under the ground. More pathetic even than Jerry's efforts to escape from the universal doom of his race was his ignorance that even if he could, by some strange alchemy, bleach his skin and straighten his hair, there would still remain, underneath it all, only the unbleached darky,—the ass in the lion's skin.

When the general had finished his facetious lecture, Jerry backed out of the room shamefacedly, though affecting a greater confusion than he really felt. Jerry had not reasoned so closely as Carteret, but he had realized that it was a distinct advantage to be white,—an advantage which white people had utilized to secure all the best things in the world; and he had entertained the vague hope that by changing his complexion he might share this prerogative. While he suspected the general's sincerity, he nevertheless felt a little apprehensive lest the general's prediction about the effects of the face-bleach and other preparations might prove true,—the general was a white gentleman and ought to know,—and decided to abandon their use.

This purpose was strengthened by his next interview with the major. When Carteret summoned him, an hour later, after the other gentlemen had taken their leave, Jerry had washed his head thoroughly and there remained no trace of the pomade. An attempt to darken the lighter spots in his cuticle by the application of printer's ink had not proved equally successful,—the retouching left the spots as much too dark as they had formerly been too light.

"Jerry," said Carteret sternly, "when I hired you to work for the Chronicle, you were black. The word 'negro' means 'black.' The best negro is a black negro, of the pure type, as it came from the hands of God. If you wish to get along well with the white people, the blacker you are the better,—white people do not like negroes who want to be white. A man should be content to remain as God made him and where God placed him. So no more of this nonsense. Are you going to vote at the next election?"

"What would you 'vise me ter do, suh?" asked Jerry cautiously.

"I do not advise you. You ought to have sense enough to see where your own interests lie. I put it to you whether you cannot trust yourself more safely in the hands of white gentlemen, who are your true friends, than in the hands of ignorant and purchasable negroes and unscrupulous white scoundrels?"

"Dere's no doubt about it, suh," assented Jerry, with a vengeance proportioned to his desire to get back into favor. "I ain' gwine ter have nothin' ter do wid de 'lection, suh! Ef I don' vote, I kin keep my job, can't I, suh?"

The major eyed Jerry with an air of supreme disgust. What could be expected of a race so utterly devoid of tact? It seemed as though this negro thought a white gentleman might want to bribe him to remain away from the polls; and the negro's willingness to accept the imaginary bribe demonstrated the venal nature of the colored race,—its entire lack of moral principle!

"You will retain your place, Jerry," he said severely, "so

long as you perform your duties to my satisfaction and behave yourself properly."

With this grandiloquent subterfuge Carteret turned to his next article on white supremacy. Jerry not delude himself with any fine-spun sophistry. He knew perfectly well that he held his job upon the condition that he stayed away from the polls at the approaching election. Jerry was a fool—

"The world of fools hath such a store,
That he who would not see an ass,
Must stay at home and shut his door
And break his looking-glass"

But while no one may be entirely wise, there are degrees of folly, and Jerry was not all kinds of a fool.

CHAPTER XXIX

Mutterings of the Storm

Events moved rapidly during the next few days. The repro-
duction, in the Chronicle, of the article from the Afro-
American Banner, with Carteret's inflammatory comment,
took immediate effect. It touched the Southern white man
in his most sensitive spot. To him such an article was an
insult to white womanhood, and must be resented by some
active steps,—mere words would be no answer at all. To meet
words with words upon such a subject would be to acknowledge the equality of the negro and his right to discuss or
criticise the conduct of the white people.

The colored people became alarmed at the murmurings of
the whites, which seemed to presage a coming storm. A number of them sought to arm themselves, but ascertained, upon
inquiring at the stores, that no white merchant would sell a
negro firearms. Since all the dealers in this sort of merchandise were white men, the negroes had to be satisfied with
oiling up the old army muskets which some of them possessed, and the few revolvers with which a small rowdy element generally managed to keep themselves supplied. Upon
an effort being made to purchase firearms from a Northern
city, the express company, controlled by local men, refused
to accept the consignment. The white people, on the other
hand, procured both arms and ammunition in large quanti-
ties, and the Wellington Grays drilled with great assiduity at
their armory.

All this went on without any public disturbance of the

677

town's tranquillity. A stranger would have seen nothing to excite his curiosity. The white people did their talking among themselves, and merely grew more distant in their manner toward the colored folks, who instinctively closed their ranks as the whites drew away. With each day that passed the feeling grew more tense. The editor of the Afro-American Banner, whose office had been quietly garrisoned for several nights by armed negroes, became frightened, and disappeared from the town between two suns.

The conspirators were jubilant at the complete success of their plans. It only remained for them to so direct this aroused public feeling that it might completely accomplish the desired end,—to change the political complexion of the city government and assure the ascendency of the whites until the amendment should go into effect. A revolution, and not a riot, was contemplated.

With this end in view, another meeting was called at Carteret's office.

"We are now ready," announced General Belmont, "for the final act of this drama. We must decide promptly, or events may run away from us."

"What do you suggest?" asked Carteret.

"Down in the American tropics," continued the general, "they have a way of doing things. I was in Nicaragua, ten years ago, when Paterno's revolution drove out Igorroto's government. It was as easy as falling off a log. Paterno had the arms and the best men. Igorroto was not looking for trouble, and the guns were at his breast before he knew it. We have the guns. The negroes are not expecting trouble, and are easy to manage compared with the fiery mixture that flourishes in the tropics."

"I should not advocate murder," returned Carteret. "We are animated by high and holy principles. We wish to right a wrong, to remedy an abuse, to save our state from anarchy and our race from humiliation. I don't object to frightening the negroes, but I am opposed to unnecessary bloodshed."

"I'm not quite so particular," struck in McBane. "They need to be taught a lesson, and a nigger more or less would n't be missed. There's too many of 'em now."

"Of course," continued Carteret, "if we should decide upon a certain mode of procedure, and the negroes should resist, a different reasoning might apply; but I will have no premeditated murder."

"In Central and South America," observed the general reflectively, "none are hurt except those who get in the way."

"There'll be no niggers hurt," said McBane contemptuously, "unless they strain themselves running. One white man can chase a hundred of 'em. I've managed five hundred at a time. I'll pay for burying all the niggers that are killed."

The conference resulted in a well-defined plan, to be put into operation the following day, by which the city government was to be wrested from the Republicans and their negro allies.

"And now," said General Belmont, "while we are cleansing the Augean stables, we may as well remove the cause as the effect. There are several negroes too many in this town, which will be much the better without them. There's that yellow lawyer, Watson. He's altogether too mouthy, and has too much business. Every nigger that gets into trouble sends for Watson, and white lawyers, with families to support and social positions to keep up, are deprived of their legitimate source of income."

"There's that damn nigger real estate agent," blurted out McBane. "Bill Kitchen used to get most of the nigger business, but this darky has almost driven him to the poorhouse. A white business man is entitled to a living in his own profession and his own home. That nigger don't belong here nohow. He came from the North a year or two ago, and is hand in glove with Barber, the nigger editor, which is enough of itself to damn him. He'll have to go!"

"How about the collector of the port?"

Tactics retired & forgotten

"We'd better not touch him. It would bring the government down upon us, which we want to avoid. We don't need to worry about the nigger preachers either. They want to stay here, where the loaves and the fishes are. We can make 'em write letters to the newspapers justifying our course, as a condition of their remaining."

"What about Billings?" asked McBane. Billings was the white Republican mayor. "Is that skunk to be allowed to stay in town?"

"No," returned the general, "every white Republican office-holder ought to be made to go. This town is only big enough for Democrats, and negroes who can be taught to keep their place."

"What about the colored doctor?" queried McBane, "with the hospital, and the diamond ring, and the carriage, and the other fallals?"

Miller of
Not in politics
MIRROR
to hospital
Outcome

"I should n't interfere with Miller," replied the general decisively. "He's a very good sort of a negro, does n't meddle with politics, nor tread on any one else's toes. His father was a good citizen, which counts in his favor. He's spending money in the community too, and contributes to its prosperity." ① *MIRROR*

"That sort of nigger, though, sets a bad example," retorted McBane. "They make it all the harder to keep the rest of 'em down."

All down or a problem

" 'One swallow does not make a summer,' " quoted the general. "When we get things arranged, there'll be no trouble. A stream cannot rise higher than its fountain, and a smart nigger without a constituency will no longer be an object of fear. I say, let the doctor alone."

"He'll have to keep mighty quiet, though," muttered McBane discontentedly. "I don't like smart niggers. I've had to shoot several of them, in the course of my life."

"Personally, I dislike the man," interposed Carteret, "and if I consulted my own inclinations, would say expel him with the rest; but my grievance is a personal one, and to gratify it in that way would be a loss to the community. I wish to be strictly impartial in this matter, and to take no step which cannot be entirely justified by a wise regard for the public welfare."

"What's the use of all this hypocrisy, gentlemen?" sneered McBane. "Every last one of us has an axe to grind! The major may as well put an edge on his. We'll never get a better chance to have things our way. If this nigger doctor annoys the major, we'll run him out with the rest. This is a white man's country, and a white man's city, and no nigger has any business here when a white man wants him gone!"

Carteret frowned darkly at this brutal characterization of their motives. It robbed the enterprise of all its poetry, and put a solemn act of revolution upon the plane of a mere vulgar theft of power. Even the general winced.

"I would not consent," he said irritably, "to Miller's being disturbed."

McBane made no further objection.

There was a discreet knock at the door.

"Come in," said Carteret.

Jerry entered. "Mistuh Ellis wants ter speak ter you a minute, suh," he said.

Carteret excused himself and left the room.

"Jerry," said the general, "you lump of ebony, the sight of you reminds me! If your master does n't want you for a minute, step across to Mr. Brown's and tell him to send me three cocktails."

"Yas, suh," responded Jerry, hesitating. The general had said nothing about paying.

"And tell him, Jerry, to charge them. I'm short of change to-day."

"Yas, suh; yas, suh," replied Jerry, as he backed out of the presence, adding, when he had reached the hall: "Dere ain' no change for Jerry dis time, sho': I'll jes make dat fo' cocktails, an' de gin'l won't never know de diffe'nce. I ain' gwine 'cross de road fer nothin', not ef I knows it."

Half an hour later, the conspirators dispersed. They had fixed the hour of the proposed revolution, the course to be pursued, the results to be obtained; but in stating their equation they had overlooked one factor,—God, or Fate, or whatever one may choose to call the Power that holds the destinies of man in the hollow of his hand.

CHAPTER XXX

The Missing Papers

Mrs. Carteret was very much disturbed. It was supposed that the shock of her aunt's death had affected her health, for since that event she had fallen into a nervous condition which gave the major grave concern. Much to the general surprise, Mrs. Ochiltree had left no will, and no property of any considerable value except her homestead, which descended to Mrs. Carteret as the natural heir. Whatever she may have had on hand in the way of ready money had undoubtedly been abstracted from the cedar chest by the midnight marauder, to whose visit her death was immediately due. Her niece's grief was held to mark a deep-seated affection for the grim old woman who had reared her.

Mrs. Carteret's present state of mind, of which her nervousness was a sufficiently accurate reflection, did in truth date from her aunt's death, and also in part from the time of the conversation with Mrs. Ochiltree, one afternoon, during and after the drive past Miller's new hospital. Mrs. Ochiltree had grown steadily more and more childish after that time, and her niece had never succeeded in making her pick up the thread of thought where it had been dropped. At any rate, Mrs. Ochiltree had made no further disclosure upon the subject.

An examination, not long after her aunt's death, of the papers found near the cedar chest on the morning after the murder had contributed to Mrs. Carteret's enlightenment, but had not promoted her peace of mind.

683

When Mrs. Carteret reached home, after her hurried exploration of the cedar chest, she thrust into a bureau drawer the envelope she had found. So fully was her mind occupied, for several days, with the funeral, and with the excitement attending the arrest of Sandy Campbell, that she deferred the examination of the contents of the envelope until near the end of the week.

One morning, while alone in her chamber, she drew the envelope from the drawer, and was holding it in her hand, hesitating as to whether or not she should open it, when the baby in the next room began to cry.

The child's cry seemed like a warning, and yielding to a vague uneasiness, she put the paper back.

"Phil," she said to her husband at luncheon, "Aunt Polly said some strange things to me one day before she died,—I don't know whether she was quite in her right mind or not; but suppose that my father had left a will by which it was provided that half his property should go to that woman and her child?"

"It would never have gone by such a will," replied the major easily. "Your Aunt Polly was in her dotage, and merely dreaming. Your father would never have been such a fool; but even if he had, no such will could have stood the test of the courts. It would clearly have been due to the improper influence of a designing woman."

"So that legally, as well as morally," said Mrs. Carteret, "the will would have been of no effect?"

"Not the slightest. A jury would soon have broken down the legal claim. As for any moral obligation, there would have been nothing moral about the affair. The only possible consideration for such a gift was an immoral one. I don't wish to speak harshly of your father, my dear, but his conduct was gravely reprehensible. The woman herself had no right or claim whatever; she would have been whipped and expelled from the town, if justice—blind, bleeding justice, then prostrate at the feet of slaves and aliens—could have had her way!"

684

"But the child"—

"The child was in the same category. Who was she, to have inherited the estate of your ancestors, of which, a few years before, she would herself have formed a part? The child of shame, it was hers to pay the penalty. But the discussion is all in the air, Olivia. Your father never did and never would have left such a will."

This conversation relieved Mrs. Carteret's uneasiness. Going to her room shortly afterwards, she took the envelope from her bureau drawer and drew out a bulky paper. The haunting fear that it might be such a will as her aunt had suggested was now removed; for such an instrument, in the light of what her husband had said confirming her own intuitions, would be of no valid effect. It might be just as well, she thought, to throw the paper in the fire without looking at it. She wished to think as well as might be of her father, and she felt that her respect for his memory would not be strengthened by the knowledge that he had meant to leave his estate away from her; for her aunt's words had been open to the construction that she was to have been left destitute. Curiosity strongly prompted her to read the paper. Perhaps the will contained no such provision as she had feared, and it might convey some request or direction which ought properly to be complied with.

She had been standing in front of the bureau while these thoughts passed through her mind, and now, dropping the envelope back into the drawer mechanically, she unfolded the document. It was written on legal paper, in her father's own hand.

Mrs. Carteret was not familiar with legal verbiage, and there were several expressions of which she did not perhaps appreciate the full effect; but a very hasty glance enabled her to ascertain the purport of the paper. It was a will, by which, in one item, her father devised to his daughter Janet, the child of the woman known as Julia Brown, the sum of ten thousand dollars, and a certain plantation or tract of land a short distance from the town of Wellington. The rest and residue of his estate, after deducting all legal charges and expenses, was bequeathed to his beloved daughter, Olivia Merkell.

Mrs. Carteret breathed a sigh of relief. Her father had not preferred another to her, but had left to his lawful daughter the bulk of his estate. She felt at the same time a growing indignation at the thought that the woman should so have wrought upon her father's weakness as to induce him to think of leaving so much valuable property to her bastard,—property which by right should go, and now would go, to her own son, to whom by every rule of law and decency it ought to descend.

A fire was burning in the next room, on account of the baby,—there had been a light frost the night before, and the air was somewhat chilly. For the moment the room was empty. Mrs. Carteret came out from her chamber and threw the offending paper into the fire, and watched it slowly burn. When it had been consumed, the carbon residue of one sheet still retained its form, and she could read the words on the charred portion. A sentence, which had escaped her eye in her rapid reading, stood out in ghostly black upon the gray background:—

"All the rest and residue of my estate I devise and bequeath to my daughter Olivia Merkell, the child of my beloved first wife."

Mrs. Carteret had not before observed the word "first." Instinctively she stretched toward the fire the poker which she held in her hand, at its touch the shadowy remnant fell to pieces, and nothing but ashes remained upon the hearth.

Not until the next morning did she think again of the envelope which had contained the paper she had burned. Opening the drawer where it lay, the oblong blue envelope confronted her. The sight of it was distasteful. The indorsed side lay uppermost, and the words seemed like a mute reproach:—

686

"The Last Will and Testament of Samuel Merkell."

Snatching up the envelope, she glanced into it mechanically as she moved toward the next room, and perceived a thin folded paper which had heretofore escaped her notice. When opened, it proved to be a certificate of marriage, in due form, between Samuel Merkell and Julia Brown. It was dated from a county in South Carolina, about two years before her father's death.

For a moment Mrs. Carteret stood gazing blankly at this faded slip of paper. Her father *had* married this woman!—at least he had gone through the form of marriage with her, for to him it had surely been no more than an empty formality. The marriage of white and colored persons was forbidden by law. Only recently she had read of a case where both the parties to such a crime, a colored man and a white woman, had been sentenced to long terms in the penitentiary. She even recalled the circumstances. The couple had been living together unlawfully,—they were very low people, whose private lives were beneath the public notice,—but influenced by a religious movement pervading the community, had sought, they said at the trial, to secure the blessing of God upon their union. The higher law, which imperiously demanded that the purity and prestige of the white race be preserved at any cost, had intervened at this point.

Mechanically she moved toward the fireplace, so dazed by this discovery as to be scarcely conscious of her own actions. She surely had not formed any definite intention of destroying this piece of paper when her fingers relaxed unconsciously and let go their hold upon it. The draught swept it toward the fireplace. Ere scarcely touching the flames it caught, blazed fiercely, and shot upward with the current of air. A moment later the record of poor Julia's marriage was scattered to the four winds of heaven, as her poor body had long since mingled with the dust of earth.

The letter remained unread. In her agitation at the discovery of the marriage certificate, Olivia had almost forgotten the existence of the letter. It was addressed to "John Delamere, Esq., as Executor of my Last Will and Testament," while the lower left-hand corner bore the direction: "To be delivered only after my death, with seal unbroken."

The seal was broken already; Mr. Delamere was dead; the letter could never be delivered. Mrs. Carteret unfolded it and read:—

MY DEAR DELAMERE,—I have taken the liberty of naming you as executor of my last will, because you are my friend, and the only man of my acquaintance whom I feel that I can trust to carry out my wishes, appreciate my motives, and preserve the silence I desire.

I have, first, a confession to make. Inclosed in this letter you will find a certificate of marriage between my child Janet's mother and myself. While I have never exactly repented of this marriage, I have never had the courage to acknowledge it openly. If I had not married Julia, I fear Polly Ochiltree would have married me by main force,—as she would marry you or any other gentleman unfortunate enough to fall in the way of this twice-widowed man-hunter. When my wife died, three years ago, her sister Polly offered to keep house for me and the child. I would sooner have had the devil in the house, and yet I trembled with alarm,—there seemed no way of escape,—it was so clearly and obviously the proper thing.

But she herself gave me my opportunity. I was on the point of consenting, when she demanded, as a condition of her coming, that I discharge Julia, my late wife's maid. She was laboring under a misapprehension in regard to the girl, but I grasped at the straw, and did everything to foster her delusion. I declared solemnly that nothing under heaven would induce me to part with Julia. The controversy resulted in my permitting Polly to take the child, while I retained the maid.

Before Polly put this idea into my head, I had scarcely looked at Julia, but this outbreak turned my attention toward her. She was a handsome girl, and, as I soon found out, a good girl. My wife, who raised her, was a Christian woman, and had taught her modesty and virtue. She was free. The air was full of liberty, and equal rights, and all the abolition clap-trap, and she made marriage a condition of her remaining longer in the house. In a moment of weakness I took her away to a place where we were not known, and married her. If she had left me, I should have fallen a victim of Polly Ochiltree,— to which any fate was preferable.

And then, old friend, my weakness kept to the fore. I was ashamed of this marriage, and my new wife saw it. Moreover, she loved me,—too well, indeed, to wish to make me un-happy. The ceremony had satisfied her conscience, had set her right, she said, with God; for the opinions of men she did not care, since I loved her,—she only wanted to compensate me, as best she could, for the great honor I had done my handmaiden,—for she had read her Bible, and I was the Abra-ham to her Hagar, compared with whom she considered her-self at a great advantage. It was her own proposition that nothing be said of this marriage. If any shame should fall on her, it would fall lightly, for it would be undeserved. When the child came, she still kept silence. No one, she argued, could blame an innocent child for the accident of birth, and in the sight of God this child had every right to exist; while among her own people illegitimacy would involve but little stigma.

I need not say that I was easily persuaded to accept this sacrifice; but touched by her fidelity, I swore to provide hand-somely for them both. This I have tried to do by the will of which I ask you to act as executor. Had I left the child more, it might serve as a ground for attacking the will; my acknowl-edgment of the tie of blood is sufficient to justify a reasonable bequest.

I have taken this course for the sake of my daughter Olivia, who is dear to me, and whom I would not wish to make ashamed; and in deference to public opinion, which it is not easy to defy. If, after my death, Julia should choose to make our secret known, I shall of course be beyond the reach of hard words; but loyalty to my memory will probably keep her silent. A strong man would long since have acknowledged her before the world and taken the consequences; but, alas! I am only myself, and the atmosphere I live in does not encourage moral heroism. I should like to be different, but it is God who hath made us, and not we ourselves!

Nevertheless, old friend, I will ask of you one favor. If in the future this child of Julia's and of mine should grow to womanhood; if she should prove to have her mother's gentleness and love of virtue; if, in the new era which is opening up for her mother's race, to which, unfortunately, she must belong, she should become, in time, an educated woman; and if the time should ever come when, by virtue of her education or the development of her people, it would be to her a source of shame or unhappiness that she was an illegitimate child,— if you are still alive, old friend, go to her and tell her, for me, that she is my lawful child, and ask her to forgive her father's weakness.

When this letter comes to you, I shall have passed to—the Beyond; but I am confident that you will accept this trust, for which I thank you now, in advance, most heartily.

The letter was signed with her father's name, the same signature which had been attached to the will.

Having firmly convinced herself of the illegality of the papers, and of her own right to destroy them, Mrs. Carteret ought to have felt relieved that she had thus removed all traces of her dead father's folly. True, the other daughter remained,—she had seen her on the street only the day before. The sight of this person she had always found offensive, and now, she felt, in view of what she had just learned, it must be even more so. Never, while this woman lived in the town, would she be able to throw the veil of forgetfulness over this blot upon her father's memory.

As the day wore on, Mrs. Carteret grew still less at ease. To herself, marriage was a serious thing,—to a right-thinking woman the most serious concern of life. A marriage certificate, rightfully procured, was scarcely less solemn, as far as it went, than the Bible itself. Her own she cherished as the apple of her eye. It was the evidence of her wifehood, the seal of her child's legitimacy, her patent of nobility,—the token of her own and her child's claim to social place and consideration. She had burned this pretended marriage certificate because it meant nothing. Nevertheless, she could not ignore the knowledge of another such marriage, of which every one in the town knew,—a celebrated case, indeed, where a white man, of a family quite as prominent as her father's, had married a colored woman during the military occupation of the state just after the civil war. The legality of the marriage had never been questioned. It had been fully consummated by twenty years of subsequent co-habitation. No amount of social persecution had ever shaken the position of the husband. With an iron will he had stayed on in the town, a living protest against the established customs of the South, so rudely interrupted for a few short years; and, though his children were negroes, though he had never appeared in public with his wife, no one had ever questioned the validity of his marriage or the legitimacy of his offspring.

The marriage certificate which Mrs. Carteret had burned dated from the period of the military occupation. Hence Mrs. Carteret, who was a good woman, and would not have done a dishonest thing, felt decidedly uncomfortable. She had destroyed the marriage certificate, but its ghost still haunted her.

Major Carteret, having just eaten a good dinner, was in a very agreeable humor when, that same evening, his wife brought up again the subject of their previous discussion.

"Phil," she asked, "Aunt Polly told me that once, long before my father died, when she went to remonstrate with him for keeping that woman in the house, he threatened to marry Julia if Aunt Polly ever said another word to him about the matter. Suppose he *had* married her, and had *then* left a will,—would the marriage have made any difference, so far as the will was concerned?"

Major Carteret laughed. "Your Aunt Polly," he said, "was

a remarkable woman, with a wonderful imagination, which seems to have grown more vivid as her memory and judgment weakened. Why should your father marry this negro housemaid? Mr. Merkell was never rated as a fool,—he had one of the clearest heads in Wellington. I saw him only a day or two before he died, and I could swear before any court in Christendom that he was of sound mind and memory to the last. These notions of your aunt were mere delusions. Your father was never capable of such a folly."

"Of course I am only supposing a case," returned Olivia. "Imagining such a case, just for the argument, would the marriage have been legal?"

"That would depend. If he had married her during the military occupation, or over in South Carolina, the marriage would have been legally valid, though morally and socially outrageous."

"And if he had died afterwards, leaving a will?"

"The will would have controlled the disposition of his estate, in all probability."

"Suppose he had left no will?"

"You are getting the matter down pretty fine, my dear! The woman would have taken one third of the real estate for life, and could have lived in the homestead until she died. She would also have had half the other property,—the money and goods and furniture, everything except the land,—and the negro child would have shared with you the balance of the estate. That, I believe, is according to the law of descent and distribution."

Mrs. Carteret lapsed into a troubled silence. Her father *had* married the woman. In her heart she had no doubt of the validity of the marriage, so far as the law was concerned; if one marriage of such a kind would stand, another contracted under similar conditions was equally as good. If the marriage had been valid, Julia's child had been legitimate. The will she had burned gave this sister of hers—she shuddered at the word—but a small part of the estate. Under the law, which intervened now that there was no will, the property should have been equally divided. If the woman had been white,—but the woman had *not* been white, and the same rule of moral conduct did not, *could* not, in the very nature of things, apply, as between white people! For, if this were not so, slavery had been, not merely an economic mistake, but a great crime against humanity. If it had been such a crime, as for a moment she dimly perceived it might have been, then through the long centuries there had been piled up a catalogue of wrong and outrage which, if the law of compensation be a law of nature, must some time, somewhere, in some way, be atoned for. She herself had not escaped the penalty, of which, she realized, this burden placed upon her conscience was but another installment.

If she should make known the facts she had learned, it would mean what?—a division of her father's estate, a recognition of the legality of her father's relations with Julia. Such a stain upon her father's memory would be infinitely worse than if he had not married her. To have lived with her without marriage was a social misdemeanor, at which society in the old days had winked, or at most had frowned. To have married her was to have committed the unpardonable social sin. Such a scandal Mrs. Carteret could not have endured. Should she seek to make restitution, it would necessarily involve the disclosure of at least some of the facts. Had she not destroyed the will, she might have compromised with her conscience by producing it and acting upon its terms, which had been so stated as not to disclose the marriage. This was now rendered impossible by her own impulsive act; she could not mention the will at all, without admitting that she had destroyed it.

Mrs. Carteret found herself in what might be called, vulgarly, a moral "pocket." She could, of course, remain silent. Mrs. Carteret was a good woman, according to her lights, with a cultivate conscience, to which she had always looked as her mentor and infallible guide.

Hence Mrs. Carteret, after this painful discovery, remained for a long time ill at ease,—so disturbed, indeed, that her mind reacted upon her nerves, which had never been strong; and her nervousness affected her strength, which had never been great, until Carteret, whose love for her had been deepened and strengthened by the advent of his son, became alarmed for her health, and spoke very seriously to Dr. Price concerning it.

CHAPTER XXXI

The Shadow of a Dream

Mrs. Carteret awoke, with a start, from a troubled dream. She had been sailing across a sunlit sea, in a beautiful boat, her child lying on a bright-colored cushion at her feet. Overhead the swelling sail served as an awning to keep off the sun's rays, which far ahead were reflected with dazzling brilliancy from the shores of a golden island. Her son, she dreamed, was a fairy prince, and yonder lay his kingdom, to which he was being borne, lying there at her feet, in this beautiful boat, across the sunlit sea.

Suddenly and without warning the sky was overcast. A squall struck the boat and tore away the sail. In the distance a huge billow—a great white wall of water—came sweeping toward their frail craft, threatening it with instant destruction. She clasped her child to her bosom, and a moment later found herself struggling in the sea, holding the child's head above the water. As she floated there, as though sustained by some unseen force, she saw in the distance a small boat approaching over the storm-tossed waves. Straight toward her it came, and she had reached out her hand to grasp its side, when the rower looked back, and she saw that it was her sister. The recognition had been mutual. With a sharp movement of one oar the boat glided by, leaving her clutching at the empty air.

She felt her strength being to fail. Despairingly she signaled with her disengaged hand; but the rower, after one mute, reproachful glance, rowed on. Mrs. Carteret's strength grew less and less. The child became heavy as lead. Herself floating in the water, as though it were her native element, she could no longer support the child. Lower and lower it sank,—she was powerless to save it or to accompany it,— until, gasping wildly for breath, it threw up its little hands and sank, the cruel water gurgling over its head,—when she awoke with a start and a chill, and lay there trembling for several minutes before she heard little Dodie in his crib, breathing heavily.

She rose softly, went to the crib, and changed the child's position to an easier one. He breathed more freely, and she went back to bed, but not to sleep.

She had tried to put aside the distressing questions raised by the discovery of her father's will and the papers accompanying it. Why should she be burdened with such a responsibility, at this late day, when the touch of time had well-nigh healed these old sores? Surely, God had put his curse not alone upon the slave, but upon the stealer of men! With other good people she had thanked Him that slavery was no more, and that those who once had borne its burden upon their consciences could stand erect and feel that they themselves were free. The weed had been cut down, but its roots remained, deeply imbedded in the soil, to spring up and trouble a new generation. Upon her weak shoulders was placed the burden of her father's weaknesses, her father's folly. It was left to her to acknowledge or not this shameful marriage and her sister's rights in their father's estate.

Balancing one consideration against another, she had almost decided that she might ignore this tie. To herself, Olivia Merkell,—Olivia Carteret,—the stigma of base birth would have meant social ostracism, social ruin, the averted face, the finger of pity or of scorn. All the traditional weight of public disapproval would have fallen upon her as the unhappy fruit of an unblessed union. To this other woman it could have had no such significance,—it had been the lot of her race. To them, twenty-five years before, sexual sin had never been imputed as more than a fault. She had lost nothing by her supported illegitimacy; she would gain nothing by the acknowledgment of her mother's marriage.

On the other hand, what would be the effect of this revelation upon Mrs. Carteret herself? To have it known that her father had married a negress would only be less dreadful than to have it appear that he had committed some terrible crime. It was a crime now, by the laws of every Southern State, for white and colored persons to intermarry. She shuddered before the possibility that at some time in the future some person, none too well informed, might learn that her father had married a colored woman, and might assume that she, Olivia Carteret, or her child, had sprung from this shocking *mésalliance*,—a fate to which she would willingly have preferred death. No, this marriage must never be made known; the secret should remain buried forever in her own heart!

But there still remained the question of her father's property and her father's will. This woman was her father's child,—of that there could be no doubt, it was written in her features no less than in her father's will. As his lawful child,— or which, alas! there could also be no question,—she was entitled by law to half his estate. Mrs. Carteret's problem had sunk from the realm of sentiment to that of material things, which, curiously enough, she found much more difficult. For, while the negro, by the traditions of her people, was barred from the world of sentiment, his rights of property were recognized. The question had become, with Mrs. Carteret, a question of *meum* and *tuum*. Had the girl Janet been poor, ignorant, or degraded, as might well have been her fate, Mrs. Carteret might have felt a vicarious remorse of her aunt's suppression of the papers; but fate had compensated Janet for the loss; she had been educated, she had married well; she had not suffered for lack of the money of which she had been defrauded, and did not need it now. She had a child, it is true, but this child's career would be so circum-

rationalizing

scribed by the accident of color that too much wealth would only be a source of unhappiness; to her own child, on the contrary, it would open every door of life.

It would be too lengthy a task to follow the mind and conscience of this much-tried lady in their intricate workings upon this difficult problem; for she had a mind as logical as any woman's, and a conscience which she wished to keep void of offense. She had to confront a situation involving the element of race, upon which the moral standards of her people were hopelessly confused. Mrs. Carteret reached the conclusion, ere daylight dawned, that she would be silent upon the subject of her father's second marriage. Neither party had wished it known,—neither Julia nor her father,— and she would respect her father's wishes. To act otherwise would be to defeat his will, to make known what he had carefully concealed, and to give Janet a claim of title to one half her father's estate, while he had only meant her to have the ten thousand dollars named in the will.

By the same reasoning, she must carry out her father's will in respect to this bequest. Here there was another difficulty. The mining investment into which they had entered shortly after the birth of little Dodie had tied up so much of her property that it would have been difficult to procure ten thousand dollars immediately; while a demand for half the property at once would mean bankruptcy and ruin. Moreover, upon what ground could she offer her sister any sum of money whatever? So sudden a change of heart, after so many years of silence, would raise the presumption of some right on the part of Janet in her father's estate. Suspicion once aroused, it might be possible to trace this bidden marriage, and establish it by legal proof. The marriage once verified, the claim for half the estate could not be denied. She could not plead her father's will to the contrary, for this would be to acknowledge the suppression of the will, in itself a criminal act.

There was, however, a way of escape. This hospital which

had recently been opened was the personal property of her sister's husband. Some time in the future, when their investments matured, she would present to the hospital a sum of money equal to the amount her father had meant his colored daughter to have. Thus indirectly both her father's will and her own conscience would be satisfied.

Mrs. Carteret had reached this comfortable conclusion, and was falling asleep, when her attention was again drawn by her child's breathing. She took it in her own arms and soon fell asleep.

"By the way, Olivia," said the major, when leaving the house next morning for the office, "if you have any business down town to-day, transact it this forenoon. Under no circumstances must you or Clara or the baby leave the house after midday."

"Why, what's the matter, Phil?"

"Nothing to alarm you, except that there may be a little political demonstration which may render the streets unsafe. You are not to say anything about it where the servants might hear."

"Will there be any danger for you, Phil?" she demanded with alarm.

"Not the slightest, Olivia dear. No one will be harmed; but it is best for ladies and children to stay indoors."

Mrs. Carteret's nerves were still more or less unstrung from her mental struggles of the night, and the memory of her dream came to her like a dim foreboding of misfortune. As though in sympathy with its mother's feelings, the baby did not seem as well as usual. The new nurse was by no means an ideal nurse,—Mammy Jane understood the child much better. If there should be any trouble with the negroes, toward which her husband's remark seemed to point,—she knew the general political situation, though not informed in regard to her husband's plans,—she would like to have Mammy Jane near her, where the old nurse might be protected from danger or alarm.

With this end in view she dispatched the nurse, shortly after breakfast, to Mammy Jane's house in the negro settlement on the other side of the town, with a message asking the old woman to come immediately to Mrs. Carteret's. Unfortunately, Mammy Jane had gone to visit a sick woman in the country, and was not expected to return for several hours.

CHAPTER XXXII

The Storm Breaks

Narrator voice

The Wellington riot began at three o'clock in the afternoon of a day as fair as was ever selected for a deed of darkness. The sky was clear, except for a few light clouds that floated, white and feathery, high in air, like distant islands in a sapphire sea. A salt-laden breeze from the ocean a few miles away lent a crisp sparkle to the air.

At three o'clock sharp the streets were filled, as if by magic, with armed white men. The negroes, going about, had noted, with uneasy curiosity, that the stores and places of business, many of which closed at noon, were unduly late in opening for the afternoon, though no one suspected the reason for the delay; but at three o'clock every passing colored man was ordered, by the first white man he met, to throw up his hands. If he complied, he was searched, more or less roughly, for firearms, and then warned to get off the street. When he met another group of white men the scene was repeated. The man thus summarily held up seldom encountered more than two groups before disappearing across lots to his own home or some convenient hiding-place. If he resisted any demand of those who halted him—But the records of the day are historical; they may be found in the newspapers of the following date, but they are more firmly engraved upon the hearts and memories of the people of Wellington. For many months there were negro families in the town whose children screamed with fear and ran to their mothers for protection at the mere sight of a white man.

Dr. Miller had received a call, about one o'clock, to attend a case at the house of a well-to-do colored farmer, who lived some three or four miles from the town, upon the very road, by the way, along which Miller had driven so furiously a few weeks before, in the few hours that intervened before Sandy Campbell would probably have been burned at the stake. The drive to his patient's home, the necessary inquiries, the filling of the prescription from his own medicine-case, which he carried along with him, the little friendly conversation about the weather and the crops, and, the farmer being an intelligent and thinking man, the inevitable subject of the future of their race,—these, added to the return journey, occupied at least two hours of Miller's time.

As he neared the town on his way back, he saw ahead of him half a dozen men and women approaching, with fear written in their faces, in every degree from apprehension to terror. Women were weeping and children crying, and all were going as fast as seemingly lay in their power, looking behind now and then as if pursued by some deadly enemy. At sight of Miller's buggy they made a dash for cover, disappearing, like a covey of frightened partridges, in the underbrush along the road.

Miller pulled up his horse and looked after them in startled wonder.

"What on earth can be the matter?" he muttered, struck with a vague feeling of alarm. A psychologist, seeking to trace the effects of slavery upon the human mind, might find in the South many a curious illustration of this curse, abiding long after the actual physical bondage has terminated. In the olden time the white South labored under the constant fear of negro insurrections. Knowing that they themselves, if in the negroes' place, would have risen in the effort to throw off the yoke, all their reiterated theories of negro subordination and inferiority could not remove that lurking fear, founding upon the obscure consciousness that the slaves ought to have risen. Conscience, it has been said, makes cowards of us all. There was never, on the continent of

America, a successful slave revolt, nor one which lasted more than a few hours, or resulted in the loss of more than a few white lives; yet never was the planter quite free from the fear that there might be one.

On the other hand, the slave had before his eyes always the fear of the master. There were good men, according to their lights,—according to their training and environment,— among the Southern slaveholders, who treated their slaves kindly, as slaves, from principle, because they recognized the claims of humanity, even under the dark skin of a human chattel. There was many a one who protected or pampered his negroes, as the case might be, just as a man fondles his dog,—because they were his; they were a part of his estate, an integral part of the entity of property and person which made up the aristocrat; but with all this kindness, there was always present, in the consciousness of the lowest slave, the knowledge that he was in his master's power, and that he could make no effectual protest against the abuse of that authority. There was also the knowledge, among those who could think at all, that the best of masters was himself a slave to a system, which hampered his movements but scarcely less than those of his bondmen.

When, therefore, Miller saw these men and women scampering into the bushes, he divined, with this slumbering race consciousness which years of culture had not obliterated, that there was some race trouble on foot. His intuition did not long remain unsupported. A black head was cautiously protruded from the shrubbery, and a black voice—if such a description be allowable—addressed him:

"Is dat you, Doctuh Miller?"

"Yes. Who are you, and what's the trouble?"

"What's de trouble, suh? Why, all hell's broke loose in town yonduh. De w'ite folks is riz 'gins' de niggers, an' say dey 're gwine ter kill eve'y nigger dey kin lay han's on."

Miller's heart leaped to his throat, as he thought of his wife and child. This story was preposterous; it could not be true, and yet there must be something in it. He tried to question his informant, but the man was so overcome with excitement and fear that Miller saw clearly that he must go farther for information. He had read in the Morning Chronicle, a few days before, the obnoxious editorial quoted from the Afro-American Banner, and had noted the comment upon it by the white editor. He had felt, as at the time of its first publication, that the editorial was ill-advised. It could do no good, and was calculated to arouse the animosity of those whose friendship, whose tolerance, at least, was necessary and almost indispensable to the colored people. They were living, at the best, in a sort of armed neutrality with the whites; such a publication, however serviceable elsewhere, could have no further effect in Wellington than to endanger this truce and defeat the hope of a possible future friendship. The right of free speech entitled Barber to publish it; a larger measure of common-sense would have made him withhold it. Whether it was the republication of this article that had stirred up anew the sleeping dogs of race prejudice and whetted their thirst for blood, he could not yet tell; but at any rate, there was mischief on foot.

"Fer God's sake, doctuh, don' go no closeter ter dat town," pleaded his informant, "er you'll be killt sho'. Come on wid us, suh, an' tek keer er yo'se'f. We're gwine ter hide in de swamps till dis thing is over!"

"God, man!" exclaimed Miller, urging his horse forward, "my wife and child are in the town!"

Fortunately, he reflected, there were no patients confined in the hospital,—if there should be anything in this preposterous story. To one unfamiliar with Southern life, it might have seemed impossible that these good Christian people, who thronged the churches on Sunday, and wept over the sufferings of the lowly Nazarene, and sent missionaries to the heathen, could be hungering and thirsting for the blood of their fellow men; but Miller cherished no such delusion. He knew the history of his country; he had the threatened lynching of Sandy Campbell vividly in mind; and he was fully persuaded that to race prejudice, once roused, any hor-

ror was possible. That women or children would be molested
of set purpose he did not believe, but that they might suffer
by accident was more than likely.

As he neared the town, dashing forward at the top of his
horse's speed, he heard his voice called in a loud and agitated
tone, and, glancing around him, saw a familiar form standing
by the roadside, gesticulating vehemently.

He drew up the horse with a suddenness that threw the
faithful and obedient animal back upon its haunches. The
colored lawyer, Watson, came up to the buggy. That he was
laboring under great and unusual excitement was quite apparent from his pale face and frightened air.

"What's the matter, Watson?" demanded Miller, hoping
now to obtain some reliable information.

"Matter!" exclaimed the other. "Everything's the matter!
The white people are up in arms. They have disarmed the
colored people, killing half a dozen in the process, and
wounding as many more. They have forced the mayor and
aldermen to resign, have formed a provisional city government *à la française*, and have ordered me and half a dozen
other fellows to leave town in forty-eight hours, under pain
of sudden death. As they seem to mean it, I shall not stay
so long. Fortunately, my wife and children are away. I knew
you were out here, however, and I thought I'd come out and
wait for you, so that we might talk the matter over. I don't
imagine they mean you any harm, personally, because you
tread on nobody's toes; but you're too valuable a man for
the race to lose, so I thought I'd give you warning. I shall
want to sell you my property, too, at a bargain. For I'm worth
too much to my family to dream of ever attempting to live
here again."

"Have you seen anything of my wife and child?" asked
Miller, intent upon the danger to which they might be
exposed.

"No; I did n't go to the house. I inquired at the drugstore
and found out where you had gone. You need n't fear for
them,—it is not a war on women and children."

"War of any kind is always hardest on the women and children," returned Miller; "I must hurry on and see that mine are safe."

"They'll not carry the war so far into Africa as that," returned Watson; "but I never saw anything like it. Yesterday I had a hundred white friends in the town, or thought I had,—men who spoke pleasantly to me on the street, and sometimes gave me their hands to shake. Not one of them said to me today: 'Watson, stay at home this afternoon.' I might have been killed, like any one of half a dozen others who have bit the dust, for any word that one of my 'friends' had said to warn me. When the race cry is started in this neck of the woods, friendship, religion, humanity, reason, all shrivel up like dry leaves in a raging furnace."

The buggy, into which Watson had climbed, was meanwhile rapidly nearing the town.

"I think I'll leave you here, Miller," said Watson, as they approached the outskirts, "and make my way home by a roundabout path, as I should like to get there unmolested. Home!—a beautiful word that, is n't it, for an exiled wanderer? It might not be well, either, for us to be seen together. If you put the hood of your buggy down, and sit well back in the shadow, you may be able to reach home without interruption; but avoid the main streets. I'll see you again this evening, if we're both alive, and I can reach you; for my time is short. A committee are to call in the morning to escort me to the train. I am to be dismissed from the community with public honors."

Watson was climbing down from the buggy, when a small party of men were seen approaching, and big Josh Green, followed by several other resolute-looking colored men, came up and addressed them.

"Dr. Miller," cried Green, "Mr. Watson,—we're lookin' fer a leader. De w'ite folks are killin' de niggers, an' we ain' gwine ter stan' up an' be shot down like dogs. We're gwine ter defen' ou' lives, an' we ain' gwine ter run away f'm no place where we've got a right ter be; an' woe be ter de w'ite man w'at lays han's on us! Dere 's two niggers in dis town ter ev'y w'ite man, an' ef we've got ter be killt, we'll take some w'ite folks 'long wid us, ez sho' ez dere's a God in heaven,—ez I s'pose dere is, dough He mus' be 'sleep, er busy somewhar e'se ter-day. Will you-all come an' lead us?''

"Gentlemen," said Watson, "what is the use? The negroes will not back you up. They have n't the arms, nor the moral courage, nor the leadership."

no arms

"We'll git de arms, an' we'll git de courage, ef you'll come an' lead us! We wants leaders,—dat's w'y we come ter you!"

"What's the use?" returned Watson despairingly. "The odds are too heavy. I've been ordered out of town; if I stayed, I'd be shot on sight, unless I had a body-guard around me."

"We'll be yo' body-guard!" shouted half a dozen voices.

"And when my body-guard was shot, what then? I have a wife and children. It is my duty to live for them. If I died, I should get no glory and no reward, and my family would be reduced to beggary,—to which they'll soon be near enough as it is. This affair will blow over in a day or two. The white people will be ashamed of themselves to-morrow, and apprehensive of the consequences for some time to come. Keep quiet, boys, and trust in God. You won't gain anything by resistance."

" 'God he'ps dem dat he'ps demselves,' " returned Josh stoutly. "Ef Mr. Watson won't lead us, will you, Dr. Miller?" said the spokesman, turning to the doctor.

urge to lead

For Miller it was an agonizing moment. He was no coward, morally or physically. Every manly instinct urged him to go forward and take up the cause of these leaderless people, and, if need be, to defend their lives and their rights with his own,—but to what end?

"Listen, men," he said. "We would only be throwing our lives away. Suppose we made a determined stand and won a temporary victory. By morning every train, every boat, every road leading into Wellington, would be crowded with white men,—as they probably will be any way,—with arms in their hands, curses on their lips, and vengeance in their hearts. In

also author voice?

the minds of those who make and administer the laws, we
have no standing in the court of conscience. They would kill
us in the fight, or they would hang us afterwards,—one way
or another, we should be doomed. I should like to lead you;
I should like to arm every colored man in this town, and
have them stand firmly in line, not for attack, but for defense; but if I attempted it, and they should stand by me,
which is questionable,—for I have met them fleeing from the
town,—my life would pay the forfeit. Alive, I may be of some
use to you, and you are welcome to my life in that way,—I
am giving it freely. Dead, I should be a mere lump of carrion.
Who remembers even the names of those who have been
done to death in the Southern States for the past twenty
years?"

"I 'members de name er one of 'em," said Josh, "an' I
'members de name er de man dat killt 'im, an' I s'pec' his
time is mighty nigh come."

"My advice is not heroic, but I think it is wise. In this
riot we are place as we should be in a war: we have no
territory, no base of supplies, no organization, no outside
sympathy,—we stand in the position of a race, in a case like
this, without money and without friends. Our time will
come,—the time when we can command respect for our
rights; but it is not yet in sight. Give it up, boys, and wait.
Good may come of this, after all."

Several of the men wavered, and looked irresolute.

"I reckon that's all so, doctuh," returned Josh, "an', de
way you put it, I don' blame you ner Mr. Watson; but all
dem reasons ain' got no weight wid me. I'm gwine in dat
town, an' ef any w'ite man 'sturbs me, dere'll be trouble,—
dere'll be trouble,—I feels it in my bones!"

"Remember your old mother, Josh," said Miller.

"Yah, suh, I'll 'member her; dat's all I kin do now. I don'
need ter wait fer her no mo', fer she died dis mo'nin'. I'd
lack ter see her buried, suh, but I may not have de chance.
Ef I gits killt, will you do me a favor?"

"Yes, Josh; what is it?"

"Ef I should git laid out in dis commotion dat's gwine on, will you collec' my wages f'm yo' brother, and see dat de ole 'oman is put away right?"

"Yes, of course."

"Wid a nice coffin, an' a nice fune'al, an' a headbo'd an' a foot-bo'd?"

"Yes."

"All right, suh! Ef I don' live ter do it, I'll know it'll be 'tended ter right. Now we're gwine out ter de cotton compress, an' git a lot er colored men tergether, an' ef de w'ite folks 'sturbs me, I should n't be s'prise' ef dere'd be a mix-up;—an' ef dere is, me an *one* w'ite man 'll stan' befo' de jedgment th'one er God dis day; an' it won't be me w'at'll be 'feared er de jedgment. Come along, boys! Dese gentlemen may have somethin' ter live fer; but ez fer my pa't, I'd ruther be a dead nigger any day dan a live dog!"

CHAPTER XXXIII

Into the Lion's Jaws

Josh leading

Not taking
a risk
+ cost

The party under Josh's leadership moved off down the road. Miller, while entirely convinced that he had acted wisely in declining to accompany them, was yet conscious of a distinct feeling of shame and envy that he, too, did not feel impelled to throw away his life in a hopeless struggle.

Watson left the buggy and disappeared by a path at the roadside. Miller drove rapidly forward. After entering the town, he passed several small parties of white men, but escaped scrutiny by sitting well back in his buggy, the presumption being that a well-dressed man with a good horse and buggy was white. Torn with anxiety, he reached home at about four o'clock. Driving the horse into the yard, he sprang down from the buggy and hastened to the house, which he found locked, front and rear.

A repeated rapping brought no response. At length he broke a window, and entered the house like a thief.

"Janet, Janet!" he called in alarm, "where are you? It is only I,—Will!"

There was no reply. He ran from room to room, only to find them all empty. Again he called his wife's name, and was about rushing from the house, when a muffled voice came faintly to his ear,—

"Is dat you, Doctuh Miller?"

"Yes. Who are you, and where are my wife and child?"

He was looking around in perplexity, when the door of a

low closet under the kitchen sink was opened from within, and a woolly head was cautiously protruded.

"Are you *sho'* dat's you, doctuh?"

"Yes, Sally; where are"—

"An' not some w'ite man come ter bu'n down de house an' kill all de niggers?"

"No, Sally, it's me all right. Where is my wife? Where is my child?"

"Dey went over ter see Mis' Butler 'long 'bout two o'clock, befo' dis fuss broke out, suh. Oh, Lawdy, Lawdy, suh! Is all de cullud folks be'n killt 'cep'n' me an' you, suh? Fer de Lawd's sake, suh, you won' let 'em kill me, will you, suh? I'll wuk fer you fer nuthin', suh, all my bawn days, ef you'll save my life, suh!"

"Calm yourself, Sally. You'll be safe enough if you stay right here, I've no doubt. They'll not harm women,—of that I'm sure enough, although I have n't yet got the bearings of this deplorable affair. Stay here and look after the house. I must find my wife and child!"

The distance across the city to the home of the Mrs. Butler whom his wife had gone to visit was exactly one mile. Though Miller had a good horse in front of him, he was two hours in reaching his destination. Never will the picture of that ride fade from his memory. In his dreams he repeats it night after night, and sees the sights that wounded his eyes, and feels the thoughts—the haunting spirits of the thoughts— that tore his heart as he rode through hell to find those whom he was seeking.

For a short distance he saw nothing, and made rapid progress. As he turned the first corner, his horse shied at the dead body of a negro, lying huddled up in the collapse which marks sudden death. What Miller shuddered at was not so much the thought of death, to the sight of which his profession had accustomed him, as the suggestion of what it signified. He had taken with allowance the wild statement of the fleeing fugitives. Watson, too, had been greatly excited, and Josh Green's group were desperate men, as much liable to be misled by their courage as the others by their fears; but here was proof that murder had been done,—and his wife and children were in the town. Distant shouts, and the sound of firearms, increased his alarm. He struck his horse with the whip, and dashed on toward the heart of the city, which he must traverse in order to reach Janet and the child.

At the next corner lay the body of another man, with the red blood oozing from a ghastly wound in the forehead. The negroes seemed to have been killed, as the band plays in circus parades, at the street intersections, where the example would be most effective. Miller, with a wild leap of the heart, had barely passed this gruesome spectacle, when a sharp voice commanded him to halt, and emphasized the order by covering him with a revolver. Forgetting the prudence he had preached to others, he had raised his whip to strike the horse, when several hands seized the bridle.

"Come down, you damn fool," growled an authoritative voice. "Don't you see we're in earnest? Do you want to get killed?"

"Why should I come down?" asked Miller.

"Because we've ordered you to come down! This is the white people's day, and when they order, a nigger must obey. We're going to search you for weapons."

"Search away. You'll find nothing but a case of surgeon's tools, which I'm more than likely to need before this day is over, from all indications."

"No matter; we'll make sure of it! That's what we're here for. Come down, if you don't want to be pulled down!"

Miller stepped down from his buggy. His interlocutor, who made no effort at disguise, was a clerk in a dry-goods store where Miller bought most of his family and hospital supplies. He made no sign of recognition, however, and Miller claimed no acquaintance. This man, who had for several years emptied Miller's pockets in the course of more or less legitimate trade, now went through them, aided by another man, more rapidly than ever before, the searchers convincing themselves that Miller carried no deadly weapon upon his person. Meanwhile, a third ransacked the buggy with like result. Miller recognized several others of the party, who made not the slightest attempt at disguise, though no names were called by any one.

"Where are you going?" demanded the leader.

"I am looking for my wife and child," replied Miller.

"Well, run along, and keep them out of the streets when you find them; and keep your hands out of this affair, if you wish to live in this town, which from now on will be a white man's town, as you niggers will be pretty firmly convinced before night."

Miller drove on as swiftly as might be.

At the next corner he was stopped again. In the white man who held him up, Miller recognized a neighbor of his own. After a short detention and a perfunctory search, the white man remarked apologetically:—

"Sorry to have had to trouble you, doctuh, but them's the o'ders. It ain't men like you that we're after, but the vicious and criminal class of niggers."

Miller smiled bitterly as he urged his horse forward. He was quite well aware that the virtuous citizen who had stopped him had only a few weeks before finished a term in the penitentiary, to which he had been sentenced for stealing. Miller knew that he could have bought all the man owned for fifty dollars, and his soul for as much more.

A few rods farther on, he came near running over the body of a wounded man who lay groaning by the wayside. Every professional instinct urged him to stop and offer aid to the sufferer; but the uncertainty concerning his wife and child proved a stronger motive and urged him resistlessly forward. Here and there the ominous sound of firearms was audible. He might have thought this merely a part of the show, like the "powder play" of the Arabs, but for the bloody confirmation of its earnestness which had already assailed his vision. Somewhere in this seething cauldron of unrestrained passions were his wife and child, and he must hurry on.

His progress was painfully slow. Three times he was stopped and searched. More than once his way was barred, and he was ordered to turn back, each such occasion requiring a detour which consumed many minutes. The man who last stopped him was a well-known Jewish merchant. A Jew— God of Moses!—had so far forgotten twenty centuries of history as to join in the persecution of another oppressed race! When almost reduced to despair by these innumerable delays, he perceived, coming toward him, Mr. Ellis, the sub-editor of the Morning Chronicle. Miller had just been stopped and questioned again, and Ellis came up as he was starting once more upon his endless ride.

"Dr. Miller," said Ellis kindly, "it is dangerous for you on the streets. Why tempt the danger?"

"I am looking for my wife and child," returned Miller in desperation. "They are somewhere in this town,—I don't know where,—and I must find them."

Ellis had been horror-stricken by the tragedy of the afternoon, the wholly superfluous slaughter of a harmless people, whom a show of force would have been quite sufficient to overawe. Elaborate explanations were afterwards given for these murders, which were said, perhaps truthfully, not to have been premeditated, and many regrets were expressed. The young man had been surprised, quite as much as the negroes themselves, at the ferocity displayed. His own thoughts and feelings were attuned to anything but slaughter. Only that morning he had received a perfumed note, calling his attention to what the writer described as a very noble deed of his, and requesting him to call that evening and receive the writer's thanks. Had he known that Miss Pemberton, several weeks after their visit to the Sound, had driven out again to the hotel and made some inquiries among the servants, he might have understood better the meaning of this missive. When Miller spoke of his wife and child, some subtle thread of suggestion coupled the note with Miller's plight.

"I'll go with you, Dr. Miller," he said, "if you'll permit me. In my company you will not be disturbed."

He took a seat in Miller's buggy, after which it was not molested.

Neither of them spoke. Miller was sick at heart; he could have wept with grief, even had the welfare of his own dear ones not been involved in this regrettable affair. With prophetic instinct he foresaw the hatreds to which this day would give birth; the long years of constraint and distrust which would still further widen the breach between two peoples whom fate had thrown together in one community.

There was nothing for Ellis to say. In his heart he could not defend the deeds of this day. The petty annoyances which the whites had felt at the spectacle of a few negroes in office; the not unnatural resentment of a proud people at what had seemed to them a presumptuous freedom of speech and lack of deference on the part of their inferiors,—these things, which he knew were to be made the excuse for overturning the city government, he realized full well were no sort of justification for the wholesale murder or other horror which might well ensue before the day was done. He could not approve the acts of his own people; neither could he, to a negro, condemn them. Hence he was silent.

"Thank you, Mr. Ellis," exclaimed Miller, when they had reached the house where he expected to find his wife. "This is the place where I was going. I am—under a great obligation to you."

"Not at all, Dr. Miller. I need not tell you how much I regret this deplorable affair."

Ellis went back down the street. Fastening his horse to the fence, Miller sprang forward to find his wife and child. They would certainly be there, for no colored woman would be foolhardy enough to venture on the streets after the riot had broken out.

As he drew nearer, he felt a sudden apprehension. The house seemed strangely silent and deserted. The doors were closed, and the venetian blinds shut tightly. Even a dog which had appeared slunk timidly back under the house, instead of barking vociferously according to the usual habit of his kind.

CHAPTER XXXIV

The Valley of the Shadow

Miller knocked at the door. There was no response. He went round to the rear of the house. The dog had slunk behind the woodpile. Miller knocked again, at the back door, and, receiving no reply, called aloud.

"Mrs. Butler! It is I, Dr. Miller. Is my wife here?"

The slats of a near-by blind opened cautiously.

"Is it really you, Dr. Miller?"

"Yes, Mrs. Butler. I am looking for my wife and child,— are they here?"

"No, sir; she became alarmed about you, soon after the shooting commenced, and I could not keep her. She left for home half an hour ago. It is coming on dusk, and she and the child are so near white that she did not expect to be molested."

"Which way did she go?"

"She meant to go by the main street. She thought it would be less dangerous than the back streets. I tried to get her to stay here, but she was frantic about you, and nothing I could say would keep her. Is the riot almost over, Dr. Miller? Do you think they will murder us all, and burn down our houses?"

"God knows," replied Miller, with a groan. "But I must find her, if I lose my own life in the attempt."

Surely, he thought, Janet would be safe. The white people of Wellington were not savages; or at least their temporary reversion to savagery would not go as far to include violence

717

CHARLES W. CHESNUTT

to delicate women and children. Then there flashed into his mind Josh Green's story of his "silly" mother, who for twenty years had walked the earth as a child, as the result of one night's terror, and his heart sank within him.

Miller realized that his buggy, by attracting attention, had been a hindrance rather than a help in his progress across the city. In order to follow his wife, he must practically retrace his steps over the very route he had come. Night was falling. It would be easier to cross the town on foot. In the dusk his own color, slight in the daytime, would not attract attention, and by dodging in the shadows he might avoid those who might wish to intercept him. But he must reach Janet and the boy at any risk. He had not been willing to throw his life away hopelessly, but he would cheerfully have sacrificed it for those whom he loved.

He had gone but a short distance, and had not yet reached the center of mob activity, when he intercepted a band of negro laborers from the cotton compress, with big Josh Green at their head.

"Hello, doctuh!" cried Josh, "does you wan' ter jine us?"

"I'm looking for my wife and child, Josh. They're somewhere in this den of murderers. Have any of you seen them?"

No one had seen them.

"You men are running a great risk," said Miller. "You are rushing on to certain death."

"Well, suh, maybe we is; but we're gwine ter die fightin'. Dey say de w'ite folks is gwine ter bu'n all de cullud schools an' chu'ches, an' kill all de niggers dey kin ketch. Dey're gwine ter bu'n yo' new hospittle, er somebody don' stop 'em."

"Josh—men—you are throwing your lives away. It is a fever; it will wear off to-morrow, or to-night. They'll not burn the schoolhouses, nor the hospital—they are not such fools, for they benefit the community; and they'll only kill the colored people who resist them. Every one of you with a gun or a pistol carries his death warrant in his own hand. I'd rather see the hospital burn then have one of you lose his life. Resistance only makes the matter worse,—the odds against you are too long."

"Things can't be any wuss, doctuh," replied one of the crowd sturdily. "A gun is mo' dange'ous ter de man in front of it dan ter de man behin' it. Dey're gwine ter kill us anyhow; an' we're tired,—we read de newspapers,—an' we're tired er bein' shot down like dogs, widout jedge er jury. We'd ruther die fightin' dan be stuck like pigs in a pen!"

"God help you!" said Miller. "As for me, I must find my wife and child."

"Good-bye, doctuh," cried Josh, brandishing a huge knife. " 'Member 'bout de ole 'oman, ef yo lives thoo dis. Don' fergit de headbo'd an' de footbo'd, an' a silver plate on de coffin, ef dere's money ernuff."

They went their way, and Miller hurried on. They might resist attack; he thought it extremely unlikely that they would begin it; but he knew perfectly well that the mere knowledge that some of the negroes contemplated resistance would only further inflame the infuriated whites. The colored men might win a momentary victory, though it was extremely doubtful; and they would as surely reap the harvest later on. The qualities which in a white man would win the applause of the world would in a negro be taken as the marks of savagery. So thoroughly diseased was public opinion in matters of race that the negro who died for the common rights of humanity might look for no meed of admiration or glory. At such a time, in the white man's eyes, a negro's courage would be mere desperation; his love of liberty, a mere animal dislike of restraint. Every finer human instinct would be interpreted in terms of savagery. Or, if forced to admire, they would none the less repress. They would applaud his courage while they stretched his neck, or carried off the fragments of his mangled body as souvenirs, in much the same way that savages preserve the scalps or eat the hearts of their enemies.

But concern for the fate of Josh and his friends occupied only a secondary place in Miller's mind for the moment. His wife and child were somewhere ahead of him. He pushed on.

He had covered about a quarter of a mile more, and far down the street could see the signs of greater animation, when he came upon the body of a woman lying upon the sidewalk. In the dusk he had almost stumbled over it, and his heart came up in his mouth. A second glance revealed that it could not be his wife. It was a fearful portent, however, of what her fate might be. The "war" had reached the women and children. Yielding to a professional instinct, he stooped, and saw that the prostrate form was that of old Aunt Jane Letlow. She was not yet quite dead, and as Miller, with a tender touch, placed her head in a more comfortable position, her lips moved with a last lingering flicker of consciousness:—

"Comin', missis, comin'!"

Mammy Jane had gone to join the old mistress upon whose memory her heart was fixed; and yet not all her reverence for her old mistress, nor all her deference to the whites, nor all their friendship for her, had been able to save her from this raging devil of race hatred which momentarily possessed the town.

Perceiving that he could do no good, Miller hastened onward, sick at heart. Whenever he saw a party of white men approaching,—these brave reformers never went singly,—he sought concealment in the shadow of a tree or the shrubbery in some yard until they had passed. He had covered about two thirds of the distance homeward, when his eyes fell upon a group beneath a lamp-post, at sight of which he turned pale with horror, and rushed forward with a terrible cry.

CHAPTER XXXV

"Mine Enemy, O Mine Enemy!"

Narrator

The proceedings of the day—planned originally as a "demonstration," dignified subsequently as a "revolution," under any name the culmination of the conspiracy formed by Carteret and his colleagues—had by seven o'clock in the afternoon developed into a murderous riot. Crowds of white men and half-grown boys, drunk with whiskey or with license, raged through the streets, beating, chasing, or killing any negro so unfortunate as to fall into their hands. Why any particular negro was assailed, no one stopped to inquire; it was merely a white mob thirsting for black blood, with no more conscience or discrimination than would be exercised by a wolf in a sheepfold. It was race against race, the whites against the negroes; and it was a one-sided affair, for until Josh Green got together his body of armed men, no effective resistance had been made by any colored person, and the individuals who had been killed had so far left no marks upon the enemy by which they might be remembered.

White mob slogan

"Kill the niggers!" rang out now and then through the dusk, and far down the street and along the intersecting thoroughfares distant voices took up the ominous refrain,—"Kill the niggers! Kill the damned niggers!"

Now, not a dark face had been seen on the street for half an hour, until the group of men headed by Josh made their appearance in the negro quarter. Armed with guns and axes, they presented quite a formidable appearance as they made their way toward the new hospital, near which stood a schoolhouse and a large church, both used by the colored people. They did not reach their destination without having met a number of white men, singly or in twos or threes; and the rumor spread with incredible swiftness that the negroes in turn were up in arms, determined to massacre all the whites and burn the town. Some of the whites became alarmed, and recognizing the power of the negroes, if armed and conscious of their strength, were impressed by the immediate necessity of overpowering and overawing them. Others, with appetites already whetted by slaughter, saw a chance, welcome rather than not, of shedding more black blood. Spontaneously the white mob flocked toward the hospital, where rumor had it that a large body of desperate negroes, breathing threats of blood and fire, had taken a determined stand.

Josh's plan It had been Josh's plan merely to remain quietly and peaceably in the neighborhood of the little ground of public institutions, molesting no one, unless first attacked, and merely letting the white people see that they meant to protect their own; but so rapidly did the rumor spread, and so promptly did the white people act, that by the time Josh and his supporters had reached the top of the rising ground where the hospital stood, a crowd of white men much more numerous than their own party were following them at a short distance.

Josh, with the eye of a general, perceived that some of his party were becoming a little nervous, and decided that they would feel safer behind shelter.

"I reckon we better go inside de hospittle, boys," he exclaimed. "Den we'll be behind brick walls, an' dem other fellows 'll be outside, an' ef dere's any fightin', we'll have de bes' show. We ain' gwine ter do no shootin' till we're pestered, an' dey'll be less likely ter pester us ef dey can't git at us widout runnin' some resk. Come along in! Be men! De gov'ner er de President is gwine ter sen' soldiers ter stop dese gwines-on, an' meantime we kin keep dem white devils f'm bu'nin' down our hospittles an' chu'ch-houses. W'en dey comes an' fin's out dat we jes' means ter pertect ou' prope'ty, dey'll go 'long 'bout deir own business. Er, ef dey wants a scrap, dey kin have it! Come erlong, boys!"

Jane + Jerry Letlow

Jerry Letlow, who had kept out of sight during the day, had started out, after night had set in, to find Major Carteret. Jerry was very much afraid. The events of the day had filled him with terror. Whatever the limitations of Jerry's mind or character may have been, Jerry had a keen appreciation of the danger to the negroes when they came in conflict with the whites, and he had no desire to imperil his own skin. He valued his life for his own sake, and not for any altruistic theory that it might be of service to others. In other words, Jerry was something of a coward. He had kept in hiding all day, but finding, toward evening, that the riot did not abate, and fearing, from the rumors which came to his ears, that all the negroes would be exterminated, he had set out, somewhat desperately, to try to find his white patron and protector. He had been cautious to avoid meeting any white men, and, anticipating no danger from those of his own race, went toward the party which he saw approaching, whose path would cross his own. When they were only a few yards apart, Josh took a step forward and caught Jerry by the arm.

"Come along, Jerry, we need you! Here's another man, boys. Come on now, and fight fer yo' race!"

In vain Jerry protested. "I don' wan' ter fight," he howled. "De w'ite folks ain' gwine ter pester me; dey're my frien's. Tu'n me loose,—tu'n me loose, er we all gwine ter git killed!"

The party paid no attention to Jerry's protestations. Indeed, with the crowd of whites following behind, they were simply considering the question of a position from which they could most effectively defend themselves and the building which they imagined to be threatened. If Josh had released his grip of Jerry, that worthy could easily have escaped from the crowd; but Josh maintained his hold almost mechanically, and, in the confusion, Jerry found himself swept with the rest into the hospital, the doors of which were promptly barricaded with the heavier pieces of furniture, and the windows manned by several men each, Josh, with the instinct of a born commander, posting his forces so that they could cover with their guns all the approaches to the building. Jerry still continuing to make himself troublesome, Josh, in a moment of impatience, gave him a terrific box on the ear, which stretched him out upon the floor unconscious.

"Shet up," he said; "ef you can't stan' up like a man, keep still, and don't interfere wid men w'at will fight!"

The hospital, when Josh and his men took possession, had been found deserted. Fortunately there were no patients for that day, except one or two convalescents, and these, with the attendants, had joined the exodus of the colored people from the town.

A white man advanced from the crowd without toward the main entrance to the hospital. Big Josh, looking out from a window, grasped his gun more firmly, as his eyes fell upon the man who had murdered his father and darkened his mother's life. Mechanically he raised his rifle, but lowered it as the white man lifted up his hand as a sign that he wished to speak.

"You niggers," called Captain McBane loudly,—it was that worthy,—"you niggers are courtin' death, an' you won't have to court her but a minute er two mo' befo' she'll have you. If you surrender and give up your arms, you'll be dealt with leniently,—you may get off with the chain-gang or the penitentiary. If you resist, you'll be shot like dogs."

"Dat's no news, Mr. White Man," replied Josh, appearing boldly at the window. "We're use' ter bein' treated like dogs by men like you. If you w'ite people will go 'long an' ten' ter you' own business an' let us alone, we'll ten' ter ou'n. You've got guns, an' we've got jest as much right ter carry 'em as you have. Lay down yo'n, an' we'll lay down ou'n,— we did n' take 'em up fust; but we ain' gwine ter let you bu'n down ou' chu'ches an' school'ouses, er dis hospittle,

724

an' we ain' comin' out er dis house, where we ain' disturbin'
nobody, fer you ter shoot us down er sen' us ter jail. You
hear me!"

"All right," responded Mcbane. "You've had fair warning. Your blood be on your"—

His speech was interrupted by a shot from the crowd,
which splintered the window-casing close to Josh's head. This
was followed by half a dozen other shots, which were replied
to, almost simultaneously, by a volley from within, by which
one of the attacking party was killed and another wounded.

This roused the mob to frenzy.

"Vengeance! vengeance!" they yelled. "Kill the niggers!"

A negro had killed a white man,—unpardonable sin, admitting neither excuse, justification, nor extenuation. From
time immemorial it had been bred in the Southern white
consciousness, and in the negro consciousness also, for that
matter, that the person of a white man was sacred from the
touch of a negro, no matter what the provocation. A dozen
colored men lay dead in the streets of Wellington, inoffensive people, slain in cold blood because they had been bold
enough to question the authority of those who had assailed
them, or frightened enough to flee when they had been ordered to stand still; but their lives counted nothing against
that of a riotous white man, who had courted death by attacking a body of armed men.

The crowd, too, surrounding the hospital, had changed
somewhat in character. The men who had acted as leaders
in the early afternoon, having accomplished their purpose of
overturning the local administration and establishing a provisional government of their own, had withdrawn from active participation in the rioting, deeming the negroes already
sufficiently overawed to render unlikely any further trouble
from that source. Several of the ringleaders had indeed begun
to exert themselves to prevent further disorder, or any loss
of property, the possibility of which had become apparent;
but those who set in motion the forces of evil cannot always
control them afterwards. The baser element of the white

population, recruited from the wharves and the saloons, was now predominant.

Captain McBane was the only one of the revolutionary committee who had remained with the mob, not with any purpose to restore or preserve order, but because he found the company and the occasion entirely congenial. He had had no opportunity, at least no tenable excuse, to kill or maim a negro since the termination of his contract with the state for convicts, and this occasion had awakened a dormant appetite for these diversions. We are all puppets in the hands of Fate, and seldom see the strings that move us. McBane had lived a life of violence and cruelty. As a man sows, so shall he reap. In works of fiction, such men are sometimes converted. More often, in real life, they do not change their natures until they are converted into dust. One does well to distrust a tamed tiger.

On the outskirts of the crowd a few of the better class, or at least of the better clad, were looking on. The double volley described had already been fired, when the number of these was augmented by the arrival of Major Carteret and Mr. Ellis, who had just come from the Chronicle office, where the next day's paper had been in hasty preparation. They pushed their way towards the front of the crowd.

"This must be stopped, Ellis," said Carteret. "They are burning houses and killing women and children. Old Jane, good old Mammy Jane, who nursed my wife at her bosom, and has waited on her and my child within a few weeks, was killed only a few rods from my house, to which she was evidently fleeing for protection. It must have been by accident,—I cannot believe that any white man in town would be dastard enough to commit such a deed intentionally! I would have defended her with my own life! We must try to stop this thing!"

"Easier said than done," returned Ellis. "It is in the fever stage, and must burn itself out. We shall be lucky if it does not burn the town out. Suppose the negroes should also take a hand at the burning? We have advised the people to put the negroes down, and they are doing the job thoroughly."

"My God!" replied the other, with a gesture of impatience, as he continued to elbow his way through the crowd; "I meant to keep them in their places,—I did not intend wholesale murder and arson."

Carteret, having reached the front of the mob, made an effort to gain their attention.

"Gentlemen!" he cried in his loudest tones. His voice, unfortunately, was neither loud nor piercing.

"Kill the niggers!" clamored the mob.

"Gentlemen, I implore you,"—

The crash of a dozen windows, broken by stones and pistol shots, drowned his voice.

"Gentlemen!" he shouted; "this is murder, it is madness; it is a disgrace to our city, to our state, to our civilization!"

"That's right!" replied several voices. The mob had recognized the speaker. "It *is* a disgrace, and we'll not put up with it a moment longer. Burn 'em out! Hurrah for Major Carteret, the champion of 'white supremacy'! Three cheers for the Morning Chronicle and 'no nigger domination'!"

"Hurrah, hurrah, hurrah!" yelled the crowd.

In vain the baffled orator gesticulated and shrieked in the effort to correct the misapprehension. Their oracle had spoken; not hearing what he said, they assumed it to mean encouragement and coöperation. Their present course was but the logical outcome of the crusade which the Morning Chronicle had preached, in season and out of season, for many months. When Carteret had spoken, and the crowd had cheered him, they felt that they had done all that courtesy required, and he was good-naturedly elbowed aside while they proceeded with the work in hand, which was now to drive out the negroes from the hospital and avenge the killing of their comrade.

Some brought hay, some kerosene, and others wood from

a pile which had been thrown into a vacant lot near by. Several safe ways of approach to the building were discovered, and the combustibles placed and fired. The flames, soon gaining a foothold, leaped upward, catching here and there at the exposed woodwork, and licking the walls hungrily with long tongues of flame.

Meanwhile a desultory firing was kept up from the outside, which was replied to scatteringly from within the hospital. Those inside were either not good marksmen, or excitement had spoiled their aim. If a face appeared at a window, a dozen pistol shots from the crowd sought the spot immediately.

Higher and higher leaped the flames. Suddenly from one of the windows sprang a black figure, waving a white handkerchief. It was Jerry Letlow. Regaining consciousness after the effect of Josh's blow had subsided, Jerry had kept quiet and watched his opportunity. From a safe vantage-ground he had scanned the crowd without in search of some white friend. When he saw Major Carteret moving disconsolately away after his futile effort to stem the torrent, Jerry made a dash for the window. He sprang forth, and, waving his handkerchief as a flag of truce, ran toward Major Carteret, shouting frantically:—

"Majah Carteret—O majah! It's me, suh, Jerry, suh! I did n' go in dere myse'f, suh,—I wuz drag' in dere! I would n' do nothin' 'g'inst de w'ite folks, suh,—no, 'ndeed, I would n', suh!"

Jerry's cries were drowned in a roar of rage and a volley of shots from the mob. Carteret, who had turned away with Ellis, did not even hear his servant's voice. Jerry's poor flag of truce, his explanations, his reliance upon his white friends, all failed him in the moment of supreme need. In that hour, as in any hour when the depths of race hatred are stirred, a negro was no more than a brute beast, set upon by other brute beasts whose only instinct was to kill and destroy.

"Let us leave this inferno, Ellis," said Carteret, sick with anger and disgust. He had just become aware that a negro was being killed, though he did not know whom. "We can do nothing. The negroes have themselves to blame,—they tempted us beyond endurance. I counseled firmness, and firm measures were taken, and our purpose was accomplished. I am not responsible for these subsequent horrors,—I wash my hands of them. Let us go!"

The flames gained headway and gradually enveloped the burning building, until it became evident to those within as well as those without that the position of the defenders was no longer tenable. Would they die in the flames, or would they be driven out? The uncertainty soon came to an end.

The besieged had been willing to fight, so long as there seemed a hope of successfully defending themselves and their property; for their purpose was purely one of defense. When they saw the case was hopeless, inspired by Josh Green's reckless courage, they were still willing to sell their lives dearly. One or two of them had already been killed, and as many more disabled. The fate of Jerry Letlow had struck terror to the hearts of several others, who could scarcely hide their fear. After the building had been fired, Josh's exhortations were no longer able to keep them in the hospital. They preferred to fight and be killed in the open, rather than to be smothered like rats in a hole.

"Boys!" exclaimed Josh,—"men!—fer nobody but men would do w'at you have done,—the day has gone 'g'inst us. We kin see ou' finish; but fer my part, I ain' gwine ter leave dis worl' widout takin' a w'ite man 'long wid me, an' I sees my man right out yonder waitin',—I be'n waitin' fer him twenty years, but he won' have ter wait fer me mo' 'n 'bout twenty seconds. Eve'y one er you pick yo' man! We'll open de do', an' we'll give some w'ite men a chance ter be sorry dey ever started dis fuss!"

The door was thrown open suddenly, and through it rushed a dozen or more black figures, armed with knives, pistols, or clubbed muskets. Taken by sudden surprise, the white people stood motionless for a moment, but the approaching negroes had scarcely covered half the distance to which the heat of the flames had driven back the mob, before they were greeted with a volley that laid them all low but two. One of these, dazed by the fate of his companions, turned instinctively to flee, but had scarcely faced around before he fell, pierced in the back by a dozen bullets.

Josh Green, the tallest and biggest of them all, had not apparently been touched. Some of the crowd paused in involuntary admiration of this black giant, famed on the wharves for his strength, sweeping down upon them, a smile upon his face, his eyes lit up with a rapt expression which seemed to take him out of mortal ken. This impression was heightened by his apparent immunity from the shower of lead which less susceptible persons had continued to pour at him.

Armed with a huge bowie-knife, a relic of the civil war, which he had carried on his person for many years for a definite purpose, and which he had kept sharpened to a razor edge, he reached the line of the crowd. All but the bravest shrank back. Like a wedge he dashed through the mob, which parted instinctively before him, and all oblivious of the rain of lead which fell around him, reached the point where Captain McBane, the bravest man in the party, stood waiting to meet him. A pistol-flame flashed in his face, but he went on, and raising his powerful right arm, buried his knife to the hilt in the heart of his enemy. When the crowd dashed forward to wreak vengeance on his dead body, they found him with a smile still upon his face.

One of the two died as the fool dieth. Which was it, or was it both? "Vengeance is mine," said the Lord, and it had not been left to Him. But they that do violence must expect to suffer violence. McBane's death was merciful, compared with the nameless horrors he had heaped upon the hundreds of helpless mortals who had fallen into his hands during his career as a contractor of convict labor.

Sobered by this culminating tragedy, the mob shortly afterwards dispersed. The flames soon completed their work, and this handsome structure, the fruit of old Adam Miller's industry, the monument of his son's philanthropy, a promise of good things for the future of the city, lay smouldering in ruins, a melancholy witness to the fact that our boasted civilization is but a thin veneer, which cracks and scales off at the first impact of primal passions.

Who is annalistic here?

CHAPTER XXXVI

Fiat Justitia

By the light of the burning building, which illuminated the street for several blocks, Major Carteret and Ellis made their way rapidly until they turned into the street where the major lived. Reaching the house, Carteret tried the door and found it locked. A vigorous ring at the bell brought no immediate response. Carteret had begun to pound impatiently upon the door, when it was cautiously opened by Miss Pemberton, who was pale, and trembled with excitement.

"Where is Olivia?" asked the major.

"She is upstairs, with Dodie and Mrs. Albright's hospital nurse. Dodie has the croup. Virgie ran away after the riot broke out. Sister Olivia had sent for Mammy Jane, but she did not come. Mrs. Albright let her white nurse come over."

"I'll go up at once," said the major anxiously. "Wait for me, Ellis,—I'll be down in a few minutes."

"Oh, Mr. Ellis," exclaimed Clara, coming toward him with both hands extended, "can nothing be done to stop this terrible affair?"

"I wish I could do something," he murmured fervently, taking both her trembling hands in his own broad palms, where they rested with a surrendering trustfulness which he has never since had occasion to doubt. "It has gone too far, already, and the end, I fear, is not yet; but it cannot grow much worse."

The editor hurried upstairs. Mrs. Carteret, wearing a

worried and haggard look, met him at the threshold of the nursery.

"Dodie is ill," she said. "At three o'clock, when the trouble began, I was over at Mrs. Albright's,—I had left Virgie with the baby. When I came back, she and all the other servants had gone. They had heard that the white people were going to kill all the negroes, and fled to seek safety. I found Dodie lying in a draught, before an open window, gasping for breath. I ran back to Mrs. Albright's,—I had found her much better to-day,—and she let her nurse come over. The nurse says that Dodie is threatened with membranous croup."

"Have you sent for Dr. Price?"

"There was no one to send,—the servants were gone, and the nurse was afraid to venture out into the street. I telephoned for Dr. Price, and found that he was out of town; that he had gone up the river this morning to attend a patient, and would not be back until to-morrow. Mrs. Price thought that he had anticipated some kind of trouble in the town to-day, and had preferred to be where he could not be called upon to assume any responsibility."

"I suppose you tried Dr. Ashe?"

"I could not get him, nor any one else, after that first call. The telephone service is disorganized on account of the riot. We need medicine and ice. The drugstores are all closed on account of the riot, and for the same reason we couldn't get any ice."

Major Carteret stood beside the brass bedstead upon which his child was lying,—his only child, around whose curly head clustered all his hopes; upon whom all his life for the past year had been centered. He stooped over the bed, beside which the nurse had stationed herself. She was wiping the child's face, which was red and swollen and covered with moisture, the nostrils working rapidly, and the little patient vainly endeavoring at intervals to cough up the obstruction to his breathing.

"Is it serious?" he inquired anxiously. He had always

733

CHARLES W. CHESNUTT

thought of the croup as a childish ailment, that yielded readily to proper treatment; but the child's evident distress impressed him with sudden fear.

"Dangerous," replied the young woman laconically. "You came none too soon. If a doctor is n't got at once, the child will die,—and it must be a good doctor."

"Whom can I call?" he asked. "You know them all, I suppose. Dr. Price, our family physician, is out of town."

"Dr. Ashe has charge of his cases when he is away," replied the nurse. "If you can't find him, try Dr. Hooper. The child is growing worse every minute. On your way back you'd better get some ice, if possible."

The major hastened downstairs.

"Don't wait for me, Ellis," he said. "I shall be needed here for a while. I'll get to the office as soon as possible. Make up the paper, and leave another stick out for me to the last minute, but fill it up in case I'm not on hand by twelve. We must get the paper out early in the morning."

Nothing but a matter of the most vital importance would have kept Major Carteret away from his office this night. Upon the presentation to the outer world of the story of this riot would depend the attitude of the great civilized public toward the events of the last ten hours. The Chronicle was the source from which the first word would be expected; it would give the people of Wellington their cue as to the position which they must take in regard to this distressful affair, which had so far transcended in ferocity the most extreme measures which the conspirators had anticipated. The burden of his own responsibility weighed heavily upon him, and could not be shaken off; but he must do first the duty nearest to him,—he must first attend to his child.

Carteret hastened from the house, and traversed rapidly the short distance to Dr. Ashe's office. Far down the street he could see the glow of the burning hospital, and he had scarcely left his own house when the fusillade of shots, fired when the colored men emerged from the building, was audible. Carteret would have hastened back to the scene of the

riot, to see what was now going on, and to make another
effort to stem the tide of bloodshed; but before the dread of
losing his child, all other interests fell into the background.
Not all the negroes in Wellington could weigh in the balance for one instant against the life of the feeble child now
gasping for breath in the house behind him.

Reaching the house, a vigorous ring brought the doctor's
wife to the door.

"Good-evening, Mrs. Ashe. Is the doctor at home?"

"No, Major Carteret. He was called to attend to Mrs.
Wells, who was taken suddenly ill, as a result of the trouble
this afternoon. He will be there all night, no doubt."

"My child is very ill, and I must find some one."

"Try Dr. Yates. His house is only four doors away."

A ring at Dr. Yates's door brought out a young man.

"Is Dr. Yates in?"

"Yes, sir."

"Can I see him?"

"You might see him, sir, but that would be all. His horse
was frightened by the shooting on the streets, and ran away
and threw the doctor, and broke his right arm. I have just
set it; he will not be able to attend any patients for several
weeks. He is old and nervous, and the shock was great."

"Are you not a physician?" asked Carteret, looking at the
young man keenly. He was a serious, gentlemanly looking
young fellow, whose word might probably be trusted.

"Yes, I am Dr. Evans, Dr. Yates's assistant. I'm really little
more than a student, but I'll do what I can."

"My only child is sick with the croup, and requires immediate attention."

"I ought to be able to handle a case of the croup," answered Dr. Evans, "at least in the first stages. I'll go with
you, and stay by the child, and if the case is beyond me, I
may keep it in check until another physician comes."

He stepped back into another room, and returning immediately with his hat, accompanied Carteret homeward.
The riot had subsided; even the glow from the smouldering

hospital was no longer visible. It seemed that the city, appalled at the tragedy, had suddenly awakened to a sense of its own crime. Here and there a dark face, emerging cautiously from some hiding-place, peered from behind fence or tree, but shrank hastily away at the sight of a white face. The negroes of Wellington, with the exception of Josh Green and his party, had not behaved bravely on this critical day in their history; but those who had fought were dead, to the last man; those who had sought safety in flight or concealment were alive to tell the tale.

"We pass right by Dr. Thompson's," said Dr. Evans. "If you have n't spoken to him, it might be well to call him for consultation, in case the child should be very bad."

"Go on ahead," said Carteret, "and I'll get him."

Evans hastened on, while Carteret sounded the old-fashioned knocker upon the doctor's door. A gray-haired negro servant, clad in a dress suit and wearing a white tie, came to the door.

"De doctuh, suh," he replied politely to Carteret's question, "has gone ter ampitate de ahm er a gent'eman who got one er his bones smashed wid a pistol bullet in de—fightin' dis atternoon, suh. He's jes' gone, suh, an' lef' wo'd dat he'd be gone a' hour er mo', suh."

Carteret hastened homeward. He could think of no other available physician. Perhaps no other would be needed, but if so, he could find out from Evans whom it was best to call.

When he reached the child's room, the young doctor was bending anxiously over the little frame. The little lips had become livid, the little nails, lying against the white sheet, were blue. The child's efforts to breathe were most distressing, and each gasp cut the father like a knife. Mrs. Carteret was weeping hysterically.

"How is he, doctor?" asked the Major.

"He is very low," replied the young man. "Nothing short of tracheotomy—an operation to open the windpipe—will relieve him. Without it, in half or three quarters of an hour he will be unable to breathe. It is a delicate operation, a mistake in which would be as fatal as the disease. I have neither the knowledge nor the experience to attempt it, and your child's life is too valuable for a student to practice upon. Neither have I the instruments here."

"What shall we do?" demanded Carteret. "We have called all the best doctors, and none are available."

The young doctor's brow was wrinkled with thought. He knew a doctor who could perform the operation. He had heard, also, of a certain event at Carteret's house some months before, when an unwelcome physician had been excluded from a consultation,—but it was the last chance.

"There is but one other doctor in town who has performed the operation, so far as I know," he declared, "and that is Dr. Miller. If you can get him, he can save your child's life."

Carteret hesitated involuntarily. All the incidents, all the arguments, of the occasion when he had refused to admit the colored doctor to his house, came up vividly before his memory. He had acted in accordance with his lifelong beliefs, and had carried his point; but the present situation was different,—this was a case of imperative necessity, and every other interest or consideration must give way before the imminence of his child's peril. That the doctor would refuse the call, he did not imagine: it would be too great an honor for a negro to decline,—unless some bitterness might have grown out of the proceedings of the afternoon. That this doctor was a man of some education he knew; and he had been told that he was a man of fine feeling,—for a negro,—and might easily have taken to heart the day's events. Nevertheless, he could hardly refuse a professional call,—professional ethics would require him to respond. Carteret had no reason to suppose that Miller had ever learned of what had occurred at the house during Dr. Burns's visit to Wellington. The major himself had never mentioned the controversy, and no doubt the other gentlemen had been equally silent.

"I'll go for him myself," said Dr. Evans, noting Carteret's hesitation and suspecting the cause. "I can do nothing here alone, for a little while, and I may be able to bring the doctor back with me. He likes a difficult operation."

It seemed an age ere the young doctor returned, though it was really only a few minutes. The nurse did what she could to relieve the child's sufferings, which grew visibly more and more acute. The mother, upon the other side of the bed, held one of the baby's hands in her own, and controlled her feelings as best she might. Carteret paced the floor anxiously, going every few seconds to the head of the stairs to listen for Evans's footsteps on the piazza without. At last the welcome sound was audible, and a few strides took him to the door.

"Dr. Miller is at home, sir," reported Evans, as he came in. "He says that he was called to your house once before, by a third person who claimed authority to act, and that he was refused admittance. He declares that he will not consider such a call unless it come from you personally."

"That is true, quite true," replied Carteret. "His position is a just one. I will go at once. Will—will—my child live until I can get Miller here?"

"He can live for half an hour without an operation. Beyond that I could give you little hope."

Seizing his hat, Carteret dashed out of the yard and ran rapidly to Miller's house; ordinarily a walk of six or seven minutes, Carteret covered it in three, and was almost out of breath when he rang the bell of Miller's front door.

The ring was answered by the doctor in person.

"Dr. Miller, I believe?" asked Carteret.

"Yes, sir."

"I am Major Carteret. My child is seriously ill, and you are the only available doctor who can perform the necessary operation."

"Ah! You have tried all the others,—and then you come to me!"

"Yes, I do not deny it," admitted the major, biting his lip. He had not counted on professional jealousy as an obstacle to be met. "But I *have* come to you, as a physician, to engage

your professional services for my child,—my only child. I have
confidence in your skill, or I should not have come to you.
I request,—nay, I implore you to lose no more time, but come
with me at once! My child's life is hanging by a thread, and
you can save it!"

"Ah!" replied the other, "as a father whose only child's
life is in danger, you implore *me*, of all men in the world, to
come and save it!"

There was a strained intensity in the doctor's low voice
that struck Carteret, in spite of his own preoccupation. He
thought he heard, too, from the adjoining room, the sound
of some one sobbing softly. There was some mystery here
which he could not fathom unaided.

Miller turned to the door behind him and threw it open.
On the white cover of a low cot lay a childish form in the
rigidity of death, and by it knelt, with her back to the door,
a woman whose shoulders were shaken by the violence of
her sobs. Absorbed in her grief, she did not turn, or give any
sign that she had recognized the intrusion.

"There, Major Carteret!" exclaimed Miller, with the tragic
eloquence of despair, "there lies a specimen of your handi-
work! There lies *my* only child, laid low by a stray bullet in
this riot which you and your paper have fomented; struck
down as much by your hand as though you had held the
weapon with which his life was taken!"

"My God!" exclaimed Carteret, struck with horror. "Is
the child dead?"

"There he lies," continued the other, "an innocent
child,—there he lies dead, his little life snuffed out like a
candle, because you and a handful of your friends thought
you must override the laws and run this town at any cost!—
and there kneels his mother, overcome by grief. We are alone
in the house. It is not safe to leave her unattended. My duty
calls me here, by the side of my dead child and my suffering
wife! I cannot go with you. There is a just God in heaven!—
as you have sown, so you may reap!"

Carteret possessed a narrow, but a logical mind, and except when confused or blinded by his prejudices, had always tried to be a just man. In the agony of his own predicament,—in the horror of the situation at Miller's house,—for a moment the veil of race prejudice was rent in twain, and he saw things as they were, in their correct proportions and relations,—saw clearly and convincingly that he had no standing here, in the presence of death, in the home of this stricken family. Miller's refusal to go with him was pure, elemental justice; he could not blame the doctor for his stand. He was indeed conscious of a certain involuntary admiration for a man who held in his hands the power of life and death, and could use it, with strict justice, to avenge his own wrongs. In Dr. Miller's place he would have done the same thing. Miller had spoken the truth,—as he had sown, so must he reap! He could not expect, could not ask, this father to leave his own household at such a moment.

Pressing his lips together with grim courage, and bowing mechanically, as though to Fate rather than the physician, Carteret turned and left the house. At a rapid pace he soon reached home. There was yet another chance for his child: perhaps some one of the other doctors had come; perhaps, after all, the disease had taken a favorable turn,—Evans was but a young doctor, and might have been mistaken. Surely, with doctors all around him, his child would not be permitted to die for lack of medical attention! He found the mother, the doctor, and the nurse still grouped, as he had left them, around the suffering child.

"How is he now?" he asked, in a voice that sounded like a groan.

"No better," replied the doctor; "steadily growing worse. He can go on probably for twenty minutes longer without an operation."

"Where is the doctor?" demanded Mrs. Carteret, looking eagerly toward the door. "You should have brought him right upstairs. There's not a minute to spare! Phil, Phil, our child will die!"

Carteret's heart swelled almost to bursting with an intense

pity. Even his own great sorrow became of secondary importance beside the grief which his wife must soon feel at the inevitable loss of her only child. And it was his fault! Would that he could risk his own life to spare her and to save the child!

Briefly, and as gently as might be, he stated the result of his errand. The doctor had refused to come, for a good reason. He could not ask him again.

Young Evans felt the logic of the situation, which Carteret had explained sufficiently. To the nurse it was even clearer. If she or any other woman had been in the doctor's place, she would have given the same answer.

Mrs. Carteret did not stop to reason. In such a crisis a mother's heart usurps the place of intellect. For her, at that moment, there were but two facts in all the world. Her child lay dying. There was within the town, and within reach, a man who could save him. With an agonized cry she rushed wildly from the room.

Carteret sought to follow her, but she flew down the long stairs like a wild thing. The least misstep might have precipitated her to the bottom; but ere Carteret, with a remonstrance on his lips, had scarcely reached the uppermost step, she had thrown open the front door and fled precipitately out into the night.

CHAPTER XXXVII

The Sisters

Miller's doorbell rang loudly, insistently, as though demanding a response. Absorbed in his own grief, into which he had relapsed upon Carteret's departure, the sound was an unwelcome intrusion. Surely the man could not be coming back! If it were some one else—What else might happen to the doomed town concerned him not. His child was dead,—his distracted wife could not be left alone.

The doorbell rang—clamorously—appealingly. Through the long hall and the closed door of the room where he sat, he could hear some one knocking and a faint voice calling.

"Open, for God's sake, open!"

It was a woman's voice,—the voice of a woman in distress. Slowly Miller rose and went to the door, which he opened mechanically.

A lady stood there, so near the image of his own wife, whom he had just left, that for a moment he was well-nigh startled. A little older, perhaps, a little fairer of complexion, but with the same form, the same features, marked by the same wild grief. She wore a loose wrapper, which clothed her like the drapery of a statue. Her long dark hair, the counterpart of his wife's, had fallen down, and hung disheveled about her shoulders. There was blood upon her knuckles, where she had beaten with them upon the door.

"Dr. Miller," she panted, breathless from her flight and laying her hand upon his arm appealingly,—when he shrank from the contact she still held it there,—"Dr. Miller, you will come and save my child? You know what it is to lose a child! I am so sorry about your little boy! You will come to mine!"

"Your sorrow comes too late, madam," he said harshly. "My child is dead. I charged your husband with his murder, and he could not deny it. Why should I save your husband's child?"

"Ah, Dr. Miller!" she cried, with his wife's voice,—she never knew how much, in that dark hour, she owed to that resemblance,—"it is *my* child, and I have never injured you. It is my child, Dr. Miller, my only child. I brought it into the world at the risk of my own life! I have nursed it, I have watched over it, I have prayed for it,—and it now lies dying! Oh, Dr. Miller, dear Dr. Miller, if you have a heart, come and save my child!"

"Madam," he answered more gently, moved in spite of himself, "my heart is broken. My people lie dead upon the streets, at the hands of yours. The work of my life is in ashes,—and, yonder, stretched out in death, lies my own child! God! woman, you ask too much of human nature! Love, duty, sorrow, *justice*, call me here. I cannot go!"

She rose to her full height. "Then you are a murderer," she cried wildly. "His blood be on your head, and a mother's curse beside!"

The next moment, with a sudden revulsion of feeling, she had thrown herself at his feet,—at the feet of a negro, this proud white woman,—and was clasping his knees wildly.

"O God!" she prayed, in tones which quivered with anguish, "pardon my husband's sins, and my own, and move this man's hard heart, by the blood of thy Son, who died to save us all!"

It was the last appeal of poor humanity. When the pride of intellect and caste is broken; when we grovel in the dust of humiliation; when sickness and sorrow come, and the shadow of death falls upon us, and there is no hope elsewhere,—we turn to God, who sometimes swallows the insult, and answers the appeal.

Miller raised the lady to her feet. He had been deeply moved,—but he had been more deeply injured. This was his wife's sister,—ah, yes! but a sister who had scorned and slighted and ignored the existence of his wife for all her life. Only Miller, of all the world, could have guessed what this had meant to Janet, and he had merely divined it through the clairvoyant sympathy of love. This woman could have no claim upon him because of this unacknowledged relationship. Yet, after all, she *was* his wife's sister, his child's kinswoman. She was a fellow creature, too, and in distress.

"Rise, madam," he said, with a sudden inspiration, lifting her gently. "I will listen to you on one condition. My child lies dead in the adjoining room, his mother by his side. Go in there, and make your request of her. I will abide by her decision."

The two women stood confronting each other across the body of the dead child, mute witness of this first meeting between two children of the same father. Standing thus face to face, each under the stress of the deepest emotions, the resemblance between them was even more striking than it had seemed to Miller when he had admitted Mrs. Carteret to the house. But Death, the great leveler, striking upon the one hand and threatening upon the other, had wrought a marvelous transformation in the bearing of the two women. The sad-eyed Janet towered erect, with menacing aspect, like an avenging goddess. The other, whose pride had been her life, stood in the attitude of a trembling suppliant.

"*You* have come here," cried Janet, pointing with a tragic gesture to the dead child,—"*you*, to gloat over your husband's work. All my life you have hated and scorned and despised me. Your presence here insults me and my dead. What are you doing here?"

"Mrs. Miller," returned Mrs. Carteret tremulously, dazed for a moment by this outburst, and clasping her hands with an imploring gesture, "my child, my only child, is dying, and your husband alone can save his life. Ah, let me have my child," she moaned, heart-rendingly. "It is my only one— my sweet child—my ewe lamb!"

"This was *my* only child!" replied the other mother; "and yours is no better to die than mine!"

"You are young," said Mrs. Carteret, "and may yet have many children,—this is my only hope! If you have a human heart, tell your husband to come with me. He leaves it to you; he will do as you command."

"Ah," cried Janet. "I have a human heart, and therefore I will not let him go. My child is dead—O God, my child, my child!"

She threw herself down by the bedside, sobbing hysteri- cally. The other woman knelt beside her, and put her arm about her neck. For a moment Janet, absorbed in her grief, did not repulse her.

"Listen," pleaded Mrs. Carteret. "You will not let my baby die? You are my sister;—the child is your own near kin!"

"My child was nearer," returned Janet, rising again to her feet and shaking off the other woman's arm. "He was my son, and I have seen him die. I have been your sister for twenty-five years, and you have only now, for the first time, called me so!"

"Listen—sister," returned Mrs. Carteret. Was there no way to move this woman? Her child lay dying, if he were not dead already. She would tell everything, and leave the rest to God. If it would save her child, she would shrink at no sacrifice. Whether the truth would still further incense Janet, or move her to mercy, she could not tell; she would leave the issue to God.

"Listen, sister!" she said. "I have a confession to make. You *are* my lawful sister. My father was married to your mother. You are entitled to his name, and to half his estate."

Janet's eyes flashed with bitter scorn.

"And you have robbed me all these years, and now tell me that as a reason why I should forgive the murder of my child?"

"No, no!" cried the other wildly, fearing the worst. "I

have known of it only a few weeks,—since my Aunt Polly's death. I had not meant to rob you,—I had meant to make restitution. Sister! for our father's sake, who did you no wrong, give me my child's life!"

Janet's eyes slowly filled with tears—bitter tears—burning tears. For a moment even her grief at her child's loss dropped to second place in her thoughts. This, then, was the recognition for which, all her life, she had longed in secret. It had come, after many days, and in larger measure than she had dreamed; but it had come, not with frank kindliness and sisterly love, but in a storm of blood and tears; not freely given, from an open heart, but extorted from a reluctant conscience by the agony of a mother's fears. Janet had obtained her heart's desire, and now that it was at her lips, found it but apples of Sodom, filled with dust and ashes!

"Listen!" she cried, dashing her tears aside. "I have but one word for you,—one last word,—and then I hope never to see your face again! My mother died of want, and I was brought up by the hand of charity. Now, when I have married a man who can supply my needs, you offer me back the money which you and your friends have robbed me of! You imagined that the shame of being a negro swallowed up every other ignominy,—and in your eyes I am a negro, though I am your sister, and you are white, and people have taken me for you on the streets,—and you, therefore, left me nameless all my life! Now, when an honest man has given me a name of which I can be proud, you offer me the one of which you robbed me, and of which I can make no use. For twenty-five years I, poor, despicable fool, would have kissed your feet for a word, a nod, a smile. Now, when this tardy recognition comes, for which I have waited so long, it is tainted with fraud and crime and blood, and I must pay for it with my child's life!"

"And I must forfeit that of mine, it seems, for withholding it so long," sobbed the other, as, tottering, she turned to go. "It is but just."

"Stay—do not go yet!" commanded Janet imperiously, her

pride still keeping back her tears. "I have not done. I throw you back your father's name, your father's wealth, your sisterly recognition. I want none of them,—they are bought too dear! ah, God, they are bought too dear! But that you may know that a woman may be foully wronged, and yet may have a heart to feel, even for one who has injured her, you may have your child's life, if my husband can save it! Will," she said, throwing open the door into the next room, "go with her!"

"God will bless you for a noble woman!" exclaimed Mrs. Carteret. "You do not mean all the cruel things you have said,—ah, no! I will see you again, and make you take them back; I cannot thank you now! Oh, doctor, let us go! I pray God we may not be too late!"

Together they went out into the night. Mrs. Carteret tottered under the stress of her emotions, and would have fallen, had not Miller caught and sustained her with his arm until they reached the house, where he turned over her fainting form to Carteret at the door.

"Is the child still alive?" asked Miller.

"Yes, thank God," answered the father, "but nearly gone."

"Come on up, Dr. Miller," called Evans from the head of the stairs. "There's time enough, but none to spare.

Giles (liaison ~ Sam merkell)   Adam Miller

Janet ——— mr   Wm   Geo

boy 4 yo.

Sandy

Jane (Aunt Jane & Mammy Jane)

child

Jerry (grandson)

Young nurse (to Felix)

Polly
Merkell
Ochiltree

Mrs. Elizabeth   Sam'n   (Leagson —)
                    Merkell   (see Julia)

Olivia ── née   1st   Mother 2nd husband
         Major   (m 1) (m 2)
         Carteret   Clara Pemberton
(Polly raised
   Olivia)

Felix (Dodie)

Dr Price   Dr Brown

Mr Delamere   (see servant, Sandy)

            Son

                  Tom Delamere (fiancé
                                   to Clara)

Gen'l Belmont
Cap'n Geo. McBane
Conductor (lower middle class?)